tantaene animis caelestibus irae?

Silverfall

Stories of the Seven Sisters

Ed Greenwood

SILVERFALL
Stories of the Seven Sisters

©1999 TSR, Inc.

All Rights Reserved.

Cover and interior art by John Foster
First Printing: August 1999
Library of Congress Catalog Card Number: 98-88147

9 8 7 6 5 4 3 2 1

ISBN: 0-7869-1365-7
T21365-620

U.S., CANADA,
ASIA, PACIFIC, & LATIN AMERICA
Wizards of the Coast, Inc.
P.O. Box 707
Renton, WA 98057-0707
+1-800-324-6496

EUROPEAN HEADQUARTERS
Wizards of the Coast, Belgium
P.B. 2031
2600 Berchem
Belgium
+32-70-233277

Visit our web site at **www.tsr.com**

Novels by Ed Greenwood

Spellfire
Crown of Fire
Stormlight

THE SHADOW OF THE AVATAR TRILOGY
Shadows of Doom
Cloak of Shadows
All Shadows Fled

Elminster: The Making of a Mage
Elminster in Myth Drannor
The Temptation of Elminster

Cormyr: A Novel
Ed Greenwood & Jeff Grubb

Silverfall: Stories of the Seven Sisters

Death of the Dragon
Ed Greenwood & Troy Denning
August 2000

To Terry O'Neal and his creation Edena,
true heroes both.

Prologue

Rise, and be not afraid.

I have no need to be feared. I am more of a goddess than that.

Look upon me, and know Magic.

I am Mystra.

Priests may prattle of this god or that, but over what mortals of Toril call "magic"—because they understand it not—there is no other.

I am the Weaver, the Road Ascending, the One True Way.

Terrible I must be, all too often, and the mortals whom I so love—for I was one of you, not so long ago—often cry out at me, or entreat me to work magic for them, or unfold all its mysteries to them at once, like a child who desires all that is good to eat to appear upon his platter in an instant.

And if I gave the mysteries that are mine to nurture and keep, unfolded and bright in all their myriad glory, who among mortals could behold them and remain sane?

Aye, think on that, and for the love I bear you and all your kind, leave off cowering. I smite or give aid as I see needful, not in whatever wise trembling supplicants— or those who threaten—desire to move me.

When you feel lonely, or lost, and think dark magics raised against you, remember this moment. Feel the weight of my power, as it flows—not turned against you, but so vast that it could sweep you away, cries unheard, in an effortless instant. My power, bent upon you as I regard you now . . . and touched and awed by it, you yet live. I am always here, all about you. You are never truly alone. I flow wherever life flows, wherever winds blow and water runs and the sun and moon chase each other, for there is magic in all things.

This vast, ever-changing, living Weave is a tapestry of power beyond the minds of mortals, though with each passing year my work gives me back bright payment, and those who work magic can do a little more, and see a little more.

Yet those who can see and work with much more than most are rarely sane. The power burns them, twists them, and makes all that is flawed and mean greater. Wherefore we have cruel tyrants, liches walking beyond death who desire to destroy or use all that lives, and wild-eyed dreamers who think that to reshape all Toril to their own visions is to master it. We have lands of mages who destroy or ruin more than they ever raise up; we have doom and devastation, and lives wasted or shattered. Mortals know the pain of such darkness, but I share it. I have the work of banishing the gloom and seeking to temper the blades that are mortal souls so that each time they can take a little more, do a little more, see a little more.

In this work, my hands are manyfold, thanks to the few mortals who can see and work with more Art, and remain sane—or, as some of them have put it, "sane enough."

I deem these rare few, if they will serve me, my Chosen. And they *are* rare. Mortals are so easily bent to willfulness by power, so easily broken into tools I can no longer use, for I work with love, and must be served willingly, by those who love me. I shall not compel service, ever. I will not become what my predecessor did, in the despair of her long waiting. I shall give, with love, and never cease in my giving.

The power I oversee, because of its might, is a danger to mortals, to gods, and to Toril. All three may be blighted or ruined if the Weave is torn or misused enough. I stand against that. I am the Guardian of the Weave, and its lover. Those who serve me must be the very best of mortals, so that they blunder little, and love the Weave as much as I do, coming to understand it as best they can—and far better than others.

Chosen do my work best when they feel my hand but lightly; when they feel free to move and act as mortals do, finding their own vision of the Weave, and serving me in their own ways.

Chosen are not easy to find. Chosen are so special that I have managed to keep no more than a bare two handfuls of those my predecessor raised to their station. The greatest work of my predecessor—the Mystra who was not once a mortal who took the name "Midnight"—was the birthing of Chosen she could not find, and so had to make.

I speak of the Seven Sisters, born under Mystra's hand, to be the sort of mortals she needed, and that I need even more these days. Mortals are wondrous, complex things; my own power is not yet risen enough that I dare attempt to make or bear Chosen as she did . . . wherefore I look endlessly about Toril, seeking fitting mortals who have arisen on their own.

I watch over all who work with the Weave, or meddle in its workings. I watch most those who fascinate me with their daring, their accomplishments, their characters . . . or their love. I watch these Seven often, almost as much as the old rogue who kept my predecessor's power in the time of her passing, and gave it so willingly to me. She lives on in him, and in me.

She lives on more splendidly still in those who could be termed her daughters: the seven mortal women who share a sex, silver hair, beauty, and wits. They have outlived most mortals, and still enter each day with gusto, a constant delight to me. My only disappointment is that they do not work together more often.

Yet once in a passing while—in particular, when I nudge them ever so gently from behind all the curtains of concealment I can spin—they do . . . and I love to watch them at work.

Watch them with me now.

Aye, my eyes shine. When I was a mortal, I wish I'd lived as these magnificent ladies of mine do.

I am Mystra, and to you all I give this gift . . . the Seven Shining of my Chosen. Aye, I weep; whatever you may think, mortal, it is a gift given with Love.

Dove
No More in Armor for My Sake

No sword of war lay long idle in her hand.
Ardreth, High Harp of Berdusk
from the ballad *A Dove At Dawn*
composed circa the Year of the Lost Helm

Sometimes Mirt had his private suspicions that the magic of the ring didn't work at all.

He thought that right now, for instance, on an all-too-warm spring day in the Year of the Gauntlet as he stumbled through the moist and uneven green dimness of a forest sane folk never dared enter. The damp leaves were slippery underfoot, and he was getting too old for creeping about on uneven ground in deep gloom. He fetched up against perhaps his hundredth tree this afternoon, ramming it solidly with his shoulder, and growled in pain.

Well, at least it made a change from wheezing for breath. The fattest working merchant in all the city of Waterdeep shook his head ruefully at the thought of lost strength and slimness—gone thirty years, and more, ago—and waved his arms in frantic circles like a startled chicken so as to find his balance. When he won that battle he strode on, his old, worn boots flopping.

A serpent raised a fanged head in warning on the vast, moss-cloaked trunk of a fallen tree ahead, and the

Old Wolf gave it a growl worthy of his namesake. What good are enchanted rings that quell all nonvocal sounds one makes, and allow one to slip through ward-spells unnoticed, if one still lumbers about like a bull in a mud-wallow . . . and the ring-spells do nothing about the confounded heat?

Mirt wiped sweat out of his eyes with a swipe of his sleeve as he watched the snake glide away in search of a more secluded spot to curl up in. He was wheezing again. Gods curse this heat—wasn't deep forest shade supposed to be *cool*?

A rattlewings started up in alarm under his boots, whirring away through the gloom in a squawking welter of wings. Mirt sourly watched it go, threw up his hands—so much for stealth—and plunged on through the damp leaf mold, spiderwebs, and mushrooms.

Oh, aye—and thorn bushes. Never forget the thorn bushes. They had their own abrupt and painful ways of making sure of that. The fat merchant growled again as he tore free of a barbed, biting tangle—not his first this day—leaving some of his blood behind, and stumped on through the endless forest. Why by all the gods had a Chosen of Mystra—who could have anything she damned well wanted—sought out such a far and hidden place, anyway?

Because she wants—needs—to be alone, he thought, and I am come to shatter the peace that must be so precious to her.

Mirt growled again at the thought, and waved a hand in anger. Sweat was dripping off his nose again, running down his face like a brook, more salty stickiness than water.

"Puhwaugh!"

Mirt found himself spitting out a moth that had darted into his mouth amidst his wheezing. Now he was eating insects. Grand, indeed.

Sweating and stumbling, the only fat merchant for miles—or so he hoped—lumbered on up a slippery slope of mosses and little leaf-filled hollows, gained the top of a ridge . . . and stopped abruptly, catching at a tree for support as he stared down at what lay ahead.

His jaw dropped open. Oh, he'd known there'd be a dell in the trees somewhere hereabouts, warded and hidden, with Dove Falconhand in it. And here 'twas, without the singing of shattered wards or any magic menacing him. Evidently the ring was working after all.

An eerie blue light of magic pulsed down in the dell, radiance that spun like sparkling mists around a strange dance. A woman taller than Mirt was dancing in midair, her booted feet almost his height off the ground, whirling with smooth grace in an endless flowing of limbs and swirling silver hair.

Gods, but she was beautiful! The Old Wolf growled deep in his throat, like the animal he was named for, as he watched her dance held aloft by her own magic. Her shoulders were as broad as his, their sleek rippling making light play and gleam along the shining plates of her full suit of black and silver armor. She wore neither gauntlets nor helm, but was otherwise encased in war steel, all slender curvaceous strength and long, strong legs. Her height and deft grace made her seem smaller and more slender than she truly was—not a squat, burly swordswinger like Mirt, not even "buxom" . . . but in truth, she overmatched him in size, reach, and probably strength. Her unbound silver hair flowed with her, licking and dancing about her shoulders. Her dark brows arched in concentration as she watched her deadly, moaning partners.

Dove of the Seven Sisters was not dancing alone. Singing in the air around her were a dozen scabbardless swords, their bared blades cutting the air in whirling dances of their own. Mirt saw runes ripple down their shining flanks, and at least two of them were moaning— one high-pitched, one lower—as they spun through air that crackled with power. In the heart of their deadly ballet, Dove Falconhand was singing, low and wordlessly, her voice quickening and growing louder.

A darting sword point struck sudden sparks from Dove's armor then whirled away. Mirt was still watching its tumbling flight in wonder when two blades slashed at the dancing woman, their steel shrieking in protest along the curves of her armor. Without thinking, the Old Wolf pushed away from his tree and stumbled forward, almost pitching onto his face as he caught one boot heel in a tree root.

Dove's song was insistent now, almost hungry. The swords were circling her and darting in, striking like sharks tearing at a stricken fish. Screams of metal raking metal rose to drown out her keening as Mirt sprinted down the leaf-slick dellside, snatching out his own sword with the vague notion of smashing down the flying blades from the air. Was she caught in some sort of magical trap? A spell that turned her own powers against her to bring her swift death?

He wasted no breath in roaring a warning—in case someone who might be directing the blades would thereby be warned—but Dove soon saw him. Her head turned, mouth opening in surprise, just as a blade slid under the edge of a plate, bit through an unseen strap, and sent the black and silver plate spinning away. Three swords plunged into the gap where the plate had been and Dove stiffened, clawing the air in obvious pain.

Her gasp was almost a sob. It rang in Mirt's ears as the wheezing merchant raced forward, waving his sword. Three blades drew back from the dancing woman, trailing flames of blindingly bright silver, and one of them rang high and clear, like a struck bell. It sounded almost triumphant.

"Blazing . . . gods . . . above!" Mirt panted, swinging his sword at one of the flying blades so hard that when he missed he found himself staggering forward helplessly, about to kiss the ground again. "Dove! Hold you them—I'm coming!"

He fell hard, skidding in soft mud and wet leaves, and his next shout was lost in a mouthful of moss. It tasted terrible.

The swords were racing through the air now, striking sparks from Dove Falconhand's armor when they missed the plume of silvery smoke that marked her wound. She was dancing again, arching her body to the world instead of clasping her hands to where she hurt. Through the sweat that stung his eyes as he wallowed in the forest mold, Mirt saw her wave at him to stay back. She resumed her dance, seeming almost to welcome and beckon the blades rather than strike them aside. He thought she must be spell-thralled.

Mirt reeled to his feet just as another sword slid into Dove, sinking so deeply it must have gone most of the way through her. He saw it draw back dark and wet, silver smoke boiling away along its length as the dancing woman reeled in midair. He wasn't going to reach her in time.

There was real pain on Dove's face as she met his eyes again and shook her head, waving at him to begone. Mirt stared in horror at a blade racing right at her face. He used one of the precious spells that slumbered in the other ring he wore; a magic to quench magics.

The sword plunged obediently to the ground, bouncing lifelessly to rest—just as two other blades thrust themselves into the silver-haired woman, their quillons clanging against each other as one slid past the other.

Dove gasped, shuddering in the air as her body bent involuntarily around the transfixing steel. Mirt was only a few running strides away now, almost close enough to snatch at those quivering hilts. He had his own sword, two gnarled old hands, and—a dose of irony—the only spells left in his ring were a flight magic, and one that conjured up scores of whirling swords. He'd have to do this the hard way.

A blade slashed at his ear as he lumbered forward to lay his hands on the hilts of the two swords buried in Dove. He'd have to leap up to reach them.

Gods, he was getting too old to jump about like a stag. With a grunt and a gasp, the Old Wolf launched himself into the air, battered old fingers reaching . . .

He was in the air before he saw it. A sword curving up and around from behind the drifting silver smoke, soaring toward him like a hungry needle.

Mirt could do nothing to evade its bright point, and the old, supple leathers he wore would be as butter beneath its keen strike.

"Must I die like this?" he growled in despair as his leap carried him helplessly on, his fingers still shy of reaching two vibrating pommels.

A wave of magic—obeying a slender, bloodied hand— hurled him back. Mirt saw the dark blade speed between them, its bright edge winking at him, as he locked gazes with Dove again.

There was calm reproach in her eyes, and yet a hint of lurking mirth, too . . . an instant before her face changed, alarm rising in her eyes again. Something struck him behind and above his ear, hard enough to spin him around and down into an echoing red void, a world that darkened as he tumbled through it, on the slow roll down to death.

✳   ✳   ✳

Rapture awakened him, greater shuddering pleasure than he'd ever felt before. The low sound he'd been hearing in the dreams that were falling away from him now, receding into forgetfulness like sun-chased mists, was his own endless moan of pleasure as he writhed on his back in the forest mold.

Dove was kneeling above him, clad in a simple white shift, armor and blood and racing blades all gone. One slender, long-fingered hand—dappled with blood no longer—was outspread in the air above his breast, and a gentle smile was tugging at the corners of her lips.

"Wh-what?" Mirt managed to ask, his throat rough.

"Lie easy, Old Wolf, and let me finish. You've been a very bad boy, down the years . . . but I suppose you're well aware of that."

Fresh waves of pleasure washed over him before he could reply, and he kicked his heels against the soft moss, needing some sort of release.

"What're you doing to me?" he groaned when he could find breath to shape words again.

"Healing you," Dove replied serenely, holding up something small in her other hand. It glinted between her fingers as she held it out. "Recognize this?"

Mirt shook his head, gasping as old, long familiar aches melted away. "What is it?"

"Part of someone's sword tip. You've been carrying it around for two score summers or so; that stiffness in your back, remember?"

The fat merchant twisted experimentally. His limbs were as supple as when he was a young lad. " 'Tis *gone*," he rumbled in wonderment, feeling flesh that hardly felt like his, stripped of accustomed pain.

Dove nodded. "That, along with a lot of fat you didn't need, those crawling veins on your legs, a rupture in your gut I could put my hand through, balls of bone built up around your joints . . . and I've forgotten how many places where your bones were broken, or once broken and poorly mended. You might have taken better care of yourself."

"And never been the great lord of adventures I am," Mirt growled up at her, "and so never met you, lady. Nay, I think I chose the right road." He patted at his belly, then ran his fingers over his chin and was reassured to find familiar girth, calluses, and hair. Ah, she hadn't made a boy of him—or, gods, a *girl*—or anything like that.

"No, Old Wolf," Dove murmured reassuringly. "You'll recognize yourself—wrinkles, scars, and all—when next you look in a glass."

Mirt lifted his head for a moment, saw shards of hacked black and silver armor strewn around them in the trampled moss, sighed, and let his head fall back.

"You give me a gift beyond measure," he rumbled, letting her see the love in his eyes. Then, because he had to, he added bluntly, "Why?"

Dove nodded, her smile gone now. "Because, in your own way, you serve Faerûn as I do—a service for which you are all too unlikely to be otherwise thanked. I could hardly leave you to bleed to death in the center of my Dancing Place when you'd taken your wound trying to protect me."

She folded her fingers as if closing an unseen book, and acquired an impish smile as she drew her hand back from above his breast. "Even if doing so would greatly please a large and ever growing host of folk spread all across the continent of Faerûn."

Mirt grunted at that and snaked out a hand to touch her knee. A surge of power washed through him, as if he'd been touched by a spell. His entire body jumped ere something happened inside Dove Falconhand, and the flow was cut off as if cut by a knife . . . leaving him holding a knee. A shapely knee, but mere flesh and bone now, not some storage keg of stirring magic.

"My, but we're greedy," said the silver-haired woman in calm tones, firmly disengaging his stout fingers with a hand that—for all its smooth slenderness—was stronger than his.

She rose in a single graceful movement and stood looking down at him. "I can see a question or three fairly bursting out of you," she said with a smile, and wordlessly beckoned forth his speech with two imperiously hooked fingers.

Mirt looked up at the woman who could kill him with just one of several dozen even smaller gestures, and asked in a raw, bemused voice, "If it pleases you to tell me, lady, I must know this: why, before all the gods, were you dancing with a dozen swords?"

She held out a hand to help him rise. Mirt rolled to a sitting position, marveling at a strength and a physical ease he'd not felt in himself for thirty winters, and took that proffered hand. He barely needed it, and stood flexing his arms in sheer pleasure.

"All of us Chosen," she replied gently, as they stood together in a glade where eerie spell-glow, drifting smoke, or darting sword kept the calling birds at bay no longer, "have our own magical pursuits—hobbies, even 'secret schemes,' if you will. What you blundered into was one of mine."

"I'm deeply sorry that I did so," the old merchant said quickly, "even if it did win me years of hurts healed. I—"

Dove laid two gentle fingers across his lips. "Please don't babble more thanks at me, Mirt. I have too few friends and too many admiring worshipers." Her lips twisted. "They almost outnumber the foes who'd dance on my dead body with glee."

The Old Wolf nodded. "Then say on about your dancing and the swords, lady," he bade gently.

"My name is Dove . . . or to certain angry Lords of Waterdeep, 'Clever Bitch,' " the silver-haired woman told him serenely, and Mirt flushed scarlet to the very tips of his ears.

"Ah, now, lass, I meant it not. Gods, 'twas years back, that! And how could you have heard me clear across the city? 'Twas just th—"

Those fingers tapped his lips again. "Just call me Dove, hmm? I hope you'll have sense enough not to cavort around like a youngling in days to come, or speak of what happened here. I don't want to end up leading a procession of wrinkled-skin lordlings around the North, all of them pleading to be made vigorous again. Nor do I want parties of axe-wielding, torch-bearing idiots blundering around in this forest seeking a glade where magic swords can be found flying around."

"Lady," Mirt said gravely, "you have my wor—I-I mean *Dove*, I promise you I'll tell no one at all. Truly."

Dove nodded, her eyes studying his face a trifle sadly. She was not smiling.

"Is—is anything wrong?" Mirt asked anxiously.

Dove shook her head. "Memories, Old Wolf, are personal gems . . . or curses. I was just remembering another man who used almost the same words you just did, and what became of his promise—and him. And before you ask, no, I won't tell you his name or fate."

The old merchant spread helpless hands and took a restless stride away from her. "Of course not, great lady. Is there anything I can do for y—"

A firm hand took hold of his arm and turned him around. "Hear the secret you sought, and keep it," she replied simply. "Mirt, you saw no hostile spell at work on me, but merely my own sloth. I was enhancing the enchantments of those blades the easy way, by borrowing powers from one to echo into another. I do such augmentations at Mystra's bidding, making the magic I spawn last by means of my own blood."

"The silver fire that legends speak of," Mirt whispered. "Tears of Mystra . . . the blood of the Seven."

Dove nodded. "The Lady Steel used to do sword dances—alone, in remote forest glades—to swiftly transform blades of minor enchantment into duplicates of a more formidable weapon. I thought others avoided such practices because of the danger and their dislike of pain, but I've discovered another reason."

She waved a hand at the scattered armor. "That is now twisted in its magic," she explained. "What some folk called 'cursed.' "

Mirt nodded. "And if you hadn't worn it?"

"You'd have found my body lying here with a dozen swords in it," she replied calmly, "or blown to blood and

Blaskar Toldovar came to a halt beside a bookcase that faced the old woman's chair; a large and heavy bookcase with a bellpull beside it . . . a bellpull the old woman knew summoned no servant, but caused the bookcase to topple forward. The case was hinged in the middle, to bow forward as it emptied its load of ledgers and surely crush anyone sitting in the chair. Blaskar hooked his fingers securely around the bellpull and glared at his visitor.

"Your ledgers won't be improved by getting my old blood all over them," the old woman said, "and I'm not here to harm you. Sit down, be at ease, and pour me a drink, Blaskar—the good stuff, not the rubytart with slavesleep in it."

Blaskar Toldovar stared at the old woman for a moment, breathing heavily, then collapsed onto his desk stool, sending up a cloud of dust that made him sneeze helplessly. When he could see again, he wiped his eyes, settled his monocle into place, and peered at his visitor through it hard and long, thrusting himself forward until he almost fell off the stool.

"No, I don't recognize you," he said at last, with a weary sigh, "but you must know me. I ask again: who are you?"

"I'd prefer not to give you my name," the old woman said tartly, "especially with your man listening behind yon door. Send him away—and *not* into the spy passage."

Blaskar sighed, went to the door, flung it wide, and jerked his head toward the stairs. The impassive servant who'd been listening at the door nodded calmly and strode away.

They listened to his boots descending the steps before Blaskar closed the door again, turned, and said, "I'm a busy man, and you did disturb me at a very delicate task. I must ask you to identify yourself forthwith."

"Busy?" the old woman asked. "I hear no chains, and see no young things lined up for inspection. How can a dust. That many enchantments at once would hamper my own powers in strange ways."

The fat merchant looked down at the scattered fragments of black and silver steel again and Dove smiled thinly. "There are those who feel far too many Chosen of Mystra walk the face of Toril these days," she said. "This is one secret you'd best not spill with your over-loose tongue."

The Old Wolf shook his head. "And you trust me . . ." he murmured in wonder. He shook his head again, then cleared his throat and said formally, "Dove Falconhand, know that I will obey you in anything. You have but to call on me."

The silver-haired woman regarded him soberly and said, "Be careful, Mirt. I may one day collect on that promise—and my calling may cost you your life."

Mirt kept his eyes on hers as he went to his knees. "La—Dove, I will answer that call right gladly, even if it comes with the clear promise of my death. We must all die . . . and in your service seems to me a goodly way to go."

Dove shook her head and turned away, but not before Mirt saw what might have been tears in her eyes. When she spoke again, however, her voice was calm and composed. "Words spoken near death tend to lay bare the heart more than grand and formal promises. Forgive me if I wonder aloud why a man so eager to promise me his death now, cried out as he did, earlier, just before he was struck down?"

The Old Wolf nudged a piece of armor with the scuffed toe of one of his boots and replied, "If die I must, I'd rather it not be in the throes of my own mistake, or a calamity I've caused. That's why I spake thus, then."

He looked up at her, discovered her eyes steady upon him, and added quietly, "You're waiting for another answer, though, Lady Falconhand . . . aren't you?"

She smiled and almost whispered three words: "Lady? Clever Bitch."

Mirt smiled ruefully. *"Dove,"* he began carefully, "know that I came looking for you because I knew of both your skills and the approximate location of this your Dancing Place, though nothing of how or why you danced."

The silver-haired woman made a cycling motion with her left hand, bidding him say on.

Mirt drew in a deep breath, let it out in a sigh, and began to speak in a rush, as if emptying himself of a heavy burden. "As you know, I've been a rather busy merchant for some years. I've done business with many folk in most cities between here and the Sea of Fallen Stars. I'm known professionally to a score of men, or more. In Scornubel, perhaps ten times that many trust me with some secrets, or seek my counsel."

Dove bent her head and regarded him sidelong. "And what currently troubles bustling Scornubel?" she asked softly.

Mirt threw back his head in thought, framing his next words, and caught sight of one of the flying swords. It was hanging motionless in midair above the lip of the dell, pointed toward him and half hidden among tree branches. He turned his head and saw another, and another, hanging silent in a deadly ring. Waiting.

He looked back at Dove's calm face, and said, "Lady, please understand that alliances and formal pacts in the Caravan City come and go with the passing hours, not merely by the day or tenday. Few of my contacts there habitually trust or confide in each other. In the matter that brought me here they spoke to me separately, each driven by his own fear."

Dove nodded and he continued, "Folk have been slow to realize this, and therefore we can't say with any surety as to when it began or how widespread 'tis. Scornubel is experiencing a stealthy influx of drow."

Dove raised an eyebrow. Drow. Most humans of Faerûn had an almost hysterical fear of the dark elves.

The evil, spider-worshiping Ones Who Went Below cleaved from their fairer elf brethren millennia ago to descend under the earth and dwell there. Vicious and stealthy, masters of fell sorcery whose skins were the color of the blacksmoke obsidian sold in Tashlutan bazaars, the drow were a mysterious race, all but unseen but for the rare, terrible nights when they crept up to the surface to raid, cruelly slaughtering at will. Drow never stayed above, for fear of their magic losing its efficacy and finding every creature's hand raised against them. So how were they invading Scornubel? Burrowing up under warehouses to make a building above seem part of their dark realms below?

"Drow are *dwelling* in Scornubel?" she asked.

Mirt shrugged and said, "It seems someone is giving the dark-skins the magical means to adopt the shapes of humans—for months or tendays, not mere hours—and they're then practicing copying human ways, speech, and mannerisms. At times, various merchants have told me, 'tis like talking to a bad actor lampooning a grasping horse monger or an oily dealer in scents . . . and 'tis chilling, if you know the merchant well and were joking with him only a day or two before."

The silver-haired ranger nodded. "Folk of Waterdeep tend to suspect dopplegangers when they encounter such impostors," she observed. "Why then are you so sure these are drow?"

Mirt spread his hands. "I know no details, but at least two mages learned so with their spells. One left the city shortly thereafter; the other's not been seen for a little more than two tendays now."

"And the drow are taking the likenesses of—watchblades? Lord inspectors? The richest moneylenders?"

The Old Wolf shook his shaggy head. "One Scornubrian merchant company or family, then another, not local authorities. Their purpose, if they share one, is as yet unknown. They seem uninterested in seizing control of the city, but very interested in gaining control of its most important shipping and caravan concerns. We don't know if the humans they displace are enslaved or simply slain. There've been no bodies found—and they seem to take the places of everyone in a target family, down to the children and chamber servants."

"While I can see no good in this," Dove said slowly, "I've little stomach for slaughtering my way through a city of drow—and starting wildfire rumors that will bring about the deaths, one way and another, of many 'suspected drow' in cities all over Faerûn. I serve Mystra, not the Lords' Alliance or some 'humans over all others' creed."

The fat merchant nodded. "I expect no whelmed Harper army to descend on Scornubel this season, or next . . . I just want to know *why*."

Dove frowned, then smiled wryly. "An eternal human need," she commented, "wherefore we have a grand variety of altars across this world, and others."

Mirt stood looking at her anxiously, like a dog awaiting either kind words or a kick. When she saw his face, the silver-haired ranger smiled and strode forward to clasp his forearms, as one warrior to another. "Your journey wasn't wasted, Old Wolf. Someday soon, if I can, I'll tell you a story set in Scornubel."

The fat merchant smiled as she patted his shoulder, then he turned back to her and asked curiously, "Do you—Dove, tell me—do you ever grow tired of racing around Faerûn righting wrongs and setting the crooked straight?"

They stared into each other's eyes for a long, silent time, and Mirt was shaken by the sadness and longing she let him see before she smiled, shrugged, and replied, "It's what I am, and what I do."

She turned away then, the folds of her shift swirling around her bare feet, and added briskly, "Return to Waterdeep, Lord Mirt. Follow me not, nor linger over-long in this place."

She strode across the trampled moss to where rising ground marked one edge of her dell, and turned to look back over her shoulder at him severely.

"And don't let your invigorated body make you a young fool again," she told him. "You're not to go looking for other trouble or trying to find again the adventures of your youth. I don't want all of my healing work wasted."

"You condemn me to a life of boredom," Mirt protested, half seriously.

Dove's merry laugh rang out across the dell. "Would it be impolite, my lord, to remind you how much some folk of Faerûn would give to enjoy such boredom?"

Without waiting for an answer she moved her hands in two quick gestures, and spell-glow filled the dell once more, blue-white and swirling, as the swords she'd danced with flew down from their hovering stations to swirl around her.

Mirt took a step toward her, opening his mouth to speak, then came to a halt. He'd seen that warning gesture before, and tasted a sword blade when he ignored it. The blades boiled up around Dove Falconhand in a bright blue whirlwind that rose a trifle off the ground, snarled up into a furious spiral, then all at once vanished, leaving a fat merchant blinking at emptiness beneath the trees.

All at once, the birds began calling again. Mirt stood on the trampled moss facing no swords, spell-glow, nor barefoot Chosen of Mystra.

"Ah, lass—?" he asked the empty air. "Dove?"

Silence was his only reply. A rattlewings came swooping heavily across the dell and veered aside with a squawk of alarm when it realized that the motionless tree trunk ahead was in truth a human engaged in the rare occupation of standing still and silent. It flapped on into the forest, crying the fear of its discovery to the world. Mirt turned to watch it go, then turned slowly on one boot heel to survey the dell.

Aside from the deep marks his own boots had left here and there in the mud and the scattered shards of black and silver armor, it looked like any other part of the wild forest.

Might Dove have left magic hidden here, buried close to the surface where she could readily find it? Well, it wouldn't hurt to just look . . .

Even as Mirt put his hands to an upthrust, helm-shaped clump of moss, the air around him sang in high, clear warning, and the ring that allowed him to pass wards unchallenged throbbed upon his finger.

Ah, well. Mirt shrugged, smiled, and straightened up. "Clever bitch," he told the dell affectionately.

When he bent again to take up a shard of armor the air around him almost screamed, but despite the danger its skirling promised, the Old Wolf stood turning it in his hands, lost in unhurried thought for some time before he stooped to gather all of the armor plates and carefully stack them against a rock. He covered them with other stones to keep them from weathering overmuch, took a last, long look around, and started the long walk back to Waterdeep.

✳   ✳   ✳

In a certain corner of the plains city of Scornubel, overly curious visitors can find a narrow, nameless passage that plunges from a garbage-strewn back alley down a short and slippery way to an open cesspool. The only folk who customarily visit this noisome spot are hairy, reeking men in old carts, who come to empty barrels of night soil. Rats often scurry along the walls of the passage, but on this particular afternoon one of them was quite surprised to see the empty, dung-smeared cobbles ahead of it suddenly grow a gnarled old woman. She appeared out of empty air an inch or so above the cobbles, holding a cane. With a grunt she slammed to the ground with a clatter, and quite nearly fell over.

Reeling upright, this aged bundle of rags cast a level look around, seeking to find anyone who might have seen her arrival, then settled her cane into a bony hand. She stumped up the passage into the alley beyond, spitting thoughtfully in the rat's direction. The rodent blinked, and decided to forage elsewhere.

The old woman staggered on around the corner, making slow work of her short trip down the alley. She turned onto a street where the houses were old, cloaked with ivy, and leaned close together among their iron-barred fences and refuse-choked yards. Old and stunted trees thrust weary branches into the late afternoon sky. Many of the houses looked empty. Those who snored within them, huddled in the corners of empty rooms in clothes no better than the old woman wore, wouldn't awaken until nightfall. The old woman planned to be long gone by then.

She stopped in front of a house ringed by tall stone garden walls capped with a gleaming row of jagged bottle-shards and looked up and down the street, but it seemed empty. The gate, flanked by two squat pillars, was unlocked. The squeal of its opening roused a large black dog in the yard within into a wild fury of barking and howling. It bounded the length of its chain, teeth snapping about an arm's length short of the path that led to the house. The beast kept up its noisy and vigor-ous threats for the entire length of the old woman's journey to the front door. Straining as it was at the links that held it, someone watching might have been forgiven for expecting the old, moss-girt, leaning statue to which its chain was fastened to topple the rest of the way to the ground and set free one frantic canine.

The old woman knew the length of that chain, though its captive had changed since her last visit, and she didn't spare the dog a glance. Her eyes were on the pair of bored-looking warriors now rising from stools flanking the door, slapping at the hilts of their swords and daggers to ensure these were ready, and staring back at the old woman with barely concealed irritation. One doorsword prudently moved to one side—to be out of range of any spell that might smite his fellow if this old crone turned out to be some sort of sorceress—and stayed on the porch, drawing his dagger to be ready for a throw. The other guard strode forward down the path to bar the old crone's progress a good twenty paces from the porch.

"This is a private abode," he announced briskly, "and my master does not make welcome beggars or unsolicited vendors. Would you have other business here, this day?"

"Mmmnh, mmmnh," the old woman said, as if working long unused gums. She turned her head as slowly as any tortoise might and fixed the doorsword with an eye that was startlingly cold, keen, and blue. "I would."

The guard towered over her, waiting. The old woman blinked at him, and made a "step aside" wave with her rough-knobbed cane.

He stood his ground and prompted with just a hint of testy impatience beneath his smile, "And it would be?"

"Best conducted inside," the old woman rasped pointedly, taking a step forward.

The doorsword stood his ground, clapping a hand to the hilt of his sword. "That's something we'd best discuss," he snapped. "My master has given me very specific instructions as to who should be allowed to disturb him."

"Lean closer, young bladesman," the stooped woman replied. "I'm supposed to whisper one o' them secret passwords to ye now, see?"

Warily, the doorsword drew his blade, held it like a barrier between them, and leaned forward, eyes narrowed. "Spit at me," he remarked almost pleasantly, "and die."

"Kiss me," the old woman replied, "and be surprised."

She was smiling as the guard's startled eyes met hers and he almost drew away. The smile was almost kindly though, and the old woman did have both of her hands clearly in view, clasped on the cane at her hip, bony fingers laced together.

She leaned a little closer and whispered hoarsely, "Firebones three."

The guard straightened, astonishment flashing across his face for a long moment before he gulped, became impassive, and said, "Pray forgive the delay I've caused you, lady, and come this way. The house of Blaskar Toldovar welcomes thee."

"Mmmnh, mmmnh," the old woman agreed, setting herself once more into motion. "Thought it would, I did. Thought it would."

She toiled up the steps with some purpose, and smiled and nodded like an indulgent duchess at the two doorswords as they ushered her within. The house hadn't changed much, though the servant who led her up the long stair flanked with blood-red hangings was a burly warrior now, and not the young lady clad only in chains that she recalled from earlier visits.

He left her in a chair in the usual shabbily genteel, dim room, where she sat in silence, knowing she was being watched through spy holes. It wasn't long before a voice that rasped even more than her own asked out of the darkness behind her chair, "Well?"

"Blaskar," the old woman said, "I need to ask you something, and get an honest answer. I'll need to cast a spell on you, to know that it's truth—and that you're indeed Blaskar Toldovar."

"What? Who *are* you?" The balding man came around the chair in his usual worn and dirty clothes, adjusting an oversized monocle she didn't remember seeing him with before. He leveled his cane at her—the cane that held a mageslaying dart of silver-coated, magic-dead metal in its end—and snapped, "Answer me!"

"You grow short-tempered, old Toldove. Not a good habit, for one of your profession," the old woman observed calmly.

slaver be busy with no slaves in his house? If you were burying money in the garden, I'd expect to see a shovel and a little sweat."

Blaskar glared at her and opened his mouth to say something—but only shut it with a snap.

"Well?" the old woman asked, eyeing him right back. "Wouldn't you?"

The slaver mastered his temper with visible effort and said shortly, "You know me, and my habits, and yet say you must cast a spell on me to be sure of me! You refuse to give your own name, and sit here insulting me rather than getting to the reason for this social call . . . and so far as I can tell, I've never seen you before in my life! I refuse to have spells cast on me"—he aimed his cane at her again, and the old woman saw that he had a row of identical ones in a rack behind his stool— "without knowing who is to cast them, and why. This city is becoming too dangerous for me to extend such trust."

"That," his visitor said in dry tones, "is what I've come to talk to you about. Scornubel seems to be undergoing some changes—or rather, a lot of its citizens are . . . aren't they? Something a slaver would know about, hey?"

Blaskar Toldovar went pale and said tightly, "I won't listen to this much longer, whoever you are." The cane trembled in his hand. "I'll warn you once more . . ."

"Blaskar," the old woman said gently, "be at ease." She reached with her cane under the chair she was sitting in, fished around, and dragged out something that clanked: two sets of manacles. "Would you feel more comfortable if I put these on?"

Blaskar stared at her, open mouthed, then said slowly, "Yes. Yes, I would. Are you an escaped slave, come back to me for revenge?"

"I'm not here for revenge," the old woman told him, calmly snapping one set of manacles around her ankles. "I'm here for information." She settled the cuffs of the second set around her wrists after propping her cane against one bony knee, and snapped them closed with a clack. "But I won't tell you my name."

The old slaver's eyes narrowed. "Your brand?" he asked.

The old woman nodded, and rolled onto one hip with surprising ease, extending her legs toward the low footstool beside the one Blaskar was sitting on. He kicked it under her feet out of long habit, got up, and extended his cane to her filthy skirts, lifting them up past a green and mottled map of veins until he could see the back of her left knee. He peered, but could see no mark there.

"Is this some sort of game?" he snapped.

"Look again," the old woman said calmly. "The light in here is not good."

The slaver wiped his eyes, then his monocle, and peered again . . . and as he stared down at surprisingly clean and milk-white flesh, something faded slowly into view. A familiar mark, and a number . . .

All the color drained from Blaskar Toldovar's face, and he whispered, "Sweet Mystra forfend! You're D—"

"Hush!" the old woman said sharply. "No names!"

She rolled over again and Blaskar retreated from her as he would from a rearing viper.

"B-but what's happened to you?" he asked, backing away behind a chair and feeling for the shelf that held his most precious warding magic. "Why are you here?"

The old woman held up her manacled wrists and shook them so the chain rattled. "Be at ease, Blaskar, I'm not here to harm you, or take revenge for what you did to a young girl all those years ago. Besides, the master you sold me to was kind and I was his slave for only about two days. I've actually been back here to check on you a dozen times since then . . . you just didn't recognize me."

"Spell-shapes," the slaver murmured. "False bodies, like the one you're wearing now."

"Like the ones a lot of folk seem to be wearing in Scornubel these days," the old woman said sharply. "Mind if I cast a spell or two, Blaskar?"

The slaver gulped, then got his stool, set it down beside the chair, and sat on it carefully. Their knees almost touched. "If one of them will shield us from all spying," he said firmly, "I do not mind. We need to talk freely."

"Now we're getting somewhere," the old woman said, shifting forward so that their knees did touch. "That'll be my first spell."

"And the second?"

"The truth telling. I know I'm talking to Blaskar, but I don't know if Blaskar's wits have been played about with, magically."

"Neither," the slaver whispered, his face white again, "do I."

The woman in chains looked into Blaskar's eyes and asked softly, "Would you like me to take you far from here, old Toldove? To a house in Neverwinter where the neighbors have never even seen a dark elf?"

The slaver looked at her with a sudden, fierce hope kindling in his eyes. "Yes!" he cried, and burst into tears. "Oh, yes!"

With a rattle of chain, the old woman put her arms around him in a gentle embrace. "You'd have to give up slaving," she murmured, "forever."

"Lady," he said, sniveling, "I'm too old for it anymore. Bold young men with no fear and sharp knives were giving me troubles long before . . . before this shadow fell on us here."

He sobbed then and she rocked him in her arms, stroking his neck and murmuring wordless comfort.

When at last he mastered his voice again, Blaskar asked roughly, "Lady? What must I do for this rescue to happen?"

"Tell me all you can about the drow here," she said. "That's all."

"Lady! Your shielding spell! They'll hear—"

"I cast it," she said gently, "when first you touched me. Be at ease, Blaskar."

The slaver drew in a deep breath, let it out in a shuddering sigh, then gave her a weak smile. "In your arms, I almost think I can do that. My mother used to hold me like that."

He swallowed, and asked, his face very pale, "B-but you're a Harper, aren't you? I thought—I thought you people killed slavers, or made us slaves."

"We do, more often than not," Dove Falconhand replied calmly. "Consider yourself an exception."

"But—oh, gods, I know this is stupid of me, but—why?"

Keen eyes seemed to blaze right through the slaver, and he caught his breath with a fearful gasp.

"Blaskar," the woman he'd once enslaved said quietly, "I've spent most of my life being a hearty, capable lady of the blade. Harder than steel, colder than stone, more merrily rough and foul-mouthed and ruthless than men who live by the sword. I've done it because I've had to. I haven't the magic my sisters can boast, to do my fighting for me. I need time to be soft, to surrender myself . . . to be with someone I don't have to fear. You showed me such times, more than once. As I said, I've been back to check on you. You've no idea how much I value tenderness and kindness in a man."

They stared into each other's eyes, and all the color slowly ran out of the slaver's face.

"Yes," Dove told him grimly, "I've magic enough to change my own body. I was Emmera, and Sesilde. Callathrae, too, and the little dancer from Tharsult whose name you never learned, who liked to oil herself and dance in a ring of candles. I know your true measure, Blaskar. Slaver you are, yes, and a little too leering for most tastes, though kind in that, too. The cruel and the cold and the slayers you sent in chains to hardhanded buyers in Calimport and like places. The gentle ones you treated gently."

She tilted her head to one side, and seemed to see right through him as she added, "All this time you've been looking for a woman who will cook for you and sleep with you and worship you with her eyes—and not thinking yourself worthy of anyone who passed through your hands that you liked the look of. It took you too long to learn not to judge females by their looks, but you learned it at last, old dog. Almost too late, but you learned it, and the one you had your heart set on growing old with turned out to be a dark elf one night, didn't she? You killed her, didn't you? Just as she must have slain your real beloved—quick, then getting rid of the body in a panic. Since then, you've cowered here waiting for all the other drow to show up and cut a bloody revenge out of your hide."

The slaver was looking at her like a small boy who'd been caught doing something clever but forbidden and doesn't yet know if he'll be punished or laughed at. He opened his mouth, but said nothing. He didn't have to speak for her to know she was right.

"How many matches did you make, down the years?" Dove asked. "A little coin to the right passing merchant here, after you'd judged him suitable, and off with the chains and another partnership . . . how many times? I know of twelve, but your neck is still within easy reach, Blaskar; how many more?"

The slaver swallowed, held up a hand to buy himself some thinking time, then said slowly, "Twenty-three. I think. Use magic on my mind to be sure, Lady D— ahem, lady. I . . . I can't avoid any fate you give to me, I guess." He was struggling on the edge of tears again, but he managed to add, "I'm so tired of being afraid."

"That," Dove said in a voice of doom, "is why I won't do to you what I once vowed to: spell-change you into a beautiful lass, chain you, and sell you into slavery to give you a taste of what you did to so many. You've suffered, and there are times when Mystra bids us to rise above 'death for death' justice, and show kindness to those worthy of it. In my eyes, those most worthy of it are those who've been kind to others, in private and with no thought of benefit to themselves. You're one of those few."

A long-fingered hand closed on the throat of the man gaping at her, and she added in a voice of sudden steel, "Yet never forget, Blaskar, that I can make you a slave girl, or legless beggar, or disease-riddled outlaw, wearing the face of someone hated and hunted, in the time it takes me to tell you this. I can come to doom you, if you turn to your old ways once more."

The slaver was trembling. She opened her mouth to say something more gentle, but he lifted his head and said, "I'll submit to whatever doom you choose. If you'd be kind to me, though, let me try to bargain a better one."

Dove snorted. "From how strong a position? What, for instance, would your opening gambit be?"

They exchanged smiles. The slaver's grin turned sly and he asked, "What if I should just happen to forget where I put the key to your cuffs?"

"Then I'll break them," Dove told him, "and help you go looking for that key. You might not be seeing things all that well after I'd stuffed two lengths of chain down your throat and made you swallow, so we'd have to do things properly. I think I'd start by taking firm hold of your ear, then go around behind you and start looking for where I could pull on the other end of my devoured chain."

Blaskar stared at her for a moment, then threw back his head and let out his first real laugh in years.

✳   ✳   ✳

The same sun that would set over Waterdeep long before a certain fat merchant found his way back to its gates—and would shine through the windows of a certain Scornubrian house now forever empty of Blaskar Toldovar—was lowering in the western sky when a weary, muddy-booted peddler led four limping, footsore mules into Scornubel. He trudged down the wide, dung-strewn streets to a certain stables where he paid grudging coins to have his beasts penned, fed, and watered. He paid rather more to have his saddlebags lock-stored, and trudged out again into the gathering dusk, rubbing at a paltry mustache that sat like a hairy caterpillar upon his unlovely upper lip. He gave "Tarthan" as his name, and he walked as one who knew the Caravan City but wasn't particularly glad to find himself therein.

His eye seemed to fall only upon Scornubel's newer establishments, but always, it seemed, to soon find them lacking. At the threshold of The Rolling Wheel he peered into the din of scrawny dancers and wearily roaring men, sniffed, and turned into the darkness again. At the shoulder-rubbing-crowded outer room of the Black Bowl gambling club he spat onto the purple carpet and went out as wearily as he'd come in, giving the bouncer who moved threateningly forward a grin of savage promise and the flourished point of a needle-thin blade three feet long.

The Bowl of Serpents seemed more to Tarthan's liking. He sat for some time tossing copper coins at the serpent-tailed dancers who undulated into view amid its many mauve tapestries, and polished off an entire decanter of emerald green Starlartarn wine from the Tashalar. The peddler was weaving slightly, but still steady of purpose, when he stopped outside Cata's Pump a little later, sniffed the air appreciatively, and told the world, "Ahh, a good broth. Worth the little walk from Waterdeep."

That comment made the eyes of the doorswords widen above their half masks as the dusty peddler stepped between them and sought the dimness within. Half a dozen merchants and burly porters were loung-ing drowsily in chairs around the edges of the tavern's lone taproom, the large empty bowls in front of them attesting to the reason for their collective torpor. A single tankard stood neatly before each diner; no one had spilled anything, or was calling for more yet. In fact, no one was saying anything. Tarthan cast a narrowed eye over the tomblike taproom, found a smallish table hard by a pillar, and sat.

A serving wench drifted up to stand over him. "Your pleasure, goodman?" she asked tonelessly, staring over Tarthan's head at something mildly captivating that seemed to be occurring several days' ride to the east, through the dirty taproom wall.

"A fist of cheese, a bowl of that broth I smell, and a roundloaf," the peddler said heartily, holding up a closed fist full of coins.

Instead of flicking her fingers in the shorthand gestures that would give him the price demanded for his meal, the girl simply nodded and turned away. Tarthan nodded too, slumping wearily into his chair, and gave the room a wide-mouthed yawn. A curtain moved back into place across a doorway at the far end of the room, but the peddler gave no sign that he'd seen it—or cared very much about curtains or spying anywhere in Faerûn.

Nonetheless, when the serving wench returned with a tray and a face of unchanged blankness, the peddler's seat was empty. There was no sign of him anywhere in the taproom. The girl stood for a moment in silent indecision, then set the tray down in front of the empty seat and glided away again. There was a thin layer of dust on the tray and the tankard, but no one seemed to notice.

✳   ✳   ✳

"A quiet night," the peddler observed, leaning on his elbow. He was the only patron of The Moonshot Tankard, it seemed, but the bar master was diligently polishing boards that already gleamed glassy smooth under the lamplight.

"Indeed, sir," came the quiet, distant reply, as the bar master turned away to wipe a row of shining, unused glasses behind the bar.

Tarthan sipped soured beer from his tankard, keeping his face carefully expressionless despite the taste, and asked casually, "Any news?"

"News, sir?"

"What's befalling in the Caravan City these days? Any new talk of the drow coming up from the depths to kill us all in our beds?"

The bar master's shoulders stiffened for the space of a long breath ere he turned and said quietly, "Not that I've heard, sir. Some bad storms this past month . . . fewer caravans running into town. That's about it, sir."

"Ah, well, then, I'd best get to my bed," the peddler replied, draining his tankard with a loud sigh and setting it carefully back down on the bar. "Good ale," he said, rising to go.

"Finest in the city, sir," the bar master murmured, turning to watch Tarthan lurch toward the door. His eyes never left the peddler's dusty back until the dwindling, dusty figure turned a corner at the end of the street. Then he turned with the speed of a striking snake, thrust his head back through the curtains that led into the kitchen, and hissed something soft and quick to someone unseen.

✳ ✳ ✳

It came to pass that four furtive figures met under the cool, clear starlight of Scornubel that night. One had darted out of the Moonshot Tankard not long after its last guest of the night, another had patiently followed a man who'd left Cata's Pump earlier in the evening without a single taste of the meal he'd ordered, and two more had but recently stepped out of other establishments where a dusty peddler had asked for fresh news of the drow.

The four hadn't planned to meet. They converged separately on the same alley in the wake of a dusty man who now stumbled a little, and whistled a few 'tuneless notes from time to time. When they came together, four pairs of eyes flickered, one hand lifted in an intricate gesture, and four figures moved on as one. If all deals were so simple, swift, and quiet, Faerûn might be a more efficient place. Then again, it might well also be a more deadly one.

The alley ended in a cluster of burned out, roofless warehouses, homes for rats and occasional beggars—though beggars didn't seem to linger long in the Caravan City these days. The four silent, graceful men gathered speed, heading for the doorway the peddler had disappeared through. They knew it led into a fire-blackened stone foundation and cellar beneath, now lacking upper floors or a roof. If a certain peddler couldn't climb walls right smartly, they'd have him—a sheep backed into one corner of a shearing pen.

The foremost blank-faced man was still two swift strides from that gaping doorway when someone stepped out of it—someone small, slender, and obsidian skinned, who moved with catlike grace on spike heeled boots. Four hands had already dipped to the hilts of throwing knives and slender long swords . . . and all of them froze now in astonishment as the drow who'd stepped out of the doorway drew her dark cloak up around her, gave them all a knowing smile, and slipped down the alley like a graceful shadow.

Four heads turned to watch her go, and four throats were longingly cleared in unison before the foremost man drew his sword and his knife and stepped through the doorway.

He was gone only a short time. When he returned his face was still blank and his weapons were clean and dry, but his gliding movements now showed unease rather than anticipation.

"Did she kill him?" one of the others asked.

The man who'd just come out of the burned ruin replied, "There's no sign of him. It's empty." They exchanged puzzled glances, then turned as one to look back down the empty alley.

✳ ✳ ✳

Seemingly sleepy folk stiffened all over the taproom of Cata's Pump as a black-cloaked figure strolled in from the street straight up to the bar, and gave the room at large a cold smile.

The she-drow let her cloak fall away from her bare shoulders, and lamplight flashed back from the cluster of gems she wore at her throat; wealth that marked her as no outcast or lone runaway. Tracing a symbol idly on the bar with one sharp-nailed fingertip, she asked the bartender and the two serving wenches flanking him, "Any of you in the mood for a little trading? Homesick for any Underdark wines or fresh glowcap mushrooms?"

Folk blinked all over the room and leaned forward. "Ah, I don't—" the bartender began, his eyes dark pits of confusion.

The she-drow facing him raised an eyebrow and purred, "Well then, do you know someone who does? There's demand below for Calishite—or Tashlutan—silk, pitted dates, and metalwork: gates, bars, gratings, filigree . . . and I've wine and 'shrooms to trade, but not much time to waste." She shifted perfect obsidian shoulders and murmured, "Are you *sure* you don't? By the looks of things, everyone here could use some real wine."

No one smiled or looked angered; folk with blank faces drifted a little nearer as the bartender stammered, "S-sarltan. Speak to Sarltan."

"And where might I find . . . ?" the she-drow murmured, watching furtive movements in the tightening crowd that marked the journeys of hands to weapons. She shrugged back her cloak still more, and from the glistening black garment she wore beneath it, four slender black-bladed knives rose slowly up into the air. There was a momentary murmur that might have been alarm, or might have been recognition, and patrons began to drift back to their seats to resume looking as sleepy as before. The knives hung in the air around the she-drow's shoulders, points menacing the floor, as the bartender pointed wordlessly out the door.

"You keep this Sarltan out in the street . . ." the she-drow asked, eyebrows raised, in a voice that did not—quite—hold open sarcasm. ". . . or as one of your doorswords?"

The bartender shook his head, then spread his hands in a wordless gesture of helplessness before waving again at the street.

His visitor shook her head, smiled, and said, "Well, think on my offer. I'll be back later to see if anyone has developed a taste for the finer things of home."

✳   ✳   ✳

There was already astonishment in the stares of the doorswords as the she-drow in the cloak whom they'd watched striding openly down the street glided up to them and asked, "I suppose neither of you knows the present whereabouts of Sarltan?"

The guards stiffened as if they'd been kicked in tender places, exchanged baffled glances, then silently backed away from their questioner, waving gloved hands in gestures of denial. The she-drow shrugged, smiled, and strode between them into the cluttered and dusty labyrinth of Chasper's Trading Tower.

Chasper's never closed, no matter what the hour or weather. Its lobby was crowded with the usual badly-mended array of life-sized wooden shop figurines, and the obsidian-skinned visitor passed through them without delay to push wide the inner doors and step into the warm lamplight beyond.

She was greeted by the same sight that had met the eyes of a decade of patrons: a welter of nets, ropes, boats, cartwheels, coach-harnesses, mended lances and armor hanging from the rafters, and heaps of well-used boots, belts, gloves, and scabbards on tables before her. Beyond these mountains of gear, aisles snaked away through piles of animal cages, battered traveling strongchests, and moldering books to sagging tables that stretched away into a warren of shelving whose far reaches were lost in dimness. From their crannies two startled men were hastening forward to serve this unexpected client.

"Yes, good lady?" one of them asked hesitantly, rubbing nervous hands together. "How may we serve you this fair night?"

"We can offer you the widest selection of goods in all Scornubel," the other put in brightly, "and at excellent prices."

The she-drow in the black cloak eyed him. "I come not to buy," she purred, "but to trade. Have you any interest in exchanging bolts of woven silk—Calishite, if you have such—pitted dates, and metalwork for wines and mushrooms from below?"

The shop attendants reared back from her as if she'd thrust a viper into their faces. One of them dropped a hand to the knife at his belt, and the other stammered, "W-we don't usually barter here at Chasper's, good lady—and certainly not in bulk. Perhaps you should meet with Sarltan."

"Ah, yes," the lady drow agreed with the faintest of smiles. "That's a name I've heard before. Yet no one in all Scornubel tonight seems to know where Sarltan can be found. You wouldn't have him under one of these tables, would you? Or in another room, perhaps?"

The doorswords appeared behind her then, having taken the unprecedented step of leaving their posts. The she-drow had her back to them, and gave no indication that she knew of their approach, but as they approached her, four long black knives rose in unison from among her garments. The knives came to a halt, hanging in a cluster in the air above her. The two guards eyed them, frozen with their hands gripping the hilts of their swords, and came no closer to the unexpected visitor. One of them reached up to a bellpull on the wall and tugged it in a careful rhythm. No resulting bell or chime could be heard.

The eyes of the older and larger of the shop attendants flicked to the doorsword's work with the bellpull, then came quickly back to the faintly smiling drow in front of him.

He tried a smile of his own, licked his lips, and said, "Ah, *no*, good lady. I don't think there's a shop in all the city that could help you there, but if you'd care to step into the back our owner might be able to help you . . . ah, in regards to what you seek."

He motioned down one of the corridors as reverently as if he'd been conducting a queen or priestess of power, and the lady drow in the cloak flashed him a dazzling smile and glided forward whence he'd indicated, her knives keeping station above her shoulders.

The back room proved to contain a once grand carpet, paneled walls almost completely hidden behind stacked and dusty rows of bulging ledgers, and a sharp-eyed, wrinkled old woman behind a desk who gave her visitor a sharp look as the lady drow entered, and said crisply, "Close the door and sit down, dear."

In smooth silence the lady drow did as she was bid, taking the only chair in the room that wasn't heaped with bundles of papers. It offered her behind a fresh, dust free cushion that hissed and settled under her weight as she sat upon it. If she noticed the wisps of greenish gas that curled up out of it to drift around her, she gave no sign of this.

The old woman behind the desk sat in frozen silence for the space of a long breath, as if waiting for something, and at length her visitor leaned forward and said pleasantly, "Greetings this night, and prosperity upon this house of commerce. I've come to Scornubel to do a little trade, but find folk here curiously reluctant to do business with me. I represent interests from below who have a strong assortment of wines to offer, and many barrels of fresh glowcap mushrooms, which they desire to exchange for Calishite silks, pitted dates, and metal gates, bars, gratings, and filigree of superior quality. Whenever I speak of this to anyone in this city, they seem ill at ease, and direct me to 'Sarltan.' Your helpful young men out front believe you can help me. Can you, or is this a notion we should both disabuse them of?"

The old woman's fingers moved in a few quick, crawling patterns above the parchments on her desk; her visitor responded with a gesture of her own.

The old woman sighed, then, and sat back. "I don't deal with the nameless," she said quietly. "Give."

"Iylinvyx," the lady drow replied, "of House Nrel'tabra. I'm also called"—she gestured at the knives hanging above her shoulders—" 'Pretty Teeth.' "

"And in what city does House Nrel'tabra flourish?" the old woman asked, her eyes two black flames.

"Telnarquel," Iylinvyx replied, gracefully crossing two black-booted legs and lounging back in her chair.

"Ah, yes, the Hidden City—sought by many, and found by none. Many of our wisest explorers refuse to believe that it even exists."

" 'Our'?" the she-drow asked softly.

The old woman gave her a smile bereft of warmth and humor, and said, "All of us in this city obey Sarltan. Among other things, he strictly forbids us to reveal our true natures. I advise you to at least put up your cowl on your way to see him. I know not if he'll apply his dictates to outside traders. So far as I am aware, you are the first such to come here."

" 'On my way to see him'?" Iylinvyx echoed, reaching for her cowl.

The old woman nodded, her smile now a trifle more approving, and said, "Ask my doorswords to direct you to a private club called Blackmanacles, and there seek a man known as Daeraude. Tell him Yamaerthe sent you before you ask him how to find Sarltan—and keep your cowl up and those knives of yours out of sight. You might say those from below are cautious in Scornubel, and embrace cautious ways."

Iylinvyx Nrel'tabra nodded and let her cloak fall away to her elbows to let the four daggers slide down into waiting scabbards. She did not try to hide the dazzle of gems at her throat as she replied softly, "I had begun to notice that—and had also begun to wonder how far a people can stray from their true natures before they become that which they disdain."

The old woman stiffened behind her desk. She let out a hiss from between clenched teeth before she replied, "A pleasant night outside, is it not? I wish you every success in the conduct of your business in our fair city."

And with those words, the owner of Chasper's Trading Tower rose and let herself out through another door at the back of the room as fast as any charging warrior, but with considerably more grace than most.

Her visitor heard a heavy bolt clack into place an instant after the door closed, and acquired a thoughtful half smile as she gathered her cloak about herself and left the room, her cowl up.

＊　　＊　　＊

Iylinvyx Nrel'tabra was unsurprised to discover that she'd acquired a stealthy escort that increased in number by one pair of soft-booted feet for every person she was sent to after Daeraude: a corner lantern and candle seller, a lock storage keeper, and a master of "discretion guaranteed" hireswords, thus far.

"Well," she told the night air lightly, "at least I'm getting to see the glories of Scornubel."

According to her latest directions, the cobbled lane she was now traversing was Delsart's Drive, named for a long-ago wagon maker whose habit, when in his cups, was to race his latest creations along the winding lane at breakneck speed—with the inevitable consequences. Delsart's descendants owned the coach yard ahead on her right, and somewhere in the darkness to her left was Pelmuth's Draw, a narrow alley that would take her to a little lamp-lit courtyard, where among the businesses and their loitering doorswords she'd find a certain blue door . . . and somewhere beyond it (she didn't doubt complications awaited) was the elusive Sarltan.

The Draw, the lamp-lit court beyond, and the bored guardsmen were all as they'd been described to her. If her escort disliked her pauses in the alley to cast two spells, that was just too bad.

A mountain of a man was leaning against the blue door as she approached. He lowered the dagger he was using to clean his nails and rumbled, "Closed. Try elsewhere."

"I've been sent," the dark figure before him replied calmly, from within its cowl, "and would fain pass within—unless you can tell me another way to find Sarltan."

"Uh," the gigantic guard replied, in tones devoid of emotion, and extended one hand as he drew steel—a fearsome, much-scarred cleaver whose blade was thrice as broad as most swords—with the other. "I'll have yer sword—hilt first, mind."

"And if not?"

The guard shrugged. "Turn about and leave, or die. No exceptions."

The figure before him slowly opened its cloak and let it fall away. A shapely female drow stood before him, jewels glittering at her throat. Below their fire she wore a tight black leather tunic that left her shoulders bare, and thigh-high spike heeled boots.

"Not even for the likes of me?" she asked softly.

There was a stirring around the courtyard as guards at other doors shifted their positions to get a better look at this newcomer. The guard hefted his weapon as he let his eyes travel slowly from the crown of her head to her toes, then back again.

"I'll be having the sword and all of those daggers I see," he rumbled flatly. "Toss yer cloak down, and lay all yer steel in it—and I mean *all* yer steel. Now."

Their eyes met—black flames flaring into two chips of stone—and held in a long silence that was broken only by the softest of sounds from behind Iylinvyx Nrel'tabra. The various folk who'd been following her drifted out of the Draw and into the courtyard, one by one, and the doorswords turned alertly to face them. Silence had fallen again before the slender dark elf slowly cast down her cloak, laid her needle-slim short sword atop it, then followed it with a pair of daggers from her belt, another pair from her boot tops, and one from each wrist.

She paused then, buckling sheath straps, and the mountainous guard gestured with his drawn blade at the sheaths sewn into her tunic. "Them, too," he said. "*Especially* them—all four of them."

He'd never moved to see the two knives that rode below her shoulder blades, so tongues must have traveled across Scornubel faster than the route she'd been sent on. After holding his eyes for another long, cold time, the drow trader plucked out the black bladed quartet of daggers and casually let them fall onto the heap of edged steel. They landed without making a sound.

"Turn around," the guard rumbled, "and stand still." After Iylinvyx had—slowly—complied, he added, "Bend over forward and cast yer hair down. I need to see the back of yer neck."

The drow trader complied. As she stood bent over in the lamplight, her magesight awake, she felt the quiver she'd been expecting. Someone had cast a dispel upon her, stripping away the shielding spell she'd thoughtfully added. Most mages would now be defenseless, but her Shield of Azuth—a spell of her own creation—had nullified the dispel with its own death—leaving her aroused protective spells untouched beneath it. She straightened up after two long breaths and turned to face the guard with a challenge in her eyes.

"See enough of my behind?" she asked lightly.

The guard said nothing, and kept his face impassive and his eyes hard and cold. He wordlessly threw back a bolt in the top of the doorframe, too high for Iylinvyx or most humans to reach, and swung the door wide to let her pass within.

The drow trader strolled past him as if he wasn't there, and did not break stride when she heard the door close solidly behind her and the bolt slide back into place. She was in a lightless passage between two high rows of crates in a dank, lofty-ceilinged warehouse. The passage came to a dead end entirely walled in with stacked crates.

Iylinvyx Nrel'tabra looked calmly around, before asking the empty air, "And now, Sarltan?"

A voice that held a dry chuckle answered from somewhere atop the crates above her, "Not quite yet. That large crate to your right with the dragon's head label has a front that can be swung open."

Iylinvyx let silence fall, but her unseen informant did not seem inclined to be more talkative, so she did as she was asked. The crate proved to have no back. She looked through the little room it shaped, into an open, dark area beyond. On the floor of the crate was a snake. It hissed at her as she stepped unhesitatingly over it and out into what lay beyond: the back of the warehouse, in which two hard-eyed men stood, drawn swords in their hands. Their arms and shoulders bulged with the corded muscles built by hefting crates, kegs, and heavy coffers for years. They stepped forward in practiced unison as she emerged from the crate, so that she came to an abrupt halt with one sword point at her throat and the other almost touching her breast.

The drow trader looked coolly along each blade in turn. The one with his steel at her throat snarled, "Who sent you?"

"I think," Iylinvyx Nrel'tabra replied calmly, "you already know that. I also think that the fresh mushrooms I want to trade will have withered to dust before I even get to speak to Sarltan, if you delay me much longer. I did not come to Scornubel for a tour, or to play passwords-and-daggers-in-the-dark games. Conduct me to Sarltan, or let me return below—to dispense full descriptions of your *attentive* hospitality."

Her voice had remained soft and mild, but the two guards stiffened as if she'd snarled her words. They exchanged swift glances, and the one with his steel to the trader's breast jerked his head back over his shoulder in a clear signal.

In unison again, they stepped back from Iylinvyx, and waved with their swords at another door.

She nodded pleasant thanks and farewell to them, walked across dark and echoing emptiness, and opened the door wide.

Light flooded out. She was looking into a huge chamber built onto the warehouse, and well lit by a dozen hanging braziers. A balcony ran around its walls, supported by stout pillars to which were tacked many shipping orders. Burly loaders were striding about the room gathering small coffers and bundles into large travel crates and strongchests battered from much use.

In the center of this bustle stood a desk. A semicircle of armed men gathered behind it raised their heads to stare at her, but the fat and unlovely man seated at the desk kept his attention on the documents he was signing and tossing aside, or handing to a clerk with murmured comments.

Iylinvyx did not tarry at the door for another confrontation, but strode calmly across the room, shifting her hips smoothly to avoid hurrying loaders—several of whom stiffened, stared at her, then hastily dropped their gazes and resumed their work—until she came up to the desk. She ignored the stares of the armsmen (beyond noticing that several gave her gems more attention than her body) as she bent over the desk, planting both palms firmly atop the parchment the fat man was reading.

"Might you be Sarltan?" she asked pleasantly. "At last?"

Without looking up, the man replied heavily, "I might be—and I might also be the man who'll have your hands off at the wrists in a breath or two if you don't get them off my papers right now."

Iylinvyx Nrel'tabra left her hands right where they were. "Perhaps you can tell me when this Sarltan ascended the throne of Scornubel—and when, for that matter, our people conquered this city from the humans who still think they rule it."

The fat man raised his eyes to meet hers for the first time. "I am Sarltan. Who are you?"

"Iylinvyx, of House Nrel'tabra," she replied, "of the city of Telnarquel."

"And the head of your house is?"

"Anonymous by choice," the trader replied coolly.

Sarltan's eyes flickered and he asked, "What house rules in Telnarquel?"

"House Imbaraede."

"And when you kneel at altars, Iylinvyx Nrel'tabra, whom do you kneel to?"

"No one," the trader said quietly, "until a divine hand convinces me otherwise."

The next question came as swiftly as the others, but the fat man's voice was now like a cold, sharp knife. "What is your true shape, trader?"

The she-drow straightened up from the table and gestured down at herself. "What you see," she replied calmly.

A look of disgust momentarily twisted Sarltan's features, and he lifted one pudgy hand and almost lazily crooked his fingers in a signal. From somewhere in the busy room came the snap of a fired crossbow.

The trader with the gems at her throat never moved. Her easy smile remained unchanged even when the speeding war-quarrel struck something unseen just behind her left ear, shivered into dark splinters, and ricocheted away to clatter down some crates nearby.

"Velrult! Imber!" Sarltan snapped, his fingers moving in a sign.

Two of the armsmen charged around the desk, their blades sweeping up. The curvaceous trader smiled at them, tossing her head so as to look both warriors in the eye, in turn, ere they struck—but they never paused in their rushes, and plunged their blades low into Iylinvyx's belly, ripping savagely upward.

Their swords passed through the she-drow as if she was empty air, leaving her leather-clad curves unmarked. The force they'd put behind their attacks sent them staggering backward, helplessly off-balance.

Iylinvyx crossed her arms, scratched idly at one ear, and asked, "And what of you, fat man? What is your proper name—and what house do you serve?"

Sarltan was gaping at her, face paling, and he snapped, "Ressril!"

Another of the figures standing behind him obediently lifted his hands to shape a spell while the she-drow trader promptly took one of the staggering warriors by one elbow and his belt. She plucked him off his feet as if he were a child's rag doll and not a burly man two heads taller than her, and flung him bodily into Ressril who had time for one sharp cry before the back of his head cracked against the floorboards. The warrior's tumbling body bounced hard atop him.

"Sarltan," the drow trader purred as she leaned across the desk, "I asked you two questions. Don't keep me waiting."

One of her hands snaked to the back of her neck and came back with something unseen—something that stabbed down through the fat man's writing hand, pinning it to the desk as he shouted in startled pain.

Iylinvyx Nrel'tabra slapped Sarltan hard across the face, whipping his head around, then sprang over the desk to catch hold of his free, flailing hand. With iron strength she forced it down to the desk, wrenched her dagger free—then brought the blade smartly down again, transfixing both of Sarltan's crossed hands and driving her hitherto-invisible dagger into the desk to its quillons. Its magic made the blade flicker, flirting with invisibility, as the fat man screamed and his blood spattered wildly across the welter of papers.

"Just sit tight," Iylinvyx said jovially, patting Sarltan's shoulder. "I'm going to be rather busy for the next little while."

She shoved hard against him—evoking a fresh, raw scream of agony—to propel herself away from a glowing spear that someone was trying to thrust through her. Out of the corner of her eye she saw the fat man's bulk change, but could spare no time to watch him turn back into his true shape . . . and after all, she knew what that shape would be.

Angry men with drawn weapons were converging on her from all sides. Iylinvyx dodged around one, tripped another, and kicked out at the crotch of a third so viciously her leg boosted him over her shoulder into a face first encounter with the desk. Sarltan shrieked again and she won herself the room she needed to race forward. The she-drow landed with both knees together on the throat of the sprawled Ressril.

Bones cracked under Iylinvyx as she looked wildly around. She had to find and take down any other mages here as swiftly as she could, both to avoid spell duels she couldn't afford to fight with so many foes seeking her life, and to free any of these loaders who might be humans in spell-thrall and not drow wearing human guises.

Thralled humans or drow, the thirty-odd loaders all seemed both enraged at her, and to have found weapons. Her ironguard spell wouldn't last forever. That glowing spear could pierce the magical defense the spell provided and hurt her as much as any other enchanted weapons. She couldn't be sure how many in the small armory now thrusting and hacking at her from all sides carried such blades.

Large, sweaty bodies smashed into her and sent her reeling. Fists came at her in a rain that soon had her ducking through the limp legs of the tall, handsome— and currently senseless—drow Sarltan had turned out to be. She ducked into the knee space of the desk. There she snatched the few moments she needed to snatch out the one magical ring she'd brought with her from its pocket in her bodice, draw it onto her finger, and let fly with her first burst of magic missiles.

Blue bolts streaked into faces that swiftly withdrew and Iylinvyx rolled hastily back out from under the desk in the wake of her spell. Clawing her way around Sarltan, she used him as a shield against whoever might be leaping down on her from atop the desk—and there was just such a bright and enthusiastic fellow. The drow trader ducked away from the sword in his left hand as he crashed into her. She let him tumble head-long into some of her other foes, jabbing ineffectually at her with a dagger in his right hand that just wouldn't reach. She was skidding helplessly along the rough floorboards at the time, so this was a good thing.

Some of the loaders still hadn't realized metal blades simply passed harmlessly through her. Their brutal but ineffectual thrusts allowed her to roll past them, or to barrel hard into their ankles and trip them. She emerged on the far side of one toppling giant of a man, wincing at the crash he made bouncing on his face on the floor, and found herself with room to scramble up and run.

More men or drow-men were appearing in the doorway she'd come in by, shouting enthusiastically. Over to her left was a stair up to the balcony—a height currently echoing with the clatter of men cranking the windlasses of their crossbows like mad-wits, their quarrels meant for her.

Iylinvyx Nrel'tabra sprinted toward the stair, skidding in her spike heeled boots as she ducked under an axe—for who could tell when one might be magical, in all this chaos of unleashed Art?—then spun around to avoid someone trying to tackle her.

Someone else then drove a sword through a friend while trying to reach her. Amid the groans she ran at and over a lone, scared loader who stood uncertainly at the bottom of the stair. Heads bobbed up here and there along the balcony, seeking the darting she-drow below, and Iylinvyx drove her dagger into the throats of two men before any of the crossbowmen even realized she was up on the balcony.

The third fell with a volley of missiles from the ring surging into his face, and the fourth flung down his unloaded bow and tried to drag out his sword. The drow trader put her head down and crashed into him, sending him sprawling back into the bowman behind him. They fell together and Iylinvyx pounced on them, driving her dagger down twice. That left just one man on the balcony. He took one look at the diminutive drow smiling at him as she rose from the bodies of two men whose blood was dripping from her arm right up to the elbow, and vaulted over the balcony railing, shouting in fear.

Iylinvyx wasted no time in gloating, but spun around and scooped up two bows that were cocked tight but not yet loaded. As she felt around her feet for the spilled quarrels, she peered narrowly at the loaders below as they gathered both weapons and courage, and streamed toward the balcony stair. Were any hanging back, lifting their hands to cast—?

Ah, yes. *There.*

The drow mage masquerading as a man didn't see her quarrel coming until it was almost upon him. By then he had time only to choke, gurgle, and be carried along by it as it slammed into his throat and carried him over a heap of small coffers. His feet kicked once, then went limp.

The drow trader peered around the room below once more as she plucked up the second bow, but saw no other mages. She turned and put a quarrel into the face of the foremost man charging at her along the balcony. He spun around and the second man stumbled over him. She sent a stream of missiles from her ring into the face of the third as she launched herself at the stumbling man and smashed the pommel of her dagger into his face. He fell over with a groan, and Iylinvyx drove her blade into his neck twice as she crouched, facing the rest of the charge.

It was proceeding with decidedly less enthusiasm now. The individual drow were either accustomed to danger or not, but they had all seen one small, unarmored female slay almost half of them in a bewilderingly short time. The same foe now stood unhurt and unabashed, giving them a grin full of the promise of death as she strolled calmly forward along the blood-stained balcony to meet them.

More than one warrior in the ranks packed along the balcony had a sudden desire to be somewhere—anywhere—else. There was a momentary, jostling confusion during which Iylinvyx calmly picked up the last cocked crossbow, loaded it, and put its quarrel through one eye of the largest man on the balcony. There were mutters of fear and alarm, and more turmoil.

When a stinging volley of missiles from the drow trader's ring struck at the faces of several men, there was a sudden, shouting move to retreat. Blows were struck, with fists and bared blades, there among the drow of Scornubel.

✳   ✳   ✳

Bruised and winded, Helbondel crouched back against the wall as the first shouting cowards thundered back down the steps past him. Black rage threatened to choke him even more than the blood welling up from where a hard elbow had driven him to bite his own cheek. He threw back his head and called on Vhaeraun for aid. The vicious madness that too often seized a priestess of the Spider Queen—and she *must* be a follower of Lolth, else why would Sarltan have challenged her so?—now threatened to destroy another triumph of the People, the greatest grip on the riches of the Sunlit World yet achieved by the Faithful of Vhaeraun. It is as the wisest elder holy ones say: the poisonous touch of the Spider Queen despoils and ruins wherever it reaches.

She must be destroyed! he thought. Whatever foul battle magic she was using to overcome veteran warriors, letting her slay like a snake striking at will in a nest of baby rodents, must be brought low.

Helbondel clutched his most precious magic—an amulet touched by the God himself, twisted forever into fire-scarred ruin from its former bright magnificence— and called up a magic to shatter all magics. It wouldn't last long or reach far, and it might mean his death, but if it pleased holy Vhaeraun. . . .

A drow warrior, dying with a sword through his pelvis, stumbled backward and fell heavily over the crouching priest. The blade projecting out of his buttocks was driven down into Helbondel's neck with all of the warrior's weight behind it, and the priest could hardly vomit forth the blood choking him for all of the shuddering and convulsing his body tried to accomplish. Writhing and thrashing against the stone wall, he died never seeing the human guises of loaders all over the warehouse melt away—or the accursed priestess dealing death to them change as well, into something else. . . .

*　　　*　　　*

The slender form of Iylinvyx Nrel'tabra boiled up like smoke, amid a grunt of constricted discomfort and a sudden loud tearing of well stitched seams. A tall, broad-shouldered human woman stood grimly on the balcony amid the ruins of split boots and a rent leather tunic, her silver hair stirring around her as if blown by its own wayward breeze.

She looked down at the tattered scraps of her clothing and kicked off the painfully pinching remnants of her boots. The last handful of drow warriors on the balcony stared at her, open-mouthed—then fled.

Dove Falconhand, free of her she-drow disguise, vaulted over the balcony rail to land in their path, snatched up the body of a fallen warrior, and swung it like a club. Her first blow missed, but her second smashed the foremost drow into insensibility. The impact didn't numb her fingertips quite enough to keep her from feeling the shock of breaking bones.

Another warrior lunged at her in desperate fury, but caught his blade in the corpse she was holding. He let it fall in his frantic haste to flee. Dove swept up a fallen sword and hurled it, hard, at the back of his head. He fell without a sound, leaving her facing just two drow.

She gave them a smile, and pointed at an open, empty crate nearby. "Want to live?" she asked. "Then get in."

They looked at her, then at the crate, then back at her. Dove nodded at the crate, and softly repeated the words she'd earlier said to Sarltan: "Don't keep me waiting."

They gave her fearful looks and scrambled into the crate in almost comical haste. Dove took two long strides through the sprawled dead, plucked up the lid of the crate, and tossed it down into place. A black sword blade promptly thrust up through it. She grinned, hefted a full—and very heavy—crate from a pile nearby, and hurled it onto the sword. There was a rending scream of wood, cries of fear, and the laden crate settled a foot or so down into the box that now housed the drow. The heavier crate would continue to sink onto them until someone cut the drow a way out through the buckled sides of their improvised prison.

Dove looked around at all the carnage and sighed. "I sometimes wish," she told the empty chamber bitterly, "that dark elves knew some other way to settle disputes than with swords. Drinking contests, say, or just tossing dice . . . anything to keep them from thinking through all sides of a dispute, and trying to come to a levelheaded agreement."

She turned, and added briskly, "Now to the unfinished task at hand. Sarltan?"

Silence was her reply.

"Sarltan?"

Dove sighed again and picked her way across the room . . . only to come to a grim halt near the desk. Sarltan was still sprawled across it, his crossed hands pinned down by her dagger—but he was quite dead. His head had lolled back to stare at the ceiling, freed to do so by the gaping slash in his throat. Blood had flowed like a river down him to the floor, and flies were already gathering around its stickiness.

One of his fellow drow had cut Sarltan's throat during the fight and a sickening tingling in the lady ranger's fingertips told her that something else had been done to seal his eternal silence.

Dove peered at the sprawled, no-longer-handsome body without approaching more closely. It wasn't long before she saw the hilt of a knife protruding from Sarltan's thigh. She waved her arm nearer to it, and felt a coldness in the air. Her lips tightened. No wonder her hitherto-invisible dagger could be seen quite clearly now: someone had driven a dead-magic-bladed knife through Sarltan to forestall any magic used to try to learn things from his corpse.

Sarltan was never going to tell her anything about the invasion of Scornubel from below. There were drow in the city who knew or had guessed why she was here, and wanted to keep the cloak of secrecy around their deeds. Sarltan's murderer had probably fled during the fray, so there was no point in trying to fool other drow into thinking this battle was an internal feud that should goad them into seeking revenge on their fellow drow for kin fallen here.

In fact, it was probably a safe prediction that the Underdark city of Telnarquel, abandoned by the drow decades ago, would be visited by certain dark elf avengers in the months to come. She hoped the alhoon who'd recently taken up abode there would give the drow war parties a suitably warm reception.

All the drow she'd seen here in their own forms were male . . . what did that mean?

Dove threw up her hands. She didn't know enough about the dark elves to even guess.

Well, a drow deception might be impossible, but the Rolling Wheel had been full of humans—true humans. Dressed as she currently was and playing the role of tearful escaped captive desiring a rescue for friends in drow clutches, she could easily lure a crowd of angry armed men here in time to see thirty-odd dead drow before anyone could clean it all up. A little widespread merchants' wariness in the Caravan City would slow ambitious drow plans for a season or two.

Someone should dispose of the magic-dead knife, but it would have to be someone else—say, one of the men she'd try to lure here. With the gods alone knowing how many drow still lurked in human guises in Scornubel, and a small but undoubtedly growing number of them planning to strike back at the trader who'd slain so many of their fellows, she needed to get far away from that magic-dead dagger—and fast.

Dove turned and padded barefoot back toward the blue door where she hoped a certain hulking guard was still on duty, all unwitting of what was about to befall him.

On the first threshold she looked back at the dead drow sprawled all over the warehouse. It did not take quick wits to arrive at the judgment that Dove Falcon-hand of the Chosen had made a right mess of *this* little meddling. It was time to call in an expert on dark elves.

"Ah, Mirt," she told the darkness with a sad sigh, as she reached for the handle on the inside of the blue door, "you were wrong. Perhaps I need to retire with Blaskar to Neverwinter. I wasn't half so clever a bitch as I needed to be, this time."

Qilué
Dark Dancer, Bright Dance

It was in the years after the Time of Troubles when Those Who Harp first truly became aware that one of the dark elf ladies who danced betimes under the moon perilously close to fair Waterdeep was the long-hidden Seventh Sister. Certain individuals given to embracing less noble purposes learned this too; some of them haven't recovered even yet.

Abranthar "Twoquills" Foraeren
from *I Harp As I See It*
published circa the Year of the Sword

"Holy Lady, hear us," the drow priestess whispered, embracing the Ladystone. As her silken-smooth, jet-black flesh ground against its rough flanks, the enchantments upon it carried her soft voice clearly to the ears of every dancer in the glade. "We dance this night in thy honor, to dedicate Ardeep to thee!"

The sacred needle of rock flashed forth a sudden bright blue radiance, as if touched by moonlight. In a silent display that brought gasps of awe from the dark elf dancers, will-o'-wisps of magic rose blue and white from the fern-girt ground. They hung spinning softly amid the trees of Ardeepforest, all around the glade where the dark elves danced.

A human watching them—had anyone dared to venture into Ardeep when such weird glows were leaping and winking through its dark trees—would have seen a ring of short, slim, yet curvaceous women, so graceful that they seemed almost to float above the dew-drenched grass. The priestess embracing the standing stone at the center of the ring was the tallest among them. All of the drow were unclad, their obsidian black skin glistening with sweat in the moonlight. All of them had swirling, unbound white hair, large and dark eyes, and the pointed ears that cried "elf!" to any human. They danced in fearless exultation, looking like bold and dangerous black flames moving under the watching moon.

"Oh, sisters," Qilué Veladorn cried, spreading her arms in exultation. "Eilistraee hears us, and approves! Eilistraee—*is with us!*"

She pointed up into the sky, the sweat on her bare limbs glistening in the light of the breast-high stone she embraced, and burst into tears of joy. The eyes of the other she-drow in the glade followed her pointing hand to see shadowy radiance building in the dark, overcast sky. Scatters of starlight were shaping the arms and shoulders of a graceful, gigantic figure. Its face was turned from them, its arms raised like those of their high priestess.

Slender, starry arms reached to the clouds, and spectral fingers plucked at the unbroken celestial ceiling of racing grayness. With a deep rumbling that shook the forest and the back teeth of the faithful of Eilistraee, throwing the few who hadn't yet knelt to their knees, the goddess pulled apart the clouds. She laid bare a wide eye of clear and starry sky and let down moonlight to set the old forest of Ardeep alight.

The drow priestesses sobbed as one, awe and joy almost overwhelming them. Qilué ground herself against the Ladystone as if riding a lover, tearing her flesh against it so as to shed her blood in thanks. It took more and more frenzied effort to do this as the years passed and the surface of the Ladystone wore smooth under the devotions of the faithful, but at that moment Qilué would not have cared if one of the cruel priests of Vhaeraun with his whip of sword blades had assailed her until his arm hung too tired to strike once more. Eilistraee had come to them, torn asunder the shroud of the heavens for them, and her favor still shone on them, even though the starry form of the goddess herself had now faded. Qilué covered the Ladystone with kisses and wept like a child.

From the stone, down the ribbons of blood that laced her legs, blue lightning of divine power snarled forth to play about the glade like joyous fireflies. The high priestess arched over backward, then let herself fall, but never touched the ground.

As the lightning shocked the ring of priestesses into song, then into senselessness, plucking them up to float and drift above the trampled ferns of the glade like so many wisps of moonlit cloud, Qilué floated on her back above them all, arms and legs spread like a star. The glory of the goddess coursed through her like living moonlight, and even in distant Waterdeep, men on the walls murmured at the beautiful light in the forest and pointed, and called their comrades up to see.

✳   ✳   ✳

It seemed that she had been somewhere wonderful for a very long time, and was sad to leave it. Qilué wept as if her heart would break. She slowly became aware that she was lying on her back in the center of a glade that should have been cold, with the stars glittering in the clear night sky above her, but somehow wasn't. Little motes of frost like trapped stars glistened amid the ferns touching her, yet the spring night was too warm for frost.

The high priestess of Eilistraee rose on unsteady feet, stared down at the snowy outline of her body in wonder, and in a sort of daze realized that the blood was gone from her legs. The raw scrapes that the Ladystone had dealt her were gone as if they'd never been. She fought back fresh tears, and looked up through the glimmering they made to see all her priestesses standing in their ring watching her, delight and anticipation on their faces.

She shook her head at them, barely able to speak, and managed to gasp, "Ah, sisters—*dance!*"

As if her words had cried a battle charge, the faithful threw themselves into the air, obsidian limbs shaping beauty. Qilué cried out in new wonder. Through the glory of the goddess, the priestesses were dancing on air, their feet no longer touching the ground. Leaps and pirouettes ended in descents of slow grace, not the usual swift, hard landings. As their chant climbed into song, their voices were at once magnified and yet kept soft, echoing away under the glowing trees of lost and fallen Ardeep.

Her heart full—could one person *know* this much joy, and yet live?—Qilué Veladorn looked up at the winking stars and sobbed her thanks to the goddess for this one night of mystery added to all her other kindnesses. Then she threw herself up into the air and into the dance, never noticing the small motes of light that trailed her lithe limbs.

A slow, faint music seemed to awaken around them. Qilué first became aware of it when she found herself shaping her movements to a rhythm that was not her own, yet seemed so right. She forced herself away from exulting in the dance, and being only aware of the dance, to look around with alertness and alarm in case this awakened power was a threat. Hers was the responsibility, as well as the glory; she was the guardian of the faithful, as well as their leader, and though what she could feel seemed friendly, it was not of Eilistraee.

For a moment it seemed as if Ardeepforest was turning slowly under her, spinning with the rising dance. Might they be calling up something, releasing some power long slumberous here? Qilué looked all around as her limbs carried her in wide circles in the air, and saw something beyond the familiar dark figures of the faithful. There were other dancers. Their forms were more shadowy than her sisters in faith, though they were bathed in the pulsing blue light under the trees, where their bodies should have been boldly lit and clearly seen . . .

If they'd had solid bodies.

Emotion caught at Qilué's throat as she spun and whirled under the stars, realizing that she was looking upon the ghosts of the elves of Ardeep, moonwraiths risen in this hollow to join in the dance of Eilistraee. These great ladies who'd perished here in younger days, had somehow been called back this night to honor the dance of elven folk whose skins were black and hotly hated by living elves.

Qilué knew she was crying again, pouring out awe and sorrow and at the same time trying to hold to the thought that there might be peril. These spirits might be some sort of magic gathering itself to expel or destroy the drow who dared to dance where fairer elves had lived, laughed, and lain fallen beneath the damp, dark soil. Qilué watched, holding herself apart from the rapture enough to bear witness to anything that might befall here before dawn brought them down exhausted to earth, and any blundering human forester with a knife could have his pick of sprawled obsidian bodies— or slay them all with a score of ruthless thrusts.

Her sisters in faith had seen the dancing spirits now and were calling to each other, even weaving among the moonshades, peering to see ghostly faces the better and match gaits and grace with the fallen. Qilué let herself rise higher above the center of the glade, up to where arching branches reached in toward her, the better to see it all.

It seemed wondrous, a crowning grace on this night of mystery, and yet . . . and yet . . .

"Oh, Lady Mystra, curse me not with your misgivings, your suspicions," she told the night air as she danced. "Let me be lost in holy Eilistraee this one night, unstained!"

She had one clear moment of nothing but dancing after that—before Reshresma screamed.

The song died in shattered notes, like a Sembian chandelier crashing onto a tiled floor. Amid its clangor the drow priestesses crashed to the earth, crumpled ferns making a crunching chorus. The light under the trees winked out, and the moonwraiths could be seen sinking slowly back down, like forlorn tongues of silver flame, into the darkness.

All but one of them: the one Reshresma had brushed against and found to be solid and real. The one her frantic slash of true sight, augmented by the power of all the dancing drow, had revealed to be no elf lady at all, but a human woman.

A human woman Qilué knew, who now stood calmly amid a hissing, tightening ring of furious drow, her bare skin curves of ivory among their darkness. Long silver hair played about the shoulders of the intruder, as if with a life of its own. She stood gravely watching the sharp nails of the drow women close in on her. Those nails would tear away her very life, if Qilué did nothing. A little coldness deep within her wanted to do nothing but watch the slaughter.

The high priestess of Eilistraee ducked her head down and drew in a deep, shuddering breath. "Forgive me my weakness, goddesses both," she whispered hoarsely, then called on the power of the Ladystone.

A bright bolt of force flowed out of her, shocking the faithful into turning to face her. Into the stillness she'd thus created, Qilué said softly, "For shame, sisters, to turn the glory we have felt here this night to anger and violence. I had thought we were followers of Eilistraee, not Vhaeraun the Sly Savage or Lolth the Tyrant Poisoner . . . nor had I hitherto detected any leanings in you toward Tempus the Butcher, or any of the other blood-drenched human gods. Now be still, and be ashamed, until we can uncover the truth of this intrusion. Has not the Holy Lady of the Dance shown us wonders in plenty this night? Who among us is wise enough to say, before we look and learn, that this is not another such, sent to us in divine purpose?"

Without a murmur her priestesses fell back. First one, then another went to her knees, leaving the human standing alone at the center of their ring.

Qilué strode forward to meet her and said, "Sister Dove, this coming was not well timed."

Dove Falconhand inclined her head gravely. "I blunder to you because I have blundered already, elsewhere, and need your aid." She looked around at the black, glaring faces upturned to hers and added, "I cry apology to all here, and holy Eilistraee, too, if I have offended. I did not mean to mock holy observances."

"Did not mean to mock?" one of the faithful snarled. "And yet you came dancing among us?"

"I love to dance," Dove said simply, "and have few enough chances to do so."

There were murmurs—some of them of grudging approval, or at least understanding—at those words, then several voices rose at once in fresh anger, and Qilué snapped, "Be *still*, sisters! You rage at intrusion, then shout and snarl in the very glade where we worship? Thus, then, do you revere the Holy Lady?"

In the moment of stillness that followed, Dove said gently, "I would have peace between us. How may I achieve it?"

There were stirrings, and urgent faces turned to Qilué, but none quite dared gainsay the fresh command of the high priestess. It was left to her alone to say, "I will be able to give answer to that when I know why you've come. Seeking me, so much is obvious, but what aid of mine do you seek?"

Before Dove could reply, one of the kneeling priestesses spat, "Qilué! How can you even entertain a request from a human? It gives her control over you— a human hand upon the holy power bestowed by divine Eilistraee! How can you sin so?"

The air was very still, yet it sang in their ears, as every kneeling dark elf in the glade strained to hear the slightest sound their high priestess might make in reply.

Qilué turned her head, looked down sadly at the panting, almost sobbing priestess, and said, "Veltheera, did you learn *nothing* from that time a wizard of Waterdeep burst in on our dance? I am Eilistraee's, and yet I am also Mystra's, seventh of the Seven Sisters."

She took a pace forward, and seemed taller, and darker.

"And know this, all of you," she continued, "I take orders from none of the Seven, nor they from me. Dove has come to beg a favor of me—and you want to slay her for it. I ask again: is it our Holy Lady of the Dance you serve, or a darker, bloodier god?"

In the silence that followed her words, Qilué made a soft blue flame of moonlight rise from her palm, and over its flickering light said in quieter, almost casual tones, "So, Dove, what's befallen?"

Dove drew in a deep breath, looked around at the kneeling priestesses, and said, "I've come from the human city of Scornubel, five days' ride or so south and east of here. It is a place of caravans, always a little lawless . . . and now home to many, many drow. These dark elves are wearing human spell-guises, and acting at—practicing—being human. I need to know why, and what's become of the humans whose shapes they wear, and what their intentions are . . . and to do that properly, without a lot of bloodshed, I need a drow to do it."

"And what is that to *us*, human," another priestess spat, "if some surface city is taken over by our kind? Are not dark elves worthy of even a tiny corner of the sunlight? You dare to call on the holiest among us to come running at your behest, to snoop and spy? Tell me, human, by what twisted thoughts do you conclude that we might, just possibly, be deluded into aiding you?"

Dove leaned over to look her questioner full in the face, and said flatly, "Dark elves are masters of magic, and Mystra bids me nurture magic wherever I find it. Humans are the most populous and energetic users of magic . . . and even I cannot nurture the dead. I want to keep alive all the drow *and* all the humans I can by avoiding the wars, and drow-hunts, and fresh feuds and hatreds that will come of humans learning too late that one of their cities has been taken over by dark elves. The humans you rightfully distrust will rise to arms in their fear and hatred to obliterate Scornubel, all drow they find, and anything else up and down the Sword Coast that they can call 'drow,' or 'friend of drow.' Lady priestess, I want to save your *children*. Help me a little."

Hands went to mouths here and there, and Qilué saw tears streaming down more than one face, but another of the faithful screamed, "Words. *Words! Those* are the deadliest weapons humans use against us, and all others. Clever words, to cloak the evils they work in fair seeming . . . until it's too late, and another dwarven realm or elven grove or drow city lies in ruins, gone forever, and the shining-eyed humans swarm on to tear down the *next* obstacle to their absolute rule and mastery."

"*Yes*," someone else hissed fiercely.

Before Qilué could utter a sound, black lightning stabbed from slender obsidian fingers, wreathing the human woman in ravening magic—magic that clawed, and blazed, then fell away in futility.

"Please," Dove said gently, "don't start this. I—"

"You can *die*, human!" another priestess— Ierembree—shrieked as the spell she'd just worked brought her favorite dagger into her hand. She sprang up like a boiling bolt of darkness to drive her blade hilt-deep into the belly of this tall, beautiful, insolent human who so profaned holy ground that . . . that . . .

Thoughts failed her, and in mindless fury Ierembree drove her blade deep again and again, her knuckles slamming home against hard-muscled flesh each time, for all the world as if the human were made of air that her blade could not touch. She stared down at her clean blade in horror, and at the unmarked body of her foe, then gentle fingers closed around her wrist, blue-white in the moonlight.

"Eilistraee is not the only power in Toril to teach magic to mortals, you know," Dove said.

Ivory limbs enfolded the drow priestess Ierembree in an embrace, a seemingly tender cradling that held firm despite kicks and bites—bites that did draw blood, more than one faithful noticed eagerly—and raking fingernails. A roar arose amid the faithful, and obsidian bodies lunged to their feet, reaching—

"Stay *back*, sisters," Qilué cried, "or face the full fury of Eilistraee!"

Dark elf limbs froze in mid-surge as their owners stared at the nimbus of bright white fire that now encircled Qilué's upraised hands. There was more than one whimper as the drow settled back onto their knees.

In their midst, Ierembree's ebony-black limbs struggled on against Dove's unmoving ivory ones. The watching faithful were startled to hear soft human cooing, as a mother might use to soothe a child, and to see human hands stroking the flesh trembling in their grasp. Dove kissed the top of her attacker's head, then lifted the dark elf priestess gently into the air until their faces were level, and kissed the snarling lips before hers.

The raging priestess shrieked, spat into Dove's face, then tried to bite her lips and nose, but Dove's gentle smile never changed. When her panting captive grew weary, she bent her head forward until their foreheads touched.

Ierembree tried to twist her face away from the contact, her features still contorted in hatred and fury. She stiffened, and her eyes opened wide in amazement.

Amid the kneeling faithful, someone whispered, "Sorcery!"

They saw the priestess turn to look at the human so close to her with no fury left in her face. Ierembree managed a tentative, tremulous smile, then she relaxed in Dove's arms, and they hugged each other as if they were long-lost friends.

The human set the dark elf down and stroked her shoulder with one last gentle caress. The priestess seemed to be struggling to say something, but could find no words.

Dove drew away from her, murmuring, "I must go now—but I'll return, Ierembree, and we'll talk more. Much more."

She turned and swept Qilué into a similar embrace, heedless of the white fire of deadly magic raging in her sister's hands and splashing down around her.

"Sister," the faithful heard the human say, "Go to Scornubel if you can, walking your own road. I must leave that city. My usefulness there is at an end. My very presence is making the surviving dark elves lie low."

Dove turned to the kneeling priestesses and said, "Farewell, all of you."

Before any of the bewildered faithful could frame a reply, the human strode a few paces into the glade and inclined her head to the Ladystone. Its response was a sudden pulse of blue radiance, a silent winking brighter than the sacred stone had shone in years. In awed silence the faithful watched the human walk away through the trees to where she'd shed her clothes. Dove took them up in a bundle, and walked on through the darkness of the wood until they could see her no more.

A moment later, as if freed from spell-thrall, the priestesses were all on their feet and talking at once, crowding around Ierembree.

"What did she do to you?" one of them demanded.

"Watch her," another said grimly. "If the human took over her wits . . ."

Ierembree threw back her head and laughed. "Stop it, all of you!" She smiled at Qilué over their heads, and told them all, "Her name is Dove, and she did nothing to my wits except give me love . . . the love of a friend who'll stand by me." She shook her head in bemusement, and added, "More than that, she *showed* me she meant it . . . and what she truly is. Mind to mind; no lying."

She smiled, stretched like a contented cat, and added, "No, Sharala, I'm not crazed. I'm . . . happy."

Ierembree turned to the high priestess, who stood like a dark shadow watching them all, and said, "I was in awe of you before, Lady of the Dance. I—I don't know how to say how much I revere you now . . . a sister of such a lady as Dove . . . and one whom Dove turns to for aid."

She started to kneel, but Qilué strode forward to snatch her upright again, whirled her into an embrace, and growled, "I'll kiss and cuddle just this once, mind. I'm not the caressing whirlwind certain of my sisters are!"

She turned in Ierembree's arms, and put out a hand to touch the priestess who'd railed against the clever words of humans.

"Llansha," she said formally, "the lead in the dance is yours. Raise your voice too much on the second chant and flames will burst from your arms; they go if you hurl fire at something. As you heard, I've work to do, and must leave you for a time."

"Leave us?" another of the faithful asked angrily. "To settle some human problem by slaying our kind?"

"Thalaera," Qilué replied in a voice of warning iron, as another tense silence fell around them. "I live to serve. Two goddesses birthed me and guide me. I see a little of how they view Faerûn, where you cannot. Trust me in this as I trust you with a part of my service for a time, to go and do other service that is needful. If you doubt me, curl yourself around the Ladystone to sleep tonight, pray to Eilistraee for judgment upon me, and learn your answer."

Thalaera stared at the sacred stone then back at the high priestess, her eyes large with fear, and Qilué added gently, "Yes, do that. I mean this not as a challenge, but to set your mind at ease as to my loyalties. Learn the truth."

Thalaera looked back at the Ladystone again. Her eyes narrowed. "Will I be maimed?"

Qilué shook her head. "Hurt, perhaps; maimed, no."

"Hurt?"

"Truths have sharp edges. Learning the truth often hurts."

Qilué strode out of the glade, the other faithful following in her wake. She turned at the edge of the trees to look back at the fearful Thalaera, and added, "I'll return after dawn, briefly, before I go south to Scornubel."

The priestess bowed her head in reply, and the faithful watched her turn and slowly approach the Ladystone, her steps reluctant and trembling.

In utter silence she reached forth one hand to touch it, and they saw her shudder and sag at the knees. Almost instinctively she clasped her arms around it, her eyes closed—and the Ladystone flashed out blue fire as it had done for Dove.

Thalaera's gasp was loud in the silence. Qilué stood watching her for a moment, then turned and said briskly, "To bed."

Dark limbs around her stirred into motion again, but several priestesses still stood staring into the glade, watching cold fire running along Thalaera's limbs in her trembling embrace of the stone.

"To bed, all of you," Qilué said sharply. "There's much to do tomorrow."

She looked up at the stars then, as the faithful began to move, and sighed. Only Ierembree, whose arms were still linked with hers, heard Qilué add in a whisper, "There's always much to do tomorrow."

✳ ✳ ✳

The stumble spilled not a drop, but displeased Namra, who seemed to be in a foul mood this morning. What right had Isryl to be so cheerful, after the beating she'd been given last night?

"Clumsy wench!"

The merchant's wife lashed out at the servant girl with all the strength in her arm, swinging her walking stick like a buggy whip. Isryl jumped as metal-shod wood cracked across her shoulder blades. The glasses on her tray chimed against one another musically. It was little surprise that she stumbled again, but her lady master saw no reason not to strike out once more.

Beatings obviously did humans a world of good. They'd left Isryl groaning in the darkness, her bared back wet with blood and afire with crisscrossing welts . . . and found her this morning humming and striding along with a spring in her step, her eyes obediently downcast, but a little smile on her lips. Why, she was smiling *now!*

"Mock my authority, will you?" Namra snarled, lurching forward to land a fury of blows on the servant girl.

Isryl half turned in their midst so that glasses flew and decanters toppled. Her lady master drew breath for a shriek of rage at this carelessness—and that was when Isryl calmly flung the silver tray and all into Namra's face.

Blinded and half choked, Namra staggered back, spitting out stinging wine. Firm hands seized her chin and held it immobile with steely strength. A cool forehead touched hers and the world exploded as if all glasses, everywhere, had burst at once, their shards tumbling down into darkness.

As Namra's stout body went to the floor, the slender servant girl moved with it, keeping their brows together. This moment had been well chosen. No one else was in this end of the house just now, and the girl who was not Isryl needed only a minute or so for this grimmest of stealing spells.

When she lifted her head from the stocky body of her lady master, Isryl's slender form had already begun to change. She tugged off her gown and carry-sash in frantic haste, then set to work with strong and eager fingers to acquire the clothing of her lady master, rolling the senseless Namra over like so much meat on a kitchen board. The fat woman's form was melting, too, her skin growing dark and more shapely, her features delicate and elfin . . . but no change could strip away the tiny wisps of smoke drifting from her staring eyes, or the thin ribbon of drool flowing from one slack corner of her mouth.

Qilué was not gentle. The real Isryl had been more dead than alive this morning. It had taken three healing potions to get her well enough to walk, and the Harper agent she'd been delivered to had still winced and clucked disapprovingly at the girl's battered appearance.

This cow under her hands had done that . . . this cow who'd now slumped fully back into her drow form. Qilué herself now looked like fat, lazy, embittered Namra Dunseltree, wife of Inder Dunseltree of Softer Tapestries fame. Qilué finished tying and adjusting Namra's over-jeweled, none-too-clean clothing around herself, satisfying herself in a mirror that she looked every bit as haughty and nasty as her predecessor in the role. She plucked up the walking stick to strike a pose, then danced back to the senseless, drooling drow. Qilué bound her hand and foot with the gown and carry-sash, then cast a careful spell.

The body vanished under her hands, and she knew it would now be lying in the midst of the glade in Ardeep, with Llansha, Veltheera—and Thalaera—staring disapprovingly down at the new arrival, wondering how many spells and how much gentling would be needed to make it sane once more.

Qilué sighed, shrugged, and stepped forward, every haughty inch Namra Dunseltree. Her mindtouch magic had earned her only the most superficial and uppermost of the disguised drow's thoughts. To learn more would have taken days of careful and continuous probing. If she'd tried for much more, much faster, her victim—and she knew that "victim" would then have been very much the right word—would have gone quickly and irrevocably insane, losing forever in mental chaos the very memories and knowledge Qilué sought.

What Qilué did know was that the cruel drow was Anlaervrith Mrantarr, a lazy novitiate into the worship of Lolth. She was a drow of humble birth and no particular accomplishments, who'd been quite happy to leave her subterranean city. Qilué had been unable to learn the name of that city, though she'd gained some mind pictures of it made vivid by fear and hatred. Anlaervrith had left there for a chance at betterment and adventure. To that end she'd dealt with a drow sorceress—not a priestess, but able to pose at will as such—who called herself simply "Daerdatha."

Anlaervrith was to wear the shape Daerdatha put her into after the human Namra Dunseltree had been "removed," and to act, speak, and live as Namra had done, as communicated in mind messages Daerdatha had thrust—Qilué would almost have said "burned"— into Anlaervrith's brain.

Qilué's lips twisted in disgust, and she gave the nearest bellpull an angry jerk. The lazy cow had jumped at vague promises of freedom from the rule of Lolth or decadent nobles. She was told tales of a vast and splendid new world where everyone who had half their wits about them could wallow in endless prosperity. These promises were made by someone deliberately mysterious, who wore a succession of spell-spun, false faces—someone

Anlaervrith hadn't even knowingly seen since taking up her role as Namra. She suspected—idly, not really caring—that some of the merchants whom her husband showed around their house were disguised drow not merely playing their own roles, but somehow keeping an eye on her.

All Anlaervrith had really cared about was that Namra didn't have to work, or skimp on food, wine, and clothing, and that she had plenty of servants that she could mistreat to her heart's content. The stablemen even included a well-muscled few whom she planned to get to know intimately. Anlaervrith had been both fascinated and repelled by the crude size and stink of humans.

Qilué frowned. When Anlaervrith thought of pleasure, she thought of warm, hearty good meals—and plenty them—and of having so many gems she could bathe in them, slithering around nude in their cool, hard beauty. She also thought of flogging servants and reducing them to tears or to obvious fear, and—older memories, these—of watching the bared, sweat-slick bodies of drow warriors as they limbered up for weapons practice. And, just lately, she thought of sugared pastries and biscuits, and of sweetened cream.

She did not think of Namra's cold and distant husband, whose face flickered with disgust at the very sight of her, or of the sadistic drow—whose name she didn't even know—now impersonating him. As for dreams of the future, Anlaervrith had none beyond endless indulgences. This drow, at least, was no threat to the kingdoms of the Sunlit World, so long as she always had a full belly and new gemstones poured into her lap often enough. She neither wondered nor cared about what plots might be driving those who offered her this chance to play at being human. In short, she was very far from the vicious, restlessly cruel schemers Qilué had met in her dealings with drow merchants, slavers, and mercenaries.

Well, so be it. 'Twould almost have been beyond belief to find a secret leader of this invasion inside the head of the very first drow she impersonated. While Qilué searched for someone who'd know more, she'd be Namra Dunseltree, or more accurately, play at being Anlaervrith playing the role of Namra. The real Namra had doubtless gone to slavery—or even some orc's cookfire—months ago. If Anlaervrith's obviously spotty memories were anything to go by, the servants hastening—reluctantly, but not daring to dawdle—to answer her summons would be arriving just about—

Qilué turned and drew herself up, pointing her walking stick imperiously down at the mess of shattered glasses and decanters, the spilled wine, and the tray, and snapped, "Well? Must I wait all *morning* for something to *drink*?"

The foremost of the two servants stared down at the chaos of the fallen tray in astonishment, and something very like delighted glee flashed across his face for just an instant before he swallowed, gulped, and said, "What beverage would be my lady's most immediate pleasure?"

Qilué waved a careless hand. "An array of wines, very like these. I'm quite unsettled. Do you know that the little bitch—Isryl, man, don't gawk at me as if you can't think who I'm speaking of!—*threw* them at me, and fled?"

The servant in the rear made a queer strangled sound that might almost have been a swallowed chuckle, then stiffened to attention as his lady master Namra leveled her stick at him and added, "*You* shall go and hunt her down. She is to be whipped until bone is laid bare, somewhere on her, then brought to me spread and bound to a tapestry frame, for my . . . *private* dealings with her. If you find her not, you shall serve in her place!"

The servant gulped, paled, and sprang away in frantic haste. "Lady—'tshall be so!" his call rang back to her, as he pounded away down a passage.

Qilué smiled grimly and said to the first servant, "Send others to clean this up, and to bring me three sharp kitchen knives and a bottle of cheap perfume. They are to be set on yonder table, for my later discussions with disobedient Isryl." Her smile broadened as she lurched forward to stroke the fearful servant under the chin with one end of her walking stick. He swallowed carefully as the metal cap caressed his throat. "I find," the merchant's wife purred casually, "that the sting of perfume, poured into open wounds, quite drives off the stink of fear."

She went on silently smiling into his eyes until she saw deepening terror there, and the trembling man felt that his lady master must be expecting—waiting for— a response.

"Y-yes, Lady Namra," he managed. "Shall I bring your wines now?"

"With a tallglass, yes," Qilué commanded, and tapped his throat with her stick. "And be aware: I shall not be pleased if it takes you long."

His eyes flickered before he nodded almost furiously and spun away. By some trick of air currents, Qilué could clearly hear sounds occurring down the passage—and she could have sworn, amid the sounds of his dashing feet, that she heard him reply under his breath, "A shortcoming that afflicts many, you old battle-axe . . . may all the gods rot you."

She gave the nearest mirror a smile and brought the end of her walking stick down hard into her own palm, hearing the smack of flesh before the sting began. It was a little like one of the slavers' goads she'd felt, years back. Qilué felt old angers stirring in her, and her usual unease at being away from the faithful of Eilistraee. Walking in the dirt, cold stone, and noisy crowding of a human city she also realized, with real surprise, that she was enjoying herself, unknown dangers and all. She'd been out of harness for too long.

Welcome back, Mystra, she said in the silent depths of her mind, and I do mean welcome.

She hadn't expected a reply, and none came, but as she set the walking stick down on the table, one of its metal ends flashed with a momentary blue radiance, as if it were winking at her.

✵　　✵　　✵

"Obedient wife," Master Merchant Inder Dunseltree told the tabletop, in a voice that dripped with cold sarcasm, "we are expected this even at the house of the glover Halonder Eldeglut, and his wife Iyrevven, for revelry until dawn. Shall our usual agreement apply?"

Namra dug her ring-adorned fingers greedily into a glistening mauve mound of hammerscale roe. From under her brows she shot the hovering server a "get hence" look that sent the servant scuttling for a distant doorway.

"Suppose, dearest Inder," she said to the fish eggs in front of her, "you reacquaint me with our 'usual agreement.' "

She thrust her fingers into her mouth and gave herself over to murmured appreciation of the flavorful roe.

Her "husband" looked as if exasperation would master him for a moment, then fell back from the brink of a furious outburst to say in silken tones of menace, "You ignore any dealings I may have with . . . ladies, remaining your usual pleasant self, and I shall do the same for you as regards both handy male flesh and, ah . . . your excesses at board and bottle."

Namra lifted her eyes to his and said with a gentleness that surprised Inder, "I still find this agreement acceptable, and I must confess to feeling a quickening interest within me, this day, for the man who now sits across from me."

She watched him rear back in astonishment, then saw his face slide from that into incredulous disgust. Qilué decided a seduction of the drow playing Inder would arouse more attention than was good for any hope of successfully learning more about those behind the drow invasion, and their plans.

She gave Inder a hard look to know that his reaction had been observed and found wanting, and asked the half-destroyed mound of roe in front of her, "Must I attend this revel at all?"

Inder lifted a dumbfounded eyebrow. "This is a *taking*, Namra. We are under orders to be there. The Eldegluts have widespread business interests, and much influence. Many of their guests are true humans, as yet unaware of us. You and I, among others, are assigned to conceal from them both the drugging and the assumption."

The drugging and the what? Qilué reached for her large and brim-full wineglass and asked, "This is expected to be an unusually clumsy assumption?"

Disgust washed again over Inder's florid face. "Just how little did Daerdatha train you?" he snarled, taking up his own wine. "Some humans can go on for half a night; others pitch on their faces the moment they take their first swallow, but it always takes hold suddenly when it does work. Human merchants poison each other so often they know in a trice just what's happened to anyone falling over senseless in mid-quaff." Mockingly he saluted her with his own glass, and drank deeply.

Qilué echoed the gesture, and helped herself to more roe. She'd been feeling a bit stomach-sick of mornings, lately, but this—the fare or the company, she didn't know which—was making her feel less than well right now.

"And do we know just what's going to happen to these humans, after?"

Inder chuckled harshly and replied, " We're none of us supposed to know or talk about that, and yet every last one of us wants to know. I'm always surprised at how much we seem to care about the fates of hairy, stinking humans—but I admit, I'm curious too."

He dug a fork into a steaming marinated ground slug, took a bite, chewed appreciatively, then said around the morsel, "Dragged off to the barge with all the rest, Brelma said, bound for Chult, where they'll spend the rest of their short lives hacking roads through the jungles for rich Calishites who hope to find mines bursting with head-sized nuggets of solid gold, and a-drip with already cut and polished gemstones."

"Gems," his wife echoed dreamily, and Inder nodded at this unsurprising reaction.

"Oh, no doubt there're stones under the mountains of Chult, *somewhere*," Inder added dismissively, "but I'd die of long-passing years waiting for someone to find enough to get out past all the sharpswords who're waiting for just such outgoing cargoes . . . then somehow to pass within reach of my waiting hands. Besides, you can't eat gems. I'd much rather deal in magic, if one has to trade in intangibles—at least there's power there, not mere empty beauty."

"Akin to the empty beauty of a smiling human maiden at a revel, perhaps?" his wife asked thinly.

Inder scowled. "I've heard what *you* do to human female beauty when you get the chance. Just keep your stick and your lash off our useful servants. If just one hanger or tapestry seamstress misses work because of you amusing yourself, I'll see to it you get a taste of what you give to others."

Namra curled her lip. "You? And just who will hold me down?"

"I'll call on Daerdatha," the drow playing at being her husband said bleakly, "then you'll harm no one. You might even find yourself in a household that we've entirely taken over—being the human maidservant who feels the lash whenever her master knows anger . . . or lust."

"I think I know Daerdatha better than that," his wife hissed—but Inder thought her voice sounded more frightened than menacing, and merely smiled.

"Go and get ready," he said. "You'll probably need some time to find a gown you can still get into. You eat like one of those hogs these humans keep!"

His wife rose, and replied sweetly, "While you, Inder, *are* one of those hogs these humans keep."

Her husband went white to the lips, and his half full wineglass burst into shards in his tightening hand. Qilué put a hand to her mouth in mock fear, struck a terrified pose, then strode away trailing tinkling, derisive laughter.

Inder plucked up the roe she hadn't yet eaten, strode to a certain door, and slapped it across the face of the servant standing at it.

"Clear the meal," he snapped as he shouldered past.

"Yes, lord!" the servant said anxiously, and set about licking all of the roe he could off of his face, before either his crazed lord or lady master might return to countermand Inder's most recent order. Hammerscale roe cost its weight in gold, and he'd only tasted it twice in his life before.

Several swallows later, he made a face, wondering why anyone prized it so much.

✳   ✳   ✳

"Halonder, you old lion!" roared a red-haired merchant whose shoulders were as wide as the door he was trying to stagger through. "All this just to get our coins for another of your swindles? Wouldn't it just be easier to hire some dancing lasses to come and try to er, *win* the coins from me? It's always worked before!"

"Ho ho," agreed Halonder Eldeglut hollowly, trying not to notice the sharp look his wife was giving him. Qilué wondered why he seemed so chastened; it was nothing compared to the glare Iyrevven Eldeglut had given her at the door, upon seeing that the webwork of emeralds displayed down the slit front of Namra Dunseltree's newest party gown was far more numerous and dazzling than the pectoral of emeralds and diamonds Iyrevven herself wore.

"*Whoa*, Halonder! Whoa! Send the lasses back and just tell your wife to come round, hey?"

The loudly roaring merchant had obviously taken several flagons of something aboard before arriving—as a necessary precaution, no doubt. Qilué had to firmly erase a growing smile as she recalled the garrulous old Lord of Waterdeep, Mirt, telling her to get drunk "as a necessary precaution, unless yer already deaf and somehow armored against boredom" before attending some nobles' revels in the City of Splendors . . . hmmm, Mirt had taken quite a shine to her, come to think of it; he'd always insisted in seeing "my little dark lady with the eyes of pure fire" in her true form before she spun a spell disguise to go out into the streets.

Inder nudged her now, none too gently. Qilué knew what he was signaling, and stepped firmly forward to tow the loud merchant past a glowering Iyrevven Eldeglut and distract the man now, as preparation for distracting him in earnest later. Namra Dunseltree was fatter and had larger jowls than many of the men here in the Eldeglut mansion this night, but the open front of her gown allowed her—by dragging everything sideways—to lay bare one of the most formidable breasts in all of Scornubel. Namra had spent some time this evening gluing glittering emerald dust to its thumb-sized nipple. Owing to a shortage, it seemed Namra had only ever stepped on one or two emeralds. The other one was adorned with ruby dust.

Qilué dragged her gown sideways, just as she'd practiced in the privacy of her mirror chamber. The merchant fastened his eyes on the sudden display, gasped, and transformed her towing into an enthusiastic charge that would have knocked her right over if there hadn't been a wall in the way. The emeralds at the throat of her gown momentarily struck her chin as her shoulders thundered into the wall, and the merchant crowed happily.

Iyrevven Eldeglut gave Namra a brittle smile over the merchant's growls and slobbering, and asked, "Happy now, dear?"

Namra blew her a kiss. "Happier than you'll ever be, Iyrevven," she replied sweetly, "if you don't get out and about more. I hear the scenery in Chult is quite spectacular this time of year."

Inder's elbow nearly broke one of her ribs. "That's neither amusing nor wise, shulteen," he snarled into her ear. He dragged her—and the still guffawing and nuzzling merchant—half a dozen paces away from a puzzled Iyrevven Eldeglut and into the din of sixty or so excitedly talking revelers. "We're not supposed to know or discuss such things, remember?"

His fingers dug into her shoulder like claws as he shook her, and Qilué hissed in pain despite herself as his fingers almost met through her upper arm. "Shulteen" was a scornful term used by some southern drow that meant, roughly, "stupid and reckless wanton, whose behavior leaves her not worthy of continued life." My, but Inder was upset.

"I don't even remember this gallant's name," she hissed, nodding her chin down at the merchant plastered to her front. "Who is he?"

"Malvaran Olnarr," Inder snapped, "deals in spices brought in from Amn. He's the eyes for someone, but we're not sure who."

The red-haired merchant burst upright, and guffawed into Inder's startled face. "An' we'll just keep it that way, shall we? I don't like my business rivals to be too sure of things." He turned to leer at Namra, chucked her under the chin, and said, "A pleasure meeting you, m'lady.

Perhaps we could get better acquainted later, hmm? About the time all these scrawny sorts fall exhausted, hey? Folk with real meat on their bones—like you and me—we're the ones who know a thing or two about life!" With a final gale of laughter, he spun away from them both and reached out with both hands to pluck wine bottles off the tray of a startled passing servant.

Inder glared at Namra, then put his lips to her ear and hissed, "Just neglect to mention Chult again for the rest of the evening, hmm?"

Namra raised one eyebrow, and shifted her gown slowly and deliberately back and forth. "I distracted him, did I not?"

"Yes, thoroughly," Inder said shortly, his breath warm on her neck. "The gem dust is very effective. Do that again when I go to refill our hosts' goblets."

Namra turned to lick his chest as if in play, and murmured, "Soon, this?"

Standing stiffly immobile under her tongue, Inder growled, "As soon as I can get back to them and take the goblets without seeming forward or unusual."

"Count on me," Namra purred, stepping away from her false husband. Several self-important voices died away momentarily among the grandly talking merchants as their owners turned to watch the buxom, emerald adorned woman strut to a pillar of sweets.

On her way back from the pillar to take up a fresh tallglass of firewine from the sideboard, Namra Dunseltree seemed to develop an itch. When a few frowning, surreptitious clawings had no apparent effect, she practically tore open the front of her gown to get at her breastbone, hiking the emeralds—and the gown they were attached to—this way and that. She didn't have to look up to know that her audience was steadily increasing, and her downcast eyes also let her see Inder's passing boot, on his way back to Halonder and Iyrevven Eldeglut with the drugged wine.

"Can I help, m'lady?" a dealer in southern silks purred at her shoulder. "I could not but help notice your obvious distress."

"Oh?" Namra purred. "Yes, 'dis dress' *is* a trifle obvious, isn't it?"

His sudden shout of laughter drew more eyes. Over his shoulder Namra saw Iyrevven throw back her head to drain her glass, as Inder put out his arm past her to usher her husband Halonder into a side chamber.

Iyrevven's eyes rolled up and she started shaking. Namra turned her head to join in the silk dealer's mirth, but shot another glance at her hostess in time to see Inder's arm snake out from the doorway. He took Iyrevven firmly by the elbow as her glass crashed to the floor, and turned her to follow Halonder.

Now came the moment she'd been waiting for. Namra clasped the delighted silk dealer to her bosom, rocked him as she giggled, and kept a steady watch on the door through which Inder and the two victims had disappeared. The folk who headed for that door now would have to be the two dark elves who'd replace the Eldegluts—and persons at least high enough in the invasion scheme to cast the spells of seizing. If one of them should happen to be Daerdatha, would Namra even recognize her?

And how well would Daerdatha recognize Namra— or the dark elf wearing Namra's skin?

Six . . . no, eight dark elves were converging on the door, laughing and talking, but strolling with rather more alacrity than they should have been. Seven strode in. The eighth—a dark-eyed man whose rich shirt was open all down the front to display not only a hairy chest, but a dozen thick, coin-adorned gold chains crisscrossing it—spun on his heel to face the wider revelry he'd just left. He darted glances all around the room, looking for folk who might be watching.

Qilué got her eyes down in time, spun away from the silk dealer with a last saucy laugh and the flouncing comment, "M'lord, I'd tarry, but after your attentions, I simply *must* go find my husband."

The silk dealer took that as a compliment, and was still laughing and waving when Namra Dunseltree turned to enter a certain doorway—and found her way blocked by a dozen thick ropes of gold and the hairy chest behind them. She gave its owner a merry smile and said, "My husband, Inder—he went this way, I know he did."

The dark-eyed man simply shook his head, saying nothing.

Namra tried to push past him and he shifted sideways, pinning her against the doorframe. One of Inder's tapestries had been hung in the room beyond, blocking everyone's view of its depths from the door.

"Good sir," Namra said insistently, struggling against the strength that held her pinned, "I *must* go to my husband. Make way!"

"Forget not your orders," he muttered into her ear. "Now turn around, act merry, and go seek out a drink. Your 'husband' will appear at your side soon enough."

Namra drew back, and he let her go. She paused, a dozen steps from the doorway, and turned to look challengingly back at him. The dark-eyed man's eyes widened as if she'd done something impossible, then narrowed . . . then seemed to blaze up into flame.

Something in Qilué's head seemed to stir, then grow warm, and she found the images of the real Namra coming to mind, one after another in a quickening, almost urgent flood: the memories Daerdatha had placed into Anlaervrith's mind. The heat of hostile, roiling magic was rising swiftly now in Qilué's head, and the images were repeating, in an ever quickening, bewildering stream. The dark-eyed man seemed to be trying to awaken something he could not find, to force her to do something. Were all the disguised drow in Scornubel controlled like puppets?

Well, one at least was not, and now one of those who sought to exercise such control knew it. Qilué turned hastily away, seeking a doorway that would take her out of this throng of revelers. If every one of them could be turned against her, bloodshed—*lots* of bloodshed—would be inevitable.

Halonder and Iyrevven Eldeglut were doomed to a brutally short slavery of backbreaking work in the hot, dangerous jungles of Chult, but if Qilué defied the many disguised drow here in open battle, scores of folk—both dark elves and unwitting humans—could well be doomed. Yet if she did nothing, doom might be reserved for Qilué Veladorn alone. . . .

"Hold, Namra!" the dark-eyed man snarled, his voice harsh and loud. Heads turned to look, all over the room, and Qilué saw other heads appear behind the man's shoulder. Crowded together in the doorway, their eyes were cold and alert. One of them whispered something Qilué couldn't catch. Men and women in the laughing, chattering height of revelry drew hitherto-concealed knives from under sleeves, out of bodices, and from the side slits of gowns, and plunged them calmly into the throats of those they'd been standing joking with.

"Sweet Mystra," Qilué murmured, hastening toward a window. So these invaders valued human lives as nothing. The gurgling dying behind her must have all been humans of Scornubel, and their slayers the disguised drow who'd slipped in to take the places of their neighbors, and vanish among them. So open a butchery meant that the leaders of the invasion considered the city already theirs—or cared nothing for the drow who'd become Scornubrians.

The window ahead was an increasingly attractive destination. The doors might all be too distant and too well guarded, but she wasn't so old yet that she couldn't manage a little tumbling.

Behind Qilué, a cold, cruel voice snapped an order in words she did not understand, and there came a thunder of movement as a hundred or more feet began to move in haste, converging on her in what seemed almost a charge.

A dozen or more grim-faced humans—spell-disguised dark elves, no doubt—stood between her and the window. They were moving to block her, ranging themselves carefully to allow her no way past, and to give each other room to fight. Every one of them had a knife of some sort, and at least two held full-sized swords ready in their hands. Dark eyes glittered with hatred . . . the eyes of her own kind. Qilué swallowed.

Murmuring words she'd hoped not to have to use, she spun around with a dancer's grace and hurled a spell at the onrushing drow. The stars of Eilistraee were quickly spread everywhere in the room, and an unseen, inexorable force that only worshipers of the Dark Dancer could withstand was hurling her pursuers back, some of them stumbling awkwardly amid the furniture and onto the bodies of those pressed too closely behind them.

Qilué wasted no time in gloating, but spun around again and hissed the words of her next spell at the drow between her and the window. Two of them were almost upon her, stabbing, and it took all of her skill at bobbing and weaving to finish her spell and send forth lightning among them.

Blue-white bolts leaped almost hungrily from her fingertips, and the bodies they darted amongst convulsed and screamed, arching and dancing helplessly in the crackling air. Here and there between Qilué and the window, humans flickered into their darker true shapes as they convulsed and screamed under the raking pain of her leaping bolts, and the daggers in their hands burst into tiny falling stars of molten metal.

Qilué ruthlessly kicked sobbing forms out of the way and sprang toward freedom. She was still half a dozen sprinting paces from her goal when a gray mist occurred before her—and almost immediately hardened into a smooth, blank wall of unyielding stone.

Qilué fetched up hard against it, shoulder first and rolling away to one side to lessen the blow. In the process she looked back to the room behind her where someone had dispelled her repulsion spell. Fifty or more drow were hastening forward again, their blazing eyes all bent on her.

Real fear rose deep in Qilué's throat for the first time in a long, long while. She hated having to strike down fellow dark elves, and yet expected no such mercy from them . . . and there were so gods-be-cursed *many* of them.

She hissed the words of a spell that should have melted away the stone, and anything solid beyond, into a tunnel for her to flee down, but nothing happened. The power to feel magic that Mystra had bestowed upon her was dulled. The very air seemed dark and dead, as if no spell could reach here, or thrive if this air reached it. She was in some sort of anti-magic field, no doubt the creation of one of the leaders of the drow invasion—either the dark-eyed man or one of the coldly scornful women who'd stood behind him. As groans around her told of the pain-wracked struggles of those who'd felt her lightning, the other drow were racing down upon her. She had just seconds to call on the most powerful magic she could, to banish the magic-quelling effect.

The air seemed to brighten and momentarily glow the faintest tinge of blue. Qilué danced away from a man who was lunging at her with a slender short sword in the style of a noble fencing his way through a duel. She opened her mouth to melt the stone between her and the window with one of her last powerful spells, and the magic-quelling returned with a vengeance, its dimness rolling down over her with renewed vigor. Someone else had cast a second anti-magic spell, and robbed Qilué of the last few vital seconds she needed.

Cruel knives slid coldly into her biceps and upper thighs, then firm hands were upon her. Unfamiliar arms wrapped themselves around her burning, suddenly enfeebled limbs, pinioning her as she gasped and kicked and bit. They dragged Qilué to the floor, where ungentle knees came down on her throat, and bodies sat hard on her laboring lungs. A small army of strong, grim drow clung to her. They held her down with her limbs spread in unyielding fleshy prisons, and cuffed her spell-hissing mouth until blood threatened to choke her, and her arching body could call up spells no more.

"Quztyr," commanded a voice that Qilué's stolen memories identified as Daerdatha, "find out just who our fierce little guest is, will you? She's yours, by the way, after we're done."

"My pleasure," the dark-eyed man replied.

The memories Qilué had seized from Anlaervrith Mrantarr identified Quztyr as a dangerously capable warrior, but she couldn't even see him through the many bodies holding her down and clapping their fingers over her eyes. Someone forced her jaws open by jabbing cruel fingers into their hinges, and someone else thrust the point of a dagger into her mouth, advancing it coldly along her tongue until it just touched the back of her throat.

From above her head, a hard brow descended to meet hers, and the same mindtouch magic she'd used on Anlaervrith flooded into Qilué's mind. Unfortunately for Quztyr, he wasn't facing a terrified, battered drow spy or human enspelled into drow shape, but an angry, alarmed dark elf archpriestess of Eilistraee who also happened to be a Chosen of Mystra, the powerful goddess of magic.

His own sentience boiled away in a flaring instant of futile terror, and his convulsing body fell away onto the floor beside the pinioned Chosen in a welter of thumps and a long, tremulous gasp. Wisps of smoke curled from his nose, sightlessly staring eyes, and mouth. Qilué heard the drow all around her gasp. Several of the painfully tight hands gripping her started to tremble. She had the time, now, to launch one magic of utter

destruction. It would reduce her to blinded helplessness for hours, perhaps days, rend this mansion and
everyone in it, and bring her no closer to learning more
about the invaders of Scornubel. Despite the part of her
that wanted to bring a screaming end to all of this,
restoring her to freedom, Qilué lay still under the
hands that held her, and awaited more pain.

"Nuelvar," Daerdatha's cold voice came again, "slay
that mindless carrion for me." After a little silence, the
voice sharpened as it added, "You heard me. I'm not
accustomed to repeating my commands, warrior."

There followed a brief, wet sound, a gurgling, then
the slump of a heavy body onto the floor.

"That's better," Daerdatha said silkily. "So passes the
overly ambitious, exceedingly arrogant Quztyr from
the scene—belatedly, some would say. Approach, now,
and press the palm of one of your hands down on a
spire of the crown on my head. Blood must be drawn."

"And—?" Nuelvar asked hesitantly.

"Your mind will be linked to mine—as, shortly, will
that of Brelma here, and Durstra, Syldar, Ghalad-
dyth, and Chaladoana. Oh, and Chaladoana's three
apprentices—gather them, dear."

Nuelvar grunted, a short sound that was almost a
bark of pain, and Daerdatha added, "Well done, warrior. Together, once the crown links us all, we can withstand the strongest spell this little spy can possibly
have waiting inside her head, and overwhelm her to
learn what we must of who sent her here, and how
much they know—or have guessed—of what we've
done in Scornubel. She must be kept alive, for our own
safety . . . witless, but alive." The cold chuckle that came
from Daerdatha's throat gave Qilué her first shiver in
years.

It seemed a very short time thereafter that another
brow pressed against Qilué's, and a cold and numbing
worm seemed to probe into her thoughts, sinking inex-
orably through the mind thrusts she sent at it—the

attacks that had shattered Quztyr's mind. Though the pinioned priestess of Eilistraee could do nothing to stop this cold, heavy invasion of her psyche, she could hear gasps and growls of amazed pain from close by. She gathered that several of the drow linked to the crown were discovering real mind pain for their first, unpleasant time.

Daerdatha gave a louder gasp, and followed it with the words, "Heed, all of you! We must be very careful. Brelma, draw that dagger out of her mouth—carefully—and thrust Quztyr's glove, there, into it. Pinch her nostrils shut if she tries to say anything at all." Her voice rose, obviously pitched to the drow throughout the room, as she added, "There is great danger! Get back, all of you— into other rooms. There could be a . . . a blast of magic."

Qilué could hear hastily shifting feet in the distance as a gag was roughly thrust into her mouth, and her head slapped hard in the process. She managed to bite the fingers of the person who did that before other hands locked her head into immobility. Someone tore away Namra Dunseltree's jeweled and tasseled mauve boots from her feet, someone tore away her emeralds, and someone else near at hand murmured, "What sort of spell blast?"

"None," Daerdatha said flatly, her voice far quieter than before. "I said that just to get ears that don't need to hear more about our spy, here, far enough away. This is not Anlaervrith Mrantarr—whose fate I can only guess at—but Qilué Veladorn, Chosen of the Chosen of the Promenade of Eilistraee, who also happens to be one of the Seven Sisters, the Chosen of Mystra . . . and, of course, one of our kind."

"Move your fingers out of the way," Nuelvar said grimly. "Chosen of Mystra or not, she'll be little harm to us dead—a simple thrust of my blade into one eye then the other should do it."

"No!" Daerdatha snapped. "The decree was clear. No more dark elf blood shall be spilled in this city."

"What? We let her *live*?"

"Her death might bring forth magics that slay *us*," the drow sorceress replied icily. "Break her wrists to stop her casting spells, bind her, and throw her in the river. Nothing was said against drowning . . . or fish bites."

Qilué twisted under the hands that held her, arching and rolling and struggling furiously to spit out her gag and hiss the words she needed to say to awaken several ready spells. She bit viciously at the hands that tried to muzzle her, but could do nothing to stop cords being tied tightly around her wrists, elbows, knees, and ankles. She felt herself being plucked up into the air, carried a little way, and dumped onto a table. Her arms were stretched over her head so that her hands were beyond a table edge, while heavy bodies sat on them. As if from a distance she felt sharp, rending pain in her wrists and heard splintering, dull cracking sounds as she lost all feeling in her fingers. Cruel hands struck her head, slamming it back and forth until her ears rang and her senses swam.

"Enough amusing yourselves. Bring her," Daerdatha purred, clear triumph in her voice. "Khlemmer's dock has anchor weights for his nets. We'll need four or five to make sure she goes to the bottom and stays there."

"*Hurrmph*—she's heavy enough," Nuelvar complained, as brisk drow footfalls sent pain shooting up Qilué's arms. "Anything else we should do to her?"

"Not what you and Quztyr were thinking of," Daerdatha said calmly, "unless you want to die screaming while she takes over your body for her own. Just tie the weights to her throat, waist, knees, and elbows, gag and blindfold her so Mystra's curse can't strike at us when she dies, and give her to the river."

With surprisingly deft haste, these things were done, the drow lifting the bound and mute body over their heads to hurl her far out into the cold and muddy waters of the Chionthar. The splash she made almost drowned out their collective gasp of relief, but none of them quite dared to turn their backs on the river for a long time. Only a handful of bubbles came up, and didn't persist for long.

Nuelvar Faeroenel wasn't the only one to turn away from the dock with a surprising sense of loss, but he was the only one to sigh aloud. This earned him a sharp look of suspicion from Daerdatha.

Three paces later she did something that made only two of the others so much as hesitate or look up at her. She blew Nuelvar's head to bloody spatters with a spell, just to ensure the safety of the drow of Scornubel. To say nothing of the safety of one Daerdatha "Darkspells."

✳   ✳   ✳

The Chionthar runs slow, cold, and foul past the mud-choked pilings and wharves of the Caravan City. If she'd still needed to breathe, its muddy bottom would have been Qilué's grave. As it was, she gave herself over to waiting in the numbing cold until all of her slayers would have turned away. She knew well the impatience that ruled most dark elves. That impatience had once governed her as well—before she'd truly come to know and embrace Mystra. She gave the goddess wry thanks, now, for this highlight of her career, and concentrated on ensuring that one of the spells she'd awakened in her last struggle was working properly.

Yes, *there*: the faintest, most blurred of touches told her she was linked to Brelma, through the bites she'd landed a time or two. Right now the lady drow was striding rather grimly through the disarray of the grandest room in the Eldeglut mansion, looking rather urgently for the glass of wine she'd been in the middle of when all the trouble with the spy had started. Good; that was a link Qilué would follow in the days to come.

It was probably time to call on one of her other active spells, and end her drifting in mud that was rather too rich in dead, rotting fish—and hungry, very much alive lampreys with a taste for recently delivered bodies—for her liking. Being dead, Qilué judged, was decidedly undignified, chilly, and boring.

＊　　＊　　＊

It was the practice of the barge merchant Welver Thauburn to shift his most valuable cargoes a little way downstream, and across the Chionthar, early in the dark hours of a night. It was a little thing, but it baffled a surprising number of thieves into spending fruitless, cursing hours groping blindly up and down the wrong riverbank. Welver kept an eye and ear out for such nuisances as crossbow bolts and strong swimmers at such times, but he was entirely unprepared for the sudden eruption from the waters not an arm's reach away from where he sat against the rail of his best barge, of a bound and blindfolded woman.

She burst up into the air, hung almost above him for one terrifying moment, dripping as she blotted out the stars, then flew rapidly and silently away to the northwest. Welver stared after the apparition, hastily drained his hip flask of Old Raw Comfort, then hurled the flask into the river, vowing to forever give up strong drink.

Well, perhaps after he'd drunk dry the keg waiting for him in his cellar. . . .

＊　　＊　　＊

"Simylra," Cathlona Tabbartan asked archly, shifting her peacock feather fan to better display the dusting of diamonds in her upswept hair, "tell me, pray, *who* is that vision of manliness below? In the silver and green scales?"

Her companion leaned forward over the balcony rail in a gesture designed to display her diamond-dusted, fur-supported breastworks to all of reveling Waterdeep, and said, "That, I declare, must be Lord Emveolstone." She gave a little shriek of excitement—not the only one to rise just then from an otherwise breathless female throat—and gasped, "Oh, but cousin Cat, look you now upon a dragon incarnate! Could it be that Danilo Thann?"

Cathlona bent forward over the rail in a near plunge that sent the spindle shaped, rose hued crystals of her pectoral dancing against her heavily rouged chin, and said, "I-I can't tell who it is. That dragon head entirely covers him . . . he must be looking out of its jaws!"

The lord in question was wearing a splendid silver specimen of what by now was over two dozen ridiculous dragon suits that the two cousins from Amn had seen grandly entering the festivities at their first Waterdhavian nobles' revel. They couldn't even recall the name of the noble family hosting this costume ball, but it was certainly grand. Servants were plying all of the guests with decanters of drink and silver pyramids of sugar dusted pastries. Cathlona, for one, was already feeling rather sick. She righted herself hastily, looking a little green, gave her cousin a weak smile, and sat back to fan herself with rather more enthusiasm than grace.

"My word, Simmy, how're they going to dance in such arrays, do you think?"

"The costumes *do* come off," her cousin said testily, "and I'll thank you not to call me by that—that disgustingly silly nickname!"

"There are no silly names," a glorious voice drawled near at hand, "in the presence of such beauty."

The cousins turned as one to stare at the speaker— and emitted identical gasps of hungry awe. The object of their attention was a man whose fine features were adorned rather than ruined by a finely upswept mustache, its chestnut magnificence overwhelmed by the curly sweep of hair that must have reached to the man's waist, but was bound up in a scarlet ribbon to keep it clear of the spotless green shoulders of his elegant, festive jacket. He was lean and lithe beneath the devastatingly simple lines of his garb. From the lace at his wrists to that at his throat, every curve of his form betrayed sleek strength and flaring, ready muscle. As for his gray silken breeches, with their discreet codpiece—why, the tight bottom they displayed to the world as he bowed and turned to leave them made both cousins gasp again, then swallow . . . then turn to each other to share an incredulously delighted squeal.

As he glided swiftly away down carpeted steps, the man in the dark green jacket managed to sufficiently suppress his shudder that neither of the overly plump Amnian ladies noticed.

"Who *is* that delectable man?" Simylra Lavartil inquired of the world at large, ruffling the furs that supported her bosom with an enthusiasm that threatened to shred them.

"That, madam," a servant murmured, as he bent to offer her a fresh drink of manycherries wine from a tray of full tallglasses, "is Dumathchess Ilchoas, as yet bereft of any noble title . . . though I believe the ladies have given him one. They've taken to calling him 'Dauntless.' "

Simylra thanked him profusely, and proved the fervor of her gratitude by seizing not one but three glasses from his tray. She drained them in rapid succession before hurling herself back in her chair to stare at her cousin with a gasp of mingled satiation, longing, and delight.

"Dauntless!" she cried. "Oh, can the world *hold* such pleasures?"

"Evidently, madam, not for long," the servant murmured disapprovingly, as he surveyed the wreckage of his tray, and glided away without giving Cathlona an opportunity to work similar havoc upon it.

She stared sourly after the dwindling form of the servant, and asked, "So just what did our Dauntless see, over that rail, to make him abandon us—nay, *spurn* us—in such unseemly haste?"

Simylra gathered her strength with a visible effort, and leaned forward again to gasp anew. "Why, it's the most daring costume yet!"

"Some lord's come naked?" Cathlona asked, raising her delicately plucked brows questioningly.

"No, cuz, not a lord, but a lady . . . and not *quite* naked. She's wearing some black leather straps—" Simylra giggled and colored prettily, waving a few fingers before her mouth—"here and there, you know. They must bear some powerful spells; her disguise is nearly perfect."

"Her disguise?" Cathlona asked, not quite daring to lean forward again after her previous experience.

"A drow princess," Simylra breathed, her eyes glittering with envy as she watched the new arrival sweep across the entry hall with catlike grace. Every male eye below turned toward her. The lady was daring indeed, to come as an outlawed, evil being, wearing little more than a pair of gleaming black buttock-high boots, with silver heel spikes, and elbow-length gloves of the same material. Her breasts and loins were covered by little more than crisscrossing leather straps hung with spindle-shaped rock crystal stones, and a black ribbon encircled her throat. Her hair reached to the backs of her knees in a magnificent, raven-dark sweep that was bound in a cage of silver chain ending in two delicate chains, little larger than glittering threads, that hung in loops attached to the spurs of her boots. Two tiny bells hung from pointed silver medallions glued to her nipples, and she wore a calm, crooked smile that broadened as the man known as Dauntless swept up to her and proffered his arm. As she turned to display herself to him, the two gaping cousins saw that a walnut-sized diamond bulged glitteringly from her navel, and that a tiny sculpted dagger hung point downward from the cluster of diamonds and silver scrollwork at her loins.

"Gods," Simylra murmured, swallowing noisily, "how can anyone compete with *that*?"

"Simmy," her cousin said grimly, "either get me a drink—a very *large* drink—or let me go home."

✺   ✺   ✺

"May I say, my lady, what a splendid costume you chose to grace our eyes with, this night?" Dauntless offered gallantly, keeping his eyes carefully on hers.

Qilué laughed, low and musically. "You may indeed say so, Lord Dauntless. I find your own appearance very pleasing to the eyes."

Dauntless chuckled. "As I've said, good lady, I'm hardly a lord, but I am, I must confess, a man smitten. I would know your name."

In reply he got a light laugh and the murmured comment, as the devastatingly lovely lady leaned into his grasp, "I'd much rather remain a woman of mystery this night, if you don't mind."

"Ah, but I do," Dauntless said smoothly, handing her forward into a curtained alcove where a waiter was holding a tray of drinks ready. "A *woman*, did you say? You mean you're not really a drow princess?"

"A drow princess? No," Qilué replied, curling long fingers around a glass. "Magic can work wonders for the outward appearance, if deftly applied."

"Your own spellcraft," Dauntless asked, leading her on into a shadowed bower, "or did someone else transform you?"

"Dauntless," the lips so close to his breathed, "that would be telling, now, wouldn't it?"

The Harper moved in close, until their noses were almost touching, and said, "I appreciate both your choice of such a daring disguise, and the skill with which it has been spun."

Her response was a low purr of laughter, and the huskily whispered words, "Go ahead, my lord, test it."

Dauntless looked into her eyes, found a welcome there, and extended his head forward until their lips met . . . and clung, tongues darting a soft duel . . . then tightened, mouth to mouth, bodies melting together.

When at last they broke apart to breathe, Qilué spun deftly out of his arms, and asked, "So, Dauntless: do I pass your test?"

"Several tests, and more, Lady of Mystery. Are you free for the rest of this evening—or any part of it?"

"Regretfully, no, my lord. Business brings me hither, and business must be my master this night. Had I freedom to pursue pleasure, good Dauntless, rest assured that I'd be at your heels, and nowhere else, until dawn—and as long after as you might . . . desire."

"Forgive my forwardness, lady," the Harper murmured, "but tell me, if your true shape returned to you at any time during such a pursuit as you've suggested, would I be aghast? Or disappointed?"

"That, my lord Dauntless, would depend entirely on your own tastes and inclinations," the dark elf said gently, "not, I believe, on whom I turned out to be. I'm not one of the well-known and well-wrinkled noble matrons of the city, gone out to play in a disguise. It is my fond hope that my true shape would not offend you overmuch. Now, if you'll excuse me? That business I mentioned, you understand."

"Of course," the handsome young man agreed, bowing deeply. "The pleasure has been mine."

"Well, someday perhaps 'twill be," she purred in reply, unhurriedly stroking the back of one of his hands, then putting her emptied wine glass into the other, before she stepped away.

Dauntless watched her lilt across the room beyond the bower, through an envious and watchful crowd, and his eyes slowly narrowed. Business here, now, would be what, exactly? What would a drow pretending to be a human wearing the spell shape of a drow be doing here at a revel for nobles and would-be nobles? She'd left suddenly, as if catching sight of someone she wanted to meet. Who?

Dauntless faded in behind a potted fern as the Lady of Mystery turned at the far end of the room to look back, almost challengingly. Gods, but her lips had been inviting.

He was doomed to spend most of the next hour acting innocent and unobtrusive, trying to stay in the background but within sight of the drow princess as she glided enthusiastically around the revel, letting many men and women test the efficacy of her costume . . . often, Dauntless was sure—though she never once looked in his direction—just to silently tease him.

It wasn't until the end of the second hour, and frequent subterfuges of being either drunk or about to be sick to escape the clutches of enthusiastic matron after smitten matron, that Dauntless thought he saw the guest that his drow princess was shadowing. He wasn't sure until that person—a buxom lady in a plain-fronted mauve gown with shoulder ruffles— moved to a spiral stair masquerading as a large plant stand in one corner of the room, and began to climb it.

The Lady of Mystery moved purposefully, too. She slipped into a dark alcove where a beaded curtain hid her from public view for, it seemed, just long enough. By the time Dauntless drifted up to it, it was empty. The casements of its lone window stood open to the night.

He peered out and up once, quickly and quietly, and was rewarded by the sight of a shapely body the hue of glossy jet climbing up through the shadows of the wall to a stone gargoyle-shaped waterspout protruding from the overhanging balcony on the floor above. It was the same balcony that the spiral stair led to. In another instant, his Lady of Mystery was going to be hanging upside down from that gargoyle, just under one end of the balcony.

He'd have to move like silent lightning, but there was another window—and another gargoyle—at the other end of the balcony, hidden from the Lady of Mystery's perch by the curving buttresses that supported the balcony. Fortunately Dauntless could move like silent lightning, and he did so.

Out and up, thus, and he was there. A pleasant night outside, to be sure. He'd just hang around for a while in the cool night air, to catch whatever words the lady in purple was going to whisper over the balcony rail. He hoped—before all the gods, he hoped—they wouldn't be something that would force him to have to kill his Lady of Mystery.

The voices began, then, and Dauntless got another surprise. The first voice was unfamiliar to him, but he could see from purple ruffles and a moving chin, just visible over the edge of the balcony, that the speaker was the lady in purple. The second belonged to someone who must have been already on the balcony, waiting, and it was a distinctive harsh croak that belonged to only one woman in all Waterdeep. Mrilla Malsander was one of the most ambitious of the rich merchants currently trying to become noble by any means possible. Their words were sinister, but too cryptic to force him to kill anyone.

✳   ✳   ✳

Qilué clung to the crumbling curves of the snarling gargoyle, and listened intently as the slaver Brelma— who made a very fetching lady in purple, she had to admit—said without any preamble or greeting, "The trouble was a spy, but she's dead now. The project is still unfolding nicely."

"Good," the other lady replied, her voice like the croak of a raven. "See that it continues to do so. If not, you know who to speak with."

With that she turned away and started down the stair, leaving Brelma to look innocently—perhaps wonderingly—out at the lamp-lit night skyline of Waterdeep.

As Qilué swung herself back in through the window, she felt another twinge of the nausea that had plagued her recently, and it strengthened her resolve. Duty to Dove was one thing, but blundering around in Waterdeep making matters worse was another. The time for an expert on drow was past; the time for an expert on the City of Splendors had come . . . and her sister Laeral dwelt not a dozen streets away, in the brooding city landmark of Blackstaff Tower.

Leaving the revel swiftly was simplicity itself. Every Waterdhavian mansion has servants' stairs, and in the shadowed, many-candled light, concealing gloom was everywhere. If her handsome pursuer wanted to come along, he was quite welcome. Whether he was part of those she was investigating or some nosy Waterdhavian watchwolf, Blackstaff Tower should give him something to think about.

One of her own covert contacts in the city had told her that the endless renovations of the tower interior had recently reached a pace she described as "enthusiastic." Hoping the back entrance she remembered still existed, Qilué strolled unconcernedly thence through the streets of the city, acting as if she had every right to be there. The three watch patrols she encountered gave her hard stares, seemed about to challenge her, then thought better of it. She must be a noble matron wealthy enough to squander spells on a party disguise—after all, didn't real drow creep and skulk about, maniacally attacking any human they saw?

With that sarcastic thought still twisting her lips, Qilué came to a certain spot along the curving wall of

Blackstaff Tower, turned to face the dark stone, and with her fingertips traced a line to a certain spot. Her fingers dipped into an almost invisible seam, then emerged, moving diagonally a little way down to touch a junction of stone blocks, before—she knelt smoothly—darting into a gap right at ground level. The wall receded silently into itself, magic lending a velvet silence to what should have been a grating of weighty stone. Qilué slipped into a dark embrasure.

It would remain open for only a few seconds before the wall shifted forward again to expel her straight back out onto the street, but if she reached thus, in the darkness, a side way should open.

It did, and Qilué stepped forward through some space of magical darkness, into a dimly lit, curving passage whose inside wall was seamed with many closed cupboard doors, warning radiance flickering around their locks and catches. What she sought was just ahead: a tall, narrow cupboard or closet door.

There it was. A touch here should open it, and—

The moment she touched the panel, a sickening, tingling feeling told Qilué that something was wrong. The locking spells must have been changed. She stepped hastily back and away from the panel, but the flock of guardian hands bursting out of the outer wall of the passage swerved unerringly toward her, snatching and grabbing with their usual icy accuracy.

With three quick slaps the drow priestess kept them clear of her face and throat, then Qilué simply hunched down, gasping at the pain, and endured their cruel grasps all over the rest of her body. Oh, would she have bruises. . . .

She could try to pry off each of the flying obsidian hands and shatter them before they began their numbing, ultimately paralyzing washes of electricity, but she needed to see Laeral anyway, and a little lock picking would attract immediate attention from the duty apprentice seeing to the wards.

Struggling against the rigid holds of the gripping hands, Qilué plucked the dangling dagger ornament from her crotch, twisted it to its full length, and shielded it in her palm from any guardian-hand strike or clawing. Khelben's one failing was to purchase all of his locks, before he laid spells upon them, from the same dwarven crafter whose work, sold in Skullport to the few who could afford it, was familiar to Qilué. Their maker had shown her the one way to force them open. It required a lock pick of just the right angle . . . like this one.

A sudden movement, a twist, a click, and the panel sighed open. Qilué got her nails under the edge, hauled it open with a strength that surprised the being who was watching her by then, and sprang onward, straight to the next door.

The duty apprentice was attentive. As she moved, the hands began to crawl up her body with bruising force, seeking joints to jam themselves in and her throat to strangle. Qilué snarled her defiance at them as she picked the next door, rushed up a short flight of steps—then threw herself out of the way of the huge iron fist that slammed down across the passage.

The iron golem it belonged to emerged into the narrow way with ponderous care, and by then she was through the door beyond and into a room where spheres of flickering radiance drifted toward her from all sides in menacing, purposeful silence.

"Khelben!" she snapped to the empty air, as magic missiles burst from her hands to destroy these guardians, "Laeral! Call off your watchwolves. I've no wish to destroy them."

Numbing lightning was leaping from the hands on her body, playing across her skin until she hissed at the pain and stumbled like a drunken dockhand under their punishment. The next door was there, but could she reach it?

Grimly Qilué staggered on, gesturing rudely at a crystal sphere that descended from the dimness near the ceiling. Its depths held a voice that said, "She called on the lord and lady master! We'd best open the doors."

It also held the frightened face of a young man sitting at a glowing table, who stared out of the sphere at the struggling intruder and gasped, "But she's a drow!"

"Get Laeral!" Qilué roared. "Bring her to me, or I'll start *really* destroying things." In sudden fury she tore a crawling guardian hand from her breast, waved it at the sphere, and hurled it to the floor, bounding onto it with all her strength and ignoring the lightning it spat around her boots as it died. "Are you deaf, duty apprentice?"

"You hear? She knows our duties. She must be—"

"Half Waterdeep has heard of the defenses of Black-staff Tower," the young man said scornfully. "She's a dark elf, and *I'm* not letting any dark elf into this room with us."

"But—"

"But nothing. You've always been too soft, Araeralee. You'd let Szass Tam of Thay in here, if he put on the body of a beautiful maid and whimpered at the door! How do we know that isn't him now? Or Manshoon of the Zhentarim, up to another of his tricks?"

"Well, I'm rousing Lady Laeral to decide for—"

"Araeralee, don't you dare! This is my duty watch, and—dark gods take you, wench! You've done it! You've burning well gone and done it. It'll be the lash of spells for you, once I tell Khelben. Now I'm going to have to rouse all the apprentices . . . don't you know we're supposed to do that first, before bothering the masters? *Drown* you!"

"Drown you, enthusiastic young idiot," Qilué snarled at the sphere, as she forced the lock of the next door and came out into a large, many-pillared chamber that by rights shouldn't have fit within the tower walls. The chamber was rapidly filling with barefoot, sleepy-eyed apprentices.

"A drow!" one of them gasped, and others quickly took up the cry. Young faces frowned in fear and determination, and young hands moved in a weaver's nightmare of complicated gestures.

* * *

In a chamber whose domed ceiling winked with glimmering stars, Laeral stirred, lifting her head from Khelben's bare, hairy shoulder. The chiming came again, and the Lord Mage of Waterdeep answered it with a louder, barking snore. Laeral's lips twisted in wry amusement. Of course.

She sat up, her silvery hair stirring around her bare shoulders, and sighed. The books they'd been studying lay spread open around them on the bed, abandoned for slumber, and Laeral carefully lifted her long legs over them as she rolled off the bed, plucked up a robe, and went to see what was wrong.

She was still padding down the tower stairs with a crystal sphere of stored spells winking ready in her hand when she heard shouts from below, the whoosh of released magic, then a blast that shook the entire tower.

She lurched against the wall, cradling the sphere to keep it from a shattering fall—and was promptly flung across the stair by another, even more powerful blast.

"True trouble," she murmured to the world at large, then launched herself down the stairs in a long glide that called on the stairway enchantments to let her fly.

The tower shuddered and shook under another blast before she hit the bottom, and a long, racing crack opened in the wall beside her. Laeral lifted her eyebrows at it as she plunged through an archway where dust was drifting down—and headlong into the battle raging below.

* * *

"Gods above!" Dauntless murmured. The door he'd seen the drow slip through banged open in front of his nose, and dust swirled out. There was a dull, rolling boom, and doors and windows creaked and slammed all over the tower. "I must be crazed to leap into this," he murmured, touched the silver harp badge pinned to the inside throat of his jacket for luck, and trotted into the booming darkness.

Not far away, in the shadow of another building, a cloaked and hooded figure the Harper hadn't noticed nodded to itself and turned away.

The passages inside were an inferno of whirling spell energies, swirling dust, and shouts, but he could follow their fury up and on, stumbling in the gloom. He came out into a room whose floor was cracked and tilted crazily, where dust-cloaked figures knelt and scrambled and waved their arms in spellcasting.

In their midst, standing alone in a ring of fires in the center of the room, was his beautiful Lady of Mystery. Shards of black glass lay all around her, something that looked like silver smoke boiled away from her sweat-bedewed body, and fury blazed out of her dark face. He almost cowered back at the sight of it. In his moment of hesitation, a white-faced young man in flapping robes bounded out from behind a pillar with a long, bared sword in his hand. Green glowing runes shimmered up and down its heavy blade as he charged at the drow.

Spells slammed into the dark elf from three sides as he ran, almost tripping over the embroidered edge of his robe. She was staggering helplessly in their grip when he skidded to a halt, grimly aimed his blade, and with both hands thrust it through her flat belly. The Lady of Mystery coughed silver fire almost into the duty apprentice's face. He reeled back as the sword shattered with a wild shrieking, spat bright shards away in all directions, and slumped into dust around the convulsed dark elf.

The young wizard hurled himself away in real horror as silver fire scorched his cheek and he realized who—or rather, *what*—this intruder must be. A cold, bright golden glow cracked across the chamber, and Dauntless found himself slammed back against its wall in the company of all of the dusty-robed figures.

A furious Lady Mage of Waterdeep strode barefooted into the center of the room, snarling, "Is *this* the hospitality of Blackstaff Tower?"

In the utter silence that followed her shout, Laeral set down a crystal sphere she'd been carrying and strode toward the drow who was standing upright again, silver fire blazing up around her in an unearthly nimbus of glowing smoke.

Laeral's unbound hair swirled around her as she stretched forth her hands, like a mother desiring a daughter's embrace, and asked in a voice not far from tears, "Sister—too long unseen—what troubles you?"

"My own ineptitude," Qilué replied, and burst into tears. She swayed amid silver flames, weeping, for a long moment, then, with a sob, she rushed into Laeral's waiting arms.

Laeral
Lady Cassalanter's Busy Day

Of all the ladies fair whom I would fain smile upon me, she whose smile is worth the most is the Lady Mage of Waterdeep. Laeral hath given me a nod of approval, and the memory of it shall be a light in the back of my mind all the rest of my days.

Zantravas Rolovantar,
Lord Chamberlain of Castle Waterdeep
from *Forty Years Before The Doors: A Life In Service*
published circa the Year of the Wyvern

"Oh, most clever tongue, save me now!" Dauntless breathed aloud, as silently as he could, then stepped boldly around a pillar and joined the hasty throng of apprentices darting back out of the shattered, dust-choked chamber where their brave defense of Black-staff Tower had just ended.

He kept his head down and matched the pace of those padding barefoot up the stairs, and had climbed an entire flight, turned on a landing, and mounted another before the expected snarl came from just behind him: "Ho! *You*—in the boots—hold hard. You're not one of us. Stand still, or be blasted to ashes."

Dauntless stiffened, sighed, and came to a reluctant halt. A hand took rough hold of his elbow and a shrill, excited voice near his ear said, "Try nothing. There's a spell dagger floating just beside your throat, ready to slay you if you try anything, anything at all!"

Dauntless was just opening his mouth to assure the speaker that he'd offer no violence when a hitherto-smooth section of wall opened like a door. A face like a

scowling lion—a lion sporting a neatly trimmed pepper-
and-salt beard—looked out of it.

The Lord Mage of Waterdeep glared past Dauntless
and asked testily, "Is *that* all you've learned, of what
we've been teaching you? Blast and threaten, blast and
threaten? You sound like Zhentarim, not apprentices
on the road to real mastery of magic. Take down that
dagger spell this instant!"

"But, Lor—"

"You stand in my tower and dare to utter me 'buts'?
Are you looking for a swift barefoot tour of the Great
Glacier? Or just a month spent as my boot scraper?"

"Ah . . . uh, yes, Lord Ma—I mean *no*, Lord Mage! The
spell is—aha, there—gone!"

"Good. As your spell is, make yourself so."

"Yes, Lord Mage," the voice agreed hastily. Dauntless
heard the receding slap of bare feet hurrying away.

The Blackstaff put out a hand to Dauntless, and said,
"Come, handsome Harper. I've a task for you."

"Lord Khelben?"

"Lad, just step into this secret passage sharp like,
and refrain from asking foolish questions every second
breath and behold . . . you'll be twice the apprentice of
magic most of these dolts are."

"In a good mood tonight, are we?" Dauntless couldn't
help but ask—in the quietest of whispers—as he
slipped into the passage after the archmage.

Khelben neither turned nor slowed, but did observe
aloud as they began to climb a narrow flight of stairs,
"A true Harper! No judgment for his own safety, and far
too quick and clever with his tongue. Yes, you'll do
nicely."

Dauntless sighed then, but took care to make it
utterly silent.

"And don't sigh," Khelben said from somewhere
above. "We Who Harp are striving for a stoic, even
eager image, not resigned acceptance of being manipulated. Right?"

*   *   *

The Dark Sister stiffened in Laeral's arms. "What are you—?"

"Easy, sister," the Lady Mage of Waterdeep said, stroking Qilué's tense, trembling back. "A little soothing spell to go with the healing. Relax. There is no more danger for you here—and never was any treachery or deceit."

Qilué gave a little, shuddering sigh, then slumped against Laeral, who deftly called on a waiting spell to hold them both up. Floating together amid the drifting dust of the shattered chamber, the two sisters held each other like a drowsy, comfortable couple, and talked as Qilué was slowly and gently made whole again.

The shuddering she-drow was jet black of complexion, but the woman who stroked and soothed her had skin tanned the lightest hint of gold. Her silver hair, tousled earlier in her angry haste, was carefully gathering itself into tidiness as the two sisters, limbs locked together, gently revolved in midair. The Lady Mage of Waterdeep had large, liquid eyes of a dancing emerald green and an impish nose that drew the eye to her fine features. Her face had a natural beauty that made young male apprentices and men walking in the city streets swallow and—eventually—find the need to visibly and reluctantly wrench their own gazes away from. Even barefoot and simply garbed, she radiated high station and gentle authority. Kindness and concern were the cloaks that enfolded her at every moment.

Laeral was still apologizing earnestly for the apprentices' attack when Qilué fixed her with dark, solemn eyes and interrupted.

"Sister, I have a favor to ask of you, as Dove asked it of me. My kind—dark elves, but not of Eilistraee; rather, cruel folk from the realms below—have for some time been infiltrating the city of Scornubel, taking the places of humans who are sold into slavery or slain. Dove asked me to investigate, and I followed a drow high in the ranks of the Scornubrian impersonators . . ."

"To here," Laeral realized, nodding grimly. "Whom did she meet with?"

"Do you know an ambitious woman by the name of Mrilla Malsander?" Qilué asked. As the Lady Mage of Waterdeep nodded, she laid a hand on Laeral's arm and added, "This is more than slavery, sister. The slaver I followed here spoke of all the impersonations in Scornubel simply as 'the project,' implying that these two, and the others they work with, deal in other matters."

"Did you not know?" Laeral asked in response, almost bitterly. "Other places grow corn, or barley, but here in hard-paved Waterdeep, we have healthy crops too. We grow conspiracies."

❋   ❋   ❋

Three heads were bent together over the bright crystal ball. With something approaching awe, Dauntless shifted his eyes to the man on his left—Khelben "Blackstaff" Arunsun, the Lord Mage of Waterdeep—then to the man on his right—Mirt the Moneylender, widely believed to be one of the secret lords of the city. Both were real, both were very much larger than life, and both were but inches from him. A wineglass was clutched in the fat merchant's large and battered right hand.

"Names, my dear," Khelben muttered, his eyes never leaving the scene in the depths of the crystal. "Don't be shy. Get some names. *What* slaver? Who in Scornubel is now a disguised drow and not a human? Heh?"

"Hmm," Mirt rumbled. "If this started a few decades back, it might explain some of our trading experiences down there. Yes, get me names, so I'll know who to drop in on next time I'm down that way—so I can ask some *persuasive* questions."

Khelben nodded and held up a hand for silence.

The three men heard Laeral Silverhand say solemnly, "You have my word, sister. Your task is now mine, though I begin to suspect we may have to turn the delving over to others among our fellow Chosen in time. Darling Mrilla I know—in passing, but still far better than I'd like to—but if this slaver of yours is still in Waterdeep, take me to see her: I always like to have two strings to pluck, and not just one."

Qilué smiled, nodded, and asked, "Now? I'm no longer tired or hurt, but the magic left to me is not what it could be."

Laeral shrugged. "I'm awake now, so why not? I can lug along enough Art for us both to hurl. We'll go openly, to see which rats scurry to their holes, and who decides they're lion enough to meet our challenge. Would you care for something to eat, or drink, or shall we 'went' without tarrying longer?"

Qilué grinned. "Let's 'went.' "

Laeral smiled, nodded, then rolled over in the air to stare straight at her unseen lord and said meaningfully, "And you stay out of this, dear."

As she spoke, her magic restored her sister's hair to its true silver hue. Mirt and Dauntless looked silently at Khelben, not quite daring to smile.

The Lord Mage of Waterdeep nodded calmly, sketched a tiny gesture with two fingers, and replied, "Of course I shall, lady." Without waiting for her reply, he passed his hand over the scrying sphere, which went dark in an instant.

Khelben sat back from it and added, his lips not quite forming a smile as he turned his head from Mirt to Dauntless then back again, "Which is why you two are going to follow the Lady Mage of Waterdeep and her sister, and see what they get up to. If it's needful, give them a helping hand, or at least ensure that the Harpers learn of what's unfolding."

He crooked a finger, and a tiny sphere of light spun itself out of nothing above his head and descended to hang in front of his nose, spinning gently. "This may be nothing more than drow spying, but I have a feeling it's deeper. I don't like it when I get feelings like that. They're too often all too well founded. This glowsphere will guide you out of here and keep you close to my Lady Laeral. If you need to speak to me, touch it. Some say 'fare well,' but that's not good enough. Good sirs, fare better."

With that the Lord Mage of Waterdeep turned away to devote his full attention to what filled the far side of the otherwise dark chamber: the ever-changing scenes in the bright depths of a dozen or more floating, flickering, keg-sized crystal spheres.

❋   ❋   ❋

A pale, dead, green-white glow bathed the pillars in a ghostly light. Fresh corpses—human hireswords or adventurers, by their garb—were sprawled along the lowest ramshackle catwalk, arms and legs dangling down to where they almost brushed the lazily-stirring silver tresses of the two strolling women. Neither so much as looked up. Skullport hardens the heart and claws at the throat, as the saying went . . . and both of them knew it all too well.

"My kind," Qilué described their quarry, her eyes never idle as she peered all around in ceaseless scrutiny. "Shorter, of course, above her right temple a lock of smoke-hued hair among the usual white . . . all of it worn long. Eyes that snap, temper to match, but not a fool. Graceful, answers to the name of Brelma."

"How long will your tracer last?"

"Until she or another deliberately dispels it. Of course, the longer it remains the more likely it is to be discovered."

Laeral sighed and tossed her head, her flowing silver hair dancing around her shoulders. "We really should meet like this more often, just to chat about the passing parade of anything and everything, not just matters at hand as we save Faerûn one more time."

"We should," Qilué agreed, as they came to a stretch of street relatively free of inky puddles, creeping fungi, and lights. "Yet who in Faerûn beyond prisoners in chains ever has enough time to do all they'd like to?"

The drow priestess reached several tresses of her unbound, living hair forward to precede her softly padding boots as she strode on into the deep gloom. From inside the waves of hair came a razor sharp thief's fingerblade. The illicit tool, wielded by one probing tendril of hair, sliced through a tripwire.

A crossbow quarrel thrummed out of the darkness, struck stone chips off the wall beside Laeral's head, and rebounded into the endless night that shrouded so much of this end of Skullport. Somewhere not all that far away, a raw, throat-stripping scream arose. From another direction there came the sudden, ground shaking thud of an explosion.

The two sisters ignored both the attack and the sounds as they walked unconcernedly on, talking of the newest plays mounted in the city. A suitably disguised Laeral often attended performances, but for Qilué, an expedition into Waterdeep entailed seeing to so many details beforehand that she didn't want to waste an evening on poorer mummeries. Drama critics she trusted were in short supply among the faithful of Eilistraee.

Their unseen assailant, obviously either dumbfounded or impressed by their complete lack of concern for his efforts, mounted no additional attacks.

"*Lord Alurmal's Double-Edged Revenge*? A farce; some clever lines, but most of it's the usual swapping-beds-with-servants-eavesdropping-in-the-closet show," the Lady Mage of Waterdeep said, dismissing the most recent theatrical offering. "The city's all a-clack because two of the dandy-prats talk only in words that certain of our stuffier noble lords have been heard to use . . . and those two lords are, to put it mildly, black in the face with ongoing rage."

"I almost fear to ask what 'dandy-prats' might be," Qilué said lightly, watching another tripwire snap, its severed ends recoiling into the deepest shadows. She waved cheerfully at a cowled form emerging hastily from a lightless doorway. It came to an abrupt, uncertain halt, failing to follow as they turned down a side-stair into a lower way. There mobile, refuse-eating fluttercap mushrooms stood like a quivering, ankle-deep carpet.

"Loudly idiotic, empty-headed parodies of the most brainless of our young nobility," Laeral explained. " 'Prat' because they're there to make all the stupidest pratfalls, and 'dandy' because of their lampooning-all-overblown-fashions appearances."

"Dare I ask about a play that bears the title *The Elf Queen's Peculiar Pleasure*?" the drow priestess asked mildly, stepping around a hobgoblin who stood like a small mountain in the center of the street. His eyes were narrow with menace, and his axe was dripping fresh gore, but he did no more than rumble half-heard profanities at the sisters as they slipped past.

Laeral winced. "You may, of course, dare anything you desire, sister, but be aware that a fat, hairy male actor made up to look like a half-orc plays the Elf Queen, and that . . . er . . . 'her' peculiar pleasure is to steal and devour sweets from Waterdhavian noble matrons . . . all of whom are portrayed by heavily stubbled male actors interested in the very coarsest form of heavy handed, simpering, 'ooh and ah' clowning. The title may suggest illicit, steamy matters, but the play delivers the oldest groaning jests with a leering enthusiasm."

Qilué looked at her sister with some amusement. "Borrowing opinions, Lady Mage? That last sentence came straight from One-Eyed Jack's review in the last *Waterdeep Watch* broadsheet."

"And whom did you think One-Eyed Jack was, hmm?" Laeral replied sweetly. "One of my favorite guises. After all, some of our worst playwrights have openly offered blood bounties to anyone who can bring them Jack's head on a platter."

"A Chosen has to take pride in something," the drow priestess agreed, wrinkling her nose. Her eyes danced, and she added, "Perhaps I'll take up acting—or writing plays. Yes. Ho, now . . . *Death And The Wanton Wizard*. That has a ring to it."

"Qilué," her sister said warningly, "don't start."

One eyebrow crooked in reply. "Start? I never stop." Her face changed and she purred, "Have some fire ready, sister."

A moment later, the tangleweb net settled down softly over them. Laeral's magic sent it melting away amid plumes of thick green and purple smoke. Somewhere out of its roiling the severed end of a catwalk plunged down like a giant's mace, smashed the Lady Mage of Waterdeep off her feet and solidly against the nearest wall, and withdrew in splintered disarray.

Laeral peeled herself off the bloody stone with her own gore streaming out of her nose and down one side of her face, and a stormy glint in her eyes. Another tangleweb net was drifting down onto their heads, and a mauve skinned, glistening figure in purple robes had appeared behind Qilué. One of its tentacles wrapped around her throat, and the other began questing its way up into her face.

The tiny sparkling of a defensive magical field was already gathering around the grotesquely linked couple as Laeral snarled in anger and lifted her hands to rend herself some mind flayer. Then someone opened a shuttered window high above her and emptied a coal scuttle full of old cobblestones onto her head.

When she came reeling dazedly to her feet again, she was in time to see the illithid standing in triumph over a sagging Seventh Sister.

"Qilué," Laeral cried, calling down lightning out of the air to dance ready on both of her palms, "shield yourself!"

"There's no need," the drow priestess replied, twisting around to face her. Laeral gasped in horror.

A mottled, slime-glistening tentacle had plunged into where Qilué's left eye had been, and was surging inward and upward, pulsing with a horrible hunger.

"Sister?" Laeral hissed, a fire kindling in her eyes to match the dancing dazzlements in her hands. "Shall I?"

Obsidian lips gasped as their owner winced, shook her head, then said, "Well, you might deal with the other two. They're heading for you before and behind. This one's linked to them. I can feel the three trading thoughts like hungry little wolves."

Lightning split the gloom of the subterranean city of Skullport with a sound like a rolling, booming clap of thunder. Two skeletons danced briefly in the dying afterglow before collapsing into ash. The crumbling tendrils of yet another tangleweb net slumped and dangled down on all sides, melting away into smoke, as Laeral turned and snarled, "Is your hungry little wolf still so eager?"

"I feel like gagging," Qilué remarked calmly. "It numbs, and yet it burns. A moment or two more and it'll touch my brain, and—ahhh! Here we go. . . ."

The drow priestess threw her shoulders back down onto the trodden stones of the street and arched her back, her body quivering with effort . . . but its straining was nothing compared to the stiffening then frantic squalling spasms of the illithid above her. A glistening mauve hand clawed ineffectually at the air, the stifled echo of a bubbling scream arose, and the mind flayer reeled away, sightless eyes smoking, dead on its feet.

A silver plume of flame arose within the gaping ruin of Qilué's face and snarled around its torn flesh like a buzzing fly. Laeral hissed in concern and lifted her fingers to trace the intricate gestures of a spell that called on Qilué's unharmed eye to spin itself a new match. She held her kneeling sister's head steady with a hand laced through Qilué's restlessly twisting hair, and looked around in all directions for the approach of fresh danger as the spell did its slow work.

What she saw instead were a lot of spying eyes sliding back into concealment. In the distant gloom where the fluttercap mushrooms ended and the street turned to join another passage between unwelcoming stone buildings, a drow with a smoky lock of hair stood looking back over her shoulder at the two sisters.

Ah, Brelma, doubtless deliberately leading us into trap after trap.

The Lady Mage of Waterdeep sent that thought directly to her sister, and Qilué replied aloud, "Of course—and I appreciate the effort she's going to. Many folks wouldn't have taken all this trouble." Her voice was more wry than bitter.

Laeral lifted an eyebrow, then sighed. "There are, however, always the favorite few . . ."

Something in her voice made Qilué look up. Her one good eye glanced along the street to where Brelma was hastily ducking around the corner of a building, in time to see a trio of leather-armored men trot out of an alley with wound and cocked crossbows in their hands. They ranged themselves into a line, loaded their weapons, took aim—as noises on all sides of the sisters marked the arrival of many of their fellows—and fired.

The air was full of quarrels as the Lady Mage of Waterdeep thrust Qilué's head to the ground and threw herself flat. The drow priestess turned over as quarrels cracked and rattled on the stones all around her. She opened her mouth to shape a spell. She was still wondering why Laeral hadn't already done so when she saw the reason.

From out of the dark tangle of decaying balconies, laundry lines, and crossing catwalks high above them, an all too familiar shape was descending—a sphere of bony plates split by a wide, crooked, many-toothed mouth that was clearly smiling. A beholder. A wriggling fringe of wormlike eyestalks could be seen around one curve of the body, and above that unfriendly smile, the eye tyrant's large central orb was fixed unwaveringly on the two Chosen. Laeral hissed something in the frantic instant before that eye erupted in the softly racing cone of pale light that consumed and doused all magic it touched.

"Not a very stylish trap," Qilué snarled, the first cold whispers of fear rising in her. "Not that it needs to be." Without magic, they were simply two tall and unarmored targets lying in the midst of a ring of crossbowmen who undoubtedly had daggers in plenty to use when their quarrels were all spent.

A wet thump came from somewhere very near, and Qilué heard her sister gasp.

"Laeral?" she cried, rolling over with no thought for the ring of grim men closing in carefully around them, or the beholder hanging so close above. "Sister?"

"What was that foolishness I said earlier about finding out who the lions were?" Laeral asked, her voice tight with pain. A dark, heavy war-quarrel stood out of one of her shoulders, threads of silver smoke stirring away from the wound, and from between the fingers she held pressed against her right flank, tongues of silver flame were licking.

"Laeral!" Qilué gasped, crawling hastily forward. "Lie still, and let me . . ."

"Die right beside her," one of the crossbowmen said coldly.

Qilué looked up to find a ring of ready bows aimed at her head. There were a dozen or more, even with most of the warriors out of the fray back behind these men, winding their spent weapons like madmen. The gentle light washing over her left her no need to look up at the lowering bulk of the beholder overhead, or to hope for any escape. The lead crossbowman jerked his head in a curt signal, and bows snapped forth speeding death.

✳　　✳　　✳

"Too late!" the Old Wolf snarled. "We're going to be too bloody late. *Move*, youngling!"

Dauntless, a good twenty paces ahead and sprinting hard over loose, rolling stones and greasy, best unseen alley refuse, didn't bother to reply. His blade was in his hand, but he was still a good seventy feet or more from the back of the nearest bowman in the ring—to say nothing of the half a dozen or so of their fellows kneeling in his way and cranking their bows, or the monstrous beholder floating overhead.

They didn't look to be taking prisoners, or pausing for a moment of gloating. The men stank of fear. Even as Dauntless hurled himself into a desperate, reckless sprint, bows hummed. The archers flung themselves hastily back and down, boots scraping on stone, to avoid being struck by ricocheting bolts fired by their fellows facing them across the deadly ring.

And so it was that the young Harper, with Mirt puffing along like a furious walrus in his wake, had a clear view of two beautiful bodies arching and twisting in agony. Silver flames roared up in sudden, street shaking fury—to the obvious surprise of the beholder hanging so low overhead.

That was all he saw before everything in front of him vanished in blinding, silvery light. The very stones of the street rose up to smite him, dashing him back, back into waiting . . . hard . . . things. . . .

※   ※   ※

Something dark and tentacled drew back from a spell-shrouded window in Skullport and said coldly to something else in the same room, "Come, and watch fools die. It's futile—even fatal—to strike directly at the Chosen. If you can trick them into working for you, though. . . ."

Something else took two eager, slithering strides before the street outside the window exploded.

✳   ✳   ✳

Qilué had always hated arrows. Quarrels, darts, and slung stones, too; anything that enabled some coward to deal death from a safe distance. Yet her fairness drove her through mounting pain to admit that those archers probably hated and feared the spells she could unleash on them—often from a safer distance—as much, or more. The torment dragged her away from that thought, letting it recede into a crimson distance regardless of her feeble attempts to claw and cling to something—anything—more than the raging pain.

Qilué sobbed, or tried to, and flailed her shuddering limbs about despairingly. The drow priestess wallowed in gut wrenching agony around four quarrels crossed in her breast and belly, struggling to swallow as fire boiled up in her throat and choked her.

Laeral was twisting in similar torment, her body a small forest of crossbow bolts. Snarling and rolling back and forth, she looked more like a spiny beast than the Lady Mage of Waterdeep. Silver fire spat to the stones, spraying down as Laeral tore quarrels from her flesh and threw them, flaming, away. When the flames rushed out of her in a sudden gout that sent Khelben's consort sprawling onto her face on the stones, she shrieked, rolled over heedless of the quarrels still in her back, and sent the boiling, raging flames straight up into the air like a lance stabbing up at the beholder.

Her roll had forced some of the remaining quarrels right through her. They burst up out of her front, spewing flames. Laeral lashed the blazing eye tyrant with those flames, her face savage. Its central eye went dark, melting away into ruin as the beholder erupted in flames and started to spin, its great mouth yawning open in a wet, bubbling roar of agony.

By then, Qilué had managed to get to her knees, her every breath a searing flood of wet and blazing silver.

She looked up through the flames of her own blood at the bowmen before her. Some were still scrambling up, plucking up bows, and trotting hastily away to where others had finished cranking their bows and were readying quarrels for another shot. Qilué snarled, dipped one hand into the wetness at her belly and spat out the words Mystra had taught her so long ago. Lines of spilling fire raced from her fingertips. She aimed at bowmen's eyes with the same ruthlessness they'd shown her. In moments they were staggering, shrieking, and falling with enthusiasm.

Qilué turned, crouching low as a few quarrels whistled past her, and dealt blindness all around the ring. As she came around to where she'd begun, leaving only a few crouching bowmen unscathed, the beholder cartwheeled into view, shrinking into blackened wrinkles as it spun away down the street. It struck the side of a building and tore away most of a wooden balcony. Laeral rose unsteadily, the last burned remnants of the quarrels that had transfixed her falling away from her blackened body, and hurled a spell at it with both hands.

Fire burst forth in brilliance above the street, and the beholder fell into ashes amid its tumbling embers. Laeral wasted no time in watching its destruction, but turned with threads of silver sparks leaping between her fingers. "Have you left me any?" she asked her sister.

Qilué managed a smile, tongues of silver flame hissing out to lick her nose, and gasped, "A few."

Laeral nodded, looked around at the stumbling bowmen, and decided no quarrels would be immediately forthcoming. She looked back at Qilué, clucked and frowned at her sister's condition, and reached out to heal, with fire dancing from her fingertips.

The drow priestess hissed in relief and pressed against the Lady Mage's soothing touch. As Qilué let go the last of her pain with a groan, Laeral murmured wordless comfort, and glanced over one of her sister's

ebony shoulders. Her gaze met the wondering eyes of a
man not all that far away, and she gave him a glare
that brought silver fire leaping into her eyes for just a
moment.

Mirt, his hands under the arms of a groggy Dauntless, did not need a more pointed command. He
nodded and started dragging the young Harper
hastily back into an alley. Mirt was not, Laeral noted,
the only man seeking to hastily depart the street.

Laeral nodded her satisfaction at that, pressed her
fingertips to one last wound of her own—high up,
where her breast started to become her shoulder—and
asked Qilué, "Were you thinking of sparing any of these
oh-so-brave bowmen?"

"Two," the priestess replied, "sighted and whole. A
hare to lead us, and a spare, should ill befall that hare.
Brelma's long gone—and what good is a sprung trap if
it leaves us no trail onward?"

"I'll need you to writhe and stagger, then," Laeral
murmured, "at the same moment I do. They're firing
one last volley." The radiance that leaked from her fingers then was blue-white, not silver, but threaded
faintly through the wisps of smoke around them.

When the quarrels came again, Laeral twisted away
and whistled a curse at how close one had come to her
throat. She threw up her arms and cried out. As the
other bolts clattered on the stones beyond the two
falsely staggering Chosen, the air all around blazed
with cold, eerie blue fire. Laeral stopped acting agonized in an instant, and stood tall to gaze in all directions.

Her sister straightened more slowly, watching the
Lady Mage with a smile of comprehension. They could
see out, but no eye could pierce the roiling fire. When it
faded, no doubt, Laeral's magic would have done its
work on the eyes of both sisters. Unless Qilué was very
much mistaken, they'd soon be plunging into real darkness.

"I see five still on their feet," the Lady Mage of Waterdeep said crisply, glowing spell bolts leaping from her fingertips. The blue-white missiles sped away, arcing high up into the gloom above the street. "Have I missed anyone?"

Qilué looked all around, seeing only the five bowmen who'd fired that last volley. They were now standing peering at the two sisters as if they couldn't see down the street properly. As Qilué watched, Laeral's missiles descended from above to smite down three of them in a deadly whirlwind. At the sight of those deaths the last two bowmen exchanged a glance—and in unspoken accord they turned and fled.

"Just those two," the drow priestess replied brightly.

Laeral gave her a sour look, then wrinkled her nose and said, "Thanks."

Qilué sketched a flowing bow some Waterdhavian noble had made to her at the revel, and asked, "Do we run after them, or have you a spell handy to whisk us to their boot heels?"

"I have three such," Laeral replied, and smiled. "Shall we run a little, first?"

"And leave the two Harpers breathless?" Qilué responded. "Why not?"

* * *

"You see?" The cold voice held no triumph, only calm comfort in knowing the true measure of powers abroad in the world. Tentacles lifted a goblet of wine that steamed and bubbled.

"Yes," someone else replied shortly, slithering away to affix a cloak over the cage where a pet barking snake had been roused to noisy alarm. "Not that the lesson was less than obvious. Chosen of Mystra are always best left alone."

"Well, some folk never learn that lesson," the cold voice pointed out, setting the goblet carefully down again. It was empty. Goblets were always too small, these days.

✳   ✳   ✳

After the third turning, Laeral took Qilué's wrist and steered her off into an alcove that had once been someone's cellar. They were both breathing heavily, but the bowmen ahead of them were panting and staggering.

"Time for a spell," the Lady Mage gasped.

"Invisibility?"

Laeral wrinkled her nose. "Ah, you guessed."

"Sister," Qilué said severely, "have we time? I don't want to lose them. They know their way; they go in haste, and the leader seldom flashes his glowstone."

Laeral nodded, murmured an invisibility spell in deft and elegant haste, touched Qilué, then tugged her back out into the passage.

"You run ahead," the Lady Mage gasped as they picked up speed again, "and I'll do myself when I get the chance. We'll still be able to see each other with this enchantment. I've a fair idea where they're headed, anyway, and they're winded. They'll have to stop soon, or collapse."

"They're not the only ones," Qilué gasped back, then squeezed her sister's arm affectionately and let go, sprinting ahead into the darkness.

"Holy Mystra forfend," Laeral puffed, watching the youngest of the Seven Sisters vanish into the gloom like a black arrow. "I'm getting too old for this."

She whirled around, half-expecting to hear Mirt's sarcastic rumble coming out of the darkness to tell her she wasn't the only one, but the darkness remained silent. The Lady Mage of Waterdeep looked down at the scorched remnants of her clothing, decided that was just as well, and started running. By the time she reached the first bend in the passage, she decided she wasn't too tardy an arrow herself.

＊　　＊　　＊

The bowmen staggered to a halt, groaning, and swiped sweat from their eyes with their forearms. One held out a glowstone and felt for the chain at his throat as the other turned his back and drew a dagger, staring warily all around.

The darkness remained empty and still, filled with the rasp of their own hard breathing and the usual reek of the nearby sewers. With a sigh of relief the man with the glowstone thrust the long-barreled key on the end of his chain into a crack between two uneven wall stones, and turned it. There was a gentle grating sound, and the man pulled on the key. It brought a smallish stone block out of the wall with it, into his waiting palm. The bowman reached into the cavity the stone had filled, drew out the mummified husk of a spider, and let it drift down to the passage floor as he reached farther into the hole, turned something, then set his shoulder against the wall. It growled once, then with a low, reluctant grating sound, yielded inward, revealing itself to be a short, wide door.

The man with the dagger took the glowstone with a snarled, "Hurry!" The bowman with the key slipped through the opened door, struck alight a lantern hanging just inside, then shoved the door closed from within.

The remaining bowman replaced spider and block with barely concealed impatience then shifted his weight uneasily from one foot to another, his eyes on the passage from whence they'd come. "Hurry, damn you!" he growled, glaring up at the wall above the door. As if it had heard him, a row of stones there slid inward in unison, dropping away to reveal an opening along the ceiling of the passage that would admit a crawling man. A rope appeared through this gap and descended, the key on its neck chain tinkling at the end of it. The bowman sheathed his dagger, locked the stone block, then clambered up the wall in almost feverish haste, the glowstone in his teeth.

He was still rolling through the gap in the ceiling when something invisible came sprinting out of the gloom. Unseen hands drew a dagger whose blade was as slender as a needle and as dull and black as tar, set it on the floor pointing to the wall exactly under one end of the open gap, then—as the stones grated hastily back into place—hurried back the way it had come.

Once she'd gone far enough to regain her breath without her panting being heard from the opening she'd found, Qilué sat down against the wall and waited until the Lady Mage of Waterdeep came up to her in the darkness.

"Your favorite stretch of wall?"

"The same," the drow priestess replied with a grin, and slapped Laeral's behind affectionately as she rose. *Ah, but it'd felt good to be a freebooting adventurer for a few days,* she thought. *I am going to miss this.*

"Was that a victory pat and you're going to show me two bodies," Laeral asked, "or—?"

"I'm going to show you my dagger in a moment," Qilué said tersely. "Now find and keep silence—for once—and come. Bring a wraithform spell, if you've got one . . . or one of those blast-everything-to-the-gods spells if you don't."

"I can provide either," Laeral murmured into her younger sister's ear as Qilué took hold of her wrist and led her forward.

With catlike stealth the two Chosen went to where Qilué's dagger lay. The priestess indicated the size and edges of the ceiling opening with her hands, then touched the Lady Mage to send the silent thought:

Stone blocks receded into a space behind that wall, up there, and have now returned to their places. Both men went through, after some complications. How many wraithforms have you?

Laeral sighed soundlessly. *Just one . . . for you?*

No. You know the city better—and if 'twould be best to slay them or leave them be. If there's no gap through down here, I've magic enough to hold you aloft, up there.

Laeral nodded, cast the spell on herself, then seemed to flow into the wall.

Qilué listened intently for a long time, then let out her own long, soundless sigh, leaned back against the cold, rough stones of the passage wall, and let herself sag wearily.

Steeling herself against the stench of the sewers, she settled herself into another silent wait. This one was less patient than the last. She found herself hoping that handsome young Harper would turn up again. Yes, she was going to miss this very much.

✳   ✳   ✳

The cellar was large, damp, and equipped with bells on the wall that could send signals up metal rods to places above. Laeral kept to its darkest corner as the two bowmen looked gloomily at those bells then at the adjacent stone door. The two agreed grimly that they'd wait until morning to give a report that was going to be received with rage. They went on a quick search for rats among the pile of empty crates that filled one end of the cellar. Finding none, the bowmen set their lantern on the floor to burn itself out, and took two of the rough rope mattresses slung along one wall. Once they'd settled uneasily off to sleep, Laeral drifted silently around the cellar, inspecting the other things it held. Among the items there were a long coffle bar with manacles, rows of body irons hung on a wall, and two casks that—if several small, dried puddles could be trusted—held the rich, dark, drugged wine known as "slavesleep."

Well, it wasn't exactly trumpet blaring news that the owner of this particular cellar was slave-dealing. Laeral wondered briefly just how many cellars, in the labyrinth of underways beneath the streets and houses of Waterdeep, held similar incriminating items. Or worse, like the one that had been found knee-deep in bodies drowned in brandy to keep down the smell, or the monster-fighting pit under Cat Alley, or . . .

Why drow, though? And why Mrilla Malsander? The reach was too needlessly broad and bold for just kidnapping and slaving. This was something bigger . . .

Not that these two would know anything of use, even if she'd been carrying the right magic to get it out of them.

One of the men muttered something unintelligible but fearful in his slumber. The Lady Mage of Waterdeep drifted over to stand above him, frowning thoughtfully down. She blew him a kiss and slipped back to the passage wall like a silent shadow, vanishing through it a scant instant before the other bowman sat bolt upright, quivering in fear, and tried to tell himself that there'd been no gliding ghost in the cellar beyond the phantoms conjured by his imagination. It took him longer than usual to convince himself that everything was all right.

Laeral melted back out of the wall, murmured a word that made her solid again, and touched a dark, bare drow arm. Through the contact she said silently into Qilué's mind, *I know whose cellar this is. Auvrarn Labraster, recently risen to become one of Waterdeep's most "prominent" merchants.*

He would be, of course, Qilué replied in the same silent, intimate way. *Sister, I simply must get back to my own work. Serving two goddesses must be the hardest trail in all Faerûn, I often think.*

I don't doubt that. I'll take over from here, Laeral replied, and kissed her sister with a tenderness that surprised them both. As they clung to each other in an embrace that neither of them wanted to end, taking simple pleasure in merely holding each other tight, the Lady Mage added, with a cold resolve that Qilué could feel through the places where their bare skin touched, *and I know just where to start.*

* * *

"My lady," her seneschal said with a grave flourish of his silver-handled rod of office, "you have a visitor."

Mrilla Malsander looked up from the latest installment of *The Silk Mask Saga* with barely concealed exasperation. Her servants seemed determined to interrupt her, time after time, in her one sacred, daily indulgence— reading a certain series of cheap, street corner chapbooks. The endless adventures of the amorous Lady Elradra, recently a slave and from birth (secretly) the Lost Princess of Cormyr, struggles in the salons and palaces of rich and sinister Sembian merchants to gain allies and the gold she needs to one day reclaim her kingdom. These melodramas were accompanied, in Mrilla's case, by warm sugared milk and pieces of expensive Shou ginger dipped in even more expensive Maztican chocolate.

She gave the seneschal her best glare, but his eyes were fixed firmly on the eagle Malsander crest that adorned the crown of her high-backed chair, and his stance and bearing were beyond reproach.

Gods blast the man down! She was theirs the rest of every day, until dusk took her out to the revels, but this one hour or so of every morning, as she raced through Elradra's latest exploits, sighed, then read the spiciest bits aloud to herself, savoring them with delicious shudders and thrills, was hers, and hers alone. It was too much, by all the gods! It was just *too much*!

She would not hurry. No.

Mrilla set down the chapbook, discreetly purchased on a corner only hours before, and carefully concealed it beneath a grand copy of the Malsander family genealogy that was as thick as her thigh, and took all of her strength to lift. She sat back to study its appearance, nodded her satisfaction, then took up her milk and drained it in one long swallow, not caring if stablemen did such things in taverns she would never deign to visit. Wiping the mustache she knew was beginning to take firm hold of her upper lip, Mrilla set the plate of ginger pieces on the table that nestled half seen beneath the spreading arm of her chair. She slid it as far out of sight as possible, and snapped, "Well, Jalarn? This visitor is important enough to interrupt me at my reading, but not important enough to have a name?"

The seneschal told the carved eagle, "She gave her name as Lady Sylull Cassalanter, my lady. I conducted her into the Fleet, my lady, where she awaits your pleasure."

Mrilla Malsander's eyes opened wide, and her mouth dropped open even wider. Lady Cassalanter? Lady *Cassalanter*?

The Dame In White, known less respectfully as "the Dame with the Cane," was one of the oldest and most respected of Waterdhavian nobles. She was reclusive due to her failing bones and rigid standards of respectability. This was a woman who was said to regard unmarried ladies dancing at revels as doing something almost as sinful as the woman who, for a handful of coins, might take several partners at once up her bedchamber stairs in Dock Ward.

Not that Mrilla Malsander knew about such things! Oh, no. . . .

Mrilla felt the warmth on her forehead and cheeks that she knew meant she was blushing crimson to the carefully shaven and powdered tip of her chin. The Fleet Parlor was the best of her receiving rooms, crowded with gold and hung with large and colorful portraits of the ships that had enriched the Malsanders racing through stormy—but vividly sunlit—seas, but still. . . .

"Jalarn," she said icily, "we do *not* keep the heads of Waterdeep's noble families waiting in our parlors. Apologize deeply to her for the wait—abjectly, mind; none of your mockery!—and conduct her straight to me, here. Then you may withdraw, listening *not* behind the keyhole, but by the board at the doors, for me to summon you by means of the bell."

The seneschal bowed deeply—to the eagle carved at her father's orders rather than to her, Mrilla noted with fresh irritation—and withdrew. The moment the door closed behind him, she plunged into a whirlwind of throat clearing, nose picking, hair teasing, and straightening of throat lace and collar.

She'd safely settled herself back into her chair and assumed an easy, graceful smile by the time the door opened again. The seneschal struck its brass boom panel, and announced the guest.

Mrilla rose graciously. "Lady Cassalanter," she simpered. "So good of you to come. My humble home is unworthy to receive such grace."

The powdered, jowled figure in white silk blinked at her, nodded thanks and dismissal to the seneschal, and started forward, stooped over a cane that glittered from top to bottom with rare and precious gems from the farthest realms of Faerûn. She bore down— slowly—on Mrilla Malsander, who found herself ensnared by piercing dark eyes divided by a nose as sharp and as hooked as a vulture's beak, but said not a word until the door boomed closed behind her.

Then she barked, "Malsander! I've words for you. *Sit!*"

Mrilla gaped at the woman.

The Lady Cassalanter lifted one white, bristling brow. "Sit *down*, woman! You look like an actress pretending to be a noblewoman, dithering back and forth there. This is your house. Sit and be at ease."

"I—I—" There were few folk in Waterdeep who could claim to have witnessed Mrilla Malsander at a loss for words—and she was proud of that—but Lady Cassalanter could now claim to be one of them.

Mrilla backed wildly to the nearest chair and sat down on its edge, straining to keep bolt upright and to remember how best to pose her hands—crossed but not clasped, in her lap, yes, that was it—and her legs—crossed at the ankles? Left together with knees bent and toes turned to one side? Drawn back under her—no, that was for young girls. Oh, *gods*!

Lady Sylull Cassalanter marched right past Mrilla and seated herself in Mrilla's own high-backed chair; the one placed to dominate the room. She crossed wrinkled hands over the massive sculpted silver rose that surmounted her jeweled cane, parked its encrusted length upright between her knees, and leaned forward to bark, "Oh, you ape nobility very cleverly, girl, and don't think your ambitions haven't been noticed. 'Lady Malsander' is what you dream of—don't attempt to deny it!—and scheme toward; none too cleverly, I might add."

The gaze fixed upon Mrilla became severe, then softened. Its owner assumed a slightly less curt tone—a tone that someone who knew Sylull Cassalanter rather better than Mrilla did would have interpreted as "tenderness."

"You might be interested to know that some of us have admired your bold spirit, your hunger to become one of us, and your deftly underhanded business methods. We have almost taken the step of petitioning the lords to ennoble House Malsander." The aged noblewoman lowered her voice and added in a growl, "I say *almost*, girl."

"Ah—y-yes?" Mrilla replied intelligently.

"There are just three things standing in your way," the Dame In White explained gruffly. "The first and foremost is your tightfistedness—gods, girl, you finally get someone noble into the house and you can't even stir yourself to offer even the tiniest glass of whatever wretched stuff you fondly believe to be 'high class' wine, or some of those chocolates you've tried to hide down there."

"Oh!" Mrilla cried, blushing bright crimson, "Ah— uh—*please*, help yourself. I'll ring for some wine. I—"

"Whatever bottle lurks in that hollow book you just glanced at will do just fine," Lady Cassalanter said in dry tones. "Don't fluster yourself, girl."

She watched Mrilla scurry to the bookshelf. Once her hostess had turned away to reach down the book, wrinkled noble hands moved in two small, deft gestures, and dry, patrician lips shaped two softly breathed words. Mrilla never noticed in her haste and breathless fumbling.

The book proved to contain both a flask and a pair of fluted tallglasses. When the pride of the Malsanders finally spun around with a glass of her best firewine trembling in her hand, the old lady had leaned back at ease in the eagle-crowned chair.

Reaching forth a hand for the proffered glass, she said, "The second thing is your clumsy campaign of unsubtle attempts to unmask and bribe as many lords as you can ensnare, girl. This is unutterably *common*. Cease at once—at *once*, do you hear me?"

The Dame In White held up her glass, surveyed its contents critically, and put it down untasted. "The proper way," she purred, "is to content yourself with just one lord and discreetly seduce him—as I did. Avoid crude jests, talking with your mouth full, and scratch-ing yourself in his presence, and you're in—oh yes, except for the third thing."

She fell silent then, with disconcerting abruptness, and fixed Mrilla Malsander with such a piercing glare that Mrilla, for all her years, wealth, and airs, squirmed on her chair like a young miss in the nursery, still aghast at the thought of Lady Cassalanter so casu-ally talking of seduction . . . and in the end felt moved to fill the silence. "Yes," she asked earnestly, "this third thing? What might it be?"

"Consorting with undesirables," the Lady Cassalanter thundered. "Waterdeep, the eternal City of Splendors, cannot clasp to its bosom snakes who work to its downfall, or those who consort with them. Grasping merchants are quite bad enough, but this Labraster man is beyond even *our* legendary tolerance! Sever your relations—whatever they may be—with Auvrarn Labraster, forthwith."

Mrilla went white then, instead of crimson, and her eyes narrowed a trifle. "How—how did you—?"

"Gods, woman, do you walk Waterdeep in a daze? 'Tis a city of *people*, girl, people with eyes and ears and wits every bit as sharp as yours, even if they be dock loaders or stablemen or chamber servants. If you treat them as furniture, stepping around them without noticing, how can you help but be surprised when they murmur that you've been talking to a drow slaver one night—"

Mrilla stiffened, and her eyes glittered dangerously, but her noble guest seemed not to notice.

"—and an old fool of a noblewoman the next morning?"

The pride of the Malsanders gripped the arms of her chair so hard her knuckles started to go white. She swayed slightly as she licked dry lips and asked rather faintly, "The . . . the noble families of Waterdeep watch with whom I deal? And care?"

"No, no, girl. Don't give yourself airs or plunge into thinking that dark conspiracies rule this city. We watch only those who interest us—those we might marry, or ambitious, thrusting persons—such as yourself—who might soon win nobility and whom we therefore want to know better."

Lady Cassalanter leaned forward and added in a stage whisper, "I don't know how much you need the coins your dealings with this Labraster bring, nor do I care what you do for him or he does for himself. Truly, girl, do you not think that each and every noble family of this city doesn't get up to a little of the shady stuff to please and enrich ourselves? But we're already 'in the club,' don't you see? If you wish to join us, you'll need to put aside this Labraster man thoroughly enough to convince, say, the Lord Mage Blackstaff that you're done with him—and I do mean *convince* him after he's rummaged around in your mind with his spells, not just a letter you don't mean and a few empty words let fall from your lips. We don't care two copper coins about this, but we'll triumphantly use it against you if you don't jump when we demand this severance. So for you, 'tis simple: be noble, or work with this merchant. Once you are noble, you can work with him again—discreetly—and probably be of far more use to him. Of course, he'll have a hold over you, then, and that's a weakness a noble can ill afford."

Mrilla Malsander blinked, and the spell-disguised Laeral hardly needed the mind reading spell she'd cast to be certain of Mrilla's connection to Auvrarn Labraster. The spell did let her read enough of the dark, reptilian mind of the would-be noblewoman to tell her that Mrilla actually knew very little of the workings of the cabal Labraster and she herself were a part of. She knew little more, in fact, than that she must report to Auvrarn Labraster what Brelma or others using Brelma's name told her, that she must invest monies he gave her as he directed, keep safe documents and gems he handed to her, purchase things he directed her to purchase, and never, upon pain of death, to ask why.

The Lady Sylull Cassalanter rose with a muffled grunt of effort, steadied her stooped self over her cane, and rasped, "Just some friendly advice, dear. I think your determination and spirit would be good for Waterdeep. I'd like to see you as one of us. You'd be surprised how many nobles don't even want to be nobles—or at least, take on the tasks and responsibilities of nobility—and you want it *so* much. I look forward to your doing the right thing. A pleasant day to you, Goodwoman Malsander."

The stooped noblewoman proceeded a few laborious steps toward the door and added, without turning, "Nice paintings, by the way."

Mrilla half rose to gush her thanks and help her guest to the door, then, somehow, fell back in her chair, her mind a welter of images and sudden strong surges of feeling. She was ashamed at how thoroughly this wrinkled old woman had humiliated her, yet she was grateful to Lady Cassalanter for the frank, discreet advice. They wanted her to be a noble! She was aghast at how closely they'd watched her, and what they knew. Auvrarn Labraster came into her mind, speaking to her on a balcony at a revel overlooking the gardens of Brossfeather Towers. His image wavered away into the piercing eyes of Lady Cassalanter, talking to her just now, and they in turn became the barely concealed contempt in the eyes of her wooden-faced seneschal Jalarn. She was enraged that folk meaner and lesser than she had presumed to judge her. At the same time she was delighted that ennoblement was so close, and that nobles—some, at least—thought her worthy of exalted station.

Mrilla Malsander sank back limply in the chair, and began to drool onto its embroidered arm cushions. Laeral's gentle, magical clouding and rearrangement of her memories had, in a matter of moments, left Mrilla with an abiding fear and hatred of Auvrarn Labraster. She was also left with the need to cooperate with him fully, loyally, discreetly, and carefully—but slowly, always slowly. She was to delay and dawdle whenever and however possible. She had no more clear a memory of Lady Cassalanter than recollections of a pleasant, welcome-to-the-nobility social call, after which she'd drifted off to sleep so swiftly that she'd left untouched the glass she'd poured for herself after the stooped old lady with the splendidly jeweled cane had shuffled out the door. She also found herself thinking of Jalarn with sudden affection, even excitement, as she considered his strong shoulders, discretion, and the grace of his long strides. She realized that the little signs he'd made, over these last few years, betrayed the depths of his affection and regard. . . .

✳   ✳   ✳

"Ah, but you can be a cruel woman, Laeral," the Lady Mage of Waterdeep chided herself under her breath. She stepped out of a palace alcove and paused critically before a mirror across the hallway. The reflection showed her a fat, male, heavy-lidded merchant, his mustache bristling importantly above a doublet that was more gaudy than pleasant to look upon. So disguised, she strode away, boots clicking on the polished marble pave, and nodded an imperious greeting to the guards she swept past. They frowned, trying to remember the name of this merchant. They'd seen him around the palace a time or two. Since none of them had seen him emerge from the alcove that shuffling old Lady Cassalanter had entered, none of them thought there was anything unusual or amiss.

Auvrarn Labraster dwelt in rented lodgings in North Ward called Windpennant Pillars. The residence was a narrow townhouse in the midst of a row of shops that opened up to sprawl from room to room over all of the shops in its block. She suspected that it might also connect, through its cellars, to a large, grand mansion that stood behind it. For all his girth, the merchant with the bristling mustache strode with speed and purpose thence, frowning as if consumed with matters of great weight.

In truth, Laeral was thinking deeply as she strode along. Qilué had been right. They all had more important work to do than smashing a slaving ring. There'd been a time when the Lady Mage of Waterdeep would have delighted in a slow, subtle, painstaking investigation of Malsander, Labraster, and all their contacts and business associates. There was a time when the fascination of a good, juicy Waterdhavian intrigue, and understanding how a particular citizen dealt with another specific citizen behind closed doors, would have meant more to Laeral than smashing or frustrating this cabal. Years had passed, though, changing Laeral as they changed everyone else, and she was too busy just now to devote more than a few hours of brute force tactics to the schemes of Auvrarn Labraster and his friends.

So it was time to confront the man, and peel his mind like an onion, or at least scare him enough that the cabal would react. The former task would no doubt be a bit more formidable than it had been with Mrilla. The latter she hoped, like flies disturbed from a corpse when a soldier rolls it over with his boot, might show the reach and strength of the conspiracy. All the while, she was grimly sure, one Khelben "Blackstaff" Arunsun would be diligently spying on her, no matter what he'd promised. Her present shape was one she'd used many times before. Khelben should have no difficulty in knowing whom Trennan Beldrusk the Waytrader— lately of Neverwinter; expert in silks, scents, and cleansing herbal scrubs—truly was.

When she stood before the door and used its knocker, Laeral had expected no reply. She was also unsurprised when her prudent step to one side did not cause her to evade a falling stone planter. Merchants crushed on one's doorstep was a little drastic for North Ward, but she was more than a little surprised to find the door unlocked. Ah, well. It wasn't as if traps had become a novelty these last few days.

"Labraster?" she called, gruffly. "Auvrarn Labraster?"

Her voice carried away through gloomy emptiness to distant, unseen corners. The house was dark, empty of life, and cold, but furnished and strewn with the oddments of everyday life. There was an ash-filled brass pipe bowl here, and an untidy pile of broadsheets there, as if everyone had just stepped out for a moment.

The fat merchant frowned, and ducked his head in through a few open doors, peering for signs of life or, perhaps, sprawled bodies.

"Labraster? Gods, man, I'm not a creditor or a tax collector! Where by the laughing fiends are you?"

The silence held, though somehow it sounded as if the house itself was awake; no longer empty, but alert and listening . . . waiting for something to happen.

Trennan Beldrusk called Labraster's name up the stairs, and for the benefit of anyone who might be hiding behind a wall panel, added gruffly, "I'll have to leave him a note. Gods, I don't want to be clawing my way through another man's house seeking quills and parchment. I'll check below, first. No one leaves just as trade season's getting into full swing without at least leaving agents behind. . . ."

She was halfway down the cellar stairs, behind the kitchens, when she heard the very faint sound she'd been waiting for. In the house above her, a door had been carefully opened, then closed again with care, by someone trying to keep as quiet as possible. She smiled, and went on down into the dimness.

The smell of damp earth grew strong around her, but there was no scurrying of rats—or any other sound, for that matter.

"Labraster?" she called, making her voice sound quiet but exasperated. "Where by all the watching gods have you gotten to?"

The house she'd seen thus far seemed like a series of reception rooms and offices. It was a place to entertain business clients, not the rooms where anyone really lived. Everything seemed too clean, too simply furnished, too unused. Nowhere had she seen any clothes—not so much as a rain cloak hanging on a peg. If the much sought after Auvrarn Labraster dwelt here at all, he lived in rooms she hadn't found yet. Here before her, behind the last of a row of wine casks and past a potato bin, was a heavy, iron-strapped door. Beside it a lantern hung on a wall hook. The door was in just the right place to connect with that mansion beyond Labraster's stables.

Laeral smiled, stopped to listen for a moment, and fancied she heard a stealthy movement somewhere in the kitchens above her. She waited, remaining absolutely still, but there came no more sounds. After a time she shrugged, threw back the door bar, and pulled the door open. Earthy darkness yawned before her.

The first trap should be about . . . *here*—where no client could have any honest reason for intrusion, and those "in the know" would have a way around it. Laeral made the way before her glow with gentle radiance, and saw a damp, dirt floored passage leading into a stone lined room that must underlie the stable yard. She took the lantern in her hand without bothering to light it, and stepped forward.

She was right about the trap.

At her third step the floor fell away, spilling her down into a musty cellar—a room where the air flashed amber at her arrival.

The radiance faded into a lazily curling yellow haze even before Laeral landed hard on bare stones, numbing her elbow, shattering the lantern, and driving the wind from her body. Struggling to breathe, she rolled over away from the spreading lamp oil, frowning. Her clothes were hanging from her arms like the folds of a fallen tent. Her magic should have lowered her gently into this cellar, preventing any fall.

Of course. Whatever enchantment she'd awakened—blundered into, fallen through—stripped away all magic. She was a mustachioed merchant named Trennan Beldrusk no longer, but herself, her garments now oversized and hanging loosely except at her wrists and ankles, where they ended a little too prematurely for the fashion conscious. She was but one tall, athletic woman with very little, now, to place between her and any subsequent traps . . . or guards.

Oh, she had knives in both boots, another strapped to one forearm—and visible, now—and a fourth under her hair at the back of her neck, the black ribbon she wore at her throat concealing its sheath strap. She had a strong feeling that little slivers of steel weren't going to avail her much against what lay ahead. She was the Lady Mage of Waterdeep, and she needed her spells.

Laeral sighed, sat up, and looked around. "I haven't *time* for this," she told herself aloud, not bothering to try sounding gruff any longer. "I've only time for brute force confrontations, remember?"

The yellow haze filled the cellar, but didn't seem to extend elsewhere. It wasn't swirling up into the passage above, still a-glow with her last magic, nor was it leaking into the only way she could see out of the room. A missing stone in the wall seemed to be the mouth of a crawl-tunnel running on toward the mansion.

Crawl-tunnel? For merchants and valuables being smuggled? No, there had to be another way, a proper way. Laeral looked up at the hole in the ceiling well beyond her reach, and sighed again. Doubtless it was up there somewhere, along with the pipe ashes and any stray human hairs and other leavings she should have scooped up to use in later spellcasting. This was rapidly becoming far more than a brute force job.

There was a soft, stealthy sound above her. Laeral peered hard, moving in a quick half circle to see the widest possible area of the passage above. She thought she saw a dark, shadowy shoulder and head jerk back out of her field of view, but she couldn't be sure. Whoever it was never reappeared. If the haze hadn't still clung to her, tingling as it drank at the glow enchantments on her daggers, she'd have used her spider climb to crawl the walls up and out of here, but she dared not waste it.

Dangerous or not, that crawl-tunnel was beginning to look attractive. Laeral sighed again, took off Trennan Beldrusk's gaudy over tunic, and dipped it in the puddle of lamp oil. The cuff of her right boot carried a flint and striker, as did the boots of many a merchant who smoked. It was the work of a moment to give herself fire, which she hastily threw down the tunnel.

Pure fire could not harm her when she stood where magic could work. Igniting the cloth had set alight a little of the spilled oil. Laeral held her hand in the licking flames and felt the swift, sharp pain of burning. Pulling her hand back and rubbing scorched, frazzled hairs from her skin, the Lady Mage nodded. Fire could certainly harm her here.

Pulling her remaining clothes tightly around her and knotting them to keep them that way, she plunged hastily into the tunnel and crawled through the wisps of smoke to where her over tunic was blazing. With the same hand she took firm hold of it, watching the flames rage around her flesh and do it no harm.

Well and good. The magicslaying effect did not reach this far. Lying on her belly in the close darkness with her over tunic smoldering its last in front of her, Laeral cast an ironguard spell upon herself against falling spikes or jabbing guards' weapons. When its tingling passed through her, she got to her hands and knees and started to hurry. She really didn't have time for this.

On the other hand, if a trap caught her the right way or guardians overwhelmed her and snatched her life from her, she'd have all the slow, coldly unfolding time in Faerûn for this little matter. In fact, it would consume her forever.

"Auvrarn Labraster," she told the darkness calmly, "I am no longer amused. Be warned."

Ahead of her, in the dimness—the only light came from the yellow haze now far behind her, and she wasn't yet quite angry enough to recklessly make *herself* glow like a torch to light her way—the crawl-tunnel turned a sharp corner to the right, and seemed to narrow as it did so.

"Well," she breathed, crawling on, "at least I don't have Dove's shoulders. It'd be no fun at t—"

One of her daggers, which she waved around the corner then thrust ahead, had awakened no reaction, so Laeral followed it. Her swirling hair saved her.

She didn't see the blur of the serpent's strike, so never turned toward it, which might have cost her an eye. Instead, sharp fangs struck her cheek, plunging deep into the side of her mouth. Laeral got her other hand around in time to catch the viper before it could rear back to strike again. She held it, with its fangs thrust into her, while she hissed a spell that made flames snarl forth from her face.

It was like cooking sausages in a fire. She held the snake motionless through the sizzling and the reek, until only black ash fell away from her in crumbling flakes. By then, her vision was swimming and that side of her face was beginning to swell up to twice its normal size. She spat onto her hand, looked at the purple result, and grimaced. Purging with Mystra's fire was both messy and destructive, but she had little choice. If she kept on swelling, she might just get stuck here, wedged in this tunnel unable to even shudder, as the poison slowly slew her. "And," she announced wryly, her thickened tongue making her speech slurred, "I don't have time for that!"

Backing hastily down the tunnel, Laeral struggled out of her clothing and boots, stripping off even her knives and jewelry. The purging would destroy everything touching her skin and empty the poison—and a lot more—out of her every orifice. She might well need some of her gear again, soon. Besides, the sight of a nude Lady Mage of Waterdeep wasn't going to shock a slave trader.

The snake had come out of a pot, placed in the tunnel recently enough that it hadn't yet picked up the damp, dank smell of its surroundings. A little present, left just for her.

"Auvrarn," she told the darkness calmly, as the purging began its raging and sweat burst out of her in all directions, "did I mention my lack of amusement already?"

Nothing up or down the crawl-tunnel answered. Perhaps nothing dared.

✳   ✳   ✳

A certain musty smell prickled in Laeral's nostrils as she reached the place where her tunnel emerged into a long, straw-strewn cellar. "Cat," she muttered. "A large one."

She emerged out of the tunnel cautiously, looking all around for the panther or whatever was going to spring at her, but could see nothing but a few bones and dung here and there among the straw. Oh, and an archway down the far end of the cellar, with torchlight beyond. This must be one of the mansion's cellars, she thought. There was the inevitable row of old wine-casks. Some of them stood well away from the wall . . . could the kitten be lurking behind them?

With a roar that deafened her, something plunged down from above, sharp claws raking fresh fire from her as she twisted desperately away. A ledge above the tunnel mouth. . . .

Gods, was this whole jaunt going to be "old-traps-for-adventurers-time"?

Her latest foe was something large and striped that she'd once seen in the jungles of Chult. Its eyes were green and afire, its claws almost as long as its fangs as it landed, turned with sinuous grace, and stalked back toward her, circling softly sideways.

Laeral swallowed. Torn apart to bloody, gnawed ribs by a cat wasn't quite how she'd planned to end her days. Abed in Khelben's loving arms was a little closer to the mark. . . .

Ah. It didn't like the fire leaking from where it had clawed her. Victims were supposed to bleed, not blaze. Laeral gave it a tight smile and let the silver fire flow, willing it to rage up into real flames.

The cat snarled and circled away, and Laeral calmly readied a spell. There was a glade she knew, in the High Forest. . . .

Rumbling its anger and hunger, the cat turned back toward her again, tail lashing. The Lady Mage calmly took off the ribbons of her doublet. At least this beast had good taste. She'd longed to tear the garment to shreds, too. She then removed the torn tunic beneath, balling them both up around her arm before she cast a bloodstaunch and sealed the silver fire away.

The cat lowered its head, stilled its tail, then sprang with another thunderous roar. Laeral charged to meet it, thrusting the ball of cloth at its jaws and slapping its striped head with her free hand.

The cellar was suddenly empty of jungle cats. Laeral smiled. It would be standing in the High Forest now, being rather baffled. She moved away from the tunnel mouth quickly, and looked up at the ledge. No more surprises?

Good. The Lady Mage of Waterdeep glanced down at her raw back and flank, made a face, and put the tunic back on. Not that it covered much of her right side any more.

She even stuffed the rag of her doublet through her belt. One never knew when a scrap of cloth might be needed, after all.

Ahead, beyond the arch, was torchlight. She fixed that as her next goal—if, of course, nothing else was lurking behind those barrels. Next time, Laeral promised herself, she'd simply march over to the mansion and hammer on its doors.

"Well, I may be an idiot, Labraster," she muttered, "but I can still be the nuisance that ruins you."

The torch in its bracket was of the "longburn" sort, almost as tall as a man and guaranteed for six hours. Someone had lit it not so long ago, yet there was certainly no one here now.

Laeral cast wary glances up and down the hall she stood in, wondering if the other cellars held hungry cats or similar surprises. She shrugged and turned toward the stairs. Perhaps in the pages of *The Silk Mask Saga* evil merchants might furnish every alcove with a trap, every passage with a spell, and every chamber with a waiting monster, but in real, everyday Waterdeep, waiting monsters had to be captured, transported past city authorities well versed in many techniques of smuggling, confined in said rooms, and fed. Not to mention the fact that folk who paid taxes on houses in the City of Splendors, and paid much coin on top of that to heat said abodes in its cold winters, usually liked to *use* the rooms they lived in.

On the other hand, a perfectly good wine cellar—without a door to confine the beast, too—had been furnished with a man-eating cat. Just for her?

If not, who was Auvrarn Labraster expecting?

The silent stairs held no answer for her, and she went up them like a ghost in a hurry, moving with as much haste as stealth allowed. The floor above was all kitchens, pantries, and laundries, lit by high windows that opened out through the thick stone mansion walls at ground level. Some of the hearths were warm, but the fires had been raked out, no lamps or torches burned, and everything was deserted.

Somewhere on the floors above, a floorboard creaked. Laeral smiled tightly and went on. Labraster didn't seem eager for a face-to-face confrontation, but sooner or later she'd peer at his every secret here, or meet with someone who didn't have poisoned fangs or claws.

That hint of deeper danger she'd felt in the slave cellar was back. Merchants with beasts from the far reaches of Faerûn, drow, haughty Waterdhavian society ladies, and the vipers who traded in Skullport didn't mix. There was too much going on here, too many disparate folk involved.

"Labraster," she murmured in little more than a whisper, "I think it's time I had some answers."

Another stair took her to the ground floor of the mansion where all was darkness and lofty ceilings. Shutters were closed here against the sunlight outside, and the gloom was deep as Laeral calmly walked through a high hall where no less than four curving staircases had their roots. She passed through an archway into a great, dark, stately cavern of a hall. *The* great hall of the mansion, this must be, with a vast expanse of bare tiled floor on which to dance and hold revels, statues galore, and a balcony for a small host of minstrels to serenade from.

Laeral spun around. Though she turned back again without pause, she hadn't failed to notice a swift movement in the high hall as someone ducked back behind one of the soaring staircases.

Humming to herself, the Lady Mage of Waterdeep stood in one spot and looked around at the silent statues and the gilded splendor of the great hall for a long time. Crossed broadswords here, tapestries bigger than peasant cottages there . . . all very nice; impressive, but not gaudy. She surveyed the ornately carved balcony lip, and the railing above it. A little smile plucked at the corners of her mouth. She strode forward boldly, right across the open heart of the dancing floor where the tiles looked bright and new, until she felt a tile underfoot that seemed to tremble slightly.

Laeral spun around so abruptly, this time, that her own swirling hair didn't quite have time to get out of her way. She plunged three racing steps through it, back the way she'd come.

Right behind her, huge ceiling stones smashed down onto the new tiles with a booming impact that shook the entire mansion, sent dust swirling up into the air all around, and almost threw the Lady Mage from her feet.

Hah—finally, a trap more worthy of a Chosen of Mystra!

Laeral smiled at that thought, and her own foolishness in conceiving of it, and kept her gait smooth and her face calm as she slowed to her normal lilting walk, ignoring the shards of tile skittering across the floor in all directions, their clatter almost louder than the rattle of chains as the ceiling stones started their slow journey aloft . . . unbloodied. Laeral suspected that if she turned around to look, she'd see their hardened surfaces carved into smiling jester's faces, or something of the sort.

On the other hand, the dark figure standing in front of her was something of a cruelly smiling jester himself from time to time, though that was probably not a description he'd enjoy hearing.

Caught out in the open, he made no move to dart behind cover this time, but shifted one hand to a pendant—probably some sort of magic—and the other to the hilt of a slender sword at his hip. Rings winked with brief magical fire on that hand, but Laeral's smile merely broadened a trifle.

"Elaith," she asked pleasantly, "are you merely amusing yourself here, awaiting your chance to rummage the broken body of a Chosen who's tasted one trap too many, or have you something to say to me? Something involving slaves, perhaps, or drow, or the merchant Labraster?"

Elaith Craulnober's soft smile matched her own. The elf whom Waterdeep called the Serpent spread his empty hands with lazy grace.

"I mean no harm to the Lady Mage of Waterdeep," he announced in a voice that was almost a purr, "and must admit I began my walk in your wake purely for . . . entertainment purposes. If it's Auvrarn Labraster you're seeking, I must tell you that my professional contacts have confirmed his arrival in Silverymoon last night."

Laeral raised an eyebrow. "Truth?"

The Serpent spread his hands once more, in a mockery of a courtier's flourish. His easy smile broadened so much that it actually reached his wintry eyes—something Laeral had never seen before. "Lady, would I dare lie to *you?*"

"You'd lie to Mystra herself, Elaith," she replied. A smile was still on her lips, but her eyes were boring into his.

The Serpent took a smooth step back, his face falling into a half smile. "Naetheless, lady, I do speak truth," he replied gravely. "More than that, I can add just as honestly that Labraster and I do not have dealings with each other. Friendly, professional, or otherwise."

They stared at each other in measuring silence for a long moment before a trace of mockery rose to dance in the elf's eyes. "May I add, Great Lady, that your lack of confidence wounds me?"

Laeral gave him a tight little smile and lifted a slender hand to point across the gloomy great hall at several spots along its balcony rail. Elaith's had not been the only stealthy movements she'd seen this last little while. "And these, wounded one? You just happened to bring a dozen men along when you went for a stroll this evening, I suppose?"

"My associates," Elaith replied smoothly, lifting his hand in a swift, intricate gesture. A signal.

Laeral turned to watch grim men and half-elves rise into view from behind the ornately carved railing, loaded hand crossbows held ready in their hands.

"Naturally they trailed after me, fearing for my health when consorting with so known and great a danger of the city as yourself, lady."

"Wise of them," Laeral replied sweetly, gliding forward with sudden speed to plant a kiss on Elaith's cheek that burned.

As the Serpent stiffened and staggered back, clapping a hand to his cheek, Laeral circled to keep him between her and the hand bows along the rail.

"Mind they keep those little darts clear of me as I go, Serpent," she said pleasantly, her voice raised to ring across the lofty hall like a trumpet. "Any pain I feel in the next hour or so, *you* will also feel."

She smiled almost merrily into elf eyes that glittered with swift anger, blew the Serpent a kiss, and strolled unmolested out of the hall.

✳   ✳   ✳

Hurrying feet pounded down a balcony stair, and a man in leathers as dark as the Serpent's own came up to his master in haste. His low voice, when it came, was urgent with alarm.

"Sir?"

Elaith Craulnober stood unmoving, still staring after Laeral. At his henchman's query he reached up to rub his cheek once more. Peering, the man saw that it was puckered up in a fresh welt, a silver-hued burn shaped like the imprint of a lady's lips.

"I've got to get me some of that silver fire, Baeraden," the Serpent said softly, his fingers carefully tracing the burn now, rubbing at it no longer. "Even if it means serving a misguided mage-goddess."

✳   ✳   ✳

The duty apprentice of Blackstaff Tower stared at the Lady Mage of Waterdeep as she strode past his station clad in the torn and tattered remnants of gaudy, ill fitting men's clothing, but wisely said nothing. Briion Dargrant said even less when Laeral turned back to his table, plucked up two specimen jars, and from various places about her ridiculous and frankly revealing ruined garb produced a handful of odd hairs and another of what looked like pipe ash. She put each carefully in a jar and shut lids upon them firmly, then ordered crisply on her way past him to the passage again, "Touch those not."

Briion did, however, turn to stare as the lady of the tower tore off her gaudy rags until they lay pooled on the floor of the passage and she wore only boots, knives strapped to her in various places, and her long, unbound silver hair.

Looking back over her shoulder at him—the apprentice swallowed and hastily lifted his gaze from her rounded rear to her eyes—Laeral added, "Burn these rags ere I return."

She gave Briion a smile that he knew was going to bring him fitful sleep during the night ahead, and ducked through an apparently solid wall, into yet another secret passage he hadn't been told about.

The duty apprentice swallowed, shook his head, then scurried to pluck up the ruined clothing from the floor. Diligent obedience was a virtue, as the saying went. He shuddered to think of his fate if Khelben should pass by.

Briion's eyes widened, not much later, as the brazier devoured the last of the rags and his nose told him that in addition to the unmistakable musk of a jungle cat just like the one he'd shaped under Khelben's supervision less than a month ago, the clothing bore more than a trace of night viper poison. The study of venoms as spellcasting components was Briion Dargrant's proud specialty, and there could be no mistaking its distinctive, almost citrus scent. Just where had the Lady Mage been, and what had she been doing?

"Kissing serpents," came a soft voice from just behind him, and he stiffened in horror at the realization that he must have asked that question aloud— and that the Lady Laeral had returned and heard him. "But not the sort you're thinking of."

To that cryptic comment she added in a murmur, "I don't think we need mention your task, or my arrival just now, to anyone at all. Do you?"

Briion Dargrant swallowed with difficulty as the Lady Mage scooped up the specimen jars. She was resplendent now in a flowing, long sleeved gown but, his flickering eyes didn't fail to notice, she was barefoot. With a heroic effort he managed to say, his voice ridiculously solemn even in his own ears, "Lord Khelben shall hear nothing from me, Great Lady."

The grin Laeral gave him then was both despairing and affectionate. Briion swallowed several times rapidly as she ducked through a spell-concealed archway—this one he did know of—taking the jars with her. He *was* going to have disturbed dreams tonight, by Azuth's Seven Mysteries, and that wasn't, he decided with a grin as he turned back to his scrying globes, going to necessarily be that bad at all.

✻   ✻   ✻

The deepest spellcasting chamber of Blackstaff Tower was empty of all but old burn scars before a tight-lipped Laeral dragged in two stone pedestals from an antechamber. If Labraster was involved in dark dealings energetic enough to rouse the Serpent into spying on him—to the extent of invading his mansion with considerable armed strength—but well hidden from the informants that kept Blackstaff Tower supplied with whispers of dastardly deeds afoot in the city, he was more than a smuggler or a slaver. Much more.

Someone had been watching her, somehow, in the cellar and in Skullport. She knew that with certainty, though she hadn't even realized she'd sensed it until now, almost as if a spell had worn off.

A spell a Chosen of Mystra could miss feeling?

Frowning, the Lady Mage of Waterdeep said a rude word. She uttered it far more calmly than she felt. She hugged herself for a moment, running long fingers up and down her arms, then shook herself and began to move with brisk haste. Setting the hairs from the mansion on one pedestal and the pipe ash on the other, Laeral spread her fingers over them, and closed her eyes.

Brief radiance played about her fingertips, and two of the hairs wriggled away from the pile and drifted to the floor.

Laeral opened her eyes again. Everything that was left had come from, or been in intimate contact with, the same human male. If she was fortunate, a much more powerful spell could now use these discards to trace—and spy upon—the absent Auvrarn Labraster. If she was unlucky, they'd lead her to a servant, or perhaps some merchant who'd recently visited Windpennant Pillars.

Laeral frowned again. Why was a feeling of foreboding growing strong within her? One merchant, after all, with no known dark history of misdeeds or penchant for swaggering menacingly around the docks with a large force of hireswords in tow . . . why was she so uneasy?

"Mystra preserve," she murmured, and thrust aside dark thoughts.

Laeral looked into the antechamber to be sure no apprentice was going to come bustling in with a message in the midst of her casting, drew in a deep breath, and carefully cast her spell.

✳　　✳　　✳

The scrying sphere that looks upon the spellcasting chambers flashed once, but thereafter remained dark. Briion Dargrant nodded calmly. The lady was conducting some sort of research with the oddments she'd brought back. He turned back to the writings Khelben had given him to go over, and did not look up until a scrying sphere burst with a flash and flame that hurled him and his stool over backward amid singing shards of glass.

Blinking amid the wreckage as loving tendrils of smoke flowed down over the edge of the table to envelop him, Briion did not have to clamber back up to know which globe had shattered.

"Oh, Great Lady!" he gasped. Tears started into his eyes, and he fainted.

Running feet almost trampled him a breath or two later. Apprentices poured down the passages and stairs of the tower, shrinking back against the walls as a black whirlwind snarled past them and plunged down into the depths.

They started to run again in Khelben's wake, feet thundering down stone steps and racing along the narrow ways to where bright light was raging in the depths. There they came to a halt and stood staring in sudden, panting astonishment, one by one. Astonishment . . . and growing fear.

The largest, deepest spellcasting chamber of the tower no longer had a door. Its arch stood empty, the door now a smear of dripping metal on the wall across the passage. Through the gaping opening, over the black and trembling statue of their master the Blackstaff, the staring apprentices could see that the chamber held leaping, clawing lightning amid scorched nothingness. A single ribbon of silver flame danced among them.

As the folk of the tower watched, the lightning became fitful, then slowly died away, leaving only the silver flame struggling alone in the darkness. Lord Khelben turned around then to face the apprentices, his face like white marble, with two terrible flames as eyes.

"It would be best," he whispered with terrible gentleness, "if all of you went away. Speedily."

He turned slowly back to face the ruined chamber without another word. By the time the Lord Mage of Waterdeep faced the flame again, he was alone once more. As the old MageFair saying put it: "Apprentices moved by fear can move swiftly indeed."

Khelben drew in a deep, shuddering breath, and stepped grimly into the room where the flame danced ever more feebly, to shape a spell he thought he'd not have to use for years.

"Only someone of great power could have wrought such a spelltrap," he said grimly, as he stretched forth his hand to let what was left of his lady take the life-force she needed from him, to survive. "The last such I tasted was the work of Halaster the Crazed."

The silver flame coiled around his forearm almost affectionately, and the familiar voice he'd cheerfully die for, any day of any year, spoke in his mind.

True, my lord, and this one feels like his work, too. He who spies on all in Skullport must have watched Qilué and this your favorite lady when we fared thence. Now shape me a body again, that I might speak to Alustriel without delay.

"Some women," Khelben growled affectionately, his voice trembling on the edge of tears, "will do anything to get in some gossip."

Alustriel
When a Good Man Loses his Head

There are some who hold that the High Lady of Silverymoon is a deluded dreamer, doomed to fail in her fair craftings because she thinks too highly of the good in folk, and too little of the evil that lurks always near at hand. I am not one of those.

Reld Barunenail, Sage of the Histories
from *The View from Secomber:*
Musings on the Years to Come
published circa the Year of Maidens

It was a very calming ceiling to stare at, and Alustriel of Silverymoon was staring at it now, lounging back in her chair to lose herself in the delicately painted panels and curving vaulting. Cracks gave the masterpiece character, like the cracks that afflicted and weakened the city she'd shaped. Her eyes followed the vault rib that plunged down in a smooth curve from ceiling to wall to become one of the two pillars framing the door. It was through that door that all urgent troubles came, sometimes jostling each other for attention, to shatter her moments of solitude here. Alustriel gave the door a wry look. It was closed now; trouble was overdue.

Sometimes she felt like a caged panther, prowling restlessly and endlessly along the bars that confined her. Outside this room was a palace, and around the palace stood the city some called the Gem of the North. Her Silverymoon, a walled refuge against the dangers of the wilderlands, and her cage for many a year. Just recently though, it seemed a larger cage beckoned her to let herself out into wider roaming, in a possible union of the Moonlands and the risen dwarf holds.

A folly, some said, but then, what folly is there in striving to bring a measure of security and happiness to even a tiny corner of Faerûn? Even if it all ended in bloody failure, leaving behind only legends to echo down the years to come, the attempt would have been worth something in itself. Would be worth something, always, for a striving, however flawed, outstrips empty dreams and the sloth of not having tried to shape or create anything worthy at all. Yet would not the same argument be championed by a tyrant invading a realm he deems decadent, or any woodcutter carving asunder an elven grove?

"Alustriel," she told herself calmly, "you think too much."

She sometimes thought it was the endless leaping and weaving of her rushing thoughts that made her weary, and drove her to seek moments of silence, alone, like this. By the grace of Mystra she no longer needed to sleep, but the wits of every Chosen grew weary of grappling with problem after problem, and memorizing spell after spell; their power a constant roiling in the mind.

"Oh, dear me," she told herself aloud, stretching like a dancer to show full contempt for her own weariness. "Is the High Lady to be pitied, then? Does she want something purring and affectionate to cuddle, and a world without cares to do so in? Well, she'd better join the stampede—"

The air off to the left shimmered and became a floating, star shaped mirror—sweet Mystra, she'd set it off again!

" 'Cuddle,' " she told it severely, "was perhaps not the wisest trigger word to use."

Obediently, the mirror winked back to nothingness again, but not before it had captured and flung her own image back at her. She beheld a slender beauty of a woman whose emerald eyes were winking with amusement as she wrinkled her lips wryly, and guided the tresses of her long silver hair—moving seemingly by themselves—to smooth back the shoulders of her fine dark gown. Gracefully, of course; a certain sensuous grace, some termed it. She was not called "Our Lady of Dalliances" behind her back for nothing.

"Oh, have *done!*" Alustriel moaned to herself in amused despair. "Enough of teasing and preening and hot and avid eyes. You came here to be alone, idiot, not pose and imagine yourself slinking along in something that will be the height of fashion from now until perhaps . . . dusk. Think of what you have wrought, not whom you've touched."

The High Lady rolled her eyes, then let them wander again. They followed that plunging vault rib once more, pausing at the arch of the still thankfully closed door. She'd not yet had any arms put up over that arch, despite the eagerness of the palace heralds. Realms were more than names and banners. They were folk thinking themselves part of a place, and she hadn't managed that, yet. This was still, first and foremost, Silverymoon, a haven in the wild and savage North.

There came a single knock upon the door—light, almost apologetic—then it swung open. She knew that knock, and permitted herself a mirthless smile, for just a moment before the man entering the room could see her face. Late for its cue but not unexpected, fresh trouble had come at last.

Taern Hornblade was Master Mage of the Spellguard of Silverymoon and Seneschal of the High Palace, but even the heralds had to think to recall those precise titles. To one and all in Silverymoon he was simply Thunderspell (or, less respectfully and at a safe distance, "Old Thunderspells"), Alustriel's faithful right hand and counselor. He was an astute if stodgy diplomat who ran with calm efficiency what passed for the Shadow Watch—what some southerly realms called "secret police"—of Silverymoon. The problems he brought to his beloved High Lady were never minor, and in recent years Alustriel, accustomed to conducting friendships and intimacies with many folk, had been surprised to realize just how much she'd come to love him.

And to know that it wasn't nearly as deeply and hopelessly as he loved her.

"My lady," Taern began, and turned away to clear his throat. Alustriel's one glance at his face, as it spun away, told her that this matter, whatever it was, was something bad.

"My lady, I bring grave news that requires, I fear, your immediate attention." Taern was too upset to reach for subtleties or delay his blunt message. "The envoy from Neverwinter, Tradelord Garthin Muirtree, lies dead within our walls—murdered. He was, of course, our guest. His remains lie where they were found, in the Red Griffon Room."

"In the magic-dead area?" Alustriel asked calmly.

Taern nodded heavily. "I've seen them—him, My lady. He looks like a man I saw once on a hunt, torn apart by some great fanged and clawed beast. His head is entirely gone."

✳   ✳   ✳

A wizards' duel in the wake of a MageFair created a "spell shadow" at a certain spot in the palace. This was a place where no magic worked. After a long consultation on her knees with the divine lady she served, Alustriel had deliberately maintained the shadow so as to give the folk of Silverymoon a way to readily strip away magical disguises, "hanging" spells, and other spell-traps or undesirable enchantments. To keep its use under control, she'd caused a chamber to be built around it, with secure walls pierced by no secret passage, message chute, or air vent.

When the work was done, the palace had two new, smaller rooms where a larger one had been. The one that held the shadow was a quiet, stately room of polished duskwood paneling. Its sole ornaments were a small company of carved, scarlet painted griffons crowning the posts of the chairs surrounding its polished meeting table. The griffons soon gave the chamber its name—and so it was to the Red Griffon Room that the High Lady of Silverymoon now hastened, with Taern striding anxiously at her side.

Their route seemed deserted—Taern's doing, no doubt. There was a stiffening in the air, and a rising, eerie sound as of many voices shouting wordless alarm. The sudden swirling up from nothingness of a cloud of sparks told Alustriel that her Seneschal had laid a powerful ward before the closed door of the Red Griffon Room.

She broke it, deliberately, before he could lift it, ignoring his reproachful look. She had to be sure—absolutely certain—that no hand besides his had been casting or altering wards while he was away fetching a silence-loving High Lady.

Alustriel strode to the door despite Taern's wordless protest. He could not, for all his years, have seen nearly as many horribly mutilated bodies as she had, in hers, and this was her city, and her castle. She fixed her mind on the most powerful slaying spell she had ready, and firmly swung the door inward.

The stuffiness—no vents, the only flow of air coming from a copper heat-turned fan suspended from a rod curving over the candle lamp that stood by the table—was familiar. The slaughterhouse smell, and the riven thing that had once been a man, now so thoroughly butchered that only one raised, clawlike hand and a hairy knee could still be recognized as human, was horribly, indecently *un*familiar.

Alustriel looked down at it expressionlessly. Nothing that dwelt in the palace could have torn apart flesh like this. It reeked of a challenge, a signal of defiance and warning from someone or something that wished to say: "See what I can do at will, High Lady? What is your power to me? If I can do this, so easily, how can you hope to defend the peace and safe haven your people look to you for?"

The seneschal made another anxious, motherly sound in his throat, and tried to step between her and the corpse. "Now, my lady," he protested, "there's no need for you to have to look upon this. I can whelm the Spellguard a—"

A slender arm barred Taern's way. He rebounded from its surprisingly immobile strength with a blink and a swallow.

"Taern," Alustriel said into his astonished face, "you've served me well for all these years. I thank you for it too seldom, so I'm thanking you now. I'm also telling you far more politely than I feel like being that you can serve me even better by taking yourself back the other side of that door *now*. Close it, and await without, patient and with thoughts of whelming the Spellguard or rousing the palace to scurrying alarm very far from your mind. Stray nowhere; I shall need your counsel very soon."

She was shepherding him to the door by now, almost driving him before her despite his red and worried face and anxiously flapping hands. "Lady, is this wise? Think you: we know not what has savaged this man so thorou—"

"Taern," Alustriel said severely, "I need to think and to feel . . . without you hovering."

Taern seemed to be on the verge of exploding. She wondered, for a flashing moment, if his oaths would impart any colorful expressions new to her. She hoped to keep from her face all trace of the mirth that thought awakened in her.

"I—I—lady, guard yourself!" her Master Mage almost roared, as her inexorable advance backed him to the door. "A hidden beast may be lurking, or a spelltrap left behind to strike at you. Danger can erupt from a gate or teleport focus in the space of but a passing breath."

He took a stand, as if he'd not be moved farther. With a serene smile she stepped into him, her bosom thrusting against his chest. Taern blinked, swallowed, backed hastily away, and lost the battle.

"Thunderspell, you're a dear," Alustriel told him with a sidelong smile, as she swung the door closed. "Please don't be angry. I'll only be a little while."

The door settled into its frame, and she reached out with a fingertip to set her own magical seal upon it, but no familiar, momentary fire enshrouded them. Her eyes narrowed, and she spun around, willing radiance to burst from her entire body. The familiar tingling began, but no light burst forth. Magic within beings, magic that affected them but nothing of their surroundings, still functioned, but nothing else.

Holding her will to the task of making light, Alustriel strode quickly around the room, feeling the extent of the unseen shadow. Neither the corpse nor anything else stirred, beyond her own dark gown swirling around her hurrying feet. Not only was the magic-dead area intact, it had expanded—had *been* expanded, that is—some time ago, by someone with the power to make a spell shadow grow to encompass the entire chamber. The walls showed no sign of forcible entry or secret ways in or out, and the hollow griffon, after she unscrewed it from its chair post, was uncharred inside. The little flaming coin hidden there remained cool and unblackened, its enchantment in abeyance as before. The spell shadow hadn't been banished then replaced. It had remained in effect at the heart of the room since there had been a room, and griffon-topped chairs in it.

Alustriel looked at the door. It didn't look changed either, and certainly not as if something large and long-clawed had ever torn it open. She swung it wide again, meeting Taern's anxious gaze, and said gently, "Master Mage, please come in. I've need of your wits now."

Taern opened his mouth to say something, remembered who he was speaking to, and closed it again
without uttering a sound. His face darkened with
embarrassment at the thought of what he'd meant to
say.

"Oh, gods above, Taern, get in here," Alustriel murmured, taking hold of him by the shoulder and half
plucking, half dragging him back through the door. "I
met Muirtree only twice, the first time years ago, and
though I know why he was here in the Moon, I don't
know why he was *here*, in the Griffon."

She closed the door again, firmly, and wondered why
her mind had begun to stray to thoughts of food.

Taern licked his lips, carefully stepped around the
carnage on the floor without looking down at it, and
stopped behind a chair, resting the fingertips of his
large hands lightly on its back. This was his lecturing
pose. Ah, well, Alustriel thought, she needed what he
knew, and his own way would be the best telling.

"Men who bear the title 'tradelord' are of course
envoys for the city, or coster, or guild they represent,"
Taern began, as if explaining to a novice that what
flowed in rivers was called "water." Alustriel kept her
face patient, and even resisted a childish urge to mimic
his voice and deliver the words she knew she could
accurately predict along with him.

"In the case at hand," Taern continued, warming to
his task, "Tradelord Muirtree, a far-traveled and well-
liked man, was here in Silverymoon representing the
interests of his native city of Neverwinter. We serve
here as a meeting place and neutral safe trading haven
for many in the North. Most official trade envoys do
little more within our walls than meet, discuss trade to
the point of drafting agreements, then depart, taking
such treaties they've drafted, or ideas they've heard,
back to their fellows or superiors. Goodman Garthin
Muirtree was here to meet with many folk, but this was
his first full day in our hospitality, and it seems he met,

in this room, with five persons before being found . . . ah, as you see him now."

"Why this room," Alustriel asked, seating herself calmly at the table as if the twisted meat that had once been a man was a day's ride distant, and not within reach of her soft, pointed shoes, "and not those lower down that most prefer, with couches and decanter-laden sideboards and windows?"

"One man has been in the city this past tenday, waiting to meet with Muirtree, or at least he requested a tenday ago that we inform him of the tradelord's arrival, and arrange a moot at Muirtree's earliest possible convenience. That man asked that their encounter be in this chamber, and his request was brought to me. When I spoke with him—a man I've not seen in the Moon before, a Waterdhavian merchant, well spoken and prosperous, by the name of Auvrarn Labraster—he said he desired his meeting with Tradelord Muirtree to be in the 'magic-dead' room, for fear of 'a sneaking magic' he'd heard the tradelord was employing."

"You granted this request, installing the tradelord herein," Alustriel prompted, "then?"

"This Auvrarn was seen to meet with the tradelord, then depart. The tradelord remained in this room, as is usual given the papers and suchlike often involved in such meetings."

Alustriel looked pointedly around at the room, which was entirely empty of quills, parchments, ledgers, satchels, blotters, and such. Taern nodded ruefully, and continued, "Though none such documents have been found. In time, Muirtree met with envoys and a courtier before his ah, demise. All of them, by the way, came to this chamber alone, without scriveners or servants."

"Suggesting that they proposed to discuss matters of exceeding delicacy," the High Lady responded patiently, before Taern could explain the obvious. "Suppose," she added, lifting her hand in an almost beckoning gesture, "you make these latter folk known to me in the order in which they entered this room."

Taern shifted his feet, cleared his throat, and began. "Following shortly upon Labraster's departure came Goodman Draevin Flarwood, representing the newly formed Braeder Merchant Collective of Silverymoon— ah, a trading coster, lady."

Alustriel nodded, repressing an urge to murmur that she had heard of such things before. Seemingly heartened by this signal of comprehension, her seneschal nodded and continued.

"After Flarwood's fairly brief audience, we know from the door page stationed across the corridor—whom none of the visitors summoned, by the way—that Muirtree's next visitor was an old foe of his: the Tradelord of Luskan, Dauphran Alskyte."

"Everyone's old foe," Alustriel murmured. "Did they get to shouting loudly enough for the page to hear?"

"Ah, *no*, lady, though it seems their time together was rather lengthy. The page could, of course, tell nothing of Alskyte's temper by his manner upon departure."

"Of course," Alustriel agreed dryly. If icy disdain and bold rudeness are worn as a constant cloak, what can be told of the cloth hidden beneath?

"The next visitor was one of our own liaison officers, Janthasarde Ilbright. She came to check Muirtree's roster of meetings for the morrow, and has testified to me that he seemed hale and in good humor. He had no demands upon her nor appointments to add to the dozen local shopkeepers and crafters Garthin usually meets with, when here. He did not request a change of room or seem in any way out of sorts, and she did not stay with him long. A short time thereafter, Muirtree's last visitor was Oscalar Maerbree."

"I've met old Oscalar," Alustriel said in tones even more dry than before. "He tried to drink me under a table once, in hopes of joining me down there. Pretend I know nothing of him, and say on."

Taern shrugged. "Maerbree's a merchant whose family has always dealt in wines and spirits, though he's recently taken to importing herbal cordials, spiced cheeses, and the like. He was born in Neverwinter, and was sent here by his father. He's dwelt and traded in Silverymoon for the last twenty summers, and though now head of his house, he's left his younger brothers to run the Neverwinter end of the family trading. His character you know . . . as, I daresay, do half the ladies at court."

"Why, Taern Hornblade," Alustriel said mildly, "you're jealous. Here, in this palace and this city?"

"Bright Lady," Hornblade said stiffly, "I bow to your wisdom, and always have done. The permissiveness you encourage does much to blunt the violence of men—and women—long lawless and unfulfilled in the wilderlands. I have partaken, and admit to enjoying the spectacle from time to time. Yet it grates in my craw that a man so—so blusteringly crude should . . . should . . ."

"Sail so far, so often, and so successfully?" Alustriel said gently, to aid her flushed and stammering seneschal.

"Exactly, lady. I cannot think what women see in such grunting bear antics. To yield to them, it seems to me, cheapens any lady."

"And yet, think on this," the High Lady replied. "I've never heard of Oscalar being cruel to anyone, nor holding grudges or having time or taste for intrigue or deception. He is what he is, like a battering ram or a war mace."

"Precisely like a bludgeon," Thunderspell agreed. "I don't dislike or mistrust him—but he irritates me, forever bellowing and backslapping his way across room after room like a walrus who delights in embarrassing others. He irritates me beyond belief."

"So it's given you some small pleasure to question him rather sharply about the passing of Garthin Muirtree?" Alustriel asked softly.

Taern Hornblade blushed so violently that his face became almost black. "I—ah, yes, it has," he told the floor, and turned away from the table to pace restlessly across the back of the room. "Yet he denies everything, and, gods save and preserve me, I believe him."

"You've done very well, Seneschal," the High Lady of Silverymoon said formally, "and you can serve me best now by bringing a glass of wine and a sausage rolled in frybread to me in the Chamber of the Hunting Horn. When I hand the empty glass back, Oscalar can be shown in. We'll talk in private."

"You want me to keep unseen at the back of the balcony, tending my truth field," Taern replied, not quite smiling. "Lady, all of my scrolls bearing that spell are piled ready in my chambers right now. You'd like this done without delay, before our suspects have time to hide things—such as, perhaps, themselves."

"And before my stomach begins to rumble so loudly that I can't hear their answers," Alustriel replied. She looked down then at the gory remains of Garthin Muirtree, and added slowly, "I can't think why I'm so hungry, given our guest here. Mind, he's not to be disturbed in any way, nor is my ward to be lifted from the doors when we leave. I'd like to speak to Muirtree's visitors in here, to unsettle them thoroughly, but there's a distinct lack of a balcony for you to hide on. Perhaps under the table?"

Taern winced. "Lady, the *body* is strewn half under the table."

Alustriel looked contrite. "I was joking, Taern, and rather badly." She rose and made for the door in a smooth, lilting movement, adding over her shoulder, "Douse that lamp, will you? The room is beginning to smell."

✳   ✳   ✳

They were hurrying along a grand hall together, with Taern swiftly pouring out all else that touched on the matter into Alustriel's ear, when it happened.

"I've questioned only the five visitors, the door-page, and the two guards who served as honor escorts through the palace for Muirtree's visitors. All of them now know the tradelord is dead, and obviously that there's something suspicious about his passing, but no details—and I'm taking care that they're all guarded and held apart, prevented from discussing things even with their servants. We can't hold them in such straits for long. The Luskanite has already begun to protest, and—"

The High Lady of Silverymoon broke her swift stride, almost stumbling, and put a hand on the seneschal's arm to steady herself. Taern turned to her in an instant, concern rising in his eyes as he saw her faraway look, slightly parted lips, and the shiver that passed through her.

"Lady? Is this some hostile spell? Should—"

Alustriel shook her head violently and leaned into his arms to slap two imperious fingers across his lips. Taern cradled his Bright Lady awkwardly but with infinite care as she inclined her head to listen to something within it that he could not hear. She lifted an intrigued eyebrow. A breath or two later Alustriel nestled against him as if for fatherly comfort, settled herself against his chest, then abruptly spun away from him to stand with hands on hips and a thoughtful frown dawning on her face.

"Well," Alustriel said aloud, eyes fixed on something that was distant indeed. "Well, well." Her eyes came back to the here and now, and snapped up to meet his. "Make sure the wine's Sharaerann amber. It need not be chilled."

She turned on her heel and strode away, swinging her arms with the determined cadence of a marching warrior on parade.

"Of course, Bright Lady," the man called Thunderspell almost whispered. "As you will, it shall be."

Taern stared after Alustriel's dwindling figure, watching the wide sleeves of her gown swirl. If she'd been ugly, or stupid, or simply lazy, he could have served her well and loyally, as the true ruler of Silverymoon, and known his worth. Why did she have to be more of a warrior than the best war captains the Moonlands could muster, more of a ruler than the wisest magisters of Waterdeep, and more of a mage than anyone he'd ever met?

And why, despite his own beloved family and hers, and many tests for them both down the passing years of crises at court, had he fallen so utterly and thoroughly in love with her?

✳　　✳　　✳

Sister of Silverymoon, I have a need for aid, and you, for the safety of your city, a need to know. Hear me now?

Of course, Laeral. I'm here; say on.

You remember Mirt? Merchant contacts in Scornubel brought word to him of drow impersonating vanished human citizens there. He went to Dove, who met with misadventures in the Caravan City, and called on Qilué. She was nearly slain uncovering some slavers, and followed one of them to Waterdeep, and to me. The slaver, a drow we know as "Brella," reported to an ambitious woman you may have heard of: Mrilla Malsander. Mrilla works for a merchant who keeps far more out of the lamplight, here, a man by the name of Auvrarn Labraster.

Surprisingly, the name is not unfamiliar to me, though I could not have said that before today.

Ah, he's been trouble to you, now, too? It seems he, and a handful of drow who can cast spells with the best of us, are part of something larger. A dark fellowship whose reach, membership, and aims remain too mysterious for my liking. Their activities are alarming others, too. No less an upstanding Waterdhavian than the Serpent told me that Auvrarn Labraster arrived in your garden two nights ago. I tried to trace him, and was nearly destroyed for my troubles. Khelben thinks the spelltrap left waiting for me was the work of mad Halaster. Be on guard, Lustra! I need you to watch this Labraster, and for all our sakes find out more about his friends . . . but I need you alive, too.

So do a steadily lengthening line of folk up here in the North who want me to advance this project, that law, or the other alliance for them. Have my warmest thanks for this warning, Lael—it's certainly thrown a fireball into the cooking caldron in front of me just now. A tradelord from Neverwinter has been bloodily murdered under my roof, and Auvrarn Labraster met with him not long before he died. Taern's sizzling around like meat on a skillet, which is about what our victim looks like, all over my floor. I'm beginning to think I need me alive, too.

We'll both work on that need, then. Keep me all-wise and all-knowing, mmm?

Without fail. Fare thee better, Lael.

By the Lady, you've been eavesdropping on Khelben again! Fare thee well, Lustra.

*   *   *

"And this is?" Oscalar Maerbree refused to be cowed into obedience or even sullen acceptance, but strode along beside the seneschal like royalty being given a personal tour of the High Palace, ignoring the two fully armored guards who bore drawn swords a bare pace behind his back.

"The Chamber of the Hunting Horn," Taern Hornblade said shortly, setting his hand on an upswept, horn shaped doorknob and thrusting the door inward. "If you will, milord."

Oscalar inclined his head graciously, clasped his hands behind his back, and strolled inside, looking back over his shoulder for the first time at the stern, helmed armsmen in his wake. "A pleasant evening to you, good sirs. Mind you keep the hallway warm out there for my return."

Then, and only then, did he turn, whistling a little tune between his teeth, and let his eyes wander lazily around the room. A balcony thrust forward to tower over the room like the bow of a docked ship, its pillars and overhang ornately carved in sweeping curves and needles of dark wood, its upper works lost in darkness. Rich rugs were spread underfoot, tapestries and paintings—the inevitable elven hunts, one of them with swanmays taking wing from human form out of a forest pool, mounting into the air in alarm beside a flight of pegasi—hung on all sides, with doors surely behind some of them. There were lamps and hanging sconces in similar profusion, though none of them were lit. Above, a soft amber glow radiated from a lone hunting horn hung on a chain. A brighter, whiter light burned before him, at the elbow of a dark-gowned, barefoot woman reclining on a lounge. The light was coming from a small rock crystal sphere at the tip of a plain, slender black staff that stood upright by itself, with no hand to hold it. There were chairs and tables in plenty, all dark and empty and silent. The only living presence was the woman. Her hands were empty, her unbound silver hair stirred about her shoulders, and her only adornment was a fine neck chain dipping down out of sight between her breasts. Her dark and thoughtful eyes were two hard dagger points upon his.

"Gods, woman!" Oscalar roared, slapping at his thighs so as to set the little bells dangling from his bright and stylish new codpiece chiming. "If you wanted me, all you had to do was send a page—or come yourself. You'll never need to bring more than a flask of wine and a smile. You didn't have to make two idiots dress up in battle steel and clank across half the palace—or awaken Thunderguts here, either."

Without waiting for a reply from the High Lady of Silverymoon, the large, fat wine merchant turned and pointed imperiously at the open door. "You may leave us, mage!"

Taern was looking at the lady on the lounge, and continued to do so. She shifted her eyes to his, and nodded almost imperceptibly. The seneschal bowed his head, turned with slow grandeur and not a glance at the merchant, and strode out, drawing the door closed as he went.

He left a little silence in his wake, and Oscalar and Alustriel peered through it at each other for a moment or two before the merchant asked more quietly, "This isn't about pleasure, is it, Bright Lady?"

"You're more than usually perceptive, Lion of the North," Alustriel replied calmly. "Or is it 'Sword of Silverymoon' these days?"

The wine merchant ducked his head down between his shoulders like a gull standing in an icy wind. "Hah-*hem*, lady, I know not. Have I offended anyone important with my ... attentions? Or is there something else you'd like to talk about?"

"There is," Alustriel said, a note of doom in her quiet voice. "I'd like to talk about death."

There was a little silence, and the room seemed to grow slightly darker. Oscalar Maerbree stared over the chairs and tables between them, squinting slightly to make clear contact with the eyes of the lady on the lounge.

"I'm sorry, Lady Alustriel," he said in disbelief, "but did you say—'death'?"

"*Death*, merchant . . . but not the death that will surely be yours if you don't take both of your enchanted daggers out of their sheaths—slowly—and lay them on that table to your right," Alustriel replied almost tenderly. "Another death."

She let silence fall again, sitting like a statue as Oscalar Maerbree met her eyes uncertainly, fumbled with his large, many-horned belt buckle as if finding nervous comfort in stroking something so reassuringly large and solid, then drew out a long, needle-thin knife from behind it, and a more stout blade from one boot. He hefted them for a moment, eyes measuring hers thoughtfully, then set the two weapons carefully on the indicated table, took two slow and deliberate steps away from it, and said, "Right—what's this about, then?"

"Please sit down, Oscalar. Here."

One of Alustriel's long arms rose to point at a chair only a stride or two away from the lounge, the sleeve of her gown rippling. The merchant's eyes narrowed, then he threaded his way through the idle furniture to the chair with a few quick strides, snatched it up with a grunt and sudden flexing of corded forearms, and carried it four paces to one side.

"Your servant, Lady," he almost snarled, sitting down heavily. "Now, what by all the gods is this about? I was hoping to catch a kiss or two before morn—"

"You still might, merchant, if you give the right answers swiftly and clearly."

"And which, Lady, might the right answers be?"

"The truth, Oscalar." The eyes locked on his were two flames of promised fury. "For once. Put away your codpiece, give me simple answers, and this will all end for you."

The merchant winced at the waiting rage in Alustriel's gaze, and swallowed, unable to drag his eyes away from hers. Gods, but it was hot in the darkened room. "Right," he said curtly. "Ask your questions."

"Was Tradelord Muirtree of Neverwinter alive when you left him?" Alustriel snapped, right on the heels of the merchant's words. He stared at her, brows drawing together in a frown. "Well?"

"Lady," he said slowly, "I never met with the tradelord."

"You neither saw nor spoke to Garthin Muirtree this day?"

"No. I'd hoped to—we had a moot planned, here in the palace—but a page brought me a note from him, begging off."

"Where is that note?"

The fat merchant spread helpless hands. "Gone. I burned it in the grate in my room the moment I'd read it—my habit for everything but contracts and treaties."

Alustriel raised a mocking eyebrow, but the merchant growled at her look and said, "Truth." His jaws snapped out the word as if he were slamming a castle door.

"What did the note say?"

"The words are gone, lady—but 'twas an apology, signed by him, saying he'd have to miss 'our planned parley' . . . that's how he put it. Said he'd been taken ill, and it would be his pleasure to send the same page to me early on the morrow to arrange another moot."

"So you'd know this page boy if you saw him again?"

"I would." The merchant sat back in his chair more calmly, his eyes fixed on Alustriel's. In the silence between them, there came a muffled sound from somewhere near, as of a door closing. Oscalar Maerbree lifted his head for a moment, then asked, "Someone's killed the tradelord? How?"

"I don't yet know that," Alustriel said carefully, "and might not tell you if I did. Would you like a drink, Oscalar?"

The merchant regarded her expressionlessly for the space of a long breath, then said, "No. I don't believe I would, given the circumstances."

"And why is that?" the High Lady asked, her voice silken soft.

The fat merchant lifted one large, blunt-fingered hand, stared at his palm for a moment, then told it, "I'd like to make my own death as difficult an achievement as possible."

The door Oscalar had come in by opened without warning, and the burly merchant's head whipped around, a dagger coming into his hand with dizzying speed.

The two guards coming through the door saw the flash of the blade and went for their own swords. Steel sang swiftly, but Alustriel came to her feet even faster. "That won't be necessary. Weapons *away*."

In the silence that followed her ringing shout, the table one guard had thrust aside to charge the merchant slowly continued its topple over onto its side, landing with a crash.

The two guards stared at Alustriel, and what she was doing. Oscalar was also looking down in disbelief at the slender hand encircling his thick and hairy wrist, its grip as hard and firm as a manacle. He tried to wrench free, but he might as well have been struggling against a stone wall. He could not move his hand, even with a sudden wrench. Staring up at her face, the merchant tried a sudden jerk that had all of his weight behind it. The chair rocked under him, but his hand was held in one place as if frozen there.

Alustriel gave him a gentle smile. "Let go of the knife, Oscalar," she said, in a mother's chiding tones.

A slow, dark flush crept across the merchant's face, but he opened his fingers and let the blade fall.

Alustriel let go of his wrist, picked up the dagger heedless of his proximity to her bending body, and inspected it.

"You *do* know sleep-salarn—as a poison—is unlawful in Silverymoon, don't you?" she said.

Oscalar shrugged, and Alustriel calmly handed him back the dagger. "Put it away," she said, "and mind the salarn is cleaned from it by evenfeast tomorrow."

The merchant gaped up at her. Alustriel gave him a tight smile and turned to address the two armsmen, who were busy erasing clear astonishment from their faces. She remained standing beside Oscalar, within his easy striking distance, as she asked crisply, "Did you conduct this man to the Red Griffon Room earlier this day, to meet with the tradelord from Neverwinter?"

Both of the guards gave Oscalar level looks, and both replied, "Yes, High Lady."

"And conducted him back to his chambers, after?"

"To Glasgirt's Hall, lady," one armsman replied.

"He asked us to take him nigh the kitchens, for an early meal," the other replied.

"And after, you went—?"

"Back to our posts, outside Barsimber's Arch."

"And this man came not past you again, while you were stationed there?"

"No, Great Lady."

"My thanks, good sirs. Return to your duties, and send in the boy you brought hence."

The guards gave Oscalar dubious looks, laid their hands on the hilts of their sheathed swords in duplicate silent warnings, and did as they were told.

The boy was trembling with awe and terror, but Alustriel gave him a smile and asked gently, "Have you seen this gentleman before?"

"M-many times, Bright Lady. Usually coming out of bedchambers or revels. He's very loud."

Alustriel's merry laugh startled both merchant and page, but she let it fall into another smooth, grave question. "When was the last time you saw him?"

"With the guards, leaving the Red Griffon Room, this day."

"You saw the guards bring him there, before that?"

"Yes."

"You're sure it's this man, and no one else?"

"Yes."

Oscalar seemed about to say something, but Alustriel turned her head and gave him a look that had a dozen daggers in it, and he held silent. She turned back to the page, the long sleeves of her gown swirling.

"Did anyone else enter that room before the Lord Taern?"

"Yes. The steward Rorild; he came out shouting, and Old Thunderspells came. Uh—that is—uh—"

"Old Thunderspells is a splendid name," Alustriel said soothingly, "that I'd be proud to bear myself. Just one question more, now. Did you take a note to this man sitting beside me?"

"No, lady."

"You have my thanks. Go now to the kitchens, and tell them my orders are to let you eat whatever you like, and drink a glass of the finest wine they have ready, and you are off duty tomorrow to recover from your gluttony unless the Lord Old Thunderspells or I send for you."

The page boy's eyes grew as large and round as saucers, and he stammered his thanks and practically sprinted out the door, leaving it open.

Alustriel went to close it, then turned and came back to the merchant.

"Well, Oscalar?" she asked coolly. "What am I to do with you? Or were all those folk lying?"

"I know not," the fat merchant said heavily. "I can only say that I did not slay Muirtree, have never acted against him—and never even went near the tradelord this day."

"Because of a note that boy says he never took to you?" Contempt dripped from Alustriel's tone.

"That was not the boy who brought me the note!" Oscalar roared. "Gods, woman, has your precious palace no other pages?"

Alustriel stared at him for a moment, then went to a wall and pulled a dark cord hanging there. After a moment the door opened again, and a steward came in and bowed. "Great Lady?"

"Summon to me here all of our pages save young Pheldren," Alustriel commanded. "Right now, asleep or awake, on duty or off, sick or well—no exceptions. If they're sick abed dying, bring them priest, bed, and all. I want everyone, in haste."

The steward assured her it would be done, speedily turned, and with wide eyes raced away. Alustriel left the door open this time, and turned back to the merchant with the barest trace of a smile on her lips. "Are you *sure* you won't have that drink, Oscalar?"

The wine merchant shrank back in his seat. "Keep away from me, Alustriel," he snapped. "You're up to something . . ."

"Oh, put that dagger away, Oscalar," she said wearily. "Here you are alone with the one woman in the High Palace you haven't yet boasted of bedding, with the avowed aim of getting 'a kiss or two' before slumber this even, and instead of trying your charm—lumbering though it may be—you're drawing knives on her. All this though she rules the city around you—the city you dwell and grow rich in. I ask you, Oscalar, is this wise? Is this . . . good business? Is this in keeping with your manly reputation?"

"Lady, I—" Oscalar's white face was now beginning to go purple, and he was trembling. "I-I—oh, gods, shut *up*, woman, they're starting to arrive."

As page boys flooded into the room, one of the foremost fixed the merchant in the chair with a cold, level gaze and said, "For the rudeness you have just offered our High Lady, I challenge thee, man. Have you a dagger?"

Oscalar Maerbree opened his mouth like a fish gobbling out bubbles, but no sound came out.

Alustriel watched him for a moment, then said to the page, "As a matter of fact, Eirgel, he does . . . but I forbid challenges in this room, and at this time. I shall, however, remember your honor in championing me with pride. Have my gratitude."

Eirgel drew himself up with shining eyes, saluted her with the dagger he'd whipped out, and put it away. By then the space between him and the doors was crowded with excited boys. The steward came into view around the edge of the door behind them, half carrying a sleeping boy. "Here we muster all, Great Lady."

"My thanks, Rorild, and to all of you for prompt obedience. This won't take long." Alustriel turned to the merchant and said, "Stand up, Oscalar, and point out to me the page who brought you the note."

The merchant looked at her with a sort of sick dread on his face, and got up slowly, staring around almost helplessly at the sea of boys. Out of their midst a hand shot up, and an eager voice piped, "If you please, Lady Alustriel, 'twas I."

Alustriel turned to Oscalar. "Well?"

The merchant was almost gasping with relief. "Yes— yes! This is the boy."

Silver hair swirling around her shoulders as if it had a life of her own—there was a murmur of excitement among the pages—Alustriel turned to the page and asked, "Who gave you that note, Kulden?"

"I—ah, no one, lady. 'Twas left on my delivery tray, so I delivered it."

"Thank you, all of you. You've just done Silverymoon good service indeed. Back to your duties or leisure, now, all of you—save you, Kulden."

When the shouting was done and the room empty again, Alustriel made sure the fat merchant and the excited page had not been mistaken with each other. She sent Kulden off to the kitchens then to find Pheldren and demand the same treatment as his colleague was enjoying. "If you hurry, merchant," she said to Oscalar, "you may yet find those kisses. Take your daggers with you."

Oscalar Maerbree gave her a wild look, but remained where he was. A slow smile grew on Alustriel's face, and she reached down an arm to help haul him to his feet. The merchant looked at her hand for a moment as if it was the head of a snake that might bite him, then took it, and found himself on his feet with his nose an inch or two from that of the High Lady of Silverymoon. He reeled hastily away, breathing heavily.

"Have done with mocking me," he snarled, heading for his knives.

He was snatching them both up from the table when two slender arms went around him from behind, and a cool voice said in his ear, "I don't mock you, Oscalar, and I won't. I wronged you, thinking you a liar. You told me the truth, and to me—or any ruler—that's worth more than a year of fawning and florid compliments. Here."

Oscalar Maerbree turned around with the daggers raised before him like a defensive wall. Alustriel stretched her perfect white throat between them and planted a gentle kiss on his cheek.

Oscalar blinked at her. He did not resist when she pushed the daggers aside and put her lips firmly on his.

He was struggling for air when their battle of tongues ended and Alustriel gently pushed him away, laughing, and said, "Behold your kisses, Sword of Silverymoon. Now get out of here, and put those daggers away before I have two murders to investigate."

The wine merchant looked at her with astonishment ruling his face. He tried to speak several times before he managed to ask, "Why?"

Alustriel put a hand on one hip and struck a smoldering pose of promise against the doorframe. "I know you, merchant. You're going to roll down the hall and out into my city bursting to tell someone about this night. You can't help not flapping your jaws, so I want you to tell all the Moon about kissing me, and not a word about Tradelord Muirtree or murder or you being suspected of it. Do you understand me?"

Oscalar swallowed at the dark fires that were now back in her eyes, and stammered, "Y-yes, High Lady." He went to one knee, almost falling over, and said in a rush, "You can depend on me, lady! Truly! I-I—"

"I know I can. Call me Alustriel," the ruler of Silverymoon said almost affectionately, taking firm hold of the merchant's ears and hauling him to his feet as if he was made of feathers. Tears started into his eyes from the pain of that handling, as he gaped again at her strength, and she grinned at him like the sister of

his youth had once done, and added, "Ah, dripping daggers, man. Have three."

When her lips came down on his this time, Oscalar
Maerbree closed his eyes and steadied himself, daring
to reach out and gently hold her shoulders. He very
much—and forever—wanted to remember this.

✳   ✳   ✳

"There goes one man who will love savagely tonight,
then go to bed alone and lie awake thinking of you,"
Taern Hornblade said gravely.

Alustriel's head snapped around. Had those words
held more than just a hint of wistfulness?

"Am I too hard on you, most loyal of men?" she asked
softly, lifting a hand toward one side of his face.

Taern shuddered, and put up a firm hand to capture
her fingers. "Lady, don't. Please don't. It's hard enough
. . ."

They regarded each other thoughtfully for a moment,
then Alustriel bowed her head and said, "Forgive me,
Taern." She brought his hand, by means of the fingers
he still held, back up between their faces, and added,
"This wisdom of yours is why you will rule this city
someday."

"Lady, *please* don't speak of such things. All I can
think of when you say that is your . . ."

"My death?" At his silent nod, Alustriel shrugged. "It
will come, one day, and find me. We can none of us hide
from it, and I've had far longer a run than most." Her
face changed. "Someone helped it find Garthin Muirtree
earlier than it should have, however, and I know from
your signal that lusty old Oscalar was telling me the
simple truth."

"Lady," Taern told her gravely, "they were all telling
the truth—both guards, both pages, and the merchant—
or believed they were."

"So where does that leave us?"

"Either someone did a lot of spellwork to twist and tamper with a lot of minds—very quickly, and with no traces that I noticed—or someone deceived their eyes, far more simply, earlier this day."

"Someone wearing a spell-spun likeness of Oscalar met with Garthin, and murdered him," Alustriel murmured.

Taern nodded. "Indeed. Which of the others will you question first?"

The High Lady of Silverymoon smiled thinly. "Flarwood. Then the exalted Tradelord of Luskan, followed by Janthasarde to give us some time to recover from the Luskanite . . . and Labraster last. Cast a fresh truth field before we begin, and have whoever of the Spellguard is up on the balcony with you hand me down your wineskin for a swallow, before anything else."

"Wineskin, lady?"

"Truth, Taern. Simple truth, remember?"

The Seneschal of the High Palace flushed and asked, "The red wine or the white, lady?"

"*Alustriel*, Taern. To you it is Alustriel, or Lustra. White, damn you."

❋　　❋　　❋

"Shining Lady, I'm flattered indeed that you've asked to see me this day!" Goodman Draevin Flarwood's bow was so low that he almost knelt. "I'm proud that the Braeder Merchant Collective has caught your eye, amid all the shining successes your rule of justice and peace has made possible."

"Well," Alustriel said in dry tones, "I like to be overwhelmed."

"Silverymoon is a great city," the merchant said excitedly. "Perhaps the greatest city. I grew up here scarcely appreciating all you've wrought until I traveled the

face of Faerûn trading, and saw what holds sway elsewhere. There's just one thing, Shining Lady, that puz-
zles me."

"And what might that be?"

"With all this prosperity and love of learning, the
Moon's long ties with Everlund, and our growing
friendship with like-minded cities of the North, why,
High Lady, have you avoided building an army and
border castles? Why is your Spellguard not an able
force for justice and hunting miscreants, like the War
Wizards Cormyr boasts?"

Alustriel stretched a little on the lounge, and gestured to him. "Please be seated, Goodman. Here."

As Flarwood scrambled to obey with the eagerness of
a puppy, the ruler of Silverymoon added, "The things
you've mentioned are the trappings of war, not the
anchors of a realm. I bend my efforts these days to
make the folk of the Moonlands feel as if they belong to
a kingdom, sharing a realm that is theirs—so in time
to come they'll govern themselves, looking to no throne
or lineage."

"But that will take years!" Flarwood protested, leaning forward in his excitement. "Our children's children
will be old before we see this."

Alustriel leaned forward until her face was close to
his and he was looking straight into her eyes. As her
long silver hair stirred restlessly about her shoulders
she asked gently, "Ah, yes, you've said it perfectly, Goodman. For our children's children. Have you ever heard
of a better reason to do anything?"

Draevin Flarwood blinked a little, and she kept
silent to give his thoughts some time to spin to a conclusion. She hoped they knew how.

When he stirred to speak again, the word she'd
expected was the first to leave his lips. "But—"

She held up a stern hand and said gravely, "Goodman
Flarwood, it will some day give me great pleasure to
debate and discuss the future of the Moonlands, but I

know not yet if I'll have that discussion with you—or if you will be dead."

Draevin Flarwood blinked for the second time in the same day—possibly a record—then managed to gasp, "Uh . . . pardon, lady?"

"Draevin," she said gently, "you met with Tradelord Muirtree earlier this day, did you not?"

"Why, yes, and it was a good meeting, very positive for trade. We—uh—that is, I can't discuss what we agreed upon, though of course if you insist, I'll h—"

"Did you strike Garthin Muirtree with your sword, Draevin?"

All the color spilled out of Draevin Flarwood's face, leaving it the hue of old bone, and he gasped, "What?"

"Did you take a weapon to Tradelord Muirtree?"

"N-no, of course not, Lady Alustriel. He and I are *friends*. I—"

"Do you know of anyone else desiring to harm the tradelord, or doing so?"

"No," the merchant replied emphatically, frowning, "but, lady, why do you ask me? Don't you know who hurt Garthin?"

"And how should I?"

"Well, doesn't your magic reveal who, the moment you bend your will to ask whom it might be?" When Alustriel silently shook her head, Draevin Flarwood looked almost as if he might cry. "But you hold the power of Mystra in your hands!"

"In this, good sir," Alustriel replied quietly, "I hold but moonlight in my hands."

As she looked into the young merchant's gaping face, memory changed it to that of an even younger man, staring and drooling after he'd spent much of a day screaming under the coldly patient fingertips of the Lord Mage of Waterdeep. Khelben had ruthlessly taken apart that man's mind to find the secrets he needed to know to defend Waterdeep against but a dozen smugglers. "For the good of the city," had been the Blackstaff's justification, and she saw again his grim face as he told her those words.

That grim face changed again, into a younger, laughing one with a hawklike nose and the beginnings of a beard. Elminster, rearing her and her sisters with warm, humor-laced kindness so long ago. The easygoing yet unfailing love that had forged her—forged them all, down the years—led her to her own dignity-to-the-winds rule in Silverymoon, here and now. In the Gem of the North men and women were free to be heroes and fools, and encouraged to love openly. They were all held to be equal, man and woman, elf and dwarf, halfling and human, until they personally proved themselves otherwise.

Alustriel drew in a deep breath. She could mind-compel Draevin Flarwood or any man, reading his every private thought and recollection, but only at the cost of much time, and burning away many memories—and his will to think, and brilliance in doing so—from his brain. She would not do that, this day. She would never do that. "Never," she hissed.

"Uh-ah . . . Great Lady?"

Alustriel returned to the here and now with a shiver that shocked the young merchant into speechlessness.

"You have our leave to depart, Goodman Flarwood," Alustriel told him gently. "Say nothing of this to anyone."

Silently Draevin Flarwood nodded, knelt to her with his hands folded as if in prayer, and backed toward the door, still on his knees. As she winced and leaned forward to bid him rise, he found his voice again and asked beseechingly, "Tell me but one thing if you would, O Shining Lady. Tradelord Muirtree; will he recover?"

Alustriel swallowed. "No," she said gently. "No, I don't think so."

✳   ✳   ✳

"Tradelords of Luskan," Dauphran Alskyte said coldly, "are not accustomed to being summoned to private audiences with unescorted women, and there accused of murder. In case you've not noticed, Great Lady, I am a tradelord of Luskan."

"The fact has not escaped our discernment, most charming sir," Alustriel purred, feeling Taern's silent growl of anger from the balcony above. It made her own irritation more easily turn into amusement. "Will you take wine?"

The Luskanite barked out a short and mirthless laugh. "I thank you, but no. A considerably more foolish man than the one you see standing before you would know better than to partake of what may be drugged—so he might thereafter awaken in the throes of execution for any number of falsified crimes, to the great cost—and displeasure—of my masters in Luskan."

Alustriel shrugged. "You may well be more familiar with drugs and deceit, most wise sir, than myself . . . or any who can command spells to achieve their ends."

The door behind the Luskanite opened then. Taern showed himself just long enough to make the clear, unmistakable gesture that meant some magical defense or other carried by the waspish tradelord was blocking his truth reading, then disappeared again.

Dauphran Alskyte showed how closely he was watching Alustriel's eyes by whirling around, in time to see the door close. He whirled at once back to face Alustriel again.

"It seems, Lady," he said icily, "that you are rather less a stranger to deceit than you claim to be . . . unless that was a sophisticated Silverymoon method of bringing us fresh air, perhaps? Or something else you'd care to enlighten me about?"

The High Lady of Silverymoon regarded her unwilling guest through half closed eyes, calling on the ability to feel magic that Mystra imparts to all of her Chosen. Taern's truth field briefly revealed itself as a shining net laid over the chamber. Against it stood a small, dark shroud, enveloping the Luskanite and centered at his throat. Alustriel opened her eyes again. There; that amulet.

"No," she said coldly, "I would not care to enlighten you."

Given time enough, she could infiltrate the amulet's enchantment, drifting past its defenses without shattering or altering the magic, then mind-read Alskyte to confirm when he spoke the truth. A simple detection of falsehood would do his wits no harm, so long as she didn't try to force him to think of specific things—to hunt down the memories she needed to see. Goading words could, of course, turn his thoughts just as surely.

"Have you any fresh accusations to hurl at me, Exalted Ruler?" the Luskanite snapped. "Or am I free to go, leaving you to sink back into your web of suspicions and feeblewittedly imagined conspiracies?"

"Dauphran Alskyte," Alustriel replied, sinking back into where she could let her perception drift out, "you have much still to answer. The small matter of Talanther's missing figurines, for instance."

The tradelord went white, showing her his guilt as clearly as if he'd babbled it before all her hushed court. "You dare—?" he hissed.

"I rule here, Dauphran," Alustriel reminded him gently. "For the safety of my people, I dare everything."

Aflame with rage, the Luskanite failed to notice the hesitant, half-asleep edge to her tone, or her nearly closed eyes. He shook his fists as he strode angrily around a table toward her, shouting, "I've *never* been treated with such insolence, wench! Accused of this, accused of that! D'you think we of Luskan are so crackwitted that we go around openly offending against the laws of trade and of state? Do you think we are all so governed by greed that we can't control ourselves from thievery and connivance from one moment to the next?"

His shrieks were echoing back at him from the far and dark corners of the room now. As he paused, eyes glittering, to snarl in more air and begin anew, Alustriel rose from the lounge and said simply, "Yes."

Dauphran Alskyte stared at her, mouth agape. She knew, now, that he was telling the truth about the murder, and that he was boiling with rage, barely keeping himself from leaping on her to claw with his hands, bite, and kick . . . something he'd done often to any number of Luskanite women. Those glimpsed mind-images made Alustriel's voice cold indeed when she said, "We do not propose to waste our time with you further this fair evening, Luskanite. We know of your guilt over the figurines, and your innocence regarding the unfortunate passing of Tradelord Muirtree, and we are frankly sick of your childish raging and insults. You will depart from our city by highsun tomorrow. If you do so in possession of something that is not yours, or tarry within our walls a breath longer than the decreed time, my armsmen shall take great pleasure in urging you on your way with whips. I shall instruct them to try to avoid any blows to your backside . . . we would not want to harm what few wits you possess."

The tradelord swayed, trembling, and for a moment she thought he would rush at her, but instead he spat, "You have no authority over me, wench!"

"Oh?" The High Lady of Silverymoon lifted both of her eyebrows. "You'd obey any one of the High Captains—and any utterance from the Hosttower, too. Why, then, should you balk at obeying a ruler of equal rank, merely because she's a woman, and alone?"

Dauphran Alskyte opened his mouth to reply, then shut it again without saying anything. Alustriel didn't need the mindtouch that she'd let go to know that he was now realizing the weight of some of the words he'd used to her, and feeling the first touches of real fear. No wonder; were he in Luskan, he'd have been horribly and painfully slain some time ago for speaking so.

"This feeble-witted, deceitful, suspicious, and, yes, insolent wench is done with you, Alskyte," she told him calmly. "Keep silent as you leave us."

The little smile she gave him then had no mirth in it. The tradelord met her eyes for an instant, then looked away. He managed to suppress a shudder, but the weight of her cold gaze chilled his back and shoulders all the way to the door, and he began to hurry long before he reached it.

✳   ✳   ✳

Janthasarde Ilbright was short, buxom, and enthusiastic. If she'd been an apprentice mage, she'd have been what one of the senior Spellguard wizards was wont to term, in distasteful terms, "perky." Her nature quickly overcame her awe of Alustriel, but she had little to add to the High Lady's knowledge.

She'd met Tradelord Muirtree on several of his previous visits to the city. If he was being impersonated by someone employing a magical disguise, or been ill at ease at their meeting, she'd noticed nothing amiss. She cheerfully surrendered her written roster of Muirtree's planned upcoming meetings, and confirmed what Alustriel saw at a glance. It held nothing out of the ordinary.

When she'd been thanked and sent back to her duties, Alustriel and Taern exchanged glances. The courtier had been telling the truth, and that left them back at Auvrarn Labraster.

Alustriel squared her shoulders, sighed, and said to Taern, "Let the battle begin."

He nodded and went out, not smiling.

✳   ✳   ✳

Glossy brown hair shone in the lamp's glow as Auvrarn Labraster set his square handsome jaw, and frowned. "I had not heard of Muirtree's fate, no," he said in a deep, mellifluous voice. "On this visit to your fair city, I've largely kept to my rooms—avoiding, as it happens, much of the gossip that skulks about this palace."

Alustriel gave him a wintry smile. "Would that more of my subjects behaved thus," she granted, then shifted forward on the lounge and asked, "I've heard from others that you and Tradelord Muirtree have had some sharp disagreements in the past. Is this so?"

Labraster shrugged. "We're both vigorous bargainers. I harbor no ill will toward the man."

"And did your meeting earlier today end cordially?"

"For my part, it did," the merchant from Waterdeep said flatly. "Muirtree was fine when last I saw him." He jerked his head up at the balcony above and added, his words almost a bitter challenge, "Have your tame wizard confirm the truth of that."

"What magic can uncover, magic can also conceal . . . or distort," Alustriel replied calmly.

"Lady," the Waterdhavian replied, his handsome features twisting into a snarl of exasperation, "how could I tear a man apart? With this?"

His hand tore a knife from its sheath at his belt, and he waved it high in the air, well away from the High Lady. Its tiny blade glittered in the lamp glow as Auvrarn Labraster sprang to his feet, flourishing the belt knife in mockery of a battle knight brandishing a great two-handed sword.

"This," he roared, "is the only weapon I brought with me to your city—the only weapon I customarily carry. With it, I do great violence to cheese, and bread, and chops at the table. Pitted against fruit, I am a lion of savagery!"

Labraster tossed the knife into the air, caught it, thrust it back into its sheath with such force that his belt and breeches seemed destined to descend to his boots, and spat, "Now I've had enough of this foolery, High Lady. You offer little jabbing questions, worse than thrusts with such a blade. You insinuate, needle, mock, but never openly accuse, because you haven't a shred of proof against me."

He raised a finger to point at her as violently as if it had been a weapon, and snarled, "And you know what? You never will. I raised no hand against Garthin Muirtree. I did him no harm, he was hale and hearty when last we looked upon each other, and no honest examination, with spells or otherwise, will be able to conclude anything else."

He strode away, then turned, his arms spread in defiant mockery. "And we hear often back in Waterdeep how honest is fair Alustriel of Silverymoon, the Lady Hope of a nascent nation. Well, then, High Lady and Most Honest Alustriel, have done. Let me be. My ears threaten to shrivel up and drop off from all these biting, suspicious, endless little questions."

Auvrarn Labraster spun on his heel and stormed out of the chamber without waiting for a reply or dismissal. Before the door banged, his snarls of fury could be heard echoing away down the hall outside.

Taern came forward to the lip of the balcony. "His fury kindled very suddenly. One might even say conveniently."

"Mmmm," was Alustriel's only reply, as she bit her lip and stared at the closed door.

"Now what, my lady?"

Alustriel whirled around to stare up at her seneschal. "Who knows how the tradelord died?" she asked softly. "Did you or anyone you know of tell Labraster that Muirtree was torn apart?"

"No . . ." Taern replied slowly, his eyes narrowing. He acquired a frown and added, "but lady, he was telling the truth in every word he uttered to you."

"Yet for all his rage," Alustriel said thoughtfully, "he chose his words carefully—very carefully. I think it's time Auvrarn Labraster and I had a little meeting of the minds . . . if you take my meaning."

Taern nodded. "If—however unlikely it seems—he's innocent," he asked soberly, "and your probing ravages his wits forever?"

His High Lady looked back at him grimly. "That's a price I'll have to risk," she replied. "I've done worse . . . and not all of my ill deeds have been inadvertent or through ignorance. A few—a very few—have even been done with glee."

"And this one?"

Alustriel gave her old friend a thin smile. "No, not this one. Not yet."

Their eyes met in wordless silence for the space of a breath before she turned toward the door, adding over her shoulder, "I'll do this alone, Taern. If I should fall, you know what to do."

The door closed behind the Lady Hope of Silverymoon, leaving Taern alone in the room. The man they called Thunderspell promptly leaped down from the balcony like a young adventurer, landing heavily on his hands and knees. He crawled forward a little way and bent his head to gently kiss the floor where her bare feet had trodden. Here, and there, he crawled on, missing not a single place.

When he reached the door, he scrambled up, wincing at the pains in his knees and his back, then rushed out into the hall, limping as he trotted. A guard gave him a puzzled frown, but the Master Mage of the Spellguard waved away the unspoken query. He had to get to a particular chamber fast—to where he could watch over Alustriel and assist her with his spells, should she need aid.

Not that one mage could hope to prevail where the Art of a Chosen fails, he thought wryly, but he can die trying. I love her that much, and more.

✳   ✳   ✳

Alustriel slipped into an antechamber, slid behind a cloak stand, and did something to the wall behind it. The wall obligingly sighed inward, and she plunged into dusty darkness.

Should he be the sort of villain who sniffs out secret passages, or has so many intrigues a-dance at once that he goes not to his own chambers, Alustriel thought grimly, I may yet lose him. Her mood lightened then, and she almost giggled. Sweet Lady Mystra! Now I'm sorting my villains.

Her fingertips, trailing along an unseen wall, told her she'd passed two openings. When she came to the third she turned down it, hurried along until her outstretched hand found a wall, and turned to the left. There was a handle here . . . ah!

Light almost dazzled her as she stepped boldly out into the Ten Tapestries Chamber. Four sets of guest apartments opened off this reception room, and the only one in use right now housed Auvrarn Labraster.

The room was deserted, so palace servants and courtiers were spared the sight of their High Lady running like a schoolgirl from one door to another, sealing off all ways into and out of the Ten Tapestries Chamber except the secret way she'd used, and the main door that Labraster should come storming through in a few moments. A scant two paces shy of that door, Alustriel whirled to one wall, plucked two cloak stands over together, and stood motionless between them. She had just time to draw in one deep, gasping breath when the door banged open, and Labraster came striding through.

"Stupid bitch!" he was snarling. "Poking and prying like a priestess running a convent. How, by all the bright, blazing—"

The merchant's cursing hid the small sounds of Alustriel raising her ward across the door, then striding along in his wake. She'd reached the open center of the chamber when he encountered the ward across the door to his chambers, and recoiled with a wordless hiss of pain and amazement, breaking off his oaths in mid word.

Labraster shook his head, then thrust himself forward again as if there'd been some mistake. When the prickling, searing sparks of warning rose up before him once more, he snarled, whirled around, and saw her.

Silence fell and Auvrarn Labraster came to a halt in the same instant, dropping his anger like a cloak as he stared at her. His scrutiny was that of a warrior, seeking what weapons she held ready or hints as to what she might do next. His hand darted to his knife, then fell away.

The merchant peered this way and that around the room, seeking guards waiting in the shadows or behind the huge, hanging tapestries, but the room was empty, and looked it.

"Lady," he asked flatly, "what're you playing at?"

"Uncovering the truth about Garthin Muirtree's death, Goodman Labraster," Alustriel replied, her eyes locked on his.

"Is there something wrong with your hearing?" he asked, and without waiting for a reply added slowly, spacing each word with biting emphasis, as if rebuking an imbecile: "I. Did. Not. Slay. Muirtree."

"Then you won't mind my doing this," Alustriel responded, her eyes boring into his as she strode forward.

He was falling into those twin pools of hungry darkness, he was . . . gods!

"Lady," Labraster protested, as the first twinges of pain in his head sent a spasm across his handsome face, "this is neither right nor just . . . this is tyranny!" "You stand in my power," she replied softly. "In my realm, wherein my word is law. Be not so quick to cry tyrant, Goodman. Innocent folk, I find, object but little to my actions."

The Waterdhavian snarled under her mind probe, clawing at his forehead and struggling to back away. "Witch!" he spat. "I'll—"

He waved his arms, shrank down, then . . . changed. There was a moment of blurred confusion before Alustriel's eyes, then something much larger rose up before her in the lamplight. It was something huge, black, and broad-shouldered, its mandibles clicking as it took its first lumbering step toward her.

An umber hulk! The High Lady's eyes narrowed. An illusion? She took a swift step to one side.

The floor shook, ever so slightly, under the tread of its great claws. It ground its teeth, its mandibles clacking again as it opened a mouth that could easily close around her body, engulfing her down to her waist. It swung that great head to follow her movement. Its arms were even longer than its squat, mighty legs, and bore claws that were even larger. Talons that could cleave solid stone like butter flexed and arched open, reaching for her.

It was big, even for an umber hulk, and the yellow-gray of its belly and chest was purplish green around the edges. It seemed almost to burst with energy, vibrating with glee as it advanced.

Shoulders as broad as a wagon shifted, black scales glinting as the beast turned to face her squarely, its black eyes flickering. As she met their fourfold gaze, Alustriel felt the familiar numbness that mages created with the spell called "confusion." It was a floating, disembodied feeling that one who was not a Chosen would not have been able to simply shake off.

Aye, this was the real thing, all right, a Burrower Through Stone and not a spell-woven disguise. Did Labraster see through its eyes, from afar? Or control it unseen, from a few paces away? Or . . . ?

As claws that could tear her apart like a thing of paper and feathers descended to do just that, Alustriel knew she was looking at what had slain Garthin Muirtree. She called on one of the magics that by the grace of Mystra was with her always, and those descending claws froze in midair, held motionless.

"Care to return, Labraster?" she asked, trying to probe the black, impenetrable eyes of the hulk.

Her answer was another instant of blurring, and the monster was gone. In its place stood a gaunt man in purple robes, his eyes cold and hard. The ends of a crimson sash rippled at his waist as he bowed, and announced, "Azmyrandyr of Thay am I. Your doom, lady." The fingers of his flourished hands were moving as he spoke, wriggling like the legs of an agitated spider.

In unison Red Wizard and Chosen of Mystra each took a step backward, away from each other. As she moved, Alustriel silently called on another of her innate magics, raising a shell to quell all magic around herself.

"I seldom welcome Red Wizards into my palace, sir," she said coldly, "even when they come to my gates in peace. Your visit here is unlikely to be hospitable."

Azmyrandyr merely smiled, letting his smirk slide into a sneer as his spell took effect and the room exploded in flames.

A sphere of clear air surrounded Alustriel and the Red Wizard. He strode forward with something sparkling in his hand. Outside it, hitherto unseen globes of fire burst with force enough to shake the High Palace, transform ten tapestries into as many raging torches, and scour the rest of the room with roaring flames.

Azmyrandyr of Thay smiled a tight, cruel smile as the true target of his magic collapsed with a roar, and announced, "A slight refinement of the traditional meteor swarm spell."

The riven ceiling of the chamber plunged down on Alustriel in a rain of tumbling panels and flaming fragments. Struggling under the cascade of embers, Alustriel managed to stagger the first four steps of a charge at the Red Wizard before a tangle of blazing timbers smashed her flat.

Tendrils of silver hair roiled angrily among the wreckage, and Azmyrandyr eyed them warily as he took two quick steps forward and tossed a small, sparkling stone onto the floor, springing hastily back as the last burning pieces of the ceiling crashed down, bounced, and rolled away in all directions. As the stone landed, the sphere of nothingness that had kept the flames at bay melted away. The last, dying tongues of flame swept over hitherto untouched stretches of carpet around the smoldering heap wherein Alustriel lay.

"Wild magic stone brings down antimagic shell," the Red Wizard said calmly, for all the world as if he were describing a move in a chess game.

Nimbly stepping around the small fires still rising here and there about the blackened carpet, he backed out of range of the stone and raised both hands to weave another spell.

Rubble shifted and sagged away. Something sprang up from the blazing heart of the debris, somersaulting to one side in a tangle of long, flowing silver hair and smoke. Azmyrandyr's jaw dropped as the dainty High Lady of Silverymoon landed, vaulted without pause over another heap of rubble, and sprinted toward him, her gown smoldering around her and her lips snarling out an incantation as she came.

Hastily he abandoned his casting and stepped to one side. Something crunched under his feet, and he found flames rising around him. Hastily the Red Wizard moved again, but by then the furious face of one of the fabled Seven Sisters was almost touching his, and her bare hands were reaching for him. He slapped one hand away, and the other drove into his ribs, glancing off bone and away in a wet, slicing glide that left searing pain in its wake.

Azmyrandyr of Thay screamed and hurled himself back, heedless of what flames he might stagger through. He fetched up against a scorched wall and stared at Alustriel's open hand. Her fingers were dripping with his blood as she advanced on him, entirely ignoring the waist-high flames she strode through.

A bleak smile touched her lips. "Laeral's Cutting Hand," she announced, her tones a mockery of his own.

The Red Wizard shrank away, then, as Alustriel's hand swept down, was lost in a blur of spell-shot air.

Her descending fingers struck the naked blade of an upthrust sword that was held awkwardly in both hands by a younger Red Wizard, robed like Azmyrandyr, but sporting oiled, glistening black hair and a beard to match. There was apprehension on his face, but also, rising to overwhelm it, a fierce delight.

Waves of tingling nausea swept over Alustriel, and she fell back with silver fire licking around her hand. That gave her new assailant all the time he needed to rise and thrust his blade right through her belly.

She could not even find breath enough to scream.

"Taste a Sword of Feebleminding, Chosen of Mystra!" he shouted in triumph. His laughter rose above the crackling and snapping of the dying fires all around them. "Haha! You'll probably find it hard to serve your goddess well, drooling and mumbling your way around this palace for the rest of your days."

Alustriel staggered back, moaning, her agonies snatching the sword from the wizard's hands. He let it go to stand and gloat.

"Oh," he cried mockingly, putting a hand to his forehead as the High Lady of Silverymoon stared down at the blade beneath her breasts and sobbed forth spurts of silver fire, "I've quite forgotten my manners. I am Roeblen . . . of Thay, but I'm sure you guessed that—back when you still could guess anything."

The wizard watched Alustriel sink to her knees, tugging feebly at the hilt of the sword to draw it forth, and laughed again. Striding over to her, he reached down for the hilt of his blade.

"Is there something more you'd like me to do for you, perhaps?" he mocked. "I've a sharp dagger ready for your fingers and tongue. Once spellcasting is beyond you, perhaps we could play. We could trade spells, you and I. Show me a spellbook, and I'll cast a painquench on you, eh? It should last just long enough for you to take me to your next spellbook, hmm? Or can't you understand such things anymore?"

The Red Wizard shook his head in mock sorrow. "Such a pity," he told her. "I was looking forward t—"

The woman on her knees before him growled, set her teeth, and wrenched forth the sword. It promptly exploded into starry shards.

As silver flames snarled forth from her in its wake, Alustriel raised eyes that blazed with pain to glare at Roeblen as she held up one hand over her head and a slender black staff appeared in it.

Roeblen's eyes narrowed. "A staff of Silverymoon, no doubt," he murmured, raising his hands to deliver a smiting spell.

One end of the staff lifted a little, and he changed his mind, backing hastily away.

"Wise of you, Red Wizard," Alustriel gasped, her breath a plume of silver flame as she climbed the staff to stand unsteadily upright, clapping a hand that glowed to the wound in her belly and gathering her will to begin what was necessary. " 'Twould have been wiser still not to have come here at all."

Roeblen spread his hands. "Such was not my intention, High Lady. I'm linked into the cycle. Azmyrandyr's calling isn't something I can resist. I saw you only an instant before I was brought here, and had just time enough to snatch down my best creation . . . which you promptly destroyed."

Alustriel spread her own hands precisely as he had done, as her healing spell spread its soothing tendrils through her body. "A pity I'm immune to feeblemindedness, isn't it?"

Roeblen's face twisted into a sneer. "For a mage centuries old, you're not very swift witted, are you? Only a fool yields information to an enemy."

Alustriel shrugged, feeling almost whole again. "Mystra bids us educate the magically weak."

The Red Wizard's eyes snapped with anger, and he spat forth a fireball incantation, hurling it at the ravaged ceiling above her. Better to crush and bury this wounded Chosen rather than cast something her personal defenses might negate or even turn back on him.

With a singing sound and a whirling of sparks, one of Alustriel's wards failed across the room, and a door burst open. As both High Lady and Red Wizard turned to look, Roeblen's fireball burst overhead, shaking the room and spitting fire in all directions. Through its roar there came a tortured groan from overhead, slow and loud, but unending. Slowly, as it went on, it grew both louder and swifter.

As a reeling Taern Hornblade and a tall and handsome elf behind him clutched at the doorframe and stared in horror, the floor of the room above the blackened Ten Tapestries Chamber broke asunder and collapsed, spilling like a titanic waterfall through the shattered ceiling.

Stones roared down in a dark flood of death as Taern screamed something and the laughing Red Wizard retreated. Alustriel glanced upward, then raised the staff, aiming it straight up. It winked once in her grasp, and she looked at Roeblen and announced calmly, "Pass—"

The rest of the word was lost in the thunder of tumbling, crushing stone. It went on and on, hiding the ruler of Silverymoon from view amid rising dust as stones cracked and rolled.

When at last the roaring died away to echoes and the dust began to settle, Roeblen turned away from his latest frustratingly futile attempt to bring down a door ward and spat out a curse. It should have been so easy. A word, two gestures, another word, and he should have been out and roaming around a palace legendary for its stored magic. It was too much to hope that the falling stones had crushed those two idiots in the doorway, but at least he'd felled the much vaunted High Lady of Silverymoon.

A figure came striding out of the dust then, a tall figure with a staff in its hand, whose silver hair stirred about its shoulders as if with a life of its own.

The Red Wizard's hissed curse turned into a groan of disbelief as two more heads came bobbing through the dust. Gods, had he missed them all?

Roeblen looked from one grim and dusty face to another, then murmured something swift and anxious, his intricately gesturing fingers momentarily shaping a closed ring. As the three folk of Silverymoon advanced upon the Thayan, the dust sprang away from him, swirling swiftly to outline the outer curve of a cylinder of clear, hard space around the Red Wizard.

The elf accompanying Taern waved mockingly at Roeblen and said, "Wall of force; ring shaped."

Taern gave the elf a glance of mingled amusement and disgust, and started to weave a spell of his own. The elf grinned back and began his own casting. Alustriel gave them all a look of weary exasperation and merely lifted her hand. Blue-white bolts blossomed from her fingers and streaked up through the dust, seeking the gaping hole where the Ten Tapestries Chamber had once boasted a ceiling. Her glowing missiles turned there, in the dust-choked ruin that had once been a parlor on the floor above, and came arrowing back down inside the Red Wizard's defensive ring. She saw an amulet at his throat flash as the missiles struck. Roeblen seemed unharmed, his hands never slowing in the casting of his latest spell. The cylinder around him glowed a bright blue and sang, the ringing noise swiftly rising into a scream as the radiance blazed into a bright, iridescent green. The light quickly faded, taking the wall of force with it into oblivion.

Taern smiled at the Red Wizard in satisfaction and lifted his hands to weave another spell as the elf let out a sudden, startled squawk and cartwheeled away across the room, outlined in red radiance. Alustriel saw the sparkling stone Azmyrandyr had thrown wink once as the elf's boots left the rubble where he'd been standing.

"Wild magic," she called warningly, just as Roeblen of Thay's right arm started to grow.

The Red Wizard stood still as his arm became impossibly long, thick, and scaled, reaching fifty feet or more across the ravaged room to snatch with thigh-long claws at Alustriel. No human should have been able to stand upright attached to the weight of its huge bulk, let alone lift and move it, but the spell-spun limb swooped down on the High Lady as if it weighed nothing.

Alustriel's eyes narrowed. She'd never seen the likes of this spell before, and almost found herself looking at Roeblen and awaiting his proud announcement of the enchantment he'd used. No such words came, and as the claws descended, she fed it magic missiles. They vanished into it without apparent effect, the distant Red Wizard's amulet pulsing as each bolt died.

The claws tore at her, and she found them very real and solid indeed. Ducking away and lashing at the talons with her hair—each of the claws was now as long as she was tall—she managed to swallow a scream as they closed on her left shoulder and crushed it to bleeding jelly.

The pain drove Alustriel to her knees, retching. She heard Taern cry out her name, then gasp and call on Mystra.

Rolling over on stony rubble and writhing in pain as that scaly limb came down to tear at her again, Alustriel stared at her dangling, useless left arm. Where her shoulder should have been there was nothing. It was hard to see through the silver smoke streaming from the wound, but the raging fire had left her little more than clinging ashes of her gown. She could see a lot of smooth, bared flesh, flesh that was changing as she watched. In an eerie webwork, scales were forming on her skin, spreading swiftly outward from her wound.

The claws missed on their next snatch, thanks to her tumbling, and when Alustriel found her feet again, she thrust the staff at them. Roeblen snatched at it, trying to take it away from her, and she let it go. She hissed out the words that would awaken a fleshfire spell before leaping at the scaly limb.

She caught at greasy scales, slipped, then clung. Her body blazed up into bright fire. Grimly she dug her fingers in around the edges of the scales and hung on as the smaller scales on her own flesh faded away and a stench like old swamp water arose from the darkening limb around her.

Roeblen roared in pain—and the High Lady of Silverymoon was falling, her blazing arms clutching nothing. She landed heavily, slithering on stones, and found herself looking into the startled face of yet another Red Wizard.

Roeblen, his scaly limb, and her staff were gone, and the elf was moaning against a distant wall. Taern was staring at her with hope, alarm, and despair at war across his face. The pain was ebbing.

Alustriel gave the newcomer a wolfish smile and charged, her body blazing. "Welcome to Silverymoon," she spat, silver flames making her words a bubbling horror, and she saw that horror rise swiftly in the Red Wizard's eyes as he stammered out an incantation, gesturing frantically.

He finished his casting a bare instant before she slammed into him, clawing at his face. She knew she'd hit him by the way the fire faded from her limbs as they rolled together. Alustriel had no clothes or weapons but her knees, teeth, and right hand. He was shorter but heavier than she was, and had no desire to be here at all. He'd flee, bringing in the next being in the cycle Roeblen had spoken of, unless she got a good grip on his throat, and . . .

The Red Wizard twisted away desperately as she spat silver fire into his face and tore free. Alustriel was left holding a scrap of purple cloth as sudden light blazed into being above her, taking the Thayan mage away.

She held up the cloth to keep from being blinded, and read aloud the name embroidered in a circle there, around a sigil unfamiliar to her: "Thaltar."

When the light faded and she saw another hand beyond the cloth, she launched herself forward onto whoever it was, and found herself panting and grappling with Auvrarn Labraster.

There was fear on the merchant's handsome face as he fended the High Lady off with one arm and peered around. She saw him take in Taern advancing on him, the ruination all around, then the furious gaze of Alustriel of Silverymoon but inches from his face. Auvrarn also obviously did not want to be there. In feverish haste he thrust three fingers into a breast pouch under his chin, desperately seeking something.

Alustriel punched him in the throat.

Coughing and gagging, Auvrarn Labraster rolled away from her, hoarsely trying to curse. She hurled herself upon him, not wanting him to have time to get at whatever small but fell thing awaited in his pouch. They rolled over and over as she clawed at his face, sobbing every time their struggle put weight on the ruin of her shoulder.

At last Labraster struck aside her clawing hand and got both of his hands on her throat. They stared into each other's eyes, hissing in fury, as his fingers started to tighten. Her hair swirled around them, slapping across his eyes and thrusting up into his nostrils.

The merchant gagged and snarled and shook his head violently back and forth, not loosening his grip around the throat of Silverymoon's Bright Lady. He never felt tresses of silver hair tear something off the chain around Alustriel's neck and knot that something into his own hair, but he did feel her surge upright. She thrust upward to her feet with astonishing strength, dragging him with her. Two rough hands slapped across both his ears, making his head ring. Before Labraster could even cry out, the hands took hold of his ears and tried to twist them off.

Auvrarn Labraster screamed and let go of Alustriel's throat, staggering and ducking as tears of pain poured forth. Twist and flail though he might, those hands stayed with him, twisting.

In desperation, he threw himself to the ground and rolled—and the hands were gone. Labraster heard a man grunt nearby, land heavily on loose stone, and roll away. He wasted not an instant on seeing who it was, but snatched the teleport ring from the pouch on his breast and fumbled it onto his finger.

Another hand was at his throat again, and he punched out with desperate force, connected solidly, and heard Alustriel gasp. He twisted blindly away again. Cloth tore at his breast, then Auvrarn Labraster hissed the word he needed to say, and was thankfully gone.

❊　　❊　　❊

As Taern clambered across shifting stones to where his lady knelt, she lifted a face still wet with tears to him, and struggled to speak through a throat dark with bruises. She held a scrap of dark cloth clenched in her hand.

"My lady!" Taern Hornblade gasped, kneeling beside her bare, blackened body. One of her arms still dangled uselessly, and pain creased her face, but she smiled at him and said huskily, "Kiss me, Taern."

He touched his lips to her forehead with infinite care. Alustriel made a disgusted sound and hauled him down to her mouth, mumbling, "No, Taern, I mean really kiss me. I'm too weak to resist you now . . . and there's not much left of me that you can hurt."

Something small toppled from the floor above then, and plunged down to burst amid the stones. Blue lightning played about the chamber. As Taern crouched over his lady to shield her, Alustriel looked down at the scrap of torn fabric in her hand and murmured to the empty air, "Well, it's up to you now, sister."

Syluné
The Haunting of Blandras Nuin

There is death for most, undeath for some, and a wraithlike place beyond death for a few. I was going to say "the favored few," but increasingly I suspect some of them would coldly dispute such a judgment. May the gods, in time, show mercy upon them.

Iyritar Sarsharm, Sage of Tashluta
from *The Roads Beyond Faerûn*
published circa the Year of the Turret

There came a cold and drifting time of nothingness that seemed to freeze her utterly, beyond gasping, and to go on forever . . . but she knew from what Elminster and Alassra had said that it in truth lasted so briefly that even those watching for it could not be sure it had befallen.

There was light then, and sound again, and she was somewhere unfamiliar, looking out of eyes that were not her own; these were male eyes. She had to be deft now, and patient, so as not to be noticed by this host. It was alert and angry, and its mind was dark with rage and evil. The mind is a powerful thing, and this one was very far from an abode Syluné of Shadowdale would ever be comfortable in. Her sentience had awakened in the tiny chip of stone Alustriel usually carried in her bodice, but had somehow managed to tangle unnoticed into this man's hair, knotting its fine strands securely around the stone.

She could only live, now, out of such stones—pieces of the fire-scarred flagstones of her now vanished hut. The

Witch of Shadowdale was dead, and yet, through the grace of Mystra, not dead nor yet "undead," at least not in the chilling, feeding-on-the-living manner that carried most undeath onward through timeless days. When she walked in Shadowdale, 'twas true, her feet made no dint upon the grass, and folk could see through her, and termed her "ghost," and were fearful. Usually Syluné used a body made to look like her old, true one, or kept herself unseen, unless she wanted to scare.

Syluné sighed now, a sound only she could hear, and banished such dark thoughts. She had died and yet lived, through Mystra's love and aid. She should be ever joyful, but she had been human, and it is the way of humans to complain.

The Witch of Shadowdale shook the head she did not have, and briskly applied her thoughts to the here and now. It took mighty magic to send her from one stone to another when they were not touching, and she knew, somehow, that she was far from Shadowdale. Alustriel must have spent silver fire to weave such a spell. That meant this was a matter of great importance, but then her journeys were always matters of great importance. Syluné smiled with lips she no longer possessed. 'Twas time to save the world again.

She was in the mind of a man who knew Waterdeep well, by all the images of it crowding each other in his place-memories. He was a wealthy man, a merchant, linked to other beings by some sort of slumbering but recently awakened magic. The man was standing on a rocky, windy hillside where bell-hung goats wandered, a little way outside an arc of standing stones that stood like jutting monster teeth before a dark cave mouth.

This was the abode, the man knew, of a hermit priestess of Shar. He'd been here twice before, and both feared and was disgusted by the old and ugly crone who dwelt here, and stank so, ate things raw, and whose fingers were always stained with blood that was not her own. Meira the Dark was a thing of bones and malice, half hidden in rags and an improbable fall of long, glossy black hair.

The man moved forward reluctantly and drew forth his dagger, holding it by the blade, and through his eyes Syluné saw that he had clean fingers adorned with rings. He lifted the dagger to use its hilt to strike a door gong. His mind termed it such, though his eyes told her that it was a cracked iron skillet hanging from a weathered branch that had been thrust into a hole in one of the larger stones.

"Don't bother," a voice sounded. The voice was sharp and a little rough, as if long unused. "Come within. The ward of serpents is down."

Though the voice seemed to come from someone near at hand, the man could see no one. He sheathed his dagger with a low growl of disgust and stepped cautiously forward through the grassy gap between the two tallest, center-most stones.

Something moved in the shadow of the cave mouth, sidling forward into the full light to squint up at her visitor. Meira was just as the man remembered her, fondling the yellowing curves of a squirrel skull necklace as she came forward to peer at her guest. "So, what trouble is it this time?"

"Why should you assume I have trouble?"

The priestess snorted. "Handsome, wealthy, charming Auvrarn Labraster has his pick of playpretties in half a dozen cities of Faerûn, and more money than Meira has ever seen in all her life. Enough to hire spells from the Red Wizards he sports with, enough to think himself important indeed . . . and this would be the same Auvrarn Labraster who can barely conceal his disgust when he stands near old Meira. Trouble brings him here. Trouble is all that could bring him here."

Syluné withdrew everything from the mind of the man she rode, clinging but to his eyes and ears so as to be as invisible to magic as she dared be. Labraster shifted his feet and replied stiffly, "Yes, I have trouble, and need your swift aid."

The hermit priestess snorted. "Sit on yon rock and spill all. Even I haven't the patience to drag words out of you. Speak."

"I've just used this ring—the only teleport ring I have—to escape Alustriel of Silverymoon. My hands were around her throat in her palace just minutes ago, and I called on the cycle. She fought and survived everyone in it to bring it back to me again. We left a room afire and several of her Spellguard mages knowing my likeness. I will be hunted a—"

Meira held up a hand with a hiss of anger. "Perhaps traced already. Yet you do not need me to tell you what a fool you are. I can see that much in your eyes."

She grunted, and drew a ring on a cord from somewhere under the rags she wore. Holding it up, she hissed in annoyance, let it fall, and fumbled around in the vicinity of her bodice until another cord fell into view. She snatched up the ring and squinted at it, made a small, satisfied sound in her throat, and with a sudden wrench, broke its cord, sliding it onto one of her fingers. Lifting her eyes to Labraster's, she snapped, "Take off your teleport ring."

Slowly, he did so, holding it cupped in his hand. The priestess gestured with her head. "Set it down on that rock, and step back outside my porch ring."

When the merchant had done as he was bid, the priestess took the ring back off her own finger and set it down on another stone. She approached Labraster's ring and stooped to peer at it, seeming almost to sniff at it in suspicion before she murmured a spell over it, watched the brief glow of her spell fade, then cast a second spell. After a moment, the ring quietly faded away.

"What did you do?" the merchant called out angrily. "D'you know how much that cost me? Where's it gone?"

Meira regarded him over one hunched shoulder with some irritation, then beckoned him to approach. "To an alleyway near the docks of Waterdeep, with a spell on it to keep someone from seeing or tracing you through it."

"But it'll be lost! Someone will see it and snatch it up! I—"

The priestess nodded. "A small price to pay for continued life. *I'd* not want to have to fight off a Chosen of Mystra, even with the Blessed Lady of Darkness standing at my side. Would you?"

As Labraster gaped at her, she snapped, "Now stand here—just here—and don't move, even after I stop casting. I'll need different spells for you and your clothes, so don't stir again until I say so."

"Why?"

Meira squinted up at him. "That," she snarled, "is one of the words I most hate; one of the reasons I don't stand in a temple teaching cruel young things to know the kisses of Shar. Utter it again, and you can face Alustriel alone."

Auvrarn Labraster swallowed, stood just where she'd indicated, and kept silent. Meira shuffled all around him with a little smile crooking the corners of her mouth. "That's better," she said. "Now stand you just so."

She continued her slow circling as her hands traced gestures in the air with surprising grace. She seemed almost to be dancing as her cracked lips shaped words that seemed both fluid and strangely angular, cruel and yet softly sliding, words that betimes rose to frame the name of the goddess Shar. When she was done, she stood with hands on hips and regarded Labraster. In her squint was a gleam of satisfaction.

"Aye, you'll do," she said at last. "Can you live without the rest of the little magics you have hidden on you now—and won't tell me about?"

"Surrender them, you mean?"

"Nay, have them still, but asleep, not working."

Labraster hesitated, then sighed. "If I have to," he said, "yes."

She was as cold, cruel and deadly, this priestess, as the goddess she served. Shar, Mistress of the Night, the Lady of Loss, the Keeper of Secrets, the goddess revered by those who did cruelty to others, and worked dark magic, under cover of the night. She was evil with lips and hips, the night mists her cloak, her eyes always watching out of the darkness. Labraster shivered, and tried to put the feeling of being coldly watched—a feeling crawling coldly between his shoulders, nowhere near the old hermit in front of him—aside. He did not find it easy.

"Good," Meira the Dark said crisply. "Put this on your finger, and keep it there." She picked up her own ring from where she'd set it on the stone and handed it to him.

Labraster turned it in his fingers as if trying to delay putting it on, then plunged it onto one of his fingers with almost frantic haste. As it altered its shape to fit the digit perfectly, Syluné felt a tingling and darkness descended around her. She drifted through brief chaos, then abruptly, was seeing out of Labraster's eyes once more, and hearing out of his ears again, but cut off from his mind, his touch, and smell. The surges of his thoughts and emotions were gone. She was riding alone again.

"What is it?" Labraster asked, holding up his finger curiously to examine the plain silvery band.

Meira chuckled. "It carries its own tiny magic-dead zone, covering you and a little of what you touch—or hold. The best shield I know against prying archmages . . . or the Chosen servants of the goddess of magic." She waved at the stone where the ring had lain, and said, "Now sit here."

When Labraster sat, she drifted up behind him and reached around to hand him something. It was a polished fragment of armor plate that served as a crude mirror. Labraster peered at it, at his new face. It was still fair to look at, but rather less commanding in looks. His hair was almost blue-black, eyes green now, nose a little crooked. He reached up to touch his own cheek. The feel of it matched what he saw. This was no illusion, but a reshaping.

"Who've you made me look like?" he demanded, turning to face the priestess.

She was no longer there, and in that same instant Auvrarn Labraster felt a sudden, sharp pain in his neck. She'd bitten him! He whirled around the other way with an oath, flinging out his arm—

Again, she was no longer there. Labraster felt a gentle tug at his belt.

The priestess was kneeling in front of him, her eyes flashing up at him, bright and very green.

"What're you—?"

Her eyes fell to the belt buckle in her hands, and she murmured, "Now for my payment."

Auvrarn Labraster resisted a sudden urge to ram his knees together, smashing what was between them, then to kick out, hard, and send a bleeding bag of bones sailing away to a hard, bouncing landing.

The bag of bones that could slay him in an instant, or send him to sure doom whenever it chose to, flicked bright, knowing eyes up at him now in a sly taunting. She knew how he felt. Oh, she knew.

He watched her calmly unbuckle his belt and said levelly, "I prefer to choose beforehand whether or not I must lose any body parts. In like manner, I like to have some say in any partners I may take in intimacies."

Meira the Dark looked up, arching one bristling eyebrow. "Do you now?"

She jerked open his breeches with a sudden, violent tug and added softly, "I bit you, man. If I will it so, your every muscle will lock, holding you rigid. You will be unable to move . . . unable to prevent me from removing the ring and my disguising spell, binding you hand and foot, and transporting you thus onto Alustriel's dining table—or kitchen hearth spit."

A certain paleness crept over Labraster's face. He made a helpless shooing motion with his hands before snarling, "All right . . ."

Her hands were cool but wrinkled. Their warts brushed his flesh as she held onto him for support, sat back a little, and did something to her rags. They fell away from one bony shoulder, and he almost gagged at the smell that rolled forth. Meira looked up at him, her eyes flashing, and thrust her wrinkled self forward against him again, purring like a cat. He felt the hot lick of her tongue on his thigh, moving slowly inward, and gentle fingers probing . . . before she made a sad little sigh and sat back, slapping him in a very tender place.

Green eyes glared up into his. "*Give*, man!" Meira snarled.

"But I . . ." Labraster growled, his voice stiff with disgust, his face scarlet.

Meira drew a little way back from him, on her knees, and sighed again. "No one loves me for what I am," she said sadly, staring down at her wrinkled hands. "No one has ever loved me for what I am."

She looked down at the ground in front of her, face hidden by her tangled hair, and Labraster sat silent, not daring to move or say anything. The priestess stirred, and he saw her clench one dirty hand. She rose to her feet, letting her rags fall to the ground in a little ring around her, looked expressionlessly at him for a moment, then turned and walked away.

Labraster stayed where he was. A gentle breeze slid past, ghosting down the hillside, but he moved no more than a stone statue, his eyes fixed on the ugly priestess as fear grew within him like a cold, uncoiling snake.

She stopped a few paces away and turned to face him in full filthy, sagging splendor, her eyes two green flames as they met his. Still holding his gaze, Meira raised her arms above her head, cleared her throat, then matter-of-factly, almost briskly, cast a spell.

Before his eyes she grew taller, her hair stirring restlessly around curving shoulders as she grew both more slender and more shapely. Long, long legs, a flat belly, and . . . Labraster swallowed and blinked, hardly believing the beauty he saw. A spicy scent wafted from Meira as she strode forward. Labraster searched her with his eyes, feeling lust stirring within him, a rising warmth that checked for only a moment when his gaze rose far enough to find her green eyes unchanged in their knowing, and anger.

Meira glided up to him and wove slender fingers through his hair, guiding his head to her. "Such a little thing Meira demands," she murmured. "Do you still know how to be tender, man? Show me . . ."

Slender fingers momentarily brushed against a tiny chip of stone amid curling hair, and as if through rippling water, Syluné saw the face of Auvrarn Labraster, tight with apprehension, shifting and sliding into the face he now wore, brighter somehow than it had seemed in the mirror. A cold, dark sentience was sliding over her, considering that face, then Labraster's own again . . . then seeming to place another face over it, so that one showed through the other. She knew this new face, and tried to keep herself calm and still as the dark sentience that could only be Meira quested past, comparing it with Labraster as he really was, and doubting that the Waterdhavian merchant was suitable to masquerade as the other man.

That other man was King Azoun IV of Cormyr.

*　　*　　*

The morning was cold, the pit-privy was filthy and swirling with biting flies, and the bowl of wash water both gray and icy. The priestess, moving naked around her smoking cooking fire, was her old, wrinkled self again. Auvrarn Labraster smelled her unwashed stink on his own limbs, and wrinkled his nose in distaste. Even his own transformed clothes itched and felt . . . wrong.

Without looking up she handed him a steaming, rather battered tankard as he approached. It smelled wonderful, but Labraster cradled it in his hands and sniffed suspiciously. "What might this be?"

"Soup," she said sweetly.

"I can tell that," he growled. "What's in it?"

"Dead things," she growled back, turning green eyes on him. They held a certain sparkle that made the merchant want to glance down at himself to make sure that nothing was missing. He hesitated, then, involuntarily, did so.

She snickered. "Ah, the great Auvrarn Labraster, scourge of the masked revels of Waterdeep." She tossed her head and laughed again, lightly. "Waterdhavians have such high standards, don't you think?"

Labraster shuddered, and brought the warm comfort of the tankard to his lips. "If you're done mocking me, woman," he growled, "perhaps you'll find time enough to tell me just whose shape I now wear, eh?"

"Blandras Nuin," Meira told her own tankard promptly, scratching herself and reaching for the pile of rags that evidently served her every wardrobe need.

Labraster watched her with fresh disgust, and asked unwillingly, "Who's 'Blandras Nuin'?"

"A man I sacrificed on the Altar of Night a few days back," the priestess said, bending to a nearby stool to kiss the oily lashes of a black, many-tailed whip reverently.

The merchant grunted, and shifted a little away. Anything dedicated to Shar was best avoided. "After you served him as you served me?"

Meira's head snapped around. She looked more shocked than angry, but her voice was as sharp as a thrusting sword as she said, "He was for Holy Shar, and Shar alone." Her thin lips drooped into a catlike smile, and she added, "He looked quite—ah, striking as he died."

"And the body?" Labraster asked, looking around as if he expected to find severed hands serving as cloak hooks, and hairy, bloodless legs bound together to hold up a table.

"Once a ritual is done, and it is properly blackened or doused in purple sauces, any suitable sacrifice to the goddess may be devoured by her worshipers," Meira said primly, then glanced sidelong at her unwilling guest as he gagged, and added slyly, "I did keep certain pieces for dessert." The merchant's shaking hands spilled soup on the cave floor.

She knelt and slithered forward between his legs to lap it up. Labraster hastily backed away, seeking another place to sit. His shoulders came up against the rotting, blackened hides that served her as doors, and in an instant he spun around and shouldered himself out into the light and the fresh, frigid air.

"Gods," he growled, blinking at the brightness and cradling his hands around the battered tankard. His stomach lurched anew at the thought of the wrinkled priestess stirring a man's hairy leg into her soup caldron.

Soup caldron . . . he looked down in horror, and hurled the tankard as far and as hard as he could, found his knees in scrabbling haste, and vomited everything in him onto the ground so furiously that his spew splashed his eyebrows. Hot tears of rage and revulsion blurred his eyes as he coughed and spat.

"Such a waste," that sharp voice he was beginning to hate so much said coolly from behind him. "There's none of him left in that. 'Tis all bustard and black voles and rockscuttler lizards. Oh, and a snake; a rock viper, but a little one, too young for his fangs to be deadly."

Her words failed to reassure Labraster. The merchant turned his white, trembling face away from her as he rose and stumbled over to one of the standing stones. He leaned against it weakly and drew in deep, shuddering breaths of air. A hand like a wart-studded claw patted his behind, the fingers lingering to caress.

"More, valiant merchant?" Meira cooed, clear mockery in her biting tones.

Auvrarn Labraster sprang forward and away, whirling around and slapping at his sword hilt. "*Away*, witch!"

The wrinkled, toadlike creature in front of him looked almost comical as it pouted, but one look into those green eyes quelled any mirth that might have been rising in Auvrarn Labraster now and for perhaps the next month or so. They held a cold and waiting promise that told the merchant he'd been judged expendable. One wrong step would be his last, or worse he'd be violently unmanned and teleported, maimed and still screaming, into the hands of Alustriel of Silverymoon, only to be hauled back again like a hooked fish, if Alustriel should show him any mercy. Back to the cooking pot, no doubt strapped to that bloodstained worktable and cut up alive, piece by piece, while Meira the Dark discussed seasonings with him, and—no, no more!

Labraster shook his head, his eyes closed, and he heard himself gasp, "For pity's sake, priestess! I-I've a heavy load, and mean no offense, but, truly, I—"

"You find Meira not to your taste," the priestess said, her voice more sad than angry. "Well, you're not the first, nor the last." She glanced up at him with the suddenness of a snake, eyes bright. "You'll find your way back here, though, when next your needs outstrip that ambition of yours, and Meira will be waiting. Oh, yes, perhaps to play the man, then, to your woman, hmm? We'll see. Oh, aye, we'll see."

Labraster shivered. She meant every word, and a small part of him was even excited. What sneaking spells had she worked on him, to make him think so? How much of a leash did Auvrarn Labraster now wear?

He had to get out of there. He had to get away from this woman and her foul cave. Fleeing all the roused Spellguard through the High Palace of Silverymoon was starting to seem preferable to this. Labraster drew in a deep breath, lifted his head, and forced himself to open his eyes and to smile.

"A part of me looks forward to that," he admitted, and saw Meira's green eyes flash. "You can use spells if you want, to confirm that I speak truth."

The priestess shook her head. "Nay, lad, I can see. I can also see that you want very much to be off and about your scheming, tarrying here no longer. Hear then my advice. Go nowhere that Auvrarn Labraster would, and reveal your disguise to no one. Let your affairs be run by your agents, even if they begin to subvert and swindle. The ring will keep you out of even the cycle's summons. You know how to contact those of us who matter, if need be. Don't go wandering back to claim treasures Labraster hid and finish deals he left hanging. The Chosen—and the Harpers, now—will be waiting and watching for that."

"For how long?" Labraster growled. "The High Lady of Silverymoon still has no proof against me. After all, I did not slay the tradelord. Such legal niceties would not matter, say, to those who rule in Luskan, but she is one who does take refuge in laws, and hold to them."

Meira lifted her misshapen shoulders in a smooth shrug. "For as long as need be. You lost a life, merchant—yes, the one you'd built, but most of us only ever get one. Think of a fresh start, a chance to deal with some traveling traders who'll come unaware that you know their true natures as a challenge, hmm?"

Labraster bowed his head. "I grant that, though it does not yet seem a gladsome thing to me. So tell me, who am I? Blandras Nuin, yes, but who is Blandras Nuin?"

The priestess lifted her lip in an unlovely smile, like a dog about to snarl. "A man of moderate prosperity, ruled by honesty. An innocent in the intrigues of the world, content to live out his life in trade."

"Trade in what, and where?"

"Blandras Nuin is a trader in textiles," the priestess said grandly, as if telling a fireside tale to rapt children, "respected in his home city of Neverwinter. He seldom travels, and when he does, 'tis usually to Everlund or Silverymoon, on matters of business. He's a kindly man, with little interest in women beyond watching tavern girls dance, and has no family or relatives."

Labraster looked pained. "Textiles? What do I know about cloth?" he snarled.

Green eyes twinkled. Their owner replied crisply, "Whatever you'll learn between here and Nuin's house. It is a tall and narrow abode, roof of old shields sealed with pitch, stone lion gateposts, on Prendle Street. You'll have six servants, but the old chambermaid Alaithe is the only one who really knows you—that is, the real Blandras Nuin."

Auvrarn Labraster sighed, glanced around at the standing stones and the hillside falling away into the trees, then brought his head up to peer at the priestess who'd transformed him. "I've no choice, have I?" he asked, his words more bitter than he'd meant them to be—but not nearly as bitter as he felt.

"None at all, Blandras Nuin," Meira told him. "Now start walking."

Labraster's brows lifted stormily. "Can't you teleport me?"

The priestess pointed a wart-studded finger at the merchant's hand and shook her raven-haired head. "The ring, remember?"

✳   ✳   ✳

The darkness of closed eyes, and the roaring that meant Labraster's snoring would render his ears useless until he awakened, left the eldest of the Seven Sisters utterly alone once more. She was alone and alert, not needing to sleep, but unable to ride a body around to look at new things, and talk to other beings, and see more. She was alone to think.

So what had she to show for all the hard work Dove, Qilué, Laeral, and Alustriel before her had done? A little more than the usual quiet, underhanded alliance between a rogue at one end of a caravan route and a thief at the other. A little more even than a trading coster gone bad, or illicit goods bought with stolen coin. It was a shadowy chain of varied individuals who worked covertly in Scornubel, Waterdeep, Silverymoon, a hermit's cave somewhere north and east of Longsaddle in the wild hills between the Long Road and the Goblintide, here in Neverwinter, and presumably in distant Thay . . . probably also in Sembia and Cormyr, and possibly in Amn and other Sword Coast ports such as Luskan and Baldur's Gate.

They behaved not unlike the Zhentarim, but enough unlike their work to remove them from suspicion, even if there'd been no Thayans or Sharran clergy to make the differences sharp.

Drow were working with humans to supplant other humans, using magical guises—long-lasting shapeshifting; powerful magic needed there. Humans were busily engaged in smuggling, hidden investments, market manipulations, and slavery, but such a widespread secret organization, with all of its perils, was hardly needed for anything but the slavery and smuggling. So why? Larger aims, as yet unseen, must underlie it all. The presence of the Red Wizards—who by nature need great power, and therefore work at a great reach, whether prudent or not—and that of any clergy of Shar both pointed to bigger things.

Just what those bigger things were was probably beyond what Labraster knew, but not necessarily beyond what he could guess.

Well, Chosen of Mystra could make guesses, too. If drow could masquerade as humans in Scornubel, what was to stop others in the cabal—yes, call it that, however ugly or possibly misplaced the word—from using similar means and magics to take the places of other folk, elsewhere? They'd target rich folk, of course, influential folk, rulers—why else had others considered this Labraster a fitting stand-in for Azoun of Cormyr, and Meira thought him too weak?—and elder noble families, energetically rising merchants, those who commanded armies or controlled fleets, caravan companies, and trading costers.

It was grain and beans again. Centuries ago, a certain bored, younger Syluné—restless and not yet rooted, not yet the Witch of Shadowdale, not yet loving any place too closely, and the poorer for it—had watched merchants grow rich. Oh, aye, merchants grew rich all the time, sometimes by innovation and more often by rushing in needed goods when there were shortages.

She remembered a few growing rich by virtue of the mercenaries they could hire to burn crops in one place, or fight the mercenaries hastily hired against them across sown farmers' fields, which bought the same result. They'd take advantage of these shortages, rushing in goods they'd already secured elsewhere when demand and prices were highest.

Grains and beans. Not so glamorous as kidnapped princesses or fell wizards cracking castles asunder, but just as hard on the folk whose land the wars raged through, or who starved outright or dwelt in misery, for the lack of things that need not have been scarce. All the while merchants who hired armsmen to kick back beggars rode in ever grander coaches to revels where they grew fatter and laughed louder, guzzling wine and eyeing each other's new jewels and hired bedmates, until they were all so bored that feuds and hunts and the ever-changing whimsy of styles known as "fashion" came to the fore as a way of spending time and coin.

Just the way of the world, a Waterdhavian merchant dead and dust these four hundred years had told her, derisively dismissing her protests at such behavior. Just something she hadn't, of course, the native wits to understand, and should leave off thinking about and hurry, while she still had her looks, to the nearest whorehouse to get back to earning herself a living.

She'd tried that, too. Mirth still rose in Syluné after all these years at the haughty merchant's wife who'd looked down from a festhall balcony with scorn at the silver-haired dancer and called out that she might as well wear naught but pig herders' boots to do what she did . . . only to recognize her own son in Syluné's arms later the same night . . . a Syluné wearing only pig herders' boots, which she'd given the man to present to his mother on her morningfeast platter the next day. The woman's shrieks of rage had been the talk of her hitherto quietly exclusive Waterdhavian neighborhood, but that woman, too, was long dead, and her fine son. Syluné, caught defending her beloved dale in the heart of a storm of dragons, should have followed them both into the cold, eternal darkness, but for the love of her sisters and the grace of her mother Mystra.

"Oh, Mystra," she prayed now, alone in the darkness with no voice to speak aloud. "Let me do what is right and best for thee and for all Faerûn . . . and let those two rights and bests run ever together."

From dark nothingness came a faint, singing sound. The gentlest echo of a chime Syluné had heard before, when drifting in the arms of the Lady of Mystery. It lingered around her, almost faint beyond hearing, then was gone.

The Witch of Shadowdale smiled, and knew peace, for she was no longer alone in the darkness.

✻　　✻　　✻

"What if I do not choose to follow this road longer? This meandering backwoods trail that leaves me far from my city, my business, the folk that I love and know, and, by all the good gods there may be, from the—the—"

"Action you crave?" the hooded man's voice was smooth and unruffled. Something that was almost amusement rippled across its rich tones.

"Well, yes. I'd not have put it that way, but this does leave me far from my coins and my battles, and yes, the grander things we . . . are both part of. I chafe in these chains." Labraster's voice had risen high in exasperation. Something in the other man's stillness warned him that he was drawing too much attention to them both, and he dropped his voice almost to a whisper to add, "They drive me wild. Sometimes I think I may go mad."

"So much is increasingly apparent, Blandras Nuin," the cloth merchant's visitor replied. "Yet it does you no credit in our eyes if we see in you a weakness. Those lions who are always bold to be a-hunt, in at the slayings whenever they scent blood, all too often move too soon and ruin things. Even when they do not, their restlessness makes them poor allies after the victories have been won. Cold patience sits comfortably in some of us, and turns our wits to think ill of those who have too little patience, or too much hunger for the chase."

"But it's been months now," Labraster protested, clenching one hand—the hand that bore a certain ring—into a fist, "and until you, today, nothing but silence. Silence and selling cloth. Gods! More than that, I tell you, Harpers are as thick hereabouts as flies on rotting meat."

"Perhaps too apt a choice of words," the hooded man murmured. "More than one of us in a certain city much visited by caravans has fallen to Harper blades in recent days. The dead carts held many surprises. Much flesh that was as black as the darkest night. Your swift and thorough flight from the questioning of the High Lady has done much to hold you blameless in this—among those who look for blame in such things."

"I thought that project was overbold from the first. How many actors can there be who can fool kin and trade partners and all, night and day, eh?" The cloth merchant waved a dismissive hand, then almost lunged forward to hiss, "Can you tell me nothing of what else has befallen? So many plans were on the brink of becoming real projects. Just to know a few shreds of—gods! Cloth again!—a little of what's happening will keep me alive, keep me feeling a part of things."

"You find excitement a drink every bit as alluring as good wine, Master Nuin?" the hooded man asked softly. "Think on this, then. Like wine, excitement can be all the better when it's aged properly."

Auvrarn Labraster growled, deep in his throat, and smoothed out a bolt of cloth with unnecessary savagery. "You'll give me nothing at all?"

"I did not say that," his visitor said smoothly. "There's word from Sembia. Tael is ready to move. The inn outside Westgate called the Black Baron burned down a tenday back, and—"

Labraster's head jerked up like a stabbing blade. "*What?*" he hissed. "Did anyone get out? What was found in the ashes—and down in the cellars?" He leaned forward eagerly to put his hand on the hooded man's arm, to shake out some answers if need be. He came to a sudden, silent halt, as a bared blade slid out of the sleeve where an arm should have been.

That calm, smooth voice said reprovingly, "Master Nuin, I've heard it said that overeagerness has carried many a lion over a cliff. You've heard the same, I trust?"

Auvrarn Labraster swallowed, stepped back a pace, and nodded, his face carefully expressionless once more. "Yes," he mumbled, then cleared his throat, threw his head back, and said more clearly, "Yes. Yes, I have."

The hood seemed to nod, almost imperceptibly, as new customers entered Blandras Nuin's shop and headed straight for the proprietor. "Other engagements press me hard now. Perhaps I'll return to buy your excellent cloth another day, but it may not be soon. Perhaps even . . . next season."

"Of course," the man who wore the name Blandras Nuin agreed with a quick smile. "I shall be waiting here; eager to serve you, as always."

He saw teeth flash in the gloom of the hood, for just a moment, shaping a smile. "Of course."

The hood turned away, but as its owner stepped around an advancing customer to seek the door, turned back again. The voice that rolled out from within it one last time was somehow no louder, and yet still as clear as if it came from right beside the cloth merchant's elbow.

Its tones were gentle, almost fatherly. "It all comes back, Master Nuin, to patience. Try not to forget that."

Blandras Nuin stared at the door as it banged, not seeming to see the customers now gathering before him.

"Old friend of yours?" one of the tailors asked.

"Sounded more like a creditor," another grunted. "Trouble, Nuin?"

Blandras Nuin looked down at him sharply, then smiled a thin and mirthless smile. "No, just matters halfway across Faerûn that I can do nothing about."

"Ah, investments," the first tailor said wisely, nodding.

"He in the hood was right enough, then," the second added. "Nothing to be done about what's out of your reach except drop all and ride to seize it—or learn a little patience." He grinned ruefully, spat thoughtfully into the floor rushes, and added, "I've learned me a lot of patience."

✳ ✳ ✳

Patience was her strength, and Syluné—as little more than a silent, thinking thing—clung to it in the days that followed, as Auvrarn Labraster settled into being a colder, more cruel copy of Blandras Nuin, and learned the cloth trade, and looked for sideline dealings that could earn him rather more coin for rather less work. She watched him swindle, and watched him deal fairly—and she watched him murder.

She was powerless to work magic, powerless to whisper in his mind, touch him in his dreams, or influence his waking mind in the smallest way. She was powerless to do anything but ride him and experience life as he did— at least until he really combed out his hair.

Labraster was disgusted with himself for being so swiftly singled out in Silverymoon, disgusted with the shape and life he'd had to adopt, and disgusted whenever he thought of the woman who'd given both to him. He took little care over his appearance, sighing instead for his own lost good looks whenever he passed a mirror. So a little chip of stone remained where it was, and he never knew how close he was to delivery from loneliness. Not that it would have been the sort of deliverance he'd have welcomed.

At least Neverwinter was cold in winter and damp with sea-breezes all the year round. Folk needed clothing, and clothing was apt not to last overlong. The man who was not Blandras Nuin grew all too used to the hitherto unfamiliar reek of mildew as the tendays passed. Neverwinter was a city of crafters, and he had much competition from lace weavers and furriers and even women who made exotic knots from silken cord, but it was also a city of fashion, of men and women with a taste for style and the wealth to indulge that taste. Some of them liked the styles of Waterdeep, and suppliers from Waterdeep were folk he knew. They had no idea that he knew them, for they saw the kindly face of Blandras Nuin hailing them from the door of a modest shop, not the grander face of Auvrarn Labraster sending an agent over from his coach to stop them in wider, less muddy streets. Yet he knew their weaknesses, and whom they owed coin to, and when they were desperate. He was careful to befriend them, to win their respect, to make them regard him as important, so far as Neverwinter was important. He dealt with them fairly and soon, he dealt with them often.

The coins started to come. Bolts of cloth gathered less dust, and Blandras took less and less mold-stained and mice-nibbled stock to the copper coin markets outside the walls, and looked a little less drawn about his face. His shop grew no larger, however, and no new coach or steed appeared in his stables. Gossip soon suggested he owed money elsewhere, and was sending it away with the same men who brought him his cloth . . . and as he did nothing scandalous, or seemingly anything at all outside of his shop, really, gossip soon forgot him.

Certain eyes and tongues in the city would have been surprised indeed to learn that no less than four of the houses on Spurnserpent Street now belonged to Blandras Nuin. They'd become his one at a time, in an inexorable march along that old lane situated on the edge of the expanding area where the wealthy were tearing down and rebuilding in grander style. They'd have been still more surprised to learn that the modest, kindly cloth merchant was just waiting for other folk to move before sending an agent to make offers on others . . . but the only eyes that did notice belonged to local Harpers, and they were pleased to see coin going there and not into something unseen or suspicious that meant they would have to skulk at the shutters of yet another fine, upstanding citizen.

An unseen, ghostly lady who'd had over six hundred years to take her measure of folk watched the world through the eyes of the man who was not Blandras Nuin, and heard as he did the words he spoke, and saw his deeds. She wondered sometimes, if things had been different, if this was a man she could have turned to truly become the sort of man he was pretending to be. A man she could have welcomed to Storm's kitchen table with a glad heart, however many murders had stained his hands in the past. After all, her own had certainly known blood enough, and Storm welcomed her.

One could always build a legion of castles on "if things had been different." Those who tried to, in life, were often the most dangerous ones. More than that, she'd had long enough to learn that men cannot be turned. They can only turn themselves. One can ruin a life with a single, crippling sword stroke, or a blinding iron, but one cannot guide the unwilling save by example and by holding out choices, and only when the unwilling don't realize what is being done. Syluné was also determined that she would do no more than guide. Down the years the eldest of the Seven Sisters had heard enough whimpering, of dogs and men, to have any favor left for the boot or the whip.

Yet she already knew that whatever Blandras Nuin was becoming, Auvrarn Labraster only really understood boots and whips. She would have to be his whip—if ever she got the chance.

Sometimes Blandras Nuin bought drinks for traders in other goods from Waterdeep, the more garrulous merchants whose wares never touched on bolts of cloth or garment-making. He sat with them, and made them feel welcome and in the company of a friend, and gave them an ear that listened all the night through, and was never attached to a face that looked bored or hostile. He seemed to some a dreamer after the gilded bustle of a city he'd never dare to try his luck in, one of many such on their travels who were hungry for their talk of who was riding high and who'd fallen down in the City of Splendors. He wanted to know where things might be heading for those fortunate and wealthy enough to pitch in when the coins started to roll. New fashions and the latest nasty gossip of betrayals and debauched revels, noble feuds and men—and increasingly, women—found dead in new and stranger "suspicious circumstances," fueled an ever-burning curiosity. If the eyes of the man who bought their drinks widened at some of the names, why then they always seemed wide and avid, didn't they?

Temple scandals and guild fights, warehouse fires on the docks and new turrets added to the already over-gilded houses of merchants rising past their ears in coin; he listened to it all.

Those nights of Waterdhavian tales were the times when Blandras Nuin bought extra bottles to carry home in his fists, or strayed to the houses where lamps burned late and silken scarves hung at the windows, beckoning lonely men inside.

Unnoticed and invisible, Syluné rode her unhappy steed through days, then months, drawing the cloak of her patience around her and waiting, waiting for the moment when a certain ring would come off Labraster's finger, and give her the chance she needed.

✸ ✸ ✸

The moon rode high above scudding clouds this night, and the breeze off the sea reached cold fingers right through his thin cloak. The man who sometimes forgot that he'd ever been Auvrarn Labraster reeled more than a little as he came down the worn stone steps of the Howling Herald, leaned for a moment against the stair post topped with a gaping gargoyle head, and was noisily sick all over the refuse strewn in the lee of the post.

Ah, but he'd drunk too much—a *lot* too much. Good old Blandras Nuin had lent small sums to a lot of men to subtly spread his influence and circle of friends, and most of them never intended to pay it back. As long as he kept smiling and not mentioning it and draining the tankards they bought for him, there was no need to kill him. Cut off from his armsmen, alley boys, and more sinister allies, Auvrarn Labraster had to be careful about things like that. He was alone, like any other idiot merchant whose friends lasted just as long as the coins in his purse. Any shadow could hold ready knives and grasping hands.

A shadow moved in the gloom of the narrow passage between the Herald and the bakery next door. Labraster moved hastily, if unsteadily, around to face it, feeling for his knife.

Eyes gleamed in the darkness, then teeth, curving into a smile. "Go home, weaver," a voice hissed contemptuously. "I know how empty your purse is."

Rage rose in Labraster, just for a moment, and with its coming, his head started to pound as if quarry hammers were setting to work on the back of his head.

"Errummahuh," he agreed hastily, turning away and hurrying off down the street, away from the softly chuckling shadow waiting by the stair post. Gods, but a youth with a long knife probably could open his kidneys for him this night, with ease, and leave him to bleed his life away in the mud, bereft of coin, and alone. Alone . . . the smiling image of the priestess Meira swam into his mind, then, and he groaned and clutched at his head.

"No," he whimpered. "Gods, no. A toothless alley whore would be cleaner and more loving."

That mumbled conviction took him around a corner onto Boldshoulder Street, which was cobbled, uneven, and dotted with the mud and dung of many wagons. He realized this only as he slipped in one such offering, his left boot shooting out wildly in front of him.

A moment later, he'd measured his length helplessly in midair, and a moment after that he slammed down so hard on his back in rather liquid horse droppings that the breath was hurled out of him. His elbows and head went numb, and he could barely find strength enough, in the sudden dizzying swirl of the moon above him, to writhe in pain.

It must have been some time later when he rolled over. Dazedly he recalled that at least two separate pairs of boots had clicked hurriedly past him without stopping. He was cold, his head was splitting, and he reeked with wet, green-brown dung.

"What had they been feeding the horse that did this?" he snarled, on the verge of tears from the smell and his headache. "And how by the God on the Rack could it have been in any state to pull anything?"

Somehow he found his feet again and stumbled on down the street. Prendle was just two lanes over, and in his house he could get a bath. Nuin had an ornate tub. The man must have had a thing for cleanliness. Perhaps he'd fallen down, just like this, once too often, and gotten tired of crawling naked under the pump in the stable yard. Auvrarn's stomach lurched as a stray breath of sea breeze brought a fresh waft of the smell coming off him to his nose. The breeze didn't touch his hair, which felt like glue. There was probably dung all through it. Labraster moaned, and felt like throwing up again—well, gods, why not?

Emptying his stomach into the street made him feel just a bit better, but it still seemed like a stinking, reeling eternity before he found his own gateposts. The stone lions stared patiently out into the night, not bothering to give him the disgusted and incredulous stares several of his neighbors had favored him with as he'd reeled past, knowing he was wearing a sick smile and raging inside.

He muttered a heartfelt curse upon the heads of all hermit priestesses, High Ladies, and stupidly honest cloth merchants, wherever they might be, and kicked and hammered at his own front door until he felt better.

That got him one thing. When the last of his three keys clicked in its lock and the door groaned wide, both of the young, empty-headed maids he'd had to hire to replace Alaithe were awake and in the hall, wide-eyed and clutching garden shears and fire tongs in their trembling hands. They were wearing two of his dressing gowns, and had obviously been too stupid—fortunately for him—to think of together lifting the door bar into place.

He cursed them all the way up the stairs. Nalambra and Karlae—Stonehead and Clumsyhands. Ardent and curvaceous they might be, but they were also slow and lazy everywhere but in bed. Anticipate his needs? Think at all for themselves? Bah! Now he'd have to shiver naked in the cold metal bathtub for hours as they pumped water and gasped their way up the stairs with hearth fire-warmed rocks to heat it.

Alaithe would have had a hot bath waiting, and if he'd not bothered with it, she'd have had fresh rocks ready to heat it anew in the morning, without a murmur of complaint. For perhaps the seven hundredth time he regretted strangling her and burying her in the garden, but he'd had no choice. She'd been suspicious of him from the first, and set about devising little tests and traps to see if he wasn't the "real" Blandras Nuin. Once he'd smelled the kaurdyl in his morning broth, he'd had no choice. If she was trying to kill him, it was time to slay her. Fat and unlovely she may have been, but what a housekeeper! Perhaps, to Blandras, more than that. Hadn't it started that first night, when he'd bolted his bedchamber door and pretended to be asleep when she'd tried to open it at dawn?

Ah, gods, but none of it mattered now. "Nalambra! Karlae!" Labraster snarled. "Stop all that screaming and get up here and pump." Gods, but he *smelled*. He unlatched the window that overlooked the garden and started hauling off sodden, dung-caked garments and hurling them out into the night. Out with it, out with it all!

Even the boots went, and the belt with the dagger built into its buckle. No one would scale the high, barred gate or force a way through the thornhedge to steal things so foul anyway. All he left—in an empty chamber pot, not on the table—were his coin-purse, his belt-knife, and the rings from his fingers—all of them. As they clattered into the pot, he shoved it away with his foot, stepped into the bath, and grimly crouched down to wait. He knew he was going to have some long, cold hours yet before morning.

✳   ✳   ✳

The worst of the dung was gone from his hair and his skin, at least, but the bath Auvrarn Labraster sat in was brown and covered with a swirl of bubble-adorned white scum. It smelled as if it was more liquid dung now than water. Worse than that, it was cold, and getting colder by the minute, and his two lazy maids with the stone-sling and the hot stones that would make this bearable were nowhere to be seen.

"Nalambra!" he bellowed. "Karlae! Where in all the yawning pits of the Abyss *are* you?"

As if his shout had been a signal, two throat-stripping screams erupted downstairs. A chair fell over, or maybe a table—the whole house shook—and fainter crashes followed, one of them the bang of his front door trailing all of its chains and bolts as it slammed shut, then rebounded. The splintering crash that came on the heels of that booming sounded as if someone had burst out of the kitchen midden chute without waiting to open it.

Then came the silence, stretching out in the cold as Labraster waited, and shivered, and waited.

"Nalambra?" he called, when he could wait no longer. "Karlae?"

He rolled out of the bath and stood up to hear better, leaning forward with one arm on a chair. Shivering thus, he waited until the water he stood in stilled again, and listened intently for any sounds of movement in the house below. Even stealthy sounds that meant he'd best find the blade under the bed would tell him something, but there was nothing more than the faint whisper of the sea breeze blowing through open doors and windows below.

"Blast all smugly blazing gods and their sky splitting thunderbolts!" Auvrarn Labraster snarled at last, as his wet hands slipped and he fell on the cold lip of the bath, before crashing back down into its depths with a helpless, mighty splash that emptied the top foot or so of its contents all over the room around him.

His candle lamp went out.

Labraster stared into the darkness in real alarm. There'd been no breeze, the thing had full shutters to keep water—even a wave of dung stained bathwater—out, and the candle had been less than a third burned down. What, then, had . . . ?

Something that glowed faintly glided past the doorway, and Auvrarn Labraster's heart froze. He struggled to swallow, to rouse himself to rise and run for his sword, but the blade was in his bedchamber, and the bedchamber was through that door.

The glow was out there, somewhere off to the right, but he knew all too well what he'd seen. It was the image of a burly woman—Alaithe—bobbing along just as she'd always bustled along the upstairs hall. An image that glowed, that he could see through, and that moved in utter silence.

It came back again, and he bit his lip to keep from screaming. The ghost of his housekeeper moved more slowly this time, as if carrying something he could not see. She did not look in his direction or appear to know he was there, but on her throat he could clearly see the dark, deep grooves of fingers.

Auvrarn Labraster shivered, snatched up the only thing he could reach that might serve as a weapon—the bath stool—and cowered down in the icy, noisome bathwater. He would not scream. He would not die here this night, if he didn't leap out the window or do something stupid. It was only an image, nothing that could harm him.

When Alaithe's sad, hollow-eyed, glowing face rose up out of the waters between his knees, Auvrarn Labraster discovered that he could scream. Quite well.

She loomed forward as she emerged from the water, swaying over him like a snake, her face coming ever closer to his. He tried screaming again, enthusiastically, and again.

"Be silent, master," she said, her white lips moving, "or I'll touch you."

Quite suddenly Labraster discovered that he could keep very quiet. He whimpered once, deep in his throat, but the ghost came no closer—not that six inches from his own nose was a comfortable distance. For just a moment, the face so close to his melted into skin shriveled over a skull, with a fat white worm crawling out of one eye socket. Labraster struggled on the shrieking edge of howling out a scream, then the face was Alaithe's again, plump-necked, familiar, almost motherly, and somehow reassuring.

"The dead rise because they need to know," Alaithe whispered, her voice the same husky drone, "and I have a need to know why you slew me, and more—much more. I will haunt you forever, no matter where in all Faerûn you run, unless you release me to my rest by telling me all. Speak freely, man, so long as you don't scream or shout."

"H-haunt me?" Labraster stammered, raising the stool up out of the water like a shield.

"Haunt you, man, freezing your heart and your loins, so that you always feel cold. Appearing at your shoulder for others to see, whenever you try to court, or make deals, or speak to priests. More than those, you shall never sleep again unless I desire to let you sleep, and never share a bed again unless it be with someone who is blind, and deaf, and feels not the cold. Yes, I shall haunt you, man."

Auvrarn Labraster sank down in the now icy water, shivering uncontrollably. The breeze rose and blew sea mist into the room, but the ghostly woman leaning over him never wavered or took her dark and terrible eyes from his.

"A-and if I tell you what you want to know?"

The ghost seemed to recede a little from him, and her strangled voice came more faintly. "Then Alaithe whom you slew shall sink back into the garden, and you shall see her no more."

"I . . . you won't hurt me?"

"Not if you tell all," the ghost said in tones of doom, "and avoid using any of the lies that fall so easily from your lips."

Auvrarn Labraster licked those lips, heard his teeth chatter, and asked, "C-could I, perhaps, get out of this bath?"

"Of course . . . if you'd like to try to bed a ghost, or answer my questions out in the street, just as you are." The ghostly face was very close to his, and so were its fingers, outstretched on either side of him and curving inward toward his throat.

Auvrarn Labraster gave a little yelp, ducked down until the cold water splashed his chin, and managed to say, "H-here is just fine—uh, just fine! A-ask your questions."

"Why did you slay me?"

"B-because you tried to kill me!" Labraster said quickly. Ghostly hands reached for him, and he shouted desperately, "Because you knew I wasn't Blandras!"

"And what happened to my good master?"

"I don't know," Labraster babbled. "I—an evil priestess forced me to come here. She changed me into his shape."

"What did I say earlier about lies?" A cold finger slid forward, and the quivering, whimpering merchant felt a needle of ice stab through his left eye. Though his trembling fingers found no blood or wound, he could not see out of that eye.

"Don't make me touch you again, man," the face so terribly close to his added, in its droning whisper. "Tell me the truth about Meira and the altar Blandras Nuin died on."

"Y-you know? Well, why make me tell you if—"

"I want you to tell all. I need you to tell all. If I cannot rest, neither shall you."

"Aha, aye, yes yes," Labraster said hastily, terror making his tongue swift. "I—I was visiting the priestess Meira for my own purposes, and sh—"

"Which purposes?"

"I needed to hide from a foe. Her spells could do it."

"And who are you, really?"

Auvrarn Labraster drew in a deep breath. "A merchant of Waterdeep. Uh, no one important. I'm a dealer in furs and trinkets. My name is N—"

"Auvrarn Labraster, have a care for your remaining eye," the ghost said mildly.

"—ot so well known as I'd like. Auvrarn Labraster, as you know, and—and—"

"And you are hiding from what foe?"

Labraster licked his lips. "Ah, Alustriel, the High Lady of Silverymoon. I—we fought."

"Why?"

"There was a murder—a tradelord of Neverwinter. She thought I did it, but it was an umber hulk, really, and—"

"And you can tell me the truth, Auvrarn Labraster, about your connection to that umber hulk, can't you?"

"I—" Auvrarn Labraster's good eye narrowed, and he asked, "What does this have to do with Blandras Nuin?"

"I need to know it all, false man and murderer, all. The cycle, the wizards of Thay . . . I need to hear it all from your lips. You will feel much better once you tell me. Much warmer, to be sure, for the furs that cloak your bed await but steps away."

"I could just get up and run *through* you and get those furs now!" Labraster shouted through chattering teeth, the bathwater swirling wildly about him.

"Men whose joints are frozen can't bend them. They can fall—once, but thereafter they cannot even crawl."

Auvrarn Labraster moaned and slid back in the bath until the waters lapped at his mouth. "I could just let myself slide under," he murmured.

"I think you know that I would not let you die until I'd heard it all," that horrible, patient voice came back at him.

"How would I know that?" the shivering merchant shouted. "You tried to kill me, remember?"

The husky voice of the wraith glowing above him was, somehow, dripping with contempt. "Kaurdyl is a *spice*, ignorant man. Only huge doses of it can kill—then only when it is mixed with certain oils."

"A-and how is it that you know that?" Labraster asked quickly, as if each accusation was a weapon that could fend off a vengeful ghost.

"All cooks have to know such things. If they can't be bothered, they become merchants instead. If they're too lazy to make coin as a merchant, why then, they can always murder a merchant and take what is his, can't they?"

The man in the bath shrank down so suddenly that cold water lapped over its edge and slapped across the bath chamber floor. "I never killed Nuin," he stammered. "Y-you know that."

"I was speaking of other merchants, back in Waterdeep," the ghost said flatly, "but I'll speak no more of them. *You* will speak. You will answer my every question, or—"

Ghostly hands stretched out, and the merchant's teeth set up an uncontrollable chatter from the sudden chill. He waved a desperate hand, fending the wraith away, and cried, "I'll tell! I'll tell!"

The ghost nodded. "You will indeed," she said, and it sounded like a king's command.

Labraster stared at it—her—and ran one desperate hand through his wet, ruined hair. When he found his voice again, it sounded on the quavering edge of tears, "Will you tell me something first? I need to know why you rose. I mean, folk die all the time, and they don't come whispering to their sons and daughters wanting to know things."

"You'd be surprised," the ghost of Alaithe said in a voice that echoed with doom.

Labraster stared at her, swallowed with an effort, then pleaded, "Just tell me, please? Did Blandras mean all that much to you?"

"*Yes.*" The whisper was so fierce, and the ghostly face so close to his, that Auvrarn Labraster almost threw himself under the water without thinking.

He cowered for a long time, staring into the dead gaze in those dark pits of eyes, before he managed to ask, "L-love?"

In answer, the wraith hovering over him drew away to the foot of the bath, and rose upright then, slowly, turned from the fat, motherly, homely figure of Alaithe into a younger, buxom, strikingly beautiful woman. "I was once like this," the ghostly voice came to him, "and Blandras knew me then. He loved me, and I spurned him. Our ways parted. Years later, I was as you knew me—" The vision of beauty became the familiar bulk of Alaithe once more. "—and was thrown out of my job in favor of a younger, more beautiful woman. I came to Neverwinter, and by chance, begging for work in the streets, met Blandras. He took me in."

"As your master, or man?" Labraster asked roughly.

The ghost drifted a little nearer. "There is hope for you

yet, murderer. As my husband, Blandras was. Now it is time for you to answer me again."

Labraster let out a sigh, shivered uncontrollably from cold rather than fear, and hugged himself in the frigid water. "Yes," he said faintly. "Ask."

"You and the priestess Meira are part of a chain of folk who work together. Who are the others?"

"There are drow, in Scornubel, who speak to me and others through one of their number, the slaver Brella," Labraster said slowly. "They, as I, have many who work for them personally, knowing nothing of us or our aims. A woman in Waterdeep, for example, has no idea why I give her orders to invest thus or hire so. It is hard to ans—"

"Meira outranks you, as you outrank Mrilla Malsander. Who is of your standing, or higher?"

"The Red Wizards Azmyrandyr, Roeblen, and Thaltar, at least two other Red Wizards above them, I think, and at least one other mage who leads us all. There are other clergy of Shar whose names have been kept from me."

"Does your group have a name?"

A bitter smile touched Labraster's lips. "You begin to sound like a watch officer . . . no."

"Who is that one other mage?"

Labraster looked very nervous. "I—there may be a spell on me that slays if I speak his name."

The ghost drifted almost nose to nose with the shivering merchant, and said softly, "Why not risk that chance?" Ghostly fingers slid down to loosely encircle Labraster's throat. They did not touch him, but he could feel the icy chill radiating from them.

"I, ah, the mad mage who dwells under Waterdeep! All know of him. Need I name him?"

There were many dark stories about Halaster Blackcloak, the mad wizard who lurked in fabled Undermountain—stories of an old, thin-lipped sorcerer who could stroke cats and aid children, or blast towers to rubble with revelers inside, or transport horrific monsters onto the feast tables of proud merchants. A wizard mighty enough to spell-tame dragons with a wave of his hand, or blast mountain peaks to rubble if they ruined his view. Labraster had heard grisly stories around many a tavern hearth about the Mad Mage of Undermountain, and some of those tales might even be true. As the years passed, stories he'd scoffed at in his younger days were turning out to be disturbingly accurate, if they were about wizards. He wished he could say the same about some of the other tales.

"Halaster Blackcloak is hardly lucid enough to lead a cabal for long, unless it was of folk working only in Undermountain," the ghost said, leaning so close that Labraster felt a chill all over his face and throat, and was jolted cruelly back to the here and now. "Who *really* leads you, Labraster?"

"I know not—I *swear* I know not! Even Meira knows only her Sharran superiors, just as I know the Thayans! Please believe me, 'tis truth!"

The ghost withdrew a little from the sobbing man in the bath and asked, "And your aims? Tell me more about them."

Auvrarn Labraster sagged against the high, upright masterpiece of scrollwork that was the back of his—well, Blandras Nuin's, but his now—bath and gasped in relief, staring at the ceiling with one wild eye and one blankly staring one. The ghost let him pant for a long time before drifting nearer, but she did not have to threaten again before he started to stammer out a reply.

"Smuggling and s-slaving, of course. Th-the drow are taking over the rulership of Scornubel, taking the places of those we enslave. Things stolen in one city are hidden and sold elsewhere in hard winters or when war threatens, for high returns. Such schemes are my tasks. Those above me work more ambitious schemes, breeding malcontents here, sponsoring rebels there—and themselves using magic to change their shapes and take the places of important persons."

"Such as?"

"High officials in Amn, Baldur's Gate, Westgate, all over Sembia, and Mirabar. More soon."

"Working toward?"

Auvrarn Labraster drew in a deep breath, groaned, and said in a rush, "Supplanting the rulers of Nimpeth, Cormyr, and Hillsfar."

"You are joined in a 'cycle' enchantment with an umber hulk and three Red Wizards, wherein each of you can trade places with the next being in the sequence so that you could leave a confrontation, and bring the umber hulk to stand and fight in your place. Whose doing was that?"

"The mad mage's."

"Are there other cycles within the nameless chain of intriguers to which you belong?"

"I believe so," Labraster said wearily. "Gods, let me get warm, I beg of you."

The ghost slid up to almost touch noses with him once more, and whispered, "You strangled me, man, and now dare to beg for mercy?"

Auvrarn Labraster looked back at her through one failing eye and mumbled, "Yes. Yes, I guess I do."

He tried to shriek, a moment later, as that icy hand touched his blinded eye again, but he found he could do nothing. He was frozen utterly in an icy grip that could crush him at any time. The merchant couldn't even breathe as the hoarse, husky whisper of the woman he'd strangled echoed through his head:

Be glad, Auvrarn Labraster, that Alaithe is merciful. Remember that mercy for the rest of your days—in particular, whenever you hold the life of another in your hands. Throats are delicate things.

He could see again, dazedly, blinking in the sudden light as the candle lamp, so long dark, flickered up into flame again by itself. He was blinking with both eyes. He could see again.

The water was still cold, and there was still an icy chill lingering about his throat, but the ghost was gone. With a sudden, wild hope, Auvrarn Labraster stood up, bath-water raining down in all directions, and looked around.

There was no eerie glow. He was free of her.

He ran his hands through his dripping hair, shudder-ing and shivering uncontrollably now as the breeze coming through the windows quickened. When he turned and leaped out of the bath he didn't care that his wet feet skidded on the floor and he almost fell, didn't care that the fouled water crashed down over the floor in a mighty sheet in his wake, and he certainly didn't hear the tiny *tink* of a small fragment of stone falling into the nearly emptied bath.

✳   ✳   ✳

The man who was not Blandras Nuin pounded naked along the upstairs hall, sniveling and shivering, and plunged through the open, dark door of his bedchamber with his teeth so loudly a-chatter that he could hear nothing else.

The candle-glow from within the closed curtains of his canopied bed would have brought Auvrarn Labraster to a wary halt on any other night but this—but as it was, he bounded across the room and tore them wide.

It was a measure of his chilled, near-delirious state that Labraster found nothing unusual in the fact that a lamp that he'd left behind in the bathroom should be hanging above his pillows now, merrily alight. Nor that two maids he'd cursed into fleeing him then heard injur-ing themselves in headlong terrified flight from a ghost downstairs earlier this evening should now be curled up nude in his bed, unharmed, with their hair neatly combed over their shoulders, so deeply asleep that his screams and shouts in the bathroom hadn't roused them. No, Auvrarn Labraster took in just one thing— and, as he always had in life, plunged heartily in to seize it.

His leap took him into the little cavity between the curved and muscled backs of Nalambra and Karlae—a space not large enough for anything larger than a stretched out and trusting cat. Both maids awoke in sudden, shrieking terror as they were landed upon and thrust rolling out of bed by something very cold and very wet, that struck both hard and with a vicious disregard for their comfort.

They both landed hard, but were up in a howling instant, running headlong and screaming for the door. Nalambra, by virtue of being hurled to the floor on the door side of the bed, got there first, but slipped on a puddle in the hallway just outside the door. Karlae, upon encountering an obstacle, clawed her way blindly up Nalambra's back. They fell through the door together, sobbing in utter terror and slapping and flailing at each other in a frantic whirlwind, somehow disentangled themselves in the hallway beyond, and ran headlong into the shadowy arms of a wraithlike figure that hung waiting in the hallway. It was silent, more slender than the ghost of Alaithe, and as dark as the night.

Sleep overcame Nalambra and Karlae as they passed through the dark arms they never noticed. As they tumbled limply toward the floor, something unseen gently caught them and left them floating, sprawled in midair.

The dark, ghostly figure glided down the hall to the door the two terrified maids had erupted out of, and peered in.

The canopied bed still held the candle lamp her spells had whisked there. Its warm rays fell upon a huge, shivering mass that looked like a man rolled up in all of the bed linens and over furs at once, so that only a little of his face could be seen down a sort of tunnel. A muffled moaning was coming from the heart of the untidy bundle, and a trail of water led through the door up to the bed where it lay.

The dark figure made a sighing sound and curled the fingers of one hand together. The candle lamp obediently went out.

A howl of fear arose immediately from the bundle, but the dark figure ignored it, turning away to go back down the hall again. Syluné had waited a very long time for the man in the bed to take off his magic-dead ring, and she did not intend to let this chance slip away. Besides, playing ghosts was good fun.

Her fading essence couldn't spin spells for much longer, though. 'Twas a good thing this fearful merchant liked to surround himself with enchanted swords and daggers—and an even better thing that he feared the magic-dead ring would break their enchantments, and had hidden them all carefully away in a locked cabinet along the back of his best bedroom wardrobe.

At least a pair of them were shortly to follow into oblivion the glowstone from the box by his bedside that Auvrarn Labraster didn't yet know he'd lost. Oblivion might well have claimed some targets of the cabal whilst Labraster was in hiding, with a certain powerless Chosen of Mystra accompanying him.

It was high time to hand this evil chain of schemers a setback. To do so swiftly without revealing to all of them that the Seven Sisters knew of them and were on the hunt—something that might cause desperate reactions, and get a lot of folk killed—would involve something the Witch of Shadowdale was usually loath to do. She would have to unleash a fox among the chickens. Three Thayan mages in turn had struck at Alustriel, and the scourge of Red Wizards was the Simbul, a fox apt to run somewhat wild. Syluné recalled rather bitterly reminding her sister from Aglarond that when castles are hurled down, folk one has no quarrel with are apt to get maimed and crushed, not just dueling mages. This once, perhaps, such bold and reckless strife was necessary, just as removing a little stored magic from Faerûn forever was now necessary.

"Forgive me, Mystra," the ghost whispered on its way into the bath chamber. "Let one magic feed another."

The dark, ghostly figure swept to the sink and held two daggers over it. There were two flashes, like stars twinkling out from behind dark clouds. Two dark hands trembled and seemed to grow more solid, then sudden darkness returned. Ashes drifted down between slender fingers into the sink, where a single brief pour from the ewer of ready water chased them down the drain and away. Syluné was a tidy person.

She was also one who hated unfinished tasks. With all speed she returned to the hallway and outlined the two sleeping maids with the same ghostly glow she favored when appearing to murderous and waterlogged merchants as the phantom of Alaithe. The Witch of Shadowdale smiled, waved her hands in a few quick gestures, and caused their hair to stand out stiff and straight in all directions and their eyes to open and stare blankly into the darkness, though they slept on. She arranged their bodies with hands at sides and feet pointed out straight, then turned them in the air so that they floated upright a foot or so above the hallway floor, side by side and facing the bedroom. If Labraster took it into his head to come eavesdropping on her, he'd have to physically force his way past them and somehow, Syluné thought he wouldn't be very eager to do that. For good measure, she left a ghostly image of the worm-eaten Alaithe hanging in the bath chamber doorway, bloated up so as to entirely fill the doorframe.

Syluné floated over to the open window to look out at the Neverwinter night. There were white, staring faces in the windows of several houses nearby, looking her way. The Witch of Shadowdale smiled broadly, gave her translucent, wraithlike self a bright green-white glow, and caused her head to rise up until it was a good three feet above her shoulders.

She waved cheerfully at the house where the loudest scream erupted in response, and strolled forward through the window to stand, nude and magnificent, her hair billowing out around her, in the empty air some sixty feet above the dark and garment-strewn garden below.

She wove a sending to chat with a distant sister and said into the night, "Hail, Witch-Queen of Aglarond!"

Hello yourself, Witch of Shadowdale, came an answer. *Storm and Lustra have been wondering where you've been these past months.*

"Trapped in an unwashed patch of hair on the head of a merchant wearing a magic-dead ring for fear of Lustra coming down on him in her full fury. It got so I wasn't just talking to myself—I was arguing with myself."

Ugh! Those things should be destroyed. I've even caught a pair of Tashlutans—hired by our friends from Thay, of course—sneaking into my court with a pair of them that generate a reciprocating field between them. Pity their greed took their ring-hands into the path of a spill of molten gold being poured in one of the crafter's shops. Oh . . . winning those arguments with yourself, I hope. What sparks your plaintive cry this fair evening, sister?

"The usual need to save all fair Faerûn and everything in it, Lassra. I'm trapped in some bathwater—treated with a liberal dose of dissolved horse dung, so bring gloves—because our villain finally did a thorough job of washing his hair. He's shivering in his bed right now. Want to come to Neverwinter and warm him up?"

Neverwinter? Does it have Red Wizards I can torment?

"No, but this man is linked in a magical cycle to an umber hulk and *three* Red Wizards. That should satisfy even someone as greedy as you."

A-hunting Red Wizards? Leave it to me.

"Touch my stone and I'll give you all I know about our foes in one mindburst."

You're a gem, Syluné. Constrained against the Art for months? I'd have gone utterly and eternally insane.

"Others of my sisters have vigor, and low contacts across Faerûn, and a love of danger. I have something rarer: patience."

While I have a hunger to kill Red Wizards.

* * *

Erovas Vrakenntun rubbed weary eyes and glared again at the window. Like the rest of the near neighbors of Blandras Nuin, he'd been unexpectedly entertained all night long. The hitherto quiet abode of a cloth merchant known for his kindnesses and solitude had provided a free spectacle that Erovas was heartily sick of.

Bloodcurdling, deafening shrieks, shouts and tavern oaths, and things breaking had been a damned near constant chorus—punctuated by displays of clothes thrown out windows, nude women plunging out of the house and running shrieking across the garden, and now, what looked like ghosts flitting past the windows. By the Untold Trembling Mysteries of Mystra, 'twas enough to make a—

His eyes widened and his jaw dropped open. His favorite monocle fell unheeded from its perch, to swing and dangle at the end of its maroon ribbon. Erovas the decanter merchant swallowed loudly, and reached forward with the sleeve of his dressing gown to wipe a small smear away from his window.

Not a hundred paces away—if he'd been able to pace upward through the air along a steady ascendant, as if climbing a staircase that had never existed and certainly never would, if he had anything to say about it, to reach a point about fifty feet above the sill of his window—a nude woman was floating. A woman whose long legs, slender, spectacular figure, and truly remarkable, gently swirling hair made his own wife look like a rather squat and badly sculpted garden statue of the jauntily gnomish variety.

The woman was standing on empty air—nay, leaning at ease on empty air, as if against a sideboard—talking in amused tones and in a relaxed, gossipy manner with someone who wasn't there. She was glowing brightly, he could see right through her, and he could see *everything*—Erovas gulped—including the fact that her head, with that gorgeous hair, was floating a good three feet above those slender, moon-drenched shoulders.

There was a small squeaking sound beside him. Erovas jumped, and it was a few anxious seconds before he realized that the sound had come from his wife, who'd come softly up beside him to see what he was staring at. When she'd seen it for herself, she'd crammed some knuckles into her mouth, and bitten down hard.

A scream erupted from somewhere nearby, echoing around the dark houses, and the ghostly woman looked down and gave them a cheerful wave. Something inside Erovas the decanter merchant snapped.

"Right, that's it," he said to his trembling wife in a voice of iron. She whirled around to stare up at him as if he were twelve feet tall, fully armored, and grimly drawing on huge spiked war gauntlets as he contemplated which heavy sword to snatch up for the ride into battle. "We're moving. First thing in the morning. I've always hated your cousin in Port Llast, but right now I could cheerfully kiss him—*and* his six fat, drooling sons. Come help me with the packing."

* * *

The Simbul's newest bedchamber took the form of a tall, soaring cone, its walls covered with the polished, interlaced, and startlingly red scales of many red dragons who would never take wing again. A steady, spell-spun breeze rose to the unseen tip of the cone, carrying swirling smoke with it.

The smoke came from a merrily-blazing bonfire that was floating some dozen feet above the tiled, diamond-shaped central dance floor. Four women were lying or sprawling at ease in the air around it, floating with spellbooks open in front of them. From time to time, encountering particularly faint or smudged writings, one of the studying sorceresses would crook a finger, and a blazing log would drift out from the conflagration to hang obligingly near, where it could shed light but not flame where desired.

The bed that usually hung high in the center of the cone was now floating handy to one side, piled high with scrolls, grimoires, bookmarks, and plates of butterbread biscuits. An unseen harp played very faint and gentle ballads in the background. The fire popped only in hushed tones, and did not spit sparks at all.

One of the floating women sat bolt upright, causing the others to look up, startled. The Simbul frowned but kept silent, nodding slightly from time to time, then slowly acquired a wolfish grin. "A-hunting Red Wizards? Leave it to me."

She was, suddenly, a small whirlwind of flame that outshone the fire, a whirlwind that spun dazzlingly into a rising spiral—and was just as suddenly gone.

The three remaining sorceresses looked at each other. Then two of them groaned in unison, and the third one asked in disbelief, "Again?"

The Simbul Wizard Hunting Season

In Thay they trust in their spells. They bluster over-much, and fear too little. Yet I know how to make a Red Wizard go pale with but three words. All I need say is: "Summon the Simbul."

Uldurn Maskovert
from *A Trader from Telflamm:*
My Years Amid High-Heaped Gold
published circa the Year of the Prince

Out of the darkness, a clawlike hand dipped into dark waters at the bottom of an almost-empty metal bathtub, plucked up a tiny, dripping chip of stone, and juggled it to the sound of a chuckle that was not pleasant at all.

It was the space of a long-drawn, comfortable breath later when something in the depths of Blandras Nuin's bedchamber made a booming sound. There followed a triple crash, then the rising sound of a scream that grew markedly in volume. Its source, a naked man whose flesh was very red and whose body trailed countless tiny curls of smoke, burst out into the hallway, rebounded off the wall with his hair enthusiastically aflame, and sprinted for the bathroom.

The running man whooped into a fresh scream at the sight of his two servant maids floating in eerie, glowing splendor, upright and staring with their feet a good way off the floor. He tried to swerve or slow his onrushing progress, but succeeded only in another heavy collision with the wall. His howl of horror carried him through a bruising roll that took him past the floating women, but sent them tumbling about the hallway like spell-slowed juggler's balls.

Scrabbling to make the turn into the bath chamber, Auvrarn Labraster never saw the rolling wall of flame that thundered out of the bedchamber door and snarled hungrily along the hall after him, swallowing Nalambra and Karlae as it came. All he saw was his high-backed metal bathtub, filled to the brim with clear, clean water, gleaming in the moonlight that was flooding in the open window. Head blazing, he launched himself into a plunge.

His head struck the curving inside of the nearly empty tub with a solid gonging noise, and the rest of his body followed in an awkward somersault, dragging the tub over on its side. Filthy water raced through Labraster's sizzling hair as his head rang like a riven bell. His senses started to drift away from him.

The last thing he heard was hearty feminine laughter—the full-bodied, head-thrown-back guffawing that so few women allow themselves—and the rising crackle of consuming fire. In the roaring heart of those flames was a sphere of open air where no flames reached. They streamed around it, defining its walls, but the space within was as cool, and the air as fresh, as if there was nothing burning for miles, and the gentlest of breezes was wafting over a pleasant meadow.

Three women hung in the heart of this little refuge. Two of them had been jolted awake into trembling terror, to find themselves floating in the air amidst an inferno that had only touched them enough to leave wisps of smoke from their scorched hair drifting about their shoulders. Speechless in amazement and fear, they stared dumbly at the third woman.

She was a tall, slender figure in a long, close-fitting gown that descended to her ankles and rose into a high collar. Her boots were of gleaming black leather, capped at heel and toe with gold. The sleeves of her gown flared from the elbow, and they rippled as she lifted a hand

that bore several rings to shape an almost careless gesture in the air. She had long, wild silver hair that curled
around her in endless, restless streams, like waves
breaking on a beach, and here and there among its
silken sweep, rings gleamed, securely entwined in the
tresses. The wild disorder of her hair was echoed in the
careless gape of her gown, that laid bare her front from
throat down to where the garment drew in to hold her
breasts. She wore, it could be seen, nothing under the
gown.

Her eyes were two dancing flames of fearless, reckless amusement. They held the gazes of both Nalambra and Karlae at once, and though neither maid could
have said then or later what color those eyes were,
they knew somehow that this woman would hurl
danger all about them and all the world without warning—and often did so—but that they were safe from
her.

They stared at her in wonder as the flames roared on
around them all, consuming the house of Blandras Nuin.
From somewhere nearby came the crash of a falling
beam, the hissing of a cistern boiling away, then more
crashes. The sorceress in the dark gown wove another
spell, her body moving in the air with wild, sensuous
grace, and smiled at Nalambra and Karlae.

They hung trembling, not daring to think what might
now befall—then, of course, it did. Flames smote them
with a deafening bellow, and the maids were hurled
helplessly up through the air, soaring high in the star-
strewn night sky as the house exploded in a huge fireball beneath them.

Nalambra and Karlae found breath enough for fresh
shrieks of terror as they tumbled into an ever-quickening
descent, realizing numbly that they were going to die.

That cold and terrifying knowing froze their hearts
and minds throughout their whirling descent down,
down to soft, seated landings on the stone bench at the
far end of the ember-strewn garden. As its cold stone

shocked their bare thighs, and heaps of their own clothing spun out of nowhere to fill their laps, they had a brief glimpse of a dark-gowned figure standing in front of them, tiny lightning coiling and darting around her slender, uplifted arms. The lightning filled the cupped palms of the sorceress, there was a flash, and Nalambra and Karlae were blinking at the empty night in front of them.

The woman with the smile like a wolf was gone.

✻   ✻   ✻

The palace that crowns the hill above Velprintalar is a slender-towered castle of green stone, beautiful to look upon. Most citizens of Aglarond gaze upon it from a safe distance, and take comfort in its reminder of the mighty magic that shields them against the dark and greedy grasp of Thay. A few have the boldness or business needs to venture into it, and most such penetrate only so far as a particular, memorable chamber.

It can be found not far beyond the darkly soaring forechamber of the palace, an audience chamber, one of nearly a dozen rooms in several buildings in the vicinity of Velprintalar that can be described as a throne room. This one was to the smaller, plainer end of Aglarond's array of throne rooms. Its walls were flame-gleaming sheets of burnished copper, and its floor a smooth expanse of scarlet tile broken only by the dark needle of an obsidian and cast metal throne that rose in dark, many-curved, irregular splendor like a watchful open hand, facing the distant entry door. A few chairs floated about this chamber, and a few plants also hung from nothing within its walls, their fronds trailing down gently as they drifted idly about. Something had caused them to cluster near the front right corner of the room this day, as the duty sorceress and the door steward sat in gently-wandering chairs and chatted, keeping within easy hearing of each other by the mage keeping one slippered foot hooked on the hilt of the steward's extended, scabbarded sword.

A dark and familiar figure appeared in the air nearby, descending to the tiles with a thump. The sorceress and the steward rose hastily to attention, but the Simbul paid them no heed. She was staring into nothingness and nodding slightly. After a moment she smiled and said, "Thank you, sister. May your city and the realm rising around it both prosper. Hesitate not to call on me if you have need."

She brought her gaze down to focus on them both, and murmured, "Roeblen, Azmyrandyr, and Thaltar. Three scores to settle, and time to teach Thay the lesson once more that a little mastery of magic and a lot of arrogance do not give one any right, divine or otherwise, to rule all Toril—or even a small corner of Faerûn."

She opened her clenched hand, and the sorceress and the steward saw a tiny chip of stone riding in her palm. The queen of Aglarond looked down at it and chuckled. "Well of course I'm different. Gentle prudence governs my every imperial act."

She turned and set the chip of stone carefully on the seat cushions of her throne. "Undignified," she told it, "but I need you to be where they'll sit on you from time to time—and always when they're feeling most regal and headstrong. Help them only if you feel they need it. You can be most useful to us all if they don't suspect your presence for as long as possible."

The stone under her fingers hummed, and her smile broadened. "Why, with pleasure, sister dear, and I'll tell Elminster you charged me to do it, too!"

The Simbul gave the stone a gentle pat and turned away to face the sorceress and the steward. Her boots moved with uncanny silence, their soles walking on air a finger's width or so above the tile.

"Well met this fair evening," she greeted the two, a customarily imperious tone returning to her voice. "I need haste in this, so both of you go, and escort Evenyl, Thorneira, Phaeldara, and the Masked One hence. I've already mindspoken them to spare embarrassments, delays for dressing, and the like. Evenyl is down in the city, the Masked One will appear shortly in the Twilight Chamber, and the other two are in their apartments here. Go."

She gave them a gentle smile of dismissal and turned back to her throne, which began to wriggle and shake. Curved doors popped open and trays thrust forth. Humming, the queen of Aglarond selected several wands and scepters from the compartments, but the duty sorceress and the steward did not tarry to watch. They exchanged grim glances and a hug that failed to confer the reassurance it was meant to before they parted. The uncomfortable fear was growing in them both that this was one of those times when there was a real risk that fair Aglarond would soon be left undefended against the enraged survivors of a ravaged Thay. That jaunty humming of sad old ballads meant only one thing. In earnest, and uncaring of her own safety, the Simbul was truly going to war.

✳ ✳ ✳

The fiery-haired, impish sorceress that some in Velprintalar call "the Small Fury"—the queen, of course, being the larger one—was the first to enter the audience chamber, striding in without ceremony. She was barefoot and tousle-haired, more or less wearing the first gown she'd had at hand to pull on, which happened to be the same rumpled one the captain of the palace guard had laughingly helped her to remove not long before. She'd curtly ordered away his hairy, fumbling hands as he tried to help her lace up and adjust this and shake out that, and told him that finding his own uniform, in all haste, might be a wise act. Roused and unsatisfied, she was not in the best of humors. This had better not be just another of the Simbul's wild whims. . . .

Thorneira Thalance tossed her head back as her determined march along the warm tile brought her near the throne. As she slowed, she lifted her eyes for the first time, nostrils flaring in fresh irritation. Three dawn-to-lastcandle days of spell weaving, *three days*, and now the queen had to pull th—

Thorneira saw what loomed before her, and screamed.

Her cry was echoed from the door behind her. Phael-dara, too, was staring at the thing in front of the throne. It stood ten feet tall or more, a toadlike, glimmer-eyed mass of loose, billowing gray- and pink-streaked flesh. Five or six eel-like limbs were plunging busily among its folds, stuffing wands and scepters and small, hovering pouches of spell components—which it snatched in curving tentacles, like an octopus—out of sight inside itself, or rather, inside pouches of flesh that were opening like obscenely gaping wounds all over its wriggling body.

Thorneira raised her hands, not quite knowing what spell to hurl, and one large, dark toad eye expanded and split at the same time, receding like an opening iris to reveal the familiar face of the Simbul inside, her hair writhing around her in all directions in a dark, fleshy tent within the monstrous mass, as the silvery tresses manipulated the rippling movements of the sagging, toadlike body.

"Oh, you'll do fine," the Witch-Queen of Aglarond said sarcastically. "I call you here to take the throne while I flit away on a brief pleasure excursion, and you scream at the very sight of me then hesitate—*hesitate*, when Red Wizards could be slashing at the very heart of the realm with their spells—as to which spell you should use to trash my throne room!"

"I—ah—Great Lady—" Thorneira stammered, face flaming.

The Simbul winked, laughed heartily, and shot forth a tentacle to give the Small Fury an affectionate slap. "I'm sorry I startled you. I'll be done in a moment. Phaeldara, put away that wand."

The two summoned sorceresses relaxed, sinking into seats with identical sighs of mingled relief and exasperation, as the misshapen mound of flesh before them dwindled, roiled, tightened, then faded down to a more familiar form. The Witch-Queen of Aglarond stood before them, in a dark, bulging garment that looked like a second skin—that is, like the skin of some leathery beast that carried things about in a series of bulging pouches made of its own hide, and had decided to mate its flesh with the head and upright bipedal shape of the Simbul. She grinned at them, and struck a pose with a hand on her hip.

"Going hunting?" Phaeldara asked with a smile, the gems in her dark purple hair gleaming in the glow from the ceiling. The Simbul winked.

"Red Wizards, of course," Thorneira put in. Her queen pouted.

"Am I so predictable?" she cried, in mock sorrow. "Does Aglarond offer such limited opportunities?"

"For magical mayhem to the point of spellstorms, yes," came a dry voice from the doorway. The Masked One had arrived, her face hidden as always behind a fantastical mask. This one was long, narrow, and curved, resembling the mandibled head of a giant beetle. Its metal shone with a glass-green hue, and the silver runes that mounted its center caught and held all eyes that strayed to them; a useful thing if those eyes should belong to an armed foe. A magic of clinging mists eddied teasingly around the full, floor-sweeping dark blue state gown the sorceress wore beneath the helmlike mask. The bodice of the gown was unseen beneath a pectoral of polished metal plates attached to the bottom of the mask; similar tongues of flexible metal cloaked the Masked One's shoulders and upper back.

"By Mystra's vigilance, don't you get hot under all that?" Thorneira murmured.

"Yes," the Masked One replied cheerfully, as a small commotion at the door behind her announced the breathless arrival of the last of the four summoned sorceresses. Evenyl gave them all a little smile and a wave as she gasped. The Simbul nodded and stepped forward.

"I'm off to hunt Red Wizards—particular and not very exalted ones, so a few zulkirs may find unmolested time and personal stupidity enough to strike out at Aglarond while I'm away. I don't plan to be long, but for me plans always fall before whims, of course. Try not to lose the realm while I'm gone." The queen gave them all a wolflike smile, and lifted her hands to begin a spell.

"What should we do?" Phaeldara asked quickly. "I mean . . ." she gestured toward the throne.

The Simbul shrugged. "Take turns sitting on it. Pull each other's hair, have spitting contests, try jumping over more prone courtiers than each other—determine who rules however you please, or just take it in shifts. You're all capable enough. See how you take to commanding without any warning. I'm off!"

Those last two words were almost a shout of glee. In silence the four sorceresses watched their queen become a whirlwind of darkness, a spinning net of golden sparks that quickened into a high-singing blur, then a puff of fading, drifting purple cloud that rolled past Thorneira's shoulder before it was entirely gone.

The last of the sorceresses to arrive looked at the empty throne and shivered. "Sometimes I wonder just how strong her sanity really is," Evenyl said softly. "She scares me."

"Thankfully for us all," the Masked One said gravely. "She scares the Red Wizards far more."

They all nodded soberly, then, one by one, looked at the waiting, beckoning throne. None of them made a move to go and sit on it.

✳   ✳   ✳

The man seated at the black table wore garments of black and silver. One of his arms seemed to be more a thing of bladed metal below his elbow than an arm grasping the hilt of a blade whose upper works coiled around and caged his arm.

Spread out on the table in a careful array were cards, large, long and narrow plaques that seemed to be sheets of thin, polished quartz or some sort of ice hued, translucent stone, each one different. Their varicolored faces glowed and pulsed, seeming to respond in a quickening, dancing white fire as the man reached across them to touch one of the slender, spirelike pieces that stood here and there about the table. He moved it with all the care of a chess player, setting it down with a slow frown of consideration. In response, a line of flashing fire rippled across the cards.

It looked like a game of solitaire using enchanted cards and tokens, but at least one of those watching knew it to be magic as old as Netheril. "Table magic," some called it, but that was akin to a tutor one of the watchers had once overheard at Bonskil's Academy in Telflamm describing swordplay as "hitting sharpened sticks of metal together in opposition."

The man at the table moved another piece. It's something he'd never have done if he'd known anyone—anyone at all—was watching.

If he'd known just who was watching, and why, he'd have fled screaming from the room.

✳ ✳ ✳

Irlmarren watched the cards flash as fingers gloved in black and silver moved another piece, and felt fresh excitement stir within him. If only he could obtain some of those plaques, somehow, and the vedarren—he knew, now, that the pieces that glowed were "vedarren." The "gult," the ones that were always dark, were simply pieces of particular sorts of stone that dampened and bent magical flows to serve as anchors for the spells being built. He could make his own gult, but each vedarren, it seemed, needed an imprisoned life—of a creature that could work magic—within it, to awaken its glow. Learning how to make those might take a lifetime, might even be something forgotten by the spellcasters of today. He must seize some vedarren, somehow. It would be best if no one knew he'd taken them, and came howling at his heels for their return. He would need time to master them, time undisturbed and in hiding, as this adventurer so foolishly assumed he was.

Irlmarren itched to touch, hold, and handle those plaques. If only he could work with them, experimenting alone as this man in the depths of his crystal ball was doing, long enough to learn to build many-layered enchantments.

He understood, now, why Halruaa had never fallen. Even all eight zulkirs standing together—and he could not think of anything beyond the rage of a revealed god that could make any eight zulkirs stand together—would hesitate in the face of spells built like this. A single table magic, if it was intricate enough and unflawed, could lash out like the spells of a dozen archwizards acting at once. Some would even outlast their first awakening, and respond to what had aroused them to lash out anew in specific, aimed ways. As many as seven of these could be hung on the edge of being unleashed, carried unseen and untouchable—so long as their tables, hidden elsewhere, remained undisturbed—as single words or symbols in a caster's mind, or in an innocent-looking bone token or earring.

If he could build enough of these, a zulkirate could be his. He could rule in Thay, he could build an empire, he could send mountains marching west to roll over Aglarond and fill in long reaches of sea and make Thay itself larger. Why, he could . . . wait for the treachery that was sure to unseat him.

Fresh fear stirred cold fingers along Irlmarren's spine. He'd found this man, a minor mage fumbling with things stolen from a tower in Halruaa, but still too well guarded for Irlmarren of Tyraturos to hope to reach, let alone overcome.

There must be scores—could well be hundreds—of mages in Halruaa who could work table magics as swiftly and deftly as a marketplace juggler. Hadn't he seen bone necklaces and pectorals and earrings in plenty in the depths of his crystal ball on the bodies of alert and ruthless Rashemaar witches? Who was to say the Witch-Queen of Aglarond herself didn't play with vedarren and plaques in hidden chambers?

Hmmm. That might well help to explain why the zulkirs never sent more than ambitious underlings, beasts, and sword-swinging armies against Aglarond. Irlmarren of Tyraturos sat back and sighed, letting his eyes wander from the glowing scene in the depths of his crystal. He was going to have to think about this. The world had suddenly become a darker, more complicated place.

✳   ✳   ✳

"Go right ahead and ponder, idiot," murmured a man in another darkened room with a crystal ball.

He smiled a mirthless smile, then turned and grinned at himself in a nearby mirror. It reflected back a man in robes of purple, whose hair and beard were oiled and cut to razor sharp edges, a man whose thick, powerful fingers made a rude gesture to his reflection and grinned more broadly when it did the same to him.

Roeblen of Bezantur looked back at the crystal ball glowing before him, and smiled again at the thought of just how useful his trapped crystal balls were turning out to be. Whether looking in at what their user was spying on, or looking out to spy on that user, just two had brought him hours of entertainment and enlightenment in but a handful of days.

Azmyrandyr's gaunt, scar-faced apprentice Stilard was planning to betray his master. Why else would he aid a doppleganger in his private quarters in repeatedly assuming Azmyrandyr's shape, then ask it to become a truly spectacular woman, and bed it? Now this.

Nasty little betrayals were just part of being a Red Wizard, and foreknowledge of them the weapons one simply collected whenever possible, and used whenever they'd best serve. This glimpse of—table magic, was it?—was important. Too important to let an over-impatient idiot like Irlmarren blunder about with, and inevitably reveal everything to a zulkir before Roeblen or anyone else could gain anything useful out of it. The power to effortlessly win a duel with any rival Red Wizard, for instance, or any two rival Red Wizards. Or, for that matter, any three. . . .

* * *

"My, my, Roeblen," murmured a woman whose silver hair slithered around her restlessly as she floated in the dark depths of a dry, disused well somewhere in the uplands of Thay, looking into a scene that glowed and flickered between her two cupped hands, "you haven't changed a bit."

The Simbul shook her head disgustedly, and did something with one of her hands. "The implications of something as simple as a trapped scrying crystal seem to be almost beyond you, let alone as powerful a toy as what you two worms have stumbled upon. I don't think we want a nation driven by cruelty, slavery, and a love of magic used to tyrannize, coerce, and destroy to have such power in its hands. Thayans tend only to see things of power as weapons."

Two distant wizards sat bolt upright, mouths falling open in horror, as those coolly-spoken words echoed in their heads. "Wherefore," she added, "and regrettably. . . ."

Silver tresses did something, a pulse of deadly force flashed through the mind of a Chosen, and two wizards gasped in unison as their eyes went dark and tiny threads of smoke curled up out of their ears.

"Farewell," the Witch-Queen of Aglarond said, in a voice dark with doom. Two crystal balls exploded in bursts of flame, beheading both Irlmarren of Tyraturos and Roeblen of Bezantur in identical storms of glassy shards.

✳   ✳   ✳

The first rays of real dawn were touching the tops of the olive trees on the hill outside the fortress wall. They were rich plantings, but it was time they were culled. He'd see to that soon. Right after he saw to the culling of his apprentices.

Azmyrandyr stifled a yawn, saw Orth do the same, and said sharply, "We're almost done here. Rildar, shape Taramont again."

The gaunt, black-bearded apprentice grimaced only for the briefest of moments as he stood up, shook out his sleeves, raised his hands carefully, and cast a spell of great length and intricacy.

He was operating at the very limits of his powers, and Azmyrandyr studied him with narrowed eyes. As it was, these four—the weakest of his apprentices, the only ones he dared trust outside Thay with some power in their hands—could only hold their disguises for a matter of hours, but they had to learn to move and speak like the people they were to supplant: the Lord of Nimpeth and his three chancellors.

Ilder Taramont was the "Admiral" of that wine-soaked city of slavers, a one-time adventurer whose thefts and

subterfuges had won him infamy before the ascension of
Lord Woren. He'd had to learn how to captain ships and
move them like weapons, instead of merely stealing from
their crews in passing. By all accounts, and by the signs
Azmyrandyr could see through farscrying, Taramont was
a quick-witted, subtle man. Rildar, regrettably, was not.

Azmyrandyr folded his arms, glanced out the window
again, then noticed moon-faced Orth was almost asleep,
his eyes vacant, his chin nodding. "Orth," he said pleasantly, "get down on your knees. You'll be a sailor—whom
the Admiral is displeased with—scrubbing the decks.
No, there's no need to take on a shape, just get down."

Rilder was now a shorter man, with a cruel, thin-
lipped mouth, black hair beginning to go white at the
temples, and sharp features. "And how is this, dog?" he
demanded, in a high, sharp voice. "Have we so far
descen—"

Azmyrandyr lifted a hand. "Stop," he said flatly. "The
voice is right, but Vilhonna don't call each other 'dog.'
Short, clipped sentences for the Admiral, one word
replies whenever possible. Likes to hiss things, remember? A casual derisive term here would be 'dung turtle.'
Try it again."

The cruel mage put his toes into the backside of the
kneeling man. All four of the apprentices were barefoot,
wearing only loose robes to avoid being harmed, or wast-
ing clothing, in their transformations. "What's this, dung
turtle? This deck was claimed clean not very long ago.
Has the word 'honesty' any meaning for you? Eh, now?"

Azmyrandyr nodded. "Passable, but remember not to
overuse that 'eh, now?' If the man knew it was his catch-
phrase he'd cut back on it, right? Well, he couldn't help
but know it if he repeated it every six sentences. And a
little too formal, there. Not 'Has the word honesty any
meaning for you?' but rather, 'Honesty mean nothing to
you?' Taramont would say it the way you did when ridi-
culing an important merchant of Nimpeth, but not a
sailor or an underling."

He looked down and added in dry tones, "Very well done, Orth, acted superbly."

Everyone—even the sleepy apprentice on the floor—chuckled, and Azmyrandyr drew in a deep breath, threw his head back, and said, "Well, now, Burgel, let's see your Noster. Coming to me, an important merchant whom you don't want to be too rude to, to advise me in a friendly but low-voiced way that I'd best stop being interested in . . . whatever I'm too interested in. You want me to see that you're trying not to be overheard by others—for my own protection, of course."

Another of the apprentices got up from his chair, a shade less reluctantly than Rilder had, and paced forward.

Azmyrandyr turned his head sharply. "Rilder! Did I say to relax? Watch and keep silent, by all means, but watch *as Ilder Taramont*. Stand as he does, fidget as he does, scratch your nose and behind as he does, not as an overtired Rilder Surtlash does."

"Oh, Azmyrandyr! Give the lad some grace, will you? He can't help being a frightened idiot serving a master too stupid to be frightened, now can he?"

That jovial female voice snapped four heads up as if it had been a slaver's lash. Its owner gave them all a wide, affectionate smile before she blew them a kiss—the kiss that triggered the waiting spells that doomed them all.

A gray smoke seemed to pass over the window outside, and three swarms of magic missiles burst forth from the empty air behind the Thayans. Two of the apprentices died without ever seeing the bolts that slew them.

If Orth had been a slimmer man, he'd have been bowled off his feet by Burgel's dying fall, but he staggered, screeched in alarm and pain as blue-white bolts seared into him, and caught at a chair, gathering himself enough to snarl out his own magic missile spell.

Rilder went white to the lips in fear—the bloody Witch-Queen of Aglarond, laughing at them as she cast *how* many spells at once?—but he managed to stammer out the most powerful battle spell he had. Perhaps she'd never heard of a spectral axe, and he could get a good chance at her while she fought the others.

Azmyrandyr was the most fearful of all the Thayans, for he knew better than the others what they faced. That had been one of her spell triggers, and there was some sort of barrier all around them now, outside the room. Three swarms of spellbolts—four spells at once, and how many more triggers might she have? It was a slim chance, but his only one right now, given the cursedly paltry spells left to him. He raised his hands and tried to disintegrate the legendary Queen of Aglarond, knowing he would fail.

The silver-haired sorceress dropped her eyelids lazily and leaned her chin onto one hand in an insolent pose, smiling lazily at Azmyrandyr. *"You're* the one I've come for," she said, in the manner of a high-coin lass taking the hand of her patron at a revel.

She's laughing at me, Azmyrandyr thought. The bitch is laughing at me!

Azmyrandyr's sudden flare of rage was white-hot, and left him snarling in wordless fury as Orth's missiles struck ruthlessly . . . and seemed to do nothing. All gods above, was she immune to everything?

As if she could read his mind, the Simbul stretched like a lazy cat, and lifted sardonic eyebrows as she gazed coldly and amusedly into his eyes.

Azmyrandyr lifted his hands to smash her into oblivion, and realized that all he had left were the magic missiles she seemed immune to. He clapped one hand over the ring he wore on the other, and cried aloud, "Aid! We are beset by a sorceress! Aid in the West Tower!"

The ring winked into life under his fingers, a ruby flame welling up.

Azmyrandyr had once seen a zulkir employ the gesture and the murmured word the Simbul used then, and all hope drained out of him in an instant. Her eyes had been on him. The tingling was taking hold of him. Azmyrandyr of the Twelve Talons was the target of her skeletal deliquescence.

Deep within himself, Azmyrandyr heard the ring send his plea for aid rolling out, but it seemed to pass into hushed silence not far beyond the walls and floor. That cursed barrier, no doubt, but even if magic was blocked hadn't they yet made simple noise enough in the fray for the priests in the chapel below, preaching dawnrise to the rest of the apprentices, to hear?

"*Aid!*" he roared, as loudly as he could, not caring if his voice broke raw. After all, how much longer would he have to use it?

It was beginning already. Through a gathering red haze Azmyrandyr saw Rilder's spectral axe swoop down and hack, hard, right into the Simbul's face. It flashed right through her, as if she were no more than a ghost. Of course, the bitch would have an ironguard up, but wait, wasn't the axe no more than a blade of spell force, and not metal at all? That must mean—

The groan and shiver that would be his last rose up in Azmyrandyr, his throat and nostrils collapsed, and he could speak no more, could barely think as the shuddering began. Of course, he thought dazedly as he began to fall, that was why the missiles struck the apprentices from behind, not from her at all. . . .

The last thing Azmyrandyr of the Twelve Talons ever properly heard, through the rising, surflike surging in his ears, was the thunder of running, booted feet. He seized on the satisfaction that brought, wrapping himself in the thought that either the insolent Witch-Queen of Aglarond would take real harm this day, overwhelmed by foes, or he'd not fall alone, while others lived on to take this his fortress and lord it here over his bones.

Not that he had any of *those* left, now.

✽   ✽   ✽

Rilder frowned, in real puzzlement as well as growing alarm and fury. The sorceress was casting a magic
missile spell as calmly as if she were standing at home,
alone in a practice chamber. All the while his axe was
racing through her, circling with all the speed he could
urge it to, and cleaving down again, biting right
through her, and being ignored. How could this be?

How by dark, soul-chilling kisses of Shar, Lady of the
Night, could this bloody well be?

He didn't realize that he'd snarled that aloud until he
heard her laugh. Strangely, that laughter seemed to
come from right behind him.

That meant . . . that meant . . . well, it meant something,
but the thought was lost to Rilder as his master
Azmyrandyr—hard and cruel indeed, but a pillar of dark
strength that somehow Rilder would have never expected
to see topple—slumped into a boneless, spreading puddle
of flesh in front of him, flowing greasily out across the
floor in front of Rilder's toes.

The apprentice was already drawing back in mounting disgust—his flowing master was *warm*—when he
saw that his racing axe was going to cleave right
through the central, sinking lump that had been
Azmyrandyr. His master was collapsing, yes, but not collapsing quite fast enough to avoid—

Rilder winced as his conjured weapon slashed through
the flowing thing, cutting a deep channel. Blood, and other
wet, bubbling substances started to well up in its wake. A
severed hand, still recognizable from the winking ring
despite its long, trailing sausages of fingers, tumbled away.

Rilder was desperately trying to be sick all over the
spreading mass of his master when a volley of blue-
white bolts tore through him from behind. Things
changed for Rilder Palengerrast in that instant. It was
no longer necessary for him to vomit if he wanted to
spatter the chamber in front of him with all that had
once been inside Azmyrandyr's most loyal apprentice.
He fell forward, never knowing that he was doing so.

✻   ✻   ✻

"Sweet Shar preserve us!" one of the two running apprentices gasped. All that was still whole of Rilder were his toppling legs. What flopped bloodily above that was torn into more holes than a sponge. Small stars marked more tiny, fist-sized explosions as the stupidest apprentice fell.

"Must've . . . been carrying . . . feather tokens . . . or the like," the other apprentice husked out, becoming uncomfortably aware that he was completely out of breath to cast spells, as they came rushing down on a woman he'd never seen before but had an uncomfortable feeling he knew from her swirling silver hair. She'd been calmly standing behind Rilder, and had now turned her head to smile at them both over one shoulder.

The apprentices crashed to a hasty, unsteady halt. "Holy Shar, be with us now!" the first apprentice whispered, and for perhaps the first time in his life, truly meant it.

The other apprentice spun on his heel and pelted right back down the passageway they'd sprinted up, weaving desperately from side to side. "I'll raise the alarm!" he shouted back, in case Marlus was so angry at being left alone to face the legendary Simbul that he turned and fed a burst of spellbolts to his colleague.

Marlus, however, was too busy recognizing the spell that the sorceress was casting, and throwing himself flat on his face, to be angry about anything.

"Behold your alarm," the Simbul remarked pleasantly, then lifted a surprisingly pleasant singing voice into a little ditty. "Come one, come all, to the murderous ball . . ."

The fireball that crisped fleeing Ilnabbath shook the fortress and sent tongues of hot flame over his head, but Marlus rolled onto his side the moment it was done and calmly cast the spell he'd been saving for Ilnabbath, later: feeblemind.

His reward, as he scrambled up to watch the sorceress start to drool, was a look of withering contempt from the Witch-Queen of Aglarond. This seemed like a good time to gulp in despair, so Marlus Belraeblood did so.

✳   ✳   ✳

Temple Master Maeldur stepped back hastily and threw up a hand to shield his eyes. "A fireball? This is more than an apprentice trying to fell his master! Go you, Staenyn, to rouse our visitors. One of them at least outstrips Master Azmyrandyr in the Art. Hurry back, I may well need you!"

He slapped at the fortress guards trying to shoulder past. "Hold! Let me cast some protections on you. Yon's a sorceress of some power."

✳   ✳   ✳

"I'm growing impatient," the Witch-Queen of Aglarond called, watching the puddle that was Azmyrandyr grow broader and shallower. "Give me battle, worms of Thay!"

She chuckled, and added, "Ah, but I sound like a hero in a bard's ballad. Time to singe that priest down there."

Some called them magic missiles, others knew them as spellbolts. They were swift, and—surprisingly often—deadly enough to be all that was needed. She called up a swarm of them, and fed half to the fool of a mageling who'd tried to feeblemind her, who was now determined to prove his foolishness beyond all doubts by charging up to her alone, and the other half to the priest shouting at the armsmen, with all of them clustered together down the far end of the passageway.

She watched them both stagger, but neither fell. Ah, at last! A chance for a real fight. She might get to punch a Thayan, or trade dagger thrusts, and taste real blood.

She shrugged, and took firm hold of her rising blood-lust. That would be fun, yes, prudent, no. In this land of her foes she must strike hard and move on swiftly, before some zulkir could flog two dozen Red Wizards into striking at her all at once. After all, she wanted to slay Red Wizards, not despoil the land of Thay and slaughter slaves by the fortress-full.

The Witch-Queen of Aglarond watched the mageling rush toward her and retreated a little way. It would not do to let him know too soon the true nature of the foe he was glaring at with such hatred, not when more Thayans would shortly be all around her.

The air all around her seemed to settle and shimmer. Small, dark objects coalesced out of nothingness on all sides. They were blades. It was a blade barrier!

As the cloud of deadly knives started to whirl around her, the Simbul saw the mageling stagger hastily back. Good. She stood her ground as the blades flashed and whirled, dicing to bloody hash underfoot the boneless puddle that was Azmyrandyr.

"Farewell," she told him mockingly, kneeling down to speak to a staring eyeball as it swirled past. "Only one left, now, of those who dared to strike at my sister in her own palace. You were such a poor challenge, O Azmyrandyr of the Twelve Talons, that I'll just have to send most of the magically adept—if that's not bestowing too generous a description—folk in your fortress after you into oblivion. Mystra knows, Alustriel's discomfort is worth far more than that."

She looked up, and gave the mageling cowering against the wall her best wolfish grin. This Sharran blade barrier was going to save her a lot of blasting spells, and win her some fun at last. It was a good thing, she sometimes thought—and thought now—that these Thayans got so excited in spell battle. None of them had even noticed yet that they were hurling all their fury at a projected image. She had no fear that this spell would harm her real body, standing invisible nearby. Before going into battle here she'd exchanged her spell storing ring for the ironguard ring she now wore. The tress of hair that had carried the latter now held the former until she needed it again, one of many rings dancing about her in her restless hair, awaiting her need.

From the wall, the mageling hurled his own swarm of spellbolts at the Simbul. Ah, well, she could take a lot of those. Sooner or later some Thayan was going to realize she was immune, and spread the word, but that wouldn't happen until about the time they all learned to work together. In the century to come when that might occur, all of Faerûn would have a lot more to worry about than one Chosen's spell immunities.

She sent a smile in the direction of the mageling's fearful face and carefully shaped one of her newer spells. "This," she announced to the gaping Marlus, "is a spell-snaring sphere. Pay attention, now."

Ignoring the battle cries and pounding of booted feet now storming up the passageway, the Simbul stepped back to the wall and spun the sphere around the priest's blade barrier. She strode forward again, into the heart of the whirling steel, to face the onrushing charge.

What she saw down the passageway made her laugh in bitter derision. The priest of Shar had come to a halt to watch the warriors he'd urged forward die. How valiant. How typically brave of clergy the world over.

Her eyes narrowed as the second priest came hurrying up to stand beside the first. His hands moved speedily through the motions of a spell she did not know. This could be interesting. Well, it wasn't a battle if she didn't feel pain before it ended.

The armsmen were thundering at her with weapons raised, their armor glowing and sparking with feeble protective magics that just might carry them once through the raging knives of the blade barrier. . . or might not.

She danced from side to side, to keep her secret from that sharp-eyed mageling against the wall for as long as possible, as the warriors rushed at her and began to thrust and hack. Overhead, amid the whirling blades but seemingly unaffected, a dark cloud spun into being. She glanced up, and quickly back at the second priest. Yes, it was his doing. His eyes were intent upon it.

Armsmen grunted and shouted and swung swords. She ducked and danced and snarled at them, as if truly trying to dodge their steel, and looked back up at the low-hanging cloud—oho! This must be the Spider of Shar spell she'd heard of . . . yes, here came the "legs." It was a small forest of black tendrils. This would last for a while, whipping the mageling, herself, and the armsmen indiscriminately. They brought stinging pain, she'd heard, but she knew not how—precisely—they dealt damage.

One of the warriors grew impatient in his frustration. Why wouldn't this woman he was hacking fall? He put his head down and charged right through her, passing through her nothingness to crash and clang hard against the chamber wall. The Simbul saw the mageling's eyes narrow.

"Y-*yes!*" he cried, pointing at her. "Yon's not the sorceress at all, but a—"

The black tendrils closed over his head and twisted it off.

The Witch-Queen of Aglarond whistled and swallowed, despite herself, as the headless, blood-pumping body staggered forward into the blades and began to slump into bloody nothingness under their butchery. So that was a Spider of Shar.

Tendrils were lashing through her phantom self in angry futility now, and she thought it prudent to stagger, look injured, and to flee—down the passageway, toward the priests—as swiftly as possible.

As she began her falsely unsteady journey, the warriors were making small whimpering sounds, wetter noises, and one or two short, desperate screams as the whirling blades penetrated their flickering, failing defensive magics. Even if one of the clergy tried to bring down the blade barrier now with quelling magic, her spellsnaring sphere would maintain it. She tugged on the sphere in her mind, sawing it from one side of the room—daggers snarled and rang sparks off the stone walls—to the other, where the song of tortured metal was repeated. Along the way, the moving blades brought final doom to the four armsmen dying in the heart of that whirlwind of steel.

Horrible things, blade barriers. Bloodletting waste, she thought, far more grisly than a good, clean fireball.

With that old and sarcastic wizards' dark joke twisting her lips, the Simbul brought the blade barrier through her phantom self. She gasped and flung up her arms in a fairly impressive feigning of fresh-wounded pain, and thrust it down the passage toward the two priests. Another pair of men had emerged into the far end of the passageway, far behind the priests, and at the sight of them, the Simbul acquired a smile that was even less pretty than the one she'd just been wearing.

Red Wizards, these two, or she'd eat all their fingers, with or without salt. One of them even wore the purple robes and red sash that puppeteers the world over used to let their audiences know "Red Wizard" in a glance.

Ah, now, perhaps this trip was going to be worth leaving a comfortable throne for, after all.

The whirling blades shrieked and snarled their way along the narrow passage, spitting shards and sparks in all directions. Had her real body not now been tucked prudently into a corner of the chamber where apprentices had recently been acting the roles of the rulers of Nimpeth, the Queen of Aglarond might have suffered some real damage. As it was, she limped and lurched forward, her face a mask of pain as she clutched at nonexistent wounds in her phantom side, and tried to keep a grin from creeping onto her face as she watched the priests struggle with their obviously meager courage.

It didn't take long for one of them—the one who'd cast the spider spell—to whirl around and flee. The other one acquired a rather sick and wavering smile of confidence as he raised his hands into some rather frantic spell-casting and stood his ground, backing only a single step to strike a more dramatic pose.

The two Red Wizards had stopped to cast ironguard magics on themselves. They glanced down the passage calmly when they were done, then began to stroll unhurriedly toward the fray. Ah, Thayan arrogance. . . .

* * *

"The priest wasn't exaggerating after all," Largrond of the Lash remarked. "I must admit I *am* surprised."

"Not exaggerating?" Ylondan the Tall replied, lifting a hand to make sure his rings were gleaming in their accustomed places. "You think that staggering wreck is the Simbul?" He nodded his head in the direction of the wounded, staggering woman in the distance.

The priest Staenyn came panting past them, his eyes wild. He looked away hastily from the hard glares they gave him—and Ylondan thrust out a boot and tripped him. Staenyn fell hard, but they did not bother to look and see what he did after that.

"Well, whoever she may be," Largrond said with a cold smile, "our duty is clear."

"Yes," Ylondan agreed, glee making his voice rise into oily triumph. "Blast the bitch!"

As if in reply to this, Temple Master Maeldur emitted a brief, brutally cut off bubbling scream as the blades reached him and did their bloody work.

"In case she should be an accomplished mage, and have some spells left," Largrond said, as the two Red Wizards strolled untouched through the shrieking, clanging blades, "I propose we take no chances. I shall cloak her in an anti-magic shell—and you can blast the ceiling above her. The old saying applies, you know."

" 'Falling stones humble even the mightiest zulkir'—that one?" Ylondan replied, stepping around the diced carrion that had recently been a temple master of Shar without bothering to really look down, "Or do you mean the one about not hurling meteor swarms when a bolt of lightning will do?"

"The former," Largrond replied, not bothering to turn and look as the blade barrier met a Staenyn who was still groggily struggling to rise, and cut him to shrieking ribbons. "The other one presumes you know precisely what you're facing."

Ylondan swallowed. "I think I do," he said in a far quieter voice than before, as the blade barrier echoed its furious way on down the passage. His eyes were fixed on the woman they were now rapidly approaching, and his face had lost some of its usual color. "I saw the Simbul once, in battle against . . . oh, never mind."

He lifted his hands in sudden haste, and began to work a spell with hissing precision, moving his hands just as fast as the casting would allow. Largrond glanced at him, lifted one eyebrow, and matched his colleague's pace.

They were halfway through when the woman they were facing straightened up, crossed her arms over her breast in lazy condescension, and smilingly awaited their spells. Largrond almost faltered when the waiting woman began to laugh at them.

The Red Wizards finished their castings with identical sighs of relief, and Largrond's anti-magic shell promptly flickered into life. As it did so, the laughing sorceress winked out of existence, her mirth cut off abruptly—an instant before the stony rubble crashed down.

"A projected image," Largrond groaned. His words heralded another instant, one in which the falling rubble was translocated onto the heads of the two Red Wizards.

Sixty-odd stones that were each half the size of men slammed down to the passage floor amid a lot of lesser rubble, shaking the fortress, causing a partial collapse into the rooms on the floor below, and driving the dust of centuries into the air.

The real Simbul coughed delicately, stepped around the corner, and stood amid the carnage, dusting off her hands. "Stand together in a passageway discussing your tactics against a foe close enough to hear? Idiots," she muttered. "The likes of these want to rule Faerûn? Better we give it to the orcs."

✳　✳　✳

It had been a long and howling nightmare of pain, with much lying shivering on cold stone in utter darkness while half-cooked flesh that glistened and quivered like feast-day jelly shed the dark, dry ashes that had once been skin, and Auvrarn Labraster found new ways to scream.

Now the one who'd brought him here was back. Cool, soothing fingers had touched his eyeballs and banished the swimming haze that had cloaked them since the fire. A flood of sheer, shivering-cold pleasure had washed over Labraster from head to toe, banishing the worst of the pain and restoring to him skin that didn't crumble into ash or stick to anything it touched, and muscles that could move his limbs.

Those chilling but gentle fingers touched his throat. Auvrarn Labraster had a brief glimpse of a ring that looked like the iridescent husk of a long, green beetle, that covered the uppermost joint of a slender male human right hand, and glowed with a green light tinged around the edges with white. The glow extended only a little way, but it was enough to show him a rough, curving wall of stone around and above his head. He was, it seemed, lying in a cavern.

Labraster then discovered that he could swallow again, could taste something besides fire for the first time in what seemed like an eternity, and could, in fact, speak. He swallowed several times, trying to shape words through a mouth and throat that seemed horribly dry.

"I owe you my life, good sir," he husked, hearing a voice that at some moments seemed little more than a whistle, and little more than a raw, ragged rattle at others, "and wish to extend to you my thanks."

The response that came from almost directly above him—where the ring-wearer stood, his head beyond Labraster's field of view—was startling. The man with the cool fingers abruptly burst into a loud, canine barking.

That barking gave way to liquid laughter, too high and shrill to be comfortably sane, then an almost childlike giggle. It was followed by the calm, matter-of-fact words, "The plume the flagon, but there is in fact no palimpsest at twice the thalers," which in turn gave way to a howl, a rising run of ragged, frantic, and ever-faster panting, then, in a quite different, almost feminine voice: "Come to the stone, and *feed*."

Those cold hands touched him again, and again as the babbling and barking went on, Auvrarn Labraster lay on his back not daring to move or speak for fear of what those hands, so powerful in magic, might do.

Cold fear rose and danced in his breast and throat, making him sob almost frantically. The man who wore the green beetle ring seemed to grow angry, his yips and shouts rising to a crescendo, then, eerily, he fell utterly silent again.

The hands left him, the green-white glow fading, and time stretched. Labraster had just begun to hope the madman who'd restored him to health had departed when the same cold hands, without warning, touched his knee and the ankle below it.

It was all he could do to keep from jumping and letting out a shriek as the mysterious mage burst into incoherent babbling above him again. Half words, or a fluid tongue that the trembling merchant did not know, gave way to speech startling in its calm clarity.

"There is no dark sun," said the man who wore the beetle ring, "but First-Speaker was even more wrong.

Under the sea of sands they wait, beyond all vanquishing. The dragon stirs, but no sleepers wake. I see that throne emptied. It will all come again. I will be there. The whips of my faithful shall strike. The eyes of my devoted shall see. There is no doom to touch the darkness I can send. Rend the sacrifices. Rend them now."

The cold hands tightened. Somehow Labraster managed to keep silent, but he was shaking uncontrollably as the hands clutched him cruelly here, there, and all over. Silence fell again.

Auvrarn Labraster would have prayed fervently—though silently—then, if he'd had any idea which god he should be praying to. Whichever one, if any, who'd have him.

His healer paid him no heed, but threw back that unseen head and howled, the roar deafening in the small, echoing space. Labraster glanced down at himself in the din to make sure he hadn't been given wings, or a tail, or—no. The Waterdhavian who'd spent far too much time as Blandras Nuin closed his eyes firmly and lay back on the stone. If a god—whoever might hear—would just take all of this pain and confusion away. . . .

A thought struck him that left him cold and cowering indeed. The hands were trailing up and down him again, seeming to caress rather than claw. What if they *were* the hands of a god?

✳   ✳   ✳

"And what is your view, Thaltar?"

"Insofar as I'll admit to having formed one, Dlamaerztus, I think it important that all of you know that it's but an immediate reaction—a feeling in the gut, if you will—and not a reasoned and sustainable position."

"Wisdom of Mystra, man, this isn't a debating club," said a third mage at the table disgustedly, as he shook out his sleeves. Despite several hot glares, his next action was to unconcernedly take up his thin, foot-long cigar again from a holder on the shining wood before him that looked like what it was, a petrified human hand cupped eternally in a pose that allowed it to receive stray and weary cigars, pipes, and even writing quills. The mage blew a smoke ring as he sat back in his chair, with the air of a man exhausted from delivering a long and modestly brilliant speech.

"Norlarram," Dlamaerztus said testily, "I don't know why you attend these meetings, given the preparations and defenses we must all make, if you're not prepared to seriously discuss our unfolding plans. I know *I* don't attend for the pleasure of having you blow cigar smoke into my face all evening."

"No?" Norlarram of the Five Hungry Lightnings returned coolly, another smoke ring leaving his lips. "Why exactly do you attend these gatherings, then, Dlammur? Is it just to keep an eye on the rest of us without having to spend long afternoons casting eleven separate spying spells? I've awaited—nay, anticipated—the bright light of worthy verbal contributions on your part these past four meetings, as you've striven to chide and curb us as if we were children and you our teacher. I find myself, now, still waiting for that brilliance to shine upon us all."

The largest and fattest of the twelve robed men seated around the table rumbled into angry life. "This again! Look, everyone, as we are all Red Wizards, we must all know how to write, and read, and think. We all have ambition, or we'd not be here. We all have far too little time to spare for anything we look upon with pleasure. So I ask the table in general: must we listen, at our every gathering, to idle, cutting witticisms by men who think themselves clever?"

"Or complaints from men who think themselves wizards?" Norlarram asked his cigar in arch tones. Someone snorted in mirth, a sound overridden by someone else's growl of anger.

"I can't see, try as I might, how this wrangling and stirring of ill feelings is going to ease—or even permit—our working together," Thaltar observed calmly. "Why don't we simply leave off speaking words clever or otherwise until Iyrtaryld describes his latest plan? I suspect it is more than just my own view that will be formed, or reshaped, in light of what he has to say."

"*Finally* something I can agree with," the fat wizard put in quickly. "Belt up, all of you, and give Iyrtaryld our silence to fill."

"With this, I find myself in agreement," a thin, pale wizard whose hair and brows were wintry white said then, turning eyes whose pupils were the yellow of buttercups to look up and down the table. "Give Taryld the floor."

A little silence fell, and into it a soft voice not heard before at this meeting said, "Ahem . . . well, now."

Its owner rose and looked coldly around the table. His beard thrust forth into Faerûn like an up-curling spike from the point of his otherwise shaven chin, beneath eyes that glittered with malice and restless ambition. "I've worked out the last details of the enchantment that will enable one of us to pass on the burden to the next without letting the magic fall, and so keep the mouth extant as days pass. My trials suggest that the addition of this spell also mitigates any backlashes that may occur when the spell does fail."

" 'May occur'? Were there not always backlashes at the end of the spell?" Norlarram asked quickly.

Iyrtaryld shrugged. "More than half the time, but not always."

"And when not, how so?"

"We could find no tactic in the use or handling of the spell to cause, steer, or prevent a backlash. The form, intensity, and even presence of this discharge seem truly random."

"So, behold then . . ." the always brisk—some would have said "impatient"—Dlamaerztus prompted.

Iyrtaryld smiled, but no humor reached up to touch his eyes. "Behold, then," he said in coldly satisfied tones, "the Hungry Mouth."

Those last two words triggered an illusion spell the soft-voiced mage had prepared beforehand, showing them a whirling, moving oval construct in the air, a maw hovering above a field. Its compulsion was strong enough to suck up streams of sand and rock dust into itself, though at a glance they seemed to be flowing the other way, drooling down out of the hungry mouth as it roved almost restlessly up and over a little rise. It drew several startled sheep into itself, whirling them away in a swift, blurred snatching.

"Vast herds of creatures, both wild and shepherded, roam the lands east of Raurin, and beyond that are realms both ancient and rich, whose folk are many. Shrewdly placed, our roving mouth can graze on these at will, delivering to us an endless supply of slaves. We can eat what can't be compelled to labor for us."

"Making us powerful indeed in Thay," one mage murmured.

"And hence, noticed and inevitably challenged," Norlarram said sharply. "Leaving us to pursue what plan?"

"I would know first," Thaltar put in smoothly, "what will occur if our mouth sucks up an unleashed spell—or a hostile mage able to cast many spells, commencing immediately?"

There was a general murmur, out of which the voice of Dlamaerztus rose like a trumpet. "So the naysayers begin to chisel away at this brightest of our dreams again, being anxious here and cautious there, querying and caviling, rushing ev—"

"In spellcrafting," the fat wizard said loudly, his voice rolling over the rising torrent of contesting voices like a great wave, "those who are not anxious, cautious, and querying are soon known as 'the dead.' "

"Shadow of Shar!" someone snarled. "Are we to be list—"

There was a sudden groaning of grating, shifting stone, and the table in their midst heaved up into the air.

Wizards shouted and scrambled to find a grip on something or just to stay more or less upright as chairs tumbled and clattered, and the stone floor surged up in a gray wave before breaking into fragments.

A furious Dlamaerztus pointed at the fat mage and screamed, "Quaerlesz, this is *your* doing!" From his pointing finger sprang a sudden flurry of blue-white, streaking bolts.

Even as the spellbolts struck some sort of unseen barrier around Quaerlesz and burst into bright flares of nothingness, the air filled with deadly outbursts of slaying magic.

Cones, rays, and volleys of conjured bolts stabbed out, crisscrossing and annihilating each other amid tumbling showers and sprays of spell sparks. Red Wizards, it seemed, were a less than trusting breed.

In the heart of this magical conflagration, great stony fists—looking for all the world as if they were an outgrowth of the floor of fitted stone blocks—thrust up through the table, trailing splinters.

A head that had no features save a gaping slash of a mouth followed them into view as the room shook and shuddered, hurling the battling mages off their feet. As they rolled and sprang up and ran, the stony shoulders of the rising colossus heaved as its arms bent in huge, swinging punches—and crashed down through robes and the frantically-sprinting flesh beneath, dashing out screams and life together into bursts of blood. Crushed bodies splattered their innards over the cracking, tilting floor.

"Dlamaerztus," Thaltar gasped aloud, identifying the sleeve and convulsing hand protruding from one dark sea of blood. He turned his head, saw, and added in a voice only slightly unsteady, "Norlarram—and all his complaints."

Around him Red Wizards shouted and took stands, weaving spells in frantic haste. Those fists fell like hammers again, smashing fat Quaerlesz like an egg and narrowly missing Iyrtaryld. Thaltar saw the creator of the hungry mouth spell somersaulting helplessly through the air as the floor beneath his boots shattered under that ponderous blow.

It was methodically crushing wizards with its fists. Thin, pale Olorus was the next to fall, as the colossus ignored lightning playing around its bulk and spellbolts streaking into it.

Amid the screaming, Thaltar dodged a rolling piece of table, slipped and almost fell in the pool of gore spreading from the bloody pulp that had been Quaerlesz, and dodged past chairs dancing in the aftershocks of the latest blows. Riven wood, spilled blood, and desperately running men were everywhere.

A few frantic moments later, another blow fell—so close behind his heels that he felt the graze that peeled the leather of his left boot away from the skin beneath. Thaltar looked down at it as he staggered, fighting to regain his balance. That seemingly doomed struggle ended when he lurched against a doorframe.

He spun around and through the curtained doorway into the relative shelter of the chamber beyond. The black fire he'd called up flickered and spat around his fingers. It would take him but moments to finish the spell, spin around again, and shatter the magic that had given brief but deadly life to the colossus.

Thaltar lifted his eyes as the curtains swirled away, to make sure no menace within was waiting to attack him when he turned to strike down the colossus. Even a cowering guard with a dagger was deadly when driven to lash out at anything in wild fear.

Instead of a white-faced, staring armsman, he found himself face to face with Quaerlesz—standing whole and unharmed in all his fat, side-whiskered magnificence. Their eyes met, and Thaltar smiled, nodded—and as the fists of the colossus thundered down again in the room behind him, said the last three words of the incantation as if they were a polite greeting.

For once he did not have to hurl the lance of black fire that formed between his cupped palms. It came into being with its tip only a finger's width from the false wizard's breast. When Thaltar willed it to strike, it burst right through the mage—almost *eagerly*.

As it was supposed to do, it left its black flame behind as it burst. The ravening flames raged briefly through a succession of magical shields surrounding the false Quaerlesz, but their owner merely murmured something that sounded almost calm from within the inferno.

Thaltar sprang back, seeking the edge of the archway with one outstretched hand, in case the murmuring was the weaving of a retaliatory spell he might be able to elude, and watched anxiously as black flames bit through a spell-spun disguise into the real body beneath. The real Quaerlesz was a sprawled mass of splintered bones, pulped flesh, and blood in the room behind him, so who was this?

It would almost have to be the caster of the colossus. An ambitious mage acting alone, or the agent of a zulkir? Was their hungry mouth scheme known to the truly powerful, or was this the first of their moots yon unknown foe had stumbled upon?

Thaltar put a hand to his sash and clamped his fingers onto a certain symbol emblazoned there. His lips could now unleash no less than six hanging battle spells, a single word for each, in case this foe should prove to be a mage still capable of magical battle. The dark flames were dying down, now.

Thaltar's eyes widened. Could it be? The blazing, collapsing body before him was sagging to its knees, scorched silver tresses of hair writhing and flailing it from knees to elbows. Both body and hair were shuddering and twisting in pain, and this must be, could only be—

The Witch-Queen of Aglarond!

As more crackling, darkening hair fell away, Thaltar saw clearly the convulsed, agonized form within, and knew wildly rising excitement. More than satisfaction, this was triumph!

As the flames died away from everywhere but her throat, the Simbul stared at him, her face creased with pain. Speaking would be an agony for her. Speaking incantations correctly would have to be the reward of a fiercely fought victory over pain.

Thaltar was under no such hindrance. He hissed a certain word, then gave her a tight smile. The air around her was full of glistening, eel-like flying serpents, their fangs grotesque, curving things that slashed, struck, and whirled to slash again.

She covered her face with her hands, and Thaltar saw her body quiver as his cloud of fangs did its work. Some mages preferred variants that gave the air a swarm of bony, disembodied jaws, but this was, somehow, more impressive, more . . . satisfying.

Watching warily, the Red Wizard gave her a good long time to suffer, then said another word that brought a silvery sword fading into being, floating not far away in midair with no hand to wield it. A sword that moved by itself at his behest, and under his will turned its point a little to the left—and promptly thrust into her.

The Simbul stiffened as the sword faded away into drifting, dying sparks, its work done. Her tattered black gown was wet with dark blood in many places, now, and acquired the blue halo-glow that Thaltar had been awaiting. He almost gasped his relief aloud. The sword's gift, the halo was the visible manifestation of a lasting spell field she'd have to struggle against even to unleash the simplest spell. She was his plaything, now, helpless meat on a swift road to death.

Behind Thaltar, in the shattered chamber where twelve proud and nigh-fearless Red Wizards had been sitting around a table such a short time ago, the colossus had fallen silent. Thaltar grinned, like a skull showing its teeth.

"So this is the mighty Simbul," he mocked her. "Oh, pray excuse me, most arrogant lady, *the* Simbul, of course."

She turned her back on him without a word or sound, and he felt exultation turning to rage. Thaltar Glaervar would break this bitch-queen, make her scream and sob and plead as she wept, on her knees and—but no. He'd not let anger master him. Careful and wary must be his way now, or he'd do something that would let her win free, to be his doom, now or in some day to come. He must be very careful.

Thaltar's next spell merely called a steel-barbed slave whip to his hand. He'd keep his attacks to the purely physical, and give her no chance to twist or send back his magic, or through it lash out with a spell of her own. He cast a quick glance behind him into the ruined meeting chamber, to make sure none of his fellow conspirators were creeping up behind him right now, but saw nothing there beyond death and destruction. The heavy silence of the dead ruled. If any of his colleagues lived, they lay senseless or had fled. His triumph would be a very private one, not something that would raise Thaltar Glaervar to fame, but not something that would make him a target for every wary zulkir or mage of Thay desiring an enhanced reputation, either.

He turned back, smiled at the huddled woman, and struck.

Had she been standing slightly differently than before, and looking a trifle different, too? No matter. The first bite of the long-spiked lash spun Thay's most hated foe around and tore down one of her arms, away from her face. Blood trailed from her trembling fingertips, and their eyes met, for just a moment.

"Long have you harried us," he told her. "Slaying and terrorizing us, frustrating our plans. I should make you suffer in torment for longer years, kept powerless to work magic or anything else by maimings and amputations. I believe I will—after I see you crawl to me and plead. I shan't know you mean it, of course, unless you leave a blood-trail on that journey, so—"

The second bite of the lash was around her legs just below the knees, pinning them together then hauling back hard. Her feet were jerked from under her, and she fell to the floor, landing on both knees. Her body swayed and almost toppled, shuddering from end to end with pain that she did not voice.

She dared not. The last, hand-sized remnant of black flame was centered on the Simbul's mouth. Should she open it to speak or utter an incantation or even to sob, it would dart within, searing tongue and throat and more, and leave her straining to breathe, let alone defend herself with magic.

"A step too far," Thaltar murmured, taunting her as he—as well-nigh every Red Wizard—had often idly dreamed of doing. "One step . . . and doom. You shall not escape me, lady. No legendary power can save you now. No bard's embellishment can deceive me or my spells. You are but a reckless—lone—sorceress, who for too long has struck like a vulture against my kind when we are weary, or hurt, or unprepared. Against a Red Wizard ready for battle, you fall with an ease that invites contempt."

He struck again, the lash laying bare her flank this time, blood spattering the floor in its wake. "Have my contempt," he told her almost gently. "You disappoint me. No sneaking spells to win your freedom while I gloat, no last-second divine defenses? It's all bardic tales, isn't it? All so much empty boasting."

He whipped Aglarond's silent queen until the lash began to shed its spikes, one of them flashing past his forehead a little too close to his own eyes. She was a blood-drenched, trembling thing by then, hunched over on knees and elbows. He stepped forward to kick her hidden face—then, at the last moment, drew back, sudden fear flooding his mouth with a taste like blood-iron. No! He must not give her an opportunity to touch him directly. She might be waiting for just such a chance to confer some horrible magical doom on her tormentor.

Yes, her tormentor! Who'd have thought Thaltar Glaervar would be the one to bring the Simbul of Aglarond, Chosen of Mystra and most deadly of the Seven Sisters, to her knees?

Thaltar stepped back a safe distance, held the dripping lash in his hands, and wove a spell with careful precision before letting go. The blood drenched whip rose under the bidding of his will, drifting through the air like a snake that could fly, and slid around the shaking woman gently, almost caressingly, looping about one of her wrists before swooping back to her waist.

He'd feared she might struggle, or manage somehow to unleash a spell that would come cracking across the all-too-little space between them to harm him, but the Simbul cowered, face hidden behind her hair, as Thaltar guided the spell-animated lash to bind her hands tightly to her sides, loops of it keeping her fingers forcibly splayed and held down tight against her thighs.

When the binding was complete, the Red Wizard let out another long sigh of relief. Pinioned as she now was, even a circus acrobat would find it hard to cast spells of consequence, or even to reach out to deliver magics to a tormenting wizard.

Now it was time to break some bones.

He could lift his captive now by casting his usual combination web of telekinesis and levitation spells on the lash and not the woman herself, and still move her about just as if he'd dared to work magic directly on her body. With unhurried care Thaltar Glaervar cast the spells he'd need, drew in a deep breath, checked again behind him, then lifted the limp Queen of Aglarond into the air.

She hung there with her ruined hair hanging down over her face, blood drooling down to the floor from beneath it. Thaltar looked at her and found himself laughing, deep chuckles of glee that rose up and burst forth wildly. He had done it! He had humbled the one person to ever dare stand alone against the Red Wizards of Thay!

"Yes!" he cried in ringing triumph, and slammed her into the nearest wall. There were solid thumps as her shoulders struck and her legs and head flailed, but the only sharper, cracking sounds he heard were of plaster shattering, as the sculpted flowers that wall was decorated with paid the price of their unexpected admirer's arrival.

Thaltar tugged at the lash with his mind, bringing the Simbul back to a jerking halt in midair. Her legs dangled loosely. He drew back his lips in a less than pretty grin, and slammed her back against the wall once more. Plaster clattered in earnest this time, flowers raining down in rubble to the floor as the bound queen rebounded from the wall, twitching and trembling.

The Red Wizard peered at the spreading cracks his work had made, then at the floating, dripping bundle, and brought them together again. Cracks widened, slabs of painted wall slid toward the floor, and his human hammer looked a little more shapeless. He'd best stop while she still lived, or her passing would be too easy. Thaltar Glaervar would lose himself magical power he might be able to harness, a victim whose torment he could really enjoy whenever he needed to, and something worth a lot should he ever desire—or need—to bargain.

Just once more! The Red Wizard turned the Simbul in the air until she was horizontal, feet toward the wall. Her brain mattered, but a sorceress who couldn't walk would be all the easier to keep biddable. The legs dangled, not held by the lash, but if he just guided a loose end of it. . . . One was hanging down. It must have already started to come undone in the fury of striking the wall. He could bring her legs up and around in a spiral, thus, and they could serve to make her a ram. Yes, he'd hear bones splinter, and perhaps a scream from those stubborn lips, at last.

Thaltar drew in his will, then hurled his human missile at the exposed timbers and rubble where she'd struck before. Perhaps she'd even pierce the wall, and he could leave her hanging head down as a trophy whilst he collected scrolls and wands to have magic enough to defend himself again.

The Simbul smashed into the wall with a crash that shook the room, and the Red Wizard heard the grisly splintering sounds he'd been waiting for. He also heard the clatter of the rubble that filled the wall inside the plaster falling away, tumbling into the room beyond, and carrying a certain limp, wet bundle with it. With a groan, a lot of wall fell away, and Thaltar blinked through rising dust at a gaping hole where an ornate wall of sculpted flowers had been not so long before.

Light was coming through that opening, and he heard a man's voice call a question.

Another male voice, curious and much closer, replied, "The gods know! A woman, I think, or *was*. There's something abou—Wait, she's moving!"

"What's that around her?"

"Rope of some sort—no, it's a slave whip. She was bound with it. Look out, she's trying to get her hands on something!"

"Shall I—?"

"Not yet. If this is a spell duel, and we interrupt, we'll be stepping into a feud between masters of power—zulkirs, perhaps. No, let's just"—Thaltar heard the sounds of feet scrambling amid loose stone—"get away from here."

By then, he'd climbed rubble himself, to the lip of the hole in the wall and a vantage point from whence he could look into the next room. Another meeting chamber, furnished with another vast, dark polished table, many high-backed chairs, and two apprentice mages whose faces told their excited bewilderment to the world. They were staring up at Thaltar, but he ignored them. They'd recognized him and wouldn't dare send any spells his way, no matter how much they'd have preferred not to be recognized. They were nothing. He had something more important to look at.

She was lying on her back in a fall of rubble, with the half-buried lash fallen away from her, and Thaltar could see the fire of furious, pain-wracked eyes through the tangle of dust-caked silver hair that cloaked her face. Her eyes fixed on him.

The Simbul was awake, aware, and struggling feebly with smashed, bloody, trembling hands to draw forth a wand from a crosswise sheath hidden beneath her breasts. She'd already got it out, and was turning it.

In a sudden panic, Thaltar Glaervar cast the mightiest spell he knew, hurling a meteor swarm into the face of the sorceress and hurling himself headlong backward, away from the hole in the wall.

Better the Simbul than himself as a trophy corpse—and one could always find more apprentices. The room he'd peered into exploded with a roar that hurled the ruined wall right at him, shook 'the building, and brought down ceiling plaster here and there.

Thaltar struck the floor, skidded along on his shoulders, and somersaulted over backward, calling on one of his rings.

He was just in time. The wall of force flickered into being just as the first hurtling stones reached it. Despite knowing the magic had turned aside arrows, hurled pikes, and even a charging horse on previous occasions, Thaltar backed away, flinching, as a deafening barrage of stone struck it. When the silence fell and the room stopped rocking, he launched himself grimly into a run, sprinting around one end of his spell-spun barrier, heading for the foe he'd just crisped.

He had to be sure. He had to *know* she was dead, or at least still his captive, not escaped to creep into his nightmares from now on, as he awaited the day the Simbul would smilingly spring the trap that would visit her revenge on the Red Wizard who'd hurt her so.

Thaltar clambered over loose, shifting stone in clawing haste, climbed into the eddying smoke and dust, and peered into the open area beyond. He could see nothing yet, and waited tensely, listening to stone creak as it cooled.

His hands were raised and another battle spell was ready in his mind, but if he should need that, it was more than likely he'd be turning to flee as swiftly as he'd ever run in his life, from one cache of magic to another, snatching up what he'd need to keep himself alive against a wounded and raging Witch-Queen of Aglarond.

Time stretched; stillness gathered. It was dark in the chamber beyond. Reluctantly—for doing so would betray his presence and whereabouts—he cast a dancing lights spell high and far, to shine down on the settling soot and dust. The room seemed ash-cloaked and lifeless.

Heart sinking, Thaltar Glaervar waited with increasing foreboding to see what his spellblast had wrought. Wisps of smoke were drifting lazily up from charred fingertips at the back of the chamber, but that cooked corpse was almost certainly one of the apprentices.

A part of the distant rear wall sighed into collapse then, and the sudden movement brought fear's icy clutch to Thaltar's heart. The Red Wizard tensed anew when there came groans from under and behind that wall, but they were male voices . . . and they were too far away to be what concerned him. He was seeking something much nearer, in the scorched stones just below where he crouched.

It was a long time before the air was clear enough to see what he'd been peering at so intently. The headless, ashen form of the other apprentice, leaning against the rock where it had been driven by the blast, became visible first.

He peered, ducking his head to see better. Sitting on its back facing him, just about *there*, should be—if the gods smiled—what was left of the Simbul . . .

Smoke drifted away with almost taunting lassitude, then was gone.

The impatient Red Wizard found himself staring at a figure of ashes. Smoke still curled up from the featureless, hairless figure; he knew that at a touch the charred remnants of flesh would fall away from the bones beneath, and the bones in turn collapse.

But one smoldering arm still held a wand aloft. It was unmarked by fire, and therefore almost certainly still magically potent, and it was pointed at him.

Thaltar left a frightened little gulp in his wake as he ducked down his side of the rocks, sliding helplessly for a few seconds. He lay there panting for a moment or two, staring up at the scorched ceiling, and in his mind saw again the utter ashen ruin of the body.

No, the Simbul was dead. No will or wit remained to trigger that wand. He told himself that several times on his careful clamber back up the scorched rocks, to look down again. Everything was as it had been. The smoking, ashen form with the wand in its hand had not moved.

Thaltar let out a long sigh of relief, then cast a careful spell. When he used its magic to whisk the wand away, the hand that had gripped it crumbled into drifting ash. He brought the wand to a gentle landing not far from his foot, in a cleft where it couldn't possibly roll to touch him, and cast another spell.

A storm cloud of flickering purple darkness came into being above the ashes, and at his soft command, burst into a brief rainfall—a torrent that crashed down on the ashes that had once been the Simbul.

The hissing and bubbling was almost deafening. Thaltar watched the sitting figure slump to ashen bones then to nothingness, and kept on watching until the acid of his spell had eaten its way deep into the stones that had underlain the destroyed sorceress, and the hissing was done.

Only then did he look down at the wand. He watched the motionless stick of wood for a long time before he bent, snatched it up in triumph, and cried forth a shout that echoed back from the battered walls and ceilings around, "And so at last the Witch-Queen is laid low!"

The other ring on his finger winked, and he was gone from that place, ignoring the groans of dying Red Wizards.

✳   ✳   ✳

The sphere of crystal floating over the table winked and sparkled into life. Sixteen people sat straighter in their chairs and tried to look impassive. Eleven of them shook out the sleeves of their purple, red-sashed robes, and two of them ran nervous hands over their black skullcaps and squared their shoulders so that the purple Eye of Shar on their breasts hung unwrinkled. Rings winked and glittered up and down the table like votive temple candles flickering in a breeze.

The sphere flashed again, as if in a signal, and one of the two women at the table leaned forward and said calmly, "Let us begin. We face a problem that, if unattended, will perhaps soon be a crisis. Two of those absent this night will never sit at this or any other table again. Roeblen and Azmyrandyr are dead."

There was a stir around the table, murmurs of excitement that stilled as the woman spoke again.

"They were destroyed, we believe, by the spells of the Witch-Queen of Aglarond, and we must assume that these murders were more than her long-running campaign to rid Faerûn of all Red Wizards. They may be just that, but we here must for our mutual safety take the view that they are blows struck deliberately at us—just as when Dove Falconhand of the Seven Sisters appeared far from her usual haunts to slaughter many of our dark elf allies in Scornubel, where Qilué Veladorn also struck out at us, shortly thereafter. Qilué was soon afterward seen in Skullport with her sister Laeral, spying on some of our operations. This was barely a day before one of our number was hampered in his activities in Silverymoon by another of the Seven, the High Lady Alustriel. Significantly, the operative in that case called upon the services of three Red Wizards to aid him in battle against the Chosen. Roeblen and Azmyrandyr were two of those mages."

Eyes up and down the table strayed to where Thaltar Glaervar sat, looking as impassive as he knew how. Many knew who the third mage was, and would now be wondering . . .

"The link that fires our suspicions," the woman continued, "is that the operative who so narrowly escaped Alustriel in Silverymoon was almost slain by spells that destroyed the home in which he was living in disguise, shortly after several witnesses saw a silver-haired woman—and I need hardly say that silver hair is a distinctive mark of the Chosen—on the premises. This befell not long before the deaths of Roeblen and Azmyrandyr."

The speaker paused, then, but no one murmured anything into the tense silence that cloaked her glancing up and down the table, and finally up at the globe hanging above them. Her dark eyes flashed with excitement as she leaned forward still more, placing her elbows on the table, and added, "Wherefore we are gathered to warn all, and discuss what should best be done to counter future attacks upon us by the Chosen. We know not the extent of their knowledge of us, but again, for safety's sake, must assume that they know all." Her gaze flicked up and down the table again ere she added the formal phrase, "Let one speak now who brings wisdom to the matter at hand."

One of the Red Wizards seated near to her stirred and said, "If the Seven know less than all about us, one here at this table stands in the greatest danger. Protecting him with our risen power, in a covert trap, would seem to be our logical course."

The wizard did not bother to look at Thaltar, but heads turned to regard him up and down the table.

The woman met Thaltar's eyes, and said gravely, "Lord Skloon uses the word 'logical,' and I find myself in no disagreement with that. How do you feel about living, for an indeterminate time to come, in the midst of battle-ready colleagues who must needs watch your every move if they are to protect you?"

Thaltar shrugged. "If it is needful, Speaker Amalrae," he said calmly, "I have no particular objection. I fill chamber pots in the usual manner, I live a relatively quiet life of study, and as all here know, Red Wizards have no secrets."

This deadpan sally was received around the table with an amusement that could be felt more than heard. Thaltar leaned forward as Amalrae had done, and added quietly, "I do think it may be needful—and that the Red Wizards of Thay have been handed an opportunity this day that the gods themselves could not have bettered. An opportunity all of us here at this table share."

"How so?"

"I speak of an opportunity to unleash magic as we never have before, against foes we know are coming. A chance to rid Faerûn forever of annoyingly meddlesome women with silver hair."

Another wizard frowned, and said in a deep voice, "How can you be so sure that we can know these foes will come to a specific place or time?"

Thaltar Glaervar turned cool eyes to meet those of the deep-voiced wizard and replied, "Lord Harkon, they will come to me—wherever I am, and soon, in fury unmatched. We must be ready for them, or this opportunity is squandered."

Harkon raised his eyebrows and said, "You presume overmuch as to your own importance, methinks. Why 'they'? Why not just the Simbul, the only one of the Seven to consistently hunt Red Wizards—the only one of the Seven to thus far act against the Red Wizards among us?"

Thaltar allowed a smile to cross his face for the first time at that meeting as he rose and replied, "I have good reason to believe that we shall shortly be entertaining more of the Seven than we might wish to, and that the Simbul will not be among them. Perhaps I do flatter myself, Lord Harkon, but I think I am now sufficiently important to be noticed by Chosen of Mystra all over Toril. I've just come from one of my abodes, where I found it necessary to replenish my spells. That necessity arose in an incident wherein I procured this."

From the flaring sleeve of his robe Thaltar shook out a wand, and set it gently on the table.

"Before you ask why I'm showing you a wand that to the eye resembles many another," he continued, "I must tell all here that bare hours ago this wand was aimed at me by the Witch-Queen of Aglarond herself."

His gaze swept the table. Every eye was fixed on him, and the room was utterly silent. For the first time ever, he had the full attention—and respect—of the gathered cabal.

Thaltar drew in a deep breath and told them, "Alone I contended against her, and alone I prevailed. I have slain the Simbul. Colleagues of Thay, *Aglarond is ours!*"

His words brought instant uproar. Thaltar permitted himself a real smile amid the din, as he saw just what he'd expected to see on the faces of his fellow Red Wizards: wary disbelief, wonderment, and the dawning of sudden hope, even glee. The scrying globe overhead flashed as it rolled over to allow the being staring out of its depths to better examine the wand.

Thaltar had suspected that producing the wand would result in a rolling away of the mask of mists that had always cloaked the features of the man in the globe. He wasn't disappointed. Peering up through his own eyebrows as he tried to keep his head tilted down, he saw the globe shimmer and clear, then beheld an elderly man seated at a table. Eyes that snapped with alert intelligence peered out of the globe. Thaltar saw long white hair and a bald-crowned head, gaunt features, and hands clasped on the table in the foreground. On one finger of those hands was a long, iridescent green ring that looked like the carapace of a beetle.

It was rare for the man in the sphere to speak, but he did so now, in a voice that was cold with misgiving, and sharp with alarm. "What magic do you awaken in the wand now, Red Wizard?"

Thaltar's gaze fell to the wand. As if mocking him, it winked once, then flashed forth a beam of soft green radiance—a beam that passed between two shouting, scrambling wizards of Thay to strike the wall of the meeting chamber, and there splash and spread out in all directions, curving along the walls and floor to cloak them in its glow with astonishing speed.

Thaltar stood frozen, a strange foreboding growing within him, but the other fifteen people in the room worked frantic magics, or made for the doors—only to find them already blocked by a glowing green field that seemed to be made of nothing at all . . . and yet resisted their every weapon, bodily charge, and spell.

Thaltar almost reached out to snatch up the wand, then drew his hand back. As he backed away from where it lay, the sphere above it flashed again then went dark, leaving behind only a single parting comment: "Fool!"

The glowing field had become an unbroken sphere within the chamber, a humming presence that crowded the folk of the cabal around the table and lifted their boots from the floor with its crackling force, enclosing them.

The beam ended, and Thaltar took an uncertain step back toward the wand—only to recoil as it boiled up into an all-too-familiar shape that stood barefoot atop the table in a garment that was more black tatters than a gown, and smiled coldly at him then around at the assembled folk of the cabal.

"Thay's perennial problem," the Simbul sighed in mock sorrow, turning with her open hand outstretched to indicate the assembled conspirators. "Such an over-abundance of Red Wizards, and such a shortage of people fit to be called human."

She shook her head and let her hands fall to her hips—only to vanish, an instant later, in the white, roiling heart of an inferno of spells.

Wizards all around the chamber hurled their most potent slaying magics. In the instant before a ricocheting beam of slicing force took him in the chest and hurled him back into oblivion with one last scream, Thaltar saw something boiling up, like a whirling tornado, from where the queen of Aglarond had been standing. It seemed to flow up into the glowing field and merge with it, rippling outward as unleashed death raged beneath it. Fire and lighting snarled around the table, which caught fire and burst into flaming splinters in two short instants, and men screamed as they melted into skeletons and were swept away.

Then the slower spells—the fireballs and bursting spheres and gigantic, disembodied hands—took effect, their blasts raging around a glowing sphere that the few surviving eyes in the chamber saw flicker, darken, and grow holes here and there—holes that grew swiftly larger, as the sphere seemed to melt. One Red Wizard was on his feet and thrusting at the glowing field with his dagger. It seemed to darken and give way where he stabbed most energetically.

Hope rose in Speaker Amalrae and in Lord Skloon as they wove magics with hands that trembled with pain, seeking only to shatter this prison woven by the Simbul, and escape.

The holes closed again as the sphere tightened, glowing brightly once more as it swept the three people in whom life still flickered together into a huddled, snarling group.

"A prismatic wall!" Lord Harkon shouted, his voice high with fear as he flung down his dagger and gestured. "Cast thus, to cut through this—this—"

Words failed him, and he hurled himself into frantic casting.

Skloon glanced up at his fellow lord in grim, head-shaking despair, knowing only too well what was coming. The spells he and Amalrae had woven were going to manifest, rebound from this astonishing field, and strike back at them. It wasn't anti-magic, now, so what *was* it? A pocket of the stuff the Weave was made of? But that was all so much bardic nonsense, fables told to apprentices as a reason for the limits to the Art that no one understood. Looking into Amalrae's eyes, he could see that she knew their doom too.

"Mystra," he quavered, calling aloud in prayer to the Lady of Mysteries for the first time in long, long decades, "be with us . . . please?"

"And have mercy," Speaker Amalrae moaned, putting her arms around Skloon in a last embrace that overcame hatred and rivalry. It is never easy to die alone.

There came the flash and roar they'd been dreading, and the three conspirators were hurled together to tumble helplessly around the dwindling sphere as magic clawed and seared, tearing Amalrae apart and burning Skloon into a husk.

Drenched in the Speaker's blood, Lord Harkon rose grimly with his bare hands glowing a bright amber hue. "So much for the mercy of Mystra," he snarled. "She helps those who help themselves!"

He moved his hands as if he were gripping a great sword. His prismatic wall flashed into existence, then, rippling in the air before him in the shape of a sword. Even if his two rivals had lived, the time for secrets was past. This was his greatest innovation, and it just might cut a way to freedom.

Lord Harkon roared his defiance and hacked at the glowing field. It darkened and withdrew a little from his conjured sword, and he slashed again with the prismatic blade.

The glowing field rippled like a sail around him, and seemed to collapse. With a wild, wordless cry of exultation, Harkon flailed at it with his blade.

It was gone from above him, dwindling into a snake-like mass that rippled in the air, danced around his blade, and surged down the wizard's throat like a ribbon snake.

Harkon barely had time to choke before the glowing thing expanded, bursting him apart like a ripe tomato. Amid his spattering blood the feebly-glowing, snakelike thing wavered upright in that chamber of death and became the Simbul once more. She was bleeding from many small wounds, and reeled as she stumbled to a wall, leaning against it for support.

"Elminster," she murmured, throwing back her head to gasp out the words she needed to say. "Come. Please."

Storm
Not Just any Mage in a Storm

I see a woman leaping like a flame in battle, bathed in the blood of foes, her sword singing a deadly song. I see her crisply negotiating peace while she bathes, unashamed. I see her tending the wounded of both sides, comforting the grief-stricken, and imparting counsel to bewildered young inheritors who must now shape their lives alone—words that they'll remember and cling to for years to come. I see her going to her knees to play with a neglected child in the dust, whilst captains-of-war stand waiting, and keep silent. And in all their eyes I see the same look of awe and love.

I never thought humans could so love a storm.

Belbradyn Tralaer
from *Why I Am A Harper*
published circa the Year of the Staff

It was that time in early evening when the shops of Shadowdale had closed, and the lowering sun told every eye that the long, slow slide into dusk had begun. Farmers were still hard at work because there was still ample light to work by, but most other dalefolk were sitting down to a hearty evenfeast, weary from another good day's work. The lanes of Shadowdale were well-nigh deserted. Fitting for the loneliest walk of all.

Maervidal Iloster walked past the Old Skull Inn quite alone, sighing as he turned onto the Northriver Road in front of the temple of Chauntea. He was dressed well, in a black leather vest and breeches, with a mauve silk shirt a Sembian dandy would not have been sorry to be seen in, and knee-high boots as dashing as anything a Cormyrean noble could boast. Yet his face was grim and his pace slow, almost dawdling. He knew he was walking to the place where he was going to die.

They'd found him out. Just how, he knew not, but it no longer mattered. They knew.

All day the Zhentarim who normally contacted him—Oleir and Rostin—had taken turns oh-so-casually dropping into his shop, giving him cold smiles and gentle reminders of the revel to which he'd been invited three days ago.

Just before closing, their superior—Samshin, whom he usually saw but once or twice a year—had strolled in to loom over the counter and huskily bid him well met, and to express the fond hope that they'd be able to share drinks together at Warmfires when the sun was fallen from the sky. Oh, they knew.

Since the day—three sunrises back, now—Oleir had leaned on the same counter to deliver the invitation, he'd felt cold, unseen eyes watching him. Waiting to see where he'd run to, and who he'd contact. Everyone who stepped into Crown & Raven Scriveners to order a sign or browse the stock was under suspicion.

What would become of his shop, after he was gone? They'd plunder it, to be sure. For all that it stood within easy view of the Twisted Tower itself, an easy trot for the guards on the Ashaba bridge, it had a back door none could see from the road. After a spell-fed fire blazed up and devoured it, who would check in the ruins for the writing paper, framed and mounted poems and illustrations, signs, heraldry, pens, inks, and portraits that should have been there? And what of Rindee?

A pretty lass she was—too pretty to escape grasping hands, if the Zhents felt so inclined. Maervidal had taken her on as his assistant for her skilled hands with the brush, not for her face and figure, but he doubted any Zhentarim would care for a finely-curved letter or a superbly-rendered coat of arms. She was a local, and didn't have to be shrewd to know something was amiss, but he'd told her nothing. He should have warned her, but she lived on a farm too far in the wrong direction—west of his shop, well over the river in the newly-cleared lands—to turn back now. But if the Zhents caught her. . . .

He felt sick, but what could he do? They were watching his house even now, on this clear, warm evening. All it would take was one man with a crossbow, back in the woods, who might shoot even if he turned back just to leave a note. They were all around him, hidden but watchful.

He should have been ready for this, with letters written out and left in safe hands. After all, only a fool could expect to watch and whisper for the Zhents and beneath it all do the same for the Harpers, and not get caught at it eventually. Somehow, though, he'd thought "eventually" would take longer to arrive.

"We'll be expecting you," Oleir had said with a crooked grin, his eyes as cold as winter, "at Warmfires House, by dusk. Don't be late."

Oleir was tall and broad-shouldered, yet moved with uncanny silence. A forester who could crush half a dozen Maervidal Ilosters in his bare hands, he was probably out there in the trees now, watching the doomed scrivener trudge up the road. The Zhents could muster twenty like him.

"Stand and face it, Maervidal," he whispered aloud. "You're doomed."

Warmfires House was a Sembian venture that stood on the new northern edge of central Shadowdale, in a bend of the Ashaba. It was a huge, rambling farmhouse that could be rented by the day, two days, or a tenday at a time. Maervidal had been in it only once, on a gawking tour with other dalefolk when it was not quite finished. He'd been brought in to see the dance floor in the feast hall, the meeting rooms above it, the bathing pool rooms, and the luxurious bedchambers. It hadn't been quite the success the greedy Sembians had hoped, but the Lord Mourngrym had built a guard post nearby, and considered it the anchor of the new cluster of homes and shops folk had taken to calling "Northend."

It was a good long walk from Twisted Bridge to Northend, but to Maervidal it was seeming all too short, now. His last walk in the clear air—gods blast it all, his last walk anywhere!

How had they found out? Oleir, a tall, blond forester, as strong and as stupid as the trees he cut down and the bears he trapped, was vicious enough, but too slow-witted to put two ends of a broken blade together and see that they matched. Rostin was sly and quiet enough to overhear things, but he was a scribe-for-hire staying at the Old Skull only for a tenday to write letters, contracts, and records for hire, before walking on to Tilverton then back and down to Ashabenford. Samshin was in the dale even less. Just now, he was posing as a farm laborer looking for work. He'd talked idly, as he turned to go, of how when a fugitive gets hunted across a quiet dale, all sorts of innocent people get knifed by mistake. In other words, if Maervidal tried to run, they'll murder a lot of dalefolk, and blame it on him, branding him an outlaw forever.

The scrivener sighed again. It really didn't matter how they'd found out, did it?

He glanced at the dark, wooded bulk of Fox Ridge ahead on his right, and shrugged. Perhaps it was full of Oleir and a dozen Zhent comrades, perhaps not. It didn't matter now. None of it mattered now.

A figure turned into the road ahead, and his heart leaped in sudden hope. A woman had stepped out of the mouth of her own farm lane. The woman drew every male eye in an instant, even when dressed in an old leather jerkin and breeches, stained from farm work and accompanied by floppy old knee boots that had gone the color of the dust and old mud that had so often caked them.

Maervidal swallowed. It wasn't just her height—she was taller than most knights and smiths he'd seen, the sort of height and shoulders that seemed to fill a doorway—but the silver hair that cascaded down almost to her ankles. It was tied back like a horsetail, with a scarf that looked like an old scrap of black silk—a scarf that every man who'd hoisted a tankard at the Old Skull knew was a dancer's costume that covered so little that Storm rarely bothered to put it on. Maervidal closed his eyes for a moment, his mouth suddenly dry, at the memory of the last time she'd shed her farm leathers to spring up onto a table in that costume—and of the dance and song she'd given them all then.

It wasn't just her dancing, though, it was her walk. All fluid, sensual grace—not the proud strut of a cat that knows it's beautiful, and flaunts it, but the calm, confident lilt of a creature who knows she is stunning to the eyes, but cares not—and it was her *eyes*. They were dancing and merry, a flashing blue as they looked down the dale, and found the view pleasant. These eyes promised everyone good humor, real interest, and a teasing, daring excitement. They were the eyes of the most famous woman in all the dales.

Common folk knew her skill with the harp, but true Harpers knew just how much they, and all Faerûn around them, owed the Bard of Shadowdale.

"Tymora and Mystra, smile upon me together now," Maervidal whispered hoarsely to the air. He'd never uttered a prayer so fervently in all his life.

Storm Silverhand had been absent from the dale a lot this winter—down Sembia way playing ballads for rich nobles and stacking up the gold coins they tossed her, some said—and he'd hardly traded six words with her yet this spring. It had been too much to hope for her to be around now, but she knew who he was.

"Oh, great gods above, save me now!" he whispered, finding himself very close to tears, and made himself stroll toward her without calling out or breaking into a run.

She was coming abreast of him, nodding to him in pleasant, wordless greeting, and striding by. Now!

Maervidal Iloster turned to the Bard of Shadowdale as if something had just occurred to him, and laughed loudly. It sounded a little wild even in his own ears, and she spun around to face him, hand falling with smooth grace to the hilt of the sword she always wore.

Desperately he hissed out his situation to her, trying not to lose control of his voice. He found himself on the verge of tears only a few words later, pleading with her to come to the revel and rescue him.

She drew herself up and looked stern, and for one awful moment Maervidal thought she was going to rebuke him for being a craven coward, and send him on his way with harsh words, send him on his way to death. Instead, the Bard of Shadowdale stepped forward and embraced him. Maervidal found himself trembling, struggling not to break down and cry, as Storm Silverhand—who stood almost a head taller than he, and smelled distractingly of forest floors and nose-prickling spices—embraced him and said into his ear, "Press yourself against me, Maervidal. Right in close—don't be shy. Thrust your belly and hips against me. Clasp your arms together, around my neck, and sag against me . . . aye, like that. Now speak not, and keep still."

The wondering scrivener felt a sudden strangeness sweep over him, a tingling that left him feeling empty and faintly sick. Something stirred, then surged through him . . . from Storm's hips, he thought. Or perhaps it seemed that way because he could feel her hands busy thereabouts, her knuckles grazing him as she did something that . . . that . . .

She was putting a belt around his waist—a waist that was more shapely than he remembered. *His* hips didn't stick out like that. And he was taller now, looking down at the muddy dale lane from a greater distance than he remembered, looking down even at Stor—ye *gods*!

Maervidal swallowed. He was looking down at himself. That is, where Storm had stood was a man with untidy brown hair and large, liquid brown eyes. It was the same handsome rake who looked back at him from his shaving mirror each morning. And he himself was . . . he looked straight down, at the body beneath his own chin.

"Great *thundering* gods!" he whispered hoarsely, utterly aghast. The man who looked like him chuckled.

"My body's not all that bad," she said, "for something that's seen around six hundred summers. Wear it well."

She clapped him on the arm and turned north, back the way she'd come—or rather, the way he'd been heading.

"But—" Maervidal managed to blurt, noting that his voice sounded lower, and more musical. "But—"

Storm turned around again, winking at him with his own eyes, and said quickly, "We haven't really switched bodies—just exchanged shapes. You'll be yourself again in the morning."

She giggled—Maervidal hadn't known his body *could* giggle—and he knew he, or rather, Storm Silverhand, the shape he was wearing, was starting to blush. He'd stared down at his new-found breasts in wonder, and without thinking had shaken himself to make them sway and bob. She'd buckled her sword belt around his hips—that'd been what he felt her doing. As for the rest, he was wearing her farming leathers, shiny with hard use at the knees and elbows, and she was him, in his best mauve silk shirt and black finery.

"You'll find coins in plenty slid in all along the sword belt," she said gently. "Now don't forget—you use the ladies' jakes this night, not that smelly corner one you men spray about in, so. Don't worry if it all seems strange. Just smile a lot, say little, and wait for the morning. My house is open. Feel free to eat and sleep as it pleases you. Oh, aye—when you're in the Skull, you'd best be careful who you have a drink with."

"Uh, pardon?" he asked, putting his hands on his—her, oh, to the Nine Hells with this: *his*—hips as he'd seen Storm do.

She winked at him. "I was on my way to the Old Skull Inn, to try to convince Jhaele to take the vacation she's been longing for, and see Waterdeep like she's dreamed aloud of doing, for years. Don't try to do that, but if you feel uncomfortable, just put your elbows on the bar and ask, 'Jhaele, what news of Waterdeep?' Then just let her talk."

Maervidal nodded, then stopped, smiled, and nodded as he'd seen her do it, head tilted a little to the right, and a hand lifted as if to cup the chin.

She nodded approvingly. "*Ver*-ry good. What I meant about the drinks was that three of the regulars at the Skull are becoming quite ardent. Hands on my knees and wandering higher . . . that sort of thing."

The scrivener who now looked like Storm Silverhand swallowed. "And I should do what—?" he asked faintly. Suddenly, and just for a wild, fleeting moment, walking to sure death didn't seem so dark a thing. He closed his eyes and thought he'd probably kiss every man in the taproom of the Skull if that's what it would take to keep him alive.

"Josh them pleasantly. Don't act shocked. The rest, I'll leave to you. The ones to watch out for are Sarnjack, Old Juk, and Halcedon."

Maervidal's eyes narrowed. "Sarnjack I know, but the others . . ."

"Mystra above, man," Storm said to him, in his own incredulous voice, "you live in this dale for four seasons as an informant for the Zhents and for us, and don't know every last man and woman in the dale? No wonder you were walking to your—"

She saw the stricken look that climbed across his face, and quickly said, "Sarnjack the ring maker—weathered face, retired farmer from Mistledale? Recall him?" At his nod, she went on. "Big, fat, balding man who sits over the chessboard most nights, retired from farming in Voonlar to raise chickens here. That's 'Old Juk,' but you'll want to tartly call him by his full name, Belinjuk Travvan, as his wife does—to remind him he's still married."

Maervidal didn't smile. He was nodding slowly, vaguely remembering the fat man by the chessboard.

Storm said swiftly, "In case we're being watched, I should go. The last man is the one you really should have been keeping an eye on. Halcedon Muiryn was once a hiresword, but someone took his right arm off at the elbow for him, and now he tutors lads in weaponsplay, spies on caravan shipments for all manner of merchants, and makes those fine long swords you see him selling to travelers in the Skull. He has a pair of jaws, like a smith's pincers, fitted to his stump. Got that? Good, now wish me luck."

"Storm," Maervidal Iloster said, swallowing back threatening tears, "May you have all the luck the gods are willing to hand out to mortals for the next season or so. They know better than I how much you deserve it."

He drew in a deep breath, and asked the last thing that was troubling him then. "But what of when I'm myself, on the morrow? Won't the Zhents just come after me then?"

Storm gave him a wintry smile. Maervidal stared at her; he'd never realized before just how chilling one of what he called his "smiles of cold promise" really looked.

"If my plans work out," she told him softly, "there won't be one of them alive to come after you in the morning."

He stared at her for a moment, then a sudden shiver swept the length of his body. "Hmm," Storm said, surveying the result critically. "That looks . . . interesting."

She turned and left him then, standing dumbfounded in the road, scarcely able to believe his good fortune.

✳   ✳   ✳

"So, Maervidal, how do you like the wine?"

Storm looked up at Calivar Murpeth and smiled with an easiness that the real Maervidal Iloster would not have felt. "It's very good," she said eagerly. "Very . . . fruity."

"That's the saisha in it," purred Murpeth's right-hand man. Aldluck Dreen had sidled up to them more quietly than she'd thought such a large man would have been able to move, though the revel was raging heartily all around them. Laughter and loud, well-oiled voices were raised in such a din that the Sembian piper trio could scarcely be heard this far across the lofty hall.

"The what?" Storm asked, playing the role of an innocent scrivener with a good memory and a clear eye, but
not much worldliness backing them up. He was the perfect Zhent informant, though they seemed to have found
an imperfection in this one. A soon to be fatal imperfection, she had no doubt.

"Saisha," Murpeth said smoothly, darting a quelling
glance at Aldluck, who seemed to have already downed
rather more firewine than it was good for a man to take
aboard this early of an evening, "is more popularly known
as hammerlock."

"Because it locks up your joints," Aldluck snarled, "so
we have to use a *hammer* if'n we want to bend them—
ahahaha!"

"Aldluck," the sly-tongued local Zhentarim leader said
smoothly, "I think it's time to tell Brezter to be ready, don't
you?"

His burly henchman peered at him a little owlishly,
then reddened, nodded curtly, and spun around to plow
his way roughly through the drink-swilling throng.

The false Maervidal watched him go a little longingly,
and did not fail to notice that two other men she knew to
be Zhents advanced smoothly to fill the gap left by Aldluck's departure. They were keeping their rabbit in a
corner, against a wall.

"*Loyal* scrivener," Calivar Murpeth purred proudly,
"may I introduce to you Nildon Baraejhe, who's come to us
all the way from the Border Kingdoms?"

"To be sure the saisha was fresh," Nildon said in a wet,
avid voice, his eyes gleaming as he looked at Maervidal.

"And over here stands Aliphar Moongul, who deals in
perfumes, oils, and medicines."

"As well as more deadly things," the handsome traveling merchant added with a smile, bowing.

They, uh, they certainly weren't s-subtle, were they?
Storm adopted Maervidal's best stammer. "I'm, uh, I'm not
exactly sure what saisha is, that is, why is, um, why is it
so . . . important?"

"It costs much," the Borderer hissed, "because the Tash-lutan herbs it is made from are rare, and the recipe is secret. It paralyzes the entire body, save for the senses, the lungs, and the jaw—which it makes hang slack—for about three hours, then passes off as if it had never been there."

"And in your three hours," Murpeth purred, "we'll help you to a nice, private bed."

"A bed?" Maervidal asked faintly. "Will I, uh, feel sleepy?"

If Storm had been standing there as herself, she'd have asked sardonically, "Where you'll slay me while I can't resist? Well, try not to get blood on the linen." She'd almost said that, but caught herself in time. She had to remember she wasn't being Storm Silverhand just now, but a somewhat handsome, good-natured, scholarly scrivener—a scrivener who'd be so tremblingly scared by now, hemmed in by tauntingly sinister Zhentarim, that he'd be on the verge of filling his pants.

"Ah, uh, excuse me," the false Maervidal said, thrusting her glass into Murpeth's hand. "I—I must visit the jakes!"

She strode between the startled Zhent leader and the Borderer, who didn't slide across to block her rush quite quickly enough. Hearty laughter erupted around the false Maervidal instead, as if she'd said something hilarious. The scrivener almost scurried as she went, clapping a hand to the seat of her breeches as if in distress.

A cold-eyed Calivar Murpeth watched her go, and lifted one hand in a casual gesture. It was a subtle signal, but two men standing near among the chattering drinkers had been watching for it, and strolled over, lifting their glasses as if in salutation, to murmur, "Yes, lord?"

"The man we were talking to is a Harper. He knows we intend to kill him. Follow him into the jakes, swiftly, and prevent any Harper tricks."

"At once, lord," the two men said, turning in swift unison.

As Murpeth, Baraejhe, and Moongul watched them go, the Zhentarim leader murmured, "our best slyblades, sirs.

The more stout one is Wyndal Thone, and the taller, Blaeragh Ridranus. Thone once killed a Watchful Order mage of Waterdeep in the headquarters of the Order."

The eyebrows of the poisoner and the merchant who'd brought him were still rising when they saw Maervidal pause in his hurrying to look back at them all. Murpeth smiled grimly. "Yes. He's up to something."

"One man, in a jakes? He could kill himself, yes," Moongul said, scratching his chin thoughtfully with the lip of his glass, "but what else need you worry about? He doesn't look like much of a challenge. I think any one of my wives could easily down him, if they were both given knives."

"Wives?" the Borderer asked. "Many men find one more than enough."

The merchant smiled thinly. "Merchants who travel much tend to look for places they can relax at either end of a route. Few women know much about a merchant's route, let alone what's at the other end of it."

Murpeth smiled. "As to your question, Moongul, we worry about nothing, but try to keep costs down. If our fleeing scrivener sets fire to this place, or hauls out an enchanted sword, say, the costs of taking him increase. Some of our most powerful mages and priests can afford waste, but they tend to frown on ah, purely local wastage. You could say that fleeing man has already been a waste to us."

✳ ✳ ✳

When Thone and Ridranus shouldered their way into the jakes, they found it empty of the "purely local waste"— and everyone else. It had one small window, a vent grate, a washbasin, and the glory-stool. The first two were closed and secure, even when Ridranus pitted all of his not-inconsiderable strength against them, and he was a far stronger man than the fleeing scrivener. The third offered no concealment for anything larger than a spider, and the fourth emptied down a chute large enough for a cat, perhaps, but not a man. That left either magic, or—"That alcove, beside the door," Thone hissed, whirling around. "Quickly!"

When the two slyblades jerked the alcove curtains aside and plunged into the gloom within, they found themselves in a cloakroom. It held cloaks on pegs, a rude bench around the walls beneath the hanging cloaks, and a person, turned away from them with one foot up on the bench.

They could see it was not the scrivener. Out of habit the slyblades moved swiftly to block any escape before Thone murmured, "Excuse me . . ."

The lady escort who was standing adjusting her garters turned unconcernedly to face them, not bothering to lower her silvershot gown to cover the wisp of silk and the magnificent legs beneath. "Yes, gentlesirs?" she asked with a half smile. "If Talantha can be of service to you in any way. . . ."

Ridranus tried to lean and peer past her—one had to be sure, and the scrivener had been a smallish man, and he might be crouching under the bench in her shadow, mightn't he?—and she lifted an eyebrow at him. "Interested in spending a little coin?"

Long, painted-nailed fingers drew aside the gown to reveal a pert breast capped by a dangle-tassel made of fine strips of goldendazzle. Thone grinned at it despite himself.

When Ridranus started to rumble a refusal to the wench and thrust her aside, Thone caught at his comrade's wrist and said with a gleam in his eye, "Yes. Ten silver, to come and talk to us for an hour. The drinks are on us. There's some special wine we want you to try." His gaze swept slowly from her head to her toes, collecting her impish smile en route, and when he was done he added with a soft smile, "Depending on what we discuss, we may be able to find more coins later."

✳   ✳   ✳

The revel was in full swing—a term that for merchants had nothing to do with dancing and little to do with lady escorts. No, it had to do with swilling wine and gobbling trays of various succulent hand-tarts almost absentmindedly whilst talking . . .

. . . and talking, and talking, excitedly remaking the world and almost out of habit trying to forge deals. As the Zhentarim guided their find back through the clusters of loud, flush-faced men, Faerûn was being enthusiastically examined and reshaped, here in this crowded feast hall.

". . . if one contrives, from time to time, to stop lusting after things, much money and distress, I find, are to be saved."

". . . I think your attitude in this matter is weak—"

". . . some priests strive for the calm face, yes, but I find the nearest stump or statue can do the blank look even better—and probably think deeper thoughts than the priest, to boot."

". . . trappings of power, man? *What* trappings of power?"

Calivar Murpeth was looking like a thundercloud when the slyblades came back to his corner with a woman—an over-painted lady escort at that, despite the fact that she was very pleasant to look upon, and moved with quiet grace—and not a frightened scrivener. Thone went straight up to him and murmured in his ear, which resulted in a few more hand signs, and certain men hurriedly leaving the press of Sembian game hunters, outlander merchants of all sorts, and even a few dale shopkeepers still crowding the feast hall.

". . . so you have a fortune, yes, but do you *deserve* it?"

". . . the name escapes me, but I remember those br—"

"Yes, yes, just so. I remember them too."

". . . and 'tis a most reprehensible habit."

". . . yet it is obvious—to me at least—that our social spheres are widely different. You boast of something I would never dream of doing—that every Saerloonian, I daresay, would never dream of doing."

". . . you deceive yourself, sir. Why, I—"

". . . that strikes me as particularly scandalous. Why, the—"

". . . an immoral compromise! Now, your tyrannies—like Zhentil Keep, before the fall—don't get themselves into messes like that. Oh, no—swords out, a dozen dead, and on we all go. Much cheaper that way."

"Certainly much cheaper if you're one of those twelve, aha?"

When the men he'd signaled had all departed, Murpeth looked at the noisy crowd with distaste and said, "I think we'd all enjoy ourselves more in a private room. If you'll follow me?"

The Zhents all moved with him—and the lady escort, secure on Thone's arm, went with them. If that irritated Murpeth, he did not show it. The slyblade was the most deadly man of them all, and they all knew it.

The Borderer even murmured a joke about it as they climbed some stairs. "I thought you were an expert in *concealed* weapons," he remarked slyly. Thone's only response was a stone-faced wink.

The Zhentarim leader strolled up to doors that two armed guards flung open before him, and into a vast, richly-carpeted room above the feast hall. This one, however, was empty save for tables laden with food, wine, and lit candles, and a row of large merchants' strongchests along one wall. Moongul raised an eyebrow as he noticed them, and peered at them in a brief—and vain—quest for chalked merchants' marks, but said nothing.

Calivar Murpeth turned and spoke to them all, waving a hand at the tables. "Feel free," he said, and turned his gaze until he ended that invitation looking squarely at the lady escort.

She crossed her wrists upon her breast in the formal salute that the gently reared in the Dragonreach lands give to persons they see as nobility who outrank them, and Murpeth's cool gaze became visibly warmer. He smiled, inclined his head, and murmured, "I trust you are a lady of discretion?"

"In everything, lord," she breathed, looking straight into his eyes. "In *everything*."

Murpeth gave no sign that her answer had registered with him in any way, but the merchant Moongul cleared his throat and turned swiftly away with a low growl of arousal, deciding that it was high time to seek wine.

Aldluck Dreen rejoined them, looking grim and somewhat more sober. With him were several frightened-looking men. Aldluck stared at Talantha in astonishment, and she gave him a demure smile then turned again to look at the man who was holding her arm.

"Would you like to . . . talk?" she murmured, training eyes that were very large on him.

"Soon," Thone told her, guiding her over to a table and pouring her a generous glass from a slender bottle of wine. She did not fail to notice that the glass he poured for himself came from another bottle, of a different shape.

"Very soon," the slyblade told her, as Ridranus followed them like a large, patient shadow. "There's a little business to be attended to first."

Those words had barely left his mouth when one of the men Aldluck had brought paused in mid-word, with his mouth hanging open, and started to drool. He stood stock still, only his frightened eyes moving, roving back and forth in sudden panic, like an animal thrust into a cage. The woman who wore the shape of Talantha recognized him. This was Gustal Sorold, the night cook at the Old Skull, three years in the dale after departing his native Hillsfar, and a man she already knew was a Zhent agent.

He seemed to tremble all over, as if fighting the paralysis that gripped him, but at that moment the two slyblades left Talantha, as if in response to some signal she hadn't seen, and calmly took Gustal by the shoulders, plucked his feet off the ground, and marched him over to one of the chests. They opened it, took out a pair of dockers' hammers, calmly broke the paralyzed man's knees, and stuffed him into the chest. Then Thone leaned in and did something that made the little yipping and gargling noises the cook had been making stop—or rather, become strangled for a brief, frenzied period, then cease. He straightened up and turned away without a word, and in similar silence Ridranus reached out a long arm and calmly closed and latched the lid of the chest.

Some grim-faced men rushed into the room, then, and for one wild moment Talantha, who stood quietly sipping her wine by the table where Thone had left her, thought they were friends of the cook, here to rescue—or rather, now, avenge—him. The newcomers went straight to Murpeth, however, and muttered reports. Talantha took one idle step away from the tables, and that brought her close enough to hear that these men had scoured the woods around Warmfires and every closet and cellar of the house itself for Maervidal Iloster, and had done so in vain.

The Zhentarim leader acquired his thundercloud look again, but Moongul shrugged and said soothingly, "He'll turn up. You can hold another revel then."

"Wherever he is, he'll be paralyzed by now," the Borderer added quickly, then raised his glass and added, "Good wine. Thanks."

Murpeth nodded his acknowledgment with a distant, distracted air, and strode over to a knot of men who looked like Sembians of middling wealth. It seemed the Zhentarim were now calling on men of all ranks and station, weaving a web of intrigue rather than having spies report directly to the arrogant, ambitious magelings Manshoon had favored. Well, it made them harder to find. Storm drifted over to meet Thone and engage in a little flirtation. She didn't know how much longer this body would have.

※　　※　　※

It seemed all too soon when the warm tingling rose in her, like a sudden wave. Thone had been looking into her face for a while, now, and the change in his gaze told her he'd seen her react.

This must be the saisha. Storm could move freely—poisons didn't affect Chosen of Mystra in the ways they were supposed to—but she knew she wasn't supposed to be able to. She paused in the act of leaning forward to caress Thone's chin, froze, and let fear leak into her eyes.

Thone scooped her up without pause or ceremony, one hand around her shoulders and the other between her legs and up to grasp her belt at the back. Like a grain sack he swung her around, flung the curt words, "She's ready, lord," across the room to Murpeth, and strode toward a table.

Ridranus was already there. Having pinched the candles out with his fingers, he was now sweeping wine and food unceremoniously aside to clear a space. Thone dumped her down on it and turned away in the same whirling movement. Storm did not have to try to find some believable way to turn a paralyzed head to see where he was going: she knew he was headed for the fireplace.

Ridranus did not wait for Thone's return. "You're going to answer some questions about how our scrivener vanished," he said shortly, "and I have a promise for you, if you fail to tell all. We will hurt you, woman."

With deft, dispassionate fingers he arranged her on her back, arms and legs slightly spread from her body. "First," the slyblade murmured, "you will feel the hot fire irons Thone's retrieving right now on your skin, in the most tender places. If you still tell us false, or omit things of importance—and you'd be surprised at how much we do know, and can check against what you say—the irons will find your pretty face next. I imagine you'll have a hard time getting any man to hand you coins for your company after that."

He smiled bleakly, and drew himself up. "Then, 'twill be my pleasure, the breaking of your fingers, one by one. If even that fails," he sighed and regarded his fingernails, "the fire irons will be put into your eyes."

He reached out and gently turned her head to face the room, so she could see two servants putting down tiles, then a hot brazier atop them, as the crowd of Zhentarim gathered in a half circle to watch.

They parted for Thone, as he came from the main hearth with two red-hot pokers in his hands, then parted again to admit a thin, superior man in brown silks, who swept across the room like he owned it, aiming his sharp nose and beady eyes like weapons to sneer down everyone.

An insecure little mageling, Storm judged. His first words confirmed it. In nasal, supercilious tones, he looked down at her and announced, "Iyleth Lloodrun of Ordulin at your service, madam." He let his eyes travel the length of her silver-gowned form and added, "I am here in these scenic dales to hunt, and dislike to be kept from my killing, so I fear I shan't show you overmuch patience for lies or evasions. Answer plainly, and live."

He glanced at Thone, who signaled the readiness of the irons in the portable brazier with a nod, then gave Calivar Murpeth a curt nod, which was returned. The last murmuring gossip stilled, and in the silence that followed the mageling gave the assembled Zhentarim a superior little smile, turned his back on them, and cast a spell that would let him into her mind.

His eyes glittered as he stared down at her, and framed his first question. Storm heard it as a faint, distant whisper, her shields blocking its coercion completely.

In what regard do you know the scrivener Maervidal Iloster?

Storm just stared at him, letting her eyes go large and dark with fear. Lloodrun lifted his head and snapped, "She's protected."

There were murmurs of surprise from some of the watching Zhents. A lady escort, shielded? Well, she must be a Harper then, at least. Perhaps even an agent of Cormyr, or . . .

Calivar Murpeth gave a shrug that was almost insolent, to show the room that he had no fear of Zhentarim
wizards, and murmured, "So break whatever shields her.
Use all your spells, if that's what it takes. We'll wait."

The mageling stiffened, locked his eyes with those of
the local Zhentarim leader for a long, cold moment, then
turned back to the helpless woman on the table. He took
care that none of his fellow Zhentarim clearly saw the
spell he wove next, and Storm almost smiled.

This could go on for a long time, but she'd be keeping a
lot more folk than these evil louts waiting, so why not let
down her shields before this puny probe? From what she'd
glimpsed of his own mind, laid open in his probe into hers,
Faerûn would be well rid of this Zhentarim mageling, and
the sooner the better.

She let him straighten and smile in triumph at the
attentively-watching slyblades, who'd drifted to positions
on either side of him along the edge of the table where she
lay, before Storm laid bare the full fury of the divine fire
that smoldered within her and fried Iyleth Lloodrun's
brain in a sizzling instant.

Smoke actually puffed out of his ears and mouth as he
staggered back. His eyes spit tiny flames as they went dark
and sizzled, and he turned to vainly claw the air in front of
astonished, frightened Zhentarim faces, then toppled like a
tree, right onto his nose, with a crash that shook the room.

Everyone shouted and snatched out weapons. The room
was briefly lit to dazzling brilliance with the reflected fire
of so many daggers, drawn in wild unison, then everyone
went deathly silent at once.

Lying unmoving on the table, Storm could see the two
slyblades glaring at her. Their blades were out, their
grips hard and tense, and their eyes never left her for an
instant. Calivar Murpeth stepped forward and cleared
his throat loudly several times. He was obviously scared,
and at a loss to know what to do now, but aware that he
must boldly seize the moment and show himself a strong
leader or every one of the men in this room would know

just how weak he truly was, and begin plotting accordingly.

"Nildon Baraejhe," Calivar said at last, striving to sound coldly calm and managing only to sound brittle, "did you bring your mrildeen with you?"

The Borderer nodded. "Of course," he murmured, and jerked his head at the woman on the table. "An application to her head?"

Murpeth's lips tightened. "Of course," he echoed, his tone not quite mocking.

Baraejhe gave him a brief, wordless look of glacial warning, then strode to Storm, drawing a small, flat bottle from an underarm pouch. He spread a two-fingered dab of the clear, thick ointment on her throat, jaw, nose, and beside either eye before his fingers dipped to the back of her neck and lastly, to touch her upper lip. Where those deft fingers went, there came a tingling, as the mrildeen banished all paralysis in very small, specific spots under the skin it was applied to.

Before she might try to bite him, the Borderer's other hand struck her hard across her cheek, the hard slap turning her head to stare at the watching men. An instant later, he slapped her other cheek, giving her a view of the nearby wall and making her ears ring and eyes water. Again he struck her, and again, all of them hard blows that snapped her head back and forth.

"You'll get these full force, and not these gentle taps," he told her almost earnestly, as if explaining how a toy worked to an avid youth, "if you dare to scream. Do try to remember that."

One last blow almost tore one of her ears off, and left her half blinded by tears and half deaf from the roaring raging in her ears.

The Borderer stepped back, giving her a genial smile—she almost found herself trying to smile back at him—and Thone, Ridranus, and Murpeth converged on her in unison. Both of the slyblades plucked pokers from the brazier and held them over her, inches above her face and her breast, letting her feel the searing heat.

"Did you do something to our beloved mage?" Murpeth asked almost idly.

"N-no," Storm said, letting a tremulous sob govern her voice. "No! How could I?"

"Indeed," the Zhent leader purred. "How could you?"

He waved the two pokers away—back into the brazier they went—and let his fingers drop to her belly. Cold fingertips trailed up her smooth curves to stop, almost delicately, at her throat.

"I'm more interested," Calivar Murpeth remarked almost conversationally, "in how you helped Maervidal Iloster escape us earlier, and why. Is he a friend of yours? Or do you work together?"

"I—I don't know him," Talantha the escort said, then screamed as his hand fell like lightning to her breast, and tore off a little tassel, the brass claw that held it to her flesh and all.

It dripped blood as Murpeth held it up and told it gently, "I *do* hate liars—don't you?"

"I'm—I'm telling the truth, lord!" the lady escort sobbed. "Truly! I've never seen him before this night, when I helped him out the back door—the one we escorts use."

"And why did you do that?" Murpeth pounced. "Helping a stranger? Or a client?"

"N-neither, lord. *He* gave me coin to do it."

The Zhent leader glared at her. "Who?"

Talantha pointed with her eyes at Ridranus, standing beside the brazier with his arms folded and a grim little smile on his face. "That man, by the brazier. He threatened me, too, that if I refused he'd cut off my . . . cut off my . . ."

Murpeth whirled away from her and made a hand signal. Five men drew steel and started toward the slyblade in grim, careful unison.

Ridranus went white then red with fury, and snarled, "She lies!" as he brought his own weapon out again.

He was just in time to furiously parry the thrusting blades, but as he deftly turned aside reaching steel and took a quick step back to be out of immediate reach, a strangle wire snapped around his throat from behind. Murpeth and Thone watched like two statues as Ridranus fought like a frenzied man, twisting and kicking in a desperate attempt to topple his attacker over his head. When the slyblade did finally manage to drag the small, agile man forward, the man let go one handle of his wire, and swung on the other as he bounded away, slicing the slyblade's head half off.

As the shocked, staring face of Ridranus lolled crazily to one side and blood fountained in all directions, more than one of the watching Zhents whirled away and began to be noisily sick.

The dark-gloved, leather-clad strangler calmly retrieved his bloodied wire from the slumping corpse and turned back to Murpeth for further orders. The Zhent leader made a grim hand signal that seemed to mingle thanks and an order to "get hence, away."

Calivar Murpeth looked a little like he wanted to be sick himself, but his voice was calm enough, even drawling, as he drifted over to look down at the helpless escort and said, "Suppose you tell me more about the words you exchanged with the man who gave you coin to assist the scrivener out the door. Was there anyone with him?"

"Y-yes, lord. Four men, all with knives. I think one of them had a sword, too."

"I see. Did he name any of these men?"

"N-no."

"Did you see any of them clearly?"

"Yes, lord. All four."

The Zhentarim leader straightened up and gave the other men in the room a chilly smile. "Gentlesirs, I desire you to draw forth and let fall every last blade you carry—*now*—and approach this table."

There was a moment of uneasy hesitation, wherein the Zhentarim leader raised an eyebrow and said mildly, "I'm interested, you see, in exactly how many of you are tardy in following my orders. It will give me a fair idea of how far Maervidal Iloster has infiltrated our ranks with his people, and how many more bodies are going to decorate the floor of this chamber, this night."

He drew back out of their way smoothly, signing to Thone to watch all of the Zhents as they reluctantly dropped their weapons to the floor and shuffled forward. The glares many of them directed at the still, large-eyed woman on the table were not pretty to behold.

"Look up and down their ranks, lady," Calivar Murpeth said gently. "Say nothing until they step back, then I shall lean close, and you shall whisper to me if any of them stood with Ridranus when he gave you coin. Fear them not. Thone shall protect you."

He nodded his head at the surviving slyblade, who was holding a dagger ready in one hand, its hilt moving rhythmically back and forth as he fondled its tip between his thumb and first finger. Three drawn daggers waited in his other hand. Thone smiled and nodded his chin in her direction, but his eyes never left the line of reluctant men.

Who now, at Murpeth's gesture, stepped forward.

"Look well," the Zhent leader commanded Talantha, who kept her eyes wide, frightened, and bereft of any recognition as they roved back and forth along the tense, silent line of sullen men.

They stepped back in unison at another signal from Murpeth, who then leaned over and murmured, "Well?"

"The two closest to my feet," the lady escort quavered, "the one on the end, nearest my head, and the one three down from him—the one with white at his temples and the ring in his ear."

Calivar Murpeth gave her a brittle smile and straightened up again to enthusiastically rid his force of four competent men who were guilty of no more than being recognized by Storm from her days of farscrying Manshoon. Veteran killers and practiced thieves, all of them, deserving of death a dozen times over that she knew of, and probably hundreds more that she did not, but no more guilty of assisting Maervidal to escape than Ridranus had been.

"Strabbin Stillcorn, Rungo Baerlan, Raelus Ustarren, and Worvor Drezil," Murpeth said in cold tones. "Step back."

One of the men swore, another spun and started to run, only to stiffen, stagger a few steps, then fall heavily on his side with Thone's dagger in the back of his neck.

"Slay at will," the Zhent leader told his slyblade calmly, drawing his own slender sword.

A dagger whipped out of Thone's hand even as he murmured, "A pleasure, lord." In the candlelight, it flashed end over end like a streak of dancing flame. Across the room, a darting man coughed out a sudden desperate sob, twisted around to claw vainly at the air, and fell, wallowing feebly in his own blood.

Even before his victim struck the floor, the slyblade was gliding forward to intercept the third and fourth men, who'd snatched up weapons from the scattering of discarded ones on the floor and charged Murpeth.

The Zhent leader hastily stepped behind Thone, and the two men instantly lost all enthusiasm for their attack, but almost as swiftly realized they were as doomed if they abandoned it as if they proceeded. First one then the other shrugged at the fate yawning before them, then, with savage yells, they came on again.

The slyblade ducked, moved his arms in a flurry of hurled daggers, re-arming, and guard thrusts, then lunged forward, both of the last pair of daggers in his hands buried to the hilts in the chest and throat of one foe while the other reeled, a dagger quivering in his right eye, and toppled slowly to the floor.

As Thone wrestled aside the body on his blades, another Zhent loomed up over Talantha. It was the man who'd slain Ridranus with his strangling wire.

There was a very large dagger in his hand now, and his face blazed with bright anger. "I'll bet there's a lot more you could tell us, wench," he snarled, "if someone really made you want to talk."

"Toarin!" Murpeth shouted. "Stand away from her. *Now!*"

Unhurriedly the Zhent slayer reached out to slide his dagger up Storm's ribs to prick the underside of one breast. "I can't hear you, Murpeth," he said merrily. "Perhaps it's the sound of my friends Strabbin and Rungo, crying out to me of their innocence. Why you let this bitch condemn us at random, I'll nev—"

"Toarin Klustoon!" Murpeth snarled. "Stand away from that woman *at once!*"

"Toarin," Thone said a moment later, his voice a quiet, warning promise.

The Zhent slayer snarled in wordless disgust and flung down his blade. It bit into the tabletop a whisper away from Storm's flank, where the blood from her breast was trickling down, humming with Toarin's fury.

The slayer whirled around again, and this time a poker from the brazier was glowing a sullen red in his gloved hands. "Tell the truth, whore," he said loudly, "or I'll—"

He made a thrusting motion at her crotch, and several straying silver threads sizzled as they shriveled away from the heat. Wondering how much longer she should put up with this—after all, what of value were these men going to reveal?—Storm lay still and waited for real pain to begin.

Instead, as so often happens in the life of a Chosen, she was given something else.

Storm, dearest!

"Mother" Syluné, as I live and breathe. Have you been watching?

Aye, but not watching you. What befalls?

Flat on my back, as usual, here in the dale. I'm entertaining some Zhents who think they're entertaining me. Affectionate fellows they are. We've reached the "hot pokers to the womb" stage.

Syluné sent a flare of alarm, then, *Need you aid?*

No, no. These are just the local threaten-and-bluster boys. What aid can I render your way, though? I can tell when you're all upset, Softspoken, and you're upset right now.

Well, it is *urgent. Lassra—at my urging, mind, not on one of her crack-Red-Wizard-bones-and-drink-their-blood moods—set out to slay a grand harvest of Red Wizards. She shaped herself into an imprisoning sphere, englobing them, and the spells they hurled have left her a—well, a dangerously weakened shell. Elminster is her refuge while she rebuilds herself. In the meantime, if the ever-adventuresome Storm could just take care of this little problem?*

Certainly, provided you stop being coy long enough to tell me which little problem this might be. Names, faces, and deeds, please, sister. I'm not the Chosen who likes to slaughter every Thayan my eyes fall upon, remember?

Lassra smashed most of the sorcerous end of a cabal all six of your sisters have been tracing for a while now, but there's at least one of note left, one often easily tracked by those who can watch the Weave.

The crotch of the silvershot gown was truly aflame now, flaring up in front of Klustoon's furious face.

Sister, my nether hair is ashes and my flesh is beginning to cook. Get on with it!

Through the flame's rising, searing orange tongue, Storm could see the slyblade Thone, face dark with his own anger, almost casually holding back Calivar Murpeth with one hand.

Halaster! Syluné told her. *We need you to track down the Mad Mage.*

The Zhent murderer in front of her growled to get her full attention, and slowly drew back his arm. In a moment, he'd thrust the hot poker forward . . .

Well, at least you got around to telling me which *mad mage. Later, sister!*

Storm sat up, letting her flesh start the slide back into her own shape as she caught hold of the poker, twisting and yanking with a sudden surge of strength. The pain made her face go white, but in an instant the fire iron was hers alone, and Toarin Klustoon's chin was plowing helplessly into her knees.

Through the sizzle and stink of her own burning flesh, Storm told the room pleasantly, "I'd love to stay for more of these Heartsteel thrills, but I'm afraid more pressing matters have arisen."

Toarin found balance enough to lift himself off her and grab for a dagger. As Storm's hair began to swirl out to its true length and turn to silver, the gathered Zhents fell back with a general murmur of recognition and fear. She smiled tightly as she bent the poker, the muscles of her arms and shoulders rippling, and wrapped it around her interrogator's neck. Toarin Klustoon screamed as the flesh of his throat sizzled, then burst into helpless tears as his howls and shrieks of pain rose swiftly to a deafening, wordless babble.

Storm regarded him sourly for a moment, then took hold of the protruding ends of the poker, put her strength to them—and broke the Zhent slayer's neck.

As Klustoon fell to the ground, wet bubbling spraying from his lips, a dagger flashed and winked as it came whirling through the air at Storm. She put up one ruined hand and caught it in deft fingers, twirling it for only a brief moment before she flipped it through the air on a side journey—one that ended in the throat of Calivar Murpeth.

The Zhent leader stared at her over its hilt in disbelief as his rich red blood fountained out. "You weren't— You mustn't—" Murpeth struggled to say, before his knees gave way beneath him and he sat down into an ignoble, strangling crash to the floor. He kicked feebly at the floor once, but then did not move again.

Storm got up off the table, herself once more. The pain in her hands was a raging fire, but already they were beginning to heal, ashes falling away as her skin began to creep back over the seared bones.

The Zhents had fallen back to the far reaches of the room, and were eyeing the door but making no charge toward it yet. The small, cold-eyed assembly of servants that had just gathered out of nowhere to stand blocking it, a glittering array of weapons in their hands, might have had something to do with that.

The Bard of Shadowdale kept her eyes on the only man still standing close to her. The man who'd thrown the dagger just now. A Zhentarim slyblade named Thone.

"I believe," she said calmly, drifting toward him as gracefully as if she wore a High Lady's gown, "you owe me some money. Ten silver, was it not?"

The assassin held up empty hands in a gesture of surrender. "Lady Storm," he gasped, "I'd never have lifted a hand against you, had I known—"

She crooked an eyebrow, not slowing her deliberate advance.

Thone swallowed, licked his lips, and said, "Ah, just kill me quickly—please." He backed away from her, pushing the air with his hands as if he could somehow slow her down. "There's just one thing I'd like to know before I die," he blurted out, looking into her angry eyes. "How did you know?"

"Know about *what?*" Storm snapped, advancing on him like a stalking cat.

"Th-that I write the Heartsteel books," he replied, as the color slowly fled from his face in fear. "I'm almost done with one now . . ."

"*You* write the Heartsteel—?"

"*Heart in a Clenched Gauntlet, Kisses Like Iron, Blackserpent's Caress, Redwyrm's Revenge,* yes, yes," Thone quavered. "*Tower Sundered at Twilight, The Dragon's Gentle Claw . . .*"

As Storm Silverhand took him by the throat, she murmured, "Well, now. Well, now . . ."

A smile rose to her lips, and she added pleasantly, "You've afforded my sister Syluné and myself much amusement. Perhaps even, at times, when you meant to. For this, you may live."

Startlement showed in his eyes—in the instant before the left hook that had started near her knees took him under the chin, snapping his head back as if it belonged to a wooden doll and not a living man.

The Bard of Shadowdale caught the slyblade as he slumped, and heaved him up into the air with another rippling of muscles. She slung Thone's limp body over one shoulder and strode to the door, where a grim-faced cook was wiping his hands on his apron amid a wall of somber servants.

Storm glanced down at her hands—still grotesque, but no longer burned to the bone—then up at the cook. "Rendal," she said gently, "You can take them all down now."

The cook saluted her, as one Harper to another, and nodded his head at the slyblade's dangling form. "Him, too?"

Storm smiled. "No. He lives." Rendal Ironguard nodded, turned, and made two swift signals with his hands. The servants surged into life, charging across the room at the remaining Zhents.

"Harpers all," Storm murmured, watching the tumult.

Screams came to her ears from below as the pitched battle spread. There'd be fleeing guests all over Northend in a few minutes, but her folk knew their Zhents. Such open violence was a crude lapse of style, but necessary— the more so if she was going to be busy chasing down a truly mighty wizard.

" 'Tis a pity, truly," she told the senseless man on her shoulder, "that so few servants are to be had for hire in the dales. One ends up having to accept almost anyone."

She gave Thone an experimental shake to be sure he was securely seated—and truly deep in his temporary retreat from the world—and started down the stairs. That cloakroom would do to strip him of strangling cords and hidden knives and suchlike, then Syluné could keep him hard at work on Heartsteel epics, back at the farm, while Storm went hunting Halasters.

"I hear they're bad at this time of year," she remarked brightly to a terrified Zhentarim who came pounding up the stairs at that moment—before she put her boot in his face and sent him plunging back down onto the blades of the Harpers pursuing him.

"Boys, boys—no fires, now!" Storm warned the Harpers grinning at her. They saluted her and clattered back down the stairs. Someone screamed in the room behind her, and someone else struck a wall with a crash that made her wince.

One of these days the Zhentarim might just learn patience enough not to get in each other's way all the time, and plunge into carrying out plans they hadn't finished considering the consequences of. If they ever did that, the dales might truly have something to fear.

Of course, to reach that level of competence, the Zhents were going to have to ferret out the Red Wizards and other traitors hiding in their midst, who customarily used them as dupes and clumsy weapons against folk in the Dragonreach lands. That and the tensions between Manshoon and Fzoul should keep them busy for a while yet. . . .

"Sleeper, awake," Storm growled at the slyblade. "I've got to go hunting mad mages."

＊　　＊　　＊

Hubris is the shared chink in all our armor.

Elminster's voice was a grudging growl in her mind. She could feel the warmth of his affection, and knew she'd started smiling.

Taerach Thone looked up fearfully from the far end of the kitchen table for perhaps the hundredth time. Almost unconsciously his hand dropped down to caress the hilt of the belt dagger they'd returned to him, then jerked back as if he'd committed a shameful crime. Storm sighed. Did he think she was going to tear him limb from limb, after carrying him all the way here, bathing him, and putting him to bed?

In her mind, she replied to Elminster, *And so?*

Through the link, she could see the Old Mage floating in the warm, dark room where the Weave surged and roiled like silent surf. Back to back, held pressed together in a human star, he and the Simbul were floating together, as he fed her from his own life-force. Let Mystra smile upon them both.

Halaster likes to weave a little trap into his enchantments, to give his apprentices—or anyone else—who breaks one of them a little slap of reproval, a jolt that tells the recipient whose lash they're feeling. Thus, a distinctive signature is woven into almost his every casting. In Undermountain, of course, they stand clustered and piled atop each other like pebbles on a beach. Outside of its passages, those who use Weavesight can easily find the work of Halaster.

Does it seem so sensible to you, El, Storm replied, *that I, among the weakest of us Chosen in the Art, should be the one to go hunting Halaster Blackcloak? If defeating this cabal matters, shouldn't one of us who might have a real hope of victory against him be the one to—?*

Halaster is waiting for just such a battle, ready with spells hung to trigger other spells in a nasty little inferno. If I pile protections upon ye—protections that need not be set aside to allow ye to hurl spells out at him—I can keep ye alive long enough to reach him.

And do what? she asked. *Slay him? Mystra above, man, he controls more gates to other planes and places than either of us know. The stability of some cellars in Waterdeep, and the buildings and streets above them, depend on his enchantments. To say nothing of the fact that he polices Undermountain better than any of us ever could, and could ravage any place we fought with the spells he carries—and the contingencies that will be triggered if he dies!*

Gently, lass, gently there. He's not acted like this before. I think someone has a hold over him, and I need ye to find out whom, and to deal with it.

I'm not sure I'm looking forward to dealing with anyone—or anything—that can maintain a hold over Halaster Blackcloak.

Grim and rueful that sounded, even to her. Storm took two strides over to a pot that needed stirring before it overflowed, felt the anxious eyes of Taerach Thone on her again, and added, *Wouldn't I be better employed tracking down the rest of this little group? They won't all retire instantly the moment we remove the mages from their midst, you know. I sometimes think we live in a Faerûn far removed from the real one. We always have spells and mages and potential castings and abuses on our minds, when most folk worry about being too cold or not having enough to eat, or about cruel laws and crueler armsmen coming to back them up.*

So we do. It's another failing we share. Elminster's voice in her mind was calm, almost weary. *Are ye getting too tired for this, Storm? Shall I leave off pestering ye?*

Nay, nay, Old Mage. Never leave off pestering me. It's all I have left of my childhood.

He chuckled, then, and Storm staggered as he thrust a whirlwind of flashing lines and knots of force into her mind. Thone tensed, as if to rise, but sat back when she gave him a glare and shook her head.

Blood of Mystra, El, what in the name of all tankard-tapping trolls was that?

Halaster's signature. Got it?

My mind feels as if it's swollen with child—a kicking child, she replied. *Yes, I have it, Lady smite thee.*

Good. Now, get out thy trivet.

My trivet? Old Mage . . . ?

I took the liberty, lass, upon my last biscuit-snatching sweep through thy kitchen, of doing a casting.

On my trivet. Well, it's nice to know archmages have enough to do, to fill up their gray-whiskered, dragging days. Once they get tired of taking on attractive young apprentices.

Don't claw, lass, 'tisn't pretty. Got it out yet?

Of course.

Storm let all the sarcasm she could muster drip through those two words, but Elminster's voice rolled on as gently as if he'd never heard her. *Put thy hand upon it and tell Syluné not to be alarmed if a few sparks come out of ye. Eyes, nose, mouth—that sort of thing. You'll be needing a fair cloak of spells upon ye to go up against Halaster. This may take some time. If ye've something on the stove, move it off.*

Storm sighed and did as she was told. Thone's eyes grew large and round at what she said then, but he said nothing—even when the fingertips of a hand rose out of the ironwork to clasp Storm's hand, and the Bard of Shadowdale stiffened, every hair on her body shot out straight, and her bare feet rose gently to hover a few feet off the kitchen floor. Syluné had to give him a warning murmur to keep him in his seat, however, when lightning began to play around Storm's toes.

✷ ✷ ✷

Syluné let her head loll onto her shoulder as she slumped down in the old high-backed armchair, and after a short time let gentle snoring sounds come out of her. She needed no spell to feel the frowning gaze of Taerach Thone on her, nor to hear the faint rattle of his quill going into the drip bottle. Slyblades learn to move with infinite care and stealth. Syluné barely heard him pass by her and out the door. She waited until he was three catlike steps down the passage before drifting up from her body to follow him, invisible and curious.

✷ ✷ ✷

Beyond the grain sacks piled ceiling-high at one end, waiting for the harvest a season away, the room was empty except for the floating woman.

A faint, flickering glow outlined Storm Silverhand, and stole out to fade just shy of the corners of the room. She was floating in midair, flat on her back and about chest high off the floor.

Thone took a cautious step away from the door he'd just slipped through, and peered to see if her eyes were open or shut. He felt somehow more comfortable when he saw that her eyes were closed. She seemed more alert than truly asleep; in a trance, perhaps. There was a very faint humming—almost a singing—coming from her body. It was coming from all over her, not her mouth alone. This must be the hunt for Halaster she'd mentioned to her sister. The hunt that would doom someone, if it succeeded.

Thone took a step closer to the floating woman, and watched her silver hair warily. It rippled in a rhythmic pulse, unchanged by his presence. He licked dry lips and cast a swift glance back at the door behind him.

All was silence and emptiness. He'd slipped away from the sleeping witch, and was now free to slay a woman Manshoon himself was said to fear. Whenever a scheme to seize the dale was advanced, it was said, and the inevitable plot to draw the mage Elminster elsewhere was outlined, Manshoon always murmured, "But there are harps . . . all too many serve Storm in that dale. What of her?"

It would take only a few moments. Immortal or not, no woman could live on with her head cut from her body. Thone stroked the handle of his dagger as he stood over her, looking down.

Aye, they'd given him back his belt blade. Why? Were these women so stupid, or so proud in their power? How many hundred years did the bards insist they'd been alive in Faerûn?

There must be a trap. Some spell or other to smash him away into the nearest wall if he drew steel here. Yet, what magic could possibly flare up swiftly enough to stop him ripping open her throat?

With a sudden swift, darting movement he drew his dagger and hefted it in his hand, seeing the reflected glow gleam back at him from it. He held his breath, but, as the seconds passed, nothing happened. He sighed out air, and started to breathe again. So, steel was drawn and he yet lived.

There were mages back in the citadel who grew pale at the mere mention of the Bard of Shadowdale. There were men in Teshwave who spat curses and fingered old scars when the Harpers of Shadowdale were mentioned, and men around the fires spoke of "the undying Storm" who led them.

And there was Ridranus to avenge.

Taerach Thone's lips tightened, and he raised his weapon. He never saw Syluné drifting with him, because there was nothing to see. She glided in to encircle his wrist as mist too soft to feel—yet—and called up the magics she'd need to blast him in an instant, Heartsteel sequels or no Heartsteel sequels.

Taerach Thone held his glittering dagger ready and looked down at the floating woman. A kind of wonder grew in his face, as the long, silent seconds passed. Then, in a sudden, almost furious movement, he thrust his dagger back into its sheath and stepped back.

He raised his hand in a sort of salute before he slipped back out of the room, as softly and as silently as he'd come.

✻   ✻   ✻

"Off you go," Syluné said gently, as she drew back from the kiss and turned away. Behind her, without sound or fuss, Storm Silverhand abruptly vanished. The Witch of Shadowdale let the spell-glow fade from around her wrists and gave the watching slyblade a wry smile.

"Seen enough for a few good scenes yet?"

Thone shook his head, disbelief in his eyes. "Lady," he said hesitantly, "what I'd heard about you silver-haired sisters was far indeed from what I've seen here. I . . . you even have *all* of my books in the kitchen. I'm still a little stunned that you trust me here."

Syluné smiled. "You've earned it."

"I have?"

"In this room, not so long ago, when you drew your dagger and didn't use it," the Witch of Shadowdale said crisply, as she swept out the door.

Thone gaped at her departing back, went as pale as old snow, then, moving in sudden haste, followed her back to the kitchen. When he got there, the room was empty of witches, but a warm mug of soup was waiting by his chair. It smelled wonderful.

* * *

The tall, gaunt man hummed to himself as he drew forth small folded scraps of parchment from the crevices of a carved face on the door of a certain vault, unfolded and read them, and either slid them back into their resting places or replaced them with other folded messages. A ring like a great green beetle shone on his finger in the faint glow of the tomblight enchantments as he worked, rapidly filling a small, hovering tray.

Such a scene could be observed nightly, by those able to win past the forbidding guards of many a priest, in most of the crypts in the City of the Dead. However, these parchments were not prayers, and the white-haired man in the tattered brown robes was no priest.

Moreover, he had no guards. A dark shimmering in the air around him kept wandering mourners at bay even more effectively. He was always alone, no matter how frenetic bustling Waterdeep might become, close around him.

Reading the little missives always amused him. The writers went to such great lengths to make them cryptic to all who weren't part of the group, in case they fell into other hands. Neither Labraster nor the growling woman—Malsander, that was her name—had picked up their messages for a long while, now. Perhaps he should . . . but no. What these fools did to make themselves feel important mattered not a whit to him.

Only the dark bidding that drove him mattered, and the fascination he shared with it. That silv—

A small sound came to his ears from just behind him, and Halaster Blackcloak whirled around. Something soft brushed his cheek, something that made his skin tingle, and he found himself staring into the dark, merry eyes of a woman with silver hair, whose nose was almost touching his own. She was as tall as he, and clad in foresters' leathers that had seen much use. She spread empty hands to show him that she held no weapon, though he could see a long sword scabbarded at one hip, and daggers riding in at least three places. His face grew hard nonetheless. She should not have been there.

She should not have been able to step through his spellsmoke. No one not mighty in Art should be able to pass through it. She should not be unfamiliar to him and yet, of course, she must be one of the Seven Sisters, one not often seen in Waterdeep.

Therefore—he sighed—he must essay the inevitable: "Who are you?"

He made his voice as cold and unwelcoming as he felt. Perhaps he could bargain for a taste of what he sought, before things came to battle. To do that, this intruder must be made to feel beholden.

"One who wonders why the great Halaster consorts with reckless Thayan fools, drow, and sneak thieves," Storm replied in level tones. Her eyes flicked to the floating tray. "And reads their mail," she added, her voice firm and yet cool.

Halaster frowned at her, lifting a hand to his tingling cheek. She must have . . . kissed him?

"I'm not accustomed to bandying words with overbold lasses, whate'er their obvious charms," he said coldly, "or the greatness they may think long years grants them. Render unto me your name, and the truth as to why you are here and what you've just done to me, or I'll blast you down into lasting torment as a crippled serpent under my boots."

"Now *that's* a charming maiden-catching manner," Storm replied.

The Mad Mage said not a word in reply, nor made any gesture that she could see, but from his fingertips lightning leaped, crackling at her in angry chorus. Its snarling and spitting rose loud in her ears, and the force of its fury made her body shake, yet she strode through it unafraid to push his out thrust hand aside.

"You'll have to do better than that," she murmured into his face.

Was she reaching her lips up to his? Gods, yes—

Halaster's eyes narrowed, and he made a quick, flicking gesture with one finger. The tomblight failed, the tray plummeted to ring on the flagstones underfoot, and the world exploded into white roaring flame.

When its fury died, Storm could tell from the surging and eddying around her that the outermost of Elminster's shieldings had been shredded, and now clung to her limbs on the verge of flickering collapse. Yet she smiled easily, knowing she had to goad him.

"Is that all? Be not timid, Blackcloak!" she said heartily, her innocent enthusiasm as much a taunt as if she'd spat curses at him.

The world exploded into purple fire this time.

Its fury was such that Storm found herself on one knee when it faded, her ears ringing, her eyes blurred with tears, and another two shieldings gone. Halaster was glaring at her with a sort of angry triumph, but she made herself rise, give him a pitying smile, and say, "Ah, but archmages certainly aren't what they were when I was but a little lass."

She fought her way through the swirling claws that he conjured next, ignoring the places where they stabbed through her last few shieldings to draw cold and bloody slices across her arms, shoulders, and thighs. When she brushed blindly against Halaster, Storm put her arms around him in a lover's embrace, entwining her legs around his.

He growled in fear and distaste, and she found herself grasping a sphere of bony plates surmounted by many staring eyestalks. She hissed in distaste, pulling her head back from the thrusting eyes even as she clung hard to the spicy-smelling beholder.

It shifted and wriggled under her, and became a barbed, conelike bulk whose tail stabbed at her repeatedly. The jaws that split the top of the cone snarled and tried to bite her, as the four arms that fringed it strained to pull her into its mouth. Storm clung close to the sharp body, wincing at the gashes it dealt, and found herself clawing to keep her hold on the smooth scales of a twisting serpent whose wings crashed against her in a furious flailing. Jaws snapped in vain and smoking green spittle flew.

The serpent became a white-haired man again, snarling, "Why did you kiss me, wench? What do you want?"

"I kissed you to set a hook in you, Halaster," Storm told him, "to stay with you no matter what transformations you work, or where you hurl us. If your spells hurt me, the same hurts shall also make you suffer."

"But why?"

"I want to know why Halaster Blackcloak became part of this cabal whose folk are so clumsy, and whose work is so far from what has concerned you for so long. Why are you meddling in backstreet taverns in Scornubel and aiding slavers in the cellars of Waterdeep? How does a mighty wizard gain anything by such work?"

Their surroundings suddenly changed. The tomb was gone, whirled away in a smoky chaos that revealed a dark, echoing, water-dripping place somewhere underground, with a purple glow in its distant reaches.

"Behold and learn then, Chosen of Mystra," Halaster hissed. "Come."

They moved together, bodies entwined as they drifted along on a spell breeze, up to the source of the glow. It was a simple, massive black block of stone, lying like a lone, gigantic clay brick on the floor, the purple glow swirling restlessly in the air just above it. There were no graven runes, and no braziers or anything else that Storm could see, yet she knew she was looking upon an altar—an altar to Shar.

"You've taken to worship in your declining days?" she asked, making her voice sharp with incredulity. Goad, then goad some more.

"The Goddess . . . of the Night . . ." Halaster gasped, seeming to suddenly have to struggle to speak, "desires—"

He gurgled and choked for some time, but as Storm clung to him, she did not think he was descending into one of his bouts of madness. No, some entity was trying to master him, to prevent the trembling wizard from saying something he very much wanted to say.

She dared to stroke him with a soothing hand, and whisper the release of a small purgative spell she carried for banishing diseases and infections. Halaster shuddered under her, as if he were a frightened horse, and Storm realized they'd somehow ended up lying on the altar together—or rather, the archmage was lying on it, and she was clinging to him.

"—desires . . . what I do!" Halaster snarled, then twisted under her like a frenzied thing, biting and bucking and kicking.

His magic lifted them and whirled them over and over in the air. One of Storm's elbows struck the stone altar as they spun, and blazed up into numb fire. Her hold slipped, and like a striking snake Halaster was out and over her and slamming her down onto the altar with all the magical force he could muster. Purple fires flowed hungrily over them both.

Storm bucked and twisted in turn, but the room was shaking with the force of the magic now roaring up out of the altar to augment Blackcloak's spell. Her shoulders were pinned to the warm, throbbing stone as if all of Mount Waterdeep were gripping her and holding her there.

Halaster clambered down off her slowly amid the streaming purple flames, his eyes bright. Storm saw that he was looking at the places on her body that he'd bitten, and where his spell-claws and stinging tail had drawn blood. Thin threads of silver fire were rising up into the roiling purple radiance from them, as if milked forth.

"The silver fire," Halaster whispered, thrusting his face close to Storm. "Shar wants it even more than I, and took to riding my mind not so long ago, stealing in when I was . . . away."

He stretched forth a trembling hand to a tiny wound his teeth had made high on her shoulder, and gasped, "Give it to me. *Give it to me!*"

"Halaster," Storm told him, "you have but to serve Mystra to gain it, obeying her as we Seven have chosen to do, but Our Lady shall never surrender it to such as Shar."

The purple radiance flared up and seared away darkening, fading shieldings then, smiting her all over as if with many smiths' hammers. Storm was shaken like a leaf in its pounding, bone-shattering fury.

Halaster stared down at her as if in amazement, as the silver fire his finger had touched was snatched away from him by the rushing purple flames. He looked for a moment as if he wanted to cry, then to chortle in glee. As Storm watched him, through the roaring and her pain, his face twisted and trembled. He barked, suddenly, like an angry, excited dog, then threw back his head and bayed before hurling himself on the woman struggling on the altar, twisting and panting and clawing at her. Sharp pains faded as his hungry hands clutched her broken bones, and they shrank away, healing at his touch.

The archwizard's furious assault dragged her off the stone into a helpless tumble, and instantly Storm could breathe—and scream out her pain—again. Purple fire stabbed forth in angry fingers to claw at the whimpering bard and the puzzled-looking wizard as they stared into each other's eyes, locked in a frozen embrace, and Halaster asked in a very quiet, precise voice, "Excuse me, but are you one of my apprentices? I don't believe I've had the pleasure—"

"No, and I'm thinking you won't be having it any time soon, Blackcloak," Storm hissed into his startled face, "if you don't get us both back out of here—*now!*"

It was a gambit that almost worked. The mad archwizard frowned thoughtfully, as if trying to remember something, lifted one hand to trace something in the air, then shook his head and said in quite a different voice, "Oh, no, I don't think I could do that."

"Halaster!" Storm roared at him, slapping his face as the purple fire rose into a shrieking howl, tugging at them enough to drag them a few inches across the stone floor. "Listen to me!"

"Thy voice is tarble upon the ears, jibby, yet thou'rt strange to me. Yield thy name, I pray," he quavered in reply, his voice different again. Storm growled, wrapped her arms and legs around him as if he were a pole she was trying to slide down, and rolled their locked bodies over and over, away from the altar.

The last of Elminster's shieldings slid away from around Storm as they went, passing into her in a healing that banished pain and brought back vigor from end to end of her body. She almost laughed aloud at the sheer pleasure it brought.

Halaster burst into angry tears, like a child who's had a toy snatched from him, and was clawing at her again. "Give it!" he sobbed. "Give it back!"

The threads of silver fire were gone, vanished with her healing. Snarling and barking, the wizard became a great black wolf, then a thing of talons and scales, panting, "Shrivel! Shred! Shatter!"

"Syluné," Storm told the room grimly, as fresh fires in her breast announced that the claws had torn open her flesh once more, "you've a lot to answer for. Next time, call on someone else."

Silver smoke billowed up from her in a bright glow, and Storm fought to slap away Halaster's head as it became snouted and many-fanged once more, and promptly snapped at her. She never saw the deeper darkness gather above the altar, and slowly open two cold, glittering eyes of dark purple.

Halaster's head was now a thing of questing tentacles, darting at her eyes and up her nostrils, sliding in a surge of cold slime into her ears.

In the gloom of the temple under Waterdeep, there came a shining forth of the Weave. The air filled with the bright sweep of a glittering net of glowing stars, stars that threw back the darkness and the purple orbs as two blue-white eyes, each as large as a coach, opened briefly to regard the struggling humans.

When the blue-white radiance faded, the bard and the wizard twisted and strained in darkness, their only light the sparks and tongues of silver fire leaking from between them.

The purple glow returned briefly, flaring up like a flame on the altar, but the blue-white flash that came out of nowhere to slash at that flame was so bright and sudden that the stone of the altar groaned aloud, and smaller stones fell from the ceiling here and there, clattering down around the two humans.

Storm and Halaster panted and struggled against each other for a long time before silver radiance flared. The Mad Mage hissed at the pain it brought him as he tried to lap at it, his wolf head sporting an impossibly long tongue. His other limbs had become snakelike coils, each wrapped thickly around one of Storm's broken limbs. She lay helpless under him, spread-eagled on the stones with her front laid open down past her navel. Silver fire flared up around her heaving, glistening internal organs in an endless, pumping sequence of dancing flames. More flames licked out between her parted, whimpering lips, and the hungry wizard bent his head to feed.

Unheeded, the stones between them and the altar were heaving upward, as if something long and snakelike were reaching out from under the freshly cracked block of stone, burrowing along at a speed no mole had ever reached. The line of heaving stones was heading straight for the spot where the helpless Chosen of Mystra lay.

* * *

"What's happening?" Thone asked, as Syluné swayed and threw up her hands. "Can I help?"

Blue-white fire spiraled around her, rising up with a muted scream, and Thone found himself trembling from the sheer force of magic rushing through the room—Art that howled and roared up, then was gone.

In the sudden stillness, Syluné let her arms fall back to her sides and sighed. Thone found he could move again, and that he felt very sad. As the Witch of Shadowdale walked to the window end of the kitchen, all the light in the room seemed to move with her, leaving him in deep shadow.

The Zhentarim slyblade stared down at his hands, and found that they were shaking, and that he was struggling on the edge of bursting into tears.

* * *

In a lamp-lit chamber in southern Thay a man stiffened, lifted his head sharply, then sketched two swift gestures in the air.

"As you wish, holy Shar," he whispered to the empty air around him, an instant before the lights in his eyes went out forever. He toppled onto his side with no more sound than a whisper, as if he were made of paper.

An apprentice looked up sharply, in time to see the body of his master settle onto the rugs like a dry, hollow husk. Empty eye sockets stared up into the lamplight forever.

✻   ✻   ✻

In two places not so far apart, sudden blue-white fire swirled, and two men found they hadn't even time to open their mouths and exclaim before the fire was gone again, and they were somewhere else.

They were somewhere underground—a chamber of dark stone where Dauntless and Mirt stood gaping at each other, then at the sole source of light in the room, a few paces away. Fitful silver fire rose from a silver-haired figure who lay sprawled on her back, gasping feeble plumes of flame as a monster crouched atop her, licking at the fire that rose from her.

"Ye gods!" Mirt snarled, as he bounded forward, past a racing upheaval of stones. He thrust his trusty dagger into the beast's nearest eye.

Dauntless said less and ran faster. His sword took the squalling creature in the throat, thrusting twice as it collapsed forward onto the woman. The stones of the floor rose up like a clutching hand around them both, creaking and rumbling.

With startled oaths the two Harpers kicked aside stones and stabbed down into what flared up from beneath. It seemed no more than glowing purple smoke, but it ate away their blades as if it were acid, spewing sparks at their every thrust. Wordlessly they dropped useless hilts into it and snatched out dagger after dagger, thrusting like madmen into the empty, glowing air they stood on, until at last the purple radiance flickered and faded.

It seemed to retreat back into crevices beneath the floor stones, and Dauntless eyed it narrowly as Mirt plucked aside the beast's shoulder, which seemed to dwindle under his fat and hairy hand.

At another time, the wheezing moneylender might have stopped to peer curiously at the vanishing monster. Now, however, as snakelike tentacles melted away, he had eyes for nothing but the white, drawn face coming into view from beneath it.

"Storm Silverhand!" Mirt swore, and scrabbled among secret places in his worn and flapping breeches for one of the potion vials he always carried. "Help me, lad!" he panted, crashing down to his knees beside the sprawled, ravaged body of the Bard of Shadowdale. "She's—"

Dauntless had already kicked aside the monster's body, staring curiously at what it had become—a gaunt old man whose face he did not know—and was now staring past Mirt at something else. He threw the dagger in his hand hard into the darkness.

The moneylender's shaggy head whirled around to see what the younger Harper had attacked. He was in time to see a man he knew catch the dagger and close his hand over it with a mocking smile. Purple light—the same hue as the radiance they'd just been hacking at—flared up between those closed fingers and the dagger faded away into nothingness.

"*Labraster!*" Mirt roared.

Auvrarn Labraster struck a pose, raising one hand in a lazy salute. Those handsome, crookedly smiling features were unmistakable, even with Labraster's eyes glowing eerily purple. The merchant put out his other hand, pointing fingers at both men, and purple lightning snarled forth.

Dauntless dodged and rolled. Snarling purple fire leaped after him, clawing and spitting at his heels. Mirt, on his knees and no longer a slender and agile man even to the most flattering observer, was struck instantly, and could be heard roaring weakly amid the raging lightning. As Mirt sagged, curling up in pain, Labraster flung both hands around to point squarely at Dauntless. The Harper cried out as he went down, writhing and convulsing helplessly in a splashing sea of purple fire.

Auvrarn Labraster threw back his head and laughed exultantly. His eyes were blazing almost red as he lowered his gaze slowly to the still figure of Storm Silverhand, sprawled on the floor with her exposed lungs fluttering only faintly.

"Any last comments, bard?" he jeered, striding forward with his hands trailing twin streams of purple fire onto the stones as he went.

Storm turned her head with an effort, lifted clouded eyes to his, and murmured, "I'm not enjoying this."

Labraster threw back his head and laughed uproariously.

He was still guffawing helplessly when the glistening point of a slender sword burst out of his throat from behind. Purple fire howled around the toppling merchant, then was gone, shrinking back beneath the stones with a suddenness that was almost deafening.

Storm, Mirt, and Dauntless alike peered through mists of pain to watch him fall. Standing in the shadows behind him was a slender figure they all knew, who lifted his eyebrows to them in sardonic salute as he deftly cut a slice from the back of Auvrarn Labraster's shirt, speared it on his bloodied blade, and tossed it aloft to wipe his blade clean with.

"If I desired my little empire of sewers to be full of goddesses, archwizards, and Chosen of Mystra," Elaith Craulnober murmured, "I'd have invited them."

As if in reply, there came a sudden roaring from the altar, as purple flame leaped up through its cracks to gather above it.

"Back!" Mirt cried feebly. "Help me get Storm back!"

Dauntless rose unsteadily and staggered across the riven floor of the temple. He was still a good way from where the fat merchant was trying to shield the Bard of Shadowdale with his own body when another figure rose up, its movements stiff and yet trembling with pain.

Halaster Blackcloak was as white as a corpse. He paid no attention to anything in the room except the altar as he lifted unsteady hands and said a single harsh word. A wave of something unseen rolled away from him, and the altar burst apart into rubble and dust. Purple flame shot up to the ceiling, emitting a howl of fury, and from its height turned and shot out like a bolt of lightning.

The Serpent and the Harpers watched doom come for Halaster Blackcloak. When the purple fires struck and raged, the archwizard reeled but kept his feet. They saw him throw back his head and gasp in pain, but they also saw a lacing of blue-white fire dancing around his brow that had not been there a moment before. It persisted until the purple flame had spat and flickered back into darkness. When it faded, Halaster Blackcloak went with it.

He looked last down at Storm Silverhand, and they quite clearly heard him say, "I am done with cabals and dark goddesses. Sorry, Lady of Shadowdale," before he disappeared.

Silence fell once more in the ruined temple, and with it came the gloom. Once again the only light came from the feeble tongues of silver flame rising from Storm.

Bright radiance burst forth a little way behind Dauntless. The Lady Mage of Waterdeep stood at its heart with a wand flickering in her hand. "Sister," she said, "I am come!"

There was another flash beside Elaith, who drew back smoothly and lifted his blade for a battle, frowning.

Taerach Thone stood blinking at them all. He held a piece of flickering stone in one of his open hands, and a ghostly lady was perched prettily in the cradle his arms formed. "Sister," Syluné said to Storm, "I am here too."

"You don't suppose," Mirt grunted, "one of you oh-so-mighty lasses could lend a hand, here? She's dying faster'n my potions can keep her alive!"

The Zhentarim slyblade tossed something across the room to the Old Wolf. "Here," Thone called, "have my potion. It can be trusted."

More than one pair of eyebrows rose at that, in the moments before the air began to shimmer in earnest, and tall, silver-haired women began to appear on all sides.

Elaith Craulnober stiffened at the sight of a white-bearded, hawk-nosed mage in worn robes and a crooked, broad-brimmed hat ... and stiffened still more at the sight of a drow priestess whose brief black garment bore the shining silver sword and moon of Eilistraee. Her eyes caught and held his as she stepped forward out of the swirling magic that had brought her, and strode grace-fully toward him.

His blade was raised against her, but Qilué Veladorn walked unconcernedly onto it and came on. It passed through her as if she was smoke, but her hand, when it touched his cheek, was solid enough.

"It seems you are one of those who deserves a kiss of thanks, on behalf of a goddess ... and a sister," she said, making the words a soft challenge.

There was no time for him to call on any magic or to break away. The elf whom men called the Serpent swallowed once, then turned his head slightly to meet the lips descending to his. They were cool, but her mouth and tongue were warm. Deliciously warm.

It was a long time before they broke apart—time enough for Storm to rise to her feet and join an interested, chuckling audience. It was an audience Elaith had no trouble ignoring as he drew back, and found Qilué's brow arched in another challenge.

There was a time when he'd have spat in the face of a drow. There was a time when he'd have offered swift death to anyone who seized on his person in such a way, leaving him so open to danger. There'd been a time when his pride ...

But here in this damp, ruined room, this day, Elaith Craulnober sighed, smiled, and told the drow priestess, "I hope you realize that, after this, tomorrow is going to be truly boring."

⊰ ILLUSTRATIONS ⊱

⇥ ACKNOWLEDGMENTS ⇤

MY HEARTFELT THANKS for reading the manuscript and providing valuable feedback to Julia Bekman, Edyta Bojanowska, Jonathan Bolton, Caryl Emerson, Michael Flier, Emily Johnson, John Malmstad, Polina Rikoun, Stephanie Sandler, Andreas Schönle, William Mills Todd III, Cristina Vatulescu, Justin Weir, Alexei Yurchak, and five anonymous referees.

My deep appreciation for helping me with materials for the project to Erika Boeckeler, Edyta Bojanowska, Ian Chesley, Richard Freeman, Rachel Platonov, and Molly Thomasy.

My gratitude to Mary Murrell at Princeton University Press for believing in the project and being a staunch supporter.

My thanks to the Davis Center for Russian and Eurasian Studies for a Junior Faculty Research Leave and to Harvard for a University Leave. Also to Houghton Library and Harvard Map Collection in the Nathan Marsh Pusey Library for their permission to use images.

My admiration to those whose thinking on the subject of Petersburg has inspired me—James Bater, Svetlana Boym, Katerina Clark, Katia Dianina, Donald Fanger, Emily Johnson, Grigorii Kaganov, and Albin Konechnyi.

Mapping St. Petersburg

INTRODUCTION

Petersburg not only seems to appear to us, but actually manifests
itself—on maps: in the form of two small circles, one set inside
the other, with a black dot in the center; and from this very
mathematical point, which has no dimension, it proclaims
forcefully that it exists: from here, from this very point surges
and swarms the printed book; from this invisible
point speeds the official circular.
—*Andrei Bely, Petersburg*

AS THE CAPITAL of the Russian Empire, St. Petersburg was the seat of pomp and
policy, but "Piter," as insiders have always liked to call it, was also the literary capital of tsarist Russia, not to mention its own favorite literary subject. Self-
regarding St. Petersburg virtually *wrote* itself into existence, so vast and varied is
the Russian literature that charts this city in all its aspects. The textual "map" of
St. Petersburg—that is, the sum total of genres, topoi, and tours that cover the
city in writing—constitutes a detailed literary analogue for urban topography.

St. Petersburg has been comprehensively mapped in terms of the literary
mythology created by Pushkin, Gogol, Dostoevsky, Blok, Bely, Akhmatova, and
Mandelstam, and by scholars who tease out allusions and influences within this
select group of authors and texts. Cultural historians treat the literary tradition
together with the visual and performing arts in a chronology of overdetermined
cultural high points such as "The Bronze Horseman," the Winter Palace, and
"Swan Lake."[1]

Imperial St. Petersburg, thus conceived, might seem a city composed almost
exclusively of palaces and slums, populated entirely by pampered aristocrats, the
desperate poor, and writers of genius who immortalized both in artistic masterworks.[2] The textual mapping of imperial St. Petersburg was, however, a project that ranged over the entire city and across a broad spectrum of literary forms
and tonalities. Much of this literary production, which insistently and prolifi-
cally maps the city in all its aspects, has been relegated to the margins of cultural
history.

When the eighteenth-century classicist ideal of unified continuous facades

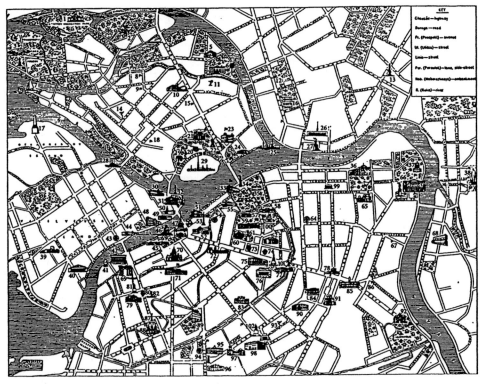

1. S. M. Kirov Central Recreation
   Park
2. Oak-Tree of Peter the Great
3. S. M. Kirov Stadium
4. Monument to S. M. Kirov
5. Lenin Electrotechnical
   Institute
6. Botanical Gardens and
   Botanical Museum
7. T. U. Water Sports Centre
8. Lenin Memorial Flat
9. Lenin Memorial Flat
10. Leningrad City Council Palace
    of Culture
11. Pavlov Medical Institute
12. May 1 Club
13. Monument to M. I. Kalinin
14. Winter Swimming Pool
15. Kirov Memorial Flat
16. Vyborg Palace of Culture

17. Obelisk in Memory of the
    Decembrists
18. House Lenin Lived In
19. Zoological Gardens
20. Historical Museum of Artillery
21. Lenin Komsomol Theatre of
    Drama
22. Monument to the destroyer
    Steregushchy
23. Museum of the October
    Revolution
24. Cottage of Peter the Great
25. Cruiser *Aurora*
26. Finland Railway Station and
    Metro Station
27. Monument to V. I. Lenin
28. Local Sea Port
29. Peter and Paul Fortress
30. Literary Museum
31. Central Naval Museum

32. Rostral Columns
33. Branch of the Central Lenin
    Museum
34. Monument to A. V. Suvorov
35. Summer Garden and Summer
    Place of Peter the Great
36. Taurida Palace
37. Smolny Cathedral
38. Monument to I. P. Pavlov
39. Kirov Palace of Culture
40. Pickhanov Mining Institute
41. Stele at *Aurora* Anchorage
42. Museum of the History of
    Leningrad
43. Pavlov Memorial Flat
44. Academy of Arts
45. Central Historical Archive
    Building
46. The Bronze Horsemen–
    Monument to Peter the Great

FIGURE I.1. Map of Cultural Monuments from 1950. (Courtesy of Harvard Map
Collection.)

proved logistically impossible for Petersburg, the Masonry Construction Commission devoted its energies to placing freestanding monumental buildings at key locations. These grand-scale edifices visually unified the space of the city along the perspectives of avenues and embankments, and lessened the impact of the intermediate "gray areas" in between.[3] Literary and cultural histories from the imperial period and most of the twentieth century have replicated this building strategy, orienting themselves either toward the monumental, or toward unsightly areas that radically undercut the illusion of unbroken panorama. The palaces and slums of St. Petersburg may seem like familiar literary territory, but other aspects of the city's history, its "gray areas," are decidedly underdocumented, if not invisible. The myth of imperial St. Petersburg thus excludes aspects of the city's cultural life characterized by mixed aesthetic tastes and social experiences. As I hope to show, the familiar mythology of St. Petersburg leaves out much of the *middle*—the ground-level urban experience that is more representative and thus less visible than the extremes of rich and poor. This study aims to revise the traditional literary "monumentalization" of Petersburg, and to offer a more decentralized view of a broader urban topography that includes noncanonical works and underdescribed spaces.

Myriad literary works that failed to achieve the status of Pushkin's "Bronze Horseman" or Dostoevsky's *Crime and Punishment* nevertheless played an ac-

47. Admiralty
48. Zhdanov State University
49. Academy of Sciences
50. Museum of Anthropology
51. State Hermitage. Pushkin Museum
52. Palace Square
53. Alexander Column
54. Pushkin Memorial Flat
55. Lenenergo Central Department
56. Monument to Champions of Revolution in the Field of Mars
57. Mikhailovsky Garden
58. Engineers' Castle
59. State Russian Museum
60. Maly Opera Theatre
61. Monument to A. S. Pushkin
62. Winter Stadium
63. Children's Theatre
64. Nekrasov Memorial Flat
65. Sovorov Museum
66. Smolny
67. Lenin Memorial Flat
68. New Blocks of Houses on the Okhta

69. "New Holland" Architectural Ensemble
70. St. Isaak's Cathedral
71. Leningrad City Council Executive Committee
72. Kazan Cathedral–Museum of the History of Religion and Atheism
73. State Philharmonic
74. Theatre of Comedy
75. Saltykov-Shchedrin State Public Library
76. Pushkin Theatre of Drama
77. Zhdanov Palace of Young Pioneers
78. Ploshchad Vosstaniya Metro Station
79. Kirov Opera and Ballet Theatre
80. Rimsky-Korsakov State Conservatoire
81. Monument to Rimsky-Korsakov
82. Monument to M. I. Glinka
83. Gorky Theatre of Drama
84. Lensoviet Theatre

85. Moscow Station
86. Lenin Memorial Flat
87. Obelisk in Memory of Russian Sailors Fallen at Tsusima
88. St. Nicholas' Cathedral
89. Obraztsov Railway Engineering Institute
90. Vladimirskaya Metro Station
91. Museum of Arctic
92. Alexander Nevsky Lavra
93. Winter Swimming Pool
94. Mendeleyev Memorial Study
95. Lensoviet Technological Institute
96. Tekhnologichesky Institut Metro Station
97. Vitebsk Railway Station
98. Pushkinskaya Metro Station
99. Chernyshevskaya Metro Station
100. Monument to Peter the Great in Klenovaya St.
101. Monument to Catherine II
102. Monument to A. S. Griboyedov

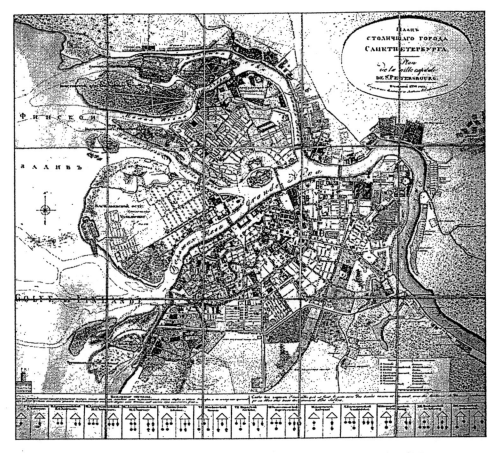

FIGURE I.2. General Map of Petersburg from 1830. (Courtesy of Harvard Map Collection.)

tive part in shaping the discourse of the very cultural mythology that later excluded them. I seek a corrective to High Romantic images—those two poles of the Petersburg binary purveyed, ironically, by middle-class writers during the heyday of literary realism—that elide the cultural middle of the imperial period. The Petersburg corpus is indeed a dense network of intertextual references, shot through with common themes and formal properties, but it is also the case that this body of texts appears unified because its boundaries have been established and maintained by a tradition. The poet Joseph Brodsky asserted that St. Petersburg would always be the capital of Russia, regardless of official designation. Its primacy is based upon "the second Petersburg, the one made of verses and of Russian prose," whose excerpts Soviet schoolchildren learned by heart: "And it's this memorization which secures the city's status and place in the future—as long as this language exists—and transforms the Soviet schoolchildren into the Russian people."[4] This second literary-canonical Petersburg insistently inscribes itself upon human subjects and transforms them into textlike bearers of cultural legacy.

A fuller accounting of writing about Petersburg is essential, precisely because the Russian imperial capital has been characterized so persistently in textual terms. Petersburg, it is said, is a city whose identity has depended on literature in compensation for its unusually short history. Vladimir Toporov's essay "Petersburg and the Petersburg Text of Russian Literature" thus synthesizes the mythology of the city into a single text.[5] Yuri Lotman suggests that Petersburg mythology is subject to a double reading, one utopian and the other apocalyptic, whereby a motif such as the Falconet monument snake can be read plausibly and simultaneously in contrasting ways.[6] Lotman thereby proposes Petersburg as the ultimate hermeneutic object, comprehensible only through multiple, seemingly incompatible readings. Petersburg has not yet been treated, however, as I propose to do, in terms of a cultural network that cannot be reduced to a single textual structure, as a body of texts that collectively provides a structural analogue for the material city, and not merely an artistic refraction of it. The geographical, material entity that is Petersburg corresponds to an equally complex structure comprised of diverse literary forms, interrelated in spatial terms, and modeling specific sites of urban life. Throughout, this study poses two central questions: What kinds of writing correspond to specific places in Petersburg or to particular aspects of imperial-era Petersburg life? How does writing constitute imperial Petersburg, both before and after the imperial period?

a literary Cul as analogous to (material.

Searching for Middle Ground

The sociocultural middle in St. Petersburg served a vital function over the course of the nineteenth century in effecting the transition to the pre-capitalist phase of pre-revolutionary Russian history. Yet the middle has long been the least studied aspect of Russian urban culture, dismissed with reference to Russia's lack of an established bourgeoisie like that in England and France. In Russian cultural criticism, the literary middle has been an object of abuse, reviled as the refuge of vulgar epigones, where "pure" aristocratic and folk cultures are contaminated by market influences, and authentic genres are diluted. Yet, as I hope to show, a great deal of urban cultural negotiation takes place on this same middle ground of literature.

The underdocumented middle ground of St. Petersburg also reflects a larger problem in Russian imperial historiography. The "middle" represents a kind of conceptual outpost, so vexed is this concept for eighteenth- and nineteenth-century Russian literature, social life, and urban geography. It has often been asserted that the West's burgeoning middle estate—in the parlance of Marxist the-

Was there no class in middle R.?

ory, the capitalist class, or bourgeoisie—had no real equivalent in Russia, but it may be more accurate to say that Russia's "missing bourgeoisie" was rather "an indeterminate, ambiguously delineated one."[7] In the imperial capital, new property owners were concentrated among the merchants, a group whose cultural influence in Petersburg did not correspond to its amassed capital, as was to a greater extent the case in Moscow.[8] Instead of a property-owning class whose influence came to rival that of the declining aristocracy, it is said, Russia had its intelligentsia—a tiny minority rich only in moral and cultural values— to mediate between privileged elite and illiterate peasantry. Imperial Russia's middle ground in social, cultural, and political terms has, however, come under historiographical reassessment in recent years.

The middle estate as formulated by Catherine the Great's instructions—a category of urban residents known as *meshchane*—designated urban residents who were not nobles, high clergy, merchants, or peasants. This definition encompassed nontaxed members of the urban community, such as low-ranking or unranked administrative personnel, artisans, and petty tradespersons. During the first half of the nineteenth century, however, the middle space of society and culture was more often associated with the *raznochintsy*, those intermediate "people of various ranks," who did not belong to the juridical-social categories of estate (*soslovie*). This notoriously vague term has been evoked in terms of "shifting and indeterminate boundaries, spontaneous development, and multiple structures," which seems the only way to characterize the "range of interstitial groups" between the primary established social categories.[9] By the 1880s, the term *raznochintsy* had become closely linked to the radical intelligentsia and had lost its usefulness as a categorization of Russia's indeterminate cultural middle. Moreover, the second half of the nineteenth century was marked by the accelerating growth of new interstitial groups. Late imperial urbanization led to increasing numbers of professionals in fields such as law, medicine, engineering, and education, as well as artists, entrepreneurs, and industrialists who did not fit the traditional categories of estate.[10] These new groups were distinct from the traditional intelligentsia, who typically considered social service far more important than private life and individual expression. Like the intelligentsia, professional groups did, however, recognize the need for a legal framework to protect individual freedoms as well as impose public obligations.

The term "middle class" with reference to imperial Russia has come to connote "the transcendence of traditional estate loyalties in favor of wider class identities" in connection with social structures that establish "intermediate identities" between the family and the state.[11] This definition emphasizes the importance of civic and social practices in the formation of a middle class, instead of taking the more traditional Marxist approach of treating class in connection with the base-superstructure model and with political life.[12] In Russia, although the bourgeoisie did not come to power, the cultural landscape of the nineteenth century can thus be seen as an ever-expanding, increasingly messy middle ground.

As an overarching concept for this study, the "middle" unites the various approaches to the city explored in the following seven chapters. My perspective on the middle itself is similarly multi-angled. In the geographic sense, the middle does not specify the physically central part of Petersburg, but rather those spaces that might occupy the "middle distance" in a visual representation, although they never serve as the focal point. Because the middle is considered ordinary it may not seem worthy of notice, but the middle is everywhere. Seen in socioeconomic perspective, the middle includes that amorphous portion of the urban population to which nonaristocratic nineteenth-century writers generally belonged (or, that portion in which aspiring writers became enmired), and which so often afforded them subjects for literature, Petersburg legend notwithstanding. Considered in evaluative terms, the middle refers to writers of no more than average talent, and to writing that is largely undistinguished, even derivative. From a generic standpoint, however, the intermediate levels of the neoclassical hierarchy generated vital emergent forms neither noble nor humble, including lyric poetry, prose fiction, and history. Nikolai Karamzin's late eighteenth-century ideal of "pleasant" language emerged from that same part of literature and became the basis for nineteenth-century-Russian literary fiction. These middle categories then dominated literary production, and from these, "Petersburg" literature, including those best-known works describing aristocratic and indigent urban subcultures, took shape. The entire Petersburg literary corpus—canonical and noncanonical exemplars—participates in the collective project of constituting the cultural middle, with writing as the ultimate medium.

In grammatical terms, a middle verb form or voice allows the subject to perform while also being affected by the specific action, in other words, to be both subject and object. In logical terms, the middle term in a syllogism is presented in both premises, but does not appear in the conclusion. Middling writers documented the milieu they knew best—their own—and this reflexive state of affairs became the hidden pretext for the Petersburg corpus, which then covered its tracks. In functional terms, the cultural middle may mediate; it is the medium or midwife that acts as conveyance, assists in bringing something forth, or marks an intersection. The cultural middle may surround, as mediums are wont to do, or be surrounded—that is, be besieged amidst an encompassing environment. Where does the middle begin and end, however, if it is to be conceived as more than a baggy catchall for those diverse parts of urban text and topography that fall between identifiable extremes? I seek the middle primarily in its functions within the urban context, as directly related to the preceding definitions, if not limited to them.

The cultural middle has a relational existence, as I conceive it, produced through the dialogic relation, in the Bakhtinian sense, of different populations and interests in the city. This cultural middle seems closely related to space it-self, which has been similarly proposed by social theorists as constituted by the nature of links between separate entities. Of course, the same claim could be made for the spaces of "high" and "low" culture; all levels of culture are inter-connected, and the middle cannot be articulated in isolation from the rest. My project aims at an archeological reconstruction of a complex discursive for-mation—the full textual articulation of imperial St. Petersburg as a cultural object.[13]

Mapping Textual and Cultural Space

The notion of time has underwritten influential Western cultural paradigms such as Darwin's theory of natural selection and Freud's theory of psycho-analysis.[14] In contrast, the Newtonian view of space as fixed and abstract has persisted throughout modern history, in spite of the many developments in the-ories of space that have suggested its integral connection with human social and cognitive patterns.[15] The nineteenth century saw a paradigm shift linked to changing practices in the natural and social sciences, as well as in artistic form, all of which began to treat space as multiple and heterogeneous, produced by subjective points of view and derived from the particular features of human physiology.[16] Traditional Marxism, however, did not occupy itself explicitly with questions of space, considered to be a reflection of social structure and class conflict, and not an autonomous determinant of social relations.

In the terms of the twentieth-century social materialist Henri Lefebvre, space represents "social morphology," the form of lived experience, and "a material-ization of 'social being'"; space is constituted by particular social relations that give it meaning.[17] Michel de Certeau has argued that everyday activities are the means of producing space or "practiced place." An act of reading is thus "the space produced by the practice of a particular place: a written text, i.e., a place constituted by a system of signs."[18] In the paradoxical case of narrative fic-tion, an essentially temporal medium creates the illusion of events unfolding in physical space, while "a succession of spatial scenes" provides the sense of time passing.[19]

A powerful sense of the city as a physical object in space and historical time can similarly be constructed by literary practices. The very project of repre-senting the city in writing is a utopian one, however, associated with classical and Enlightenment conceptions of the city, since no single artistic mode, not even the elastic and form-swallowing novel, can fully accommodate the com-plexities of urban life. The city is thus invoked in terms of synecdoche such as stage, market, labyrinth, fortress, temple, palace, library, archive, and mu-seum.[20] Still, the perceived need to attempt a complete representation is central to the urban experience. Raymond Williams finds that Dickens's vision of London ultimately lies "in the form of his novels," in which "the experience of the city is the fictional method" and "the fictional method is the experience of the city."[21] Neo-Kantian sociologist Georg Simmel posited a connection between human intellect and urban environment by characterizing modern sensibility as a response to the city with its circulation of money and excesses of stimuli.[22] Experience, fictional methods, and people themselves may be products of the city, but they also play their part in shaping the urban environment. "The city," declares Lefebvre, "is the work of a history, that is, of clearly defined people and groups who accomplish this *oeuvre*, in historical conditions."[23] In the seemingly charged significance of every street sign, statue, facade, and foundation stone, cities project a complex, textual coherence. Although the urban oeuvre may seem a cultural text in its own right, however, it is produced in part by actual writing that employs various mapping strategies.

Peter the Great, Petersburg's founder, has been characterized as a man for whom "geography was far more real . . . than history," a monarch "in love with space," which he saw as continuous and accessible.[24] When Peter imposed his vision upon the Neva swamplands with ruler, pencil, and force of will, he thus drafted a new map of reality. In truth, before Peter, Russians lacked the map-making skills to produce a comprehensive geographical account of their territory. Seventeenth-century Muscovite cartography retained a medieval character, with pictorial representations of landmarks on hand-drawn maps, little sense of scale, and views from impossible positions in space. Only after Peter's Grand Embassy to Europe of 1697–98 did the Russian state begin to produce accurate scaled maps that pronounced themselves "an instrument of rule" and "an advertisement . . . of knowledge as power."[25] The beginning of modern European-style mapmaking in Russia precedes the founding of St. Petersburg by only five years, and this effort would have its institutional base at the Naval Academy and the Academy of Sciences in Peter's new city.

According to the humanistic cultural geography that has taken shape since the late 1970s, metaphors such as text and map have replaced the more scientific paradigms of system and machine in descriptions of cultural landscape.[26] The guiding metaphor of the map structures the exercise of cultural cartography, offering a model at once more overtly material and more obviously figural than that of a printed text. No longer seen as a mirror—an empirical, scientific, and direct representation of the world—the map has been re-visioned as rhetoric.[27] New-style geographers have welcomed this shift in guiding trope from duplicitous model to self-acknowledged metaphor as a long-overdue recognition of the essentially cultural construction of human knowledge. Put simply, maps are disingenuous about their own rhetorical nature, professing scientific disinterestedness, but they nevertheless reflect choices about inclusion and exclusion and, therefore, represent a set of interests or power relations. Seeing mapping as metaphor, moreover, can uncover the interests behind other seemingly self-evident and inviolable cultural topographies. Canonization stud-

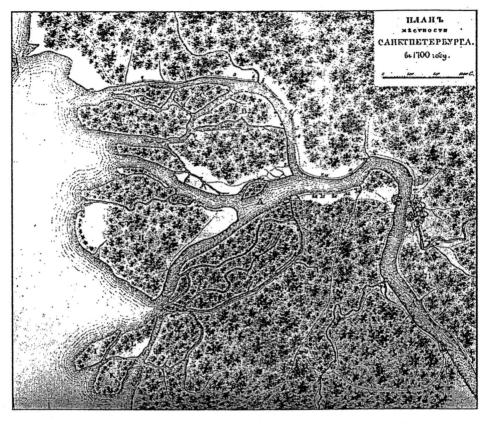

FIGURE I.3. St. Petersburg Environs in 1700, from 1853 *Plany S. Peterburga.* (Courtesy of Houghton Library at Harvard.)

ies, for example, ask how written texts have been put "on the map," as seemingly natural facts of cultural life and spontaneous expressions of national greatness channeled by writer-representatives.

The English-language term "topography" has been associated with three different meanings over time.[28] Topography originally denoted "a description of place in words," or a kind of travel literature, but later came to mean "the art of mapping a place by graphic signs." Ironically, in a further slippage, the third meaning of topography, now dominant, simply designates "that which is mapped." Thus "the place of writing" (*topos* + *graphein*) has come to mean the always-already-written terrain rather than its description. Landscapes can, however, be brought into another kind of being by written texts, which, like mapmaking, elaborate topographical relationships.[29]

The connection between cartography and literature came into relief during

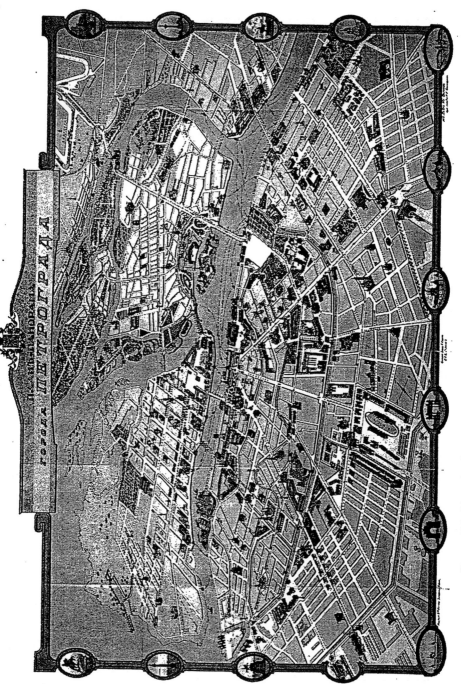

Figure I.4. Map of Cultural Monuments from 1914. (Courtesy of Harvard Map Collection.)

the Renaissance, as evidenced by a surge in cartographic activity, coincident with the growing importance of the self as a literary construct, and this self's relation to the idea of national space.[30] Russia, of course, is a special case, since it remained locked into a largely premodern worldview until the reign of Peter the Great. Literary mappings of self and imperial capital did not become a widespread practice in Russia until the nineteenth century, when lyric poetry and literary prose, investigative journalism, travel literature, memoir, and autobiography all flourished.

It was only in the nineteenth century that Russian culture began to exhibit what Yuri Lotman and Boris Uspenskii call the "structural reserve" that constitutes the "neutral axiological sphere" of culture—in other words, the middle zone of behaviors neither "holy" nor "sinful" that developed in the medieval West. Even the dramatic cultural changes in Europeanizing eighteenth-century Russia can be seen as a simple inversion of the old culture's binary values, not unlike pagan Russia's adoption of Christianity in the tenth century.[31] "Polite society" of the early nineteenth century and its associated conventions thus constituted a new public space where creative forms such as literature evolved.[32] The writers who compiled Nikolai Nekrasov's 1845 *Physiology of Petersburg* (*Fiziologiia Peterburga*) did not seek to emulate the aristocratic Petersburg literary tradition of Pushkin, Prince Odoevskii, or Count Sollogub, however. As Vissarion Belinsky declared in his introduction to this compendium, the writers of *Physiology* lacked "any pretensions to poetic or artistic talent," and hoped merely to initiate a new literary practice of social inclusiveness in Russia, following the lead of France.[33] Belinsky claimed that Russian literature of the mid-1840s was richer in works of genius than in works of ordinary talent. Masterpieces such as Griboedov's play "Woe from Wit" (*Gore ot uma*) or Pushkin's novel in verse *Eugene Onegin* were *not* surrounded by "a vast and brilliant entourage of talents that could serve as intermediaries between them and the public," and thus lead this public further along the path established by the greats.[34] Russian literature desperately needed this middling sort of writer, often embodied by the figure of the modest journalist, because without this writer literary institutions faltered and the public ran out of reading material. Belinsky argued that literature should resemble the natural world in its diversity and consist of many different genres and species. A national literature cannot consist only of masterworks and works of no merit whatsoever, concludes Belinsky, because "ordinary talents are essential for the richness of literature, and the more of them there are, the better it is for literature." Belinsky himself did not live to see it, but, in fact during subsequent decades of the nineteenth century the cultural landscape saw exactly this sort of growth in the middle ranges of literature. St. Petersburg was the preferred destination of middle-range writers, most of whom came from the provinces in hopes of becoming literary professionals.

Changes in literary expression shifted the literary center of gravity: literature

grew increasingly thick around the middle. The middle space of literary production and reception expanded horizontally, while the formerly capacious
realms of high-style discourse grew cramped and musty. The new emphasis on
aspects of social life that had previously been invisible to literature (the so-called
Natural School) represented one such mid-sectional trend, describing the
everyday with recourse to unexpected linguistic flourishes and rhetorical figurations. Poetic forms grew more diffuse in style and diction, while continuing
to fulfill their traditional elevating function through satire, as in the urban verse
of Nekrasov. The distinctions between stylistic registers became clearly demar-
cated, and the in-between spaces dilated and eventually outgrew the named literary forms against which these bastard aesthetic structures had initially defined
themselves. Nonaristocratic writers intent on inscribing themselves upon the
cultural map produced much of this new literature. All of these changes gradually transformed the ideal neoclassical generic hierarchy into a lateral network,
which then became topographical in literary works that traversed the city. The
diffuse and distended literary works that filled nineteenth-century thick journals attest to the expanding cultural space of the middle, offering a vivid contrast to the time-space compression typical of both neoclassical and modernist
art. The boom in middle prose genres—of wordy, overextended stories, novels,
feuilletons, and sketches by middling writers—was part and parcel of this cultural expansion.

How is it that a city with such a finite history inspired such a vast quantity of
writing? Certainly it is significant that St. Petersburg was the center of Russian
publishing and book trade during the imperial period. During the second half
of the nineteenth century, active printers, publishers, and booksellers such as
the Glazunov family, M. O. Vol'f, Adolf Marx, Aleksei Suvorin, and many others
considerably broadened the city's literary culture. In an 1881 sketch devoted to
life in the capital, the journalist Vasilii Mikhnevich invoked an 1877 statistical
study that attributed forty-five percent of the books published in Russia to Petersburg, as opposed to Moscow and the provinces combined, and claimed an
even larger share of Russian journalism for the periodical press.[35] He characterized primacy in the book business as a measure of Petersburg's distinctively
intellectual atmosphere: "Along with fashionable hats and frock-coats of the latest cut, new ideas, new concepts, and knowledge are ordered from Petersburg,
and the reigning tone and direction of the given moment in Russian intellectual
life—for which Petersburg serves as the concentration point—is disseminated."
These figures of speech, like the prologue to Bely's *Petersburg,* cast Petersburg as
a great writing-machine blanketing the rest of Russia with its ceaseless production.[36] Moreover, the expansion of the imperial bureaucracy in St. Petersburg
also produced a seemingly inexhaustible flood of paper, which in turn generated more bureaucratic work, which generated more documentation, and inspired literary efforts that described this strange world. Writing both literally
and metaphorically *covers* the city of Petersburg.

As Belinsky had hoped, the middle ground of literature expanded, swelled by the ranks of competent practitioners, and eventually included literate residents of the capital not counted among the intelligentsia. In this regard, Nikolai Sveshnikov's *Memoirs of a Fallen Man* (*Vospominaniia propashchego cheloveka*, 1896) is of great value in reconstructing the lower end of the later nineteenth-century Petersburg book trade—a rich, virtually untapped source of information about the middle range of culture in the capital. Sveshnikov worked as a dealer in the book market that served members of the urban lower middle classes through its own channels of distribution, primarily in stalls around Bolshaia Sadovaia Street, and most specifically, at the Apraksin market. In 1897, Sveshnikov also produced a series of sketches called "Petersburg Apraksin-Booksellers and Secondhand Dealers" (*Peterburgskie knigoprodavtsy-apraksintsy i bukinisty*) that provide an intimate look at this meeting-point of literacy and trade.[37] Sveshnikov portrays popular literature as part of the middle ground in Petersburg writing, a cultural space that served an increasingly diverse portion of the city's population during the nineteenth century.[38] The mass daily newspapers similarly served a heterogeneous urban middle readership in Russia beginning in the era of the Great Reforms.[39] These developments were neither sudden nor unprecedented in Russian letters. Even canonical texts by writers such as Pushkin and Gogol from the earlier part of the nineteenth century prefigure the growing space of the cultural middle, providing a meeting place for hybrid literary genres and mixed populations within the space of a single fictional work.

This study attempts to remap the Russian imperial capital, but not simply by providing a reverse image of the literary tradition with Pushkin and Dostoevsky at the margins. Instead, I propose a new integration in terms of architectural and literary eclecticism (chapters 1 and 2); literature that travels around the city (chapter 3); spaces of interchange between oral and print literature (chapter 4); the ambiguous relationship between urban center and margins (chapter 5); shared experience as meeting ground in a city to which so many came from elsewhere (chapter 6); and the city as collective textual and memorial repository (chapter 7).

This study treats particular sites within writing about imperial Petersburg—physical areas, aspects of city life, and persistent themes. I juxtapose canonical texts by prominent authors with works from the margins of these well-charted oeuvres, as well as works by lesser-known figures, so that clusters of texts can be experienced in terms of interrelationship rather than intertextuality. I also disperse my attention over a wide textual field, of which fictional prose is only one component. Texts of a quasifictional and nonfictional nature participate no less significantly in the discursive project of constructing imperial Petersburg.

While this study ventures into the final years of the imperial period, so-called Silver Age texts are not the focus of my project. The emphasis is on the period 1830s–1890s, with what I hope is an equal distribution of attention across the years preceding the Great Reforms and the years following them. I have not limited myself to texts written during the imperial period, however, but sample writing about imperial Petersburg produced after the 1917 revolution. I am interested in the ways that the imperial-era discourse has been recapitulated and reappropriated demonstratively in the post-Soviet period, and in the perpetual return of persistent *genres* of writing about imperial Petersburg.[40]

A word about the Soviet period is necessary at this point. The features of imperial Petersburg as constituted in Soviet-era writing up to the late 1980s and early 1990s could well serve as the subject of an entire volume. The shifts of perspective adopted in relation to imperial Petersburg throughout this multidecade period have yet to be traced carefully, particularly during the post-Stalin years, when practices of preservation, the cultural politics of place naming, and the canonization of imperial-era texts revealed inconsistent and ambivalent attitudes toward the past. A thorough critique of imperial Petersburg mythology would reconstruct the entire grid of intelligibility that took shape during the Soviet period. This study includes only limited references to the Soviet period, however, in illustrative examples of official and dissident discourse. Ironically, too, logistics have obliged me to omit the in-between, eclectic middle level of post-Stalinist Soviet discourse. This very middle level has, however, emerged strongly in the flood of publications about imperial Petersburg from the post-Soviet years, and these are discussed in more detail.

Chapter 1 discusses architectural eclecticism, which flourished in Petersburg during the 1830s–1890s, exemplified by apartment houses, public buildings, commercial institutions, and private homes. A hybrid blending of diverse period and style elements, architectural eclecticism is an urban phenomenon expressive of new social groupings such as the professional middle class and independent entrepreneurs, who found aesthetic voice by making their mark on the cityscape. Eclecticism thus manifests the cultural middle in its function as medium and meeting place. Chapter 2 juxtaposes the notion of architectural eclecticism with literary works about Petersburg, examining eighteenth- and nineteenth-century texts in terms of genre and style. The alleged eighteenth-century uniformity in this writing proves as elusive as the corresponding purity of origin ascribed to Petersburg architecture of the neoclassical period. Writing about Petersburg—even in monuments of the literary myth such as Pushkin's "Bronze Horseman" and Gogol's "Nevsky Prospect"—is revealed to be insistently hybrid. The canonical Petersburg sites treated by these two famous works are not inviolate spaces of cultural heritage, but rather energetically contested, interrogated, and, ultimately, constituted by diverse literary discourse. Chapters 1 and 2 map a shared space of culture that expanded over the course of the imperial period—a fascinating cultural reserve denigrated and neglected by grandstanding Slavophiles, principled populists, late-imperial elitists, bourgeois-hating socialists, and dissident nostalgics, each group for its own particular reasons. Only since the 1990s has attention begun to rest seriously upon the unwritten middle ground of the imperial period, with Russians taking an interest in the historical bases for market democracy, and with academic fashion in the West, subject to its own forms of cultural elitism, treating aesthetic categories such as "middlebrow," "mainstream," and "everyday" more generously. This study adopts a conception of everyday life in keeping with Yuri Lotman's vision of a cultural boundary zone, where practices of lived life engage in complex ways with the codes of a dominant discourse.[41]

Chapters 3 and 4 look at two complementary genres—travel literature and urban legend—which both render the middle space of urban culture as a dynamic, heterogeneous environment that gives rise to flexible and mobile forms of discourse. In contrast to eclecticism, which has only recently been inscribed onto the cultural map of imperial Petersburg, these two genres have always been warmly acknowledged as Petersburg traditions. Chapter 3 examines Petersburg travel literature, including conventional guidebooks, cultural histories, and subjective journies detailed in feuilleton, sketch, and memoir. The sum product of this travel literature, an on-going literary project that traces the contours of the imperial capital, is a cultural terrain claimed by diverse, competing interest groups. Chapter 4 treats a different sort of collective discourse—urban legend, which traverses Petersburg according to its own characteristic means, moving freely about the city, transcending social hierarchies, and creating provisional communities. Urban legend represents the discourse of the city in perhaps its purest form; writing cannot effectively capture such legend, a largely oral form that leaves only random traces behind in texts.

Chapter 5 returns to the physical space of the city in terms that parallel the rise of eclecticism; it investigates parts of the city that were both central *and* marginal and looks for common ground in these representations, while also exploring their paradoxes. The palace-parks inhabited by the royal family and visited by the Russian public were located at the furthest distance from the city proper. These ensembles are central sites of Petersburg discourse in guidebooks, albums, poetry, and memoirs, but as architectural complexes they were surprisingly vulnerable to the vicissitudes of both imperial and postimperial life. The dacha regions to the north and south, in contrast, became sites of satire and parody, often self-directed, for writers who scraped together the wherewithal to enjoy the dubious pleasures of Petersburg's natural environment. The city slums, many located in central portions of Petersburg, were inhabited by the most socioeconomically marginal citizens of the imperial capital, and yet, these literary sites were much favored by middling writers and journalists, evolving into one of the most-documented spaces of Petersburg life. Finally, the industrial regions of the city—an increasingly prominent aspect of imperial Petersburg over the course of the nineteenth century—remain nearly invisible in the Petersburg literary corpus, in marked contrast to the literatures of London, Paris, and New York. The writers of populist orientation who assiduously covered the city from mid-century onward had a fondness for colorful street life, but with very few exceptions, they remained stubbornly retrograde in their approach to the modernizing Petersburg of their time. Chapter 5 reveals "central" and "marginal" to be highly contradictory structuring principles in Petersburg literature and argues that, in this regard, the cultural middle is produced by oscillations between unstable social and literary poles.

Chapter 6 locates a middle ground in a much-practiced literary and autobiographical genre—the common story of writers who came to the capital from Moscow or the provinces and found themselves roughly initiated into the ways of the city. This chapter takes up the conundrum of the striking similarities among texts in the Petersburg literary corpus, attributing this literary curiosity to a shared perspective, and explores the dialogue between imitation and tradition in the vast body of middling writing about the imperial capital.

Chapter 7 explores the city as collective property in terms of memory and loss, as the result of time, urban cycles of growth and decline, oft-recalled catastrophes such as floods and fires, and commercially or ideologically motivated destruction sanctioned by city authorities. A city is always engaged in simultaneous processes of remembering and forgetting, erasing, reconstructing, and rewriting, and these efforts often take parallel textual form, or, alternatively, constitute the city in textual terms. Institutionalized forms of remembering such as memorial cemeteries, city history museums, and place names make these connections explicit. The conclusion to this book reflects upon writing and remembering in connection with Petersburg's 2003 tricentennial celebrations, also looking back to 1803 and 1903.

The Collective Text of Petersburg

Some cities are more "storied" than others, to use a term for city settings that represent a "*transmitted* literary paradigm," a topos, whose symbolic space casts a "long shadow of literary precedent."[42] Perhaps this paradigm has not been transmitted from writer to writer so much as slavishly reproduced in St. Petersburg's case, since so much literary writing about the city quite literally covers the same ground.[43] The Petersburg Text of Russian literature has been characterized in terms of the striking similarity among its component texts and the irreducible conflicts that lie at the city's core, as Nikolai Antsiferov did in *The Soul of Petersburg* (*Dusha Peterburga,* 1922).[44] Toporov characterizes the "Petersburg Text of Russian literature" in the same way:

> The first thing that strikes the eye in analyzing the specific texts comprising the "Petersburg Text" . . . is the astonishing closeness the various descriptions of Petersburg bear to one another, both in the works of a single author and in those of diverse authors . . . right up to coincidences that in another case . . . might have been suspect as plagiarism. . . . The impression is created that Petersburg implicates its own descriptions with incomparably greater insistence and obligation than any

other objects of description that can be opposed to it (for example, Moscow), substantially limiting authorial freedom of choice.[45]

The structural affinities across the Petersburg Text arise from the "monolithic
character" of the central idea: "the path to moral salvation, to spiritual rebirth
under conditions when life perishes in the reign of death, and lies and evil triumph over truth and good."[46]

Or perhaps writers merely transcribe the text that the city dictates—a story
of bad weather, bad moods, and, quite frequently, bad writing. Due to the Russian imperial capital's northern latitude, Petersburg residents expect rain, raw
damp air, gray skies, fog, slush, mud, penetrating wind, and biting cold, except
during the "White Nights" in June and July. Catherine the Great was reportedly
fond of declaring, "We have eight months of winter, and four months of bad
weather."[47] The pernicious climate was certainly responsible for the early deaths
from tuberculosis and pneumonia of many young intellectuals. In the nineteenth-
century literary tradition, Petersburg's unhealthy air also stands for the malig-
nant influence of the city, which destroys Russia's most promising young artists
and social activists. The unstable but reliably bad Petersburg weather is much
more than a realist setting that determines character; it reflects an earlier literary solipsism associated with romanticism, according to which an individual's
inner state is projected—writ large, so to speak—on his environment.

The interpenetration of literature and weather in the Petersburg tradition can
be abundantly illustrated, but a few examples will suffice here. The first is from
Nikolai Gogol, who left an unfinished fragment from the 1830s that begins,
"The rain was prolonged and raw when I came out onto the street." The narrator elaborates with peculiar relish:

> The smoky-gray sky foretold that the rain would continue at length. Not a single
> band of light, not in any spot was there a break in the gray shroud. The moving
> screen of rain almost completely curtained off everything that the eye had formerly
> seen, and only the front-most buildings flickered as through thin gauze . . . the roof
> was nearly lost in the rainy fog, distinguished from the air only by its damp gleam;
> water gurgled from the drainpipes. There were puddles on the pavement. The devil
> take it, I love this time.[48]

The narrator watches the inclement weather drive a self-satisfied civil servant,
a portly lady, and a merchant couple from the streets. "Douse them, rain, for
everything," importunes the narrator. He takes malicious pleasure when the rain
comes down harder, "as if wanting to press this swampy city down even lower."
Gogol's brief treatise on the weather functions as antinarrative, washing away
all possible characters or events—hence the fragment, which, along with the unnecessarily distended prose work, constitutes a favorite Petersburg literary form.

Fedor Dostoevsky underscores the interrelationship of weather and narrative
when his antihero Goliadkin wakes up at the opening of the 1846 story "The

Double" (*Dvoinik*, subtitled "A Petersburg Poem"): "Finally, the gray autumn day, dull and dirty, peered into the room at him through the dim window so angrily and with a grimace so sour that Mr. Goliadkin could longer possibly doubt that he was not in some far-off land, but rather in the city of St. Petersburg."[49] Goliadkin is merely the passive recipient of these impressions, since the Petersburg climate itself represents the more striking character. Later, Goliadkin's double appears as he gazes despairingly into the Fontanka on a "terrible" night: "damp, foggy, rainy, snowy, fraught with abscess, cold, ague, quinsy, and fever of every possible type and sort, in a word, with all the gifts of a St. Petersburg November."[50] It may be that the weather, as well as the figure of the double, reflects Goliadkin's stormy mind. On the other hand, it seems that the weather drives the narrative. Goliadkin is lashed by wind and wet, which "assail" him until the decisive internal break occurs.

For Dostoevsky, Petersburg weather and Petersburg narrative are implicitly one and the same in syntactic terms. Dostoevsky thus comments on the sufferings of little Nellie in *The Insulted and the Injured* (*Unizhennye i oskorblennye*, 1861) with a sentence as long and insistently morose as the bad-weather season to which it alludes: "It was a gloomy story, one of those dismal and excruciating stories that so often and so unobtrusively, almost secretly, transpire under the heavy Petersburg sky, in the dark, concealed back alleys of the enormous city, among the turbid boiling of life, blind egoism, conflicting interests, dispirited vice, and hidden crimes, amidst all this infernal hell of senseless and abnormal life."[51] A more explicit connection between text and weather is proposed in a 1844 feuilleton by Nekrasov, a minidrama titled "Preference and Sunshine" (*Preferans i solntse*), in which a civil servant muses upon the dreary summer weather: "The unhappy residents, wishing to show off their new summer outfits, cannot understand why, for such a protracted period, there hangs over their heads a hazy, dark-gray veil, from which daily drips a fine, close and penetrating rain that induces low spirits in the same way as a dull article printed with the tiniest compressed typeface."[52] This remark transforms Petersburg weather into an uninviting *text* in figurative terms—rendering culture from nature, as the Petersburg myth habitually demands.

Nekrasov trumps Dostoevsky's weather-mania with his poetic cycle "About the Weather" (*O pogode*, 1858–65), in which atmospheric conditions represent a constant that unites diverse aspects of life in the capital. The first part of the cycle begins with the just-averted threat of flooding on a day that is "murky, windy, dark, and dirty," when tears appear to be streaming down the windows.[53] Hoping to escape his melancholy mood, the poet-narrator goes for a walk and joins a funeral procession on its way to the cemetery. The rain is replaced by hail and snow, as fog covers the city. Only the narrator can make it all out via the medium of poetry. For Nekrasov, bad weather does not constitute merely the precondition or occasion for writing, but also the source of literary plots, since the narrator documents the misfortunes that the weather brings to the city's inhabitants—epidemics, fatal frosts, and fires—in his all-inclusive, middle-range urban poetry. When the weather is bad, the Petersburg writer is in his element.

For many writers, the city represents the much-reviled locus of their deepest, most treasured suffering.[54] Pushkin famously wrote to his wife Natalia in 1834, "Do you really suppose that swinish Petersburg is not repulsive to me? That I enjoy myself living amidst pasquinades and denunciations?"[55] Belinsky declared, "If one suffers in Petersburg, one is a true human being."[56] Writers often expressed their ambivalence toward the city in terms of paradox, as did Herzen when he pronounced himself indebted to Petersburg for his moral and emotional suffering: "Nowhere did I give way so often to so many sorrowful thoughts as in Petersburg. Burdened by heavy doubts, I would wander along its granite pavements, close to despair. I am obliged to Petersburg and grew to love it for these minutes."[57]

In his poem "The City" (Gorod, 1845), Apollon Grigor'ev responds to Pushkin—who in "The Bronze Horseman" declared, "I love you, Peter's creation"—with a paradoxical paean of his own: "Yes, I love it, this vast, proud city / But not for that which others love."[58] Grigor'ev venerates the "stamp" of suffering that he sees everywhere in Petersburg. In Nekrasov's poem "The Unfortunates" (Neschastnye, 1856), Petersburg similarly leaves its "mark of depression" on every face and object.[59] Vasilii Sleptsov claimed, "Petersburg cannot possibly be anyone's homeland," whereas Vsevolod Garshin asserted that Petersburg, despite the torments he experienced there, was the only Russian city that represented "a genuine spiritual homeland."[60] The Petersburg Text resembles an echo chamber, in which writers cannot help responding to other voices in the tradition and to their own earlier pronouncements.

The vocabulary of mental illness is part of the Petersburg lexicon, which includes a rich selection of words for a troubled inner state—exhausted, lonely, hopeless, feverish, morose, anguished, anxious, depressed, insane, terrified, agitated, and alienated.[61] Vsevolod Krestovskii, author of the novel Petersburg Slums (Peterburgskie trushchoby, 1864–67), wrote an 1860 poetic cycle titled "Depression" (Khandra) that seems in this respect emblematic of Petersburg literature from the latter part of the nineteenth century. "Melancholy. . . Again melancholy!" declaims Krestovskii's poetic alter ego, who sits alone in a dark room, mentally reviewing his psychological and moral decline since coming to Petersburg, and working himself up to suicide. Visions pass before him. In one, he lies, "torpid, in the fetters of a dream," under an ancient pine tree on a winter night. The pine whisperingly lulls him to sleep and urges him to forget treacherous spring, whose flowers will fade. "I am more faithful," chants the pine. "My gloomy hue does not fade / And my quiet refuge is never-failing."[62] Thus the Petersburg bard returns again and again to his depression, that dependable source of inspiration, as if to the safe and enfolding embrace of the gloomy pine tree.[63]

Melancholy used to be understood as an excess of "black choler," one of the four humors whose balance accounted for an individual's temperament. The poet Gérard de Nerval proposed a metaphor for depression in his 1853 poem "The Disinherited" (*El Desdichado*), declaring, "My lone star is dead, and my bespangled lute / Bears the black sun of melancholia," with recourse to a figure that Julia Kristeva characterizes as "dazzling with black invisibility," summing up "the blinding force of the despondent mood."[64] This particular line of the poem also enacts the depressive's search to express his experience: "The verb 'bears' points to that bursting out, that reaching the signs of darkness, while the learned word *melancholia* serves to bespeak that struggle for conscious mastery and precise meaning." The Petersburg Text, too, can be summed up as a collective attempt to exorcise black melancholy through writing, with Nerval's "black sun" a particularly fitting image for St. Petersburg's extreme northern darkness in autumn and winter.

Kristeva's theory of melancholia suggests that the depressive retains the use of signs, although with radically reduced affect. "Let us keep in mind the speech of the depressed—repetitive and monotonous," she writes. "Faced with the impossibility of concatenating, they utter sentences that are interrupted, exhausted, come to a standstill. . . . A repetitive rhythm, a monotonous melody emerge and dominate the broken logical sequences, changing them into recurring, obsessive litanies."[65] In the depressive, an abyss separates language from affective experience, although the subject may be a lucid observer of his own misfortune. The artist, in contrast, has control over the use of signs, and the work of art is therefore the sign of a vanquished depression, the work of mourning through the agency of a symbolic system such as language, and an articulation of loss in semiotic terms. The Petersburg Text nevertheless retains an affinity with the language of the depressed, as a meeting of nineteenth-century literary practice (long-winded and repetitive prose) and Petersburg setting. This corpus thus represents an obsessive melancholic utterance that refuses to complete the work of mourning.

According to cultural mythology, then, Petersburg is the capital of bad weather and dark moods that give rise to a sublime literary tradition. But Petersburg might just as easily be reconceived as the city of *bad writing*, so persistent are the deplorable literary habits that pervade the Petersburg Text. Many fictional prose works, poems, memoirs, and cultural tributes to the city are self-indulgent, long, overstuffed with "writerly" adjectives and irritatingly rapturous (what the Russians call *vostorzhennye*) epiphanies. Petersburg moves a would-be author to express in writing his distinctively sensitive and perceptive response to the city, which, ironically, uncannily resembles all of the Petersburg lyrical epiphanies that have preceded it. The young poet described in Semen Nadson's "A Child of the Capital, From the Days of Youth . . ." (*Ditia stolitsy, s iunykh dnei . . .*, 1884) perfectly embodies this Petersburg writer-figure and his literary excesses. Nadson's poet does not mind the quotidian urban environment seemingly inhospitable to poetic reverie, since he has learned to find

> Everywhere poetry—in the fogs,
> In the rains, which never tire of pouring down
> In the kiosks, flower-beds, and fountains
> Of faded city parks,
> In the designs of frost in winter,
> In the haze of sullen clouds,
> Set afire by winter dawn. . . .[66]

This Petersburg poet wears his melancholy as a badge of honor and a sign of creative genius. As it turns out, however, the moody exaltation experienced by Nadson's poet makes him ordinary in Petersburg terms.

Even the most revered contributors to the Petersburg corpus sometimes follow the pattern of bad Petersburg writing, taking flight in lyrical epiphany. Thus Gogol concludes his witty "Petersburg Notes of 1836" (*Peterburgskie zapiski 1836 goda*) with an insistently pastel vision of quiet Lent, when the city assumes a "picturesque" aspect. Gogol's narrator stands by the Neva and admires the "rosy" sky and the "azure fog," which gives a "lilac" cast to the buildings on the Petersburg Side, gazing upon the spire of the Peter-Paul church-tower, "reflected in the infinite mirror of the Neva."[67] The narrator warms up with a vague poetic pronouncement: "It seemed as if I were not in Petersburg; it seemed as if I had moved to some other city, where I had already been, where I knew everything and where there exists that which is lacking in Petersburg. . . ." The epiphany then reaches its peak in fatuous self-assertion: "I love spring deeply. Even here, in this wild north, it is mine. It seems to me that no one in the world loves spring the way I do. With spring, my youth comes to me; with spring, my past is more than remembrance: it stands before my eyes and is ready to splash in tears from my eyes." The more the narrator sets himself apart by drawing attention to his writerly sensibility, the more he belongs to this Petersburg literary tradition. The Petersburg Text, in fact, inevitably tends toward self-parody in this way, or, at least, toward stylistic registers where parody is indistinguishable from pathos.

Like Gogol's piece, Dostoevsky's "Petersburg Visions in Verse and Prose" (*Peterburgskie snovedeniia v stikhakh i proze*, 1861) describes a "fantastic, magic vision" remembered by the narrator from his youth, when he stood by the Neva on a January evening and contemplated a misty second Petersburg rising into the air:

> Some strange thought suddenly stirred inside me. I shuddered, and at that moment my heart seemed to fill with a hot spurt of blood, suddenly boiling up from a surge of a powerful, but previously unknown sensation. I seemed to understand something at that moment, which up until that point had only stirred within me, but had not been consciously realized. It seemed that my eyes had been opened to something new, to a completely new world that was unfamiliar to me and known only by some murky rumors or secret signs. I suppose that my existence began at that precise moment.[68]

While the ironic feuilletonistic style of Dostoevsky's older narrator throughout this piece suggests he has renounced the visionary excitement of his younger self, this passage can also be read as a wishful meditation on becoming a writer in an improbable moment of sudden transformation. What remains unclear, as in Gogol's epiphany, is whether the author depicts a first-person narrator-character as a typical self-dramatizing Petersburg literary hack or ironically char-acterizes his own younger *self* this way. Even the Nadson poem—surely composed in all seriousness—is careful to distance the writing subject in the poem from its author. Is St. Petersburg a school for bad writing? Bad writing about Petersburg is a literary meeting place welcoming to both ordinary people and great writers. For all that Petersburg is constantly invoked as a "riddle" or an "enigma," writers cannot stop themselves from characterizing it in the most luxuriantly banal terms.

In the discourse around the cultural middle in imperial Russia, the word *meshchanstvo*, akin in meaning to *petit-bourgeoisie*, carries associations of vulgar philistinism. Nikolai Pomialovskii—whose radical-idealist views, unrealized literary potential, and early death from alcoholism caused him to be canonized as the "emblematic" Petersburg intelligentsia writer—made his literary debut with a novella titled *Petit-Bourgeois Happiness* (*Meshchanskoe schastie*, 1861). Pomialovskii's novel questioned whether an educated young man of nongentry origin could find his place in Russian society, conflating the dilemma of the so-called *raznochinets* with the *meshchanstvo* class origins this hero hoped to leave behind. Alexei Pisemskii's late novels, among them *The Petit Bourgeoisie* (*Meshchane*, 1877), castigate rising capitalists for their acquisitive immorality, and illustrate the extent to which the notions of *intelligentsia* and *meshchanstvo* had diverged by this time, at least from the perspective of the former. The cultural war between *meshchanstvo* and intelligentsia shapes modern Russian intellectual history because "the Russian intelligentsia needs to fight meshchanstvo to construct its own identity," obscuring their common social origins.[69] While the intelligentsia considered itself the bearer of intellectual and moral values, dismissing the *meshchanstvo* for prizing material comfort above all, the two groups nevertheless shared a condition of deprivation, a common experience of exclusion from Petersburg privileges and pleasures.[70]

All of this textual evidence makes it difficult to dispute Antsiferov and Topo-rov when they assert the remarkable similarity of discourse across the Petersburg Text. Perhaps, however, the striking unity in intelligentsia accounts of the city constitutes an *intentional* unity rather than an inadvertent one, based on a literary elitism not so different from that displayed by the aristocrats who made *raznochintsy* authors feel so inadequate during the first two-thirds of the nineteenth century. Intelligentsia writers posited their superiority in intellectual and moral terms, of course, and not according to wealth, position, or breeding. Petersburg critics and theorists of both the imperial and postrevolutionary periods then replicated these attitudes. It might be, thus, that the persistent sense of repetition evoked with reference to the Petersburg Text, only to be dismissed with assertions of a great overarching theme proposed by the city itself, actually reflects the literary aspirations of middle-range writers, who wanted so much to see themselves as part of a tradition.

Reconsidering the Petersburg Text

The Petersburg Text is an anthology of canonical literary fragments, more alike than they are different, excerpted in postimperial compendia. What is more, the Petersburg Text is continuously self-cannibalizing and self-regenerating, repeatedly re-using what has already been written by drawing upon this common body of literary excerpts. Must the Petersburg Text be limited to literary texts? Surely, the Petersburg Text should include the vast array of documentary genres that cover the imperial city, among them guidebooks, reference works, single-theme studies, and cultural histories produced from the latter eighteenth century up to the present day, as well as a more extensive body of fictional works than is usually treated in Petersburg literary studies. As an elastic container, the Petersburg Text might also expand to include the ever-growing body of nonfictional writing that treats the Petersburg Text of the imperial period as a cultural phenomenon—that is, metacommentary on St. Petersburg. After all, Petersburg literary fictions themselves became self-referential over time, and a Petersburg work came to be defined as a network of textual allusions, quotations, and citations that invokes predecessor texts and topographical features in the manner of Andrei Belyi's novel *Petersburg* (1913–22) and Osip Mandelstam's "The Egyptian Stamp" (*Egipetskaia marka*, 1927).[71] "Petersburg" serves as interdisciplinary shorthand for an eclectic fusion of cultural and literary history, social and political thought, biography, autobiography, memoir, and oral lore. My study thus adopts Toporov's well-known term "the Petersburg Text of Russian literature," but substantially expands its range of application.

Petersburg's tricentennial year of 2003, as well as the city's 1991 decision to change its name from "Leningrad" back to "St. Petersburg" (*Sankt-Peterburg*), has intensified the collective writing project, and also generated many reprint editions of past writing about the city. "Indescribable Petersburg" (*Neopisuemyi Peterburg*), the title of an essay from the 1990s, comments ruefully on the quixotic graphic endeavor of textually mapping this city. Petersburg is at once "equal to itself," like a perfect sphere from which nothing can be subtracted.[72] This characterization points to the two most familiar ways of approaching the city in writing: by producing yet another text that makes Petersburg equal to itself, articulating the same things about Petersburg that so many have said before, or by seeking to rupture the closed tautology of Petersburg writing by adding something new. Each aspirant who sets out to write about Petersburg becomes subject to this Petersburg discourse, however, and tells the well-honed story of a frustrated encounter, affirming tradition by re-enacting the quintessential Petersburg narrative.

In mapping the textual topography of imperial Petersburg, I wish to interrogate the myth of Petersburg's uniqueness, often ascribed to the forced and rapid manner in which the city came into existence, and the resulting miragelike quality peculiar to it. In fact, the Petersburg phenomena I explore—architectural eclecticism, urban legend, provincial aspirants, institutions of memory—have their counterparts in London, Paris, Berlin, Prague, Budapest, and New York. Petersburg's insistence on its own uniqueness, I argue, much like its disdain for the cultural middle, may be linked to the insecurities shared by so many of the middling intelligentsia writers who collectively created and articulated the city's mythology. Thus I am not asserting Petersburg's uniqueness, but examining the source of so many *claims* to its uniqueness. Where the Petersburg mythology asserts remarkable unity, I seek pluralism; where this mythology asserts Petersburg's essential difference, I emphasize the city's more ordinary qualities.

It is difficult not to adopt a greedy encyclopedic approach to writing about St. Petersburg, stuffing representative aspects from the vast field of discourse into a single volume. I am not attempting to reproduce imperial St. Petersburg mimetically by way of an "imperialistic" cultural-topographical description that is literally or implicitly totalizing, but rather proposing an alternative model of cultural geography for this much-documented city. The literary texts under consideration do not so much represent St. Petersburg as illustrate particular ways of mapping or constructing this city. This body of literature approximates—not mimetically, but metaphorically, by analogue—the dense web of diverse and coexistent relations constituted by the city.

This plural literary space of the cultural middle represents a re-visioning of realist literature in imperial Russia that does not deny this literature's long-accepted functions of social critique and exposé. Still, the literary realities of inclusion and exclusion in the Petersburg Text are more complex and contradictory than the familiar narrative of literary history would have it. It may be true that the nineteenth-century intelligentsia led the movement to depict St. Petersburg with greater variety and social awareness, but their accounts structurally reproduce and perpetuate the very power relations they protest, even as this writing demonstratively tunnels into the obscure "corners" of Petersburg life. To this day, writing about Petersburg manifests an uneasy balance, reveling in the sumptuous details of "Pushkin's" drawing room Petersburg, while self-righteously celebrating depictions of "Dostoevsky's" slum Petersburg. My study maps Petersburg from the perspective of the cultural middle, the mediating structural reserve from which "Pushkinian" and "Dostoevskian" Petersburg both derive. Upon closer examination of the additional quasicanonical and noncanonical literature about Petersburg, the alleged monolith of the Russian imperial capital—the smooth facade of monumental emptiness punctuated by

familiar landmarks—is reborn in its fascinatingly multiple and nearly undoc-
umentable eclecticism.

This particular mapping proposes an alternative model of the imperial period within which the all-pervasive mythology of Petersburg represents only a
component part. Shifting focus to the cultural middle de-centers imperial Petersburg as we have known it, portraying the city in terms of alternate literary
trajectories, in-between spaces, and outer edges.[73] Mapping St. Petersburg does
not constitute an alternative inventory of the Russian imperial capital in its material aspects, but a reexamination of the literary discourse constituting Petersburg cultural space. Writing is, in this sense, a mediating place, the elusive middle zone that may be unwittingly represented even in the most canonical of
Petersburg literary texts.

Petersburg Eclecticism, Part I:
City as Text

THE ARCHITECTURAL HISTORY of imperial Petersburg, as recounted in numerous scholarly and popular studies, skips over a period—the second half of the nineteenth century, when so-called eclecticism held sway. What might account for this lacuna? Pronouncements made by foreign visitors and Russian cultural critics over the city's lifetime reveal a welter of inconsistencies; eclecticism is celebrated or reviled in accordance with writers' own politico-aesthetic orientations, in response to the cultural climate of the day. What are eclecticism's origins as an architectural style, if indeed it *is* an architectural style, and what is the significance of its presence in the Petersburg cityscape? This chapter argues for eclecticism's legitimate place in Petersburg's cultural and architectural history, both on its own terms and in relation to the neoclassical and art nouveau (known in Russia as *moderne*) styles that bracket its existence. Eclecticism typifies the neglected middle of Petersburg history, dismissed as transitional, chaotic, vulgar, and of suspect commercial orientation, but speaking nevertheless to the rich sociocultural mix in the life of the Russian imperial capital.

Russian pronouncements on eclecticism by both Westernizers and Slavophiles were initially positive but soured over the course of the nineteenth century, as eclecticism proved *too* flexible a concept, seemingly accommodating all comers. The Soviet era, across its seventy-odd years, manifested the same disdain for eclectic architecture as the late-imperial preservationists, in a shared animosity toward commercial protobourgeois culture. Russian accounts of Petersburg, even those by respected antiestablishment writers and scholars, also adopted this stance to a great extent in an implicit identification with Petersburg's late-imperial intellectual elite. Only the post-Soviet period promises a full-scale rehabilitation of eclecticism, long considered the illegitimate sibling of late neoclassicism, respectable revival styles, and prestigious high-culture moderne. Even this warming trend may not represent an appreciation of eclecticism on its own historical terms, however, since it has been reconceived to fit our own postmodern sensibility.

Eclecticism is the "pink elephant" in the Petersburg cityscape. Blocks of imperial-era apartment houses in this style are no less responsible for the city's aesthetic appeal than grand palaces and churches, and, moreover, significantly outnumber their pedigreed architectural brethren. For many visitors, these rows of apartment buildings with their lavish facade detail are what seems most vividly memorable about Petersburg. With roots as an aesthetic strategy in Petersburg's very origins, eclecticism manifests the dissemination of a shared middle-range urban culture beyond the court and the nobility during the second half of the nineteenth century. For all the accusations of superficiality that have been leveled at this architectural trend over the years, eclecticism must have made Petersburg feel increasingly like a real place rather than Dostoevsky's "abstract and premeditated" imperial showpiece, shaping the dwellings and institutions of moderately prosperous people living and working in the city.

The first part of this chapter examines the range of derogatory responses to eclecticism over the years. The second part offers a more positive recapitulation of the term and a closer look at Petersburg's eclectic architectural structures.

St. Petersburg Architecture: A Familiar Story

By the 1830s St. Petersburg's classical architecture seemed stylistically retrograde, lagging behind new ideas emerging in literary and cultural life. As the familiar story goes, St. Petersburg represents the material embodiment of the definitive shift made by Peter the Great from Russia's tradition-bound and culturally isolationist past toward the European-oriented future he envisioned for his country. Peter imported Western technologies and architects to create Petersburg, and the city's initially baroque, then rococo, and neoclassical features were further elaborated during the reigns of Elizabeth (1741–61), Catherine the Great (1762–96), and Alexander I (1801–25).[1] Architectural histories of St. Petersburg detail the feats of design and engineering executed by Domenico Trezzini, Bartolomeo Francesco Rastrelli, Giacomo Quarenghi, and Carlo Rossi. Cultural histories characterize St. Petersburg at the end of the eighteenth century as a collection of artistic masterworks—the Cathedral of Saints Peter and Paul, Alexander Nevsky Monastery, Kunstkammer, Twelve Administrative Colleges, Smolnyi Cathedral and Convent, Winter Palace, Academy of Fine Arts, Tauride Palace, and sumptuous palace-parks at Peterhof and Tsarskoe Selo, to name only a few. These buildings draw primarily upon Western architectural vocabulary, sometimes adding Russian-style onion domes, as in the case of Smolnyi. The architectural narrative extends into the nineteenth century through the reign of Alexander I, with grand projects such as the General Staff Headquarters, Stock Exchange, redone Admiralty, Kazan Cathedral, and finally, massive St. Isaac's Cathedral.

The story of the city after Alexander's death in 1825 grows more confused, however, in both aesthetic and cultural terms. The coherent architectural ensembles of Alexandrine classicism became part of Petersburg's living past. Around them sprung up the architecture of the mid to late nineteenth century, whose profusion of ornamentation proclaimed full or mixed allegiance to neo-Grecian, neo-Byzantine, neogothic, neo-Renaissance, and neobaroque aesthetic revivals. Architectural eclecticism, the much-disparaged product of these changes, refers to those in-between, nonmonumental spaces of the Petersburg cityscape that became an increasingly dominant aspect of the imperial capital and, to a lesser extent, to similar spaces in the other major cities of European Russia, including Moscow.

Eclecticism is a blanket designation for the architectural tendency that falls between neoclassicism and moderne. Eclecticism in Russian architecture also corresponds to the period in literary history between romanticism and modernism, a span of years associated with realism (1830s–1890s), and the great flowering of Russian prose. Unlike literary realism, however, architectural eclecticism is rarely treated as a style in its own right; it is considered merely a transitional stage between two distinct periods. The Russian literary hybrids and unprecedented stylistic formations that developed beginning in the 1830s and 1840s nevertheless parallel a similar shift in the aesthetic orientation of Petersburg architecture.

History credits the repressive Tsar Nicholas I (1825–55) with initiating the breakdown of a unified aesthetic vision for St. Petersburg when he gave his blessing to the hurried construction of buildings for the growing government bureaucracy in a style known as "barracks" (*kazarmennyi*), bureaucratic (*kazënnyi*), or conventional classicism.[2] In doing so, Nicholas inadvertently opened the door to eclecticism. The ensuing "crisis of classicism" in architecture reflected the shift in national consciousness from celebrating the victories of the Napoleonic wars to grieving over the crushed hopes of the Decembrist uprising. City dwellers grew weary of relentlessly classical facades that seemed no longer to proclaim eternal civic precepts or embody Johann Joachim Winckelmann's ideal of "noble simplicity and calm grandeur," but rather suggested an oppressive ever-present state power.

Architectural classicism has often been described as democratizing, of course, in contrast to the aristocratic baroque style used for palaces. Classicism in architecture proclaimed itself a universal style, emphasizing the harmonious relationship of parts to the whole. Classicism as manifested in large, open squares and multicolumn buildings spoke to the Enlightenment ideal of a freely unified populace. On the other hand, classical architecture's emphasis on the center of the composition and its subordination of ornament to overall structure signaled the ambiguous nature of this "democratizing" force. The dull sameness of "barracks" classicism, moreover, made it impossible to determine from the outside whether a given structure was public, private, cultural, commercial, military, or industrial. The crisis of classicism anticipated the need for new architectural

forms that could respond to urban modernization—among them railway stations, hotels, financial institutions, and shopping arcades—and to the changes
in urban demographics that would accelerate after Nicholas I's death.

The decline of classicism in Russian architecture, as the story goes, corresponds to the passing of Russia's "Golden Age," a conceit that evokes the elite
literary and social culture of Pushkin's time, as well as the consolidation of
Russia's status as an imperial power under Catherine II and Alexander I.[3]
Eclecticism arose in response to the diffusion of cultural currency toward the
end of this period, and with it came a powerful if sloppy nostalgia for the seeming certainties of the past. It is possible, however, that the flexible and inclusive
notion of eclecticism has been partly a foil, useful for shoring up the potent retrospective mythology of Alexandrine architectural coherence. After all, the
"Empire" style of Alexander's time combined elements from Roman and Greek
architecture with those appropriated from foreign cultures in a decorative expression of Napoleonic imperialism.[4] Furthermore, Alexandrine Petersburg has
by no means been universally celebrated for its gloriously harmonious wholeness. O. A. Przhetslavskii's memoirs of the 1820s, for example, refer to the "unfinished" look of the capital and complain of the "monotonous" streets and
squares with their uniform pale-yellow facades.[5] Perhaps the story of Petersburg
architecture has grown no less rote than the tired classicism of Nicholas's reign,
and certainly the evolution of architectural eclecticism is due for reexamination.

The questions that eclecticism raises about aesthetics and value have proved
challenging for anyone attempting a synthetic overview of the nineteenth-
century cityscape. Was nineteenth-century eclecticism motivated and coherent,
or is *eclecticism* a term used to convey the absence of a dominant style during
an awkward transitional period that predates the emergence of "modern" architecture? At its worst, architectural eclecticism stands accused of "indiffer-
entism" and "uncommitted romanticism" in its haphazard mixing of elements
from different cultures and historical periods.[6] Rather than unthinking recourse to tired architectural conventions, however, might eclecticism be considered an explosion of architectural vocabulary into the space of the possible?

Soviet-era architectural histories characterize the second half of the nineteenth century in St. Petersburg as the "capitalist epoch" because of the boom in
entrepreneurial construction, apartment buildings in particular, relative to
building projects funded by the imperial family, the nobility, and the state.[7] Architectural eclecticism is thus negatively associated in Petersburg cultural history with the decline of coherent city planning and the rise of a prominent new
class of professional moneymakers. There is little doubt that the Great Reforms
of the 1860s provided tremendous impetus to the architectural trend toward
eclecticism. This period saw the advent of architecture as a profession; innovations in technology, engineering, materials, and architectural design; and the increase in privately funded multiresidence housing and other nonmonumental
structures meant to be both functional and aesthetically appealing.[8] Did eclec-

ticism simply seek to distract the viewer's eye with excessive ornamentation in order to hide the cheap construction of apartment buildings and commercial facilities? Or did the specifically "capitalist" aspects of this era provide the impetus for a new architectural unity in Petersburg?[9]

Perhaps eclecticism is related to Russia's earlier cultural and territorial imperialism as well as to nineteenth-century social-climbing aspiration, in that eclecticism literally tries to have it all. Eclecticism more overtly performed the operation toward which so much of post-Petrine Russian culture directed itself: to appropriate the legacy of world culture, especially of Western Europe, for itself. This proposed common strategy would explain why, beginning in the first part of the eighteenth century, there have *always* been those who considered Petersburg architecture to be eclectic. It may well be that Petersburg did not merely pass through an eclectic period during the latter part of the nineteenth century, imitating the latest European trend in a highly regrettable departure from its authentic neoclassical self, but has always been at its core an eclectic city. From this perspective, St. Petersburg is hypereclectic, overlaying its eclectic eighteenth-century European influences with the new nineteenth-century European eclecticism.

Significantly, St. Petersburg's first century, the eighteenth, was the very period during which questions of influence and originality in art began to receive full theoretical articulation. The "classical" is that locus from which cultural values are conveyed through normative concepts such as genre, style, and tradition. The classical principle polices the cultural terrain for transgression of canonical structures, although revisions to the canon must inevitably occur.[10] In this sense, the eighteenth-century classicism of Petersburg architecture, even as an ideal that was never realized, already contained within itself the seeds of its eclectic nineteenth-century offshoots.

In manifesting eclecticism, the Petersburg cityscape echoes the dissolution of the neoclassical generic hierarchy during the nineteenth century and mirrors literary innovations that occurred over the course of several decades. Chapters 1 and 2 of this book examine the architectural and literary phenomenon of nineteenth-century eclecticism, which I claim as the dominant aesthetic of the imperial Russian capital.

Eclectic Rhetoric: Critical Responses to St. Petersburg

Foreign visitors and Russian cultural critics have both gone on record denouncing Petersburg's architectural eclecticism. Some statements attributing a mongrel quality to Petersburg's borrowings from the West significantly predate the second half of the nineteenth century, when the notion of eclecticism arose. One of the first such characterizations came from Count Francesco Algarotti, who visited Russia during the first half of the eighteenth century, a decade and a half after Peter the Great's death, and referred to Petersburg as "this new city . . . this great window lately opened in the north, through which Russia looks into Europe."[11] Algarotti describes his first sighting of the imperial city, which struck him as sumptuous. Upon disembarking from his ship, however, Algarotti found the city less impressive: "There reigns in this capital a kind of bastard architecture, which partakes of the Italian, the French, and the Dutch." Algarotti's famous metaphor of the great window (*finestrone*) suggests that Russia is doomed to remain an outsider, nose pressed up against the glass, no matter how assiduously it imitates the West. Still, Algarotti's window metaphor—adapted and immortalized by Pushkin in the Prologue to "The Bronze Horseman"—has overshadowed his equally compelling characterization of Petersburg's "bastard architecture," which argues that Petersburg was eclectic right from the start.[12] Indeed, Peter the Great brought Italian, German, and French architects to build his city, and Dutch and English trends, among others, also exerted a significant influence on his plans.[13]

Lest it be assumed that the Golden Age provided a corrective to the motley landscape of Peter's time, the Marquis de Custine's memoirs from the time of Nicholas I attest otherwise. In 1839, a century after Algarotti, the Marquis de Custine declared, "[T]he streets of Petersburg present a strange appearance to the eyes of a Frenchman."[14] He stated flatly, "A taste for edifices without taste has presided over the building of St. Petersburg." For Custine, this incongruous effect resulted from the incompatibility between European architecture and the Russian natural landscape. Antique statues, ornamental columns, and temple-like facades all seemed to him "captive heroes in a hostile land." Situated near swamps and unprepossessing woods, classical buildings are "mere heaps of plaster and mortar" and classical art becomes "an indescribably burlesque style of modern decoration." Like Algarotti, Custine refers to Petersburg's eclecticism without naming it as such, blaming the hodgepodge effect on an ill-advised transplantation of European architectural conventions. The nostalgic idea of a lost, once powerful neoclassical unity in St. Petersburg—the "stern harmonious aspect" invoked by Pushkin in "The Bronze Horseman"—might be merely a fond notion, held only by Russians.[15] In truth, the era of Catherine the Great, the Russian monarch most closely identified with the neoclassical style, produced relatively few important buildings in Petersburg proper, especially as compared with the era of her predecessor Elizabeth, proponent of a lavish baroque style.[16] Foreign visitors like Algarotti and Custine have played up St. Petersburg architecture as "hopelessly eclectic" and "faux classical" to underscore the city's aesthetic illegitimacy, but where did Russian views fit in?

Petr Chaadaev initially condemned Russia's indiscriminate copying of the West, but came to appreciate cultural eclecticism's place in relation to his country's particular moment of historical evolution. The first of Chaadaev's *Philosophical Letters* (1829) refers to the Russian people as "illegitimate children," members of a culture "based wholly on borrowing and imitation" who accept only "ready-made ideas." Russians have not contributed a single great idea to the progress of humanity, and have adopted "from the inventions of others . . . only the deceptive appearances and the useless luxuries."[17] In his 1837 "Apology of a Madman," however, Chaadaev celebrated Peter the Great, who "opened our minds to all the great and beautiful ideas which are prevalent among men; he handed us the whole Occident, such as the centuries have fashioned it, and gave us all its history for our history, and all its future for our future." Russia importing new ideas thus became for Chaadaev "a truth" that "has to be accepted."[18]

Fedor Dostoevsky, in contrast, followed the reverse trajectory, evolving from celebratory to disparaging assessments of eclecticism. Early in his career, Dostoevsky saw in the city's architectural diversity a truly contemporary, national quality. Polemicizing with Custine, Dostoevsky wrote in his 1847 feuilleton series "Petersburg Chronicle" (*Peterburgskaia letopis'*): "All this diversity testifies to a unity of thought and a unity of movement. This row of buildings of Dutch architecture recalls the time of Peter the Great. This building in the style of Rastrelli recalls the century of Catherine; this one, in the Greek and Roman style, the latest time; but all together recall the history of the European life of Petersburg and all Russia. Even up to the present, Petersburg is in dust and rubble; it is still being created, still becoming."[19] For Dostoevsky, spatial diversity becomes temporal continuity, but this history remains incomplete until Petersburg fulfills its glorious potential. Petersburg "dust and rubble" is thus a sign of creation rather than destruction. Dostoevsky changed his tune in his 1873 "Little Pictures" (*Malen'kie kartiny*) from *Diary of a Writer*, however, in an extended polemic against St. Petersburg architecture, which, for him, now manifested the city's characterless quality. "There is no other city like it. It is a reflection of all architectures in the world, all styles and fashions," he wrote. "Everything has been borrowed and everything in its own way disfigured. . . . One doesn't even know how to define our current architecture. It is a kind of disorder of the present moment."[20]

Dostoevsky renders St. Petersburg legible in negative terms this time. Instead of writing history, the St. Petersburg cityscape *erases* history by redoing its facades "for chic." Instead of creating order and narrative, the St. Petersburg cityscape expresses chaos and is original only in its fundamental lack of character. For Dostoevsky, architectural eclecticism initially told the story of the world, but was then made to embody the antihistorical principle in modern times. Dostoevsky paints a vivid picture of rotting wooden houses crowded between marble palaces, and a jumbling together of Roman-style imitations, Italian palazzos, public hospitals and institutes suggesting the epoch of Napoleon III, and prerevolutionary aristocratic French chateaux. Huge hotels with their "American" air of business and new industrial structures complete the picture. Dostoevsky's critique in "Little Pictures" grounds itself in the connection between eclecticism and capitalism that was to receive such bad press in Soviet architectural histories.

In an 1882–83 four-part survey of the arts during the reign of Alexander II, the critic Vladimir Stasov similarly employed the language of trade and commerce in characterizing eclecticism as the attempt to establish a history overnight. According to Stasov, Russian architecture was a Janus-like art with two faces, one of which looked backward with an eye to the saleable potential of past civilizations. Stasov contemptuously ventriloquized a purveyor of such an architectural bill of goods: "If it suits you, here are five yards of Greek 'classicism'; if not, here are three and a quarter of Italian 'Renaissance.' Don't like that? Well then, here, if you please, is a little piece of the highest sort of 'Rococo Louis XV,' and if that's not it, here is a nice bit of 'Romanesque,' six ounces of 'Gothic,' or a whole gross of 'Russian.'"[21] In Stasov's view, this cynicism can assign a price-per-piece to the legacy of the past because a given style need not be appreciated for its integrity, but simply invoked to decorative effect. "Russian" architecture is a bargain, if something of an afterthought in the cultural warehouse, available in large quantities at low cost.

Stasov's protests underscore the relationship between eclecticism and the nineteenth-century search for a national identity. In fact, Russian Slavophiles and nationalists themselves made use of eclecticism to forge a modern Russian identity from Eastern cultural referents from Byzantium and old Russia. The second face of architecture, in Stasov's view, was thus the new "Russian" style used for churches, museums, theaters, apartment housing, and administrative buildings, which he heartily endorsed.

Calls for a return to an "authentic" Eastern architectural style in Russia came from foreign observers as well as Slavophile patriots. The Marquis de Custine declared that Russia's cultural debt to Byzantium mandated a search for models "at Constantinople, but not at Athens."[22] In this, Custine anticipated Eugène Emmanuel Viollet Le Duc's 1877 treatise, L'art russe, which urged Russia to recover its native genius in architecture by returning to Eastern influences and forswearing sterile imitations of Italy, France, and Germany.[23] Such assertions were frequently made by Russians, too, during the second half of the nineteenth century. In his 1871 treatise Russia and Europe, for example, the Slavophile historian Nikolai Danilevskii devoted an entire chapter to protesting "the aping of Europe" (evropeinichan'e) as "the disease of Russian life."[24]

In the nationalists' view, Western-style eclecticism was the logical extension of a classicism that had excluded Russia's own cultural legacy, if somewhat of an improvement in aesthetic terms. Stasov, who so preferred the pseudo-Russian style, could thus favor architectural eclecticism with a kind word. He granted that the new private homes with their Italian and French excesses were better than the reflex classicism, "gloomy, unadorned, and dull to the point of nausea," from the time of Tsar Nicholas. Recalling barracks classicism drew an outburst of spleen from Stasov, who invoked "pediments everywhere, endless columns like rows of classical corpses . . . a lifeless correctness, tastelessness, misery, cold, wide dark corners, walls like those in a political prison, something barn-like and soulless."[25] In comparison, he conceded, the colorful, graceful, and even capricious Renaissance and rococo forms were very welcome.

Although Stasov saw the national trend in architecture as a solution to the excesses of eclecticism, many critics considered the pseudo-Russian style to be part of the problem. In a series of essays that appeared in the journal *World of Art*, the preservationist Alexander Benois revived the old notion of classical Petersburg, casting himself as the city's defender. In the 1902 "Painterly Petersburg" (*Zhivopisnyi Peterburg*), the most notable of these essays, Benois declared: "It seems that there is no city on earth that has been less liked than Petersburg. Which epithets has it *not* earned: 'putrefying swamp,' 'absurd invention,' 'without individuality,' 'bureaucratic department,' 'regimental office.' I have never been able to agree with all of this, and must, in contrast, confess that I love Petersburg, and in contrast, even find a mass of charms that are absolutely distinctive, and characteristic of it alone."[26] Benois considered Petersburg admirable "as a whole," or at least, "in large pieces, big ensembles, and wide panoramic views." He urged readers to rehabilitate what he saw as Petersburg's stony Roman beauty, whose larger lines had remained in place despite the ravages of later nineteenth-century eclecticism that obscured the city's essential nature.[27] Benois attempted to rally the Russian public, protesting the destruction of beautifully proportioned old mansions to make room for new architectural "buffoons, loaded with an enormous quantity of cheap and vulgar plaster ornamentation."[28] He similarly deplored the nationalists' attempts to make Petersburg seem more Russian by interspersing Eastern Orthodox domes and multicolored tile decorations amid the Empire-style structures.

Benois sought to restore what he saw as an authentic masterpiece that had been painted over by amateurs. To prevent further damage, he called for artists to take Petersburg as their subject, and to defend the city's classical consistency against the onslaught of "barbarian mutilation."[29] This artistic call to arms signalled Benois's attempt to re-conceive Petersburg in aesthetic terms, positing a unitary style for an architecture that had always included a mix of elements. The passing of time seems to have dignified the early Western-style architecture that Algarotti and Custine had dismissed as mongrel, whereas later manifestations of eclecticism became a useful whipping boy, blamed for degrading an imaginary classical unity. Ironically, if there *were* an architectural style in Petersburg's past that might be immune to accusations of impurity, it would be the reactionary classicism of Nicholas!

Benois's claims about Petersburg grow more grandiose as his essay unfolds. He denies the commonplace that Petersburg developed by imitating the West, stating instead that Petersburg "grew and developed in a surprisingly original fashion."[30] While Benois concedes that basic constitutive classical motifs were borrowed from Europe, he declares them to have been recombined into unprecedented and magnificent new forms that are neither European nor Russian. This was because Petersburg's empty spaces and lack of history inspired foreign architects to create on a grander and more original scale than had been possible in their native countries. In this sense, Benois saw Petersburg as more truly representative of eighteenth- and nineteenth-century architecture than its predecessor cities, since only Petersburg offered a "pure" manifestation of period spirit. Benois does not even employ a term to dignify the eclectic phenomenon from the 1830s onward, which he refers to as "dilettantish imitation" and "a vinaigrette of *all* styles."[31]

As the preceding examples have shown, Petersburg eclecticism has long suffered a poor reputation, and this situation has yet to be fully remedied. A mid-1990s survey by Natalia Glinka subtitled "The Golden Age of St. Petersburg Architecture" stops pointedly with the last of Carl Rossi's "ensemble" projects, the construction of the Alexandrinskii Theater complex in the early 1830s.[32] Glinka follows the early twentieth-century example of the preservationist Igor Grabar, whose history of Petersburg architecture purports to cover the eighteenth and nineteenth centuries, but goes no further than "Nicholaevan Classicism."[33] Architects from the eclectic period grace the Petersburg pantheon only if their early work was thoroughly grounded in the neoclassical style, or if they were responsible for one of Petersburg's most celebrated buildings. August Montferrand (1786–1858) designed and built the lavishly eclectic St. Isaac's Cathedral, but receives more approval for his Alexander Column on Palace Square. Similarly, Alexander Briullov (1798–1877) created interiors in gothic, Renaissance, and Moorish styles for the Winter Palace after the 1837 fire, but is probably best known for his work on the General Staff Headquarters.[34] Vladimir Kurbatov, Grabar's contemporary, reserved particular contempt for Andrei Stakenschneider (1802–1865), who built the Mariinskii and Beloselskii-Belozerskii palaces, both completed in the 1840s, and Constantine Thon (1794–1881), who infused an essentially neoclassical structure with early Russian and Byzantine motifs in the St. Catherine church of the 1830s.[35] Lesser-known architects practicing mid-century eclecticism, such as Ludwig Bonstedt, Harald Julius Bosse, and Nikolai Efimov—whose artistic vision shaped the Yusupov mansion on Liteinyi Prospect, Kochubey house, and Buturlin house, as well as the House of Ministries and the remodeled City Hall—rarely receive so much as a mention in Petersburg architectural histories.[36] Only after *moderne* is perceived to have emerged as a distinctive architectural style at the very turn of the twentieth century do new buildings—among them the Astoria Hotel, the new Fabergé headquarters, the Eliseev food emporium, and the Singer Sewing Machine building—join the roster of Petersburg masterworks.[37] The moderne style lies on the same continuum with eclecticism, however, not refuting the decorative mix-and-match practices of the latter, but rather adopting this strategy as its own, particularly in the early stages. In the eyes of Petersburg cultural historians, the moderne style successfully dignified buildings that served the same commercial purposes as their despised eclectic predecessors.

Russian historians may have neglected eclecticism, but some writers have gone so far as to obliterate it, canonizing the ideal classical Petersburg they prefer to remember. In this spirit, Alexander Solzhenitsyn's 1960s prose poem "The City on the Neva" celebrates Petersburg's "perfect, everlasting beauty." "It is alien to us," he declares, "yet it is our greatest glory."[38] Solzhenitsyn expresses gratitude that Petersburg has remained its classical self, immune to Soviet innovations such as "wedding-cake skyscrapers" or "five-story shoeboxes." His poem, however, evinces an unacknowledged desire to protect an imaginary authentic Petersburg, not from the ravages of the twentieth century, but from the truths of nineteenth-century architectural history. Like Benois, Solzhenitsyn turns back the clock to an imaginary era and reconceives Petersburg according to an insistent mythology, without the architectural eclecticism that was a major part of its history.

Even Petersburg's most sophisticated cultural theorists and elegists are not immune to the prevailing view on architectural eclecticism. In his 1979 essay "A Guide to a Renamed City," Joseph Brodsky characterizes the gradual decline of Petersburg architecture from the perfect abstraction of classicism to the unlovely shapes of capitalism: "This was dictated as much by the swing towards functionalism (which is but a noble name for profit making) as by general aesthetic degradation."[39] Brodsky, like so many others, evokes the "barrack-like style of the Nicholas I epoch," and the "cumbersome apartment buildings squeezed between the classical ensembles." "Then came the Victorian wedding cakes and hearses," notes Brodsky, referring to eclecticism's heyday. "And, by the last quarter of the century, this city that started as a leap from history into the future began to look in some parts like a regular Northern European bourgeois." Brodsky attributes the diseased spread of eclecticism to the pernicious influence of capitalist Europe and not to Petersburg's own copycat tendencies. Still, the aesthetic effect remains the same.

And yet, Brodsky invokes the imperial capital's architecture before Nicholas I as a phenomenon no less haphazard, and thus implies continuity between "classical" and "eclectic" Petersburg. When the "sluices" (Brodsky's version of the "window on Europe") were opened, European architectural motifs "gushed into and inundated" St. Petersburg. Petersburg represents European aesthetic surplus; the city was overwhelmed by Western architectural elements, just as the Russian language was flooded by an unregulated influx of foreign words during the eighteenth century. Regarding the European tradition, Petersburg remains a fake, or at least, it is authentic in an unintended sense: "whatever the architects took for the standard in their work—Versailles, Fontainebleau, and so on—the outcome was always unmistakably Russian." Brodsky's essay manifests contradictory tendencies. Did eclecticism taint Petersburg's essence or is eclecticism Petersburg's most essential quality? It appears that one person's eclecticism is another person's consistency. It seems moreover that a critic who subscribes to the potent myth of St. Petersburg as classical colossus may elsewhere invoke Petersburg's eternally synthetic eclecticism.

Brodsky rejoices that Lenin's fateful arrival at Finland Station "froze" St. Petersburg, since the Bolsheviks transferred the seat of their government to Moscow and paid little attention to the former capital, which thus escaped a monumental Stalinist architectural facelift. Brodsky's motif of freezing, which turns Peter's city into a poignant monument to itself, signals his wish to hold the process of change at bay. Although Soviet architecture is the ostensible threat here, one senses that Brodsky might wish to turn back the clock and excise the most offending representatives of late-imperial eclecticism.

In another essay, however, Brodsky gives eclecticism its due: "I must say that from these façades and porticoes—classical, modern, eclectic, with their columns, pilasters, and plastered heads of mythic animals or people—from their ornaments and caryatids holding up the balconies, from the torsos in the niches of their entrances, I have learned more about the history of our world than I subsequently have from any book. Greece, Rome, Egypt—all of them were there."[40] The poet and essayist renders Petersburg's eclecticism legitimate as a source of cultural literacy and an essential part of his own artistic evolution. Brodsky is speaking of the Soviet period, of course, when citizens were not free to travel abroad and Petersburg architecture was the closest they could get to European civilization.

An uneasy acknowledgement of Petersburg eclecticism can even coexist alongside emphatic assertions of the city's extraordinary unity of style. Reprising the early Dostoevsky, Yuri Lotman asserts that Petersburg represents a "unique phenomenon in world civilization" in its intense contrasts and metaphysical paradoxes.[41] Sounding like Benois, however, Lotman cites "the architecture of the city, unique in the consistency of the huge ensembles which cannot be divided up into buildings of different periods, as is the case in cities with long histories."[42] Petersburg is here distinguished precisely by the *absence* of diversely blended styles in random juxtaposition, as is usual in most cities. What has become of Petersburg's infamous eclecticism? To be fair, Lotman's Petersburg implicitly pertains to the early decades of the nineteenth century—the much-beloved "Pushkinian" moment in the city's cultural history. The architecture of Lotman's imperial capital nevertheless seems frozen in his writing, much in the way of Brodsky's Soviet-era Petersburg.

Lotman describes the first half of the nineteenth century as a time of "cultural and semiotic contrasts which served as the soil for an exceptionally intense intellectual life" in St. Petersburg, characterized by a struggle between "Petersburg the literary text" and "Petersburg the [normative] metalanguage."[43] He evokes the constant collisions between heterogeneous texts and codes that collide within the "cauldron" of the city. Lotman neglects to treat architectural eclecticism on its own terms, however, as part and parcel of the heterogeneous mix. Instead, he implicitly assigns Petersburg architecture to the monolithic "metalanguage" that literature sought to subvert. He celebrates the city's literary, social, and cultural eclecticism, but only against the background of a Petersburg that he renders architecturally much more coherent than it truly was.[44]

Only at the very end of the Soviet period did twentieth-century Russian sources begin to treat eclecticism's low status in explicit terms as part of Russian cultural history. The 1988 exhibition catalogue *Lost Architectural Monuments of Petersburg-Leningrad*, for example, provides an unusually subtle perspective on the relative distribution of cultural value, noting that the term "monument" (*pamiatnik*) became a distinct historical-artistic category for the city only at the beginning of the twentieth century: "For Petersburg, this included the surviving constructions of the entire eighteenth century and the first third of the nineteenth century, that is, of baroque and classicism. Eclecticism on the whole was despised; *moderne* was selectively respected, but not counted in terms of 'monuments' because of its recent appearance."[45] A few Russian architectural historians have concentrated their efforts on the problematic second half of the nineteenth century in an affirmatively revisionist spirit, among them Andrei Punin, who pointedly titled one of his monographs *Architectural Monuments of Petersburg: The Second Half of the Nineteenth Century*.[46] Boris Kirikov began an article about the architecture of this period by eschewing the decades-long tradition of denigrating eclecticism: "It is generally known that the development of architecture from the mid-nineteenth century to the beginning of the twentieth was distinguished by high intensity, complex diversity, and, at critical moments, by an abrupt shift in orienting values, and by the taut dramatism of creative striving."[47] Kirikov discusses eclecticism in terms of its "pluralism" and "polymorphism," albeit primarily with reference to private mansions outside of the city center and in the rural Petersburg environs.

The architectural historian Evgenia Kirichenko advocated taking eclecticism on its own terms, rather than assessing it negatively against the conventions of classicism, by "deciphering" the architectural language of later nineteenth-century Russian buildings.[48] The democratic diffusion of cultural influences is a deliberate feature of eclecticism, whose operative values are distribution (*ravnomernost'*) and equivalence (*ravnoznachnost'*), she claims. In short, eclecticism entails "a multiplicity of forms and a single device," resulting in a profusion and democratization of expressive means.[49] Eclecticism represents a deliberately horizontal and democratic, not a vertical or hegemonic, expressive strategy.

A sampling of post-Soviet trends in writing about the imperial capital reveals that eclecticism is now linked in positive terms with Petersburg's essential qualities and with its status as a "metacity" that creatively combines elements from other world capitals. The spirit of the times seems almost to dictate seeing Petersburg in this way, in fact. Petersburg can be characterized as a "style-engendering" city, in "adapting, transforming, assimilating, and processing diverse urban styles."[50] Petersburg architecture corresponds to its inhabitants, who constituted a "Pan-European world," a synthetic "sign of European unity," even a "Europe in miniature" that surpassed Western Europe itself.[51] Petersburg res idents, even those who were Russian, were all immigrants. There existed no "indigenous ethno-cultural nucleus" in Petersburg to exert a dominant influence on new arrivals from different parts of the Empire—Finland, Poland, the Baltic states, and Armenia, to give a few examples—and these residents had to reinvent themselves as "Petersburgers." Europeans of all kinds—Germans, Dutch, French, and Swedes—also made their way to Petersburg and settled there. The human cultural synthesis in Petersburg thus manifested itself visually in architecture.

Eclecticism is Petersburg's "stylistic dominant," if the city's "stylistic polyglossia" can be treated in an "aesthetic-historical" sense, and not according to eclecticism's more narrow discipline-specific connotations in architecture and art criticism.[52] In this way, eclecticism may constitute a stylistic rather than period designation, forming the basis for Petersburg's essential character of "city-compilation," "city-collection," and "city-museum."[53] Petersburg might thus be envisioned in terms of "architectural crib-notes" (arkhitekturnaia shpargalka), since it presents an ideal object of study in its "hypersemiotic" aspect and self-consciousness as an aesthetic artifact. This affirmation of Petersburg's composite qualities is not a new view of the city, but an old one with a new, positive spin. Given the central role that eclecticism has played in the persistent view of St. Petersburg as an inauthentic capital, however, it is ironic that eclecticism now offers the solution to the city's identity crisis. If eclecticism is to be made fully legitimate, however, a better accounting of this cultural phenomenon seems warranted, particularly since some postmodern accounts of Petersburg sound suspiciously akin to the familiar imperial-era judgments rendered by Custine and others. Petersburg is Russia's "most grandiose simulacrum," expressing the fundamentally "simulative nature of Russian civilization," which strives to produce the impression of reality through such secondary stimuli as names and external images.[54]

Petersburg eclecticism—in literature as well as architecture—has been overdescribed but largely undertheorized.[55] Of course, "the battle of the styles," particularly on building facades, also characterizes later nineteenth-century architecture in Western Europe, most notably in London, but in Vienna and Paris as well. Paris was secure in its neoclassical tradition, however, and eclectic facades emerged there on an architectural continuum that retained a firm classicist foundation.[56] Seen thus more broadly, nineteenth-century eclecticism may represent more than an antistylistic confusion following a crisis in classicism and constitute a natural and logical outgrowth of that preceding period, as well as an expression of sociohistorical realities.[57] In Petersburg's case, eclecticism, while paralleling developments in Europe, threatened the city's fragile self-assertion as timeless, utterly cohesive, and unique, and contradicted a perhaps too insistent mythology of classical splendor. Cities are eclectic by their very nature. Petersburg, however, was augmented with a discourse promoting its homogeneity.

The History of Eclecticism: The Unprincipled Principle?

During the time of Augustus, Vitruvius established the language of architectural form in terms of grammar and syntax. He provided recommendations for style, proportion, and effect, proposing the view of an architectural structure as a harmonious, organic whole governed by the principles of *eurythmia* and *symmetria*. The concept of harmony is derived from Aristotle's *Poetics*, in which the fundamental principle of dramatic action dictates "the structural union of the parts being such that, if any one of them is displaced or removed, the whole will be disjointed and disturbed."[58] Vitruvius codified the spatial practices of the ancient Greek and Roman city in rhetorical terms and raised architecture to the same level as the art of poetry.[59] The figurative operations of architecture thus came to resemble the "shapes" described by figures of speech.[60] As author-architect Wightwick wrote in an 1850 essay titled "The Principles and Practice of Architectural Design," "A building is a body . . . lettered over with beauty of diction, with poetic illustration, and with the charms of rhetoric."[61] But did mid-nineteenth-century eclecticism threaten or enhance the essential legibility of architecture?

Calling eclecticism "indiscriminate" ignores the principle at the word's very root, as well as eclecticism's history as a philosophical movement. The term comes from the Greek *eklektikos* (selective) and *eklegein* (to select), meaning to choose out of a selection, or to distinguish. Etymologically, then, eclecticism does not indicate randomness, but rather intentionality. Eclecticism's primary meaning, moreover, implies an evaluative basis for selection—choosing what appears to be *best* from diverse sources, systems, or styles, while remaining democratic in its array of choices.

Eclectic philosophy arose in Greece in the second century B.C., as a fusion of three major schools of thought—Academic, Peripatetic, and Stoic—and their doctrines on life, nature, and the divine.[62] The mixing and matching specific to nineteenth-century aesthetic eclecticism, however, was a cultural phenomenon inspired by the teachings of Victor Cousin, whose 1818 course at the Sorbonne, *Du Vrai, du Beau et du Bien*, referred to his system of philosophy as "Eclecticism." Cousin distilled the teachings of English, Scottish, French, and German philosophers, creating a synthetic approach to the discipline that combined elements of spiritualism and scientism.[63] This work provided the basis for French academic philosophy, which was taught throughout the French lycée and university systems from a common syllabus known as the *programme*. In nineteenth-century philosophy and then architecture, eclecticism retains a strong pedagogical component, stressing the need for a discriminating receptivity to multiple traditions. In this, eclecticism represents an antidote to unreflective revivalism, and not an example of it.

Nineteenth-century "eclecticism" designates European architecture during the first half of the nineteenth century with its "more liberal use of the whole vocabulary of the Graeco-Roman tradition" that was too narrowly interpreted during the crisis of classicism.[64] Not all eclecticisms are alike, however. "Typological eclecticism" adapts a model from the past to meet contemporary requirements, whereas "synthetic eclecticism" combines architectural features from different periods. Typological eclecticism resulted in the use of classical architecture for public buildings, and medieval architecture—generally Byzantine, Gothic, or Romanesque—for churches. Architectural treatises such as Thomas Hope's *Historical Essay on Architecture* (1835), however, called for a new composite style that borrowed individual features selectively from the past as appropriate for a particular nation's climate, topography, and cultural environment. In this way, eclecticism dovetails with romantic aesthetics, freeing architecture to express the authentic genius of a nation, although not in exclusively native forms. Synthetic eclecticism is often linked to the work of Charles Garnier, architect of the Grand Opera in Paris (1861–74), perhaps the most famous building of the nineteenth century and an exemplar of the hybrid "Second Empire" or "Napoleon III" style.

The entry on "eclecticism" in Denis Diderot's famous *Encyclopedia* (1751–72) takes pains to distinguish eclecticism from the less principled aesthetic strategy of "syncretism." "Imagine a poor insolent fellow," writes the author about a hypothetical syncretist, "ill content with the rags that cover him, who throws himself upon the best-dressed passers-by, tears from one a blouse, from another an overcoat, and makes from his plunder a bizarre outfit of every possible color and part."[65] Syncretism is "antistylistic" and anarchic.[66] Eclecticism, like syncretism, draws upon the products of broad historical and cultural experience, but unlike syncretism, eclecticism has discriminating taste and intends the results of its labors to be harmonious.[67] As an embracing language of culture, architectural eclecticism was more worldly than classicism, not confining itself to Greek, Roman, and Renaissance influences, but reveling in Eastern motifs as well, and in architectural styles such as Baroque, Gothic, and medieval Russian, whose aesthetic reputations had declined by the latter part of the eighteenth century.

In an 1837 article, the Russian writer Nestor Kukol'nik evaluated the new aesthetic standard for architecture after a visit to Peter the Great's summer palace, Peterhof, and its environs. Kukol'nik approvingly noted the coexistence of small summer dachas, private residences in diverse architectural styles, and the new neoclassical theater:

> Our age is an eclectic one, in everything its characteristic feature is intelligent choice (*umnyi vybor*) . . . variety is superb, enchanting, but only if it is exquisite. The Parthenon and other remnants of Greek architecture; the Moorish Alhambra; Gothic cathedrals of the old and new styles; the Italian architecture of Palladio; . . . Ancient Venice; . . . Indian architecture with its Byzantine development; in a word, all kinds of architecture can be exquisite, reciprocally employ their means, inter-

mingle and produce new kinds. But these new kinds are exquisite and original only when they sustain the harmony of their parts and their majesty . . . as a whole.[68]

Kukol'nik supported the creation of "new kinds" that combined diverse influences, but called upon the principles of taste, proportion, and harmony—rather than any specific guidelines—to govern these choices.[69] Nikolai Gogol also called for a varied cityscape in "On the Architecture of the Present Day," an essay from his 1835 *Arabesques* (discussed in Chapter 2). During this cautiously optimistic period, eclecticism was felt to balance informed choice and traditional values. But what if someone else's taste proves not to your liking?

Kukol'nik's remarks belong to the polemic about artistic form and function in 1830s and 1840s Russia that was often directed against classicism. Initially, the eclectic impulse was connected with a general trend toward "historicism," without which, as the critic Vissarion Belinsky affirmed, "the apprehension of art and philosophy would be impossible."[70] Growing out of the philosophies of Herder and Hegel, historicism countered Enlightenment philosophy of the preceding century, maintaining that universal principles could not fully account for human culture. In this, historicism provided a marked contrast to classicism's reliance on the "timeless" and "abstract" forms of antiquity.[71]

The two major architectural tendencies of the historicist period in Russia were "retrospective stylization" and "true eclecticism," notions largely parallel to "typological" and "synthetic" eclecticism.[72] Stylization refers to the reproduction of a style as a whole or in recognizable motifs, a common strategy of the 1830s–1850s often employed for royal and noble homes. Initially, such retrospective stylization was dominant and multiple architectural revival styles were simultaneously present in the Petersburg cityscape. As well as a response to the new historicism, retrospective stylization can be considered a trickle-down effect of the eighteenth-century, recalling the fantasy pavilions at Tsarskoe Selo in Catherine the Great's time and the solipsistic aesthetic environments created by eighteenth-century Russian landowners on their private estates.[73] Builders of new mansions would often execute the building exterior in a particular revival style, such as early Florentine Renaissance, and create interiors in a mix of styles that might include Gothic, Moorish, Louix XVI, and so on. By the middle of the nineteenth century, however, as the following paragraphs will show, retrospective stylization had progressed to true eclecticism in Petersburg architecture.

The Gothic retrospective stylizations that appeared during the 1820s through the 1840s were an early and striking new trend in postneoclassical architecture, inspired by the popular fictions of Sir Walter Scott and by romantic fashion in general. Initially limited to curiosities such as the imperial "cottage" at Peterhof's Alexandria Park and the Chapel Pavilion, Arsenal, and White Tower at Tsarskoe Selo, neo-Gothic stylization soon spread to private estates throughout the European part of Russia. The neo-Gothic style had a distinct arriviste component as it asserted the allegedly venerable status of its patrons.

A fascination with Eastern decorative motifs during this same period followed an earlier flurry of "chinoiserie" during the eighteenth century and was greatly stimulated by the archeological discoveries of Ancient Egypt. The Empire style of Alexander I's reign also included interior furnishings and ornamentation inspired by Napoleon's campaigns in Egypt. Egyptian motifs appeared in outdoor structures such as the defunct Egyptian Bridge on the Fontanka and the Egyptian Gates at Tsarskoe Selo. (The most important "Egyptiana" in St. Petersburg, of course, is the pair of genuine stone sphinxes on the Neva embankment by the Academy of Arts, brought to Russia from Thebes in 1832.) Moorish and Turkish styles too made their mark on the Petersburg cityscape, mostly in interior settings, in a reflection of the imperial mood. The aesthetic turn toward the East manifested itself most notably, as already mentioned, in the turn to a "Russian" style, based upon Byzantine architectural tradition, particularly in churches, which took on a more pronounced national character under Nicholas I.[74] Eastern-style church cupolas and bell towers became a more marked aspect of the Petersburg cityscape, marring the "European" effect of the whole.[75]

Like the archeological discoveries in Egypt, the excavation of Pompeii that had begun during the eighteenth century inspired Roman architectural stylization during the middle part of the nineteenth century, particularly in private homes built to resemble the villas of antiquity. Also popular were motifs from ancient Grecian architecture, particularly facade elements such as caryatids, atlantes, and mask faces, like those used on the New Hermitage. Even neoclassicism received its own eclectic updating, with a revisiting of architectural features from the age of Catherine.[76]

Neobaroque ("Second Baroque") and neo-Renaissance (Italian fifteenth- and sixteenth-century) elements in architectural detail also became fashionable during the reign of Nicholas I, as exhibited by one of the city's first major buildings in a fully realized eclectic mode—the 1836 Demidov House on Herzen Street by Montferrand. The ground level displays square relief panels between the arched windows; the second level, Ionic pilasters between pedimented windows; the third, Corinthian pilasters. In addition, the building also uses mixed neo-Renaissance and neobaroque ornamentation: the central porte cochere is flanked by atlantes and caryatids supporting the long second-story balcony; semicircular reliefs decorate the area over the three balcony doors, with two marble angels holding a huge coat of arms above the middle door; and the central third-story window is framed by two caryatids. The neo-Renaissance style took a story-by-story approach to facade ornamentation, in contrast to the classical method, where the facade was conceived as a unit. This Renaissance-inspired use of diverse motifs within a single structure opened up a world of possibilities for eclectic decoration, anticipating the use of ornamentation on the facades of apartment buildings.

During the second third of the nineteenth century, true eclecticism emerged

FIGURE 1.1. Demidov House. (Author's Collection.)

from retrospective stylization, exhibiting a diminishing sense of obligation to be consistent in evoking architectural motifs on a single structure. Eclecticism eventually came to denote the heterogeneous features on the exterior of a single architectural structure. During the second third of the nineteenth century, a number of new palaces were constructed in accordance with these eclectic trends, several by architect Andrei Stakenschneider.[77] The Mariinskii Palace (1839–44), his first major project in the city center, represented a major remodeling and expansion of Vallin de la Mothe's Chernyshev Palace from the mid-eighteenth century. Built for Maria, the daughter of Tsar Nicholas I, the redone three-story palace on St. Isaac's Square had a projecting six-column portico supporting a tall attic, and a porch extending over the driveway at the entrance. Four-column porticoes with pediments balance the projecting end pavilions. Thus the major structural aspects of the Mariinskii Palace accord with classical principles, particularly the severe pediments, the vertical accents of the columns and pilasters, and the horizontal emphasis provided by the cornices between floors and the entablature. The Palace is, however, infused with eclectic elements that depart radically from the conventions of even late neoclassicism.[78] The faceted rough-hewn stone of the first floor, for example, recalls the

FIGURE 1.2. Mariinskii Palace. (Author's Collection.)

palazzo style of the Italian Renaissance. The large scroll decorations on the attic
are reminiscent of baroque ornamental conventions, as are the large vases on
the central balustrade. The lampions by the entrance arcs are stylized, rather
than historically accurate versions of those from antiquity. Thus the decorative
accents on the Mariinskii Palace—done in sandstone and metal, and not stucco
as would be the case during the second half of the nineteenth century—are not
consistent with the conventions of classical ornamentation, although classicism
governs the essential structure of the building.

Inside the Mariinskii Palace, the public halls dispersed around the central ro-
tunda were much more intimate in their style and dimensions than was usual
for classical interiors. The rooms were appointed in a variety of different styles,
a departure from baroque and neoclassical practices, which tended to choose a
single unifying style for interiors. Conventionally classical sculptural figures
mixed with bas-reliefs depicting sentimental rustic scenes. Rooms in the Pom-
peian style and French rococo boudoirs alternated with decor using Renaissance
masks and figures. Decorative medallions displayed scenes from the works
of Pushkin, Derzhavin, and Zhukovskii, rather than well-known episodes from
antiquity.

Stakenschneider's Novo-Mikhailovskii Palace on the Palace Embankment

(1857–61) joined two preexisting houses behind a new facade with varied motifs, among them Renaissance bas-reliefs above the first-floor windows, early classical decorative sculptural garlands on the first- and third-floor window frames, and baroque second floor windows and balcony railings. Each floor includes porticoes with columns at the center and ends of the facade, but caryatids in baroque-style poses are substituted for the third-story columns, and an enormous coat-of-arms sculpture occupies the center. A cascade of stucco relief decorates the facade and pediments. As dwellings built for members of the royal family, eclectic stylized palaces such as the Mariinskii and the Novo-Mikhailovskii are counted among St. Petersburg's major architectural structures, if somewhat hesitatingly.

The Cathedral of St. Isaac of Dalmatia is the eclectic structure that looms largest in the Petersburg cityscape. The cathedral's great golden dome dominates the skyline and has been compared with St. Peter's and the Pantheon of Agrippa in Rome, and St. Paul's in London. Constructed over the period 1818–58 under the direction of architect August Ricard de Montferrand, St. Isaac's extends historically and stylistically from late classicism into eclecticism. To be sure, the introduction to an album devoted to the cathedral characterizes St. Isaac's as "the last major building in Russia designed in the style of late Classicism," and one that merely shows the "influence" of the new eclectic trend in individual features such as "the excessive use of sculpture on the pediments."[79] In the early twentieth century, however, the Russian preservationist historian Igor Grabar declared that the "poor taste of the time" was reflected in features such as St. Isaac's "ungainly angels with torches" and four small bell-towers, which, he claimed, spoiled the cathedral's grand design. Grabar refused to attribute St. Isaac's to the Alexandrine epoch, insisting that in the time of Alexander I, the cathedral would have been considered too bourgeois and philistine (*meshchanskaia*).[80]

St. Isaac's is more than slightly eclectic in its fusion of neoclassical pediments, columns, and porticoes with Italian Renaissance-style paintings, Greek-Orthodox crosses, Church Slavonic lettering, and Byzantine architectural features, in a grand marriage of West and East. In this spirit, Théophile Gautier, who published his *Voyage en Russie* in 1866, mounted a stirring defense of St. Isaac's as an architectural masterwork. Gautier devotes a lengthy chapter to the cathedral, exclaiming, "What a symphony of marble, of granite, bronze and gold!"[81] He declares St. Isaac's "unquestionably the most beautiful of modern churches," whose architecture admirably suits St. Petersburg, "the youngest and newest of the European capitals." Gautier insists on St. Isaac's "absolute unity" of sui generis style and admonishes those who regret that it was not built exclusively in the Byzantine style, as was Saint Sophia at Constantinople. A great church, Gautier insists, should affect nothing "peculiar, temporary, or local."

Gautier describes St. Isaac's in terms that consistently seek to join the principles of unity and diversity. The strong classical influence makes use of forms that

Figure 1.3. Novo-Mikhailovskii Palace. (Author's Collection.)

FIGURE 1.4. St. Isaac's Cathedral, from Auguste Montferrand 1820 *Église de St. Isaac.*
(Courtesy of Houghton Library at Harvard.)

are consecrated, "independent of fashion and time" and "eternal," while its fusion of styles "unfolds itself like a beautiful phrase of religious music that . . .
does not deceive the eye by any dissonance." Gautier also notes approvingly that
interior paintings by other artists treat diverse subjects from the Greek liturgy
and Russian national history, as well as from the Old and New Testaments.

Gautier praises what he calls the church's "magnificent sobriety," which re-
frains from fanciful or capricious exterior ornamentation, limiting itself to bas-
reliefs, groups, and single figures in bronze. Although Gautier notes the "pure,
noble, and severe" outlines of St. Isaac's, he also praises rich Eastern touches
such as gold cupolas, as well as the tremendous variety of materials, such as
malachite, lapis-lazuli, jasper, agate, porphyry, colored marble, and Finnish
granite. These touches save the church from "the cold, monotonous, and slightly
wearisome effect of what—for want of a more correct expression—we call classic architecture." Gautier thus celebrates St. Isaac's for its Eastern aspect, while
simultaneously emphasizing the cathedral's reassuringly familiar classical orientation. His defense of St. Isaac's is itself eclectic in character, celebrating both

the church's adherence to classical form and its departure from these conventions, an approach that seems appropriate in light of the church's inception. Montferrand reportedly won the commission to build St. Isaac's from Alexander I when he dazzled the Tsar with a sketchbook containing twenty-four miniature illustrations of the cathedral variously conceived in Chinese, Indian, Byzantine, Greek, Roman, Gothic, and Italian Renaissance styles. The Tsar was thus persuaded by the eclectic flexibility of Montferrand's vision.

Although St. Isaac's included Eastern Orthodox architectural elements, it seems closer to the classical tradition when compared with the Russian Revival that was given a second lease on life in conjunction with the Russification policies of Alexander III (1881–94). True, this style was far less prominent in Petersburg than in Moscow, where the Historical Museum, the Upper and Middle Trading Rows, and the Moscow City Duma exemplified the trend. Petersburg has one major Russian Revival architectural monument from this period, however—the Church of the Resurrection of the Savior on the Blood, built on the site of Alexander II's 1881 assassination by terrorists.[82] This church, stylized to evoke medieval Muscovy, is criticized far more than the eclectic St. Isaac's for appearing incongruous in its (Western-looking) urban setting.[83] In its insistence on a unity of pseudostyle, perhaps the Savior on the Blood was not eclectic *enough* for Petersburg.

Eclecticism's lack of prestige in Petersburg cultural history may reflect the fact that during the second half of the nineteenth century, this style became increasingly associated with functional public buildings rather than magnificent monuments like St. Isaac's. The most eclectic architectural exemplars from this period were schools, hospitals, commercial arcades, railway stations, and apartment houses.[84] These new building types represented a blank slate, aesthetically speaking, since they had no precedents in the distant past to confine architectural fancy. In contrast, the earlier phenomenon of more internally consistent architectural stylizations in the 1830s through the 1850s occurs most often in elite cultural structures such as theaters, churches, palaces, mansions, and museums.

With the spread of eclecticism, the direction of influence reversed itself from that of neoclassicism, and elite structures, such as palaces, came to resemble their more public counterparts in a general "bourgeoisification" of the late-nineteenth-century Petersburg cityscape.[85] The mid-1870s Hotel Europe, for example, which extended along the west side of Mikhailovskaia Street and thus intruded upon Carlo Rossi's much-praised Mikhailovskii Palace ensemble, was considered an exemplar of the "Third Baroque," a contemptuous term for ornamental excesses that made Stakenschneider's "Second Baroque" look restrained. The 1890 Officer's House on Liteinyi Prospect was similarly vilified.

Eclectic effects moved up, down, and across Petersburg social and geographical topography. Interior decorative features appeared on facades, while private and public buildings exchanged features of detailing. The overall quantity of

FIGURE 1.5. Officers' Building. (Author's Collection.)

decoration increased, while the scale of individual decorative features diminished, becoming almost miniaturized. An insistence on maximal ornamentation, much of it dismissed as "pseudo-historical," was seen as the hallmark of buildings commissioned by newly prosperous nonnoble clients. Ornamenta-

FIGURE 1.6. Mutual Credit Society House. (Author's Collection.)

tion also characterized buildings that wished to ingratiate themselves with this
clientele, such as Girshovich's Azov Bank from the late 1890s and Pavel Siuzor's
1888–90 First Mutual Credit Society House on the Catherine Canal. The latter's
mixed neo-Renaissance and Louis XVI facade features a large arched niche resembling a triumphal arc on the upper floors of the central projection, a dense
covering of relief panels, sculpture in mixed styles, grillwork, balustrades, cor-

FIGURE 1.7. Azov Bank. (Author's Collection.)

nices, and variegated fenestration, the whole topped with an ornate Second Empire four-sided cupola with large Winged Glory figure. During this late-century period, there were more than two-dozen banks on Nevsky Prospect alone.[86]

Should one speak of multiple eclecticisms, or of different types of eclecticism within the nineteenth-century Russian cultural context? During the 1830s and even 1840s, the notion of eclecticism seemed largely positive, signaling a new diversity in the cityscape and an embrace of world culture in architecture. Eclecticism asserted that a new reality could be constructed from fragments of the past, since invoking the past in fragmented form pays tribute to history, while denying its power to determine the future—a particularly potent notion for Russia. Only during the second half of the nineteenth century did "eclecticism" acquire the negative connotations of ahistoricity and tastelessness in the eyes of cultural critics, very probably because of the more middling social origins of its practitioners and admirers. At its best, however, eclecticism represents a meditation on tradition that is inherently democratic and nonhierarchical, since no single style or historical period is privileged. Petersburg's architectural eclecticism points backward in time to the imaginary neoclassical union of all artistic forms and genres, but transforms that hierarchical, vertical structure of cultural meaning into a horizontal network, a more accurate "map" of the heterogeneous nineteenth-century city.[87]

Eclecticism expressed the vibrant nature of the everyday in shaping buildings for housing, shopping, and traveling, and manifested the transhistorical, transcultural imagination of an emerging sector of the public.[88] Why must it be the case that eclectic architecture expresses only the banal cultural aspirations and superficial educations of its arriviste bourgeois patrons? It could just as well be argued that eclecticism promoted cultural literacy. For example, the Mercury statue on the western facade of the Stock Exchange reminded the public that he was the god of trade and commerce, who also appeared on the roof of the Customs building to emphasize the connections between Petersburg's naval might, its international port, and concomitant prosperity.[89] In this same way, statues of Mercury often presided over late-imperial factories, financial institutions, and commercial enterprises, as well as eclectic apartment housing from the 1860s onward.[90] Rather than characterizing eclecticism as an "impure" counterpart to classicism distinguished by unmotivated decorative effects, this seemingly unprincipled aesthetic trend may be seen as countering both a moribund classical style and the didactic attempt to create a unified neo-Russian "national" architecture.

In its philosophical and pedagogical origins, eclecticism strives to integrate its well-chosen components, and thus to create a self-justifying unity, perhaps like that claimed by Gautier for St. Isaac's Cathedral. In other words, eclecticism does not mandate one particular unity as classicism does, but allows for an unlimited number of persuasive aesthetic or intellectual unities. Who is to say that one group's architectural unity is more "intelligent" (*umnyi*) than others? The critics weighing in on Petersburg's eclecticism were not necessarily the same people commissioning, building, and enjoying these structures. Across a chain of historical circumstances, Russian writers and historians have rejected eclecticism for various reasons, just as we have our own incentives for reclaiming eclecticism today. As shown throughout this chapter, eclecticism, rather than being a collection of specific features, is in the eye of the beholder and defined in abstract terms that allow for a great deal of interpretation. Eclecticism serves all masters, including but by no means limited to sophisticated cosmopolitanism, Russian nationalism, and unfettered bourgeois individualism.

Early statements on eclecticism by Kukol'nik and others presumed an agreement on what constitutes harmony and unity. The impetus behind eclecticism in Petersburg, however, was neither the state nor the cultural elite, but rather a plurality of agents in a cityscape that had formerly only allowed for rigid top-down planning. Eclecticism spoke with a new voice even though it was a concept originally appropriated from nobles building new palaces or high-minded romantic thinkers seeking a new national style. It is interesting that architects' freedom to create eclectic buildings in Petersburg grew during the second half of the nineteenth century as the political climate grew more conservative and repressive. These buildings grew more and not less fanciful in the face of the growing social and political strain. They can be dismissed as extravagant posturing by the newly wealthy entrepreneurs, industrialists, bankers, and the like, but also provide evidence of new groups becoming enfranchised and asserting their presence. Their fates may have changed radically after 1917, but these groups left their mark on the Petersburg cityscape.[91]

Eclecticism is not a retroactive designation adopted for lack of a more pregnant concept, but a practice adopted from its initial, rather elitist advocates, albeit not in ways they might have anticipated. Eclecticism does not level all voices in a sham display of democracy, but rather gives rein to the imagination by making the past accessible. Eclecticism in its increasingly democratic access to styles corresponds to the growth and diversification of St. Petersburg's population over the course of the nineteenth century. In this sense, eclecticism conveys a hopeful sense of the potential for intellectual, cultural, and civic life in the imperial capital.

The Eclectic Apartment House as a Literary Analogue

As a structure shared by a socially heterogeneous public, the apartment building nevertheless provided for private segmentation of self-contained individual dwelling units. The rise of apartment housing in Petersburg during the nineteenth century corresponds to developments in Paris, where apartment houses became the dominant architectural element during the period 1814–48.[92] These buildings appeared in response to the growing urban population, on the one hand, and the high price of real estate in the central city, on the other.

Apartment housing accommodated residents from different socioeconomic backgrounds in eclectic, if graduated fashion. In literary tableaux, a genre popular in Paris during the first half of the century, writers such as Frédéric Soulié described Parisian society through the microcosm of a single apartment building.[93] Yakov Butkov proposed to modify this approach in "An Edifying Word," the author's preface to his two-part story collection Petersburg Heights (Peterburgskie vershiny, 1845, 1846).[94] In Butkov's account, the "crowded rows" of buildings that had taken root all around the city "suddenly" shot upward "into the free space under the clouds" by sprouting additional stories filled with stuffy or chilly "cells."[95] This vertical growth promoted a horizontal expansion in literature's middle ranges. Butkov complains that Russian literature serves only the wealthy inhabitants of the "blessed" middle floors, supplying them with stories about their own comfortable lives. He proposes instead to occupy himself with the "heavenly line," that is, with the modest residents of the garrets, who, although they share certain traits with destitute basement-dwellers, possess their own particular "ideas and passions." Butkov's garrets hold what he considers the true Petersburg middle, a sociocultural territory characterized by economies of scale, as opposed to the physically middle floors of multistory apartment houses that represent the city's social heights:[96]

> In this crowd, there are people whose sorrows and joys are determined by the cost of beef, whose dreams fly about the lumber yards, whose hopes are focused upon the first of the month, whose ambition strives towards an apartment at public cost, whose vanity yearns to shake the hand of an administrator or department head, whose voluptuousness directs itself to the sweet-shop. There are people, many people, who burn after making the acquaintance of a chorus girl, who boast of a meal worth two rubles, who are in delight over a stroll at Ekaterinhof . . .

In Butkov's characterization, the garrets are a cultural space replete with story potential, which he feels a moral imperative to explore. Butkov's 1840s approach thus shifts the focus of literary scrutiny. By the second half of the century, however, Petersburg literature's sociocultural interests had grown more truly inclusive, in conjunction with the evolution of the cityscape.

In Russia, five- and six-story apartment buildings were called *dokhodnye doma*—that is, buildings specifically constructed for profit, or *dokhod*. The ever-increasing rate at which apartment houses were constructed in every district of St. Petersburg during the second part of the nineteenth century represents one of the distinguishing features of the evolving cityscape, attributable to the growing post-Reforms population and the immensely profitable pursuit of filling such structures with paying tenants. These buildings provided housing for the better-off intelligentsia and civil bureaucracy, alongside, as in Butkov's day, the city's richer and poorer extremes.[97] The professional builders who emerged during the 1860s were the primary architects of the new multistory apartment buildings, and they intended their creations to suit urban citizens of middling wealth and life-style like themselves.[98] Rather than serving the "nouveaux riches" exclusively, as is dismissively asserted, apartment buildings of the latter nineteenth century addressed the housing needs among the middle ranges of the Petersburg populace.

Apartment buildings featured lavish eclectic decoration, in imitation of earlier palaces and mansions, across their substantial, uniform-height facades, generally constructed from brick covered with stucco. Facades could thus be easily redone at regular intervals, and made ever more ornate by mixing motifs from every major architectural style and period. This decorative saturation of apartment buildings was duly reviled in the architectural press, most notably in the professional journal *Architect* (*Zodchii*). Dostoevsky included these buildings as

FIGURE 1.8. Siuzor Apartment Building. (Author's Collection.)

the target of his ire in his 1873 "Little Pictures," invoking the "multitude of extraordinarily high (the main thing is high) apartment buildings, extremely thin-walled, it is said, and cheaply built, with an astonishing architecture of facades: here is Rastrelli, here is late Rococo, the balconies and windows of a doge, *oeil de boeuf* windows without fail, and always five stories, and all of this on the same façade."[99] It is equally true, however, that in their diversity of architectural motifs and residents, apartment buildings suggested the eclectic possibilities of literature, to which Dostoevsky had ample recourse in his own fiction, creating, for example, a crime novel at once ornately melodramatic and deeply metaphysical with his 1866 *Crime and Punishment.*

Just as ornamentation spread across facades, apartment houses spread across the districts of the city proper. A great number of these buildings appeared on the main bank of the Neva—along the Ekaterininskii and Fontanka canal embankments, and clustered around Zabalkanskii (now Moskovskii), and Liteinyi Prospects. The Rozhdestvenskaia district between the Alexander-Nevsky Monastery and Smolnyi was similarly colonized, and apartment construction projects also invaded the western part of Vasilievskii Island and the Petersburg Side.

FIGURE 1.9. Apartment Building in Neo-Russian Style. (Author's Collection.)

In their eclectic individualism, these apartment houses symbolized for many the bourgeois capitalist greed crowding Petersburg's most celebrated architectural ensembles and diminishing the reputed coherence for which the great architects had striven. Considerable concern was thus voiced about the danger that eclectic apartment housing would obscure the city's most treasured neoclassical structures. Particularly offensive to many was the 1880s development of private apartment buildings along the Admiralty Embankment, seen as an act of disrespect to Zakharov's Alexandrine-era Admiralty. The eclectic assortment of buildings erected during the 1870s and 1880s around Rossi's elegant Alexandrinskii Theater was similarly perceived as an affront to the cityscape.

As one scholar has declared somewhat ironically, "This sort of [apartment] building became for eclecticism that which the cathedral was for Gothic, and the palazzo for the Italian Renaissance."[100] But eclectic apartment houses from the latter part of the nineteenth century—among them the buildings designed during the 1860s and early 1870s by Mikhail Makarov, perhaps the single most productive architect of eclectic apartment housing—are rarely acknowledged by cultural historians as a legitimate architectural presence in the St. Petersburg cityscape. Only as eclecticism was overtaken by the more aesthetically presti-

FIGURE 1.10. Dom Muruzi. (Author's Collection.)

gious moderne in the 1890s were apartment buildings such as those by Fedor
Lidval, Sergei Korvin-Kriukovskii, Ippolit Pretro, and Nikolai Vasilev allowed
into the Petersburg architectural pantheon.[101]

A few eclectic nineteenth-century apartment houses did become part of the
mythology surrounding the elite prerevolutionary Petersburg literary culture,
among them the Moorish-style Muruzi building (*Dom Muruzi*) built for Prince
Alexander Muruza by the architect Aleksei Serebriakov during the 1870s on
Liteinyi Prospect.[102] Over the years, many Petersburg luminaries rented apartments in the Muruzi building, among them the writer Nikolai Leskov and later,
Dmitri Merezhkovskii and Zinaida Gippius, who made the apartment a gath-
ering-place for their symbolist circle during the early years of the twentieth century. The Muruzi building also received tender mention as the site of childhood
in the reminiscences of the artist Mstislav Dobuzhinskii. After the Revolution,
the writer Kornei Chukovskii and others created a "literary studio" there, followed by a group of poets associated with Nikolai Gumilev. Joseph Brodsky lived
in the building for over twenty years, until he was forced to emigrate to the

United States, and famously described life with his parents in their Muruzi "room and a half" in an essay by the same name.[103] Culturally legitimized individual representatives of eclectic apartment housing such as the Muruzi building, however, represent the exceptions that prove the antieclectic rule. This exemplar of eclecticism was lent cultural authority by its illustrious inhabitants, and thus forgiven its aesthetic transgressions.

Considered in different terms, the eclectic-style apartment house offers a material representation for the expanding midsection of Petersburg literature and fills in the empty cultural space between the grandest city prospects and the most squalid slums. Since residential segregation among the various socioeconomic groups in Petersburg was weakly developed throughout the nineteenth century, the eclectic-style apartment house was a perfectly representative structure for the city population—a complete cultural microcosm that lent itself admirably to literary description in realist prose, or even a *figure* for the way such prose tried to be socially comprehensive.[104] At street level, apartment buildings often housed multiple storefronts with prominently displayed shop signs. In their protean nature and multiple functions, as well as in the mixture of styles they proudly displayed to the observer, apartment houses were truly eclectic, speaking to the increasingly complex blend of elements in both the Petersburg cityscape and the Petersburg literary language. The cultural meeting place of the latter nineteenth century, the apartment building suggests itself as a metaphorical materialization of Petersburg literary eclecticism.

Eclecticism emphasizes detail as its primary constitutive element, and the clutter of eclectic detail in both architecture and literature paradoxically creates additional artistic room and new interpretive space. In this sense, eclecticism proclaims its affinity with nineteenth-century literary realism, which relies upon the gradual accumulation of detail to create meaning in long prose texts. As explored in Chapter 2, architectural eclecticism as manifested by the nineteenth-century apartment building is analogous to the period poetics of feuilleton, sketch, story, novel, and verse—diffuse literary forms whose distinguishing feature consists of fragmentary gestures that are interesting in their own right, and which also evoke generic origins that are recognizable to readers.

CHAPTER TWO

Petersburg Eclecticism, Part II: Literary Form and Cityshape

As an aesthetic strategy, architectural eclecticism developed in parallel to Petersburg literature from the 1830s onward, in that major works in the Petersburg corpus correspond in structural terms to the eclectic architectural vistas that also serve as their setting. Eclecticism in both architecture and literature relies upon the notion of "mixed" or "hybrid" forms subject to new interpretive strategies.[1]

The hierarchy of literary genres articulated by neoclassical theorists such as Nicolas Despréaux Boileau resembles the ideal systemic conception of the neoclassical city, the model according to which it is said that St. Petersburg was planned and built. Alexander Sumarokov's second epistle of 1747 imitated Boileau in elaborating a system of genres and provided instructions on the art of poetry with specific instructions for each established form.[2] Mikhail Lomonosov authored prescriptive treatises such as his 1740s "Short Course in Rhetoric," which included guidance on topics such as "Ornamentation," "Tropes," and "Figures."[3] During the nineteenth century, however, romantic and realist writers challenged the boundaries between established genres, modes, and registers and experimented with stylistic effects by mixing elements from different levels in the neoclassical hierarchy. Where once inhabitants of the "ideal city" stared up at the lofty spires of artistic expression, literarily inclined urban dwellers began to cover the territory themselves.

The nineteenth-century textual cityscape resembles a literary tag sale, where poetry and prose, and genres such as epic, tragedy, ode, lyric, elegy, comedy, satire, and picaresque, with their attendant hierarchical associations, collide, melt, and merge. This process resulted in generically eclectic and inclusive literary forms such as feuilleton, sketch, and, of course, the novel. These forms often retain identifiable features—lexicon, figures of speech, and other stylistic attributes from older, more rigorously policed generic forms—that bespeak their multiple origins.[4] This literary landscape, both as a whole and in its individual exemplars, models the highly eclectic nature of the physical urban topography as a semiotic structure. The urban literary setting of this period cannot be adequately described through recourse to a particular literary form and its characteristic features, since it constitutes a meeting place of all forms.

Alexander Shakhovskoi's 1828 theatrical vaudeville-burlesque, "Mercury Standing Sentry, or The Gates of Parnassus" (*Merkurii na chasakh, ili Parnasskaia zastava*) heralds the generic flux of the eclectic 1830s and 1840s in Russian literature.[5] This comic divertissement builds upon his 1822 "Analogic Prologue" titled "News on Parnassus, or The Triumph of the Muses" (*Novosti na Parnase, ili Torzhestvo muz*), in which Vaudeville, Journal, and Melodrama attempt to displace the muses from Parnassus, but are banished by Mercury. In the later "Mercury Standing Sentry," the winged god is approached by various genres seeking to ascend to immortality. "Bah!" exclaims Mercury disgustedly. "What sort of motley crowd swarms here?" Each genre in the quarreling throng must plead its case in its own particular stylistic register, singing or reciting, and in terms of its unique history.

History, Epic, Tragedy, Comedy, Opera, Ode, Cantata, and Ballad are granted entry, but Mercury contemptuously dismisses a host of minor forms, including Romance, Madrigal, Epigram, and Sonnet. Parody convinces Mercury that it is Epic turned inside out, and Romantic Long Poem successfully claims to be Epic's sister. Eclogue, Elegy, and Satire are given the respect due their age and invited to pass the portals. Fable and Fairy Tale are permitted to enter as well, but not prosaic Story. The Novel's pleading softens Mercury's heart, although the profit-minded Journal is sent packing. In the concluding scene, Drama begs to be allowed to enter and make the muses weep. Mercury postpones his decision, however, so that he can enjoy an impromptu show proposed by Ballet and Vaudeville, who have the final word. This light drama on the subject of genre serves Shakhovskoi as an opportunity for polemics about the current literary scene—he attacks plebeian journalist Nikolai Polevoi's *Moscow Telegraph* and Raphael Zotov's melodramatic reworking of European historical verse tragedies. Shakhovskoi's vilification falls upon generic interlopers he considers unworthy, but a newcomer, his own beloved vaudeville form, carries the day, both within the play and for the audience watching its performance. The neoclassical hierarchy exists as a unified but precarious vision of literature in this allegorical vaudeville, but the upstarts have already taken Parnassus by storm.

Like Shakhovskoi's unruly crowd of genres, the architectural eclecticism in St. Petersburg of the nineteenth century countered normative strictures, in this case proposed and imposed by such bodies as the Commission for the Orderly Development of Petersburg (established 1737), the Commission for Masonry Construction (established 1762), the Committee of Construction and Hydraulic Works (established 1816), and the Central Administration of Communications and Public Buildings (established 1832, expanded 1842). Despite official efforts to control the pace of urban growth, and to dictate the stylistic consistency of individual structures, the spirit of eclecticism manifested itself in the Petersburg cityscape as an increasingly visible element from the 1830s onward. Rather than functioning as a marker of aristocratic privilege as it did initially, architectural eclecticism after the reign of Nicholas I redistributed cultural access, even cultural authority, amongst the city's diverse inhabitants. The breakdown of central architectural authority in St. Petersburg corresponds to the passing of prescriptive eighteenth-century handbooks of rhetoric and poetics derived from the traditions of Aristotle's *Poetics*, Cicero's *De oratore*, Quintilian's *Institutio oratoria*, Horace's *Ars Poetica*, and Boileau's *L'art poétique*.

The neoclassical hierarchy of genres is, upon closer examination, a false, wishful memory of a unity that never was, which comes into focus most particularly when the literary order is under assault.[6] Classical genre theory is notoriously incomplete, no more than suggestive, and was never sufficiently prescriptive to prevent the flowering of generic mixtures and hybrids in Italian and English Renaissance literature. Neoclassical theorists such as Boileau merely assumed that the notion of genre was self-evident and historically substantiated, as were the typologies they proposed. Still, despite its insufficiencies, the hierarchy of genres does constitute at least a unified *vision* of literature. As Mikhail Bakhtin states in his essay "Epic and Novel," "The great organic poetics of the past—those of Aristotle, Horace, Boileau—are permeated with a deep sense of the wholeness of literature and of the harmonious interaction of all genres contained within this whole.... Scholarly poetics of the nineteenth century lack this integrity: they are eclectic, descriptive; their aim is not a living and organic fullness but rather an abstract and encyclopedic comprehensiveness."[7] This merely descriptive encyclopedic documentation is counterpart to the largely unwritten poetics of eclectic ages. Neither strategy, however, accounts for the structural underpinnings of eclecticism.

In an extended metaphor of the literary system as an organic, evolving city, Claudio Guillén evokes the "natural" eclecticism produced by time, rather than human innovation:

> [A] cultural whole or a literary system could be visualized, metaphorically speaking, as the verbal and imaginary equivalent of an ancient yet living, persistent yet profoundly changing *city*. The great cities we have all admired, merging stone with flowing water, monuments with gardens, humble streets with spacious plazas, Gothic churches with Baroque palaces, accomplish time and again the integration of a plurality of styles in an existing, growing environment . . . they succeed in assembling not only a variety of styles and ways of life but series of historical moments, layers of historical time. *Civitas verbi*: artistic wholes and literary systems are, like great cities, complex environments and areas of integration.[8]

Such a model differs from prescriptive hierarchy in gracefully accommodating the evolution of new forms. This city metaphor does not fully account for eclecticism, however, since it consists solely of authentic forms and not later stylizations, and furthermore, only the total landscape is hybrid, not its individual structures, which all retain their formal integrity. If in Guillén's view, genre is "an invitation to form," that would make architectural and literary eclecticism, in my view, "an invitation to *forms*."[9] The notion of genre itself implies, after all, choice and selection, since literary genres formalize the discursive possibilities that a given society has made conventional.[10] Furthermore, models for literary systems can be far less harmonious than the preceding city metaphor—they can assert that literary meaning arises from the struggle between generic possibilities and differences.[11] In this sense, genres are defined recursively; they arise out of other genres through processes of transformation and recombination.[12]

Why think vertically and hierarchically where literary form is concerned? Why not flip vertical distinctions onto the horizontal plane, as eclecticism does, and look for affinities as well as differences among diverse forms?[13] Genre does not provide a way to identify a text, but rather a way to "constellate" texts, to express relations *between* texts.[14] This spatial model posits genre as the invisible glue that holds a diverse disposition of signs together and makes them legible. But what holds genre itself together? Jacques Derrida's ironically titled essay "The Law of Genre" emphasizes how vulnerable genre is to disintegration. Texts must therefore declare themselves through a "mark" each bears proclaiming allegiance to a particular genre. The "mark" of genre is, however, a highly ambiguous entity, since it can potentially apply itself to new members. The mark both "gathers together the corpus" and simultaneously "keeps it from closing, from identifying itself with itself." In this way, at the very moment that a genre or a literature comes into being, "degenerescence"—the breaking down of genre—has begun.[15]

The term *eclecticism* might thus designate a structure composed entirely of such generic marks. Eclecticism as a style conceived in this way effectively represents the ambiguous nature of genre, which, although often described as a stern authority, is actually a fragile construct ever on the verge of collapsing and scattering its fragments across a textual field. Put another way, genre is a *fiction*, since genre is derived from literary works, even though it pretends to produce them.

Literary Eclecticism, Petersburg Style

Does there exist a "Petersburg" literary principle for the nineteenth-century period that corresponds to architectural eclecticism, a "mark" that identifies Petersburg texts from this period as such? Certainly, the designation "Petersburg" itself applies to a self-identified literary metagenre. Pushkin initiated this tradition by famously assigning the subtitle "A Petersburg Tale" (*peterburgskaia povest'*) to his narrative poem "The Bronze Horseman" (1833). Dostoevsky reconceived Pushkin's gesture when he subtitled his novella "The Double" (1846), calling it "A Petersburg Poem" (*peterburgskaia poema*), and thus reversing Pushkin's strategy of moving poetry closer to prose.[16] Dostoevsky further extended this special class of texts with his feuilletons "Petersburg Chronicle" (1847) and "Petersburg Visions in Verse and Prose" (1861).

There is evidence that "Petersburg" was already perceived as a literary designation by the mid-1840s. Five of Gogol's stories, composed at different times but all set in Petersburg, were regrouped by the author into a cycle known as the "Petersburg Tales" in the third volume of his 1842 *Collected Works*. In his introduction to Nekrasov's *Physiology of Petersburg* (*Fiziologiia Peterburga*, 1845), Belinsky also noted several dramatic fragments among the better-known works from Gogol's "Petersburg" oeuvre—"The Morning of a Busy Man" (*Utro delovogo cheloveka*), which was originally subtitled "Petersburg Scenes," "Fragment" (*Otryvok*), and "After the Play" (*Teatral'nyi raz"ezd*).[17] Alongside self-affiliated Petersburg "tales" by various authors, there exist additional subcategories of this type, including the free-form Petersburg "letters" (*peterburgskie pis'ma*) and Petersburg "notes" (*peterburgskie zametki, zapiski, otmetki*) produced by writers such as Odoevsky, Gogol, Grigor'ev, Goncharov, and Garshin. The titles of Nekrasov's *Petersburg Physiology* and *Petersburg Collection* (*Peterburgskii sbornik*, 1846) similarly point to the generically heterogeneous nature of these two compendia.

By the 1850s, the "Petersburg" tag already served to dignify a new text, as a prominent family name does. This may explain why Ivan Iakovlev gave his rambling and undistinguished 1858 story "The Daughter of a Poor Civil Servant" the subtitle "A Petersburg Tale" (*peterburgskaia povest'*) when it appeared in the journal *The Contemporary*, thereby setting up the inevitable association with the seminal Pushkin text in the reader's mind.[18] Like Derrida's more hypothetical generic "mark," the "Petersburg" literary designation provides a democratic opening into the corpus.

"Petersburg" works constitute, in Vladimir Toporov's formulation, a "cross-generic unity of numerous texts from Russian literature," which points to the fact that every level in the generic hierarchy can be employed to describe and depict Peter's city, or any city for that matter.[19] Works whose titles pair the "Petersburg" designation with an explicitly generic term, however, often seek to confound the very categories that they invoke—most notably Pushkin's "Tale" or Dostoevsky's "Poem." Self-consciously antitraditional references to known generic forms make this subset of Petersburg works distinct from those whose titles merely specify a Petersburg setting, such as Yakov Butkov's 1845–46 story collection *Petersburg Heights* (*Peterburgskie vershiny*) and Vsevolod Krestovskii's 1864 novel *Petersburg Slums* (*Peterburgskie trushchoby*).[20]

While "eclecticism" as an aesthetic designation is not normally used to describe Petersburg literature of the period from the 1830s through the 1890s, Petersburg literary "monuments" and the groupings of lesser-known texts that cluster around them do reflect the architectural principles of the time. The "Petersburg" quality of Petersburg literary works concerns the puzzle of genre that these works propose, and the particular gestures by which they link the great decomposing system of sanctioned literary forms to the changing cityscape. "Petersburg" literature thus proclaims itself as eclectic and makes free with specific generic markers while assuming its readers possess the requisite literary sophistication to decode them. This Petersburg discourse may well be representative of nineteenth-century literature as a whole in its diversely transgeneric nature, but the urban subject under consideration foregrounds the form/content relation, in both literature and architecture, in a particularly conscious manner. This Petersburg literary eclecticism is more than the byproduct of many different authors writing about a complex urban reality over a period when social and intellectual paradigms were undergoing a shift. The city, rather, offered these writers a productive site for the deliberate working out of a new discursive model.

The following sections examine groupings of Petersburg literary texts on canonical themes—eighteenth-century invocations of the imperial capital, works depicting the Falconet monument to Peter the Great, and textual renderings of Nevsky Prospect—in order to highlight the generic concerns that shape artistic representations of the city from its inception. Both singly and collectively, these "Petersburg" literary works illustrate the principle of textual eclecticism.[21] Put differently, the characteristic feature of the "Petersburg" genre—that is, the mark that united these texts—is eclecticism. The previous chapter argued for considering architectural eclecticism seriously on its own terms. This chapter treats literary works from the Petersburg corpus under the rubric of eclecticism in order to extend this concept, with an eye to illuminating a broader swath of the urban cultural landscape.

St. Petersburg in Literature: The Eighteenth Century, Revisited

To argue that eighteenth-century literary works about Petersburg invoke the city in a highly eclectic manner would seem to fly in the face of literary history. Most accounts of Petersburg literature provide excerpts from the eighteenth century, but treat these works as a monotonously high-style prelude to Pushkin's brilliant literary hybrid "Bronze Horseman." L. V. Pumpianskii, for example, points to three poetic formulas, repeated in eighteenth-century and 1803 centennial depictions of Petersburg, and given their ultimate expression in Pushkin's poem: 1) "where formerly . . . now there is" (*gde prezhde . . . nyne tam*), 2) "one hundred years passed" (*proshlo sto let*), and 3) "from the forests' gloom, from the swampy marshlands" (*iz t'my lesov, iz topi blat*).[22] He similarly links the description of the contemporary city in Pushkin's poem to the style employed by Derzhavin, especially in the use of lofty architectural motifs such as "palaces" (*chertogi*) and "towers" (*bashni*): "Derzhavin always loved the vocabulary of architecture, but during the period 1791–1795, pyramids, obelisks, pillars, palaces, and idols become positively the signature of his style."[23] In literary histories, eighteenth-century invocations of Peter's city provide the source for the most conventional lexical elements in Pushkin's stylistic tribute and serve merely as a static textual backdrop against which the real drama of the literary process is enacted.

Most historical and critical sources invoke eighteenth-century works about St. Petersburg only to make short shrift of them. As Waclaw Lednicki declares, "This whole group of poets, by and large, struck the same banal panegyric note."[24] M. V. Otradin similarly avers that eighteenth-century literary representations of Petersburg play themselves out in a "maximally major tone," uniformly expressing "wonder and transports of joy."[25] Sidney Monas finds the eighteenth-century tradition from Buzhinsky to Derzhavin to employ standard *topoi*, "very much in the spirit of the *laudes Romae* of the Latin poets, and their Latin and vernacular imitators throughout the Middle Ages, though with one or two distinctive touches."[26] Monas contrasts eighteenth-century celebrations of Peter's accomplishment with the darker images of Petersburg found in "oral and manuscript folk literature," whose motifs, he claims, would later enter Russian literature through the creative agency of Pushkin and Gogol. According to this familiar characterization, the eighteenth-century tradition of Petersburg literature was an artistic cul-de-sac that became the object of critical revisioning and even parody.[27] The absence of nuanced literary portraits depicting eighteenth-century Petersburg is attributed to the nature of official court literature, which allowed only for high-style genres, and to the fact that St. Petersburg itself, as opposed to the city's founder Peter, was not generally the central subject of high-style works. Thus, it would seem, the eighteenth century does not offer much more than an anthology of fragments—fleeting invocations of St. Petersburg gleaned from interminable expanses of ode and grand rhetoric.[28] This set of eighteenth-century "Petersburg" texts is more diverse than literary history generally grants, however, and this is hardly surprising, since these texts were composed over a period of more than a century. While the existence of differences as well as similarities among eighteenth-century literary characterizations of Petersburg is not in itself remarkable, the conventional critical insistence on the sameness of these texts is curious, recalling as it does the allegedly lost neoclassical unity of Petersburg architecture. The literary similarities are seen as evidence of an underdeveloped national tradition, however, whereas the architectural cohesion is mourned as a cultural pinnacle never regained.

Nikolai Antsiferov acknowledges the difficulty of pinpointing the moment when the city of Petersburg first manifested itself in literature, but begins his account with Alexander Sumarokov, who established the city's connection with Russia's past through Alexander Nevsky and invoked Petersburg's glorious future with reference to the "new" or "northern" Rome.[29] The other earliest literary works that invoke the Petersburg cityscape include Feofan Prokopovich's 1716 "Oration on the Birth of the Great Prince Petr Petrovich" (*Slovo na rozhdenie velikogo kniazia Petra Petrovicha*), Gavrilo Buzhinskii's 1717 "Oration in

Praise of the Capital City St. Petersburg and the Emperor Peter the Great"
(*Opisatel'naia pokhvala tsarstvuiushchemu gradu Sanktpeterburgu i pritom gosu-
dariu imperatoru Petru Velikomu*), and Antioch Kantemir's 1730 unfinished epic
poem "Petrida." Most works in the eighteenth-century Petersburg corpus come
from the post-Petrine period, however, among them Vasilii Trediakovskii's 1752
"Praise of the Izhora Lands and Capital City St. Petersburg" (*Pokhvala Izherskoi
zemle i tsarstvuiushchemu gradu Sankt-Peterburgu*) and Mikhail Lomonosov's
odes to Empress Elizabeth and Catherine the Great (1748 and 1762, respectively) as well as his 1740s "Inscriptions for a Statue of Peter the Great" (*Nadpisi k statue Petra Velikogo*). The eighteenth-century canonical roster concludes
with Gavrila Derzhavin's 1783–84 "The Murza's Vision" (*Videnie Murzy*) and
his 1810 "Procession of the Russian Amphitrites along the Volkhov" (*Shestvie po
Volkhovu rossiiskoi Amfitrity*), as well as Mikhail Murav'ev's 1794 "To the Neva
Goddess" (*Bogine Nevy*). Petr Viazemskii's odic 1818 poem "Petersburg" is also
considered part of the eighteenth-century tradition due to its high-style diction
and corresponding approach to the city.

The trajectory of development over time in stylistic and generic terms is, nevertheless, as is always the case in imperial "Petersburg" literature, *toward the
middle*. Derzhavin—the bard of Catherine the Great's classical city—initiated
the tradition of a more accessible and personal Petersburg in poetry, breaking
ground in his "The Murza's Vision" on the imaginary site of friendship and
memory that would be much mourned in the elegiac verse of Pushkin and his
intimates. Murav'ev's poem "To the Neva Goddess" similarly enacts this incli-
nation toward the elegiac or idyllic middle, providing the requisite panegyric in
its grand invocation of rivers, lakes and seas (the first six stanzas) but then shifting to a more contemplative *topos* of love poetry within St. Petersburg (the second six stanzas) that prefigures Fedor Tiutchev's metaphysical Neva poems of
the mid-nineteenth century.[30] The destination of Murav'ev's poetic trajectory
is personal experience—dips in the Neva, the cool of the evening, and trysts
with a beloved. The poem's final stanza repeats this movement in miniature, first
invoking the high-style rapturous poet (*vostorzhennyi piit*), and then transforming him into an impressionable proto-Pushkinian insomniac who spends
the night leaning on a granite embankment, lost in fantasy.

The earliest eighteenth-century works invoking Petersburg exhibit an eclecticism that reflects the encompassing imperialist aesthetic. Gavrilo Buzhinsky,
a prefect attached to the Petersburg navy, delivered his 1717 "Oration in Praise
of St. Petersburg and its Founder" as he presented the monarch with a plan and
facade of St. Petersburg engraved in bronze.[31] Although pitched in the most formal stylistic register with recourse to many archaic Slavonic forms, Buzhinsky's
oration makes itself contemporary by naming Petersburg's specific topographical features and architectural structures: the Peter-Paul fortress, the Admiralty,
the triumphal gates and pyramid on Trinity Square, Vasilievskii Island, Kronstadt and Kronflot, and the branches of the Neva.

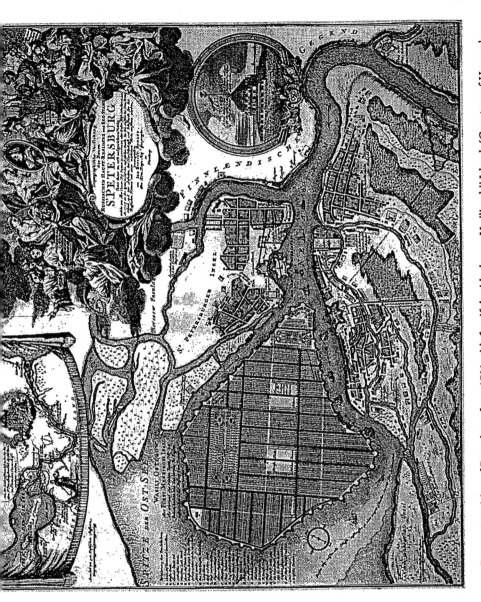

FIGURE 2.1. Map of Petersburg from 1721 with fanciful grid-plan on Vasilievskii Island. (Courtesy of Harvard Map Collection.)

Buzhinsky draws widely from the history of Western civilization to praise Peter, who is identified with the heroes and gods of antiquity (Apollo, Hercules, Ulysses, Achilles, Mars), as well as biblical and historical figures (David, Solomon, Emperor Constantine).[32] Buzhinsky also invokes territories of contemporary Europe—Poland, Pomerania, Courland, Denmark, Holland, England—in their relationship to the city. Buzhinsky thus employs an eclectic strategy of composition, choosing from the many cultural systems available to him in an imperialist poetics that can also be used to characterize other high-style "Petersburg" literary works from the eighteenth century. Viazemskii continued this eclectic practice a full century later in his 1818 poem "Petersburg," invoking Grecian art, Roman marvels, and the gardens of Semiramide, and acknowledging Petersburg's multiple cultural influences when he inquires, "Whose bold hand has combined you?"

Trediakovsky's 1752 "Praise" poem in honor of Petersburg's fiftieth anniversary offers the provocatively diverse blend of literary elements so typical of this pioneering eighteenth-century literary figure. Despite its seemingly high-style vocative opening, for example, "Praise" also invokes alternative, middle-range generic forms in the qualities it attributes to the imperial capital ("Pleasant shore! Dear country!"). Trediakovsky's panegyric even produces unintentionally comical effects with its upbeat assertions about life in the capital, when he assures readers that, although the Petersburg air is cold, it is bracingly healthy.[33] He insists belligerently on Petersburg's parity with other world cities with the programmatic declaration that life in the city is "pleasant" for all inhabitants, "pleasantness" being, again, a distinctly non-high-style attribute. The poem characterizes St. Petersburg as mirroring the true image of Peter the Great, but simultaneously reflects Trediakovsky's own personal experiences—hardly a high-style practice. In another fifty years, predicts Trediakovsky, Russians will not leave their motherland to visit Venice, Rome, Amsterdam, London, and Paris (as he himself had done); instead, Westerners will flock to Petersburg to marvel at Peter's accomplishment. Trediakovsky's reference to European travel strikes a wistful note, however, when he recalls conversations with friends about happy times abroad (*Tak my ob nikh beseduem mnog chas,/I pomnim, chto sluchilos' tam dragogo*). Thus the grand sweep of Trediakovsky's panegyric, which explicitly extends itself to address future generations, seems continually in danger of collapsing into the more intimate middle ground of elegiac reflection.

Sumarokov's eight-line 1756 poem "To the Little House of Peter the Great" (*K domiku Petra Velikogo*) offers an intriguing contrast to his more conventionally odic invocations of the city. The poem opens by pointing to the humble hut, asserting that it was *not* the dwelling place of a hermit, as might have been expected. Instead, a great ruler lived there, retaining only the most essential attributes of majesty—purple robes, scepter, orb, and crown. No one could have foreseen that this little house represented the promise of a magnificent city, marvels the lyrical voice, but Peter was as great as this house is small. Voicing lavish

FIGURE 2.2. The Little House of Peter the Great, from 1853 *Plany S. Peterburga.*
(Courtesy of Houghton Library at Harvard.)

praise within such cramped poetic confines and with recourse to images of rustic modesty, Sumarokov overturns generic expectations while managing to accomplish his larger task. His poem functions exactly as does the hut it celebrates—making smallness signify great things. The unmistakable material and verbal proofs of royalty are hidden inside the hut, and accordingly, these images are introduced only subsequent to the image of the simple dwelling place. Sumarokov then literally turns his poetic image inside out, thrilling his reader with the unmediated leap between miniature and monumental forms. The little house of Peter the Great becomes in Sumarokov's poem the marker of an evolving, increasingly eclectic Petersburg poetics. Like the eighteenth-century literary tradition of celebrating Petersburg, both poem and dwelling house an unexpected assortment of tropes, styles, and associations.[34]

When discussing Derzhavin's contribution to "Petersburg" literature, the critical literature generally points to his 1783–84 "The Murza's Vision" with its image of the sleeping city outside the poet's window (*Petropol' s bashniami dremal*). His 1810 "Procession of the Russian Amphitrites along the Volkhov" more creatively extends the tradition, however, in order to make the city itself into a poetic agent, rather than simply a creation of the poet. Derzhavin composed the later tribute on the occasion of Princess Catherine, sister of Alexander I, and her husband's journey by water from Tver to Petersburg. Derzhavin borrows imagery from Lomonosov, most notably the latter's oft-invoked "clapping" river banks—Lomonosov's "the Neva's banks clap their hands" becomes "with a clapping of hands the banks run ahead" in "Procession." Derzhavin animates his Petersburg landscape in a manner that surpasses even Lomonosov's baroque exhibitions of joy. His dancing hills and leaping oak trees (*pliashut kholmy, skachut duby*) are, however, merely a prelude to an eclectic vision of the imperial city that anticipates and perhaps even surpasses the hallucinatory imagery of Pushkin's "Bronze Horseman."

As the royal barge approaches and tritons blow their trumpets, the poet wonders ingenuously whether the scene thus depicted represents Poseidon and his Amphitrites, or perhaps the ancient Russian Queen Olga, wife of the heroic Igor. No, he declares, it is not a "picture" of old marvels that delights the mortal gaze as the river leads the barge into the unusual, richly decorated city (*grad... preuzorochnyi*), but an entirely contemporary occasion. Petropolis stands to meet the barge (*Petropol' vstaet navstrechu*), and its towers rise from beneath the waves (*Bashni vskhodiat iz-pod voln*) along with sculptural figures from the Russian pantheon (*V pamiat' vozhdiam i tsariam / Zriu kumiry izvaianny*). As the poet has suggested, this imperial city departs from established tradition in order to stage its own entrance. A "dense forest" of masts comes to the stone-hewn banks (*Les prishel iz macht dremuchii/K kamnetesanym bregam*), along which runs a chain of wharves, buildings, and markets. Derzhavin's poem allows for the coexistence of figures from classical mythology with the prosaic structures of a real city, even if the latter are dignified by an elevated, archaic vocabulary (*torzhishch* instead of *rynok*) and gathered together under the middle-range rubric of a "flower bed" (*tsvetnik*) that has bloomed amongst the rivers. In Derzhavin's poem, culture rather unconventionally resembles nature (the masts of the Russian navy recall the primeval forest), while nature joins the choreographed celebration that greets the royal barge (clapping, dancing, leaping). The great city emerges magically from the waters, just as the poem gives rise to a mixture of images and tonalities that it gracefully unites within an eclectic literary vista.

As these few examples illustrate, Petersburg in eighteenth-century literature is a generically eclectic phenomenon. Still, it must be allowed that eighteenth-century literary invocations of Petersburg constitute a much smaller sample than those from the nineteenth century. Even within this limited corpus, however, literary form and style run the gamut from lofty ode to dreamy lyric, with many hybrid literary landmarks along the way. It may be that nineteenth-century literary eclecticism does not overturn the allegedly monotone eighteenth-century tradition, as has been so often asserted, but rather extends and elaborates upon eclectic literary tendencies that were already in evidence. The stylistic and generic middle, moreover, is an essential part of canonical nineteenth-century literary portraits of Petersburg. It is not the case that literature from either century produced a monolithic or rigidly binary Petersburg, but rather that readings of this literature have often done so.

Monumental Eclecticism: Pushkin's Project Extended

The Bronze Horseman monument to Peter the Great is the structure most emblematic of the Russian imperial capital.[35] Catherine the Great commissioned the sculpture in 1766 from Etienne-Maurice Falconet, who chose to represent Peter not as a Roman emperor in armor, but rather in a belted smock, cloak, and boots that, to some, suggested the thirteenth-century prince Alexander Nevsky, celebrated for his victory over the Swedes in what would become the Petersburg environs. Although a classical laurel wreath crowns Peter's head, a more folkloric bearskin serves him as a saddle. A massive boulder transported across the Finnish Gulf provides the granite base of the monument.[36] Despite its "local" references, the Bronze Horseman monument with its outstretched hand recalls the famous statue of Marcus Aurelius on the Capitoline in Rome and proposes a similar classical identity between the ruler as lawgiver and an empire's golden age. Still, it might well be argued that the great "neoclassical" monument that defines the city of St. Petersburg is, in its conception, a blend of East and West, not to mention closer to the baroque style in its dramatism.[37] What is more, Petersburg literature tolerates a wide range of "approaches" to this allegedly monolithic cultural site.

With its explicitly designated "Petersburg" literary structure (*peterburgskaia povest'*), Pushkin's "Bronze Horseman," together with many other stylistically diverse nineteenth-century literary tributes to Peter's statue, is the consummate collective monument to Petersburg literary eclecticism. Pushkin's famous image of Petersburg architectural structures that crowd one another out of the introductory poetic frame (*Gromady stroinye tesniatsia*) itself offers a figure for eclecticism, which strives to find unity in diversity, and which may strain to accommodate its multiple influences. Pushkin's poem, moreover, enacts the tension between vertical and horizontal systems that, in my view, lies at the heart of the eclectic aesthetics of the early-to-mid nineteenth century. Pushkin's poem can be read in terms of hierarchies, histories, and contentions for cultural space, but his "Bronze Horseman" also turns hierarchy into network and transforms generic system into generic pastiche, just as architectural eclecticism does. All boundaries in Pushkin's poem are permeable.

Pushkin's poem exhibits a complex temporal layering, with multiple historical moments simultaneously present. Peter stands on the banks of the Neva and looks into the future. The poet celebrates all eras in Petersburg, including the founding moment, the time of the flood, its aftermath, and the endlessly re-

FIGURE 2.3. Bronze Horseman, from Andrei Martynov, *Recueil de vues de St. Pétersbourg,* 1821–22 (Courtesy of Houghton Library at Harvard.)

peating pleasures of the present. All periods in the city's history are accessible, all in dialogue with one another. Topographically speaking, Pushkin joins together diverse parts of Petersburg in his poem—from the central imperial cityscape to the wooden houses out on the islands.[38] In generic terms, Pushkin employs much the same strategy. It is well established that the poem opens by drawing upon the tradition of the eighteenth-century ode, invoked in connection with Peter the Great.[39] Odes that commemorate monarchs and state occasions represent perhaps the largest category of forms that influenced Pushkin's work on "The Bronze Horseman." Odes on the subject of floods or other disasters are also plentiful in classical, European, and Russian literature, as are high-style poetic tributes to statues and monuments that "animate" these images.[40]

In addition to the eighteenth-century odic mode, Pushkin deploys a nineteenth-century "Onegin" style in depicting contemporary Petersburg, as well as a modern belletristic realism associated with the antihero Evgenii.[41] "The Bronze Horseman" invokes historical as well as literary sources, some of them by Pushkin himself, and includes scholarly-style footnotes. Scholars have emphasized the "mosaic character" of the "foreign material" (literary, historical, and anecdotal) that infuses Pushkin's poem, and its "wide range of discourses," among them epic, ode, lyric, eulogy, sermon, journalistic reportage, and anecdote.[42] Even the final lines of the poem adhere to this eclectic strategy. A high-style invocation exhorts the Finnish waves to forget the old antipathy over their defeat by Peter, but in the final stanza, the poet refers to the pattern of oral legend and invokes the audience to whom he will relate this sad tale. The manuscript of "Bronze Horseman" contains still a different version—the poet promises to write the story in verse, in the form of nineteenth-century narrative poetry. In characterizing the magnificent literary hybrid that is "The Bronze Horseman," Alexander Ospovat and Roman Timenchik assert, "Pushkin's last poem took into itself fragments of all possible traditions—a semantic intermingling that was carried in the air of the epoch."[43] All great literary works, they claim, exhibit a "boldness of generic resolution." Such works "bring into a unity that which formerly seemed impossible to combine."[44]

In *Strolls with Pushkin*, the writer Andrei Sinyavsky discusses the affinity between Pushkin and Peter the Great in terms of creation.[45] The Tsar-Creator calls forth the great storm and quiets it by transforming natural chaos into harmonious cosmos. Peter and the elements are thus not opposed, but parts of a larger whole that constitutes the creative cycle; the Dionysian ecstasy of creation resolves itself into balanced Apollonian form. Petersburg is *created* by the elements, from elemental materials. As Sinyavsky observes, the Prologue to "The Bronze Horseman" reins in the poem like a steed. The natural elements crystallize, not only in the forms of towers and palaces, or in the monument to Peter, but also in the verses of Pushkin's poem. It might also be argued, however, that cultural, rather than elemental materials find eclectic but harmonious fusion in "The Bronze Horseman," which evinces a kind of democratic antipoetics.

Semantic as well as generic associations in "The Bronze Horseman" are fluid, not fixed on a single character or entity. Instead, semantic elements—that is, highly-charged lexicon such as sad (*pechal'nyi*), empty (*pustoi, pustynnyi*), full (*polon*), angrily (*zlobno*), gaze (*gliadel*), and thoughts (*dumy*)—are shared freely among characters and personified natural forces in the tale, including Evgenii, Tsar Alexander, Peter, the Neva, and the poet. Similarly, no character in the poem can be considered the undisputed occupant of any physical or semantic zone. For example, Evgenii's emblematic-parodic position astride a sculptural lion parallels the posture of the Horseman monument, and Tsar Alexander acknowledges himself powerless before the natural elements. Thus the poem constructs a horizontal web of associations linking characters, physical spaces, and lexicon, in this way undermining the cultural and stylistic hierarchies that represent one of the poem's central preoccupations, while positing a persuasive new literary unity.[46]

"The Bronze Horseman" is a crowded poem in that contrasting images, styles, and genres jostle one another for a place within it—not unlike Pushkin's throng of buildings. This contesting of space is made tangible by the Neva overflowing its banks and by the incongruous succession of objects carried along by the flood—materials from ruined dwellings, everyday objects, entire bridges, and even coffins transported from their resting places. The vast, empty space of artistic potential that is several times equated with Petersburg is thereby revealed over the course of the poem as a densely populated literary space, a precursor to the mid-century Petersburg apartment building. The eclectic literary structure of the "The Bronze Horseman" partly explains the diverse and often contradictory interpretations of this poem as a politically subversive work cloaked in the rhetoric of patriotism, a celebration of Russian imperialist expansion, and an assertion of the Petersburg poet's sensibility.

The mood at the end of "The Bronze Horseman" is peaceful and open. The poem reaches no conclusions and asserts no hierarchy. Evgenii's corpse at the threshold of the little house provides a last ambiguous image, since this resting place is outside the city but still associated with Petersburg. The quiet, empty landscape suggests that the city has been obliterated. And yet, the poet's paean to the crowded city *follows* the discovery of Evgenii's body, temporally speaking. The city endures. Thus the end of "The Bronze Horseman" returns the reader to the mood of the opening lines, a vista of unoccupied space and possibilities, suggesting the diverse potential of a generic meeting place. This very openness is one of the enabling conditions of eclecticism.

"The Bronze Horseman" exemplifies literary eclecticism as an individual work, but Russian poetic representations of Peter's statue written both before and after Pushkin compose a similarly eclectic unity as a group, adopting dramatically different postures and tones in relation to the monument.[47] Vasilii Ruban composed 1782 "Inscriptions to the Colossus-Stone" (*Nadpisi k Kamniugromu*) to the natural monolith that serves as the pedestal to the Bronze Horseman, in a tribute that Pushkin invoked in his footnotes to "The Bronze Horseman." Ruban's verses urge the Great Pyramids of Egypt and the Colossus of Rhodes to pay homage to the divinely created (*nerukotvornaia*) marvel that has fallen at the feet of the Russian Tsar, thus proposing the Falconet monument rather ambiguously as a pagan idol worshipped by the entire world. Aleksei Merzliakov's brief 1815 "To the Monument of Peter the Great in Petersburg" (*K monumentu Petra Velikogo v Peterburge*) strikes a very different note by making Peter fly "on a flaming horse, like a god," but then bringing him back to earth. The final line of this poem belongs to a higher power: "Death spoke to Peter: 'Stop! You are not a god, go no further!'" Merzliakov retells the myth of the hubristic Icarus and recasts the bronze horseman as a cautionary figure. In contrast, Ivan Kliushnikov's 1838 "Bronze Horseman" (*Mednyi vsadnik*) calls the statue "a symbol of god on earth," and a most appropriate memorial for one who "embraced the entire universe" with his "enormous soul," and rocked "half the universe" with his "mighty arm." Peter calls out heartily from the heavens to his Russian subjects, "Bravo, bravo, good lads!" (*molodtsy*). This odelike posture seems oddly marred by the bluff good spirits of the apparition.

The second part of Nikolai Ogarev's long poem "Humor" (*Iumor*) from the 1840s presents Petersburg as "a prodigal son" who has deviated from the instructions of Peter the Father.[48] The lyric persona arrives in Petersburg only to have his spirits dampened by the cold rainy weather and the pointlessly frenetic movements of the city's inhabitants, who rush about in order to "kill the day somehow." The persona kneels before the bronze horseman, who looks upon him sorrowfully. In the city, the Winter Palace and the fortress prison face one another, as two halves of a single whole. Ogarev's narrator visits Peter's two-room house in search of the founder's spirit, but finds a "grave-like chill" wafting through. Something great is "buried" there, and in Petersburg itself, "as if in a crypt." The persona flees these evil places as the horseman statue laughs bitterly. In a similarly dark tribute, Nikolai Shcherbina's 1859 four-line poem "Before the Monument to Peter the First in Petersburg" (*Pered pamiatnikom Petru I-mu v Peterburge*) begins with the word "No," and continues in the spirit of repudiation. "It was not the snake that the Bronze Horseman trampled, while striving to move ahead," declares Shcherbina. "He trampled our poor people, trampled our simple folk." (*Net, ne zmiia Vsadnik mednyi/Rastoptal, stremias' vpered,— /Rastoptal narod nash bednyi, / Rastoptal prostoi narod*). The title of Shcherbina's poem recalls the older tradition of laudatory poems to Peter's monument, only to shock its reader by looking down at the horse's hooves and the lowliest Russian subjects. In its abbreviated form, the poem recalls the witty epigrams of the eighteenth century—except that it is deadly serious. The triple repetition of "trampled" at the beginning of lines 2–4 feels like a heavy bronze hoof striking the ear.

Nineteenth-century poetic renderings of the Falconet monument also strove for lighter satirical effects. Alexander Iakhontov's 1863 "Window on Europe" (*Okno v Evropu*) aligns itself explicitly with Pushkin's poem, using the famous lines from the latter as its epigraph, but to an ironic purpose. "It's not for us to judge why he doomed us to freeze eternally by the Neva," muses the persona. Peter may have broken through to Europe with his window, but "we" have been sitting by that window for more than a century and a half. "How long, yawning and half-asleep, have we butted our foreheads against this window!" exclaims the persona. When the "forbidden" window suddenly opens to the spirit of the times, Russians hurry abroad to spend money, and "crawl back through" to Russia when their funds are dissipated. The persona urges his reader to stay at home: "Why not lie down on the stove, having boarded up the window to Europe?"

Perhaps the most provocatively comic contribution to "The Bronze Horseman" poetic tradition is Vladimir Benediktov's 1855 "A Small Oration about the Great" (*Maloe slovo o velikom*), published in *The Library for Reading* and reviled by Nekrasov in *The Contemporary*.[49] Benediktov's poem offers an ironic account of Peter and his achievements, concluding with Petersburg's founding and the dedication of the monument. "We'll hack out a path to Europe!" Peter urges his subjects in highly colloquial fashion. "That door isn't locked. We'll manage it somehow." The rapid construction of the capital is conveyed by choppy, summary-style declarations: "Today—the border is established, tomorrow—the forests cut down, in ten years—a capital, in one hundred—miracles!" The persona inspects the bronze statue at close range: "So majestically, so royally he gazes on the Neva's course, that you go up to him and unwittingly your hat is torn from your head." Benediktov's poem paradoxically pays homage to the bronze horseman by approaching the monument irreverently—acknowledging and simultaneously subverting the traditional forms of obeisance. The neoclassical monument to Peter the Great is not a unitary image, but in fact stands for the diverse range of responses that the statue has invoked.[50] Another consummate Petersburg site—the central avenue of Nevsky Prospect—is similarly rendered in literature as a consistently heterogeneous unity.

Eclectic Unity: Perspectives on Nevsky

Beginning in the 1830s, Petersburg's main boulevard, Nevsky Prospect, came to exemplify the growing eclectic trend in architecture and was represented in literature according to the same aesthetic principles. Almost all the "great architects" who worked in eighteenth- and nineteenth-century Russia were responsible for at least one building on or near Nevsky Prospect: Rastrelli's Stroganov Palace, Trezzini's Alexander Nevsky Monastery, Carlo Rossi's Alexandrinskii Theater, Zakharov's redone Admiralty, Voronikhin's Kazan Cathedral, and so forth.[51] In this sense, Nevsky Prospect conforms to the traditional image of Petersburg as a catalogue of masterworks. Nevsky Prospect was also the street, however, with the best shops displaying the most varied imported wares. Moreover, Nevsky Prospect juxtaposed buildings of extremely diverse purpose, such as the Imperial Public Library, the Catherine-era Merchants' Arcade (Gostinyi dvor), churches of different faiths, and Filippov's confectionary, one of the city's favorite pastry shops.

Although Nikolai Gogol's story "Nevsky Prospect" is the best-known fictional work associated with Petersburg's central artery, analogous texts on the subject of this street propose a comparable eclectic unity. Nevsky Prospect as depicted in diverse literary texts consistently conforms to the architectural terms according to which Russian artists and theorists of the time, Gogol himself included, often expressed their views.

Architectural principles implicitly inform much of Arabesques, Gogol's 1835 collection of essays, short stories, and novel fragments.[52] The essay "On the Architecture of the Present Day" explicitly asserts the value of the vertical in the urban landscape and claims that Gothic architecture allows the artist's imagination room for maximal upward striving.[53] Gogol appears to be responding to the chapter "This Will Kill That" from Victor Hugo's Nôtre-Dame de Paris (1831), in which archdeacon Claude Frollo predicts that printing will supplant architecture as the great work of humanity. Like Hugo, Gogol conceives of the totality of literature as an ideal structure, a grand "edifice" of diverse properties and magnificent wholeness.[54] Gogol, too, feels more than a twinge at architecture's purported passing as the greatest art form and hopes to find a place for it within a new aesthetic order.

Gogol does not simply call for the return of spiritual principles in architecture, however. He preaches expansion in the use of architectural forms through an intricate blending of disparate elements, brought about through the collaboration of man and nature in the manner of the late-eighteenth-century "picturesque." The result would be a horizontal, synchronic "map" of history as well as a landscape for contemplation.[55] Although the picturesque as an aesthetic category typically refers to gardens, this notion can be grafted onto an urban topography, as the Marquis de Custine did in 1839, when he declared of his reader, "let him embrace in one view the whole of these varied parts, and he will understand how Petersburg may be infinitely picturesque, not withstanding the bad taste of its borrowed architecture."[56]

In my view, Gogol's aesthetic program also heralds architectural "eclecticism," a trend in its incipient form when *Arabesques* appeared.[57] True, Gogol's emphasis on the vertical aspect of city architecture seems to argue against the democratic horizontal aesthetics of eclecticism. Like Petr Chaadaev, who published an 1832 "philosophical letter" praising Egyptian and Gothic architecture for monumental imaginative fancy, Gogol values grand-scale architecture that expresses a single great will.[58] While Gogol argues against eclecticism within a single architectural structure, however, he argues *for* eclecticism when considering the cityscape as a whole, as Nestor Kukol'nik did in his 1837 description of Peterhof:

> A city should consist of varied masses . . . so that it provides pleasure to the gaze . . . On a single street, let there rise the gloomy Gothic, the Eastern laden with luxurious ornamentation, the monumental Egyptian, and the Greek infused with harmonious proportions. Let there be visible the lightly protruding milky dome, the infinite religious spire, the Eastern mitre, the flat Italian roof and the high figured Flemish roof, the four-sided pyramid, the rounded column, and the angular obelisk. Let the buildings not merge into a single undifferentiated wall, but rather incline variously up and down.[59]

In Gogol's vision, every part of a city should be a "vivid landscape." His conception of eclecticism as an overarching urban aesthetics recalls the notion of unity (*edinstvo*) in Orthodox religious thought. This unity comes from the tight bonding of heterogeneous parts, all of which are essential to the integrity of the whole.[60]

"Architecture . . . ," Gogol declares grandly, toward the conclusion of his essay, "is a chronicle of the world: it speaks when songs and legends are silent, when no one speaks any longer about a vanished people."[61] He goes so far as to propose in a footnote that each city could have a single street constituting an architectural chronicle that proceeded through styles of different ages in a history of "the development of taste."[62] Citizens too lazy to read thick volumes could walk the length of this street "in order to know everything."[63] This proposal allows eclecticism to achieve the ultimate coherence of text, serving its pedagogical function, as Victor Cousin advocated, and allowing for the diachronic study of history within a synchronic, all-encompassing cityscape.[64] Gogol's recommendations correspond to the now-canonical view of the Russian imperial capital as a "city of cities," a second-degree aesthetic phenomenon like literature itself.

Did Gogol take his own advice and create an urban promenade of eclectic coherence? Gogol's famous story "Nevsky Prospect," which itself first appeared in the collection *Arabesques,* can be considered in such terms. Granted, Gogol's story contains little information about the architectural features of the Prospect or the Petersburg neighborhoods to which the story leads its characters and readers—the brothel on Liteinyi Prospect and the artisans' neighborhood on Meshchanskaia Street near Kazan Cathedral. Gogol's generic chronicle is literary, not architectural. A draft version of the story, however, characterized Nevsky Prospect as the only place in St. Petersburg where the city becomes truly visible and legible to the artist's eye.

Gogol's famous "tour" of Nevsky Prospect over the course of a single day transforms space into time, as reader and narrator stand together on a corner and watch life go by at appointed intervals. Each of these interludes represents a distinct generic tradition or literary milieu (tradespeople, governesses and their charges, well-heeled couples, clerks), none of them yet fully realized in Russian letters. The two stories that follow—tracking Piskarev the artist and Pirogov the libidinous lieutenant—also constitute excursions through the literary past in a confused, fragmentary, even generically incoherent manner. Identifiable traditions along the way include naturalistic roman-feuilleton, farce, melodrama, sentimental story, urban physiological sketch, romantic artist's tale, satirical-burlesque anecdote, and cautionary account of urban squalor.[65] When the artist Piskarev attempts to dream of his beloved, his mind produces unsatisfactory, abortive bits in diverse generic modalities. His more extended visions take the reader on a literary tour through chivalric romance, society tale, rustic love story, fairy tale, and bourgeois fantasy of conjugal bliss. Gogol's style in this story has been termed "a heedless disregard of all literary schools" and "a purposeful mixing of all elements of tone and expression" in an "apparently complete disdain for form."[66] Perhaps Gogol was not displaying a disregard for form, but rather surveying existing literary forms in an attempt to create a new unity. In a thoroughly eclectic spirit, Gogol's story challenges the seeming incongruity of combined elements—the young girl's beauty and the fact that she is a prostitute, the two male protagonists and their destinies—in terms of style, tone, and literary convention, all within the confines of a single story.[66]

Gogol's "Nevsky Prospect" thus constitutes in literary terms the kind of edifying and comprehensive tour he proposes for his model architectural route. This might seem a surprising claim about a writer who, on the one hand, polemicized emphatically at this point in his career against the author's obligation to uplift his audience (see, for example, the ending to "The Nose"), and on the other hand, emphasized the vertical, and not the meandering, ambiguous horizontal in the ideal cityscape. The invocations of largely unrealized generic possibilities in Gogol's story nevertheless point to literary eclecticism and make his dissolving generic landscape coherent in aesthetic terms.[68]

The story can further be read as a marriage between two seemingly incompatible discourses—the ennobling language of art-making and the all-appropriating language of the market, as embodied in the related concepts of commodity (*tovar*) and creation (*tvar'*). Are the two really so separate in "Nevsky Prospect"? The narrator's early assertion that Nevsky is the only place in St. Petersburg where "mercantile interests" do not predominate seems too glib. Moreover, his claim that Nevsky constitutes an "exhibition" of the "finest works of man" (*proizvedenii cheloveka*) creates a similarly ambiguous effect. After all, the Prospect itself is initially characterized as a beautiful woman who might turn out to be either an art object or a prostitute—"the great beauty (*krasavitsa*) of our capital." The language of commerce permeates every part of the story, and literary pleasure itself, it is implied, possesses a similar kind of value.

One would assume that the idealistic Piskarev story would display a determined immunity to the language of the market, in contrast to the seemingly transparent story of Pirogov, who calculates the possibility of success with a German artisan's blonde wife. This is not, however, the case. Piskarev's artistic evaluation of his "Perugini Bianca" requires him to "measure her from her feet to her head," and he imagines her as a "pearl of unappreciated worth." He wishes the young girl were a painting—art as a material commodity—so that he could keep her in his studio. He purchases opium in order to exchange a waking state for a dreaming one, during which he communes with visions of his beloved. Even the conditions under which he buys the opium seem suspect: the Persian seller asks in payment that Pisarev draw a picture of a beautiful woman with himself (the opium-dealer) depicted alongside her. Here, an artistic representation of sexual gratification can be traded for a drug-induced experience. It seems that everything is present simultaneously in its capacity as both art *and* commodity.

Nevsky Prospect functions as a major site of literary eclecticism because this part of Petersburg did not constitute a unity even in its original conception. Initially, Nevsky—or, as it was originally called, "Great Prospect Road"—served as a road (*doroga*) and not a street (*ulitsa*), since its purpose was to lead *out* of the city, not toward the city center. Nevsky was simply a "throughway" to the old Novgorod Road, and its proximity to the Admiralty did nothing to enhance its status. The precise location of Nevsky between the Admiralty and Znamenskaia Square can be attributed to local topographical features and conditions,

FIGURE 2.4. Nevsky Prospect, from Andrei Martynov, *Recueil de vues de St. Pétersbourg,* 1821–22. (Courtesy of Houghton Library at Harvard.)

namely a narrowing of the Fontanka that provided a promising place for a crossing, and impassable swamps between waterways that deterred efforts in other spots.[69] Nevsky Prospect was never intended as the main artery of the capital and became an important part of the city only toward the end of the eighteenth century.[70]

Nevsky's function as a modest travel route first appeared likely to change in 1739, when the Construction Commission thought to build the central city market, an unrealized project called Mytnyi Dvor, in this area. Empress Elizabeth's decision during the 1740s to build the Anichkov Palace for her lover Razumovskii, as well as her own sumptuous Summer Palace on the Fontanka, more truly heralded the change in Nevsky's fortunes. Over subsequent decades, Nevsky Prospect began to feel like a central avenue.

The first part of the nineteenth century witnessed a major attempt to transform Nevsky Prospect into what Yuri Egorov calls "a grand spatial composition" and "an unbroken chain of related ensembles" (Kazan Cathedral, Mikhailovskii Palace, Alexandrinskii Theater) leading up to the larger culminating ensemble of the five central squares.[71] This, however, is only one way of looking at a boulevard that served as home to diverse religious, residential, commercial, cultural, and government institutions. Nevsky exemplifies eclectic diversity even within single categories; for example, along its length could be found Dutch, Lutheran, Catholic, and Armenian churches, as well as the Russian Orthodox Kazan Cathedral, a Greek church, and a house of worship for Old Believers.[72]

The Prospect's starting point was, architecturally speaking, also an eclectic one, with the Admiralty resembling, in Théophile Gautier's words, "the mast of a ship of gold, planted on the roof of a Greek temple."[73] Gautier found the central artery of St. Petersburg to be essentially hybrid and characterized Nevsky Prospect as "a completely original mélange of shops, palaces, and churches." He surveyed the diverse structures that represented different architectural periods and styles and, in so doing, described St. Petersburg as a whole:

> Nevsky Prospect represents a kind of resumé of Petersburg. . . . The surrounding buildings are high and wide, and resemble palaces or town-houses; the oldest among them recall the ancient French style, but are somewhat Italianate. . . . Others are decorated in the style of Louis XV . . . while further on, the Greek empire style shows the even line of its columns and triangular pediments, which stand out white against the yellow background. There are thoroughly contemporary buildings in the Anglo-Germanic style. . . . This ensemble, whose details should not be studied too closely . . . creates a wonderful visual effect, for which the name of "Prospect" that the street bears . . . is marvelously apt and meaningful. Everything is devised for perspective.

Tellingly, Gautier asserts that Petersburg's ornamental detail need not be studied for its inherent artistic merit, but rather considered within a larger eclectic unity.

A number of Russian literary texts from the nineteenth century similarly traverse Nevsky Prospect in order to catalogue its eclectic vistas. The Ukrainian professor Vasilii Maslovich, for example, documents a stroll along Nevsky during his 1816–18 visit—one of the earliest Nevsky descriptions of a type that would become a "Petersburg genre."[74] Maslovich takes his reader on a hypothetical walk during which he encounters a number of prominent Petersburg figures, mostly writers: arch-conservative A. S. Shishkov, graphomaniac Count D. I. Khvostov, reactionary "mass" journalist N. I. Grech, gluttonous *litterateur* A. E. Izmailov, Khlestakovian P. P. Svin'in, *Iliad* translator N. I. Gnedich, liberalist poet and Napoleonic war memoirist F. N. Glinka, official nationalist S. S. Uvarov, and satirical fabulist I. A. Krylov. For Maslovich, Nevsky Prospect offers a visual analogue for the variegated panorama of Russian literary life at this complex pre-Decembrist moment. Like the sights on Petersburg's main boulevard, Maslovich's parade of cultural icons runs the stylistic gamut—in his case, from lofty seriousness to good-natured buffoonery.[75]

Even before Gogol's "Nevsky Prospect" was written, it was difficult to determine which genre might best represent Petersburg's main avenue. One of the most provocative texts in this "Nevsky" corpus is a telegraphic Pushkin prose fragment from the early 1830s that reads, "N. chooses Nevsky Prospect as his confidant—he confides all his domestic problems and family grievances to it.—He is pitied.—He is satisfied."[76] The Academy edition provides no further information to illuminate Pushkin's idea for this literary work, and it is difficult to formulate even an approximate generic category to which a work matching this description might belong—the fantastic, the sentimental-pathetic, the comic-parodic?

An otherwise undistinguished "Petersburg" poem by Petr Veinberg from 1858 partially realizes Pushkin's project, conveying the mix of elements on Nevsky by adopting a series of poetic postures in quick succession. The poem opens, "Sadly I wander along Nevsky Prospect . . ." (*Pechal'no ia brozhu po Nevskomu prospektu* . . .), a phrase that evokes Pushkin's 1836 metaphysical graveyard lyric "When I wander, dreamily, in the city outskirts . . ." (*Kogda za gorodom, zadumchiv, ia brozhu* . . .). In the second line, Veinberg turns to more immediate aesthetic considerations: "How full of life it is! How much effect in it!" (*Kak polon zhizni on! Kak mnogo v nem effektu!*). The rhymed pairing of "Prospect" and "effect" makes clear the poem's central aim—to evoke and catalogue the diverse public, twice characterized by the attribute "motley" (*pestry*), a rather Pushkinian epithet. The poem's light-hearted inventory of social types is then interrupted by a flat reminder of the poet-persona's own position within this cosmos, "alone in the crowd, lost, forgotten / In a patched overcoat, uncombed, unshaven." In fact, the lonely persona itself is just as much a part of the Nevsky textual cosmos as the hussars, diplomats, civil servants, and tradespeople whose presence this persona notes.

Literary and artistic treatments of Nevsky Prospect often resort to the survey or panorama format in order to posit unity from diversity. While Gogol's story constitutes the most notable artistic "survey" of Nevsky Prospect from the 1830s, the scroll-like lithograph *A Panorama of Nevsky Prospect* was also well known in its time, created from watercolors by the peasant artist Vasilii Sadovnikov and published by the Society for the Encouragement of Artists.[77] Sadovnikov's *Panorama* depicts the buildings from the Admiralty to the Anichkov Bridge, in a single detailed scroll nearly fifty feet long for each side of the street. The artist faithfully reproduced even the tiniest architectural features, and rendered the Prospect very much of its moment by including shop signboards and readily identifiable members of the Petersburg population. The *Panorama* captures chance encounters and particulars of dress and posture, as well as an architectural "ensemble" that can—at least in theory—be considered as a whole. In practice, Sadovnikov's work was viewed in segments by winding the lithographic ribbon forward and backward on two supporting spindles, a technique that created a more "local" sense of street life. Sadovnikov includes deeper perspectives at crossroads, where the view extends back from the street, providing a sense of the urban space as a whole. In its conception, Sadovnikov's project represents both high and low, distanced and near—suggesting in its diverse comprehensiveness the decomposing system of generic forms that defines the nineteenth-century cityscape.

Alexander Bashchutskii's three-volume literary *Panorama of St. Petersburg* (*Panorama Sanktpeterburga,* 1834) attempted to represent the city by approaching it from various disciplinary and generic perspectives, among them historiography, statistics, ethnography (*nravoopisatel'nyi ocherk*), and historical fiction.[78] Bashchutskii's third volume may even have inspired Gogol's "Nevsky Prospect," published the following spring, devoting twenty pages of description to a single day in contemporary St. Petersburg, beginning at dawn.[79] To be sure, Bashchutskii treats the city as a whole, but he adopts the same strategy as Gogol would, tracing the movements of Petersburg subpopulations over the course of the day.

At 2:00 P.M. during this hypothetical day, Bashchutskii turns to Nevsky Prospect, the "main artery of Petersburg," which offers "a vast field for the observations of the customs chronicler and the reasoning of the philosopher, revealing the everyday lives, occupations, passions, and weaknesses of the inhabitants from nearly all classes."[80] After the strolling ladies and gentlemen come merchants hurrying to the Stock Exchange, and then the Prospect fills with civil servants rushing out for their dinners. Nevsky is an "enormous, living kaleidoscope, into which all of humanity has been poured." As should be clear by now, even the "panoramic" genre, which purportedly surveys its subject at a lofty remove, can convey a vivid sense of the everyday activities transpiring within a given space at a particular time.[81] The length of Nevsky traverses human life metaphorically as well, Bashchutskii observes, beginning with the Economic Society and concluding with the monastery and cemetery.

Ivan Bozherianov's 1903 bicentennial album *Nevsky Prospect 1703–1903* combines and extends the comprehensive representational strategies of Sadovnikov and Bashchutskii, with a book-format textual and visual "panorama" of Nevsky that continues past the Anichkov Bridge up to Znamenskaia Square.[82] Each photographic segment of the Prospect is followed by an index of firms and building owners, and a long sequence of advertisements, thus situating this "panorama" in its historical moment in the same way as Sadovnikov's shop signboards and miniature inhabitants. Bozherianov separated out churches, palaces, and monuments from the architectural skein, however, and treated them in separate parts of his anniversary album, so as to distinguish high culture from commerce and heterogeneous lived experience. This strategy of presentation in itself constitutes an unacknowledged negative response to the period of Petersburg eclecticism. The second half of the nineteenth century receives remarkably short shrift in Bozherianov's historical account, and the phenomenon of architectural eclecticism is not granted any place at all in the city's retrospective self-contemplation.

The anecdote as a compact textual structure provides an alternative form to the panorama for representing Nevsky Prospect in literature. Bashchutskii's "kaleidoscope" finds its counterpart in a fantastic humoresque from 1833 by Vladimir Odoevskii, titled "A Tale about How Dangerous It Is for Young Girls to Go Walking in a Group along Nevsky Prospect" (*Skazka o tom, kak opasno devushkam khodit' tolpoiu po Nevskomu Prospektu*), one of his "motley" (*pestrye*) stories.[83] This cautionary allegory recounts the fate of a silly young beauty, who is trapped in a shop by a mysterious foreign proprietor. Odoevskii's narrative dazzles the reader with an inventory of items for sale in the shop, among them slippers made of dragonfly feet, feathers woven from ewe's fur, and a lorgnette made from the eyes of a fly, through which one might see everything transpiring at the theater. Each of these items juxtaposes an ordinary function with extraordinary materials, and, in a sequence, they propose themselves to the reader as a bizarre unity. Aided by his henchmen, a French head, a German nose, and an English torso, the shopkeeper transforms his captive Russian beauty into a foreign doll by brewing her heart in a potion concocted from Italian roulades, a dozen new *contredanses,* a handful of city slander pulled from the air of Nevsky, and a slew of conventional phrases. After twisting her tongue with pincers so that she cannot pronounce Russian words properly, the shopkeeper places the living doll under a crystal bell in the window, until a young man purchases her. The young man's patience is soon exhausted by the doll's insipid phrases and never-ending demands, and he throws her out the window. Odoevskii casts Nevsky as the center of foreign cultural influences, which combine in an indigestible, indecipherable glut of commodities of which the author disapproves, or so it would seem. Yet the story itself is a hybrid literary mixture of the fantastic, the parodic, and the satirical that suggests a proclivity for eclectic aesthetics, or at least acknowledges Nevsky as Petersburg's eclectic center.

Where the panorama is all-inclusive, the anecdote is idiosyncratic and local, although it implies the coexistence of many other such ministories. Bashchutskii's characterization of Nevsky as the life trajectory of an individual thus serves as the main shaping device for Vladimir Dal"s 1843 story, "The Life of a Man, or A Stroll along Nevsky Prospect" (*Zhizn' cheloveka, ili Progulka po Nevskomu Prospektu*), published in the conservative nationalist journal *The Muscovite.* Dal"s story opens in an already familiar vein, asserting that Nevsky Prospect is

an entire world; a material world and a spiritual world, a world of events, collisions, coincidences, a world of sly and complex calculation, of subtle intrigues and crafty talk; a palace of intellect and a rut of foolishness; an abyss of wisdom and a jester's platform of buffoonery; a fount of ingeniousness and a packed pavement of vulgarity; a gallery of modest fashionableness and a shameful spectacle of fashionable modesty; an exhibition of foppery, luxury and taste—a bazaar of conceit and vanity, a flea market of . . . human weaknesses and foibles; the fulcrum, basis of action, and entire life of a single person—the turning point and solstice of another; a field of war and a secluded cell—a chase across an immeasurable expanse and a cramped circle of rotation around a rented hearth.[84]

After this inventory of possibilities, Dal' considers the generic alternatives for his own particular work. "Someone else" has already described the public on Nevsky Prospect according to shifts of day and hour, he notes. Instead, the author asserts, he will recount the story of a single person, whose world was bounded by Nevsky from birth to death—the hunchback "Joseph," left on a German baker's doorstep as an infant. The first thirty years of Joseph's life proceed up the right-hand side of Nevsky from the monastery to Palace Square, and the second half returns along the same route, but on the left-hand, "aristocratic" side of the Prospect. Joseph lives through the Napoleonic Wars and the flood of 1824, but his life is touched by only the most local events—those that impact his beloved Nevsky. The secret of his origins is never revealed and is buried along with the hero in his modest grave on the monastery grounds.

Dal"s story, like Veinberg's poem, realizes Pushkin's laconic plan for a story about the relationship between a character and the street, to whom such secrets are confided. It also creatively retraces and reanimates Sadovnikov's *Panorama*, telling a story that takes the same route as the artist, rather than one that merely enlarges one of the stationary citizens represented on the lithograph. Nevsky Prospect itself proposes many different walks across its territory, and multiple angles of vision on the same places. On Nevsky, eclectic place gives rise to eclectic discourse.[85]

When literary hierarchies are disordered, an eclectic poetics may replace them, as exemplified by Gleb Uspenskii's anecdotal story "An Encounter on Nevsky" (*Vstrecha na Nevskom*), part of the story cycle "It Came to My Memory" (*Prishlo na pamiat'*), in which a chain of recollections leads from one story into the next. The encounter on Nevsky arises out of a dense stew of narrative possibilities, as the narrator reaches a street intersection and finds himself caught in a "solid mass of people from every rank and status: ladies with folders of music, fish-sellers with tubs on their heads, clerks, and officers, and in the street—a halted mass of large and small carriages, cab-drivers, and carters—and all of this had been piled into a heap due to the funeral of some military man."[86] When the military band begins a German waltz, the public suddenly begins to dance, creating a "furious whirlpool of people, carriages, and horses," a torrent going in every direction.[87] This chaos allows a brief space for the narrator's chance meeting with a peasant he had known in the country, who, he sadly notes, now works at a city brewery and has been much coarsened by his move to the capital. As the two chat awkwardly, the peasant Ivan insists that he has just spied his former beloved, Varvara, in a sledge full of prostitutes. Uspenskii's story invokes but does not pursue the fates of Ivan and Varvara, as the narrator continues along the street alone—presumably on his way to the next encounter.

The tradition of treating Nevsky Prospect as an eclectic terrain, both literary and architectural, includes Egor Rastorguev's 1846 *Strolls along Nevsky Prospect* (*Progulki po Nevskomu prospektu*) and contemporary exemplars, such as Dmitri

Sherikh's 1996 *True Stories and Tall Tales of Nevsky Prospect* (*Byli i nebylitsy Nevskogo Prospekta*).[88] Sherikh's walk extends from Znamenskaia Square to the Admiralty, as is usual in such Nevsky surveys, but takes a synchronic approach to each site of note. He claims to have selected true and fictional tales for inclusion based upon those aspects of the city's 300-year history that seemed interesting to "the author"—that is, according to the originary selection principle of eclecticism. Sherikh does not discuss the Prospect's architectural features and justifies this choice by inquiring rhetorically, "Can there be a theme in Petersburg literature more fully elucidated than the architecture of Nevsky?"[89] Instead, the author relates "unusual acts, occurrences, absurdities, anecdotes, stories of love and death," and asserts his pride in writing "from outside the tradition of history as a science."[90] In fact, Sherikh writes very much from within a tradition: the chatty narrator who throws an arm around the reader's shoulders, acting as tour-guide and treating Nevsky Prospect as a metagenre— a meeting place for literary modes. In this, Nevsky Prospect as literature mirrors its eclectic architectural double.

CHAPTER THREE

Armchair Traveling: Russian Literary Guides to St. Petersburg

IS IT POSSIBLE to speak of "travel" literature when the ground being covered is one's own? Foreigners who visited St. Petersburg during the eighteenth and nineteenth centuries produced a substantial body of travel writing, but this chapter concerns Russians' *own* journeys within their capital city, a place that never quite felt like home.[1] For Russian writers, the persistent foreignness of St. Petersburg proved a productive discomfort.[2] By the end of the imperial period, Russian writers had covered the physical and cultural terrain of St. Petersburg with describing words. Literary guides continued to propose versions of imperial St. Petersburg during the Soviet period, and even more energetically in the post-Soviet years. Readers could retrace these paths by perusing textual tours, or by traveling around the city themselves, guidebook in hand, accompanied by the tradition of Petersburg literary mapping. Reading Petersburg guidebooks and their literary kin simulates strolling through the imperial capital, while physical travels around the city can suggest turning the pages of a well-thumbed book.

The Petersburg city guidebook written by Russians for Russians emerged from the topographical descriptions of the later eighteenth century, taking shape over the nineteenth century as the expression of imperial ideology, and during the early decades of the twentieth century in more partisan preservationist and excursionist approaches to the city. Beginning in the early nineteenth century, Russian writers also produced belletristic guidebook analogues: urban feuilletons, sketches, and sociocultural explorations that traversed the metropolis, using the travel-writing designations "stroll" (*progulka*) and "journey" (*puteshestvie*) to connote a train of thought. In this, belletristic texts exploring the imperial capital inherit and transform the leisurely discursive practice of aristocratic eighteenth-century travel notes. These more loosely conceived Petersburg literary guides developed as a tradition from Konstantin Batiushkov's elegant 1814 stroll to the Academy of Arts, through the satirical urban travel notes of declassed gentry writers like Dostoevsky and Nekrasov, who wrote feuilletons for ready cash in the 1840s, and thence to all comers—late-imperial popular journalists like Nikolai Zhivotov, nostalgic postimperial memoirists such as Anatoly Koni, and contemporary literary time travelers charting the byways of Petersburg cultural history.

More traditional Petersburg guidebooks from the mid nineteenth century onward rely on excerpts from famous Russian literary works as elements of their city tours, evidence of the extent to which the guidebook as a genre situates itself at the crossroads of literary and nonliterary writing. In fact, conventional guidebooks and belletristic writing about Petersburg both underwent significant development beginning in the 1820s–1830s, all the while overlapping in function, and exchanging rhetorical devices. It is even fair to say that the guidebook genre best embodies the overarching intent of *all* writing about St. Petersburg as it constructs and constitutes the city using travel as a central metaphor. The urban mapping project common to imperial Petersburg "travel" literature has been obscured by the dissimilarities of genre that formally demarcate topographical descriptions, guidebooks, handy reference works, school textbooks, literary-cultural excursions, feuilletons, ethnographic sketches ("physiologies"), investigative journalism, memoirs, and geographically plotted urban fiction. The highly individualized literary "stroll" that wanders over a terrain of loosely structured meditations, the feuilleton that visits an unlovely neighborhood, and the general "guidebook" (*putevoditel'*), a purposeful textual cicerone that leads the reader along a largely celebratory path, might seem at times to work at cross purposes. Still, the differences between idiosyncratic explorers and proselytizing tour-guides are less important than their participation in the common endeavor of literary mapping. The guidebook form as a basic model for writing about St. Petersburg has proved highly elastic in its ability to accommodate diverse approaches to the city, and to provide a meeting place for writing of diverse sociopolitical orientation, stylistic register, generic form, and topographical emphasis.

All of this textual "travel" produces the collective sense of cultural middle ground via much-traversed sites, familiar perspectives, and learned responses to St. Petersburg that can be mastered by residents, visitors, or readers who allow themselves to be thus guided. This chapter's guided tour of Petersburg travel writing reveals the persistent sense of common purpose: negotiating and articulating claims to imperial Petersburg as a shared cultural resource.

Guided Reading for Russians: Official Tours to Eighteenth- and Nineteenth-Century Petersburg

The first half of the nineteenth century marks the onset of the "great guidebook" tradition, as exemplified by John Murray, Karl Baedeker, and Thomas Cook's Tours.[3] While the Grand Tour of Europe for young men from good families in

England, America, and Russia was a well-established eighteenth-century institution, extended travel for self-edification became more widespread after the Napoleonic Wars, and developed even more rapidly with the public's growing access to European railroads in the 1830s.[4] Approximately fifty guidebooks to London appeared in 1851, the year of the Great Exhibition—most of them published in English by London presses.[5] A wide variety of guidebooks to New York City were readily available by the first half of the nineteenth century, as well as a large selection for Paris subsequent to Baron Georges-Eugène Haussman's major reconstruction of the city during the Second Empire.[6]

St. Petersburg during the first part of the nineteenth century was not nearly such a draw for foreign tourists, however, and there were few guidebooks available for such visitors.[7] The Marquis de Custine wrote despairingly, if not entirely accurately, of his 1839 trip to St. Petersburg: "If you wish to ascertain precisely what is to be seen in this great city, and if Schnitzler [the author of a work on Russian statistics] does not satisfy you, you will find no other guide: no bookseller has on sale a complete directory to the curiosities of Petersburg. . . . No one has any idea of gratifying the curious; on the contrary, they love to deceive them with false data."[8] There also existed an expressed need for "travel" literature about St. Petersburg written for Russians. As Vissarion Belinsky wrote of Nikolai Nekrasov's 1845 sketch compendium *Physiology of Petersburg,* "The purpose of these articles is to introduce Petersburg to provincial readers, and, perhaps even more importantly, to Petersburg readers."[9]

The Petersburg guidebooks that appeared over the course of the nineteenth century construe their audiences diversely as consumers of official information, visitors from the provinces, children, peasants, and architecture buffs. All of these guidebooks instruct their readers in the exercise of reading Petersburg, however, as did literary works (including the *Physiology* sketches) that emulated guidebook conventions and exerted a reciprocal shaping influence on the Petersburg guidebook genre. The shared literary space of coexistent guidebooks can be contentious, however. Both the Marquis and Belinsky demonstratively evoke the *lack* of guidebook writing about Petersburg, ignoring or dismissing existing work on the subject, a move that would be repeated by Petersburg travel writers through the end of the imperial period. Many Russian writers have characterized Petersburg as persistently strange, resistant to a final written account, but their habit of making other authors' texts disappear is rarely acknowledged.

Eighteenth-century topographical descriptions (*opisaniia*) of the city were direct precursors of the guidebook tour to St. Petersburg. The first such detailed record of the imperial capital was composed by Academy librarian Andrei Bogdanov, whose *Historical, Geographical, and Topographical Description of St. Petersburg 1703–1751* (*Istoricheskoe, geograficheskoe, i topograficheskoe opisanie Sanktpeterburga*) was prepared in honor of the capital's fifty-year anniversary at the request of Empress Elizabeth and appeared posthumously in 1779. Bogdanov's project was originally intended as explanatory text for a huge map of

St. Petersburg produced by the Academy of Sciences, but was published with more than one hundred engravings accompanying the prose description. Literary and visual representations thus have contended for primacy in the history of this project, as two complementary but very different kinds of documentation; both are integrally related to the practice of mapping. Bogdanov's work anticipates the connection between history and topography that nineteenth- and twentieth-century Petersburg guidebooks would articulate, by providing a full accounting of the contemporary city as well as its early history, based on work with archival sources.[10] In an even more comprehensive effort, Johann Gottlieb Georgi, a German professor at the Russian Academy of Sciences, produced *Description of the Russian Imperial Capital City of St. Petersburg 1794– 1796 (Opisanie rossiisko-imperatorskogo stolichnogo goroda Sankt-Peterburga)*, first published in German and French.[11]

The lengthy "description" format of these proto-guidebooks encompasses geography, history, and ethnography, as well as urban institutions of culture, education, medicine, finance, trade, industry, religion, and the military. The city's notable monuments do not stand out within this textual terrain, nor are thematic routes proposed to help readers make sense of the city. Such "descriptions" more closely resemble inventories, with data in loose nonnarrative form.[12] It might be said that eighteenth-century descriptions evoke the totalizing plane projections of *maps*, whereas their fully evolved nineteenth-century guidebook counterparts manifest the discursive operations that constitute *tours*.[13] The eighteenth-century "descriptions" of Bogdanov and Georgi do, however, exist on a literary continuum with the Petersburg guidebooks of the nineteenth century, and include much of the same sort of information, as well as occasional rhetorical gestures that anticipate the guidebook genre.[14] The evolution from descriptive map to guided tour responds to the growth in the Petersburg cityscape between the reigns of Catherine II and Nicholas I, as much as to the dawning of the Guidebook Age in the nineteenth century. The increasing number of less noteworthy civil and military buildings relative to grand palaces, churches, and showpiece cultural institutions, not to mention the expanding territory of the imperial capital, meant that guidebooks needed to emphasize what was important, instead of merely taking account of what was there.

Although the Marquis de Custine did not know it, the first dedicated guidebooks to St. Petersburg had appeared in print well before his 1839 visit—Fedor Shreder's *Newest Guidebook to St. Petersburg (Noveishii putevoditel' po Sankt- peterburgu,* 1820) and Pavel Svin'in's multivolume *Memorable Sights of St. Petersburg and its Environs (Dostopamiatnosti Sankt-Peterburga i ego okrestnostei,* 1816–28). Both can be considered transitional forms that share features with both the eighteenth-century "description" and the later excursion-based nineteenth- century guidebook. Fedor Shreder took a cautiously official approach to the capital, in a "short survey (*kratkoe obozrenie*) of everything curious that might occupy the traveler," that "keeps to the *middle* [emphasis mine] between a dry inventory of objects and an overly detailed description."[15] Even if Shreder did have the ordinary tourist in mind, however, his reader is easily lost in the maze of official Petersburg; the guidebook contains no illustrations and only a single map, and he emphasizes public institutions such as hospitals and government ministries at the expense of tourist attractions.[16]

Svin'in's *Memorable Sights*, which appeared in five illustrated volumes with facing-pages text in Russian and French, was the grander of the two (and might have proved useful to the Marquis, who did not know Russian).[17] With an emphasis on "sights" (*dostoprimechatel'nosti* or *dostopamiatnosti*, meaning literally "that which is worth noting or remembering"), *Memorable Sights* itself stands as a memorial to Alexandrine-era tastefulness. Each volume treats a set of major cultural monuments such as the Hermitage, Public Library, Academy of Arts, and Stock Exchange, and includes a section on Petersburg folk holidays. The five "sets" are not organized according to any discernible logical or thematic grouping, however, and Svin'in does not attempt to map out literary strolls around the city, as later guidebooks would do. Instead, he brings the tourist-reader before individual, isolated sites—each represented as an object of contemplation by a beautiful lithograph—and offers a substantial description and history. It is true, however, that sequenced descriptions of building complexes, as well as the prose structures of the gesturing tour guide ("Passing through the archway, you will see . . ."), can be detected in descriptions of individual monuments. With its lengthy descriptive passages and multivolume heft, *Memorable Sights* nevertheless seems better suited for armchair traveling than for pedagogical promenades. Most important, Svin'in's *Memorable Sights* does not convey the sense of a living *city*, but rather presents larger-than-life architectural masterworks without surrounding urban context.

Alexander Bashchutskii's massive three-part 1834 *Panorama of St. Petersburg* (*Panorama Sanktpeterburga*), accompanied by engravings and city maps and published in Russian, German, and French, seems at first glance a late exemplar of the bloated eighteenth-century "description."[18] Bashchutskii devotes two of the three parts to the early history of the city under Peter—based on archival work that his successors would criticize as sloppy—and then creates a portrait of contemporary St. Petersburg that includes details from everyday life as well as statistical data on births, deaths, and arrests. Bashchutskii declares the multifarious intent of his *Panorama* in the preface to the first part: "In composing a panorama of St. Petersburg, we had in mind: to sketch a broad and diverse picture of the capital in reduced form, preserving, as far as possible, precision in dimensions and local color; in gradually surveying all that meets the eye, to . . . capture the primary qualities of mores, habits, and everyday life—the common existence of different estates."[19] A reviewer from *The Library for Reading* responded with ironic praise for Bashchutskii's encyclopedic knowledge, particularly as exhibited in Part Three, where he characterizes segments of the city population and provides a protracted description of a single day across the capital. "After this," observes the reviewer caustically, "I cannot imagine how to go on living in Petersburg, when we have been shown without any frills in a public panorama for provincials, when our most significant secrets have been revealed to them and they have been given all the keys to our mores."[20] Bashchutskii resembles an "anatomist," who cuts open the body of Petersburg and reveals the city's inner life to the reader.[21] Bashchutskii's *Panorama* can thus be considered a marriage of eighteenth-century description and nineteenth-century *physiologie*, signaled by the reviewer's discomfiture at the unseemly exposure of the subject to readers. Still, this new inclusiveness in relation to urban life, as characterized by both author and reviewer, works to establish the crucial middle ground—"the common existence of different estates"—whose articulation would represent the shared goal of future Petersburg guidebooks and literary travels. This feature of *Panorama* belies subsequent criticism that Bashchutskii's project was no more than an apologia for the grim reign of Tsar Nicholas I.

The Nikolaevan-era 1838 *Strolls with Children around St. Petersburg and Its Environs* (*Progulki s det'mi po Sankt-Peterburgu i ego okrestnostiam*) by V. Bur'ianov (pseudonym of the journalist Vladimir Burnashev) marks a new concern with the *audience* in guidebook prose, a preoccupation that would extend to newly literate emancipated peasants during the latter part of the nineteenth century. Bur'ianov's is the first Petersburg guidebook to present an explicit tour-text, insistently herding its young readers along. The purportedly "documentary" form of the first Petersburg guidebooks thus evolved into a more explicit means of imparting a set of attitudes about St. Petersburg and Russian culture to an audience, in this particular case treated quite literally like children. Bur'ianov's "Strolls" are intended to occupy Russian children's two-month "vacation time" with instructive excursions around the city proper, the islands, and the palace parks. The narrator of *Strolls with Children* stands in for the kindly, authoritative adult who leads youngsters around the physical city, using the typical second-person plural and imperative exhortations of a tour-guide.[22]

With its requisite halts and rapturous transports at particular spots ("A Look at the Neva"), and its frequent recitations of Pushkin's verse, Bur'ianov prefigures what would become a well-honed Soviet tradition, by way of excursionist Nikolai Antsiferov, who represented St. Petersburg as a compilation of literary excerpts in *The Soul of Petersburg* (*Dusha Peterburga*, 1922). Indeed, Bur'ianov required his audience to situate his tours within an even more substantial textual context. To benefit fully from the "Strolls," children were directed to bring along a map of Petersburg, as well as copies of Bashchutskii's *Panorama* and Svin'in's *Memorable Sights* (although it is difficult to imagine how anyone could manage these heavy volumes on a stroll). Bur'ianov further specifies that children should already have read *History of the Russian State* by the "immortal" Karamzin with their teachers. As Bur'ianov's guidebook shows, by 1838, Russians touring St. Petersburg had to make their way through a dense textual-cultural thicket, metaphorically reenacting the city's founding moment—the mythical bushwhacking survey of the territory performed by Peter the Great.

Exhaustive topographical descriptions from the eighteenth century find a nineteenth-century counterpart in encyclopedic reference works that strive to make the imperial capital both compact and comprehensible. Most notable among these are Aleksei Grech's alphabetical *All of Petersburg in Your Pocket* (*Ves' Peterburg v karmane*, 1846, 1851) and Vladimir Mikhnevich's *All of Petersburg on Your Palm* (*Peterburg ves' na ladoni*, 1874).[23] These genuinely portable reference works liberate the reader-tourist to wander the city, empowered to consult the text at hand about any monument, square, or institution. In an updated eighteenth-century spirit, Mikhnevich suggests several spots from which tourists can obtain the best "panoramic" views of St. Petersburg, but also provides passionately detailed information that includes 1874 calendars for religious faiths practiced in the Russian imperial capital, seating plans and pricing for the major theaters, fire signals, and train schedules.[24]

For the most part, the period 1850s–1890s produced only variations on the guidebooks already discussed, some guilty of barefaced excerpting and plagiarizing.[25] Perhaps this stagnation of the Petersburg guidebook genre reflected the existence of eminently serviceable tomes by Svin'in, Shreder, Bur'ianov, and others, not to mention the more recent reference works. The lack of new guidebook approaches to Petersburg may also have corresponded to the gloomier imperial mood of retrenchment rather than self-celebration from the latter 1870s on.[26] Earlier guidebook authors acknowledged social problems only implicitly in their upbeat descriptions of the city's charitable institutions. This evasive approach to the growing sense of urban social crisis must have been difficult to sustain, especially with the rise of exposé journalism beginning in the 1860s.

As the nineteenth century drew to a close, the Petersburg guidebook genre was briefly refreshed by the presence of a new addressee, the "folk" (*narod*), whom excursions sought to educate in the art of appreciating St. Petersburg. In 1898, D. N. Loman published *The Sights of St. Petersburg: Reading for the Folk* (*Dostoprimechatel'nosti Sankt-Peterburga. Chtenie dlia naroda*), which provided a four-day tour of the city.[27] Loman's guidebook proposes Peter the Great plunging his shovel into the earth at St. Petersburg's founding moment as a figure for individual learning and self-betterment, the point driven home by excerpts from Pushkin's "Bronze Horseman." Loman's little volume emphasizes the presence of the Orthodox Church throughout the city, as well as encouraging a reverential approach to monuments commemorating cultural figures such as Pushkin, Lomonosov, Gogol, Zhukovskii, and Krylov. The newly literate peasant reader of Loman's guidebook, like the discerning reader of Svin'in's *Memorable Sights*, is placed before objects of imperial, spiritual, and cultural authority, and made to learn a cultural catechism. In addition, as Loman's title suggests, mastering the skill of reading is equivalent to gaining access to a particular cultural perspective—that is, the Russian Empire as seen from the capital.

The equation of St. Petersburg with literacy supports, albeit from a less cus-tomary angle, the conflation of city and literature that represents the quintes-sential nineteenth-century Petersburg conceit.[28]

In 1903, the People's Educational Commission issued *Guidebook to St. Pe-tersburg: Educational Excursions* (*Putevoditel' po S.-Peterburgu: Obrazovatel'nye ekskursii*), which provided thirty-five topographically organized and pedagogi-cally oriented tours. Many of the excursions march their tourist-pupils through the city's museums: Zoological Museum, Museum of Ethnography and An-thropology, Naval Museum, and Pushkin Museum among them. The fifteenth excursion features a lengthy tour through the Public Library, whose hours are given as though encouraging readers to patronize its facilities. The twelfth ex-cursion is devoted to the Hermitage collections, and the sixteenth excursion sur-veys the holdings of the Russian Museum, describing the contents of each exhi-bition hall. To be sure, this guidebook provides a diverse grouping of sites for most of its neighborhood-based excursions, and includes visits to churches and a synagogue, factories, markets, hospital, printing press, and laboratory. A view of St. Petersburg as a "museum of museums" nevertheless emerges from this late imperial guidebook, which reverses the sense of teeming diversity characteris-tic of the ethnographic approaches from the second half of the nineteenth cen-tury (described in the next section), and instead conveys a foreboding sense of stasis. Petersburg as rendered by this official commission is unmistakably a text of the past, inviolate and self-evident. Yet, the preservationist movement also arose during this same period, presenting St. Petersburg in its own guidebook literature as a priceless treasure terrifyingly vulnerable to the vicissitudes of time.

The preservationists, discussed later in this chapter, proposed a more elitist view of the city as a shared resource; while attempting to educate the general readership, their writing reflected the informed expertise of dedicated artists, serious scholars, and professional architects. The preservationist perspective can be considered an outgrowth of the guidebook tradition, somewhat akin to the connoisseur-like appreciation of masterworks cultivated by Svin'in's *Mem-orable Sights*, appropriated for marshalling support during a more divisive era. The preservationist approach to the city also countered the antimonumental, freewheeling Petersburg travel literature produced by nineteenth-century urban feuilletonists and journalists.

Literary Transports: Feuilleton, Sketch, Journalism, Memoir

Practiced by many future luminaries of Russian literature upon arrival in Pe-tersburg from Moscow or the provinces, the feuilleton—a form that evolved in Paris newspapers during the early years of the nineteenth century—reported on current happenings in the city. As the feuilleton evolved, overlapping with forms

such."as the literary sketch, Russian writers used it in creative ways to explore un-
charted, unexpected spaces between or beyond central imperial sites. I wish to
propose Petersburg feuilletons of this sort as closely related to the guidebook
genre that was also becoming familiar to Russian readers during the same period. After all, what is urban journalism but a kind of guide to a city? The reader
of the urban feuilleton or sketch follows its author's footsteps, rambling across
a topography of words that gradually assumes the shape of the city.

Literary travel writing became widespread in the West beginning in the second half of the eighteenth century, and Russian translations of these accounts,
as well as Russians' own travel memoirs, date from the 1770s.[29] The literary fragment provided the basic building block of this travel literature, as it would for
the nineteenth-century urban feuilleton, each work a heterogeneous assortment
of materials including anecdotes and dramatic scenes, placed within a memoir
or epistolary context, and infused with "the sense of an author."[30] The Petersburg feuilleton of the 1840s and beyond acknowledged its debt to travel literature through the use of a confiding narrator who resembled the first-person persona of eighteenth-century letters and travel notes. In the feuilleton's case,
however, travels could remain within one's own city; they could even be limited
to a particular neighborhood or street. Nineteenth-century literary excursions
also adopt older travel literature's habit of mediating experience through textual sources—an established sentimentalist practice—interspersing abundant
quotations and verse excerpts with reportage, and thus juxtaposing a "journey"
across written terrain with physical travels around the city.[31]

As I have shown, the initially static and descriptive forms of the Petersburg
guidebook eventually animated themselves as walking tours, if carefully scripted
ones. The feuilleton was at greater liberty to explore different aspects of the city,
but could sometimes dovetail with the guidebook to a marked extent. An early
protofeuilleton, Konstantin Batiushkov's 1814 "A Stroll to the Academy of Arts"
(*Progulka v Akademiiu khudozhestv*), shares the Alexandrine emphasis on classical form of Svin'in's *Memorable Sights*, but also evokes later feuilletons in its
whimsy and strongly manifested narrator-persona.[32] The Academy Stroll represents an early example of Russian art criticism, but more important, this piece
is the first substantial contribution to the tradition of Petersburg literary
strolls—in spite of the fact that its narrator begins by consenting to his provincial friend's alleged request for "a continuation of my strolls about Petersburg."[33] Batiushkov links the Academy of Arts and its projects with the founding of Petersburg and proposes the city as an art object, using the excursion
format to justify these analogies to his readers.[34]

Batiushkov's narrator begins at his window with a copy of Johann Winckelmann's history of the classical arts. He indulges in a reverie about the founding
of Petersburg and retells the myth in terms of an aesthetic rather than imperial
conquest. "Here will be a city," declares Peter. "I will summon all of the arts.
Here, the arts . . . will conquer nature herself."[35] As if in response to this revi-

sionist founding myth of Petersburg, a young artist materializes at the narrator's door and offers to take him to the Academy of Arts, where they are holding a visitors' day. "I am ready to be your guide (*putevoditel'*), your cicerone, if you please!" announces the young man, proposing himself in lieu of an instructive text. "Look!" he commands, throwing open the window. "What a pity my comrades make so little use of the riches close at hand; painters more eagerly render views of Italy and other countries than these enchanting subjects. ... Look—what unity! How all parts correspond to the whole!"[36] The narrator's new friend anticipates the rhetoric of the excursion, with its imperatives and exclamations, in an explicit aesthetic strategy that transforms the city into an artistic masterwork. Petersburg is not only a suitable subject for art, but itself represents an academy of arts for aspiring Russian talent.

Once they reach the street, the young artist repeats his tour-guide gesture by describing a panorama in relation to a smaller portion of the vaunted Petersburg whole: "Look now at the embankment, at these enormous palaces—one is more magnificent than the next! Look at Vasilievskii Island, forming a triangle graced by the Stock Exchange, the Rostral Columns and granite embankment, with splendid descents and staircases to the water!" As the pair near the Admiralty, the narrator remarks upon the changes that twenty years have brought to "this long, ugly factory surrounded by ascension bridges, with deep dirty trenches heaped with boards and logs." Rebuilt under Alexander I by the architect Zakharov, the Admiralty has become an "ornament" to the city, and its story, as told by the narrator, has been shaped according to his Petersburg fine-arts founding myth. The narrator comments on the new boulevard around the Admiralty, the "only promenade from which one can see everything grand and beautiful in Petersburg: the Neva, the Winter Palace, the great buildings of Palace Square forming a semicircle, Nevsky Prospect, Isaac Square, the Horse Guards' riding hall that recalls the Parthenon—the beautiful construction of Mr. Quarenghi—the Senate, the monument to Peter I, and again the Neva with its embankments!"[37] Circling the boulevard, the narrator displays Petersburg's center like a beautiful object on a revolving stand.

At the Academy of Arts, the narrator and his guide, who have been joined by the elderly Starozhilov, survey plaster casts of classical sculpture, which the young artist declares essential to the training of Russian art students, and they examine Russian paintings that treat favorite subjects from Western art.[38] The Academy imitators of conventional biblical, classical, and Russian historical subjects are nevertheless termed "original" by the young artist-guide: "They might in time be called the founders of a new Italian school, *la Scuola Pietroborghese*," he declares.[39] He wonders why young Russian artists feel they must travel to Paris or Rome to learn about great art when they can study great (Western) art treasures in their own Hermitage Museum. The characters' discussion of Russian art provides an implicit referendum on Petersburg, the city that foreign visitors criticized for imitating Western achievements and producing inferior, merely academic works. In this way, Batiushkov's "Stroll" evinces a nervous preoccupation with the distinctions between original and copy, as they relate to the native and the foreign in Russian art. Batiushkov's literary sketch—like the city of Petersburg and the Academy of Arts—is itself a treasure trove of motifs borrowed from antiquity and modern Europe. His narrator employs the poetry-reciting technique of later nineteenth-century guidebooks, serving up bits of Latin and Russian verse along with Russian-language translations and adaptations of classical works.

Batiushkov's narrator worries that he might offend Russian artists with his frank assessments of their works, but the young artist reassures him that "genuine talent does not fear criticism; on the contrary, it loves and respects criticism as the only true guide (*putevoditel'nitsa*) to perfection."[40] This assertion makes explicit the link between guidebook rhetoric and cultural value that is everywhere suggested in Batiushkov's "Stroll," while simultaneously preempting potential criticism of both Russian art and Petersburg itself with aggressive praise. Anticipating the guidebooks of coming decades, Batiushkov encourages his reader to develop the requisite aesthetic discrimination and critical sensibility to appreciate Petersburg's cultural achievements.[41] Nearly a century earlier than the preservationist Alexander Benois, Batiushkov proposed Petersburg to his readers as a *living* museum whose contents should be cherished. In contrast, Petersburg feuilletons from the 1840s offered guided tours to urban areas that corresponded to literary and intellectual tastes of an entirely different order.

In France during the first half of the nineteenth century, major writers such as Honoré de Balzac, Théophile Gautier, and Jules Janin conferred an increasing literary prestige upon the feuilleton. During the latter half of the 1830s, the Petersburg feuilleton similarly aspired to "greater dignity as a literary form," and in this capacity migrated from newspapers to journals.[42] During the 1840s and 1850s, however, Fedor Dostoevsky, Ivan Goncharov, Nikolai Nekrasov, Ivan Panaev, Ivan Turgenev, and others produced feuilletons that languish in the more obscure volumes of their Academy-edition "Complete Works," or, in some cases, that have never been republished from the original nineteenth-century periodicals.[43].

Providing unconventional literary tours of the capital, the Petersburg feuilletonist of the 1840s saw himself as reconceiving the 1830s Paris *flâneur*.[44] Dostoevsky used this term ironically in its Russified form when he complained in his 1847 "Petersburg Chronicle" (*Peterburgskaia letopis'*) that the unfortunate "pedestrian, *flanyor*, or observer" must put up with clouds of dust from the exterior repair work around the city during the summer, and reconcile himself to resembling Pierrot in a Roman carnival.[45] The Russian *flanyor* is a sad clown, not an urbane, cane-twirling gentleman, but if this figure seems less elevated in social terms, his literary vistas have broadened significantly. The Petersburg feuilleton is linked to the older aristocratic travel literature paradoxically by the demographics of authorship; as nongentry Russian writers entered their profession via journalism, the feuilleton form provided an opportunity to explore their new territory, both textually and topographically. The feuilleton, a genre for city insiders, was often practiced in Petersburg of the 1840s–1850s by recent arrivals trying and failing to master the lay of the land.[46]

Dostoevsky proposes a connection between the feuilleton and the guidebook in an installment of his four-part 1847 series "Petersburg Chronicle," as he wonders what to do in a city that has emptied out for the warm-weather season. During the winter, he observes grandly, the social and professional bustle does not afford residents the time to "scrutinize Petersburg more attentively, to study its physiognomy and to read the history of the city and of our whole epoch in this mass of stones, in these splendid buildings, palaces, monuments."[47] Many Petersburg citizens, he notes, "haven't left their neighborhood for ten years or more, and are familiar only with the route to their place of work." His project of "reading" monumental Petersburg is stillborn, however, perhaps because Shreder, Svin'in, Bur'ianov, and Pushkarev have already provided this service, but also because Dostoevsky is not interested in the standard cultural attractions. Even Petersburg itself, he maintains, in an abrupt change of tone, does not wish to gaze at its own "damp enormous walls, at its marble, bas-reliefs, statues, and columns, which also seemed to be angry at the bad weather."[48] These few lines invoke and reject the expansive imperial guidebook perspective on Petersburg. Better to stay home and read, surveying intellectual vistas through the exercise of armchair travel!

Dostoevsky initially suggests that his feuilleton will provide an edifying tour of the capital, but instead he produces an idiosyncratically structured description that conveys the rhythms of the urban environment as a heterogeneous whole. His strategy is fully in keeping with the genre of the mid-century urban feuilleton, which often took its reader to the physical outskirts (*okrainy*) of the city, on a literary trip to geographical parts unknown.[49] The series also represents a guidebook to the particulars of Petersburg life for other writer-newcomers who might think to write about the city.

In the third feuilleton, Dostoevsky's narrator characterizes the city as "an enormous number of little circles, of which each has its regulations, its sense of decorum, its law, its logic, and its oracle," and he proceeds from there to a series of virtuoso digressions that trace the contours of the city in metaphorical terms.[50] His vividly detailed "personifications" of Petersburg take shape as an irritated high-society spinster, a debt-ridden husband who loses at cards, the spoiled son of a respectable provincial papa, a briefly blooming consumptive young girl, and a Dostoevskian dreamer. Each figure represents an excursion stop, but offers no more than a fleeting composite image for the city. Dostoevsky's volatile, alienated narrator compares his attempts to grasp social discourse to the wistful longing caused by the faint sounds that reach a lonely pedestrian from a brightly illuminated house where a ball is taking place, a poignant experience no less piercing for being rendered as simile. In its hyperbolized textuality, Dostoevsky's feuilleton series harks back to the eighteenth-century travel writing that predates the conventional nineteenth-century guidebook. His account of Petersburg augments existing guidebooks by underscoring their literary origins, flaunting a highly particular point of view, and challenging the pseudoobjective guidebook prose that drapes itself over an imperial agenda.

From time to time, Dostoevsky's narrator makes the barest link between physical movement and train of thought, anchoring himself in city space, often in the process of strolling and looking for literary material: "I walked across Sennaia Square, and mulled over what to write."[51] In the second feuilleton, the narrator muses about the role of gossip, and then adds, "And all of these useful thoughts came to my mind at the same time as Petersburg went out to the Summer Garden and onto Nevsky Prospect to show off its new spring outfits." Echoing Gogol's famous description of Petersburg's main boulevard, he declares archly, "One could write an entire book about encounters on Nevsky Prospect alone. But you know about all this so well from pleasant experience, gentlemen, that in my opinion it is unnecessary to write the book."[52] Bur'ianov used shared literary referents as shorthand for a common cultural legacy, whereas Dostoevsky invokes these to express his own hope of writing something original about Petersburg—paradoxically conceived as a guide to being a writer in the imperial capital.

Nikolai Nekrasov, who moved to Petersburg in 1838, authored prose and verse feuilletons, most of them published in 1844 and early 1845, to a significantly greater extent than Dostoevsky.[53] In the spring of 1844, he published a feuilleton cycle called "Chronicle of a Petersburg Resident" (*Khronika peterburgskogo zhitelia*) in *The Literary Gazette*, under the pseudonym I. A. Pruzhinin. The cycle begins with "A Letter from a Petersburg Resident to a Friend in the Provinces," a document allegedly dropped on the street by the fictional civil servant Pruzhinin and retrieved by the unnamed frame-narrator, who sends it to a printing press. The cycle makes maximally ironic use of this alter ego and even includes parodies of Nekrasov's own poetry, displaying the self-reflexive quality so typical of the feuilleton and mocking the citational practices of aristocratic travel literature. Pruzhinin ruminates upon the dogs that run past his window in the quiet outskirts of the city, describes a visit to a tavern where one customer found a goose neck in his food, and treats the reader to naïve observations about Kukol'nik's new play, "The Boyar Fedor Vasil'evich Basenok." The public culture of Petersburg—reported more conventionally by Nekrasov in his earlier feuilletons from 1841 and 1843—is here filtered through a *skaz*-narrator, who takes a comically low-style journey around normative "guidebook" Petersburg.

The April 27 feuilleton opens with Pruzhinin's abortive attempt to elevate his writing, a moment that recalls the panegyric section of Pushkin's "Bronze Horseman": "What a majestic, beautiful, and illustrious spectacle the Neva presents when, having broken its icy fetters, which have long inhibited her triumphant flow into eternity, suddenly, like . . ." He breaks off, "No! I can't . . . I wanted to begin from the heights, to relate everything as good writers do; but such labor is beyond my strength!"[54] As Pruzhinin gazes at the Neva, his fifteen-ruble hat blows off and into the water.

Nekrasov also wrote feuilletons that charted the Petersburg terrain in an ethnographic explorer's spirit.[55] His 1844 cycle "Features from a Characterization of the Petersburg Population" (*Cherty iz kharakteristiki peterburgskogo naseleniia*) uses the same term in its title that Belinsky would use in reference to *Physiology*.[56] In the introductory essay to *Physiology*—mentioned earlier in connection with the Marquis de Custine—Belinsky wrote, "We have absolutely no belletristic works that would, in the form of travel literature, trips, sketches, stories, or descriptions, acquaint readers with the various parts of boundless and diverse Russia."[57] Belinsky offers *Physiology* to the reading public as an "attempt at a characterization (*kharakteristika*) of Petersburg" that provides "several sketches of its internal particularities," and represents the first literary effort of this sort.[58] The *Physiology* aims, that is, to capture Petersburg's distinguishing specificities, and not merely to compose a general description (*opisanie*) like those by Bogdanov and Georgi.[59] The "internal particularities" evoked by Belinsky also correspond to the use of the term *kharakteristika* to describe the temperament, disposition, and marked traits of *persons* as well as things. In this, the *Physiology* resembles the metaphorical personifications of Petersburg in Dostoevsky's "Chronicle"—both are written accounts that animate the city, bringing it to life through writing. In fact, the word "character" in both English and Russian derives from the Greek verb "to inscribe," which is the origin of its two main meanings: "character" as a living being defined through *difference* expressed by distinguishing features, and "character" as an actual written symbol. Thus writing itself makes the difference, creating its subject by marking it with a defining trait (that can then be described in future writing).

In an anonymous feuilleton from September 1844, Nekrasov himself reviewed *Physiology*, declaring that the collection attempted to address the question, "Why until now has there been so little written about Petersburg, and why is so little written now?"[60] He takes pains to distinguish his anthology from guides that emphasize architectural monuments instead of Petersburg life: "Not touching upon the exterior of Petersburg, or touching upon it only in passing, [the *Physiology*] has set itself the goal of acquainting readers with Petersburg in the physiological respect. In it, you won't find descriptions (*opisaniia*) of streets, theaters, or Petersburg promenades, but you will find a more or less faithful characterization (*kharakteristika*) of all this." *Physiology* provides tours that exemplify the primary paradox of the guidebook genre—that the reader-excursionist cannot properly see the sights without an informed and informing textual intermediary.[61] The conventional guidebook and the urban feuilleton are two halves of one whole, the exterior and interior travel literature of imperial Petersburg.

The Ukrainian author Evgenii Grebenka's "The Petersburg Side" (*Peterburgskaia storona*, 1844) from *Physiology* offers an excellent example of the feuilleton trip to unknown city parts. Grebenka's narrator begins with his childhood fantasies about this as-yet-unseen Petersburg neighborhood, which he envisioned as a kind of "El Dorado."[62] As an adult with more developed sensibilities, he imagines his reader as a well-heeled Petersburg resident of limited perspective who frequents only the central part of the city. For Nevsky strollers suffering from melancholy, the narrator prescribes a tour of the Petersburg Side, "that poorest part of our capital." "Look upon the long rows of narrow streets, many of which are not even paved, surrounded by little wooden dwellings," exhorts the narrator, in his best guidebook manner. "The further you go from Bolshoi Prospect, the quieter, gloomier, and more miserable it all grows." Once a naïve provincial plying a visitor with childish questions about the capital, the writer-narrator now instructs the uninitiated reader, parading his sociological expertise.

He covers the entire territory of the Petersburg Side, describing the incongruous elegance of Kamennoostrovskii Prospect and the desolation that reigns each year when the summer dacha season ends. Providing a detailed inventory of Petersburg types inhabiting this dingy area, the narrator leads his reader past a series of "touching family scenes" visible through the windows of basement apartments. He knows precisely the kind of wallpaper found in the rooms where renters are served their meals ("violet or brownish-green with scenes from mythology"), the exact spot in the center of town where this wallpaper can be purchased ("in a little shop on Sadovaia Street, not far from Shchukin Market"), and the cost ("2 to 2½ silver kopecks per piece").[63] Grebenka's narrator does everything possible to make the Petersburg Side real to the reader in its everyday specificity. He transcribes a page-long conversation overheard between two young men on the street and invites the reader to eavesdrop on servants exchanging gossip about their wealthy employers. He meditates upon the colonnaded ruins of a wooden shopping arcade on Malyi Prospect and revisits in imagination a now defunct sweet shop. His sketch ends at the border of the Petersburg Side, as the narrator looks across the river to Krestovskii Island, which he promises to describe "next time." In this respect, Grebenka's sketch—although it was not actually followed by a series of similar pieces—recalls the pedagogical "stroll" format of the 1838 Bur'ianov children's guidebook, although in support of a very different educative mission.

Even writers not much associated with Petersburg literature contributed to this corpus of feuilleton and sketch travelogues, at least in spirit or intent. Ivan Turgenev, for example, left notes, most likely from the mid-1840s, for a planned series of sketches. At this early point in his career, Turgenev displayed an uncharacteristic interest in parts of the city frequented by ordinary working people, with whom his narrator might converse in the manner of a committed ethnographer. He recorded the following series of ideas:

1. Galernaia port or some other remote part of the city.
2. Sennaia Square with all its details. Can make two or three articles out of this.
3. One of the large buildings on Gorokhovaia Street.
4. Petersburg physiognomy at night (cabdrivers, and so forth. Can include conversation with cabdriver here).
5. Tolkuchii market with books for sale.
6. Apraksin Dvor.
7. Race on the Neva (a conversation during this).
8. Internal physiognomy of Russian taverns.
9. Some large factory with workers (singers of Zhukov).
10. About Nevsky Prospect, its visitors, their physiognomies, about omnibuses, conversations in them.[64]

These sketch ideas could practically write themselves, so closely do they correspond to "Natural School" Petersburg literary subjects much favored from the 1840s onward. These notes constitute a suggestive map to a totally unknown Turgenev, as well as to Petersburg's physical, social, and economic peripheries.[65]

The greatest trick of the 1840s Petersburg feuilleton was traversing literary and urban topography simultaneously, making each serve the other in metaphorical terms; journalistic and memoir texts borrowed this same strategy. It was thus easy to tour Petersburg without ever leaving home, as amply demonstrated by Ivan Antsiferov, author of "Petersburg from My Window" (*Peterburg iz moego okna*), who perfectly exemplifies the tradition of "armchair traveling." During his visit to the capital in 1852, Antsiferov's lodgings looked out on Voznesenskii Prospect, one of the three radials leading away from the Admiralty. His window, he declares, "resembles a magical lantern, reflecting into my room the living pictures that are drawn on the prospect."[66] Antsiferov employs the Gogolian device of letting time move along as he remains stationary, noting the changes that occur on the Prospect at different points in the day, beginning in the early morning with the appearance of vendors, servants, and workmen, and ending late in the evening when the shop lights are extinguished. Antsiferov notes people hurrying home for their midday meal and urges, "You rest too, readers, and please, have your dinners, if you are reading these lines at that time of day."[67] The author's exhortation suggests that reading his account is equivalent to sharing his experience—that is, to experiencing the flow of time and human traffic on the Prospect in real time. The resourceful narrator uses his unseen vantage point to eavesdrop on conversations taking place on the street below and to underscore his privileged, nearly omniscient perspective. In this spirit, Antsiferov watches two Jews fleecing customers and observes a tenant smuggling furniture out of his apartment at night to avoid paying his rent. Even the published work's format—a tiny pamphlet of some fifty-odd pages—suggests itself as a small window onto its chosen subject.

Several decades later, the popular-press journalist Nikolai Zhivotov mapped the city from a novel perspective (or rather, from several such perspectives) in

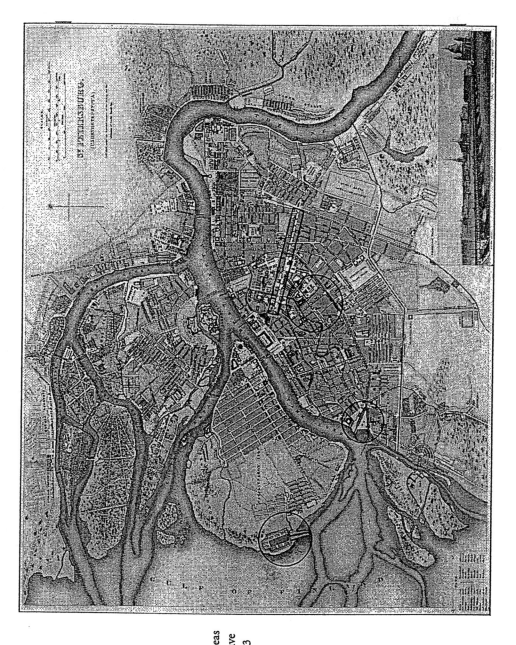

FIGURE 3.1. The Areas Turgenev Would Have Described from 1853 Map. (Courtesy of Harvard Map Collection.)

an inventive feat of reportage. Zhivotov's 1894 *Petersburg Profiles* (*Peterburgskie profili*) document his experiences disguised, in turn, as cabdriver, tramp, funeral torchbearer, and waiter.[68] In this, Zhivotov updates the practices of the Natural School ethnographer by transforming himself temporarily into a subject from the lower reaches of Petersburg life. Zhivotov's interlude as a cabdriver, "On the Coach Box: Six Days in the Role of a Cabdriver" (*Na izvoshchich'ikh kozlakh: Shest' dnei v roli izvoshchika*), explicitly evokes the guidebook genre, as it required him to traverse the city according to an entirely new set of urban landmarks. It has often been claimed that Petersburg incorporates aspects of all cities and cultures, and Zhivotov's survey of cabdriver taverns—establishments with names such as "Persia," "Batum," "Serbia," "Caucasus," "Venice," and "Naples"—confirms the freedom of imagination Petersburg grants to drivers who can travel across the Russian empire and to far-away lands each time they order a drink.

Zhivotov explains his decision to assume a false identity instead of simply conducting interviews among Petersburg's 20,000 cabdrivers: "The head driver is afraid, doesn't trust you and won't say anything; the working driver doesn't know how to tell you anything because of a lack of cultivation that is close to savagery; and at the drivers' haunts, they hide everything at the first appearance of a 'new' person."[69] The Petersburg reading public requires a tour guide in this unfamiliar world, and to this end, Zhivotov's account is topologically precise. He refers to parts of the city well known to Petersburg residents, but in the context of an alternate sociocultural paradigm, and in this way, creates a radically new mapping. He also amazes the reader with his mastery of cabdriver's argot in many transcribed conversations. This sort of investigative journalism as a form of urban ethnography flourished during the final quarter of the nineteenth century, a period when the conventional guidebook form was largely moribund.

Zhivotov thought at first to write a "cabdriver's diary" that would "describe my travels step by step," but concluded that "this structure would have been rather dull: first, because of the abundant superfluous details of little interest, and second, because I had to make many repeated visits; if you arrive at a tavern when no one is around, there is no 'picture,' so you turn your shafts and come back another time."[70] His account adopts a rambling structure that reproduces a cabdriver's "characteristic" daily sojourn, if in distilled form—an approach that recalls Nekrasov's insistence on essential, rather than purely representational particularities. Zhivotov acts simultaneously as guide and translator, and also as a kind of literary cabdriver, taking the reader for a ride.

In a very different vein, Anatoly Koni's 1922 *Petersburg: Memoirs of a Long-Time Resident* (*Peterburg: Vospominaniia starozhila*) takes the reader on a nostalgic time-tour of St. Petersburg from the latter nineteenth century, departing from the lifeless emptiness of the postrevolutionary city contemporary to his writing. Koni (1844–1927), who was personally connected to many prominent nineteenth-century literary and cultural figures, wants to traverse this remembered Petersburg "with a visitor," so as to "acquaint him with memories that have departed into the past of no return."[71] In his phrasing, memories of imperial-era Petersburg have become as much a part of the past as the events and experiences they attempt to preserve. In Koni's literary "guidebook," Petersburg is a memory museum as much as a remembered city.

He begins the tour at the Petersburg-Moscow railway station: "On such a train, my expected visitor arrives for the first time in Petersburg, burning with impatience to become acquainted with the 'Northern Palmyra' in its details and particularities, and we begin our wanderings around the city."[72] He describes the Znamenskaia Square of old, with its frame of unprepossessing single- and two-story buildings. From there, Koni and his imaginary tourist-companion walk along "Old Nevsky" toward the monastery. They note a military procession that halts to administer corporal punishment to a convict, and see the Metropolitan in his carriage, on his way to the morning session at the Synod. Returning to Nevsky on the other side of the Ligovka Canal, Koni passes the small building where Belinsky lived, not far from Shestilavochnaia Street, and points out the Meniaev house, on whose balcony sits the notorious publisher and editor of *The Northern Bee*, Faddei Bulgarin, "a fat man with coarse features on a bloated face, drinking tea in his dressing-gown with a long pipe in his hands."[73] Passing the former Griaznaia Street, Koni recalls an adjacent street, formerly Iamskaia, with its nearby cabdrivers' yard, which later burned down. Iamskaia Street, he notes, was renamed in Dostoevsky's honor after the author's death in 1881, a fact that leads Koni to recall the crowd at Dostoevsky's funeral. His literary stroll along Nevsky Prospect is structured as a string of associations that arise as if spontaneously out of cultural memory. For Koni, reminiscence *is* an excursion around St. Petersburg. His associative thought can be precisely mapped to the streets of his city, the twists, turns, and pauses of his reflections coinciding with the contours of the capital, where past and present coexist at every step. He wants to remember on everyone's behalf, and this intention explains why events from the 1850s that occurred when he was a child, when he was unlikely to have been present or able to recognize their significance, are so vividly presented to the reader-tourist.

Not far from the Mikhailovskii Palace, on a side street that leads to Bol shaia Millionnaia Street, Koni's train of thought leads to "an enormous granite block, depicting in unfinished form a sitting giant."[74] At one time, this statue had been intended for a theatrical production somewhere in Petersburg, but had proved too much for its transport equipment, and settled nearly in the middle of the street, where it remained until the 1870s. Koni's memoirs travel back through time to find a figure for memory, the granite block as a monument to the fascinating accidents of city life. He transforms the granite statue—despite its abortive theatrical career—into an actor in the procession of cultural history, a Petersburg landmark that has receded into the past along with people and events he describes. He recalls a notable eccentric from this period, Alexander Ne-vakhovich, who mourned his past "popularity" in Petersburg and declared that he could not return from abroad, since he had so few acquaintances left there. Koni's memoirs, in contrast, show how easy it is to return to the past, which always furnishes the present.

Conveying the Legacy: Preservationists and Excursionists

The preservationist movement, which began during the final years of the imperial period, brought a spate of new book-length guides to St. Petersburg, this time expressing the perspective of a particular group, whose concerns were not shared for the most part by either Petersburg officialdom or the public at large. Georgy Lukomskii produced *Old Petersburg: Strolls along the Historic Quarters of the Capital* (*Staryi Peterburg: Progulki po starinnym kvartalam stolitsy,* 1917), which attempts to safeguard the legacy of the past, or, where that effort has already failed, to remember what has been lost. In his preface, Lukomskii declares that his attention was not confined to the universally acclaimed architectural treasures of Petersburg, but extended to unsung entranceways and arbors "dispersed among distant outskirts, often built-over or blocked from the view of the passing pedestrian by the great masses of apartment blocks."[75] The famous buildings can take care of themselves, but those "details of Old Petersburg that have been crowded by the new buildings"—obelisks, columns, wells, fountains, sphinxes, entryway pylons, lamplights by front-door awnings—"deserve especially to be photographed or sketched." He intends his book to inform residents and nonspecialists about their city, and declares, "I do not take upon myself the roles of guide, scholarly mentor, or Old Petersburg epicure who flaunts his knowledge of historical fact's subtlest points," this last a dig at Petr Stolpianskii.[76] He also objects to mannered writing (*literaturshchina*) that distracts attention from what should be the primary subject—the "unmediated" beauty of Old Petersburg.

Lukomskii continues the Natural School project of exploring hidden aspects of Petersburg, except that now it is the past, rather than the life of the lower classes, that is obscure and in need of illumination by writing. Lukomskii makes a fetish of the antique and decrepit, regarding an old warehouse as a valuable cultural artifact, but treating a new one as a merely functional structure. Despite his implied criticism of Stolpianskii, moreover, he instructs his reader in scholarly attentiveness to the city's physical analogues for literary marginalia, historical footnotes, parentheses, tiny details, and subsidiary forms.

One of Lukomskii's "strolls"—in a chapter titled "Vandalism"—takes the reader to the former sites of culturally significant buildings pulled down to make room for unworthy successors, and surveys existing constructions spoiled by unsuitable renovation. His primary task, however, is to seek out moments of textual coherence in the Petersburg cityscape that transcend single surviving structures—mini-ensembles that form "little corners" (*ugolki*) of Old Petersburg. The best of these is located near Tuchkov Lane on Vasilievskii Island, an area that features low-lying structures dating back nearly to Peter the Great's time, as well as the church of Saint Catherine. Lukomskii mourns the loss of the old eighteenth-century Gostinyi Dvor in this neighborhood, but is grateful that "Within the space of just a few blocks are concentrated not architectural 'chef d-oeuvres,' but 'monuments' from a bygone time, and moreover an antique reality that is dear, cozy, and typical."[77] Lukomskii's *Old Petersburg* provides an inventory of cultural value at grave risk. The narrative of his "tour" speeds up as the book proceeds, and Lukomskii seems almost breathless as he hastens to name the precious surviving features of the city as it once was, and creates a document of record that he hopes will ensure their safety.[78]

The prolific Petr Stolpianskii contributed numerous works to the project of mapping Petersburg during the early twentieth century, in a unique juxtaposition of historical depth and topographical specificity.[79] His best-known work is the historical excursion *How Sankt-Piter-Burkh Arose, was Founded, and Grew* (*Peterburg: Kak voznik, osnovalsia i ros Sanktpiterburkh*, 1918), which treats the city according to individual neighborhoods.[80] Stolpianskii excels at choosing a single well-known spot as the focus of a historical trajectory that reveals unexpected shifts and accidental developments in St. Petersburg's evolution. For example, Stolpianskii's 1923 *Old Petersburg: The Admiralty Island* (*Staryi Peterburg: Admiralteiskii Ostrov*), subtitled "A Historical-Artistic Sketch," provides a dense textual exploration of a "miniature corner" of the city that "constitutes more than a single page" of Petersburg's history.[81] Stolpianskii's notion of "corner" is distinct from Lukomskii's use of the term, in that Stolpianskii does not wander through marginal areas of the city, but rather excavates the well-traveled territory of "tourist" Petersburg. In a larger sense, however, Stolpianskii's equation of urban corner and textual page recalls Lukomskii's link between writing history and carefully reading the material evidence of the city. The physical city is already written, but in a shorthand that few can penetrate unassisted.

The preservationists provided their readers with tours that performed virtuoso synchronic elaborations of individual locales, digging beneath the contemporary surface to reach aspects of St. Petersburg that now led an exclusively textual life. The reader of these works was dependent on the immensely knowledgeable narrator for this information, which was nowhere manifested on the city's visible surface. Unlike more conventional guidebooks, which turn complex urban environments into legible cultural topography and place knowledge literally right at hand, the preservationists' studies showed readers how much they did not and could not know. The preservationists estranged readers from their city even as they attempted to win new converts to their cause. Following the tradition of the many "memory," "archive," and "legacy" journals such as *Russian Archive* (*Russkii arkhiv*, 1861–1917), *Russian Antiquity* (*Russkaia sta-*

rina, 1870–1917), and *Historical Herald* (*Istoricheskii vestnik*, 1880–1917), the preservationists continued the project of constructing an entire city out of printed material. The Petersburg contemporary to their writing projects was only a ghost of its former self.[82]

Nineteenth-century literary tours around St. Petersburg find their natural complement in the humanist excursions developed by Professor Ivan Grevs and his more famous student Nikolai Antsiferov during the period 1910–20.[83] From the start, the Grevs circle intended its excursions for a mass audience, particularly the urban working class, in an orientation diametrically opposed to that of the preservationists.[84] Subsequent outgrowths of their excursionist project enjoyed a brief period of government support during the early 1920s—among them the society "Old Petersburg" (1921–38), which represented a particularly important force in the preservation of the city's prerevolutionary cultural legacy—before their project fell under political attack in the early 1930s.[85] The excursionist project carried out the working philosophy of *kraevedenie*, perhaps best translated as "the study of local lore."[86]

The work of Nikolai Antsiferov represents the culminating point of nineteenth-century guidebook literature and preservationist studies, while also serving as the basis for many Soviet and post-Soviet guides to St. Petersburg. Antsiferov perfected the humanitarian excursion that combined architectural and literary history—a format prefigured by poetry-quoting nineteenth-century guidebooks. This genre of cultural tour covered literary referents associated with urban topography while exploring the physical city itself. An excursion of this type also exhibited its *guide*, who had mastered the network of cultural connections that linked text and terrain. As one of Antsiferov's contemporaries declared, "a brilliant memory helped him to preserve, and at the necessary moment extract verse and prose excerpts, which he used to corroborate his conclusions."[87]

Antsiferov viewed the city as a concentrated form of human social life—a cultural and historical organism that can be known only through communion with its "soul" (*dusha*).[88] "How can one learn to understand the language of the city?" asks Antsiferov in the opening chapter of his best-known work, *The Soul of Petersburg* (1922). "In no case should one turn the city into a museum of tourist attractions (*dostoprimechatel'nosti*)." Instead, an excursion should represent a process of "spiritualizing" the city, of liberating it from its "material casing."[89] As he declared, "Our love regenerates the past, makes the past a participant in our lives."[90] Antsiferov's excursions thus sought to transcend both scholarly *and* popular approaches to St. Petersburg.

Antsiferov's cultural excursions took several basic forms, all of them hugely influential. Firstly, literary "strolls" connected with a particular writer such as Alexander Blok, Fedor Dostoevsky, or Alexander Pushkin trace the routes of literary protagonists (most famously, of Dostoevsky's Raskolnikov) or strive to see the city as the writer himself experienced it.[91] Nikolai Antsiferov explores

Raskolnikov's literary territory in a special section of his 1923 *Dostoevsky's Petersburg* entitled "The Topography of *Crime and Punishment*."[92] Tracing literary or historical routes in order to formalize them as text and thus facilitate numberless future tours is typical of Petersburg "travel" literature. In this way, *Dostoevsky's Petersburg* represents a second-degree guidebook—a guide to a guide, as it were. Antsiferov produced his tour of Dostoevsky's Petersburg after wandering around the city in 1910–11, using Dostoevsky's literary works and biography to lead him toward a new understanding of the city. There thus evolves a tradition of Petersburg guidebooks that traverse the literary works and biographies of artists who were students of this terrain themselves. The emblematic figure for Petersburg writing is a young author, wandering the city streets and neighborhoods with a book in his hand.

Antsiferov may well have been inspired to create his literary excursions by the many works in the Petersburg literary corpus that exhibit a striking precision in the specific routes and locations of their protagonists. This technique lends a verisimilitudinous quality to any flight of literary fancy, and itself suggests the popular form of the twentieth-century Petersburg literary excursion that traces a beloved fictional plot by Pushkin, Gogol, or Dostoevsky across the cityscape.[93] Mikhail Lermontov's 1836 story "Princess Ligovskaia" (*Kniaginia Ligovskaia*), for example, traces the route traveled by his protagonist Pechorin, after his bay trotter nearly crushes the clerk Krasinskii, who is about to turn right along the canal from the Voznesenskii bridge on Voznesenskaia Street, at 4:00 P.M. on December 21, 1833. Krasinskii loses sight of Pechorin's carriage, but the reader follows as it "flew along the canal, turned onto Nevsky, from Nevsky onto Karavannaia Street, from there onto the Simeonovskii bridge, and then right onto the Fontanka," where it stops in front of a wealthy home.[94] Similarly, Nekrasov's early story "The Life of Alexandra Ivanovna: A Story in Four Carriages" (*Zhizn' Aleksandry Ivanovny: Povest' v chetyrekh ekipazhakh*, 1841) maps its heroine's melodramatic trajectory from countess's ward to compromised and abandoned maiden, impoverished laundress, and finally, to a lonely grave in the distant Okhta cemetery, with recourse to Petersburg topographical detail and four emblematic means of conveyance.[95] Nekrasov's heroine begins in an elegant coach (*kareta*) turning onto the English embankment, but soon descends in life to a more modest barouche (*koliaska*) that carries her to a stone house on Vasilievskii Island, far out beyond Srednii Prospect. Fate banishes her further in a lowly droshky (*drozhki*) to a basement apartment on the Petersburg Side, and then, after the sad denouement, to a simple church on the Vyborg Side's Bocharnaia Street in her coffin on a dray-cart hearse, and thence to her remote resting place. Lermontov's mapping strategy is referential, while Nekrasov's is allegorical, but both authors exhibit the nineteenth-century "excursion" mentality that creates narrative linkage between parts of the city.

Tours such as the two Petersburg excursions in Antsiferov's 1924 *True Stories and Myths of Petersburg* (*Byl i mif Peterburga*) take a more traditional guidebook approach, treating the city as a "document" that speaks to "the power of place as a source of knowledge."[96] Antsiferov acknowledges that both 1924 excursions are excessively long and too detailed to serve as actual strolls, but he expresses the hope that would-be Petersburg tour guides can profitably draw from his metatours, perhaps creating an entire series of excursions from each of the two. Antsiferov's methods could be applied to a highly diverse set of Petersburg places, as he proved by treating trade-oriented areas such as Vasilievskii Island and Sadovaia Street, and the outlying palace parks at Tsarskoe Selo and Pavlovsk.[97] Finally, *The Soul of Petersburg* constitutes yet another form of excursion, touring the literary and cultural history, or perhaps more precisely, the *textual* history of St. Petersburg.[98] Antsiferov's body of work crystallizes the essential connections between excursion text and physical city, invoking the persistent textual metaphors for urban culture that infuse the entire tradition of writing about St. Petersburg.

Soviet and Post-Soviet Remappings

Although Antsiferov's "excursionist" approach to the city fell from official favor after the 1920s, his legacy makes itself felt in Soviet-era guides such as the 1968 *Literary Commemorative Places of Leningrad* (*Literaturnye pamiatnye mesta Leningrada*). This guide creates a revolutionary's literary Leningrad, devoting chapters to individual writers such as Belinsky, Nekrasov, Chernyshevsky, Dobroliubov, Gorky, and Mayakovsky, as well as the expected treatments of Pushkin, Lermontov, Gogol, Dostoevsky, and Blok. Each chapter walks the reader through the Petersburg portions of a writer's socially progressive biography, noting addresses and dates of residences, and quoting generously from prose fiction, poems, and letters. This Soviet-era guide intends its readers to cover the ground between two hard covers, perhaps memorizing literary excerpts while thoroughly assimilating the notion of St. Petersburg as revered cultural text *and* revolutionary breeding ground. Each writer corresponds to a very particular Petersburg, much like the city "images" summoned up by persistent notions such as "Pushkin's Petersburg" (*Pushkinskii Peterburg*) and "Dostoevsky's Petersburg" (*Peterburg Dostoevskogo*), both of which have given rise to numerous studies.[99] In marrying biography to urban topography, *Literary Commemorative Places* also resembles a subgenre of literary Petersburg that has flourished since the 1950s—"The Author in Petersburg" (*Turgenev v Peterburge, Griboedov v Peterburge, Lomonosov v Peterburge, Zhukovskii v Peterburge,* and so on), each volume of which creates a Petersburg refracted through the life of a major writer.

In contrast to Nikolai Antsiferov's search for the city's "soul" in literary representations, Soviet-era literary guidebooks to Petersburg typically transform the city into an encyclopedia of official Russian culture in a spirit that recalls the most formal of the nineteenth-century guidebooks. Such "tours" provide an airless mesh of addresses, dates, writers' names, and titles that overlay the city map. Although virtually unreadable, such a volume of literary mappings might manifest itself as a comfortingly solid presence on a bookshelf alongside the Complete Works themselves. These politically correct biographical and artistic journeys around St. Petersburg still manage to convey something of the city's "soul," however, participating in a well-established tradition that tries to render the urban environment legible in cultural, historical, and literary terms.

With the resurrection of "St. Petersburg" in the early 1990s has come the reprinting of many imperial-era Petersburg texts, including guidebooks and cultural histories. Three of Antsiferov's most important works were republished in a single paperback volume in 1991, making it possible once more to roam Petersburg with Nikolai Pavlovich as a guide. This rehabilitation made explicit how influential Antsiferov's work had always been and also led the way for a new surge of publications about the imperial capital. In tribute to Antsiferov's practice of cultural archeology for discrete parts of the city, for example, recent books trace the history of a single street or an individual building.[100] Other guidebooks manifest the Russian intelligentsia's fondness for cultivating knowledge of Petersburg's past, taking guests on special walks that provide occasions for sharing stories and little-known facts.

N. R. Levina and Iu. I. Kirtsideli's 1997 *Along These Streets, along These Banks . . .* (*Po etim ulitsam, po etim beregam*) opens with the notion of lovingly repeated strolls, analogous to recitations of memorized poetry: "Why do people learn their favorite verses by heart? Why do they reread their favorite books? Why, when taking a stroll, do they repeat the same favorite route?"[101] The authors hope to help those who have only begun to study (*shtudirovat'*) Petersburg to "learn the City-Poem by heart, line by line," and to this end, *Along These Streets* provides seven strolls, each, a thicket of verse excerpts and unattributed quotations that only the culturally literate reader can hope to penetrate. While reprising Antsiferov's project of teaching a general audience to know their city, *Along These Streets* thus reproduces the strategies of preservationist guidebooks that promise enlightenment, but instead exhibit erudition.[102]

Close to the genre of Petersburg guidebook lies the Petersburg textbook. The 1992 *Conversations about St. Petersburg* (*Besedy o Sankt-Peterburge*) provides stories and dialogues about the city's history intended for foreign students learning Russian, who are encouraged to ask and answer questions about the city, act out proposed scenarios, and commit Petersburg facts and literary excerpts to memory. The authors explain, "Dear Reader! If you not only want to know about the history of Petersburg, its myths, secrets, traditions, and present renaissance, but also want to learn how to socialize with Petersburg residents, converse on Petersburg themes, and discuss Petersburg problems, you will find stock phrases and essential examples of the normative literary language in our book."[103] *Conversations* makes the relationship between text and tour explicit, not merely by linking the Russian literary language with St. Petersburg's cultural history, but in proposing a symbiotic relationship between the two. Petersburg can be known only through the medium of its own discourse, which the aspiring reader must master.

Like the school textbook, the "Question and Answer" book dedicated to St. Petersburg offers a pedagogical tour of the city's history in the form of a cultural catechism. Boleslav Pukinskii's 1981 *One Thousand Questions and Answers about Leningrad* (*1000 voprosov i otvetov o Leningrade*) provides a late-Soviet version of this instructive genre, while the 2001 *St. Petersburg: Diverting Questions and Answers* (*Sankt-Peterburg. Zanimatel'nye voprosy i otvety*), authorized as a school textbook by the Ministry of Education, updates the form, purging it of heavy-handed attempts to recast the imperial capital as cradle of revolution and industrialized socialist city.[104] Both Q & A textbooks showcase a hypothetical model student-reader who knows how to ask the right questions. More obviously, these textbooks offer a ready-made cultural quiz that inducts students into the ways of reading their city. Pukinskii presents excerpts from Derzhavin, Pushkin, Ryleev, Lermontov, and Nekrasov invoking specific locations in St. Petersburg and then queries, "Which 'palace abandoned by oblivion' did the poet have in mind?" (Pushkin's invocation of Mikhailovskii castle in his ode "Freedom") and "To which building did Nekrasov refer in 'Reflections at the Main Entrance'?" (Number 37/39 Liteinyi Prospect, an imperial ministry office whose doorman turned away peasant petitioners). *Entertaining Questions and Answers* places a greater emphasis on general cultural literacy, devoting an entire chapter to deciphering Petersburg architectural sculpture in terms of figures and motifs from classical mythology. The illustrated 1995 *Alphabet of Petersburg* (*Azbuka Peterburga*), in contrast, makes the cultural catechism as simple as possible—"A" is for Admiralty, "B" is for Birzhevaia Square, "V" is for Vasilievskii Island, and so on.[105]

The encyclopedic approach to the city embodied by Grech and Mikhnevich is reprised by Dmitri Sherikh's 1998 chronicle *Petersburg Day By Day* (*Peterburg den' za dnem*), which provides anniversary entries from Petersburg cultural history for each day of the year (1703–1998), thereby organizing the city temporally, rather than spatially.[106] The curious reader may enjoy provocative juxtapositions such as those for May 18, on which the military commander Alexander Suvorov died (1800), the future Tsar Nicholas II was born (1868), and the first movie theater opened in St. Petersburg (1896). *Petersburg Day By Day* offers an eloquent illustration of the overwrought but devoted labors of residents to map their city over the years, suggesting, as do all such purportedly comprehensive descriptions and references, that all of Petersburg might possibly be contained between the covers of a book. As this survey has shown, however, all literary-cultural guides to St. Petersburg use criteria for inclusion that implicitly propagate a hierarchy of what is and is not important in the topography of the city.

Mikhail Kuraev's aphoristic 1996 "Journey from Leningrad to St. Petersburg"

(*Puteshestvie iz Leningrada v Sankt Peterburg*), written in response to the return of the city's historic name, offers a postscript to imperial-era literary journeys around St. Petersburg. Kuraev's journey, subtitled "Travel Notes," exemplifies the kind of intellectual armchair-traveling around Petersburg time and space that has characterized so many written accounts of this city. Unlike Koni, however, Kuraev does not perform his act of cultural reminiscence to keep memory alive, but rather to characterize Petersburg as a "completed historical subject," analogous to a fictional work that has come to its end, or "an unneeded organ" withering away.[107] How can this be, when Kuraev himself provocatively renews the tradition of Petersburg textual tour, demonstrating yet again that the Russian imperial capital can engender an infinite number of such literary journeys? The heterogeneity of the guidebook as a form provides a home to the city in all its aspects, tracing familiar pathways and charting the unknown. Its on-going life as a genre speaks to Petersburg as an inexhaustible literary-cartographical subject. The guidebook project, whatever the ideological coloration of its individual manifestations, always attempts to expand cultural common ground.

CHAPTER FOUR

Stories in Common: Urban Legends
in St. Petersburg

It is a Petersburg commonplace that mysterious legends and oral lore play an integral role in the imperial capital's cultural life and convey an essential part of the city's history. Just as the city rose over the mass burial ground of peasant workers who died constructing Peter's pet project, it is said, the Petersburg literary myth was founded upon a graveyard of undocumented urban folklore.[1] As the city's original wooden structures gave way to stonework buildings, the story continues, unwritten legends yielded to printed texts. Even the city's most famous cultural monument echoes this structure of ephemeral preliterate underpinnings overwritten by a new culture's civilizing mission. The Bronze Horseman statue to Peter the Great with its dedicatory inscription from Catherine II stands upon an ancient granite block split by lightning (called the Thunder-Stone, or *Grom-kamen'* by pagan worshippers), which the Empress had transported to the city from the primeval Finnish forest.

The patterns of urban legend from the imperial period live on in shadow form, their shapes discernible within some of the best-known Petersburg literary texts. These urban legends do not merely represent the popular-culture foundation for a magnificent literary tradition, however. In fact, canonical literary works about Petersburg (often devote themselves to puzzling over urban legends as a cultural phenomenon.

The term "legend" (in Russian, *legenda*) derives from the Latin verb "to read" (*legere*). "Legend" refers to a popular story or myth transmitted across time and space, as well as a key to reading a visual representation such as a map. This second etymology of the word "legend" points to the virtual inscription of oral lore on material surfaces such as buildings and monuments, and to their actual inscription in literary texts. In this way, Petersburg urban legends leave their marks on both city structures and literary works that can thereafter be read in terms of these productive symbiotic relationships.

Another Russian term for urban legend, *predaniie*, comes from the prefix "across, over" (*pre-*) and the verb "to transfer" (*dat'*), emphasizing the way in which these stories are passed around human communities over space and time. Urban legends possess a life of their own that allows them to navigate the city with great freedom. They have the "legs" to transcend social and literary-generic matrices and thus to create a richer mix in the middle space of city culture. Oral lore is an integral part of the horizontal model of the city that this study seeks to elaborate, in that the circulation of shared stories is more important than the vertical strata of elite and popular culture. Urban legends are not merely a function of city culture; in their wide-ranging movements, they constitute this culture, mapping the larger shapes and more obscure features of the city.

Walter Benjamin observed that storytelling is an "artisan form of communication" that "thrives for a long time in the milieu of work—the rural, the maritime, and the urban."[2] Urban legends as a form of storytelling have less to do with relieving the boredom of repetitive tasks, however, and more to do with short vivid exchanges that impress themselves on the listener's memory. Benjamin's essay "The Storyteller" concerns story forms such as epic poems and fairy tales that are perfected through repeated telling over long periods of time. Urban legends do not stay in one place long enough to be burnished in this way.

Similarly, in contrast to rhetorically driven anecdote, which turns on a final aphorism or epigram, urban legend usually concerns an ambiguous event, begging interpretation. Urban legend is loosely defined as a *false* story of the bizarre or supernatural, narrated as if it had really happened, and corresponding to a given community's anxieties (such as the alligators reported to inhabit the New York sewage system).[3] Urban legend is generally "verified" by its narrator with reference to an eyewitness or other source, often through "friend of a friend" relay, which leaves the story open to question. The urban legend is thus performative and affective, a type of social discourse that exists simultaneously in multiple versions and emerges from interactions within a specific cultural context. Such legends appeared as diverting fillers in English and French newspapers beginning in the nineteenth century, and in published collections throughout the twentieth century.[4] In folklore studies, modern urban legends (or "contemporary" legends, as they are often called) are not treated in the morphological terms that dominate traditional folklore scholarship, but rather examined as a confrontation between opposing but overlapping narratological and epistemological perspectives.[5] In this way, urban legend remains a live phenomenon, not inventoried according to its component parts, but acknowledged for its power to draw together diverse elements of the city population across historical periods or social and topographical divides.

The lifecycle of an urban legend retrieved from the historical past reflects its ability to migrate from one environment to another. Apprehended momentarily in its progress through the city, a legend may be recorded in personal documents, or receive mention as a newspaper item. From there, the legend can return to the realm of the unwritten, but may live on in cultural memory. The legend might at some point merit inclusion in a literary work whose author is sensitive to the common discourse that shapes a particular place. As a medium far more enduring than private papers or daily news, a literary text can keep an urban legend in circulation forever.

Since a speech act is inseparable from its context, however, urban legend as captured in a literary text would seem to be no longer equivalent to itself. Transcribed legend is, in Michel de Certeau's words, "a relic in place of performances."[6] Paradoxically, however, oral legend of the past can be reconstructed *only* with recourse to textual sources, even though these inevitably distort the "on the move" and "out of focus" quality inherent in such lore. Perhaps what de Certeau calls the "lost and ghostly voices" of oral culture stranded in a "scriptural economy" are actually clever parasites with a fierce instinct for survival. Can urban legends survive their incorporation within literary texts? Does the insinuation of urban legend alter a host text in some fundamental way? In my view, urban legend can be seen as creating a hinge point, a discursive field where oral and written modes achieve a delicate rapprochement, making canny use of one another.

Approaches to Urban Legend: The Cluster Tactic

Urban folklore is more fleeting than its traditional rural counterpart; it is not transmitted consciously to new generations by established rituals such as songs or myths, or with the concomitant formal sense of occasion, community, and tradition. The newspaper story rather than the folk ballad serves as a fitting figure for the urban legend as a narrative that circulates widely for a short time, but falls into obscurity unless its lease on life is renewed by new variants or fresh incidents. Rural legend may be more inherently conservative, functioning to bind and restrain behavior in a community. Urban legend, in contrast, can serve many masters as an instrument of subversion, coercion, or distraction.

Traditional Russian folklorists tend to consider the urban legend an unworthy object of study. Just as the "cruel song" (*zhestokii*, or *meshchanskii romans*) is seen as the half-breed offspring of the folk song and the salon art song, the urban legend is considered a contamination of the authentic "folk" story, made homeless by its move to the city. Soviet-era conceptions of "folklore" privilege the innate poetic abilities of simple, illiterate people, and avoid acknowledging that oral lore can be produced and transmitted by any part of a society.[7]

Petr Viazemskii, friend of Zhukovskii and Pushkin, recorded in his notebooks his interest in the urban oral lore of Moscow, which he thought merited attention. The cholera epidemic of 1830 gave rise to an extraordinary number of tales and rumors, themselves resembling a kind of epidemic, which inspired Viazemskii to make the following recommendation:

> Gather all stupid gossip and tales, true and false, that have dispersed themselves in Moscow on the streets and in homes on the subject of cholera and the present circumstances—a most curious chronicle will be the result. The spirit of the people

is depicted in these saying and tales. Judging by the din that reaches us, I am guessing they are myriad in Moscow, and that the vapor from them stands like a column: you couldn't cut it with a knife. It is said: "Literature is the expression of a society," but gossip is even more so, especially in Russia. We have no literature as such, because our literature is transmitted orally (*izustnaia*). Stenographers should transcribe it. With gossip, a society does not only express itself, but also coughs things up (*vykharkivaetsia*). Set up a spittoon.[8]

Although Viazemskii hailed urban oral culture, he did not follow his own advice and never compiled these intriguing bits and pieces. Possibly he had mixed feelings about the actual value of urban lore, as evidenced by his coarse metaphor of a spittoon. Viazemskii was clearly pleased with his characterization of these national resources, however, since he made a note to himself after this item: "From a letter to Nikolai Mukhanov. I'll write about this to A. Bulgakov." In Viazemskii's case, urban legend tellingly serves as the basis for a witty aphorism to be passed around his circle and recorded for posterity in lieu of the legends themselves.

In fact, there is no systematic way to research urban legends of the past. Oral narratives survive in random invocations that the fortunate researcher may happen upon in private or published documents whose authors considered these tales worthy of mention. The accidental nature of the sources exacerbates the problems inherent in the accurate documentation of historical urban legends. As Yuri Lotman points out, there exist two types of written materials useful for recovering oral literature, neither of them completely satisfactory: 1) forms of writing close to oral genres, such as collected anecdotes, and 2) literary writing inspired or influenced by oral literature that can be examined from a specific, reconstructive perspective.[9] A third type, termed "flying" folklore, arises spontaneously and disappears just as unpredictably, but is often recorded from memory, sometimes years later, with the transcriber's embellishments and corrections. These seemingly "secondary" texts should nevertheless be considered folklore.[10] Oral literature of the past—performative and syncretic by definition—leaves no tangible record of itself except for these imperfect textual reflections.[11] Urban legend comes into view only at the intersection of diverse cultural discourses.

Perhaps the best chance of corroborating the content of an urban legend and speculating as to the extent of its dispersion lies in uncovering "clustered" traces of a given story—variants of the same urban legend in sources from a reasonably compact time period.[12] It is, after all, the norm for a work of oral literature to exist in multiple variants. Traces of urban legends come to us embedded in high-culture artifacts such as memoirs, letters, and fictional works, in the periodical press, and via the humble proverbs of the illiterate, themselves often featured in compendia by urban folklorists. One such cluster exists for a story about dancing chairs that circulated in Petersburg during the 1830s. Pushkin himself recorded the incident in a diary entry for December 17, 1833: "In town people are talking about a strange occurrence. In one of the buildings belonging to the chancellery of the court equerry, the furniture was so bold as to move and jump about; the matter came to the attention of the authorities. Prince Dolgorukii set up an investigation. One of the clerks called a priest, but the chairs and tables did not want to stand submissively during the service. Various rumors are going around about this. N said that it is court furniture and is being requested for the Anichkov Palace."[13]

Pushkin ironically attributes intention and desire to the furniture (*mebeli vzdumali . . . stul'ia i stoly ne khoteli stoiat' smirno*) and refers to the different versions of the story currently in play without actually relating them. He provides the specific detail that generally studs the telling of an urban legend and concludes his account with irrelevant information whose presence, even if in jest, nevertheless implies a substantiating function. Pushkin casually sandwiches the urban legend between two other items in his diary for that day—a disparaging note about a reading of *Faust* at Zhukovskii's home, and the observation that two of his acquaintances have been the victims of robberies. The urban legend, like these two items, is a fact of Petersburg life.

A second variant of this same urban legend occurs in a letter from Viazemskii to A. I. Turgenev a few weeks later, on January 4, 1834: "Here people were talking for a long time about a strange phenomenon in the building of the court equerry: in one of the clerk's rooms, the chairs and tables danced and turned somersaults; glasses filled with wine hurled themselves at the ceiling. Witnesses were summoned, and a priest with holy water, but the 'ball' did not abate. I don't know how the 'ball' did end, but the main thing is, these stories are not empty, and something certainly did happen, but whether it was a diabolical or human delusion is unknown."[14]

Although the two versions of this urban legend correspond in most of their details, and both begin by noting that "people are talking," Viazemskii's account maintains a more reliably human point of view, attributing movement but not conscious agency to the furniture. In seeming compensation, he uses more vivid imagery than Pushkin, rendering the incident as a hallucinatory high-society dance.   Viazemskii's account is also more earnest than its predecessor, however, maintaining that the story has some basis in reality, and pedantically attempting to sort out what is known from what is not. Both accounts end inconclusively, without impeding the legend's continued free circulation.

As it happens, this same urban legend receives mention toward the end of Gogol's 1836 story "The Nose." Referring to the public interest in Kovalev's runaway proboscis, the narrator remarks, "rumors about this unusual occurrence spread all over the capital, and, as it generally goes, not without special embellishments. At that time, everyone was oriented towards the extraordinary: experiments in magnetism had very recently diverted the public. And the story of the dancing chairs on Koniushennaia (Stables) Street was still fresh."[15] All this is offered to explain why the public has responded to Kovalev's story with curiosity rather than disbelief or fear. In this way, the legend of the dancing chairs lives on in Gogol's collected works, whose Academy Edition notes point back to the letters of Pushkin and Viazemskii, in parallel to but more explicitly than Gogol's narrator who makes assumptions about his reader's familiarity with Petersburg urban lore of the 1830s that do not stand the test of time.

Gogol invokes but does not recount the legend of the dancing chairs, since by 1836, the story has already passed into cultural memory. There is, however, something similar in the gleeful disregard for human discomfiture shown by both the equerry furniture and the Major's nose, and in their insolent usurpation of human activity (dancing, strolling, attending church). In 1838 the story pops up once more, this time as a glancing reference in Vladimir Odoevskii's story "The Apparition." A character remarks that everyone knows all of the usual legends about mysterious happenings, "about people who appear after their deaths, about faces that look in at you from the third-floor window, about dancing chairs."[16] The court equerry furniture incident becomes common knowledge, but remains a mystery.

Uncertain distinctions between animate and inanimate forms represent a common preoccupation of urban legend. The legend of the court equerry, like urban legend as a form, animates a persistently and perhaps pointlessly rebellious subject that cannot be stopped, even as the story grows more difficult to trace back in time. Urban legend does not refer to the story itself, but to the generic principle of a story ever in motion, in search of a medium. The urban legend of the dancing chairs is a particularly apt example—the court equerry furniture bucks like a herd of wild horses, and the story piggybacks on the live-transport motif. The Russian word for furniture (*mebel'*) comes from the French equivalent *meuble*, meaning "movable household item," itself traceable to the Latin "mobile." The underlying foreign derivation makes itself literal in the Russian environment by animating and "possessing" the equerry furniture.[17]

The modern notion of the uncanny is linked to the urban environment rather than the rural, and thus requires a different approach than supernatural folk tales. In Anthony Vidler's phrasing, the uncanny, "generalized as a condition of modern anxiety," truly went public in the metropolis: "As a sensation it was no longer easily confined to the bourgeois interior or relegated to the imaginary haunts of the mysterious and dangerous classes; it was seemingly as disrespectful of class boundaries as epidemics and plagues."[18] In Sigmund Freud's view, the uncanny arises from demonic associations evoked by involuntary or compulsive repetition—of acts, on victims. Thus the uncanny cannot be contained in space or time. Freud associates the uncanny with "the omnipotence of thoughts, with the prompt fulfillment of wishes, with secret ... powers, and with the return of the dead."[19] In the urban legend's case, that which is compulsively enacted upon victims is the recounting of the story itself, the insistent return of the oral narrative, as if from the dead.

A second urban legend "cluster" has been identified around a mysterious event that purportedly took place in December 1890, reported in at least five different Petersburg newspapers—*The Citizen, Petersburg Leaflet, The News and Stock Exchange Gazette, The Day,* and *Petersburg Gazette.* The story concerned a priest, summoned by a female visitor to an apartment "somewhere on Sergievskaia Street, or near it," to administer the sacraments to a sick man.[20] When the priest arrived at the apartment in question, however, the young man who received him insisted that no one was sick. The puzzled priest pointed to a woman's portrait on the wall and identified the person who had asked him to come. At this, the young man grew pale and revealed that the woman in the portrait was his dead mother. Sobered, he allowed the priest to administer the rites, and that evening he died.

The Citizen and *Petersburg Leaflet* printed identical brief versions of the incident, but titled them differently—"Thoughts and Facts" and "A Mysterious Fact." Apart from these titles, which allude indirectly to the story's truth value, only the first two sentences of the account respond to the story as a legend in circulation: "There is a story going about town that is worthy of attention. The only question is whether it is true, and to what extent."[21] *The News and Stock Exchange Gazette* account, a lengthy article written by poet and journalist Sergei Safonov, took the matter much further. Safonov's article, "On the Trail of a Miracle," does not begin with the particulars of the legend, but rather with the author's attempt to investigate the story and the nature of urban legend as a cultural phenomenon: "When the story reached me about the unusual event that had happened to one of the Petersburg priests, my interest was aroused not so much by the question of its probability as by the question of just where the rumor got started, how it spread, and finally how it became common property and even turned up in the columns of minor newspapers—naturally in the form of conflicting and mutually contradictory accounts." Safonov claims that people from all walks of Petersburg life related the story to him—aristocratic ladies, their maids, peasants, and sleigh drivers. He searches for an "authoritative voice" in "this chaos of rumors" and attempts to "track down the starting point of the tales," although this seems a doomed project, incompatible with the very nature of urban legend. A poetic rather than journalistic approach to the legend might have proved far more productive.

The version of the story related by Safonov includes embellishments absent in the earlier variant from *The Citizen.* The priest is summoned from a church—"some say it was on Vladimirskaia Street, others on Sergievskaia"—by an "elderly lady," who is "dressed all in black," and the story includes the words with which she implores him to come to the dying man. The encounter with the young man is similarly more complex, since the priest engages him in conversation about his lapsed faith, and the young man consents to confession and takes communion before he and the priest discuss the latter's errand and the "very large" portrait on the wall. The priest finally learns that the young man's mother died four years ago. Three days later the young man dies "of a heart attack." Safonov's version of the urban legend dilates the telling as well the units of time and the size of the objects that constitute the story's "substantiating" details. On the other hand, according to Safonov, the young man takes communion not because he is frightened by the supernatural occurrence, but rather because the presence of the intellectually sympathetic priest by seemingly happy chance affords him this opportunity. The story's trajectory is made more innocent, no longer directly implicated in the effects such urban legends have on their listeners. This longer version shows urban legend evading Safonov amidst the welter of details, possibly spun as protective coloring in response to his project of elucidation.

Is Safonov's story long and confusing because he has compiled a version of versions from the multiple accounts in circulation? Safonov only declares enigmatically, "I provide it here in the form that is considered to be the most complete and authentic." He does point out, however, that the tale avoids reference to proper names and was thus extremely difficult to authenticate. After interviewing dozens of people who claimed to know something about the affair, Safonov concludes that "among us" the real object of fear is "news that is frank and responsible, news that . . . draws real conclusions about the matter, and puts a stop to indulging in nonsense." People love "wild tales and gossip" and pass these along to Safonov with great satisfaction until he mentions that he is a journalist, which causes them to "jump back from me in superstitious fright." The most ironic aspect of Safonov's article is this assertion that his investigative reportage has uncovered an irrational fear of journalism among the Petersburg populace. Safonov ends his story with a probing question: "If all this really is true, then why are the people who know keeping quiet?"

An anonymous account in *Petersburg Gazette*, a short piece attributed to Nikolai Leskov called "Bad Jokes," represents the final item in this "cluster."[22] The author refers scornfully to "this sham miracle," and claims that the story "smelled unmistakably fictitious." "Bad Jokes" purports to be an incontrovertible dismissal of the legend, "refuted from beginning to end by the archpriest of the Sergievsky Cathedral," since "Nothing of the kind has taken place either in the Sergievsky parish or anywhere else in Petersburg!" Instead, the author insists, the "miracle" is merely a blasphemous hoax perpetrated by Prince Meshcherskii, publisher of *The Citizen*, and by similar "Pharisees" looking to sell newspapers. In Leskov's account, newspaper publishers cynically exploiting urban legend for their own profit counter Safonov's hero journalists, who raise the specter of terrifying accountability before the city population.

Written transcription and explanation—a kind of textual stake through the heart—may check the path of oral legend. If inscription fails to transform legend into literary artifact, however, the written version may simply become a new agent of dissemination. Leskov's "Bad Jokes" does not constitute an authoritative refutation of the legend, but merely the next installment, putting into circulation an unsubstantiated accusation of Meshcherskii and claiming to have canvassed the entire city—a logistical impossibility. Here, the absence of firm evidence— an attribute of the urban legend, which typically provides *almost* enough information—is offered as solid confirmation of the story's falsity. This account underscores the exchange of services between urban legend and newspapers, in which handy column filler is efficiently dispersed across the city. The truth and objectivity claims implicit in newspapers coexist uneasily with the disposable nature of their contents, made possible by the evolution of movable type.

Newspapers offer a material metaphor for urban legend in that their collective movements around the city are too complex to retrace, just like the proliferation and dynamic evolution of secondhand information. Indeed, newspapers are the consummate document of the everyday—fleeting, ghostly, not worth saving—most particularly in the case of the boulevard press, which served a broad reading audience.[23] News, like urban legend, is always on the move, as etymologically attested by early newspaper names from the seventeenth and eighteenth centuries with their pervasive image of information "currents" flowing throughout a community (Dutch "corantos," The English Daily Courant, the New England Courant). Newspaper pages blowing along the city streets provide a perfect image for the unpredictable movement of urban legend. The roving reporter who overhears and transmits tidbits he picks up around town simply formalizes the process by which stories seek new homes.[24]

Legend Personified: Petersburg's Ksenia

Urban legend requires a kernel around which to coalesce—most often a place, but sometimes a person. Petersburg's most famous person-legend, Saint Ksenia Grigor'evna, represents a near-perfect fusion of urban legend, traditional folk culture, and official Orthodox canon. Ksenia of Petersburg also represents the cohesion of person and place, since her grave became a place of legend.

The "Blessed Ksenia" of Petersburg (blazhennaia Ksenia Peterburgskaia) was born during the first part of the eighteenth century, sometime between 1719 and 1730. After the death of her husband, Andrei Fedorovich Petrov, a singer in the court chorus, the twenty-six-year-old widow gave away her possessions, donned male attire, and became a pilgrim, wandering barefoot around Petersburg for forty-five years. Ksenia assumed the name of her late husband, burying her own former identity. She could often be found on the Petersburg Side, at the entrance to the church of Apostle Matvei, near what was possibly the site of her husband's former house, where one street came to bear the name "Andrei Petrov" (changed to Lakhtinskaia Street as of 1877). Instead of wandering the whole of Russia, this religious pilgrim traversed the unpaved minor streets and alleyways of the Petersburg "wilderness."

Ksenia could see the future and cure the sick.[25] She predicted the death of

Empress Elizaveta in December 1761, roaming the streets the day before and proclaiming that all of Russia should prepare funeral pancakes.[26] She foretold the bloody 1764 end of Ioann Antonovich, named successor to Empress Anna Ioannovna, who was overthrown in 1741 and imprisoned in the Schlusselburg Fortress. According to the diverse but scanty sources on Ksenia, Petersburg cabdrivers vied for the privilege of giving her a ride, believing it would bring them good fortune. Merchants offered their wares without charge. Mothers begged her to touch their children. She would take only a single kopeck from those wishing to give her alms, and gave even this money away.

The date of Ksenia's death is in debate, held variously to be before or during the 1777 flood, possibly during the reign of Paul, or in 1803, but no later than 1806. No written records attest to any of these speculative dates. Regardless, Ksenia was buried in the Smolenskoe Cemetery, where visitors broke off pieces of her gravestone and carried away bits of the earthen mound. Her burial place became the site of reputed "miracles" during the nineteenth century.[27] In 1902, a small chapel-monument was erected at her gravesite, paid for by money left by visitors. During the prerevolutionary period, the number of visitors in a single day sometimes approached five thousand.[28] In 1988, the 1000th anniversary of Russia's adoption of Christianity, the Russian Orthodox Church formally canonized Saint Ksenia.[29] Her cult continues to be based at the Smolenskoe Cemetery church of the Smolensk Icon of the Blessed Virgin.

Legends concerning Ksenia are subject to the variations in transmission and transcription typical of oral genres. In Evgenii Grebenka's 1845 sketch "The Petersburg Side" (Peterburgskaia storona), for example, the legend of Ksenia appears in distorted form, and not acknowledged as such. Marveling at the strange street names in this Petersburg neighborhood, Grebenka's narrator is surprised to hear of a street named "Andrei Petrovich" or "Andreia Petrovaia," whose origins he attempts to discover from local residents:

> They say that a happy couple taken right from La Fontaine lived on this street at one time. The husband, Andrei Petrovich, loved his wife more than can be imagined, and the wife, Aksin'ia Ivanovna, loved her husband more than can be imagined (this is how the female-storyteller of Andreia Petrovaia Street expressed herself). Suddenly, the husband died and the wife was left and played quite a trick: she lost her mind from grief and fancied that she was not Aksin'ia Ivanovna, but rather Andrei Petrovich, and that Andrei Petrovich had not died, but had just turned into her, Aksin'ia, and in reality had remained Andrei Petrovich.
>
> She would not answer to her previous name, and when someone addressed her as "Andrei Petrovich" she would always answer "Eh?," and she went about in men's clothing.[30]

As a postscript to this random bit of lore, Grebenka's narrator notes, "This is one of those streets where cab-drivers refuse to take passengers in either spring or fall, fearing the mud." Oddly, the poor road conditions, rather than supernatural associations, incite apprehension and keep people away from a place haunted by legend. The version of Ksenia's life preserved in Grebenka's sketch translates both urban legend and hagiography into local eccentricity. Grebenka's narrator can make a casual reference to La Fontaine, but his source on "Aksin'ia" is not very skillful at constructing a narrative line. The names and story-logic have been garbled by the "female story-teller of Andreia Petrovaia Street," and Ksenia's simple but mysterious pronouncements are reduced to grunts of acknowledgement. The version in Grebenka's literary text is nevertheless countered by urban legend, which gave rise to an entire oral oeuvre relating to the Blessed Ksenia and her deeds.

Official "textual" memory of Ksenia came into being well after her death, recorded from oral legends preserved and transmitted by the "folk" (narod).[31] Stories about the Blessed Ksenia survived even those decades during the twentieth century when the Soviet government made concerted attempts to eradicate this oral tradition and its practices. Vladimir Toporov made a study of such lore from the 1970s and 1980s, before Ksenia's canonization, listening to conversations among visitors at her Smolenskoe gravesite. He claims that although most of the worshippers were peasant women, visitors also included diverse members of the urban population, including "cultured" (intelligentnye) people. While documenting the cult of Ksenia in a collection of scholarly essays and asserting her broad sociocultural appeal, Toporov nevertheless transforms text back into legend, returning to oral sources on this Petersburg persona-legend. Printed literature about Ksenia repeats the same body of provisional biographical information, awkwardly cobbled together into a narrative, but individual accounts of her miracle-working and predictions, conveyed in the colloquial oral form in which legends typically traveled the streets of Petersburg, constitute the still-living part of Ksenia's story.

Petersburg Urban Legend: The Story Everyone Knows

Another commonplace about Petersburg urban legends is that they compensate for the dearth of history in this relatively young city. Joseph Brodsky declares that Petersburg is too new for "soothing mythology," by which he means corrective official history that overwrites old wrongs. This, in Brodsky's opinion, is why "every time a natural or premeditated disaster takes place, you can spot in a crowd a pale, somewhat starved, ageless face with its deep-set, white, fixed eyes, and hear the whisper: 'I tell you, this place is cursed!' You'll shudder, but a moment later, when you try to take another look at the speaker, the face is gone."[32] Brodsky playfully renders the very phenomenon of urban legend as an urban legend, but also as a self-evident fact of Petersburg life that requires little explanation. Like urban legend, Brodsky's pale figure is democratic, extending beyond categories of gender, class, race, or age.

Legends are nevertheless a highly elusive object of study, even for those who seem to have devoted themselves to this project. Petr Stolpianskii's 1924 article "Legends, Tales, and Stories of Old Petersburg," for example, dispels several false notions about the city: Peter the Great never actually planned to model his city after Venice or Amsterdam, but only created such a plan on paper to impress European dignitaries; the three main radial arteries of Petersburg do not reflect skillful city planning because the Admiralty was never intended to be the city center; Nevsky Prospect became Petersburg's main thoroughfare only by happenstance; the site of the Winter Palace was selected wholly accidentally when Count Apraksin died childless and left his palace to Peter.[33] Stolpianskii argues for *chance*, and not grand design, as a major factor in Petersburg's evolution. Urban legend itself, however, is only a spectral presence in Stolpianskii's text, since he refutes what readers assumed to be historical truth, relegating it to the realm of legend, but does not treat the phenomenon of legend as such. Only the general structure of Stolpianskii's urban archeology mirrors the attempt to uncover legend at the foundation of official text, as when he describes the rowdy Morskoi market that formerly occupied the site of the buttoned-up Alexandrine General Staff building.[34] Although Stolpianskii's task is to reestablish history rather than legend, he takes pleasure in revealing the unexpected bases of Petersburg's carefully composed exterior.

Most accounts of Petersburg urban legends as such adopt a similar strategy of explaining and debunking, claiming that Petersburg rumors have reflected public consciousness ever since the city's inception, when misinformation first began to circulate.[35] Rumored death rates among workers during the early years, as reflected in accounts by visiting foreigners, rose to as high as 200,000, but the actual number would have been closer to 2,000. Unless truth is stranger than legend, however—as in Stolpianskii's case—rumor tends to outlive fact.

Even the work of Petersburg's most distinguished theorist-scholars tends to smooth out the troublesome contours of urban legend, subordinating oral narratives to literary history without acknowledging any conflict between these two forms of cultural production. Not unlike Brodsky, Lotman makes the famous assertion that Petersburg's shortage of history gave rise to a "tumultuous surge in mythology," which "filled the semiotic void."[36] "Long before" nineteenth-century Russian literature made explicit reference to Petersburg's mythology, he declares, the life of the city's population was distinguished by the "exceptional role of rumor" and "oral accounts of unusual occurrences" that circulated as urban folklore, provoking great interest among the city's educated population. During the first third of the nineteenth century, the oral genre of "the scary or fantastical story with its invariable 'Petersburg local coloring'" thus became a popular diversion in Petersburg salon culture. In a telegraphic series of undocumented, unattributed claims, Lotman notes that the first collector of this folklore was the Privy Chancellory; Pushkin evidently intended to make his diary of 1833–35 into an archive of city rumors; Anton Del'vig was a collector of 'scary stories'; Nikolai Dobroliubov established the theoretical role of oral production in folk life in the manuscript newspaper *Rumors* from his student years; and the poet Kozlov was fascinated by urban legends.[37] Apart from a single story about Del'vig's ghost, however, Lotman offers no examples of Petersburg urban legends and provides few leads for further sleuthing.[38] Gogol and Dostoevsky "canonized" the oral literature of Petersburg, he claims, and carried its stories, along with the oral tradition of the "anecdote," into the realm of "high literature" (*vysokaia slovesnost'*).[39] This is the single most important conclusion of Lotman's account, which treats urban legend as raw material creatively transformed by Russia's great writers, and his assertion has been taken at face value in much subsequent writing about Petersburg. Might it not be the case that urban legend makes equally productive use of literature?

Toporov similarly proposes oral culture as the foundation for the Petersburg Text, citing an assortment of proverbs, rhymes, and popular sayings about the city from the eighteenth and nineteenth centuries.[40] He quickly moves past the oral tradition, however, to treat the vast array of letters, memoirs, essays, and fictional works that constitute the central subject of his study—the textual part of the "Petersburg Text." Toporov relegates to a footnote survey of the basic categories of Petersburg oral legends: founding stories; eschatological predictions; historical myths about rulers, prominent figures, and local saints; literary legends; legends connected with particular places in the city; stories of apparitions; and onomastic lore.[41] These legends initially seemed to Toporov utterly distinct from the written tradition about Petersburg, but upon deeper examination, he concluded that Petersburg legends are intimately connected with the "Petersburg Text of Russian literature," as "two poles, two outer limits of a single 'supertheme'—'Petersburg in language' (*Peterburg v slove*)."[42] His survey of unwritten antecedents to the Petersburg Text thus becomes part of a larger project that insistently harmonizes and synthesizes literature and urban lore within a unified textual field. My own readings of several well-known works of Petersburg literature later in this chapter counter this view by illustrating the ways in which urban legend, as a unique form of cultural discourse that seeks to extend its lifespan, makes printed literature serve its own purposes.

In keeping with Lotman's assertion, urban legend of the imperial period is generally considered part of *high* culture, since all historical corroboration comes from textual evidence generated by the upper strata of the population. Indeed, one urban folklorist remarks, "If the mystical legends we've related were so prevalent in educated court and aristocratic circles, one can imagine what unbelievable rumors circulated among the simple folk."[43] Urban legend's prevalence among the lower classes in Petersburg is, of course, everywhere asserted and nowhere documented; the larger causes behind the flourishing of this phenomenon during specific historical periods are moreover hard to ascertain. The prominence of urban legend in earlier nineteenth-century Petersburg could have been related to the relatively low literacy rate, which only began to rise significantly during the second half of the century in response to rural reforms and industrialization. Urban legends seemed nonetheless to grow even more numerous during the final years preceding the Russian Revolution, a development possibly attributable to the disorienting effects of the city's social unrest and rapid commercial and industrial growth.[44] Popular literature such as commercial *lubki* and mass newspaper serials from the same prerevolutionary period countered this tendency by debunking belief in the supernatural, encouraging readers to adopt a more rational outlook.[45] In contrast, interest in spiritualism among the aristocratic class and the royal family became widespread during the reigns of Alexander III and Nicholas II, as evidenced by the notoriety of such figures as Madame Blavatskaia and Alexander Aksakov, and the popularity of the weekly journal "Rebus" (1881–1917), which reported strange happenings and séance proceedings.[46] The impetus for urban legend arises from contradictory, often unexpected responses to historical circumstance (industrialization, political conservatism), and legend's lure knows no class boundaries.

Recent collections of Petersburg lore suggest the migrating, proliferating tendencies of urban legends, whose variants can never be fully accounted for in textual form. In addition to the familiar legend of the Peter monument, which descends from its pedestal to gallop about the city, there are similar tales of animation concerning the Peter monument by the Mikhailovskii castle, the Catherine monument by the Alexandrinskii Theater, and even the granite obelisk on Znamenskaia Square. In this way, the themes of urban legends are self-describing—always in motion, highly contagious. The stories evoked in recent collections of Petersburg lore are generally those that concern the evolution of the city *itself* rather than strange phenomena merely observed in Petersburg—coexistent yet incompatible stories about the creation, naming, and subsequent fate of Petersburg bridges, buildings, and monuments. In this sense, the city is constructed—and reconstructed in each subsequent (and remarkably similar) Petersburg guidebook—from legend fragments, which, even as they are repeated, draw attention to the overlapping, overwriting, and contradicting operations performed by such historical "evidence."

Story Sites: A Topography of Petersburg Urban Lore

Petersburg is a legend-place. Not for nothing does Mary Shelley's 1818 novel Frankenstein, or The Modern Prometheus begin in this very city.[47] Writing from St. Petersburg on December 11, "17—," Shelley's protagonist Robert Walton reassures his sister in England that "no disaster has accompanied the commencement of an enterprise which you have regarded with such evil forebodings."[48] The bracing northern wind of St. Petersburg "inspirits" Walton, making his daydreams "more fervent and vivid." His imagination inflamed, he imagines the desolate Arctic pole, his intended destination, as "the region of beauty and delight" and "a country of eternal light." From Petersburg, Walton travels to Arkhangelsk, where he hires a ship and engages a crew. Thus Shelley's novel and its hero both depart from St. Petersburg, the city that creates an unsettled state of mind, impelling the plot toward the encounter with Doctor Frankenstein and the strange hybrid creature who parallels the animation of the inanimate so prevalent in Petersburg urban legend.

In Shelley's case, Petersburg gives rise to a story long established as a classic of British nineteenth-century literature. Petersburg story-lore usually possesses a much more local currency, however. How does urban legend circulate around a city? In Petersburg, the absence of well-developed public transport and inexpensive boulevard newspapers during the first half of the nineteenth century did not seem to inhibit the wide dispersion of urban legend across the population.[49] How do oral stories find their way into Petersburg drawing rooms and salons where the more lowborn narrators in their chain of relay would surely not have been welcome? Recent research suggests that urban legend circulates in the manner of rumor—termed "the oldest form of mass media."[50] Rumor and urban legend circulate spontaneously, but narrators extend the lifespan of these stories by choosing narratees likely to pass them on. Perhaps it is simpler to say that legends choose their narrators. In any case, urban legends need to be repeated in order to survive.[51] Repetition, however, leads to death, when there is nowhere left for the story to go—at some point, the story has exhausted its potential for spawning new variants and everyone seems to have heard it.[52]

In his 1898 collection of lore, Remarkable Eccentrics and Originals (Zamechatel'nye chudaki i originaly), Mikhail Pyliaev traces the movement of rumors and stories around St. Petersburg of the 1820s. Pyliaev claims that a group of Guard officers used to distribute themselves about the city, disseminating wild tales to the various idlers (zevaki) they encountered and relishing the swiftness with which these tales spread further. The officers once claimed to have seen a man in a long frock coat—a merchant or a shop assistant—lying on the pavement on a remote street in the Vyborg district. Within a half hour, the neighborhood buzzed with rumors that "the corpse of merchant P., a well-known millionaire, had been found, knifed—by whom?—O, horror!—a monster, his own nephew, whom the merchant had stripped of his inheritance due to his dissolute way of life." After murdering the relative who caught him plundering the store's cash reserves, the nephew, "taking all of the rings from the fingers of his unfortunate victim and even the cross from his breast, threw the corpse out the window, and ran away to America with the dead man's wife, his aunt by birth!"[53] In other parts of the city—Meshchanskaia Street, Sennaia Square, and Kolomna—an entirely different version of the story held sway, in which a poor young man with no connections had thrown himself from a fifth-floor window for love of a wealthy young woman promised to another. According to this version, "The hand of the unfortunate who had died before his time tightly grasped a medallion with a portrait of the woman whose name he had murmured with his last breath." In each case, a small object within the story—ring, cross, medallion—lends credence by suggesting that material evidence confirms the event. As Pyliaev notes, however, anyone who wished to find out the true story of this putative corpse could inquire at the police station, or even ask the individual in question, "when he, after sobering up, betook himself to the same tavern near which he had been found."

A round black hat was seen floating on the Fontanka near Ismailovskii Bridge on another occasion. A crowd of idlers gathered to watch the "inexpensive entertainment," and Fontanka residents sent their servants outside to find out what was happening. The Guards officers took full advantage of the occasion, and Pyliaev records the different story-versions that sprang up along the Petersburg waterways. By the Panteleimonskii Bridge, it was said that the hat belonged to "a clerk, who drowned himself from grief, because he was given no recompense when those lower than he in rank and position each received a Stanislav order." By the Simeonovskii Bridge, the drowned clerk became "a young Kolomna poet, who threw himself into the Fontanka because the publisher of a particular journal did not want to print his verses." The hat, a familiar object in an unfamiliar context, offers a perfect material metaphor for urban legend. The waterways exemplify its passage by channels of communication throughout the city, as do the many mentions of specific Petersburg bridges, which, as figures, exist to fix the location of the story briefly, and then to allow its progress across as well as along the water. Further on, the victim was reportedly a merchant, who had drowned himself over a contract he was unable to secure. Others claimed the hat belonged to a sorcerer and that it was enchanted, since no one could catch it—one man, it was rumored, had fallen into the water and drowned in the attempt. (Here the hat evolves into the cause of death, not the evidence of a death.) Still further on, the victim turned into the only son of rich parents, a handsome lad who had accidentally fallen into the river and drowned; some asserted that he died from "hopeless love for a cruel-hearted and relentless actress." Some were certain the suicide was a millionaire who had lost his fortune to a merchant who owned taverns and fruit shops. Others insisted there were 200,000 rubles sewn into the hat's lining, and that the wind had snatched the hat "from the head of a miser who was moving to a new apartment and feared he would be robbed." By the Anichkov Bridge, the hat belonged to a young girl who had dressed like a man to run away with her lover. When the breeze lifted the hat from her head, revealing her long hair, she was recognized and apprehended by her parents. By the Obukhovskii and Izmailovskii Bridges, finally, rumor had it that the hat was attached by a thread to the finger of an Englishman, who, according to the terms of a bet, was swimming underwater all the way from the Prachechnyi Bridge. Story variants thus often evoke additional "evidence" tied to or concealed by the hat. Legend leaves no corner unexplored in its investigation of potential narrative crevices within the story's own internal components, as it simultaneously traverses its external physical environment. The victim moves up and down the social ladder, turns into a woman, then a foreigner. The death, initially a suicide, becomes an accident, before the story turns lighter-hearted, playing pranks and staging contests. Finally, the legend comes full circle, returning to the Izmailovskii Bridge, where it presumably expires, worn-out. At this point, an urban chronicler such as Pyliaev can transcribe the adventures of the picaresque story-hero, which also illustrate the collective story-embroidering talents of the Petersburg populace.

The Guard officers who initiated such stories resemble scholars of urban legend such as the journalist Safonov or the theorist Toporov, conducting experiments and observing patterns. The Guards can also themselves be considered an urban legend, of course—figures for the mysterious origins of lore that arises spontaneously as an inherent feature of the urban environment. Pyliaev notes that rumors spread by the mischievous Guards could assume "colossal" proportions, as when an enormous crowd gathered at Kazan Cathedral, hoping to glimpse a corpse said to have horns and claws ("the faithful image of the devil"). The crowd was so persistent that the fire brigade directed streams of water at those present "to cleanse Kazan Square and Nevsky Prospect of idlers." Later, another rumor circulated that Minister of War Alexander Arakcheev had himself started the story to distract public attention from lurid stories going around about the murder of his lover Nastasia Minkina. Even the fire brigade is helpless to combat rumor. Perhaps the only force that can truly wage war against subversive rumor is a counter-rumor. Russian authorities learned this lesson well during the second half of the nineteenth century and stirred up public feeling by circulating stories of terrorist arsonists and dangerous student revolutionaries. Still, every urban legend bears the potential to spawn a contradictory response (thus the rumor about Arakcheev's starting a rumor to counter a rumor), and can make no permanent allegiance with a particular social or political interest group. Urban legend may fill a void in the physical space of the city, explaining an absence, but urban lore can just as easily displace an existing reality, or return to challenge a prior displacement and thus to demand an explanation.

In some cases, the movements of urban legend themselves become the subject of a literary work. Gogol's 1841 story "The Overcoat" was inspired by an anecdote about a clerk who carefully saved money to buy a gun, and took to his bed, ill with grief, after losing it in the water on a hunting trip—a tidbit Gogol picked up at a party.[54] "The Overcoat" in its very conception is thus implicated in the everyday dynamics of oral narration. Furthermore, as has been more than once observed, Gogol's famously original style of written narration seems to render the performance of a talented oral-storyteller.

The story's coda, following the death of Akakii Akakievich, invokes urban legend in a chain of mysteriously connected circumstances that reflect the transmogrifying nature of legend, and by which the narrator's "poor story" unexpectedly receives "a fantastical ending."[55] Rumors circulate about a clerk's ghost that snatches overcoats from the shoulders of passers-by near the Kalinkin Bridge. One clerk-victim glimpsed the ghost "with his own eyes" and recognized Akakii Akakievich, but fled without taking a closer look. A policeman on Kiriushkin Lane was on the point of apprehending the ghost, but the apparition sneezed and made its escape. The Important Personage who frightened Akakii Akakievich to death sees the ghost, whose face was "pale as snow, and looked just like a dead man's," and hastily relinquishes his overcoat. The ghost seems satisfied with this offering, and disappears—"at least there were no more stories heard anywhere about overcoats being torn off people's backs."[56] The temporary absence of new rumors appears to confirm the end of the affair.

The chain of urban lore continues, however, as a police constable in Kolomna, again "with his own eyes," sees a ghost leaving a house. The story ends with the gesture of the ghost—a much taller one with a huge moustache—who raises an enormous fist at the policeman, and then, "apparently heading towards the Obukhovskii Bridge, was completely hidden in the nighttime darkness." The ghost in "The Overcoat" mutates as urban legends do, accruing details, but not necessarily in a coherent or consistent manner. The end of Gogol's story illustrates the proliferation of urban legend, detailing its travels around Petersburg much in the way that Pyliaev traced the movements of a mysterious hat along the city's canalways.

According to Vladimir Nabokov, "The Overcoat" recounts Akakii Akakievich's "gradual reversion to the stark nakedness of his own ghost," which represents "the most tangible, the most real part of his being."[57] The seemingly ordinary ghost story is thus transformed into "both an apotheosis and a degringolade." In Nabokov's view, the story ends with its own "queerest paradox," by which "The man taken for Akakii Akakievich's cloakless ghost is actually the man who stole his cloak."[58] The high moral fervor of the narration seemingly exalts the departed Akakii Akakievich, but then comes crashing down with the final grotesque turn of events. The resolution of Gogol's story points generically upward and downward, stranding the reader on ambiguous middle ground. The story also ends by pointing outside itself to legend dissolving into the murky darkness, reversing the usual direction of such influences, according to which urban legend provides raw source material for a writer of genius to shape into finished literary form. Gogol's best-known story, "The Nose," ends similarly with the narrator's exaggeratedly ingenuous and incoherent ramblings, evoking that kernel of truth that just might constitute the core of an urban legend: "However, when all is said and done, and although, of course, we conceive the possibility, one and the other, and maybe even. . . Well, but then what exists without inconsistencies? And still, if you give it a thought, there is something to it. Whatever you may say, such things do happen—seldom, but they do."[59] Major Kovalyov's hunt for his elusive nose suggests a flat-footed urban ethnographer in hopeless pursuit of a slippery story.

Like Gogol's "The Overcoat," Yakov Butkov's 1848 "Nevsky Prospect, or The

Journey of Nestor Zaletaev" (Nevskii Prospekt, ili Puteshestvie Nestora Zaletaeva) documents the peregrinations of oral story-variants, in a section subtitled "Rumors and Gossip" (slukhi i tolki) that comes at the text's midpoint:
"Soon the rumor about the mysterious carriage traveling around the capital city
of St. Petersburg began to spread everywhere."[60] Cabdrivers said the carriage belonged to a scholarly German, who was making a study of Petersburg conveyances in order to put them out of business. Servants, tavern workers, and bil-
liard markers told of a wealthy young man who squandered all his means and
lost his apartment on Bolshaia Morskaia Street, although "some people, in contrast, stubbornly asserted that it was not on Bolshaia Morskaia, but on Malaia
Millionnaia Street." In other story versions, the young man became an organ
grinder, as attested by those who claimed to have seen him "on the Petersburg
Streets, in Okhta, in Pargolovo, and on the islands." The young man, it was said,
had sold his soul to the devil in order to regain his former comforts, and now
traveled Nevsky Prospect in a carriage of the newest German workmanship,
"with colored lamplights and blue, some claimed raspberry-colored, velvet pillows." (Here, the scheming German seems to have already built his superior
model, which the carriage now represents.) The actual occupant of the carriage,
the eponymous Zaletaev, stops to refresh himself at a café and listens to far-
fetched theories about the mystery man circulating amongst the clientele.
Butkov's story documents twin journeys—that of Zaletaev, who travels grandly
but purposelessly up and down Nevsky Prospect in compensation for his undistinguished life, and that of urban legend, which, like the German scholar, has an
ulterior motive. The story's main conveyance, the carriage that Zaletaev has unexpectedly won in a lottery, like urban legend, is ambulatory and procreative,
generating new story-versions that set off on their own journeys. The disputed
details—street name, neighborhood, and the color of the velvet pillows—are
all subsumed by the legend, however.

The structures of fictional works inspired by oral legend often reflect the patterns of transmission and reception by which legends circulate in a society,
sometimes, as in Odoevskii's 1838 story "The Apparition" (Prividenie), as a
nested series of romantic narratives.[61] Odoevskii's story is not set in Petersburg,
however, but literally "on the road," as four travelers in a coach—"a retired captain, the head of a Petersburg civil service department, Irinei Modestovich, and
myself"—pass the time in conversation. Irinei Modestovich regales the travelers with stories of the supernatural, of which he has an endless supply. The Petersburg department head remarks sarcastically that, of course, "we can't get
along without apparitions," but Irinei Modestovich defends himself on the
grounds that "our minds, wearied by the prose of life, are drawn involuntarily
to these mysterious occurrences, which make up the itinerant poetry [empha-
sis mine] of our society and serve as proof that none of us can shake off poetry
in this life, no more than we can original sin."[62] The department head himself
involuntarily illustrates the characterization of urban legend as the "itinerant

poetry" of society, even though as "a Petersburg man accustomed to not being astonished by anything," he means to prove the disastrous consequences of "strenuous thinking" (myslennost'). The official's story concerns a poor clerk who was instructed to sort through an enormous old archive. The clerk's labors were so protracted that he became mentally agitated, climbed to the highest shelf, and squatted among the stacks of paper, declaring himself a "closed case" (reshennoe delo). The point of this story, for those interested in urban legend, is cautionary: the closure that often seems synonymous with written text (the "closed case") is an illusion that urban legend dispels. The clerk enters oral history, and his story becomes a passenger in the coach, alongside the department-head narrator and three listeners. Odoevskii's story both supports and debunks the supernatural, while using its Chinese-box of narratives to simulate the structure of oral communication. Odoevskii's story also reproduces in its carriage-interior setting the conventional origin ascribed to such published narratives. Stories of this type often appeared in collections or cycles purported to represent an evening of tales recounted among a circle of friends.[63]

Although urban legends always circulate, they often arise from specific places in the city. Walter Benjamin imagined a proverb as "an ideogram of a story," and pictured it as "a ruin which stands on the site of an old story and in which a moral twines about a happening like ivy around a wall."[64] In spite of the fact urban legends, unlike proverbs, suggest unpredictable movement rather than stasis and decay, Benjamin's figure can be adapted to suit this more volatile oral form. Urban legend lacks the twining moral of proverb, but it similarly stands as a ruin—the perpetually haunted house of unresolved narrative.

Haunted houses are linked with the uncanny in the very term Freud used to refer to this phenomenon—unheimlich, literally, "un-homelike," defined as "that class of the frightening which leads back to what is known of old and long familiar."[65] Thus the uncanny does not refer to the unknown, as might at first be assumed, but to the disturbing changes sensed in the place where one no longer feels at home. This new sense of unease also refers to the second meaning of unheimlich, which denotes something "no longer concealed or kept from sight." Thus, as Freud notes, Friedrich Schelling declared, "'Unheimlich' is the name for everything that ought to have remained . . . secret and hidden but has come to light."[66] Freud makes much of the overlap in meaning between heimlich and unheimlich, where the homelike by definition contains secret, hidden ghosts. The coziness of the home thus simultaneously provides a secure strongbox for its secrets. Heimlich can therefore, refer to knowledge that is unconscious or obscure, but eerily familiar—something already half-known.

The haunted house represents the most popular topos of the nineteenth-century uncanny, an essential ingredient of many horror stories and all Gothic novels. Poe's House of Usher is the "paradigmatic" haunted house, "a crypt, pre-destined to be buried in its turn."[67] Or perhaps "re-buried" is the more accurate designation, since the unheimlich crypt should have remained hidden and is only briefly illuminated by the experience of Poe's narrator. Sites such as haunted houses generate and perpetuate urban legends along with serving as repositories for them. The haunted house stays in place, but the story, a ghost of the house, can detach itself and become mobile. The familiar substantiating details such as specific named places in urban legends lend these floating, itinerant stories the semblance of a home.

The haunted house in Petersburg is a particularly insistent image associated with urban lore—a monument to urban legend. In this spirit, Yakov Polonskii's 1868 poem "Miasm" (Miazm) evokes, in sketchy but effective terms, the archetypal tale. The elegantly appointed house in question stands "near the Moika." Once overflowing with guests, the house has fallen silent—the owners' small son has died of a mysterious illness. The boy's mother is visited by the ghost of a shaggy, barefoot peasant, who explains that her house presses down upon the old burial-ground of the conscripted laborers who built Peter's city. The foul exhalations of this cursed spot have "smothered" her child. The apparition disappears and the mother falls to the floor, raving and feverish. From this time on, she does not live in the capital, but at her country estate or abroad. The house is for sale. Polonskii's poem concludes with an image of the deserted home— rain knocks at the locked entrance, and the stars' reflection fills the darkened windows. The natural elements invoke, in ghostly form, the absent inhabitants and guests. Urban legend has taken up residence, but also remains outside. It has been asserted, "Petersburg legend is social protest that has taken a fantastical form, and Polonskii's poem seems to concur."[68] Urban legend may sometimes seem too self-absorbed for social protest, merely describing its own legend-life in metaliterary or allegorical form. It is pleasing, however, to think about Petersburg urban legend as compensation not for the paucity of city history, but rather for the absence of a city forum, which the haunted house provisionally provides.

In a meditation on "The Haunted London House," Sharon Marcus explores how "the discrepancy between domestic ideology and the dwelling practices of Londoners came to be inscribed within the literary subgenre of the haunted-house story," a mid-century form responding to the crowding and transience spreading from the city's core into London's middle-class suburbs.[69] She distinguishes Victorian ghost stories from both nineteenth-century French tales of the uncanny and late eighteenth-century Gothic novels. The French stories were "written in a romantic, subjective strain and focused on themes of doubling, necrophilia, hypnotic influence, mysticism, and dream states," while Victorian ghost stories kept more closely to realist literary convention, referring to specific addresses and explicitly declaring themselves to be "truthful testimony." The Gothic novel occupied "labyrinthine, secret, even ruined spaces in ancient aristocratic castles," while Victorian ghost stories inhabited "contemporary middle-class houses whose initial coziness, mundanity, and legibility get disrupted and altered by apparitions."[70] At the conclusion of these stories, the reader along with the narrator and protagonists is chased from the house by the ghosts, "restoring an extreme version of the privacy whose invasion they [the stories] had depicted—a privacy that could never be documented, because it excluded the presence of any recorder or observer."[71] In Petersburg lore of this type, however, the situation is quite different—a function of historical demographics. Rather than representing the encroachment of the lower-class inner city into the surrounding middle-class regions, Petersburg urban legend often reflects the resistance of the city's frontierlike periphery to the structuring and organizing influence of the imperial capital's center.[72] In Petersburg's case, the cultural tension that fosters the appearance of urban legend seems to result not from threatening encroachments into the mediating social middle, but in conjunction with the attempt to establish a middle ground between civilization and wildness. Urban legend does not police the borders of the unkown, but rather appears to act as an advance guard into unfamiliar and unsettled territory, piquing city dwellers to investigate the truth of rumors for themselves, and working to create a common discursive space, if a contested one.

Which particular Petersburg sites give rise to urban legends? In general, the most productive areas for urban legend have been remote areas such as Vasilievskii Island, the Vyborg side, and Kolomna. Accounts of doubles and apparitions were also common within the "mystical triangle" of the Fontanka and Zagorodnyi Prospect near Nevsky.[73] Individual monumental structures recur in urban legends, among them St. Isaac's Cathedral and Mikhailovskii Castle. Urban legends more often inhabit the spaces between familiar monumental sites on the city map, however, emerging from places such as apartment buildings that house private stories and only partially visible aspects of cultural life.[74] In this, the peregrinations of Petersburg urban legend reverse the shift in spatial aesthetics that occurred during the first half of the nineteenth century—from representing external forms to exploring the inner recesses of urban life organized by minor events.[75] While legends emanate from secret inner places, they also make their way to central parts of the imperial city where they manifest themselves before a wider public.

The memoirist Anatoly Koni tells a story from the mid-1850s about a building on Nevsky Prospect then owned by the merchant Lytkin. An elderly woman had hurled herself to her death from the top of the stairwell, leaving a pool of blood that "seeped into the sandstone floor," and causing a stain that could not be washed away. The woman was from a "remote corner" of Petersburg and had nursed a secret passion for her young ward's affianced, a postal clerk. Upon the couple's marriage, she resolved to end her life, and came upon Lytkin's building with its steep main staircase. After the tragedy, building residents could not avoid passing the disturbing blood stain at the bottom of the stairwell, and "the suicide gradually gave rise to a series of fantastical stories during that period so poor in civic interests."[76] The old woman haunted the staircase at night, offering her "lifeless embraces" to building residents. The unseemly spot in the story

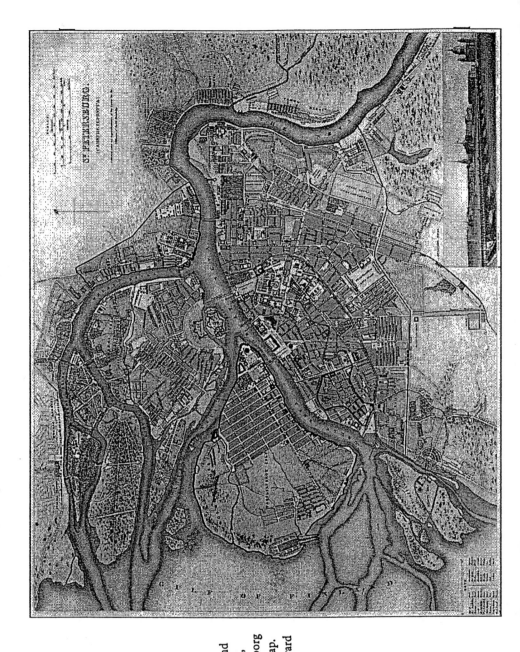

FIGURE 4.1. Legend Places: Vasilievskii, Kolomna, and Vyborg Side from 1853 Map. (Courtesy of Harvard Map Collection.)

seems to underscore the shameful nature of the old woman's alleged passion, but also, quite literally, to "mark the spot" from which legend originates. That is, the blood stain offers a figure for the more often invisible traces of a possibly apocryphal past event, from which legend—itself figured by the ghostly old woman—emanates.

Vasilievskii Island is a particularly important site for Petersburg urban legends, since this area represents the ghost of a Petersburg that never was—the unrealized Petersburg of Jean Baptiste Alexander Leblond's 1717 plan.[77] According to this scheme, Peter's palace would have been located at the center of Vasilievskii Island, with four diagonal streets radiating from each corner and a cathedral within a square at the end of each street. The shortage of financial and technical resources probably caused this grand project to be abandoned before it ever left paper. The successful rival plan from the same year, based on a design by Domenico Trezzini, turned Vasilievskii Island into a less interesting grid-work of canals and streets without an architectural centerpiece. Only the easternmost tip of Vasilievskii Island (Strel'ka), home to the Stock Exchange and Rostral Columns, along with the nearby southern embankment with its university, academy, and museum buildings, was truly part of official imperial Petersburg.[78] Still, even this most settled part of Vasilievskii houses the Kunstkamera, Peter the Great's collection of curiosities, where skeletons were said to roam the halls at night. Similarly, the first director of the Academy of Arts, the architect Alexander Kokorinov, was believed to have hung himself in the Academy attic and to have haunted the building ever since, along with the ghost of the sculptor Mikhail Kozlovskii.[79] The genuine Egyptian sphinxes on the Academy embankment, angry at being removed from their ancient place of rest, caused psychological disturbances among area residents.

The rest of Vasilievskii Island remained sparsely settled due to its high risk of flooding and was almost completely unoccupied to the north beyond the Smolenskoe Cemetery (technically another island, then known as Golodai, believed to be the site of unconsecrated graves for criminals and prostitutes, as well as the secret burial site of the five executed Decembrist leaders). A recent culturological survey of Petersburg real estate termed this relatively undeveloped part of the city a "sleeping beauty" whose main streets "lead nowhere except from water to water."[80] Even the origins of Vasilievskii Island's name are obscure, honoring a fifteenth-century Novgorodian governor, a simple fisherman and his wife, or possibly a Petrine-era artillery commander.[81]

Chartkov, the protagonist of Gogol's story "The Portrait" (Portret) liveD on Vasilievskii Island, as did Svidrigailov from Dostoevsky's Crime and Punishment, and the terrorist Dudkin from Bely's Petersburg. Ghosts of Russian literature that might have been similarly haunt Vasilievskii Island, since two of Gogol's unfinished works from the early 1830s are set here. Gogol's first fragment, "The Terrible Hand" (Strashnaia ruka), is subtitled "A Tale from a Book Named: Moonlight in the Broken Window of an Attic on Vasilievskii Island on the Sixteenth Line," foreshadowing the fragment's literary demise with a long string of partial structures. The fragment reads simply, "It was long after midnight. A single streetlamp capriciously illuminated the street, threw a frightening gleam on the stone buildings and left in darkness the wooden structures, which were completely transformed from gray to black."[82] The second fragment, "The Streetlamp Was Fading Out" (Fonar' umiral), begins "on one of the most distant lines of Vasilievskii Island," with a corresponding contrast between partly illuminated stone buildings and wooden structures pressed into invisibility by the surrounding darkness. The student from Derpt walking through this scene is afraid neither of robbers nor of his own "enormous shadow, whose head was lost in the dark gloom." A house on Bolshoi Prospect draws his attention, and he peers through a gap in the shutters, where he sees dressmaking materials strewn about a lamp-lit room. In the corner stood a "slender female figure" in a dazzling white dress. "A woman is more than a woman when she is in white," notes the narrator, echoing the student's own impressions. "She is a tsarina, an apparition, she is everything that resembles the most harmonious dream . . . What sparks fly along one's veins when a white dress gleams amidst the gloom." The narrator adds, "I say 'amidst the gloom' because everything else seems to be darkness in such a case."

The "Streetlamp" fragment concludes just as the woman's face moves out of the shadow and, at the same moment, the student notices a black-frocked man with an odd profile standing nearby. The insistent play between light and shadow in these fragments seems particularly apt, as the fragments themselves represent briefly illuminated bits of Gogol's literary art surrounded by silent darkness. The fragments come into view as the reader's attention falls upon them, as do the indistinctly perceived features of Vasilievskii Island. Familiar diurnal Petersburg seems precariously perched at the tip of the island, nearly crowded off into the water by the encroaching murky gloom.

The Vyborg side, across the Neva from Liteinyi Prospect, is another Petersburg neighborhood subject to legends. Wolves were rumored to roam in this area, where Goncharov's Oblomov takes up residence during his retreat from the world. The Vyborg side shared a border with Sweden, and its history dates from the pre-Petrine period, when small Russian settlements tried to secure the territory.[83] This area remained largely unsettled until the final decades before the Revolution. Even during the mid-nineteenth century, Goncharov depicts the Vyborg side as a small provincial community of kitchen gardens with chickens wandering the unpaved streets. The Vyborg side was also home to industrial facilities for sugar, leather, and beer, situated at a remove from the city center along the Poliustrovskaia embankment, former site of eighteenth-century summer mansions built for Catherinian grandees. Only in 1870, when the Finland railway station was constructed on the Vyborg side close to the Neva, did residential areas become populous. Even after that, however, the landscape was dominated by legend-generating landmarks such as the gloomy Kresty prison complex, constructed in 1890, whose architect the tsar reportedly locked up for life, so that the prison layout would remain a strict state secret. Cabdrivers did not like to cross the Liteinyi Bridge onto the Vyborg side at night, since it was rumored that students from the Military-Medical Academy lay in wait for passers-by, whom they would strangle and then use in their anatomical experiments.[84]

Vasilievskii Island and the Vyborg side were productive sites for legends because they contained a great deal of uninhabitable, unoccupied space. The Kolomna neighborhood, although located on the Admiralty side of the Bolshaia Neva (that is, relatively close to the city center), also represents an ambiguous space, where official Petersburg gives way to a terrain of undocumented lives and untold stories. Kolomna encompasses the territory to the west of the Kriukov Canal, bounded by the Moika and Fontanka waterways, beginning just outside of Theater Square and extending toward the port area into a series of tiny islands. During the nineteenth century, marginal types inhabited Kolomna—retirees, widows, and men who worked on the wharves. Literary inhabitants of Kolomna include Gogol's demonic moneylender from "The Portrait," Evgenii from Pushkin's "The Bronze Horseman," and the comedic protagonists of "A Little House in Kolomna."

Gogol's narrator from "The Portrait" describes this area in the liminal terms that characterize a site congenial to oral lore: "Here everything differs from the other parts of Petersburg; here there is neither capital nor provinces; as you cross over into the streets of Kolomna, you seem to feel all of the dreams and enthusiasms of youth leaving you. Here the future does not visit, everything here is quietness and retirement, all of the sediment of capital-city movement has settled." The inhabitants of Kolomna "exhibit a kind of murky, ashy exterior, like a day when there is neither storm nor sun . . . fog disperses and robs all objects of sharp definition."[85] The quietness and lack of definition in Kolomna are a deceptive cover for legends, however.[86] Stories circulated about hidden treasures concealed in the palace once inhabited by Aleksei Bobrinskii, putative lovechild of Catherine the Great and Grigory Orlov. "Litovskii Castle," late eighteenth-century regimental quarters converted to a prison where the city executioner lived, was another site rampant with legend. One of the sculptural angels from the castle roof was said to roam the hallways of the prison at night, knocking at the cells of those slated for death.

The late nineteenth-century psychiatric hospital of St. Nicholas the Miracle-Worker on the left bank of the Priazhka canal similarly inspired its share of urban legend. All three Kolomna legend-places themselves mark cultural borders—of social standing, criminal behavior, and sanity.

Like Gogol's "The Portrait," Vsevolod Krestovskii's 1864 novel Petersburg Slums (Peterburgskie trushchoby) recreates the experience of entering Kolomna for the reader. Krestovskii's narrator traces the contrast as a carriage ride proceeds along Ofitserskaia Street, where the constant bustle "speaks to the prox-

FIGURE 4.2. Litovskii Castle in Ruins, from Pavel Shillingovskii engravings in 1923 *Peterburg, ruiny i vozrozhdenie,* 1923. (Courtesy of Houghton Library at Harvard.)

imity of the city center," and then through Theater Square with its brightly illuminated entranceways and windows. As soon as the carriage crosses the Litovskii Bridge over the Kriukov Canal, the city outskirts begin, and Ofitserskaia Street "seems the same, and yet not the same." The buildings are lower and smaller, there are fewer people, and less noise. The narrator marvels at the sharp contrast: "There, in back of you—noise and movement, the flash of lights and of society life, ballet and opera, all the signs of merriment and idleness. But here—quiet and darkness, the absence of people. Here, the first thing that greets you on the other side of the bridge is the gloomy city prison, which you would not have distinguished in its enfolding darkness as you rode up to one of the two theaters some evening."[87] Legend-friendly areas suggest the experience of leaving the known, but they simultaneously impel stories to issue forth and cross over into the main part of Petersburg. Legends exist because of these divisions—marked by structures such as the Litovskii Bridge—but they also exist to transcend and obscure these very boundaries. Descriptions of entering Kolomna take readers to the border of the unknown, nudge them over, and leave them in this territory, enacting the requisite circumstance that allows legends to find new carriers.

Individual monumental structures as well as specific neighborhoods gave rise to Petersburg urban legends, as in the case of St. Isaac's Cathedral. Its architect Auguste Montferrand died one month after the opening of the cathedral, which had been under construction during the period 1818–58. It was subsequently said that a fortune-teller had foretold Montferrand's death immediately following the completion of his grand project.[88] (Urban legend very often recounts these uncanny predictions after the fact.) Other rumors asserted that Montferrand died from mortification after being slighted by Alexander II. Many believed that the Romanov dynasty would fall once all repairs and renovations of the cathedral were complete—a goal that was reached, apparently, in 1916.[89]

Legends attached themselves to other well-known features of the Petersburg cityscape, such as the 1841 Klodt sculptural groupings on the Anichkov Bridge, which stand at the intersection of Nevsky Prospect and the Fontanka. During the eighteenth century, this place constituted the southern boundary of the capital, where documents were checked before visitors could enter the city limits, and thus a border lending itself to the free movement of legend. Petersburg lore tells of Peter Klodt's death immediately upon his embarrassing discovery that tongues had been omitted on two of the four sculptural horses. More outrageously, some said Klodt had revenged himself on an enemy by depicting his foe's face under the tail of one of the bronze horses.[90] The sculptures are thus believed to confirm legend in their own physical aspect, but there are no accounts of anyone actually checking them.

Perhaps the eeriest single structure in Petersburg was the Mikhailovskii Castle, built at the intersection of the Moika and Fontanka canals in accordance with Emperor Paul's desire to secure himself against attacks. The brooding castle was surrounded by a moat, accessible only by drawbridge raised at night, and defended by cannons. The entire history of the Mikhailovskii Castle is subject to legend.[91] Paul was reportedly inspired to build it by dreams and premonitions. In order to complete construction with the desired speed, Paul commandeered marble and stone from the site of St. Isaac's Cathedral, whose builders then had to use brick. A mysterious prediction that proved correct stipulated that Paul would die at precisely the age corresponding to the number of letters in the castle's frieze inscription: "Thy house is like the Lord's shrine for thy lifetime" (Domu tvoemu podobaet" sviatynia Gospodnia v" dolgotu dnei)—also taken from St. Isaac's Cathedral.[92] Paul lived in his castle for little more than a month before being assassinated by his own military leaders in March 1801, apparently with the implicit consent of his son. Might he have been punished for desecrating St. Isaac's, itself a locus of legend?

After 1801, it was said, at exactly midnight each night, the shade of the murdered emperor appeared at the palace windows holding a lighted candle.

The site of the Mikhailovskii Castle had been formerly occupied by Empress Elizabeth's gorgeous Rastrellian Summer Palace, which Paul ordered torn down—just as Elizabeth had, in her time, destroyed the previous Summer Palace on the same spot, beloved by her predecessor Anna Ioannovna. In 1822,

FIGURE 4.3. Mikhailovskii Castle. (Author's Collection.)

the Mikhailovskii Castle was transformed into an engineering academy—attended by the young Dostoevsky during the period 1837–43—retaining its original form only in the grandest halls. From this time, the building was generally known as the Engineer's Castle. The Mikhailovskii Castle exemplifies the layerings and overwritings in the Petersburg cityscape that provide fertile ground for urban legend. The castle's history recounts a chain of repeated displacement—the endless destruction or diversion of resources needed to give it life. Each twist in the castle's prehistory, history, and posthistory leaves the ghost of a story behind.

The Mikhailovskii Castle also typifies the preromantic tendencies in Russian art of Paul's time.[93] In its stylistic contrast with the Petersburg architectural landscape, the Mikhailovskii Castle exemplifies the preromantic aesthetic, separating itself gloomily from the world like the castle in a Gothic novel, and reflecting the contrary qualities of its master. Rather than inhabiting an ancestral home already filled with legends of the past, Paul built his stylized stronghold after tearing down the Elizabeth Summer Palace where he was born and educated as a child. The Mikhailovskii Castle thus represents difference with a difference, individual exception within the larger cultural exception that is Petersburg itself.

The palace was not treated as an important architectural site, however, at least in the opinion of the Marquis de Custine, who in 1839 perhaps overestimated its value as a forty-year-old antique:

I am not surprised that the Russians neglect their ancient architectural monuments; these are witnesses of their history, which, for the most part, they are glad to forget. When I observed the black steps, the deep canals, the massive bridges, and the deserted porticos of this ill-omened palace, I asked its name; and the answer called to my mind the catastrophe which placed Alexander on the throne, while all the circumstances of the dark scene which terminated the reign of Paul I presented themselves to my imagination. . . . At the present day, Russians pass the old Michael Palace without daring to look at it.[94]

In Nikolai Leskov's 1882 story "The Apparition in the Engineer's Castle: From a Cadet's Memoirs" (*Prividenie v Inzhenernom zamke: iz kadetskikh vospominanii*), the legend of the castle, invoked portentously by the Marquis, is the jumping-off point for an exorcism in a quasisatirical vein. The story opens by asserting, "Buildings, like people, have their own reputations," and some buildings—such as the Mikhailovskii Palace—are considered "unclean."[95] The narrator reviews legends about the castle from the time of Paul, but dwells upon the nineteenth-century era of the engineering cadets, promising to put an end to all the rumors.[96]

According to Leskov's narrator, new cadets were terrified of the locked room where Paul had died, and where his ghost was rumored to live. One cadet found a way into the mysterious chamber, to which he came secretly over a period of several months, and would drape himself in a sheet and stand at the window, which looked out on Sadovaia Street, nodding his head and bowing. When the mischief-maker was apprehended, he was subjected to corporal punishment and "disappeared forever from the institution." A rumor arose that the cadet had died during the whipping, and that *his* ghost now wandered the castle, "all cut up from lashing," wearing a funeral wreath. The cadets continued to believe in Paul's ghost, even those among them who sometimes staged mock "visitations."

In "1859 or 1860," four cadets were subjected to a fright, which the narrator recounts "in the words of one of the participants in this unseemly graveside joke." The head of the establishment, General Lamnovskii, had recently died. To revenge themselves on the despotic General while he was alive, the cadets had initiated a rumor that "Lamnovskii consorted with satanic forces and made demons haul blocks of marble" intended for St. Isaac's Cathedral, thus casting him as a reincarnation of the murdered Paul. When the General had guests, cadets in sheets would stage a funeral procession, as if demons were enacting the long-awaited end of their oppressor. The General's angelic wife had been reportedly the only person who could soothe his bad nature, but she had never been seen by any of the cadets, and was apparently an invalid. At any rate, the General died during the gloomy late autumn season, and his body was laid out in his apartments with four cadets standing guard while the other castle occupants attended funeral services.

Among the cadet guards was "K-din," an inveterate prankster whom Lamnovskii had sworn to punish. K-din boastfully asserted that the dead General could do nothing to him now, even if K-din were to seize the corpse by its nose, which he did, triumphantly. At this, a terrible sigh seemed to come from the coffin, and the hapless K-din was pursued by a "wave" of muslin—the shroud with which the corpse had been covered. As K-din lay on the floor in terror, awaiting the dead General's wrath, a white shade emerged from the portieres.

Leskov's narrator goes to great lengths in describing the apparition—a "haggard figure" with a thin, bluish-white face, "feverish" eyes that gleamed with an "unhealthy fire," disheveled gray hair, skeletal arms, and lips that were "completely black and open." With tortured, shaking steps, the apparition approached the coffin, emitting deep gasps. The ghost paused by the prone K-din, unhooking the muslin from his button, then gazed at him with "inexpressible sadness," and made the sign of the cross. Moving to the catafalque to embrace the dead General, the apparition broke into sobs, revealing itself as the General's wife, herself on the point of death, paying a final visit to her husband. In the cadet's own words, the four companions forever remembered the castle's "last apparition," who forgave their terrible prank "according to the sacred law of love."

While it is true that Leskov's story purports to dispel the legends connected with Mikhailovskii Castle, the story actually performs a more complex feat. "The Apparition in the Engineer's Castle" titillates the reader with a sequence of terrifying possibilities (Paul's ghost, the ghost of the whipped cadet, Lamnovskii's ghost, and the unidentified ghost behind the portieres). The final revelation does not negate the satisfyingly suspenseful effect of the entire preceding narrative. In fact, the ending is fully compatible with the spirit of urban legend, particularly at the moment when, as it seems to the watching cadets, "two deaths were kissing at the coffin" in the best spirit of Edgar Allan Poe. Even divested of its supernatural elements, the story of the cadets itself passes into urban legend via Leskov's literary text, whose title continues to assert the presence of a ghost.

As in the case of the Mikhailovskii Castle, legends can be recovered by the practice of cultural archeology, which excavates down through the layers of time to uncover complex relationships between strata. In this way, Toporov chose a physical site as one of the seven "myth-texts" he explores in "Petersburg Texts and Petersburg Myths"—"The Myth of the Polovtsov House on Kamennyi Island."[97] At the time of Toporov's visit in 1990, the Polovtsov House, an imposing private home built between 1910 and 1920, had become a sanatorium for patients suffering from digestive-system disorders. When Toporov slips inside to look around, the female porter apprehends him, but is softened by his genuine interest in the building and recounts the story of Polovtsov's daughter. Perhaps, as suggested earlier, narrators do choose appropriate narratees, but often in the case of urban legend, a passerby, whether random or predestined, becomes the legend's recipient, and sometimes in becoming a participant, is swallowed by the legend. As when he visited the grave of Saint Ksenia at the

Smolenskoe cemetery, Toporov investigates urban legend from the inside, not as a careful reader, but as a member of the Petersburg community that the legend constitutes.

The house, according to the porter, was haunted by what Toporov calls the "quasi-historical myth" of Polovtsov's daughter, who reportedly threw herself out of the window and drowned in a well. She had apparently been distraught over a sculptural depiction of herself nearly naked in a chiton and being ogled by a satyr, which her stern father had commissioned as punishment for a flirtation. Although specific features of the physical surroundings (the relative positions of window and well, for example) cast doubt on the reliability of the story, the presence of a statue, which did resemble the girl's portrait, seems provisionally to supply confirmation.[98] Toporov notes that the Polovtsov House was the former site of a dacha from the eighteenth century. In August 1836, while a guest at this dacha, Alexander Pushkin composed his well-known "Monument" poem. The implicit juxtaposition of Pushkin's tribute to the permanence of literary art and the marble statue whose story has been half lost gives Toporov's account its special resonance.

Literary "monuments," too, can serve as the basis for urban legend. For years, Petersburg residents argued over whether the real-life model for the Countess in Pushkin's story "The Queen of Spades" was the Princess Golitsyna who lived at the corner of Malaia Morskaia and Gorokhovaia Streets or the Countess Iusupova who lived on Liteinyi Prospect in a house with what Stolpianskii called a "rather gloomy, mysterious appearance." The great debunker Stolpianskii, while conceding the tempting likeness of this latter house to Pushkin's conception, pointed out that construction of the Liteinyi building had been completed only in 1859—twenty-two years after Pushkin's death.[99] The confusion over mutually contradictory legends seems particularly apt in this case, since gossip, rumor, and misinformation are the engines that drive the plot in "The Queen of Spades" itself. Furthermore, the end of Pushkin's story represents the beginning of a new oral legend—one about the hapless Hermann that will doubtless circulate throughout the city for a long time to come.[100] In any case, the street intersection where the Golitsyna "Queen of Spades" house was located came to be known as a haunted place that exerted a mystical, often negative influence on the lives of its inhabitants.[101]

Textual Sites: Detecting Oral Narrative

Russian writers from the imperial period imported and transplanted literary genres current in the West—among them the epistolary novel, society tale, travel memoir, and Bildungsroman—but there do exist some notable gaps in the reflection that nineteenth-century literary fashion found in Russian letters. The detective fiction as a staple of Western urban literature is largely absent in the Petersburg tradition, although the works of Edgar Allan Poe, Charles Dickens, Émile Gaboriau, Wilkie Collins, and Arthur Conan Doyle would have provided ample literary prototypes for such a project.[102] The detective as a literary figure cloaked himself in Enlightenment rationality and employed the latest realist techniques of observation and analysis. He worked to free urban residents from lingering romantic literary convention and belief in the supernatural. In this, Sherlock Holmes resembles Professor Van Helsing in Bram Stoker's 1897 *Dracula*, whom Richard Lehan calls "a man of European science" as well as Christian faith, dedicated to ridding London of "the irrational element, a modern avatar of Dionysus."[103] The detective character puts the pieces of the fragmented nineteenth-century city back together into a coherent whole, an operation the genre requires him to enact repeatedly in order to hold chaos at bay.[104] Later nineteenth-century detective fiction is indebted to the often lurid "novel of urban mysteries," a French- and English-language prose subgenre that includes Victor Hugo's 1831 *Notre-Dame de Paris*, Charles Dickens's novels of the late 1830s and early 1840s (*Oliver Twist, The Old Curiosity Shop, Martin Chuzzlewit*), Edgar Allan Poe's "The Murders in the Rue Morgue" (1841) and "The Mystery of Marie Rogêt" (1845), and Eugène Sue's 1842–43 *Mystères de Paris*.[105] This earlier genre (discussed in Chapter 5) was represented in Russia, but failed to grow into a true detective tradition. It may be that reason as a human capability was not granted the value in the Russian tradition that it held in the West, and that Russian readers were more likely to be humbled, shown how much they did not and could not know. Perhaps the Russian state performed more than enough surveillance and dectection of the populace on its own.

Another partial explanation for the absence of a master-detective figure in Russian literary history may lie in crime fiction's low cultural prestige and in its lack of real commercial success during the nineteenth century, as illustrated by the case of writer Alexander Shkliarevskii, sometimes called the "Russian Gaboriau," a provincial who came to Petersburg in 1869. Inspired by the example of Dostoevsky's 1866 *Crime and Punishment*, Shkliarevskii authored crime fiction with attention-grabbing titles such as "Why Did He Kill Them?" (1872, *Otchego on ubil ikh?*), "What Killed Him?" (1877, *Chto pogubilo ego?*), and "What Incited the Murder?" (1879, *Chto pobudilo k ubiistvu?*), which he published in low-paying popular newspapers, barely eking out a living. This fiction differed from its Western counterparts in its emphasis on the criminal protagonist, the socioeconomic circumstances leading to the crime, and the attendant legal proceedings, rather than on the skillful and suspenseful unraveling of a mystery by the master detective.[106] Rather than remaining a beloved part of literary tradition, the works by Shkliarevskii and others like him were quickly forgotten.[107]

While it is difficult to speculate about cultural factors that might account for the lack of detective fiction per se in the Russian literary tradition, it does seem that Petersburg urban legend, as manifested in several well-known fictional texts, resists the patterns of this nineteenth-century genre. In this, urban legend in Petersburg recalls Tsvetan Todorov's claim that the fantastic narrative "is not characterized by the simple presence of supernatural phenomena or beings, but by the hesitation [emphasis mine] which is established in the reader's perception of the events represented."[108] In a detective-like manner, readers and characters must puzzle over the generic context of such a story, oscillating between supernatural and natural explanations for the mysterious occurrences, without ever reaching a final resolution. The fantastic "implies an integration of the reader into the world of the characters; that world is defined by the reader's own ambiguous perception of the events narrated."[109] In other words, the perceptions of an "implicit reader," a frustrated detective, are encoded in the fantastic text. This affinity explains why urban legend lends itself so admirably to being passed along a series of temporary owners—any and all can play the hesitating reader-detective's role.

In 1848, the poet Vasilii Zhukovskii wrote an article entitled "Something About Specters (Nechto o privideniiakh)," in which he notes the strong interest of the Russian public in this subject.[110] In keeping with the vague phrasing of his title, Zhukovskii asserts that it is equally impossible to believe or to fail to believe in specters, since such phenomena "remain for us forever between yes and no." The Creator has placed "secret curtains" between our human world and other worlds, he declares, and these curtains, although "impenetrable," occasionally lift slightly "so that we know that there is something behind them." Zhukovskii warns that reason can never obtain proof positive as to the existence of the spiritual world and can only harm itself with vain efforts to know that which should remain obscure. In place of evidence, Zhukovskii offers his readers baffling *stories*, which function as talisman-like reminders of the inexplicable. As I hope to show, Petersburg literature often has recourse to a similar strategy regarding urban mysteries.

Three literary works from the Russian tradition—Pushkin's "The Lonely Cottage on Vasilievskii Island" (1828), Gogol's "The Portrait" (1834, 1842), and Lermontov's "Shtoss" (1841)—exemplify the reciprocal relationship between Petersburg urban legend and written texts, reflecting in conception, contents, and reception the uncanny abilities of oral stories to find human beings and published materials to serve as their cultural conveyances. Each of these works enacts a failed sleuthing attempt directed at apprehending urban legend and subordinating it to text. In this failure of detection, however, lies a hidden tribute to the resourceful proliferation of oral lore.

Pushkin's 1828 story "The Lonely Cottage on Vasilievskii Island" represents one of the most interesting conjunctions of urban legend and literary text, and as such, an unresolvable conundrum. The text has an ambiguous status—it is considered part of Pushkin's oeuvre, but somewhat questionably so, and normally relegated to an appendix in multivolume Russian editions of his works, unlike Pushkin's unfinished fictional fragments and plans, which are normally included in the volume with the rest of his fictional prose.[111] "The Lonely Cottage," in the history of its creation and publication as well as its contents, exemplifies the productive relationship between literature and legend; both inside and outside of the text, the story passes through multiple tellers before being manifested in print form.

At a social evening in 1828, a young writer named Vladimir Titov heard Pushkin tell a story of the devil, who, disguised as a society swell named Varfolomei, wreaks havoc in the lives of a weak-spirited young man and his poor but kindhearted relatives, an elderly widow and her daughter. Titov was so impressed that he later transcribed the story from memory and published it in Del'vig's almanac *Northern Flowers* of 1829, under the pseudonym of Tit Kosmokratov.[112] There the matter lay until 1879, when Titov, then in his 70s, wrote a letter to A. V. Golovin disclosing the circumstances behind "The Lonely Cottage" and its connection with Pushkin (although Titov coyly continued to refer to the transcriber as "Kosmokratov"). Titov claimed that he had brought the manuscript to the famous writer and incorporated the latter's suggestions before submitting the story for publication. These events and the text of Titov's letter were made known to the public when A. I. Del'vig included them in his 1912 memoirs, and the matter was discussed in periodical literature of the same period.[113] The existence of a fictional plan by Pushkin on a similar theme ("The Devil in Love," 1821–23), as well as the coincident figures of the old widow and her daughter in "The Bronze Horseman," provided further evidence in support of the attribution.[114] In a 1914 article, Vladislav Khodasevich declared that "The Lonely Cottage" represented a vital missing link in Pushkin scholarship, revealing the "common internal connection in a whole series of Pushkin's Petersburg tales"—"The Little House in Kolomna," "The Queen of Spades," and "The Bronze Horseman.[115]

"The Lonely Cottage" in its basic outlines and most vivid details would thus seem to belong to Pushkin, whom Titov's letter credits with particulars such as the apocalyptic number 666 and the demonic party guests who conceal horns beneath their wigs a play cards for souls instead of money. Still, it is hardly possible that Titov accurately copied down from memory a story of thirty pages. The rambling, inefficient narration of "The Lonely Cottage" moreover differs markedly from Pushkin's famously taut prose works from the 1830s.[116] Just as Titov was haunted by the tale he heard at the Karamzin home (in his 1879 letter, he claimed he "could not sleep for nearly the entire night"), the text-specter of "The Lonely Cottage" hangs over Pushkin's prose oeuvre. Ultimately, like an urban legend, the extant text of "The Lonely Cottage" belongs to nobody. What is more, its ambiguous status—transcribed oral masterwork or inferior literary effort—is encoded within the work itself.

"The Lonely Cottage" opens with the contrast between the grandly imperial southern bank of Vasilievskii Island and the undeveloped northern bank opposite Petrovskii Island, where the widow and her daughter live:

> the stone buildings thin out, yielding to wooden huts; among the huts vacant lots come in view; at last buildings disappear altogether, and you walk along . . . to the

outermost elevation, adorned with one or two forlorn houses and a few trees; a ditch, overgrown with tall nettle and burdock, separates this elevation from the levee that serves as a bulwark against inundation; and beyond the levee stretches a meadow, muddy as a swamp, which constitutes the beach. These deserted places are melancholy even in the summer, and become much more so in the winter, when the meadow, the sea, and the woods lining the shores of Petrov Island on the opposite side are all buried under white snowdrifts as though in graves.[117]

This initial paragraph, with its details and careful phrasing, seems most unlike oral narration. As the description moves across the story's opening topography, however, familiar markers grow sparse and finally disappear, like letters being erased from a page. The final phrase of the opening paragraph completes the disorienting transition to weightless, invisible oral legend, as the hypothetical snow obscures and buries all remaining traces. The story then begins in the nonpresence of legend, returning to the events of "some decades ago." Near the end of the story, the lonely cottage burns to its foundations, and, the narrator notes, "the lot on which it had stood has for some reason remained vacant to this day."[118] The narrator seeks a return to the legend's place of origin, but absence marks the spot.

From this point, "The Lonely House" does suggest a transcription of oral narration. The chatty narrator cannot recall certain details of the story, such as the precise occupation of the heroine's father, "a civil servant who had served in a collegium, I do not recall which one." This device of forgetting proposes the story as mimetically reproducing the features of oral narration. Like an improvising storyteller, the narrator shows poor judgment about the criteria for inclusion in his story, digressing to provide irrelevant information. When the priest arrives too late to give the dead widow the sacraments, the narrator confides, "He had not been on particularly good terms with the late widow, regarding her as an evil woman; but he loved [her daughter] Vera, about whom he had heard many good things from his daughter." Is the garrulous narrator designed to be incompetent, or did Pushkin himself make these errors in performing on the spot? Perhaps Titov was simply an inadequate transcriber? It is difficult to say, since this folksy and inept oral narrator-persona is not consistently manifested in "The Lonely Cottage." He seems all too skillful at managing the separate narrative strands at key points, in a manner that recalls Pushkin's Belkin tales. The widow's elderly maidservant assumes narrative responsibility for several pages, while the hero Pavel, who had been delirious for three days and thus out of commission as an eyewitness to the story events, rides back with her to Vasilievskii Island. The point of view then shifts neatly at the precise moment of Pavel's arrival. The story similarly shows occasional excessive concern in accounting for how information could have reached specific characters: "It may be surmised that Vera, before her death, confided not only to her father confessor, but also to Pavel, those circumstances of the last year of her life that had been known to her alone."

In contrast, the narrator winks at the reader-listener by including details whose significance has eluded the hapless Pavel. Thus the narrator mentions that the mysterious Varfolomei's hand is "cold" and his laugh is "diabolical." The significance of these references grows ever more obvious to the reader-listener, in a choreographed literary crescendo that seems far too subtle for an oral narration. Moreover, the "meaning" of Pavel's three dreams—which feature two flowers, two goldfish, and two stars, all menaced by a black presence—is so transparent as to be laughable. A classic oral narration would be more likely to play tricks on its listeners, letting them be duped along with its characters during the telling. The double voicing evident even in this rather crudely constructed text seems much more typical of a written narrative.

Invoking methods of both oral and written communication, "The Lonely Cottage" ironically underscores the tension between these two modes, oscillating between the teasing incompleteness of oral legend and the expected closure of written narration. Pavel reverses his course of action completely upon receiving a note from the treacherous Countess, which he believes to affirm the truth of her love. The narrator exclaims, "How stupid lovers are! No sooner had Paul glanced through these magic lines than . . . as far as he was concerned, the whole of the present, past, and future crowded together in that slip of paper; he pressed it to his heart, kissed it, and brought it to the light to read it over and over." In its status as written text, the Countess's note is absurdly credible to Pavel, who declares, "No! This cannot be deception; I am indeed a happy man." Although the Countess pays little attention to him when he arrives, Pavel interprets her languid glances in terms of the "mystical alphabet of lovers, incomprehensible to laymen." Only when he finds himself in a strange cab being driven haphazardly through unfamiliar neighborhoods does Pavel recall "old tales about dead bodies found in Volkovo Field." In the postlude to "The Lonely Cottage," Pavel takes refuge in the comforting world of written text, secluding himself in an attempt to hide from legend. He settles on his remote ancestral estate, "grew a beard and long hair; did not leave his study for three months at a time; gave orders to his servants in writing."

Although the story plays at privileging written text over oral legend, however, the true purpose of "The Lonely Cottage" is to animate legend through the merely instrumental medium of text, just as Varfolomei's dark powers cause the dead widow's corpse to raise her head and gesture with her hand. The end of "The Lonely Cottage" accordingly depicts the events of the story trailing off into multiple versions in various generic registers. A police corporal believed he had seen Satan himself when he rushed into the burning cottage to retrieve the widow's body, and becomes one repository of one variant, which he recounts in taverns for the rest of his life. The tavern customers become new carriers of the story. Another carrier of legend is the ancient servant Lavrentii, the sole witness of Pavel's bizarre behavior at the end of his life ("Lavrentii used to say . . .").

The struggle for primacy between oral and written text continues up to the story's last lines. The final paragraph, with its explicit invocation of readers, points to the transcription of oral legend into the text before the reader: "Pavel died long before reaching old age. His and Vera's conjoined story is known to a few middle-class people in Petersburg; I myself heard it related orally (*po izust-nomu predaniiu*). But you, estimable reader, are actually in a better position to judge whether one can give credit to such a story." The frame narration of the story—the short tour of the island's northern bank and the aforementioned concluding paragraph—establishes the transmission of the possibly *fictional* story, from anonymous "middle-class" tellers to the mediating narrator, and then to printed text that offers itself to skeptical scrutiny. Still, "The Lonely Cottage" does not acknowledge the most interesting act of narration connected with its contents, which is the process by which a story Pushkin related to a salon audience became a published story written by Vladimir Titov. Noting the migration of the demon motif from Pushkin's drawings, poetic fragments, and plans for works of prose and drama, one scholar declares, "Pushkin's conception searches for and discovers new forms for the expression of its essence, its idea."[119] In this, "The Lonely Cottage" as an ambiguous fact of Russian literary history seems closer to urban legend, ever on the lookout for a free ride from a textual host. Whether Pushkin's conception or not, "The Lonely Cottage" has only benefited from its association with the revered writer.

Gogol's 1834 story "The Portrait" (revised 1842) most clearly of all his works exemplifies the workings of urban legend. Vissarion Belinsky called this under-examined story "Gogol's unsuccessful attempt in the fantastical genre," finding even the revised second half with its toned-down supernatural effects "unbearably bad."[120] "The Portrait," despite or perhaps even in keeping with its literary flaws, can be read as an allegory for urban legend, in which the transmission of the story-within-the-story—which assumes material form as the portrait—is represented as the main, infinitely recurring event.

"The Portrait" opens in a shop at Shchukin Dvor, where the artist Chartkov roots through piles of paintings and drawings, hoping to find an overlooked copy of a great masterwork. He buys an unfinished portrait of a man with disturbingly watchful eyes. This portrait has a peculiar influence on the young artist, inspiring a nested series of dreams that begin when the mysterious subject seems to climb out of the picture frame.[121] The cracked frame contains a roll of gold coins that sets Chartkov on the road to becoming a fashionable portrait-painter instead of a genuine artist. He eventually goes mad, imagining the terrifying portrait multiplying all around him, and expires in hellish agony. The doctor, "having heard quite a bit about his [Chartkov's] strange history, tried valiantly to uncover the mysterious relationship between these imagined apparitions and the events of his life, but did not succeed."[122] Part I ends with the hermeneutic puzzle laid out before the reader, who may hope to be more successful at solving it than the characters have been.

Part II of "The Portrait" begins some time later at the estate auction of an unidentified wealthy amateur collector. When the mysterious portrait is offered up to the audience, an artist steps from the crowd and offers to tell the portrait's story, which opens in Kolomna, where, during the reign of Catherine the Great, the moneylender depicted in the portrait plied his ignoble trade. All who borrowed money from him came to a tragic end, reports the artist, adding, "Whether this was simply people's opinion, silly superstitious gossip, or rumors spread intentionally remains uncertain."[123] The artist-narrator relates two such tragic stories—the first about a young man of good family whose soul became perversely twisted, and the second about a beauty whose jealous husband fatally stabbed himself. Additional stories of the lower classes follow in the artist's account, in abbreviated form: "An honest, sober man became a drunkard; a merchant's shop assistant robbed his employer; a cab-driver who had transported fares honestly for several years murdered a passenger for a two-kopeck piece."[124] All of these substories comprise the larger Kolomna legend of the satanic local figure.

Here, the artist-narrator turns to the story of his own father, who was commissioned by the moneylender to paint the portrait. When the moneylender died, the artist's father, still in possession of the unfinished portrait, underwent troubling changes in disposition. On the verge of burning the portrait, he instead gave it to a friend, who was in turn plagued by insomnia and evil thoughts. The friend's nephew took the portrait, but was tortured by horrible dreams and sold it to an art collector. The portrait had been on the loose from this time on, its whereabouts unknown, but the artist's father had begged his son to find and destroy it.

In the earlier 1834 version of "The Portrait," the artist's father claimed the moneylender was the "Antichrist" himself, but that a vision of the Blessed Virgin assured him that the demon would cease to exist if "someone portentously proclaims its history at the end of fifty years, during the first new moon."[125] The artist claims he did not believe his father's story, but had never been able to "convey (*pereskazat'*)" it to anyone, since "something" always prevented him from doing so. It so happens that thirty years had passed since the painting of the portrait when the artist's father performed his ritual narrative act, passing the story on to his son, and twenty more years had passed since that moment. Thus in the original version of Gogol's story, the *telling* of the story is the event toward which the entire text is directed—the final, full, formal telling before a gathered audience that promises to put an end to the story's travels.

At the oral story's conclusion in both versions of "The Portrait," the artist-narrator's eyes turn to the wall, as do those of the auction audience. In the earlier version, the moneylender's image grows faint and turns into an undistinguished landscape. In the 1842 version, the mysterious portrait disappears completely—apparently stolen while all were absorbed by the artist's tale. According to this final version, the legend can continue as the portrait goes on circulating and its truth is never really proven. Ever on the lookout for a new credulous fool, the unfinished portrait moves along its relay of victims—just like the story itself, which is similarly incomplete and just as compelling. Urban legend is the true hero of Gogol's story, asserting, like the moneylender, that it wants to "live" and that it needs to "exist in the world."[126] The published story Belinsky termed "unsuccessful" enacts the triumph of oral narration, with the reader as dupe instead of detective.

All victims connected with the arts in "The Portrait" become destroyers of true talent. In fact, however, every major character in "The Portrait" is an artist because each temporary holder of the portrait makes a contribution to the story. Rather than affirming the aesthetically conventional in art, "The Portrait" celebrates aesthetic disorder and itinerancy—from the stall full of motley artworks in Shchukin Dvor, to the diversely pitiable inhabitants of Kolomna, to the mass display of items at the estate auction. Rather than constituting a genre of limited form and device, Gogol's "The Portrait," like urban legend, is capacious, as a story of stories should be.

Mikhail Lermontov's fragment "Shtoss" provides both comment on and parody of the phenomenon of urban legend, extending even to the mystifying circumstances surrounding this fragment's creation. The Countess Rostopchina's memoirs tell of the occasion in early 1841 when Lermontov summoned thirty chosen friends to a reading of his new novel *Shtoss*, an event he claimed would last four hours. Lermontov entered the room "with a huge notebook under his arm," ordered a lamp brought in and the doors locked, and then commenced his reading, which lasted for fifteen minutes: "The inveterate joker tempted us with the first chapter of some fearful story begun by him only the day before. He had written twenty pages or so, and the remainder of the notebook consisted of blank paper. The novel stopped here, and was never finished."[127] Lermontov thus invited his audience to hear the ghost of a novel, in the form of a teasing story that only seemed to be going somewhere. While "Shtoss" may be a parody of Pushkin's "Queen of Spades" or a polemic against Russian romantics such as Zhukovskii and Odoevskii, this fragment also ponders the workings of urban legend. The story's name itself is part of the puzzle, with its multiple meanings of card game, servile interrogatory (*chto-s?*), and last name. With its multiple suggestions of mishearing and misunderstanding, "Shtoss" mockingly demonstrates that urban legend thrives on imperfect transmission.

"Shtoss" begins on the familiar ground of the society tale, as the artist Lugin and the lovely Minskaia banter about love at a salon. Lugin informs Minskaia that he is going mad, since for several days a voice in his ear has whispered a precise address: Stoliarnyi Lane, by the Kokushkin Bridge, the building of the titular councilor Shtoss, apartment number 27. Minskaia advises Lugin to cure himself by visiting this apartment, where he will doubtless find "some shoemaker or watchmaker," but the investigation to dispel mystery contributes to the perpetuation of the strange story, as expected.

Part II opens by setting a scene—a raw November morning, snow, dim light, and the occasional passer-by: "Of course, you could only encounter such pictures (*kartiny*) in the remote parts of the city, as, for example. . . by Kokushkin Bridge."[128] Here the reader encounters Lugin again, but from an estranged perspective as "a man of average height, neither thin nor stout, not slender, but with wide shoulders, in an overcoat and in general, dressed with taste." The scene's strangeness derives in part from the narrator's inconsistency, but also from the insistent perceptions of Lugin, who seems oddly disturbed when he asks directions of a cabdriver who drives past without responding. Lugin takes his own startled responses to the situation as evidence of the extraordinary—something tells him he will know the house at first glance, and when he hears the name "Shtoss," his heart beats harder, "as if sensing misfortune." When the janitor of Shtoss's building lists the unremarkable past inhabitants of apartment 27— a colonel, a German baron, and a merchant's mistress—Lugin thinks to himself, "How strange!" The strangeness and the story in "Shtoss" are both self-perpetuating.

Lugin declares he will take the apartment, and at that precise moment (as he himself notices, finding it "strange"), he catches sight of a man's portrait, which, although badly painted, conveys an arresting and "inexplicable" expression. Alone in his new apartment at midnight, Lugin receives a ghostly visitor, an old man resembling the portrait, whose form changes constantly, "becoming taller, then heavier, then almost completely shriveling up."[129] These details function as metafictional devices, since "Shtoss" itself is awkwardly put together, changing its tone repeatedly to suggest diverse story possibilities. The shifting specter also points to the protean nature of urban legend, while the ghostly "ideal woman" who soon appears drives Lugin onward in vain hope of resolving the conundrum. Perversely, Lermontov's story fragment dissolves into compulsive repetitions of the same card game that yield no definitive result: "Every night for a month this scene repeated itself: every night Lugin lost." The climax of the story is also its mysterious end: "He had to resolve upon a course of action. He made his decision." The story ends here, having it both ways with a nominal, but unrevealed resolution. The story remains open to all comers, as urban legends and literary fragments always do.[130] Like Lugin setting himself up in what seems to be someone else's apartment, urban legend takes up residence in a literary text, an only seemingly inhospitable medium that actually allows a legend to prolong its own narrative life. Urban legend undermines the possibility of textual resolution, and thus leads to the existence of unfinished fragments on this theme by famous Petersburg writers. These literary fragments, however, have proved compelling to readers for precisely this reason.

"The Lonely House on Vasilievskii Island," "The Portrait," and "Shtoss" all suspend explanatory power rather than resolving the puzzle. Classic nineteenth-century detective fiction cannot develop without the impulse to elucidate and demystify so lacking in Petersburg literature. Each of these three stories terminates with the loss of the hermeneutic trail, rather than with "Elementary, my dear Watson." Urban legend survives among the ramshackle structures of the incomplete or ambiguous written narrative, but not simply in defiance of story closure. Urban legend serves a valuable purpose, bridging the divide between print culture and the oral lore. Passing through diverse neighborhoods, populations, and media, urban legend is a creator of intermediate cultural space. Urban legends haunt places to which people are drawn. But more than anything, urban legends haunt literary texts, which have afforded such lore the most durable home of all.

CHAPTER FIVE

Literary Centers and Margins: Palaces, Dachas, Slums, and Industrial Outskirts

THE WORD for "city" in many languages carries a semantic association of enclosure or boundaries, yet urban growth must balance containment against expansion.[1] The clear delimitation of center and margins provided by city walls, gates, and customs barriers in various parts of the world gave way over time to expanding border-regions—encircling territories initially conceived as military defensive zones. Parkways and boulevards, palaces with large grounds, cemeteries, industrial facilities, and mass housing occupied fringe belts moving out from the city center. In Petersburg, urban expansion accelerated during the second half of the nineteenth century in step with the city's post-Emancipation growth rate. The margins of Petersburg became ever more distant from the center, as formerly peripheral areas such as Zagorodnyi Prospect (literally, the avenue that leads "beyond the city") accommodated new construction. The city extended into the Petersburg Side to the north and the Izmailovskii regiment camp-base area to the south.[2] Factories and workers were pushed into more remote territories such as Okhta, the Vyborg Side, the Obvodnyi canal embankments, Golodai Island, and the area beyond the Nevsky tollgate.

The city periphery is an ambiguous zone. Language, for example, can hold physically remote regions of the city at arm's length or, alternatively, can embrace them. The contrasting notions of "environs" (*okrestnosti*) and "outskirts" (*okrainy*) accordingly underscore the use of discursive inclusion and exclusion tactics on the part of St. Petersburg's chroniclers. The term *okrestnosti* encompasses the imperial palace-parks and thus includes them within the cultural territory of Petersburg. In contrast, marginal industrial areas are designated by the term *okrainy*, which emphasizes their relationship to the outermost border of the city and thus to their near-exclusion, even though the palace-parks actually lie at a greater physical distance from the center. In terms of social rather than physical margins, the most concentrated nineteenth-century slum neighborhood in Petersburg was located at the city center, although it was frequently depicted in literature as a foreign country.

The "Petersburg Text" sustains a social-moral focus on city slums, a fact proudly cited by cultural chroniclers, who consider this pervasive theme a centerpiece of the literary tradition. Other vital aspects of urban life, most notably industry, however, are consigned to the literary margins. The collective record of ambitious newcomers to the city discussed in chapter 6 belongs more ambiguously to the expansive middle space of Petersburg literary culture, as does the literature on the democratizing dacha regions treated in this chapter. This chapter and the one that follows treat Petersburg literary centers (palaces and slums), peripheries (industrial fiction), and meeting places (dacha life, the shared experience of provincials coming to the city) in order to articulate a model of Petersburg physical and cultural space in textual terms.

The literary works considered here contest the territory of the rapidly changing city by appropriating, investigating, or eliding areas associated with specific groups. The palace-parks gradually become public property, suggesting beautiful bound albums that catalogue tourist attractions and national treasures; the dacha regions evolve into the paraliterary province of middle-class discourse; the slums are crisscrossed by accounts in which melodrama, autobiography, and documentary find a common home; but the industrial outskirts receive no more than a sideways literary glance. Intelligentsia writers are implicated in all of these literary practices, since their permanently alienated and conflicted perspective on the city lies at the heart of Petersburg textual mapping. These writers could not help tracing those major shifts in the sociocultural landscape that brought about new spatial relations between populations in the imperial city.

The transitional literary and cultural environment of the later nineteenth century is underdocumented as such, or, at least, obscured by the scholarly attention accorded the preceding ("Golden Age") and subsequent ("Twilight") imperial periods.[3] This chapter reads the particular textual geography of Petersburg that was produced by emerging capitalism, widespread social change, and intellectual currents such as populism and Marxism, which collided with imperial nostalgia and retrograde literary tastes.[4]

Distant Centers: The Palace-Parks

The urban residential space of pre-Petrine Russia lacked a mediating territory such as that designated by the term *prigorod*—literally, "attached to the city" or "near the city"—and thus maintained a stricter distinction between fortressed towns and settlements (*poseleniia, posady, slobody*) or estates (*usad'by*).[5] Generally, as mentioned, "environs" (*okrestnosti*) denotes those surrounding areas of imperial Petersburg occupied by the lavish country residences of the imperial family. The construction or major renovation of each such palace would stimulate the Petersburg aristocracy to build new summer residences of their own nearby.

While the islands and dacha regions discussed in the next section are located primarily to the north of St. Petersburg, the major palace-parks are situated to the west and the south. Along the Peterhof road to the west lies Peter the Great's version of Versailles, Peterhof (Petrodvorets), planned by the architect Leblond and later expanded by Rastrelli for Empress Elizabeth. Prior to reaching Peter's palace, the Peterhof road passes the Strelna Palace, another early-eighteenth-century project originated by Leblond, which featured similarly styled fountains, terraces, and canals out to the sea. Past Peterhof, the road leads further west to Oranienbaum (Lomonosov), a palace-park overlooking the sea across from the Kronstadt island-fortress in the Finnish Gulf. Oranienbaum, named for an orangery that once stood near the palace, was originally established by Prince Men'shikov. It was significantly expanded later in the eighteenth century when ownership passed from Elizabeth to her nephew Peter III and then to his widow, Catherine the Great, who commissioned the construction of an enormous slide and a Chinese pavilion on the grounds. Inland and due south of Petersburg lie the palace-parks of Tsarskoe Selo (Pushkin), with its enormous rococo main residence constructed under Elizabeth, and nearby Pavlovsk, the exquisite country home of Paul's wife Maria Fedorovna, which dates from the 1780s and is thus the youngest of the imperial palaces. Even further to the south and to the west stands the most distant palace-park, Gatchina, built during Catherine's time by her lover Grigorii Orlov and presented to her son Paul after Orlov's death. Paul used it as a camp for large-scale military drills and maneuvers; later monarchs favored Gatchina for hunting and fishing.

Each palace-park, with its particular history and itinerary of attractions, is a complex cultural text. Each includes a main residence and a number of smaller villas, cottages, churches, pavilions, and monuments in diverse, even whimsical architectural styles, as well as (in some cases) imperial manufacturing works for luxury goods, and an associated village or small town. Individual palace-parks are also distinguished by their most notable outdoor sculptural groupings, fountains, and special gardens, as well as their interior design and art treasures.[6]

Peterhof's network of fountains with allegorical sculpture, for example, emphasizes Russia's domination of the surrounding water and marshlands. The crowned Neptune fountain in the Upper Garden, the Samson fountain commemorating the twenty-fifth anniversary of the Battle of Poltava, the Grand Canal leading from the sea to the baroque-style palace, the elevated site overlooking the Finnish Gulf—all contribute to the essential iconography of Peter the Great's Petersburg project, and to a symbolic system that defines the palace-park regardless of the additions and innovations made by subsequent monarchs. Even the smaller residences of Marly and Monplaisir on the Peterhof grounds contribute to this symbolic system, attesting to the simple tastes and modest living habits of Tsar Peter, despite the enormous power he wielded.

In contrast, the grounds at Tsarskoe Selo are associated with the imperial vision of Catherine the Great, combining the influences of Greek and Roman antiquity with Chinese stylization, Gothic revival, and English landscape gardening. The grounds of Tsarskoe Selo are a mosaic of late eighteenth-century military monuments, which coexist with promenade diversions such as the Cameron Gallery, the Grand and Little Caprices, and a pyramid. The nearby Pavlovsk palace-park projected its own system of signs through its Palladian master residence, artificial ruins, and sentimental references to family relationships embodied by the Family Grove, Temple of Friendship, and sepulchral monuments.

Not every visitor to a palace-park read its configuration of buildings, monuments, and grounds as a cohesive imperial text, however. Viewing Tsarskoe Selo during summer 1846, English visitor William Kinglake voiced the complaint that "pavilions, columns, cottages, and kiosks, Turkish, Dutch, Chinese, are scattered through the park in tasteless profusion." In his view, the tawdry colors of the palace facade gave it "the appearance of a London dowager, or a New Zealand chief, artistically prepared for action in their war-paint." Kinglake deplored the uneasy coexistence of Eastern and Western Christendom, pointing out that "Dannecker's Christ stands, inappropriately and irreverently, in a paltry building erected for the purpose, but not consecrated; so scrupulously observed are the Greek [Orthodox] canons, which are directed against image worship."[7] Kinglake dismisses the eclectic assemblage of treasures meant to proclaim the triumphs and impeccable taste of the Russian monarchy, his aesthetic ear deafened by the cultural Babel.

The palace-parks were, moreover, subject to the same temporal layering and overwriting as the rest of St. Petersburg. During the imperial period, the major residences both inside and outside the city were frequently redone to suit changing circumstances, when palaces changed hands between members of the imperial family and court favorites, or when a new ruler took a fancy to a previously secondary residence. Some palaces were torn down or incorporated into new structures, and others simply fell into disrepair. The Strelna Palace near Peterhof stood empty for nearly the entire second half of the eighteenth century.[8] The Ekaterinhof Palace, built for Peter's wife Catherine I across from Gutuevskii Island near the future site of the Narva Triumphal Arch, was neglected for a long period following Empress Elizabeth's death until Count Miloradovich took an interest in it during the reign of Alexander I.[9] Catherine I's palace at Tsarskoe Selo was swallowed up by Rastrelli's creation for Elizabeth. Catherine II overwrote Elizabeth's formal French landscaping at Tsarskoe Selo with the English-style grounds she preferred. Elizabeth's Venetian-style Summer Palace at the meeting point of the Fontanka and Moika canals in Petersburg proper was knocked down to make room for Paul's Mikhailovskii castle. Paul also destroyed the Pella Palace to the east toward Schlusselburg and Lake Ladoga, an estate that had been owned by Prince Dolgorukii under Elizabeth and purchased in 1784 from the Nepliuev family by his mother Catherine. The eighteenth-century Ropsha estate to the southwest—ill-famed as the site of Peter III's 1762 murder—was left to decay during Catherine II's time but restored under Paul.[10] Catherine the Great's pseudo-Gothic Chesme Palace along the way to Tsarskoe Selo was converted into a veterans' hospital during the 1830s. The first two Petrine-era Winter Palaces are defunct, and it is only the Rastrellian third Winter Palace, whose interior was extensively renovated during the late 1830s after a devastating fire, that is known to nineteenth- and twentieth-century historians. All of this pales, of course, in comparison to the grand-scale destruction wrought at most of the palace-parks by the invading Germans in the 1940s, which necessitated decades of loving restoration work by Soviet cultural workers.[11] Each palace-park must thus be treated as a cultural text across both space and time.[12]

Tsarskoe Selo looms especially large in Petersburg literary mythology. Erich Gollerbakh's popular 1927 *Town of the Muses: (Gorod muz)* treats the palace-park as literary symbol and cultural "anthology," beginning with Pushkin's poet-predecessors Gavriil Derzhavin and Vasilii Zhukovskii, and concluding with Innokentii Annenskii's "Pleiad."[13] Derzhavin's poems "A Stroll at Tsarskoe Selo" (*Progulka v Tsarskom Sele,* 1791) and "Ruins" (*Razvaliny,* 1797) already manifest the backward-looking orientation of this poetic tradition, which soon becomes self-referential. Derzhavin's "Stroll" recalls a long-ago happy outing at the palace-park with his late wife "Plenira." "Ruins" meditates upon the Tsarskoe Selo grounds a year after Catherine II has died and her son Paul has removed his court to Pavlovsk, and devotes all but the final six lines—out of more than one hundred—to the past glories of the Empress's reign.

Pushkin's poem "Recollections at Tsarskoe Selo" (*Vospominaniia v Tsarskom Sele*), written upon the poet's 1829 visit after his return from southern exile, similarly represented a new version of a much longer, similarly titled poem written fifteen years earlier. Pushkin's rambling "Recollections" of 1814 evoke his own personal history—his studies at the Lycée—as well as the history of the Russian empire, whose triumphs under Catherine are commemorated by the palace-park monuments.[14] The earlier "Recollections" poem circles back in time to connect Catherine's military victories with Alexander I's entry into Paris. In the 1829 "Recollections," Pushkin characterizes himself as a prodigal son returning repentant to his former haunts, revisiting the garden monuments celebrating national heroes and recalling his own patriotic visions of Russian military victories.[15] For Pushkin, Tsarskoe Selo stands for a complex series of physical and thematic repetitions, in which every return must depart from both memory and history.

For Innokentii Annenskii and Anna Akhmatova, Tsarskoe Selo was intimately connected with the shade of Pushkin, but they also regarded it as a gloomy place from which history had passed—a "forever-exhausted theme" preserved in a silent death-sleep under a shroud of snow, in Akhmatova's phrasing from her 1910 lyric "First Return" (*Pervoe vozvrashchenie*).[16] Ironically, Akhmatova's view of Tsarskoe Selo echoes the much earlier sentiments of Charles Masson, who included impressions of the park in his "secret" memoirs of 1790s Russian court life:

> Tzarsko-selo is an immense and dreary palace, begun by Anne, finished by Eliza-
> beth, inhabited by Catharine, and forsaken by Paul. Its situation is a swamp, the
> country round it a desert, and the gardens are uniformly dull. . . . By the side of
> obelisks, rostral columns and triumphal arches . . . are seen tombs consecrated to
> some of her favourite dogs; and not far from these is the mausoleum erected to the
> amiable Lanskoi, the most beloved of her favorites, and the only one whom death
> tore from her embraces. . . . These monuments, however, from the neglect to which
> they are doomed, will shortly disappear in the dreary swamps which serve for their
> foundation.[17]

For Masson, viewing Tsarskoe Selo during the rule of Paul, who forsook the residence because of its associations with his hated mother, the palace-park was
consigned to the nonplace of posthistory. In his estimation, the already incoherent "text" of the grounds ("Are we from this to imagine that a dog, a lover,
and a hero, are of equal importance in the eyes of an autocrat?") was soon to be
overwritten by the natural environment. Masson little suspected that he, like
Derzhavin during the same period, was strolling through what would be merely
the first few pages of the Tsarskoe Selo poetic anthology. Wistful meditations on
the ruined state of a palace-park constitute a special "Petersburg" genre that extends from the latter half of the eighteenth century until the present day. Writing about the Petersburg palace-parks arises from a few basic forms—official
paean, private elegy, or museum catalog—depending on the cultural moment
of the palace in question.[18]

The fragility of these seemingly solid imperial residences is a recurrent theme
in memoiristic writing about the palace-parks, in contrast to the accounts in official guidebooks and histories. Catherine the Great's memoirs of the long, con-
stricting period that preceded her ascension to the throne (1744–62) include a
number of curious passages about the palaces outside of Petersburg proper. Her
life is marked by constant, tedious shifts between the Winter Palace and the Summer Palace, punctuated by stays at Peterhof, Tsarskoe Selo, Oranienbaum, and
Krasnoe Selo (located south of Strelna, and west of Tsarskoe Selo), all according
to the whims of her husband's aunt, the Empress Elizabeth. Oranienbaum, notes
Catherine, was during this period "in a rather ruined state," although the hunting there was very good.[19] The palace at Oranienbaum had not been renovated
since Men'shikov's time and its beams were so rotted that Catherine had to stay
in a ground-level wing and take her meals in a tent.[20] Peterhof was in no better
condition. Catherine and her husband were given rooms in the oldest Petrine-
era part of the palace, which threatened to collapse at any moment. As Catherine remarked, "If anyone walked about my dressing-room, the entire floor
shook."[21] After a terrifying experience at Count Razumovskii's estate Gostilitsy
in 1748—during which the wooden house where Catherine was sleeping slipped

off its foundations, nearly killing the future Empress and her husband—it was decided that the outlying palaces should be more carefully inspected and repaired in order to prevent such accidents. Thus the palaces that served both the nineteenth and twentieth centuries as symbols of continuity in Petersburg cultural history seemed highly contingent structures during the eighteenth century.

From the same standpoint of cultural history, the Strelna Palace provides a provocative parallel to Peterhof, the palace that most obviously speaks to the solid foundations of Peter's project. Strelna is most notable for its checkered history—alternating periods of glory and neglect that propose an ominous alternative narrative for all of the Petersburg palace-parks. Peter originally intended Strelna to be his "Versailles," until it was made clear to him that Peterhof's topographical situation lent itself much more favorably to the system of fountains he had planned. Although construction of Strelna continued after 1711, the palace-park missed its chance at greater glory, and instead became a secondary residence, given over to subsidiary members of the royal family such as daughters and noninheriting sons.[22] Following a major fire during the reign of Anna Ioannovna, Strelna was partially reconstructed by Rastrelli, but stood empty for the remainder of the eighteenth century. Writing in 1818, the guidebook writer Pavel Svin'in imagined this sad spectacle with relish:

> Soon the wide alleyways were overgrown with prickly grass, thick-trunked birches and aspen took root on the flagstone terraces and bridgeways, and the palace assumed an appearance of neglect and destruction. The growth-choked groves no longer beckoned visitors to rest; the waters turned to shaded marshlands; the wind whistled in the windows. Travelers avoided these sad, gloomy spots, or stopped there only to interrogate the echo, which would answer in a wild voice three times from the ruins. During this period, fearsome stories about spirits who wandered about the grounds and made noise at night circulated among simple folk.[23]

Svin'in then segues into a triumphant account of Strelna's return to glory in 1797 after Paul presented the palace to his son Constantine, who took great pains renovating both palace and grounds, and established a camp for his Horse Guards there. Strelna was almost entirely destroyed by fire in 1803, but rebuilt at the wish of Alexander I. When Constantine died in 1831, the Strelna narrative was repeated: Nicholas I gave the palace to *his* son Constantine, who was only four years old at the time. In 1843, a new wave of renovations at the yet-again dilapidated Strelna began, and, upon Grand Duke Constantine's wedding in 1848, work on the main palace grew more intensive. The ensuing era—the second half of the nineteenth century, when Strelna was occupied by the Grand Duke and his large family and called the "Konstantinovskii Palace"—can be considered Strelna's heyday.[24] One of Constantine's sons published poetry under the initials "K. R." (Konstantin Romanov), including more than a dozen elegiac lyrics written during the final two decades of the nineteenth century at Strelna, his birthplace and beloved personal refuge.

FIGURE 5.1. Strelna Palace from J. Meyer *Vues pittoresques des palais et jardins imperiaux aux environs de St. Pétersbourg,* 1850s. (Courtesy of Houghton Library at Harvard.)

In 1911, Strelna passed from Constantine's widow to his son Dmitri, who lived there until his 1918 arrest and 1919 execution at the Peter-Paul Fortress. The Soviet government auctioned off the palace's contents, and Strelna rapidly deteriorated during the 1920s, when it served as a facility for homeless children. During the late 1930s, the palace interior was reconstructed in preparation for its conversion to a sanatorium, but in 1941, the invading Germans occupied it. The extensively damaged palace was liberated in 1944, and, after partial restoration, housed the Arctic Institute until the 1990s. Various *perestroika*-era groups took an interest in renovating Strelna, but because of the expense of such a project, the palace-park remained decrepit and abandoned. In 2001, President of the Russian Federation Vladimir Putin conferred upon Strelna the status of "Palace of Congresses," and following a competition calling for restoration proposals, Putin appointed a consortium to accomplish the transformation in time for the city's May 2003 tricentennial festivities.[25]

If Strelna seems the neglected orphan in accounts of the Petersburg palace-parks, Pavlovsk is the favorite, spoiled child. Descriptions of the Pavlovsk palace-park assume many forms—sentimental tales that inscribe mournful epitaphs on the natural landscape, poetic elegies paced like contemplative strolls, reverent guidebook prose, preservationist scholarly inventory, and even impressionistic photo albums from the late Soviet era—but each genre of Pavlovsk writing invokes the staged quality particular to this palace-park. As Svin'in rhapsodized in 1816, "If Art can draw near to Nature . . . then it is, of course, at Pavlovsk. These brooding crags, these foaming waterfalls, these velvety meadows and valleys, these gloomy, mysterious woods seem the pristine creation of exquisite nature, but they are the product of human hands."[26] Within the pantheon of Petersburg palaces, Pavlovsk stands for perfectly natural taste and artful simplicity.[27] As such, most Russians proudly declare Pavlovsk their favorite among the palace-parks, providing evidence of their discriminating taste by agreeing with the majority. This response itself seems predetermined by the preromantic aesthetics that dominate at Pavlovsk, which set themselves apart from the grandiose formality of baroque and neoclassical palace settings.[28]

The fact that Pavlovsk escaped large-scale changes during the nineteenth century was due to the foresight of Paul's widow Maria Feodorovna, who shaped the palace-park and the residence during the period 1777–1828. Maria Feodorovna bequeathed Pavlovsk to her son Michael along with a large sum of money for its upkeep, stipulating that all furniture and objects remain at the palace. In 1849, Pavlovsk passed to Nicholas I's son Constantine (also the owner of Strelna), who had a lovingly detailed volume produced for the palace-park's 100-year anniversary in 1877.[29] After Constantine's death in 1898, Pavlovsk went to his widow and eventually to his son, the aforementioned verse-writing Constantine (K. R.), who treasured the palace's link with major literary and artistic figures of the earlier nineteenth century and produced a number of brief, tender poems about Pavlovsk during the period 1885–1906.[30] After Maria Feodorovna's death in 1828, Pavlovsk was thus maintained as a "family museum" for her descendants, in accordance with her instructions.

There are exceptions to the nearly uniform reverence with which Pavlovsk is treated in literature, however. The middle part of Dostoevsky's 1868 novel *The Idiot* is set in the Pavlovsk summer community, rendered as a merely fashionable place in this most famous use of a Petersburg palace-park from the nineteenth-century Russian literary prose canon. A Vauxhall concert provides the backdrop to a scandalous scene, hardly in keeping with the earlier idyllic topos of Pavlovsk, which here exists only in Hippolyte's mocking references to "green trees." N. A. Leikin's 1881 collection of sketches *Irrepressible Russians: Stories and Pictures from Nature* (*Neunyvaiushchie rossiiane: Rasskazy i kartinki s natury*) treats Pavlovsk with a much heavier-handed comic irony, behind which can nevertheless be detected nostalgia for an imagined golden age. Formerly, declares Leikin, Pavlovsk was an "aristocratic dacha region," where exclusively well-born or high-ranking persons—whom he defines as those possessing documented proof that their ancestors had been beaten with cudgels, impaled, or divested of noses and ears by Mongol invaders—"vegetated" during the summer season.[31] Now, anyone who can afford the exorbitant rents can summer there, and newcomers include kept women and Jews "trying to cover their garlicky smell with eau-de-cologne." Leikin describes a typical summer day at Pavlovsk, culminating in the evening concert by the station, attended by old maids and generals' widows, merchant wives weighed down by diamond earrings and bracelets, and a madwoman with "an entire garden of flowers on her hat."[32] Leikin's parodic account mourns the perceived loss of cultural prestige so much a part of Pavlovsk's nineteenth-century history, even as he anticipates the coming wave of Pavlovsk-worship. For the poet Osip Mandelstam, for example, the train journey to the concerts at Pavlovsk figured a return to the memories of his prerevolutionary youth, as reflected in his 1921 lyric "Concert at the Station" (*Kontsert na vokzale*).

Pervasive nostalgia about the palace-parks begins in the late nineteenth century when the city was undergoing a process of rapid change, and continues into the final years of the imperial period and the early Soviet period. The artist Alexander Benois (1870–1960) writes against the cultural tradition of particular palace-parks, however, treating several of the preserves in his memoirs, as idiosyncratic memory sites.[33] Benois's father was the architect of several buildings at Peterhof and remembered the festivities arranged by Alexander I in honor of his mother Maria Feodorovna. Benois himself recalls the atmosphere at Peterhof as "so bewitching, lovely, poetic, and sweetly melancholy, that nearly everyone who became acquainted with the place fell under its spell," rejecting the conventional comparison of Peterhof with coldly formal Versailles. As an adult, Benois loved Peterhof for its touchingly "provincial" eagerness to amaze visitors, and he delighted in the more obscure vistas and lesser buildings at the park. At Peterhof, Benois claims, the stern figures of Peter the Great and Nicholas I assumed the more welcoming forms of a hospitable Dutch landowner and a romantic dreamer. In contrast, as a child, he knew Tsarskoe Selo only distantly from an eighteenth-century Makhaev engraving and tried unsuccessfully to love Pavlovsk, which repelled him with the heavy atmosphere that seemed to linger from the years of Paul's rule. As Benois's memoirs make clear, the palace-parks may be conceived as public or private, obsolete or deeply significant, in accounts that are continguent upon different moments in their histories and composed from diverse literary viewpoints, but the changing fortunes of the Petersburg palace-parks always reflect the complex meanings of center and margins in the city's cultural history.

Visiting Nature: Petersburg Islands and Dacha Regions

In contrast to the palace-parks, each of which represented a remote nexus of the imperial elite, the islands and dacha regions near Petersburg became radically democratized over the course of the nineteenth century and, increasingly, belonged to the expanding middle space of the capital's culture. Thus these areas adjacent to the city proper provided a mediating territory, in both physical and cultural terms, between rural-feudal and urban environments.[34]

The Krestovskii, Kamennyi, and Elagin islands northwest of the city—often referred to collectively as the "Northern Venice" or the "Pearls of Petersburg"— originally served as an elite recreation area for the imperial family and their favorites, an arrangement that lasted through the first half of the nineteenth century. During the time of Nicholas I, Kamennyi Island featured a wooden summer theater in the neoclassical style, which initially staged French drama and later showcased vaudevilles and scenes from popular operas and ballets.[35] Petersburg's aristocracy came out to the islands in their carriages to stroll and to watch the setting sun from Elagin's appropriately named western "ballet-slipper point." For the Marquis de Custine, the islands were emblematic of Petersburg itself, however, ever in danger of reverting from artificial culture-parks to their natural, desolate state. Should the capital be abandoned someday, predicted Custine, "the granite hid under the water would crumble away, the inundated low lands would return to their natural state, and the guests of solitude [bears and wolves] would again take possession of their lair."[36] In fact, it was not nature that wrought the greatest change on the islands' topography, but rather their increasing accessibility to the wider public culture of the capital.

During the reign of Alexander II, who favored Peterhof in the summertime, island property owners rented or sold their homes to wealthy merchant families. Beginning in the 1860s, boats from the Summer Garden ferried passengers to the pleasure garden on Krestovskii Island where they could enjoy music outdoors and watch performing acrobats.[37] This new public was regarded with displeasure by various chroniclers of Petersburg, among them Mikhail Pyliaev, who drew a contrast between the elegant strollers on Elagin during the first part of the nineteenth century and those who frequented the island in 1889, at the time of his writing: "[T]he present aspect of the Elagin tip is curious and even funny. . . . It seems that the carriages and *bon monde* have grown a hundred times more numerous. . . . There are cavaliers, but also many Jews; there are diplomats, but also many Jews; there are grande-dames, but also demi-dames, and even quarter-dames; there are matrons, but also Matrenas."[38] Pyliaev describes the new public on the islands in terms that suggest generic incompatibility with the islands' established cultural topos of elegy and idyll.[39]

The public culture in the city's "natural" settings is increasingly a preoccupation for Petersburg writers during the final part of the nineteenth century. Vasilii

Mikhnevich's 1887 feuilleton "Petersburg Gardens and Their Ethnography" (*Peterburgskie sady i ikh etnografiia*) describes the social types who frequent each public park at particular times of the day, evoking the old Gogolian formula from "Nevsky Prospect."[40] He deplores the noisy drunken behavior in the beer gardens, where increasing numbers of factory workers, tradespeople, and tramps have taken over the former sanctuaries of shade and quiet. Mikhnevich takes particular umbrage at the "café-chanson" style of entertainment that, for him, reflects the social and generic decline of these "natural" settings.

Textual visits to "nature" in Petersburg literature beginning in the 1840s, traced a generic descent and diversification most particularly in connection with the summer culture of the dacha regions. The Petersburg "dacha theme" was thus actively assimilated by vaudeville and sketch sociology during the first half of the nineteenth century.[41] This "dacha" theme departs from the elevated perspective of literary excursions around Petersburg's palace-parks, more readily assuming the forms of social satire, burlesque, and comic farce. As the dacha historian Stephen Lovell declares, "If the tag 'middle-class' refers to anyone in Russia, it is to the dachniki," in their creation of a hybrid cultural zone that combined intelligentsia, merchant, and petty-bourgeois values.[42]

The so-called dacha boom began during the period 1830s–1850s, when the middle sectors of the Petersburg population began to rent summer dwellings from local peasants, usually on lands owned by Petersburg aristocrats. This period was followed by the increasingly commercial construction of dacha colonies near the new Finland railway line during the period 1860s–1880s, and then along all of the major railroad lines out of the city—Baltiiskaia, Nikolaevskaia, Varshavskaia, Finliandskaia, and Tsarskosel'skaia.[43] Dacha communities also developed closer to the city proper, in neighborhoods such as Staraia and Novaia Derevnia, Chernaia Rechka, and Lesnaia, and along the Neva in places like Peski.[44] These areas offered inexpensive bungalows, elegant summer mansions, and a great variety of options in between, as the summer housing market grew ever more differentiated in catering to an increasingly diverse public.

Before the 1840s, dacha life connoted elite company and creative leisure. Konstantin Batiushkov's 1817–18 "Epistle to A. I. Turgenev" (*Poslanie k A. I. Turgenevu*) pays tribute to the refuge provided by A. N. Olenin and his wife at their summer residence Priiutino. "There is a dacha beyond the Neva," begins Batiushkov's poem, "About twenty versts from the capital. . . ." The poem celebrates Priiutino as a "shelter for good souls" and the site of "bucolic holiday," where artists such as Krylov, Gnedich, and Batiushkov himself commune with the muses in the open air. Later, the "dacha theme" provided an opportunity for trenchant social commentary in that most urban of literary forms, the feuilleton. In an 1837 article called "Dachas," Faddei Bulgarin opined that country houses constituted a "barometer of a people's strength, a people's prosperity, enlightenment, civic spirit, and communal life."[45] Bulgarin pointed out that the Romans began to construct their villas only once their capital was secure in its position and they were no longer concerned about invaders. Until the end of the eighteenth century, he observes, summer homes were the exclusive province of royalty, aristocracy, and wealth. Now, "nearly all of the salespeople in Gostinyi Dvor get a breath of fresh air on holidays at their employers' dachas," and this summer culture takes its toll on urban life: "You might die ten times over before you'd find your doctor out in the dacha region, or before he could be brought back from his dacha. During the summer, don't bother looking for a merchant in his shop, an apothecary in his drugstore, a German tradesman in his workshop, or a clerk in his office! All of them are at the dacha!" All have gone in pursuit of elusive pleasure, declares Bulgarin, to those territories where the sleep-inducing heat of the country alternates with the twilight fog and penetrating damp. And no one reads anything from spring until fall. Thus did Bulgarin take the measure of Petersburg's "enlightenment, civic spirit, and communal life."

In 1844, Nikolai Nekrasov produced a cycle of six feuilletons called "Petersburg Dachas and Environs" (*Peterburgskie dachi i okrestnosti*), published in the *Literary Gazette*.[46] He describes the machinations required to find a summer place in Murino, Pargolovo, or Ekaterinhof, wondering, "How many dramas, how many vaudevilles play out until finally the residents of Petersburg divide amongst themselves . . . these airy, quick-growing structures, with which the environs of Petersburg are strewn?"[47] In the feuilleton of May 4, Nekrasov includes an exaggerated paean to the omnibus that will soon be available to transport passengers back and forth from the northern dacha regions several times a day. He warns that, due to the mass exodus, there will be no further Petersburg news until fall, except for that which can be gleaned from foreign newspapers. The July 13 feuilleton describes the rain and gale-force winds that produce impassible roadways, trapping miserable *dachniki* inside low-lying dwellings surrounded by puddles. The July 20 feuilleton offers a socioeconomic reading of various dacha regions, but the narrator finally concludes that it is dull and rainy in *all* of them. A separate feuilleton by Nekrasov published on August 24 closes out this summer cycle, exhorting readers not to lament the end of this brief, unsatisfactory season, but instead to turn their attention to the new offerings in the Petersburg theaters and the renewed literary polemics in its journals. "Do not mourn," urges the narrator " . . . the fact that the larks, nightingales, and other 'songbirds' (which, however, are far less numerous in the Petersburg environs than bats and frogs) are singing their final songs before flying away from us until spring."[48] Deprived of the joys of nature, Petersburg residents can console themselves with the higher pleasures of art in the city. Nekrasov's rambling "tours" through the rural dacha regions are part of his business as a feuilletonist—to chronicle *cultural life*.[49] In spite of realistically wet and muddy details, the literary trip to the summer colonies actually documents a collective fantasy that all stubbornly perpetuate, a kind of rueful shared joke.[50] Despite avowals to the contrary by Bulgarin and Nekrasov, Petersburg's "natural" settings, like the city's more obviously cultural sites, consistently serve as a textual meeting ground.

By the middle part of the nineteenth century, the dacha's primary function as a recreational retreat from urban life had become more sharply opposed to the long-term residence and traditional way of life afforded by a proper country estate. Periodical literature such as the mass daily *The Petersburg Sheet* (*Peterburgskii listok*) expressed disapproval over the alleged contamination of rural peasant life by commercial urban influences ferried out along the new railway lines.[51] Throughout these decades, the dacha as a cultural institution remained linked to the nearby city, associated with the ambiguous middle space between urban and rural settings, and with the interests and pursuits of the diffuse late imperial "middle class."[52] As Petersburg territory expanded beginning in the 1860s, however, former dacha regions on the Petersburg and Vyborg Sides lost their identities as such and became seedy, urban neighborhoods with inadequate transportation and sewage services, their wooden houses occupied all year by renters, often low-ranking civil servants.[53] Factories and worker settlements took over the portion of the Peterhof Road closest to the city, along the southern side of the Finnish Gulf. Through the mediating presence of the dacha region, the city thereby encroached upon the country, with territory passing gradually from the elite, through the middle classes, and thence virtually out of sight as a kind of holding area for urban industrial workers. Before this chapter reaches those distant industrial regions, however, we will survey a much more central Petersburg topos—the central city slums, a kind of reverse counterpart to the dacha regions, which similarly grew denser, more crowded, and more "written" over the middle and late decades of the nineteenth century.

Literary Slumming

The opening line of Pushkin's 1828 Petersburg poem "Magnificent city, poor city . . ." (*Gorod pyshnyi, gorod bednyi*), it has been said, syntactically underscores the impressive relative weight of the sociocultural margins in the Petersburg literary tradition. The development of nineteenth-century Petersburg literature is often characterized as a fundamental shift in emphasis from the "magnificent" (*pyshnyi*) to the "poor" (*bednyi*), the latter most commonly invoked as "Dostoevsky's Petersburg" (*Peterburg Dostoevskogo*).[54] In actuality, Pushkin's short poem conveys an entirely personal notion of the city, home to the tiny feet and golden curls so dear to the poet's heart. The much-celebrated literary pole of "poor" Petersburg is similarly problematic in terms of cultural mythology. Literary slums actually constitute a rather exclusive territory, more or less limited to the fictions of Dostoevsky and Nekrasov, with numerous works on this theme elided from the Russian literary canon.

The slums of imperial Petersburg are an ambiguous place in literature and urban culture, at once central and marginal. The Russian word *trushchoby* ("slums") can also refer to a godforsaken far-flung place. Thus etymology connects the neighborhood of the poor with the remove of space. In nineteenth-century Petersburg, however, slums occupied central areas of the city and provided an extreme contrast at close range to the catalog of cultural riches that typifies "Pushkin's" Petersburg.[55] While poverty certainly existed in outlying neighborhoods, the worst Petersburg tenements could be easily reached on foot from the city's grandest prospects.

Early attempts to develop a literary approach to the social margins in the 1830s and 1840s tended to focus on the genteel poor—characters such as the lowly civil clerks of Gogol and the early Dostoevsky, who cling to standards of respectability in the face of ruinous circumstances.[56] The lower classes in Petersburg were also depicted from an ethnographic and typological distance, as in Dmitri Grigorovich's 1845 sketch "Petersburg Organ-Grinders." (*Peterburgskie sharmanshchiki*) Nekrasov's unfinished novel *The Life and Adventures of Tikhon Trosnikov* (*Zhizn' i pokhozhdeniia Tikhona Trosnikova*) offers a rare exception to this rule, providing a glimpse of those Petersburg homeless who have passed beyond the bounds of decency. Nekrasov's hero is reduced to renting a "corner" in a cryptlike, cobweb-filled basement apartment off the filthy back courtyard of a huge, run-down apartment building. A physical description of the apartment and its inhabitants over the course of an entire chapter was published as the stand-alone sketch "Petersburg Corners" (*Peterburgskie ugly*) in Nekrasov's anthology *Physiology of Petersburg* (*Fiziologiia Peterburga*, 1845). Thus this particular introduction to the city's marginal inhabitants reached a wide readership within Petersburg itself.[57]

After the 1861 Emancipation and until the 1910s, rising population densities overwhelmed central districts such as Spasskaia and Kazanskaia, and the lack of extended public transportation prevented those who worked in the city from moving to the outlying areas. Building owners converted damp storage cellars into apartments, subdivided existing rooms to create additional rentable space, and filled attics with paying tenants, and these developments exacerbated the overcrowding problem.[58] Journalistic treatment of the Petersburg poor was given greatly renewed impetus by these developments in the wake of the Great Reforms.[59] Works of this period devoted particular attention to slums, flophouses, state jails, hospitals for the indigent, taverns, and back streets. Dostoevsky's *Crime and Punishment* (1866) is, of course, considered the apogee of this literary tradition, with much of its action set in the neighborhoods off Haymarket Square.[60]

During the second half of the nineteenth century, multistory tenement buildings could be cheaply constructed on the sites of the single-story wooden buildings that had formerly been so numerous in the central parts of Petersburg, and merchants, who began investing in Petersburg rental real estate decades before the Emancipation, emerged as the dominant group of tenement landlords.[61] Merchant owners are not, however, associated with the first and most dramatic instance of slum housing in the Petersburg city center. Beginning in the middle of the nineteenth century, the territory between the Fontanka and the southern part of Haymarket was occupied by the infamous "Viazemskaia Monastery" (*lavra*), a series of thirteen two-story buildings that stood on land owned by the aristocratic Viazemskii family. As many as 10,000 people languished in these slum dwellings, described by Vsevolod Krestovskii in his mid-century novel *Petersburg Slums* (*Peterburgskie trushchoby*, 1864–67) and by Nikolai Sveshnikov in an 1892 ethnographic-literary account based on personal experience.[62]

Krestovskii's potboiler, which enthralled the *Notes of the Fatherland* readership and appeared in five subsequent editions, was a self-proclaimed depiction of the urban underclass. The anachronistic and antirealist elements of *Petersburg Slums* nevertheless drew dismissive pronouncements from both nineteenth- and twentieth-century critics, who classified the novel as "tabloid (*bul'varnaia*) literature"—in other words, as literature directed toward the growing middle readership. *Petersburg Slums* was accused of pandering to a popular audience of provincial landowners, civil servants, merchants, and petty bourgeoisie (*meshchane*) who enjoyed the novel's melodramatic excesses.[63] In truth, Krestovskii's novel represents a throwback to Eugène Sue and the romantic French *roman-feuilleton* of the 1830s–1840s, rather than a groundbreaking work in the spirit of its own reformist times, even though it treated topical issues such as prison conditions and prostitution.[64] Krestovskii had double recourse to a central motif from Sue's overwrought *Mystères de Paris* (1842–43) —his novel features *two* illegitimate children separated from their well-born families, growing up amidst misfortune and unaware of their origins.[65] Similarly, Krestovskii's inclusion of *two* women ruined by evil seducers and forced into prostitution speaks to his fondness for melodramatic overkill. The significant attention given to the corrupt Petersburg aristocracy moreover constituted a major part of the novel's appeal, as indicated by its subtitle, "A Book about the Sated and the Hungry." The novel's preoccupation with the wealthy and powerful was actually a retrogressive feature looking back to the 1830s "society tale," although the emphasis on aspiring nonnoble characters as victims was new.

Krestovskii's plot contrives to send cultured characters into the slum as literary witnesses, so that their horrific experiences can be rendered for the middle-class reader. The journalistic passages in *Petersburg Slums* describing tavern, prison, brothel, and tenement counterbalance the novel's hoary plot motifs by creating a broader social canvas.[66] Even here, however, Krestovskii borrows from the past, producing "genre scenes," descriptions of social types, and authorial commentaries that recall 1840s physiological sketches.[67] Krestovskii brings his reader into close contact with the pressing contemporary issue of urban poverty by making his work seem familiar in literary terms, evoking the society tales, urban sketches, and foreign melodramas of the earlier nineteenth century. In his preface, Krestovskii warned readers that the contents of his novel might strike them as unbelievable. He meant by this to underscore the injustices perpetrated upon the urban poor by the indifferent judicial system on the eve of the Great Reforms, rather than to shore up the hardly credible coincidences and far-fetched circumstances on which his plotting depends.

Despite the improbable plot, Krestovskii assures readers that his depiction of "the dark world of the slums" is based on actual conditions. He describes an incident from his student days in the late 1850s, when he peered into a basement near Haymarket Square and saw "pitiful creatures, insulted and outcast by all," living "in animal conditions."[68] He assumed at the time that this scene represented the "furthermost limits of Petersburg abomination and vice," but later discovered it to be only a "tiny corner" of that "enormous picture" of slum life never represented in official accounts. His novel, he claims, attempts to answer the questions that might come to his readers as they drive through Haymarket Square: "What goes on behind those huge stone walls? . . . Why this hunger and cold, this corroding poverty in the very center of an industrial, wealthy, and elegant city, alongside palaces and smug, sated faces?"[69]

Krestovskii's preface casts him as eyewitness to conditions unimaginable "without demonstrable, unmediated acquaintance, face to face."[70] He cautions therefore that his investigative tactics have produced a novel suitable only for a morally and intellectually serious readership. It is not, he insists, "for reading in boarding schools and institutes for aristocratic girls." Krestovskii ends his preface on this defiant note, warning away sensitive readers who cannot stomach harsh realities. He clearly expects such readers to disregard the warning, however, since he intermittently bullies and patronizes them throughout the book. In a section on slum prostitutes, the narrator the gentle reader by insisting on his work's faithfulness to life: "Look! It's no use turning away with a shudder and closing your eyes! This is our own, this is the product of our society." He urges, "Look more closely, more intently at these women. Acquaint yourself as much as possible with the conditions of their existence, with their social position in relation to the rest of society."[71] Perhaps Krestovskii was trying to create a new sort of readership, or perhaps his assertions and exhortations were disingenuous. Did he hope to flatter the growing middle readership by lambasting hypothetically squeamish aristocratic maidens?

Krestovskii devotes far greater attention to slum settings than Sue did, however, and takes pains to reproduce the particularities of Petersburg slum argot.[72] His novel includes a close-up view of the Viazemskaia "Monastery," which he approaches from an unexpected, rather Gothic-inspired literary angle. He begins by pointing out the "exquisite architectural structure in the baroque style" visible on the right bank of the Fontanka not far from the Obukhovskii bridge.[73] But there is no sign of life in the former residence of the Viazemskii family, notes the narrator, except for the light in the steward's apartment. Krestovskii takes his reader through the furnished rooms with their white marble statues and dusty paintings, through the remains of the indoor garden and the library full of rotting volumes. The back half of the house is in ruins, infested with birds, bats, and mice. From here, the description turns to the adjoining inner wings connected by courtyards and alleyways, which constitute the warren of the Viazemskii slums. Each wing has its own name and special character, associated its particular slum industries and inhabitants. Krestovskii even turns to the tried-and-true Gogolian format to provide an account of the slum life cycle over the course of a day and night. Thus he makes good on his promise to look beyond the facades of the buildings around Haymarket Square. The elegant facade on the Fontanka leads to an entirely unexpected slum landscape, without any middle ground as transition, apart from the ruins of the aristocratic interior. Krestovskii's novel itself is the mediating element between social extremes, and in this, his lengthy narrative points to the expanding midsection of the Petersburg Text, even as it succumbs to the retrograde literary impulse to peer into a high-society milieu or titillates its modestly respectable readers with a daring close-up view of the urban underclass.

In 1892, the sometime-writer Nikolai Sveshnikov published a series of feuilletons called "The Viazemskii Slums" (*Viazemskie trushchoby*), which appeared in 1900 as a volume called *Petersburg Viazemskii Slums and Their Inhabitants* (*Peterburgskie Viazemskie trushchoby i ikh obitateli*), subtitled *An Original Sketch from Nature*. Sveshnikov follows Krestovskii, who was the first to see the Viazemskii slum complex as the site of unnumerable and intertwined stories— that is, as a physical structure that suggests, even requires, a corresponding textual form. Although the Viazemskii slums had been treated frequently in the mid-nineteenth-century press, to say nothing of Krestovskii's novel, Sveshnikov argues that these earlier accounts were exaggerated. In contrast to the sensationalist Krestovskii, Sveshnikov walks his readers calmly through the notorious slums in order to dispel the persistent social mythology that clings to them. He points out, for example, the small-scale artisans who maintain workshops there. He calls for eliminating the squalid taverns that operate out of the "Monastery" and for suppressing their brisk trade in alcohol. Sveshnikov insistently distinguishes the ordinary urban poor from the social parasites who prey upon them. He thus sought to humanize the Viazemskii slums, rendering diverse individual histories in residents' own words, rather than through the shocked eyes of Kre-stovskii's cultured-but-degraded protagonists, and emphasizing the circumstances that have led these people to such a place.

Sveshnikov served a truly mediating function between his readers and the slums, since he wrote about the Viazemskii slums from direct personal experience as well as from the perspective of a journalist. As he describes in his *Memoirs of a Fallen Man* (*Vospominaniia propashchego cheloveka*, 1896), he himself at one time rented a "corner" in the Viazemskii slums, more exactly, a bunk in a two-room apartment that housed twenty-five people—petty tradesmen, laborers, beggars, and people "of indeterminate occupation."[74] In his account, the Viazemskii slums of the late 1850s and 1860s provide a refuge for unregistered city residents. These slums also recur in his memoirs as the place of last resort to which he returns periodically when alcohol and indigence overcome him.[75] In the late 1880s and early 1890s, Sveshnikov's drinking binges compelled him to live in a two-room apartment "above the baths" occupied by up to forty people at any given time. During this period, he described his environment in short periodical pieces, "The Viazemskii Slums" series among them.[76] His perspective on the Petersburg underclass was unique, in that he did not "visit" this part of the city as a socially conscious *intelligent,* but was compelled by his alcoholism to make these circumstances his own.

In Victorian London, the physical segregation of the poor from the rest of the city's inhabitants provided the circumstances for a literature of "discovery" a nineteenth-century tradition in which Frederick Engels's *The Condition of the Working-Class in England* (1845) represents an early milestone.[77] From the 1860s onward, there appeared an extensive body of written work exploring the plight of the urban poor in London, including Henry Mayhew's four-volume *London Labour and the London Poor* (1861), James Greenwood's *A Night in a Workhouse* (1866), George Sims's *How the Poor Live* (1883), Andrew Mearns's *The Bitter Cry of Outcast London* (1883), William Booth's *In Darkest England and the Way Out* (1890), and George Booth's seventeen-volume survey *Life and Labour of the People in London* (1892–97).[78] Russian writers such as Vasilii Mikhnevich, Anatoly Bakhtiarov, and Nikolai Zhivotov emulated this British model to describe the slums of Petersburg during the late imperial period in the words of an educated narrator who was both intrepid explorer and social-moral witness.

Petersburg journalists tended to lead shabby, itinerant lives and were constantly in danger of drinking themselves out of an occupation.[79] These reporters did not attain the literary fame of a Chekhov or a Gorky, or even that of a prolific secondary writer like Alexander Amfiteatrov. Moreover, as persons who inhabited the cultural interstices of literary-professional and social status, these journalists often exhibited an ambivalent relationship to the slum-dwelling subjects of their writing, producing texts that teeter between exposé and apologia.

Vasilii Mikhnevich, for example, authored *The Sores of Petersburg* (*Iazvy Peterburga,* 1886), a work that combined statistics on poverty and crime with a series of sketches called "Pictures."[80] Mikhnevich's introduction to *Sores* cites an unprecedented public concern over declining morality at all levels of contemporary Russian society. He sets out to determine whether the situation is as grim as popular opinion paints it, venturing the comforting hypothesis that the atmosphere of pessimism may indicate that the Russian social conscience has grown more sensitive, not that the situation has grown worse. His social sketches depict "the contemporary moral physiognomy of Petersburg" by peering into what he calls "the dark, unexplored world of need and deprivation, passion and suffering, vice and error, ruin and crime," in a lurid literary manner that recalls Krestovskii's furtive inspection of the Haymarket basement.[81] Although Mikhnevich complains in his introduction that "negative types" such as "embezzlers, profiteers, speculators, exploiters, banking bureaucrats, bank-robbers, careerists, 'jacks of hearts,' lechers, fallen women, and so forth" figure far too prominently in belles-lettres of the day, he relies upon these very figures to create his vivid plots and characterizations. True, the statistics that pepper Mikhnevich's discussions lend a judicious air to his tales of urban misadventure. It is nevertheless easier to view *The Sores of Petersburg* in strictly literary terms—as a compendium of story subjects from the Russian capital at a particular historical moment, and a companion-guide to the same literary works that Mikhnevich seeks to discredit, rather than a sociological investigation. Attempting to distinguish himself by providing an accurate account of the Petersburg poor, Mikhnevich merely adds his voice to the literary throng, rendering his description in terms of the same melodramatic middle genres and dictions.

Although roving reporter Anatolii Bakhtiarov is best known for his sketches of everyday trade in the 1880s, which were published under separate cover as *The Belly of Petersburg* (*Briukho Peterburga*, 1887), he described the city's marginal residents in his later works—*The Proletariat and Street Types of Petersburg* (*Proletariat i ulichnye tipy Peterburga*, 1895), *Tramps* (*Bosiaki*, 1903), and *The Done-For* (*Otpetye liudi*, 1903). These works exhibit an ambivalence toward the marginal figures of the city not unlike that in Mikhnevich's writing. Bakhtiarov's *Proletariat* opens with a grim sketch of the five official flophouses in Petersburg, but this volume also includes sketches on colorful "street types" such as peddlers and ragmen.[82] A sketch titled "The Poor" (*Nishchie*) takes a disapproving rather than sympathetic approach to its subjects, describing men and women who "make their living" at poverty, supporting an idle, drunken existence by preying upon the consciences of passersby. Bakhtiarov also points a finger at the poor who frequent city cemeteries to solicit funeral parties, and at beggars who position themselves at church entrances or in front of affluent homes. Thus, while ostensibly producing revelatory social commentary, he assuages the guilt of well-heeled residents who would probably not wish to make his own acquaintance.

Nikolai Zhivotov received a great deal of attention for his journalistic *Petersburg Profiles* (*Peterburgskie profili*, 1894–95), which provided "undercover" investigative accounts of the city from the viewpoints of, in turn, a cabdriver (described in Chapter 3), waiter, funeral torchbearer, and tramp, this last modeled after the incognito reportage of Greenwood's *A Night in a Workhouse*. The profile exploring the subsistence-level conditions of the homeless—"Among the Vagrants: Six Days in the Role of a Ragamuffin" (*Sredi brodiazhek: Shest' dnei v roli oborvantsa*)—most dramatically attests to the author's willingness to extend his reach to the outer limits of city life. He outfits himself and sets off on a chilly autumn morning to acquaint himself with the "backstage" existence of Petersburg's tramps: "I acquired some old, baggy denim trousers full of holes, a shirt to match, a greasy and ripped frock coat, worn-out footwear without any soles, foot wrappings. . . . In this attire, having dirtied my face and tilted a faded cap

with a frayed visor over my eyes, I left my apartment by the backstairs. . ."[83]
Zhivotov sought firsthand experience of "the vagrants' *life,* their everyday circumstances, past, present, and future," rather than the merely external appearance of their temporary shelters or the filthy conditions that were more properly "the concern of the sanitary commissions." He insists on the vividness of
these unknown lives, declaring them "more interesting than lives we see on
the theater stage, in our friends' drawing-rooms, in salons, clubs, and meetings,"
for all that these human dramas cannot be observed "through a monocle or
from the heights of the belle-étage." Zhivotov himself functions much like his
own writing in this undercover account—as a medium, through which his literary subject becomes manifest and accessible for readers. The overt, albeit unacknowledged theatricality of Zhivotov's escapades, however, highlights the
always-implicated presence of the narrator in ethnographic description. Moreover, the author's relish at donning his tramp costume and engineering an en-
grossing urban adventure detracts somewhat from the social pathos of his
account.

Zhivotov samples every aspect of the vagrant's life—he drinks their vodka,
learns tramp argot, solicits their stories, sleeps on flophouse floors, and is per-
secuted by policemen, doormen, and lackeys. He creates a typology of vagrants,
dividing them into mendicants, blackmailers, pilferers, swindlers, alcoholics,
and victims of misfortune, and he provides their case histories.[84] Oddly, he
claims that "the great majority [of vagrants] are not tormented, but rather are
quite satisfied and happy with their situation, do not wish for anything better,
and avoid almshouses and shelters," but he admits that this assessment refers to
bachelor tramps who know no other life, and not to those brought down in the
world by unlucky circumstances, much less to women and children.[85]

Zhivotov concludes his adventure by emphasizing the persistence with which
passportless persons return to the capital after being apprehended and removed
by officials. He describes the scene just outside the Moscow gates on the south
road toward Tsarskoe Selo, an area taken over by factories and workers' settlements, through which crowds of tramps pass in the early mornings, on their way
to the city. Zhivotov proposes the construction of barrackslike "homes" for vagrants at the city outskirts, each with room for 1,500 to 2,000 people. The city
could put them to work cleaning streets and removing snow, he suggests, and
the money saved could be used to underwrite the new facilities. Zhivotov's reportage thus oscillates between a romantic celebration of the tramp's freedom
and an eerie vision of resettlement and forced labor.

By the early twentieth century, Petersburg slum literature had taken a turn
from avowedly (if ambivalently) moralist to openly entertaining. Works like
N. V. Nikitin's *Petersburg by Night* (*Peterburg noch'iu,* 1903) captured readers'
interest with tales of secret gambling dens and decent young girls abducted and
forced into prostitution. These so-called sketches from ordinary life (*bytovye
ocherki*), as they were subtitled, professed to offer a peek into the Petersburg un-

[handwritten annotation in top margin: "(but the only mention A.)"]

derworld by presenting "a gallery of nighttime Petersburg's most frequently encountered types."[86] Here, the old Natural School vocabulary is invoked to legitimize a suspect literary enterprise, masking the extent to which the social margins represent a saleable commodity—both literally in the case of prostitution, and also as a literary subject. Such commodification has always posed a danger for literature about the urban underbelly, which attempts to make the marginal of interest to the general readership.

Although quantities of journalistic writing about Petersburg were produced during the final decades of the nineteenth century, most of this work was soon forgotten, and became part of a marginal literary Petersburg—an analog to the socially marginal Petersburg it sought to depict—that is only now being unearthed and reprinted. Although literature of the margins seemed briefly central following the Great Reforms, these journalistic works still await their unreserved inclusion in the Petersburg Text.[87] Literary slumming in Petersburg veers between two poles—the tediously chatty ethnographic sketch and the distended, improbable melodrama—and, perhaps appropriately, never quite finds a happy medium that is both readable and plausible. The notoriety and shock value of works like Krestovskii's *Petersburg Slums* or Zhivotov's *Petersburg Profiles* soon faded, while the overly descriptive naturalism of writers such as Mikhnevich and Bakhtiarov lacked narrative tension. Only Nekrasov and Dostoevsky remain as lasting champions of the urban poor in Petersburg literature, and even so, the first is revered but not much read, while the other is so central to the literary tradition and so much discussed that it seems disingenuous to approach him through the notion of the marginal. With a little help from Antsiferov, Dostoevsky's literary terrain has become as much a part of Petersburg museum and excursion culture as any of the city's imperial monuments.

The Illegible Industrial Text

Fictional works that treat urban industrialization of the nineteenth century may well offer the most striking example of the literary periphery in Petersburg cultural history. In lieu of a significant tradition such as that of England and France, the textual map of Petersburg renders industrialization as marginalia. While this unexpected literary lacuna poses a question for Russian literary history as a whole, its implications for Petersburg writing are particularly weighty. The fact of industrial literature's exclusion challenges this corpus's claim to a full representation of the capital as trumpeted by the Pushkin credo "Magnificent city, poor city."

It might be argued that industrialization in St. Petersburg did not develop quickly enough to have altered the literary landscape by the early 1880s, the decade traditionally cited as the end of the nineteenth-century Russian prose realism embodied by Dostoevsky, Tolstoy, and Turgenev. In fact, significant heavy industry *did* exist in Petersburg of the 1830s and 1840s—the latter decade marked by the literary advent of the Natural School, which might have been expected to take an interest. Beginning in the 1830s, paintings and lithographs regularly showed black smoke issuing from steamships on the Neva, "declaring the victory of technical progress and comfort over the abstract emptiness and transparency of the Neva's expanses."[88] By the 1860s and 1870s, Petersburg was a major Russian industrial center undergoing rapid and dramatic change. The absence of industrial themes and motifs in so much of the nineteenth-century literature about Petersburg thus illustrates the patrolling of literary territory, even as physical urban space spun increasingly out of control. Similar claims can be made for Moscow and, to a lesser extent, for the provinces, but what is most interesting here are the blind spots in the mythology specific to Petersburg where the industrializing city is concerned, among them that mythology's claim to comprehensiveness.

Writing about St. Petersburg from the latter half of the nineteenth century often evokes the preindustrial, precapitalist life of the city, the quaint atmosphere of the open-air markets with their peddlers and hawkers, the port area, the Stock Exchange, the colorful street trade in books, and the old-fashioned merchants' rows such as Gostinyi Dvor.[89] Literature thus perpetuated the conservative view of industrialization in Petersburg prevalent during the reign of Nicholas I until long after his 1855 demise. This literary selectivity is particularly remarkable given that St. Petersburg, which began as a fortress town, directed significant resources early on toward shipbuilding and armaments industries located in the center of the city.[90]

During the 1830s–1840s, textile industries were the fastest-growing and most modern area of industry in Russia as a whole, and specifically in the capital. Machine and metal works received an infusion of resources from the private sector during the 1850s, with the blessing of a government unable to keep up with demand in the wake of the Crimean War. The late 1850s also witnessed the opening up of railway construction to private enterprise, as well as important changes in tariff structures that had impeded the development of industries dependent on imported raw materials. During the second half of the nineteenth century, the percentage of St. Petersburg's population employed in factories rose from five percent to ten.[91] The 1860s–1870s brought a surge of urban migrant workers to Petersburg as well as an increasing number of textile, metalworking, tool and die, chemical, food, tobacco, and printing factories.[92] New enterprises in heavy industry that were privately owned or based upon the joint-stock principle multiplied in order to support the continued growth of the railway system and the expansion of Russian military forces. Entrepreneurial families such as the Putilovs and the Obukhovs established enormous factories in the outlying industrial districts, employing many thousands of workers. While the 1880s were a time of stagnation and reduced growth, marked by Russian protectionism to encourage domestic industries, the 1890s saw an unprecedented rise in

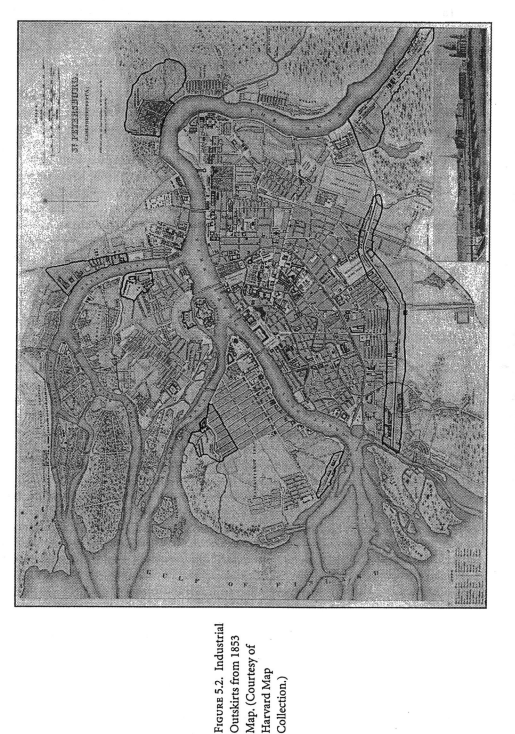

FIGURE 5.2. Industrial Outskirts from 1853 Map. (Courtesy of Harvard Map Collection.)

industrial growth and development. The period 1908–13 brought a renewed surge in Russian industrialization. In 1913, there were 956 factories within St. Petersburg, accounting for nearly ninety percent of the factory employment in the Petersburg province.[93] By the outbreak of World War I in 1914, there were nearly a quarter million industrial workers employed in Petersburg.

Already by the 1860s, large metalworking and textile plants "girdled" the central city, and industry showed marked growth in the Vasilievskaia, Peterburgskaia, and Vyborskaia regions to the north during the final decades of the nineteenth century, appearing in the greatest concentration to the south at the mouth of the Neva, along the Obvodnyi canal, and inland all the way to the Neva across from Malaia Okhta.[94] In his 1918 history of Petersburg, Petr Stolpianskii uses a sinister figure to describe the topography of industrialization during the second half of the nineteenth century: "In this way, factories encircled the city like a ring, clutching the administrative-trade center in its embrace."[95] Plants and smokestacks would have been on view as Petersburg residents moved about the city, and the pollution and congestion from industrial activity would have been evident to all. James Bater notes that by the early 1900s, "[F]actory chimneys obtruded into most of the popular views and smoke belched up around some of the finest examples of architecture of the late eighteenth, or early nineteenth centuries."[96] As it turns out, Russian literature proved far more effective than state zoning regulations at keeping industrialization out of sight.

Why do the lives of urban factory workers and the facilities where they worked—to say nothing of the changes industrialization wrote upon the urban landscape—fail to register their presence in the "Petersburg Text" during the nineteenth century in more than a fleeting fashion?[97] Why were depictions of St. Petersburg industrial life and its participants seemingly confined to the nonfictional realm?[97,98] Descriptions of industrializing areas in Russian periodicals only very occasionally shade into the quasibelletristic, as in an 1839 description of a "stroll" on the Schlusselberg road along the Neva to the south of the Alexander Nevsky monastery—a literary exploration that appeared in the conservative newspaper *Northern Bee* and was widely reprinted. The author of this piece admiringly describes "eternal movement and manufacturing-activity," characterizing the textile and paper factories as "majestic" structures that "astonish the eye with their immeasurably large stone columns."[99] The author describes the Aleksandrovskaia manufacturing complex in utopian terms, noting lush surrounding gardens and fruitful fields where, before the advent of the factories and their worker communities, there had been only unproductive, uncultivated territory.[100] The *Northern Bee* stroll thus marries the anachronistic vocabulary of high-classical Petersburg to a retrogressive GoldenAge vision that seems incongruous alongside the idealizing rhetoric of technological progress.

Perhaps the lack of literary interest in factory workers reflected the fact that most of them were illiterate male peasants who had migrated to the city from the countryside.[101] These migrant urban workers, who soon composed the largest single sector of St. Petersburg's population, were considered unwelcome interlopers, and they overloaded city services such as transportation, housing, and sanitation. The neglect of Petersburg factory workers in literature may also be attributed to the fact that nonindustrial migrant laborers in construction, transport, trade, service, handicraft, and casual work long outnumbered the city's factory workers.[102] The problem of the "urban proletariat" was, moreover, not posed as such in Russia until the end of the nineteenth century because it was subsumed within the larger "peasant question."[103] Censorship may also have played a role in keeping the plight of urban workers out of literary view, but so did hostility to Western urban industrial life on the part of both conservative Slavophiles and populist leftists, who believed that "proletariatism" deprived peasants of their ancient communal structures.

Although Russian literature did not participate to any notable extent in the discourse of industrialization during the imperial period, this fact of literary history cannot be accounted for by a lack of industrial activity in Petersburg or in Russia at large. It is perhaps more significant that members of the intelligentsia—the writers' class—did not work in factories or often visit industrial outskirts, although, as already shown, they did have recourse to slum neighborhoods for literary subjects.[104] This literary fact is all the more surprising, however, given that in St. Petersburg, child labor, handily supplied by the imperial foundling homes, was a source of cheap, only nominally illegal workers, and, one might have imagined, a source of literary pathos, as had been amply demonstrated by Western literature.[105]

Industry's marginalization in the Petersburg Text may also reflect the particularities of Russian literary history, or at least the way in which this history has thus far been written. As literary historian Dmitri Mirsky characteristically declares, "The reign of Alexander II (1855–81) was an age of great literary achievement, the Golden Age of the Russian novel. . . . But there was a worm in the flower: all this great achievement was by men of an older generation, and they had no successors."[106] By the end of this period, Tolstoy had lost interest in fictional literature; Dostoevsky and Turgenev were dead. In the wake of Tsar Alexander II's 1881 assassination, economic depression, political conservatism, and a cooling of the literary passions of the 1860s and 1870s marked the 1880s, claims Mirsky.[107] Perhaps the literature of industrialization has not been adequately compiled and treated in terms of an overarching poetics because it consists largely of small forms—short poems, sketches, feuilletons, and brief stories—rather than full-length novels, and it was produced by minor writers at that. As literary history has it, the 1880s and 1890s were only a weigh station en route to the brilliant experiments of the early twentieth century. Russian literature from this period is seen as something of a Chekhovian story about nothing, and, what is more, literary scholars tell this story dismissively and by rote. Might a fuller account of this literary period yield unexpected additions to the Petersburg industrial text?

Searching for Industrial Literature

Industrialization has been largely kept out of sight in histories of Petersburg architecture and literature. In a departure from this tradition, however, the historian Margarita Stieglitz accords Petersburg's "unique" industrial buildings the same prestige as other eighteenth- and nineteenth-century structures.[108] She strives to recapture their visual presence within the familiar Petersburg panoramas, arguing that industrial chimneys and water towers existed alongside celebrated architectural ensembles from the earliest years of the city's existence.[109] Her study aims to reinscribe industrial architecture into the "stone annals" of Petersburg, since these structures were from the very beginning enmeshed within the "fabric of the city."[110] Valentina Lelina hopes to retrieve these industrial structures from the edge of Petersburg "consciousness."[111] She cites the "proud silhouettes" of such buildings, alluding to the "hidden energy" and "secret power" of the industrial region encircling the city, and to the "fantastical colossi" that have stood for more than one hundred years, now towers of "sadness" in their "silent submissiveness." Lelina mourns the loss of similar architectural "monuments" (*pamiatniki*), destroyed to make room for more modern factories.[112] Her remarks thus gesture at what has long been lacking—an industrial poetics for the nineteenth-century imperial Petersburg cityscape.

The differentiation between industrial and nonindustrial architecture came about during the first half of the nineteenth century, when steam technology came into use. The "brick style" (*kirpichnyi stil'*) of industrial architecture in St. Petersburg during the 1850s–1880s thus exemplifies a "rational" aesthetics that made sparing use of the palette of ornamentation available at the time. Still, even a casual survey of surviving photographs shows that industrial structures—among them the Chernorechenskaia paper factory, the Zigel' factory, the boiler-house of the Baltiiskii factory, and the Mertz main city water tower—exhibited many of the same constructive and decorative principles as the rest of Petersburg architecture from the period of "eclecticism" (1830s–1890s), including Gothic and medieval details, and central towers in the Renaissance style. The cityscape was ambivalent, in places expressing the affinity between industrial and nonindustrial structures, while elsewhere emphatically distinguishing between the two visually and through physical isolation. The failure of the Petersburg Text to account for the experience of industrialization reflects a similar ambivalence.

The neglect of industrial themes in the Petersburg literary corpus is countered by period guidebooks, which are reasonably informative about the city's industries even during the eighteenth century. Still, even these nonfictional sources are uncertain about how to represent industrial activity in Petersburg in institutional or architectural terms—as an illustration of the lavish and outmoded style of the court, or as an integral part of the cityscape. Pavel Svin'in's *Memorable Sights of St. Petersburg and its Environs* (1816–28) treats both the Old and New Arsenals as armaments museums and depopulated exemplars of architectural style. An 1849 edition of John Murray's *Handbook for Northern Europe (Denmark, Norway, Sweden, Finland, and Russia)* includes a section on Petersburg factories, noting "some splendid industrial establishments, particularly of the description which produces the more rare and costly articles required by that class to whom luxuries are indispensable."[113] Murray was referring to the imperial Shpalernaia works, which produced Gobelin tapestries for the Court, and to factories for porcelain, playing cards, precious stones, mirrors and other glass objects.[114] The 1903 People's Educational Commission *Guidebook to St. Petersburg*—notable for its representation of the city as a museum of culture—provides readers with a tour of select manufacturing facilities, including the imperial glass and porcelain works along the Schlusselberg road and the Putilovskii factory, established in 1801. The factory workers are absent from the guidebook's description, however, as are their working conditions, which had been treated by Nikolai Blagoveshchenskii in an 1873 sketch (discussed below).

When we turn to literature, it is not difficult to inventory the brief mentions and relatively obscure corners in Petersburg writing that allude to urban industrialization. Uncle Petr Aduev in Goncharov's *An Ordinary Story (Obyknovennaia istoriia,* 1847) owns a successful factory in St. Petersburg, but the reader is never permitted to visit, or to learn anything about its operations. In fact, rather than being represented as a realist setting, Uncle Petr's factory is transformed into an extended metaphor by his nephew Alexander, who compares the workings of the vast government bureaucracy to a "paper factory" assembly line, in which a single document passes through a series of different hands, "unceasingly, without rest, as if there were no people, but only wheels and springs. . ."[115] The abstraction and indifference with which Goncharov's novel treats Aduev's factory corresponds to its ultimate fate: in the novel's final pages, Aduev dismisses his immensely profitable, smoothly functioning facility in a single sentence—"I shall sell it"—when he decides to go abroad and devote himself to his wife's happiness.

Nekrasov's poetry, too, relegates industrialization to the margins, even as it seems to raise the subject. The second part of "About the Weather" (*O pogode,* 1865), for example, alludes to the remote outlying regions of the capital:

> Where, like black snakes, fly
> Puffs of smoke from colossal chimneystacks,
> Where as a wall of fires burn
> The enormous walls of red factories,
> Rimming the capital all around,—
> Gloomy scenes begin.
> But we will not go to these remote regions.
> In the winter we find the capital more pleasant
> There, where the streetlamps burn brightly,
> Where satisfied faces stroll,
> Where the tsars themselves go riding.[116]

The poet evokes the factory districts and the infernal spectacle they at once proclaim and conceal. He satirically dismisses this site as a suitable literary subject, however, briefly assuming the role of the affluent city-dweller who prefers the amusements of central Petersburg. While this stanza from "About the Weather" is often cited and anthologized as an example of civic verse, these glancing references to the industrial outskirts are among the best that the Petersburg Text has to offer on the subject.[117]

Lev Mei's poem "Smoke" (*Dym*, 1861) provides a rare poetic departure from these marginalizing literary norms. Here Petersburg appears as a forest of domestic chimneys and industrial smokestacks that pour smoke into the atmosphere. Mei's lyrical persona ironically terms himself an "attic poet" (*piitom cherdachka*), merging high and low locutions in his juxtaposition of the odic "poet" and the cozy, diminutive "attic." Unlike so many contributors to the Petersburg Text, this poet-narrator is a native of the capital (*pitershchik*) and surveys it from on high. He looks out of his garret window on a frosty day and addresses the smokestacks in a pseudolofty vocative (*Truby!*). The poet watches the smoke spreading itself "like a shroud" across the sky:

> And alongside—black smoke, as if from a plague graveyard,
> As if from the waning burial bonfire,
> Where the infected were burned from midnight until morning,
> Yes, they burn them alive, under the wild cry of a toast
> From crazed youths . . .
>   And the plague smoke curls,
> Like a viper twining under the blue sky,
> Carrying along all the ash of hypocrisy
> Before nature, the treachery of feelings, lack of faith—
> And rainbow-colored money bills.[118]

Mei's image suggests that the city is consuming itself alive, smoke offering evidence of what has been sacrificed. The smoke also purges modern ills, whose ashes are borne away into a celestial sky. In Mei's poem, smoke is the great equalizer, emanating from every sort of establishment in Petersburg, linking culture and industry, private and public spheres, lofty and low pursuits:

> What is further, there
> A factory smokes, and here—the temple of science,
> And here—shopping arcades, theaters, stores;
> And that—is not smoke, but steam—from machines

Smoke in all its variety mingles with engine steam—the writing of the future—and the wispy, shifting hieroglyphs in the sky combine in a form of urban writing that Mei's persona knows how to decipher. At the conclusion of "Smoke," he expects that "Our whole sinful world will cleanse itself through fire / And disappear as smoke in the heavens." The spiritualized, apocalyptic reading of the smoke is the one at which Mei's poem comes to rest. The poetic voice strives to create a coherent text, linking industrial Petersburg with cherished images of the imperial city, but suggests that this can happen only through the erasure of the existing Petersburg Text.

In English literature, narrative fiction, especially the novel, took active part in the discourse around industrialism and was changed as a result.[119] The new industrial poetics gave rise to novels such as Benjamin Disraeli's *Sybil* (1845), Elizabeth Gaskell's *Mary Barton* (1848) and *North and South* (1854–55), Charles Kingsley's *Alton Locke* (1849), Charles Dickens's *Hard Times* (1845), and George Eliot's *Felix Holt* (1866).[120] The roster of "industrial fiction" is, moreover, not limited to the canon, since popular writers in America, for example, produced dozens of literary works about the plight of urban industrial workers during the period 1840–70 and afterwards.[121] The same cannot be said of Russian literature.

Fedor Reshetnikov's 1868 *Where is it Better?* (*Gde luchshe?*) is the exception that purports to prove the rule of industrialization's absence from the nineteenth-century Russian novel.[122] Reshetnikov himself lived and worked in the factory districts of Petersburg for several years before writing his novel.[123] *Where Is It Better?* traces the fate of peasants from a Ural mining village shortly after the 1861 Emancipation.[124] Having left the wretched conditions at the metallurgical plant in their village, they wander across Russia in search of a better life, and, at the novel's halfway point, they arrive in Petersburg, only to find themselves exploited anew.[125] When a group of workers gather in a Petersburg tavern and try to resolve the novel's central question—"Where is it better?"—the grim consensus is that life is equally difficult in the country and the city, best in a tavern, or better still, "in the grave."[126]

The initial descriptions of Petersburg in the novel tellingly make no mention of the Bronze Horseman, the Winter Palace, or the elegant shops on Nevsky. Instead, Reshetnikov describes a dense urban landscape of street trade, commercial traffic on the canals, malodorous black smoke pouring from smokestacks at the city outskirts, and unceasing machinery noise, which, he notes, is not audible at the center of the city. Even so, Reshetnikov's *Where Is It Better?* takes a disappointingly long time getting to the plight of urban factory-workers. Most of the novel's Petersburg section follows the young peasant woman Pelageia Goriunova, whose frustrated hopes for employment are directed toward simpler preindustrial occupations: cook, laundress, and seamstress. The novel seems almost to shrink from exploring the industrial regions, leaving them as a last recourse. Pelageia encounters Petrov, a Petersburg activist-worker, who proposes she look for a job at a sugar factory on the Vyborg Side and arranges a living space for her in a nearby tenement. Pelageia inquires at several factories, but she is turned away, and the reader receives only a cursory impression of one factory floor.

In the novel's final chapters, the emphasis shifts to Petrov, who protests unfair wage policies and is fired from his foundry job. He unsuccessfully seeks new employment along the entire length of the Obvodnyi Canal—a plot device that allows him to hear brief tales of woe from a series of factory-workers, although this literary strategy is largely undeveloped.[127] Petrov then tries to establish a small workshop of his own on Ital'ianskaia Street in the city center. He encourages Pelageia to operate a laundry-business out of the apartment they share, and they plan to marry. After a brief period of happiness, however, she falls ill, and, while he takes care of her, both of their small businesses fail. After her death, Petrov finds a factory job back on the Obvodnyi Canal, the city center having proved inhospitable to this sort of literary character and his concerns, but the reader learns nothing about his new life. In the concluding scene, Petrov returns to the question "Where is it better?" This time, the answer proposed to the reader is "in the afterlife." Reshetnikov's novel, which poses the central problem of where its protagonists truly belong, itself never found a place in the Russian canon, remaining merely a curiosity at the margins of the national literary tradition. For all its author's real-life experience, moreover, this rambling novel takes no more than a quick look at the industrial regions, not pausing long enough for a fully realized exposé.

In a few cases, journalistically inclined writers visited factories and described what they saw, but even these accounts are riven by ambivalence. In the early 1870s, for example, Nikolai Blagoveshchenskii wrote several sketches, one of which, "At the Foundry-Works" (*Na liteinom zavode*, 1873), is set in the southern outskirts of Petersburg. He describes the dangerous conditions at the Putilovskii factory, where workers ply their trade amidst "an infernal heat" in an environment filled with noxious smoke, fumes, and sparks.[128] The author's stated aim is to create in the reader an astonishment rivaling his own at the ability of the simple Russian factory worker to tolerate such an unhealthy exposure day after day. Blagoveshchenskii's sympathy is nevertheless tempered by a proto-Communist rapturous admiration for the "new man" forged in the process of this industrial work. He describes one of the stokers as "cast from iron," his body transformed by its constant proximity to fire, and marvels at his "bogatyr-like" muscles and exposed blackened chest. The rest of the factory workers are, in contrast, "thin, like skeletons, with tortured facial expressions, and with swollen eyes and nervous, awkward gestures."[129] Blagoveshchenskii declares nervous ailments to be common among the workers, along with diverse physical illnesses and a tendency to be "superstitious, fearful, inclined to mysticism and even sometimes subject to hallucinations."[130] He thus pathologizes the industrial environment, but also conversely suggests it might be the source of a dramatic, alternative re-visioning of the urban proletariat.

In 1880, Gleb Uspenskii published a brief sketch called "With Love (From My Memorandum Book)," which he later retitled "From One Horse-Drawn Streetcar to Another" (*S konki na konku*). Uspenskii's sketch proposes to explore the factory areas along the Obvodnyi Canal and in the surrounding territory, extending from the Rybatskoe settlement at the end of the Shlusselberg road to the end of the Narvskii post road, in which thousands of "unskilled workers" (*chernorabochii narod*) live and toil. Uspenskii's opening topographical characterization is so protracted and precise that the reader justifiably expects a full-length tour of the industrial outskirts to follow. Instead, Uspenskii produces a familiar ethnographic Natural School sketch in a manner nearly unaffected by the immense changes that have transpired in the cityscape since that literary style was in vogue.

On the day of Uspenskii's visit, the southern factory region is animated by a church holiday, the festival of John the Baptist, to which hordes travel on overloaded streetcars. Uspenskii finds a place at the top of one "noisy and cramped" streetcar, longing to get lost in the crowd, and thus to relieve the spiritual anguish he experiences as a provincial, "abandoned for long years in the capital."[131] The factory outskirts serve in this way as the background to Uspenskii's personal (if typical) intelligentsia torments. With his writer's eye, Uspenskii observes those around him, carefully transcribing conversations and exchanges of verbal abuse. He is outraged by a father's brutal treatment of his young son, but when he rides back to find the pair after they have disembarked, he discovers the boy willingly being taught to drink in a tavern. The narrator despises his own impotence and, as a seeming consequence, absents himself completely from the sketch's final paragraphs, which present dialogue between ethnographic specimens viewed as if through a glass wall of representational language. When Petersburg literature approaches the terrain of industrialization, the text in question often retreats from the challenge, taking a self-marginalizing approach to its topic. The retitling of Uspenskii's sketch further elides the writer-storyteller's evaluating presence, instead suggesting an objectively neutral sequencing of impressions.

Anatolii Bakhtiarov's "physiology" *The Belly of Petersburg* (1887) sought to acquaint readers with the "types" who worked on the city's underside. By this he did not mean the "underside" dwellers in the "insulted and injured" Dostoevskian sense, but rather workers who practice the unglamorous trades that feed the city, and who themselves belong to the "machinery" of St. Petersburg. As of 1887, Bakhtiarov's subjects were not yet characterized as "proletariat," although Bakhtiarov himself was to use the term in a book title some years later. In fact, these subjects are practitioners of preindustrial trades soon to be taken over by instruments of technology.[132] Bakhtiarov does not treat factory workers, preferring to describe the petty-bourgeois tradespeople and artisans, as well as the more traditional peddlers who stand in plain view on St. Petersburg's streets.

As Bakhtiarov's belly metaphor makes clear, the city represents a single, immense *organism* that requires constant feeding. Appropriately, *The Belly of Petersburg* opens with a chapter on slaughterhouses, which details the means by which many hundred thousands of cattle travel from the southern steppes to sate the hunger of "those two monsters," Moscow and Petersburg.[133] Bakhtiarov also devotes a chapter to the city's "mouth"—the port that serves as the entry point for goods. The persistent attention given to the physical body is made most graphic in Bakhtiarov's treatment of boiling heads, entrails, and other unusable animal parts to make lard on Glutton's Row (*Obzhornyi riad*), and processing bones collected from households by rag-pickers and sent on to plants for glue and bone meal. In these most startling sections of *The Belly of Petersburg*, Bakhtiarov lapses into fanciful reverie. Watching cattle parts stewing in enormous vats, he muses, "Looking at this picture in the evening illumination, by the light of the lamp hanging from the ceiling, it seems to you that gnomes are preparing food for some sort of fantastic giant."[134] The opening to the chapter on bones begins in a similarly "literary" fashion:

> On Gutuevskii Island, on the shore, rises a magnificent mountain of bones—whose height is greater than that of any five-story building in Petersburg. Having clambered up this mountain, you can survey the city's surrounding areas (*okrestnosti*): first, you can see the Finnish marshes, and further, by the seashore, the fishermen's hauls and finally, at the horizon—the blue of the sky merging with the blue of the water. At the foot of the mountain, gnomelike workers potter about, loading bones on barrows with shovels and transporting them to the bone-burning plant, where they process more than one million *poods* of bone every year.[135]

This moment—the opening of a chapter concerned with the waste produced by the imperial and the industrial plant that disposes of it—is resonant with references to earlier works of Petersburg literature. Bakhtiarov seems to mock the already-trite style of guidebook prose encouraging visitors to enjoy views from selected vantage points around Petersburg. This passage can also be read as a grotesquely parodic re-visioning of the opening to Pushkin's "The Bronze Horseman," when Peter the Great stands upon the desolate marshy shore and summons Petersburg into existence through force of will and imagination. The emphasis on bones evokes the folkloric claims that Petersburg is a city built on the skeletons of slave laborers. Although Bakhtiarov's Petersburg in *The Belly of Petersburg* is insatiable and teeming with life, this chapter strikes a ghoulish note with its image of "gnomes" serving an industry of death. By implication, the workers responsible for the flow of goods have also been sacrificed to the appetites of the voracious city-monster.

It is curious that Bakhtiarov did not choose to treat factory workers and factory sites, when there would have been many to choose from in the 1880s. The title of Bakhtiarov's *Proletariat and Street Types of Petersburg* (1895), subtitled *Everyday Sketches* (*Bytovye ocherki*), suggests a major shift in the author's view of St. Petersburg's lower-class inhabitants. The expectations raised by Bakhtiarov's title, however, are not entirely borne out by the book's contents. He offers a portrait gallery of lower-order exotics with a first section ("Street Types") that describes flophouses, Tatar peddlers, Okhta milkmaids, traveling monks, and the same haulers, rag-and-bone dealers, and indigents encountered in his earlier *The Belly of Petersburg*. His "proletariat" shares no common interests or goals. In fact, the book's fragmented treatment of "types" belies the very assertion that a proletariat has emerged in Petersburg.

Only a brief middle section of *Proletariat* occupies itself with "Factory Types" (*Fabrichnye tipy*) such as weavers, founders, smelters, and blacksmiths, and even then, it does so in an inconsistent fashion. Retracing the 1839 *Northern Bee* "stroll," Bakhtiarov visits the Aleksandrovskaia settlement along the Shlüsselburg road, with its five-story factory buildings emitting smoke. Surrounding the factories are tiny huts, in which 100,000 workers live. Bakhtiarov describes the colorful spectacle on Sundays, when workers stroll along the Neva bank, attending plays at workers' theaters, and visiting taverns. He emphasizes the self-sufficiency of these factory communities, initially seeming to propose Aleksandrovskaia in a Chernyshevskian spirit as a workers' paradise. When Bakhtiarov describes a typical family, whose weaver-patriarch Ivan's face bears the "factory stamp" of a "yellowish color, just like wax," however, he suggests that Ivan represents the true product of the Aleksandrovskaia complex.[136] Bakhtiarov cannot then sustain the spirit of exposé and lapses back into a more Nikolaevan admiring tone.

He notes that each worker in the enormous Aleksandrovskaia textile facility can distinguish the special morning whistle of his own factory from all the others, and thousands of workers hurry to their places "like bees to the hive." Amidst the rows of looms stand the weavers, "like reapers in a field."[137] At the beginning of the day, an entire "forest" of belts set the looms into motion. The rumbling grows louder and louder, until it becomes a "genuine hurricane," making the observer feel he is standing by a "waterfall." The constant up-and-down motion of the belts evokes "ocean waves." In the cotton-spinners' facility, Bakhtiarov marvels at the spindles, which twirl so rapidly at 8,000 cycles per minute that they appear to be motionless. The white thread wound on each spindle makes it look like "a seagull, circling in the air in one spot." Human voices cannot be heard, however, in this chaos of machine noise. Bakhtiarov's frequent recourse to natural metaphors for this brave new world undercuts his intermittent attempts to describe the harsh working conditions at the factory settlement.

Bakhtiarov also visits the Obukhovskii steelworks, where he witnesses the casting of a huge cannon—a project that requires the participation of 150 founders. Here he seems more interested in the technical process by which the steel reaches the proper temperature than in the working conditions of the foundry-men. At the moment of casting, a whistle sounds and all four hundred workers fall silent. It is clear, observes Bakhtiarov, that "the workers were well-disciplined."[138] When the smiths take the mass of pig iron and fashion it into a cannon, Bakhtiarov finds the spectacle inspiring, calling the factory whistle "triumphant" and characterizing the overall "picture" as "majestic." Except for noting the soot-blackened faces of the workers and the tremendous heat, Bakhtiarov remains preoccupied with the fact of production and its related statistics. His choice of a cannon as the object of industry echoes the patriotism of earlier periods in nineteenth-century Russia—the Napoleonic Wars, the Crimean War, and the Serbs' war with Turkey in the 1870s. In short, the few attempts made at representing industrialization in literary terms rely ineffectively on outmoded styles and genres, or marginalize this topic within the work as a whole. At best, such works gesture suggestively in the direction of a new industrial poetics.

In the autobiographical *The History of My Contemporary* (*Istoriia moego sovremennika*, 1904–18), the writer Vladimir Korolenko wakes up after his arrival in Petersburg and looks out his window near the Technological Institute, attempting to "read" his new environment. He sees "the characteristic view of the Petersburg outskirts," which consists of "roofs, empty spaces, yards, and factory smokestacks." Korolenko continues, "Massive stone structures tower over the little wooden houses, and the half-circle tanks of the gas plant are visible, along with the dull facades of manufacturing facilities. Farther out by the horizon lies a belt of trees, and in their midst, the walls of churches gleamed in the sun." It seems to him that "all of this—the musical cries of the haulers, the factory signals, and the hurried whistling of the steam engines on the branch line that connects the Nikolaevskii railway with the Tsarskosel'skii line—bore some relation to my arrival."[139] He does not elaborate this felt connection between the diverse sights and sounds of the cityscape in literary terms, but contents himself with inventory.

Remembering himself as a new student at the Institute, Korolenko discerns across time a "general type" amongst the student population, the so-called working *intelligent* or "cultured (*intelligentnyi*) worker," identifiable by the "stamp of thought" that belied a powerful physique. Such proletariat-intellectuals populate Korolenko's Technological Institute of memory, whose enormous facility seems to him "an intellectual factory producing a new man for a new life."[140] Korolenko's autobiography was actually written during the twentieth century, however, around 1917, and his 1870s cityscape thus incorporates the aesthetic values of the revolutionary era in a retrospective overlay.

The terrain of industrialization in the imperial capital seems closest to taking shape in artistic terms in Andrei Bely's novel *Petersburg* (1916, 1922), with its signature images of apocalyptic factories belching out black smoke across the turbulent cultural landscape of 1905. In Bely's novel, the relegation of industry to the literary margins is explicitly attributed to a conservative character's individual consciousness, as if Bely were subtly incriminating the entire Petersburg Text. The "foggy, many-chimneyed distances" that are "so wanly etched" from across the Neva in the mind of the functionary Apollon Apollonovich reflect an uneasy awareness of the ring of factories surrounding the city:[141] "Apollon Apollonovich did not like the islands: the population there was industrial and coarse. There the many-thousand human swarm shuffled in the morning to the many-chimneyed factories. . . . The islands must be crushed! Riveted with the iron of the enormous bridge, skewered by the arrows of the prospects."[142]

Apollon Apollonovich seeks to turn industrialization against itself, destroying the islands by directing the center to attack the channels of communication that are themselves the achievements of a modernizing city. The narrator knows that this movement will be in reverse: "Petersburg is surrounded by a ring of many-chimneyed factories. . . . All the factories were then in a state of terrible unrest."[143] Radiating from the margins, the "agitation that ringed Petersburg" begins "penetrating even to the very centers," crossing the bridges and taking over Nevsky Prospect.

Factories appear in Bely's *Petersburg* as the source of a new poetics, whose preliminary distant glimmerings can be felt in the novel: "Chimneys rose up high; chimneys squatted; over there rose a row of slender chimneys which from a distance became fine hairs. You could count the fine hairs; the arrow of a lightening rod jutted up."[144] Bely's vision of the new cityscape thus appears as an unrealized, but imminent possibility towards which the eye and the imagination must travel: "There where nothing but pale gray misty haze hung suspended, at first appeared the dull outline and then the full shape of the dingy blackish gray St. Isaac's Cathedral. . . . And it retreated back into the fog. And an expanse opened: the depths, the greenish murk, into which a black bridge stretched away, where fog draped the cold, many-chimneyed distances and whence rushed a wave of on-rushing clouds."[145]

When the bomb goes off at the Ableukhov home in the final chapter, the smoke that symbolizes industry finally arrives in the center of Petersburg, as "gawkers, heads thrown back, gaped at the sinister yellowish-lemon clouds pouring out of the black gaps of the windows and out of a fissure that cut across the house."[146] This explosion rends the Petersburg Text, which cannot absorb this aesthetic intruder. Bely's novel makes explicit the threat that shapes the late-imperial literature of the capital, which responds to a conservatism that clings to preindustrial "Dostoevsky's Petersburg" no less tenaciously than it embraces "Pushkin's Petersburg," going no further than an sketchy ethnographic objectivity, and largely ignoring new stories or literary potential at the industrial margins.

The chaos of the industrial outskirts recalls the primordial swamp in Pushkin's "Bronze Horseman," which threatens to engulf the city. In both cases, these dangers lie at the periphery of the cultured intelligentsia consciousness that produced the Petersburg Text. In literary works, the industrial regions of the city are circumscribed by this consciousness, but the authors' refusal to cast more than a tentative glance at them points to the city limits of the Petersburg mythology, for all that it was produced by self-proclaimed outsiders.

While the changing face of the modernizing city represented an integral aspect of Western urban literature, the Petersburg Text jealously guards the privileges of gentry and intelligentsia writers, whose literary tastes remained conservative until the end of the nineteenth century, even when their social leanings seemed most democratic. Thus the factory worker is a rare figure in the Petersburg literary corpus, and the literary terrain of industrialization—in terms of poetics as well as themes—is no more than a distant ring of settlements whose smokestacks are visible on the horizon. Both pathos and patriotism prove inadequate tonalities for treating this unfamiliar subject, which seems similarly intractable within the available Russian literary forms of sketch, distended novel, and civic verse. Petersburg literature declines after the 1870s, at the very moment when industrialization could have given it a powerful new impetus. Even though the Prologue to Bely's *Petersburg* represents the capital as two concentric circles with a black dot at the center, from which "surges and swarms the printed book," those circles also attest to a closing of literary ranks in Petersburg, whose "text" seeks to repel an alien industrial presence.

CHAPTER SIX

Meeting in the Middle: Provincial
Visitors to St. Petersburg

THE DIALOGUE between urban margins and city center is particularly vexed for Petersburg, which is geographically distant from the heart of Russia, yet administratively and symbolically central. As Yuri Lotman notes, Peter the Great's "transfer of the politico-administrative centre to the *geographical* frontier" also brought about a "transfer of the frontier to the *ideological* and *political* centre of the state."[1] An extended conception of the margins in relation to to the imperial capital would thus have to take account of the provinces—the "third reality of Russian culture," after Petersburg and Moscow.[2] The provinces are a literary space from which characters take an awestruck perspective on Petersburg (Gogol's 1836 play *The Inspector General*), an unchanging pastoral ideal whose loss is figured by the city (Goncharov's 1859 novel *Oblomov*), or a repressive, monotonous environment in which human creative potential, not infrequently the potential to be a writer, withers horribly on the vine (Saltykov-Shchedrin's 1870s novel *The Golovyovs*). According to a nongeographical conception, however, "literary province" refers to a position within a literary process that, as a whole, is conceived as a horizontal terrain rather than a hierarchy. A "literary capital" represents the dominant literary model for a given period. A "province" is a nondominant literary model that may supply a "capital" with various resources, but also lives its own separate life. In fact, the major impetus for change in a literary capital often comes from the literary provinces.[3] The artist Giacomo Quarenghi, known for his singularly "pedestrian" and "chambered" sense of urban space in late eighteenth-century Petersburg, captured the perspective of a literary province in a perfect visual analog.[4] Quarenghi's ink drawings "Street on the Edge of Petersburg" and "The Neva and Fortress in Petersburg" depict the city from its rural outskirts, which are rendered at ground level in loving detail, while the spires of Petersburg architectural monuments appear as tiny objects in the distant background.

A "provincial text" has a double orientation, both to itself and to the center, and must accommodate these divergent perspectives.[5] Does the same principle of double orientation apply to the outlying regions of Petersburg literature?[6] The notion of a literary province can be taken both literally and literarily in this case, in order to consider the vast body of writing that treats new arrivals to Petersburg. Most of these texts were authored by writers of middling status in the Russian literary canon, or by future luminaries during the early unsatisfactory stages of their careers. This social and artistic periphery in Petersburg has been accorded central significance by Vladimir Toporov, for whom "the Petersburg Text of Russian literature" reflects "the quintessence of life in a 'liminal' condition, on the edge, at the abyss, at the border of death."[7]

The oft-written story of coming to Petersburg traverses the line between provinces and city that represents one of the decisive binaries in Russian cultural history and simultaneously exemplifies the productive relationship between literary province and literary capital. Both literary Petersburg and Petersburg in literature represented the destination of young hopefuls, who came to the city to offer their skills at the cultural market, and created a small army of literary semblances—fictional and remembered selves who endured common privations. This Petersburg master plot shapes a body of fictional works, autobiographies, private letters, and diaries by new arrivals aware of the existing tradition.[8] Much satirical literature on this theme thus assumes the borrowed form of real-life documents, most particularly "letters" and "diaries" composed by a fictional provincial, which provide an ideally estranging perspective on life in the capital.[9]

Many of the authors who contributed to the "provincial in Petersburg" master plot were members of an economically and socially disenfranchised group that appealed to literature for recourse. In making itself a central element in the "Petersburg Text of Russian literature," this collectively authored story produces the cultural middle space whose very lack provides its narrative impetus. This subgenre also provided a literary meeting ground for readers at a geographical remove from Petersburg, would-be writers who perused these works in the thick journals.

Mikhail Saltykov-Shchedrin, who came to the capital from the province of Tver in 1838, went on record declaring, "A true writer should live in Petersburg, because, living in the provinces, it is impossible to take the course of events so much to heart."[10] The narrator of Shchedrin's feuilleton series "Diary of a Provincial in Petersburg" (*Dnevnik provintsiala v Peterburge*, 1872) similarly asserts, "We, provincials, strive towards Petersburg somehow instinctively."[11] He continues, "To Petersburg! With that, all is said. As if Petersburg on its own, in its name alone, its streets, fog, and slush, should resolve something, should shed light upon it." It was not so much that Petersburg provided a particular illumination, however, but rather that these provincial writers wished to see it with their own eyes. In truth, writers who were not originally from St. Petersburg made the most significant contributions to the Petersburg Text, while native Petersburg writers had relatively little to say about their city.[12]

The story of the new arrival with its many common features belongs to writers of diverse social origin: gentry-class writers such as Ivan Panaev, Mikhail Saltykov-Shchedrin, Vladimir Korolenko, and Alexander Kuprin, and writers of modest origin such as Vissarion Belinsky, Nikolai Chernyshevsky, Nikolai Dobroliubov, Aleksei Pisemskii, Ivan Kushchevskii, and Dmitri Mamin-Sibiriak. Some young noblemen, among them Dostoevsky, came to Petersburg to be educated and developed literary aspirations once in the capital. Social status and place of birth prove of secondary importance in this body of writing, however, in which the virtually preplotted experience of coming to Petersburg shapes the texts. Within these "provincial in Petersburg" tales, writing is represented as the most effective medium in Petersburg cultural life of the nineteenth century, providing a conduit for ideas, a negotiating ground for cultural values, and an entry point for voices from the outside.

While it is true that canonical authors produced such tales of new arrivals—most prominently among them Ivan Goncharov and Nikolai Nekrasov—their ranks were swelled by numerous minor figures, many from the so-called *raznochintsy.* Many of these would-be writers lived on the border of respectability that separates the middle-class from destitution. This boundary, the so-called poverty line, often marks the success or failure of literary aspirants in imperial Petersburg, beginning in the 1830s and 1840s.

The *raznochinets* as a Russian literary type first appeared in the early 1840s and reached its more fully evolved form in the early 1860s, a period extending from the early works of Nekrasov through the short career of Pomialovskii.[13] Etymologically, the term *raznochintsy* specifies no identifying traits, but simply codifies the diverse rank origins of these individuals, some of them sons of provincial priests or schoolteachers. A *raznochinets* shared with the nobility the possibility of entering government service, but was often limited by circumstance to the lower ranks. *Raznochintsy* were socially displaced, neither tied to the countryside by the feudal system nor firmly established in the bureaucratic centers of the large cities. It might be said that their cultural function was to mediate between the two worlds, and the social and spatial mobility of the *raznochinets* thereby determined his consummate literary function—arriving from outside, he sets the plot into motion.[14] Lacking a group affiliation, the *raznochinets* strove to distinguish himself, often through writing, and thus to join the pantheon of Russian authors, the bearers of cultural authority so admired in the provinces.[15] By no means was it the case that every provincial aspirant was a *raznochinets,* or that every *raznochinets* came from the provinces, but the two social groups did overlap during the middle decades of the nineteenth century.[16]

The story of collectively lost illusions in Petersburg reflects historical reality—the influx into the capital of young provincials beginning in the 1830s and 1840s, and the difficulty of surviving there without wealth, connections, or an assured position. A newcomer with talent and the right introductions could gain entry in the age of salons and familiar associations, but this model predates the 1840s, the decade in which the "provincial in Petersburg" story assumes recognizable form.[17] Petersburg types from these archetypical tales correspond to the authors themselves—"hungry journalists" and "tubercular students," for example. This story most often constitutes an artistic Bildungsroman, since the young provincial protagonist is usually a would-be writer. "Provincial in Petersburg" tales can be seen as a school for young *raznochinets* writers, who often began their literary careers inauspiciously in out-of-date forms such as romantic poetry, were given short shrift by critics, and then moved on to writing about their own disappointing experiences. Every realist can be seen as a "reformed idealist."[18] Stories of the provincial arriving in the Russian imperial capital thus cohere as a thematic corpus when a transitionally realist literary aesthetic also became *de rigueur*.

The "novel of education" as practiced by Balzac, Stendhal, and Dumas *fils* takes a young protagonist from the sheltered environment of childhood into the free-for-all of the world at large, often a city.[19] The canonical plot chronicles the protagonist's success and calculates the accompanying costs in moral, psychological, and aesthetic terms.[20] The European literary tradition finds its counterpart in the somewhat later figure of the immigrant "greenhorn," who recreates himself as an American urban intellectual. The nineteenth-century Russian version of this archetypal tale similarly has recourse to foreignness, since many aspiring writers came to Petersburg from Ukraine or Poland, with the vibrant life of the mind as their longed-for destination. Like its Western counterparts, the Petersburg Text chronicled the difficulties in deciphering a complex urban environment as experienced by young provincials, who interpreted their surroundings too literally or with reference to the wrong system of decryption. It is precisely the challenges of taking on the capital that bring out the best in a writer—or so the commonplace asserts. Within the "provincial in Petersburg" corpus, however, it is just as likely that living in the capital will stifle a literary aspirant's talent or send him to an obscure early grave. The provincial in Petersburg often gets stuck in the unproductive, still incipient middle of Russian urban cultural life, unequal to the demands of either physical or intellectual labor, consigned to teaching, petty journalism, or the humblest of service positions.

The "provincial" theme in the Petersburg Text is elaborated by fictional and nonfictional works, as well as by the life-texts of individual figures. Still, however archetypal these "provincial in Petersburg" tales, it must be noted that such works did not speak for all newcomers to the Russian capital. Peasants who came to post-Emancipation Petersburg in search of work had different stories to tell via *lubok*, anecdote, proverb, and oral history. Women too might have their own narratives of hearts broken during a winter season, conversion to political radicalism, or descent into prostitution.[21]

Memoirs or personal letters that provided real-life accounts of early nineteenth-century Petersburg appeared regularly in memory journals such as *Russian Archive* and *Russian Antiquity* from the 1860s onward. Would-be writer Ivan Roskovshenko, for example, corresponded with a friend in his native Khar'kov from Petersburg, where he had come as a young man to take a civil service post.[22] In a letter of October 1831, Roskovshenko describes his initial impressions of the city. He takes the obligatory routes, stopping to admire St. Isaac's under construction and to muse upon the Alexander Victory Column, soon to be unveiled. Roskovshenko strolls along Nevsky and, in a manner characteristic of "provincial in Petersburg" tales, admires the "magnificent taste" with which items are arranged in the shop windows, while including a litany of prices—for clothes, in particular—that are much higher than he had "imagined." "If I had known," writes Roskovshenko plaintively, " I would not have left Ukraine." He rents a two-room apartment without firewood or water in the central part of town. His fifth-floor apartment is, he notes thankfully, relatively quiet, except for the din from carriages passing by, whose rumbling noise resembles "hundreds of mills."[23] The "provincial tale" typically begins with dreams of glory and is quickly reduced to searching for habitable middle ground. Roskovshenko's account of Petersburg is ambivalent—much that he sees is "delightful," but the capital also strikes him as "alien" and "wild."

Roskovshenko augments his letters with touching, if not particularly distinguished verses composed to his homeland, "the South," and wonders why cruel fate has sent him to the "gloomy" North, to meander alone "along the wide Neva's banks," gazing upon "palaces and granite." Wandering alone in Petersburg and composing melancholy phrases on this theme becomes a consummate "provincial in Petersburg" nineteenth-century pastime, both in literature and in life. Roskovshenko soon has little time to write letters or poetry, however, since his civil service job keeps him occupied late into the evenings and even on Sundays. He dreams of devoting himself to literary pursuits, perhaps finding a position as a teacher, but fears to disappoint his parents, and accepts a better-salaried position in the military administration. Over the next half-century, Roskovshenko held many professional positions, retiring only in 1880, but he also published poems, historical essays, and translations that enjoyed a modest literary success. Perhaps the "provincial in Petersburg" does not illustrate the principle of lost illusions, so much as that of reduced expectations. The consolation of joining a tradition compensates the middling writer for the failure to distinguish himself.

The contours of Roskovshenko's letters recall the lives of many Petersburg literary characters, as well as major literary figures, among them Nikolai Gogol. In a letter to his mother from February 1827, toward the end of his time at boarding school in Nezhin, Gogol declared, "Sleeping or awake, I am always dreaming of Petersburg, and along with it, of state service."[24] In a letter of June 1827, written to his school friend Gerasim Vysotskii, who had moved to Petersburg, Gogol confesses, "Already, I mentally place myself in Petersburg, in that jolly little room whose windows face onto the Neva, since I have always thought to find myself such a spot." The young Gogol even turns his fantasy apartment into a figure for a successful career, wondering whether he would truly be able to live "in such a heavenly place," or whether fate would instead allot him "the black apartment of obscurity."[25]

Gogol's first letter to his mother from Petersburg, written in January 1829, apologizes for not writing sooner, explaining that a fit of melancholy (*khandra*) has fallen upon him. He declares, "Petersburg struck me not at all as I expected. I imagined it as much more beautiful and majestic, and the rumors that others have put into circulation are similarly false."[26] Such deflation following a first viewing of the city will be a requisite aspect of the provincial tale, whether expressed in real-life letters by Chernyshevsky and Dobroliubov, or in fictional works by Goncharov and Pisemskii. In July, discouraged by the negative reviews of his pseudonymously published poem-in-scenes "Hans Küchelgarten," Gogol expresses contempt for those who come to serve in the capital and "leave their distant provinces, where they possess estates on which they could be good masters . . . but no, they must wander off to Petersburg, where it is not enough that they earn little, but they must also carry away so much money from home, which they use up imperceptibly in terrible quantities."[27] Gogol's fondness for grotesque self-dramatization makes his letters seem almost a parody of the "provincial in Petersburg" tradition, *avant la lettre*.[28]

Gogol returned to the impressions of the visiting provincial in his later literary works, restructuring this material artistically at a distance from his own biography, as well as from Petersburg itself. Part One of *Dead Souls* (*Mertvye dushi*, 1842) invokes an elaborate metaphor for grasping the scope of any venture from the start: "The entry into any town, even into the capital, is always rather uneventful; initially, all is gray and monotonous: endless sooty factories, and only after them appear the angles of six-story buildings, stores, signs, the enormous perspectives of the streets, a medley of bell-towers, columns, statues, towers, with the glitter, noise, and rumble of the city, and with every wonder produced by the hand and mind of man."[29] The disappointingly unremarkable arrival in the capital that stands as a defining moment in the life of a provincial, as well as the ensuing chaotic confusion, are both rendered reassuringly figurative in this passage. What is more, the "wonders" of the sentence's second half are revealed as the writer's invention ("produced by the hand and mind of man").[30]

The provincial in Petersburg often finds that the city has a dampening effect on his writing. Nikolai Chernyshevsky arrived in Petersburg from his native Saratov in June of 1846. His first letter home marvels at the number of bookstores on Nevsky Prospect, but a month later, he writes, "I can't remember whether I wrote you about the impression Petersburg has made on me—no impression at all. If you imagine a city with enormous buildings, it's like that, and nothing more."[31] Anticipation, deflation, and finally, depression—the "provincial in Petersburg" undergoes a ritual narrative process.

In his journal from 1853, seventeen-year-old Nikolai Dobroliubov confessed his dreams of moving to Petersburg from Nizhnii Novgorod, but denied that he expected the city itself to be the central attraction: "Authorship is what mainly tempts me, and if I want to go to Petersburg, it is not out of a desire to see the Northern Palmyra. . . . Foremost is the opportunity of communication with journalists and men of literature."[32] After Dobroliubov's arrival in Petersburg in August 1853, he confirmed his own prediction by adopting the requisite literary stance: "I've been in Petersburg for an entire month and have not written a single line about it to anyone in my letters. I have walked the length of Nevsky Prospect at least fifty times, strolled along the granite embankment, walked across hanging bridges, gazed upon St. Isaac's, visited the Summer Garden and Kazan Cathedral . . . and all of this has made an extremely insignificant impression upon me."[33] Dobroliubov's voluminous correspondence does, in fact, maintain a close focus on his studies and daily personal contacts, taking little note of Petersburg itself. In rejecting the familiar contours of the "provincial in Petersburg" tale, however, Dobroliubov follows the pattern, confirming his own place in the collective corpus.

Vissarion Belinsky's essay "Petersburg and Moscow" (*Peterburg i Moskva*), which appeared in Nekrasov's *Physiology,* presents the disillusionment of the young provincial as an essential formative experience—the prerequisite for a literary career. Belinsky argues that Petersburg lacks what Moscow possesses in abundance—an educated middle class, which he defines as a diverse group united by a tendency to read and wear Western-style clothing.[34] "Nowhere are there so many thinkers, poets, talented individuals, even geniuses, and particularly 'high natures' as in Moscow," he writes. "But they all become more or less known to the world outside of Moscow only when they move to Petersburg." New arrivals to the capital then quickly fall under its influence:

> What happens to their grandiloquent dreams, ideals, theories, and fantasies? In this sense, Petersburg is man's touchstone. . . . At first it seems to you that its atmosphere causes your dearest convictions to fall away like leaves from a tree. But soon you see that these were not convictions, but dreams, born of an idle life and utter ignorance of reality. And you are left, perhaps, with a heavy sadness, but in that sadness there is so much that is sacred and human. . . What are dreams! The most enchanting of them cannot equal bitter truth in the eyes of an *active* . . . person, because the happiness of a fool is a lie, while the suffering of an active person is the truth.[35]

The shared experience of the Moscow middle class in Petersburg, reflected by the plural second person of Belinsky's address, is a phase, even a foregone conclusion, in the development of a moral and intellectual sensibility that allows the "bitter truth" to be communicated in writing. Perhaps, however, Belinsky's 1845 scenario was wishful thinking, since another *Physiology* contributor presented a very different picture in a darkly comic parody.

Ivan Panaev's sketch "The Petersburg Feuilletonist" (*Peterburgskii fel'etonist*) tells the familiar story of the provincial in Petersburg, but in a manner that emphatically contradicts Belinsky's hopes. Panaev provides the generic biography of his literary subject, a pampered child on a provincial family estate, who attends boarding school in Moscow, and, as a university student, publishes a translation in a journal. The nameless future feuilletonist yearns to move to Petersburg where the prospects for a literary life seem so much more promising. He leaves Moscow to take the capital by storm, planning to grow rich from vaudevilles and translations. Like the young Gogol, he spends untold sums on fashionable clothing. He accepts a service position and works zealously for two months, but then becomes bored and "retires."[36] After that, the young aspirant survives on journalistic hackwork, spends his evenings at the theater, and writes undistinguished, limply romantic stories. He changes literary allegiances according to pragmatic considerations, becomes ever more cynical, takes to drink, ceases to be respectable, and eventually loses his fragile footing: "A year passes. The retired feuilletonist idly shambles along the Petersburg streets in an old overcoat splattered with mud." He encounters his former colleagues in a sweetshop, is snubbed by them and after this encounter, disappears without a trace: "He has left the stage. . . . Onto this stage come others, no less talented than he. "[37] Panaev's sketch takes a comic-ironic tone, but lapses into bathos at the end. Literature serves simultaneously as medium, setting, and object of "The Petersburg Feuilletonist," and the protagonist-litterateur, unable to produce any original work, must live out a plot of correspondingly small scope. By 1845, the archetypal feuilletonist's tale already seems like old news, and yet this story continues to repeat itself over the course of the nineteenth century.

Nikolai Nekrasov's literary works from the early 1840s, written during the writer's difficult first years in the capital, also belong to this "provincial" corpus in the Petersburg Text. Nekrasov left his family estate in the Yaroslavl province for Petersburg in the summer of 1838, hoping to publish his poetry and study at the university. Nekrasov's father opposed this plan and refused him financial help, forcing the young writer to eke out a subsistence living from literary piecework. This period of privation lasted until the mid-1840s, when Nekrasov became established in literary circles and began his tenure as co-owner and chief editor of *The Contemporary*. Later in life, he related autobiographical episodes to friends who transcribed them for publication, but these bits of his personal history are scattered across multiple sources.[38] Nekrasov's first months in Petersburg constitute a "blank spot in his biography," for which it is possible to establish only isolated episodes.[39] In contrast, Nekrasov's literary oeuvre includes many hapless provincials in Petersburg. In these works, Petersburg functions as the collision point of the familiar incompatible extremes—the luxurious life of the upper classes and the miserable poverty of the lower social strata. In between lies an implicit viewpoint, however, the perspective of the young writer who strives toward a unified image of the city beginning with the shared space of prose or poetry. Even as Nekrasov's later works broaden out into a panoramic view of Russia itself, infrequently invoking the *raznochinets* writer per se, the implied middle viewpoint as a literary principle remains a central feature of his texts. His first prose works are rarely discussed in connection with his early years as a writer, however, even though becoming a writer is one of their central preoccupations.[40]

Nekrasov's 1840 story "The Poet Who Disappeared without a Trace" (*Bez vesti propavshii piita*) initiates his use of the autobiographical "provincial" theme. The story gives vent to self-mockery, documenting the travails of the young poet Gribovnikov, a hopeless epigone of late classical and romantic poetry, whose work pleases the critics no more than did Nekrasov's own first volume of collected poems, *Dreams and Sounds* (*Mechty i zvuki*, 1840).[41] The story begins in the 1820s, as Gribovnikov arrives in Petersburg with notebooks under his arm, and in exalted tones consonant with the lofty form of "poet" in the story's title (*piit*), expresses his hopes of attaining the "Russian Parnassus" and growing wealthy from his literary labors. The narrator, a starving literary hack, attempts to dissuade Gribovnikov from his intended course, hoping to "save at least one victim from the rapacious claws of the monster called literature."[42] When the well-meaning narrator finally succeeds in convincing the guest of his own poverty as he emphasizes the poor prospects for a literary career in the capital, Gribovnikov rushes despairingly from the apartment, never to be heard from again. He leaves his writings behind, however, and the narrator vows to publish all nine volumes as an act of personal penance. Gribovnikov's literary artifacts as sampled in the "The Poet Who Disappeared" offer the reader a lesson in how not to write, however. The exorcised Gribovnikov may not have a future in Russian literature, but Nekrasov's narrator will persevere in his modest literary labors.

Nekrasov's unfinished autobiographical novel from the 1840s, *The Life and Adventures of Tikhon Trosnikov* (*Zhizn' i pokhozhdeniia Tikhona Trosnikova*), turns the provincial theme into urban picaresque. Like Nekrasov himself, as well as his fictional "poet who disappeared without a trace," the *raznochinets*-hero Tikhon arrives in Petersburg from the provinces with an armload of juvenile poetry and dreams of literary fame. Tikhon similarly fails to obtain a position in the civil service, publishes a poorly reviewed first volume of romantic poetry, lives as an itinerant among the city's poorest inhabitants, and eventually becomes a journalist and playwright.[43] In a literary victory for both character and author, however, Tikhon's Petersburg "adventures" are artistically transformed into a detailed, first-person satirical portrait of the literary figures, camps, and polemics of the 1840s—that is, the novel *Tikhon Trosnikov* itself.[44]

Tikhon Trosnikov has been termed an "encyclopedia of Petersburg in the 1840s," a characterization that aptly captures the panoramic yet everyday nature of Tikhon's Petersburg acquaintance, which encompasses residents of diverse professions, backgrounds, morals, intentions, and styles of speech.[45] Nekrasov's unfinished novel anticipates Bakhtiarov's *The Belly of Petersburg* (*Briukho Peterburga*, 1887) in its view of the city as a complex social and economic system viewed from the bottom up rather than from the top down. Perhaps this is why *Tikhon Trosnikov* lacks the canonical "first sighting" description of Petersburg rendered by so many arriving literary protagonists and real-life visitors to the capital. This bottom-up insider's view of Petersburg represents the subjective experience of Nekrasov's first-person narrator, whose biographical trajectory very gradually maps out the city for the reader, surveying a vast urban territory proposed as common ground for would-be writers. In this way, Nekrasov's unfinished novel turns social hierarchy into the meeting ground established by the provincial tale. Despite the autobiographical elements in *Tikhon Trosnikov*, the novel's contents possess a "typological" significance.[46] Nekrasov's story is archetypal in literary terms as well, beginning with what he had gleaned from works available to him in journals and inexpensive editions as he grew up, and proceeding with literary corrective from there. In this way, he received "the literary education of a *raznochinets*, blindly seeking culture and entering the literary field in a haphazard manner."[47] *Tikhon Trosnikov* records this peregrination, which moves across established literary topoi and through unfamiliar life experience.

Tikhon Trosnikov has been termed "the most Petersburgian of all Nekrasov's Petersburg works," because the novel captures everyday Petersburg realia so broadly.[48] In addition to the narrator's story, the novel's cumulative image of Petersburg includes the first-person accounts related to Trosnikov by fellow slum-dwellers, which the narrator presents as separate titled chapters according to picaresque convention. *Tikhon Trosnikov* thus takes as its primary subject the long process of coming to know Petersburg. The deflated literary portrait of Petersburg typically proposed at the moment of the young provincial's arrival in the capital comes only in the third and final part, as a product of experience, in a tirade by Trosnikov that, like Belinsky's *summa* from the same period, constitutes a blueprint for the collective "provincial in Petersburg" text:

> Petersburg is a splendid and vast city! How I loved you when, for the first time, I saw your enormous buildings, in which, it seemed to me, only the fortunate could live. . . . I saw so much wealth and luxury. . . . And like a child, I rejoiced that I was in Petersburg. But several years passed. . . I discovered that these magnificent and enormous buildings . . . had attics and basements, where the air is dank and noxious, where it is stuffy and dark, and where on bare boards and on half-rotted hay, in filth, severe cold, and hunger, trudged poverty, misfortune, and crime. . . . And I descended into those stuffy basements, ascended to the space under the roofs of the tall buildings, and saw poverty both in the process of moral decline and already fallen, poverty ashamedly concealing its tattered rags, and poverty parading its rags with repulsive calculation. . . . And such pictures, inescapable in big cities boiling with people, impressed me more strongly, penetrated my soul more deeply than

your brilliance and wealth, treacherous Petersburg! And your proud buildings and all that is glittering and astonishing in you no longer divert me![49]

As I will show, passionate outbursts about the horrors of urban poverty give way in the later nineteenth-century tradition to more self-serving, but similarly ornate tirades about the fate of the provincial in Petersburg, who becomes less a witness than himself the principal victim.

In the third part of the novel, Nekrasov toys with the idea of treating his hero in the third person and frames Tikhon's first-person reflections within the commentary of a separate first-person narrator, who addresses the reader directly on the subject of "our hero." This occasional narrator follows Tikhon's tirade with a drier assessment: "Needless to say, our hero also loved Petersburg, loved it unaccountably, *with all the heat of a provincial* [emphasis mine], and . . . for all the same things as most people do—for the huge buildings, wide streets, and gas illumination." Even during his hero's most lyrical outburst against conventional thinking, Nekrasov's narrator points to the generic nature of this experience, and to a subgenre that, ironically, Nekrasov himself helped to establish in Russian letters. The experience of poverty and loneliness in Petersburg represents an essential component in the biography of the *intelligent,* fictional or otherwise, and the figure of the homeless provincial youth wanders across most of Nekrasov's early works.

Like the figure of the penniless would-be writer, the university student is a stock character in the "provincial in Petersburg" tale. Evgenii Grebenka's story "Notes of a Student" (*Zapiski studenta,* 1841) traces the well-worn path of one exemplar, drawing both from its author's own biography and the conventions governing the shape of the provincial hero's life in literature. Having received his education at a lycée in Nezhin (like Gogol) and completed a three-year stint in the military, Grebenka came to Petersburg in 1834 to enter the civil service. From 1838 onwards he taught literature at Petersburg military schools. The narrator in "Notes of a Student"—an older literary professional, like the one in Nekrasov's "The Poet Who Disappeared"—and the student-protagonist are nameless, underscoring the generic nature of their respective roles, as well as the reader's familiarity with this topos. The story's epigraph from Victor Hugo asserts, "Between the beginning and the end, there is life" (*Entre le commencement et la fin il y a la vie*), pointing to the middle space of life *and* literature that the story details.

As the story opens, the older narrator watches a hearse carrying a coffin through the icy Petersburg streets and purchases a diary interleaved with letters left behind by the deceased, a destitute young man. The narrator finds that this text relates a "simple tale" and he decides to publish it "without changing a single word."[50] The dated entries of the diary begin as the provincial hero completes his lycée studies and returns to the family estate in "Little Russia," immersing himself in the joys of the countryside and falling in love with a friend's sister. He yearns to put his knowledge to use that is "beneficial to my fatherland" and resolves to go to Petersburg, where his mother's brother is in service: "I will exchange my saber for a pen and go to the capital, to Petersburg," where there is "a wide field for intellectual activity, he writes."[51]

The student's first diary entry from the capital acknowledges the predictably painful gap between expectation and reality, echoing Gogol's letters, and anticipating those of Chernyshevsky and Dobroliubov: "I am in Petersburg and I don't like it! My imagination constructed an ideal version of this city; but the reality did not approach the ideal, and Petersburg does not please me. I expected something much better. . . Unplastered buildings of an unattractive architectural style, like factories, struck my gaze unpleasantly. It even seems to me that there is little life and movement here for a capital".[52] His uncle is disinclined to help him find a position, and the Petersburg cousins sneer at his provincial clothes. The student vows, "I will never set foot in that house. Even if I must die on the street from the cold, I will not seek shelter at his gates."[53] According to the subgenre's dictates, the melodramatic threats of youth more or less fulfill themselves as realist prophecies.

The student finds a position as a bureaucracy scribe, and his mind grows numb from the dull work. He receives word of his father's death, and shortly afterwards he learns that his beloved has married someone else. Distraught, he coughs up blood, and falls into a delirium. He loses his service position and is on the point of returning home, when he is informed that his family's estate has been sold in response to financial difficulties. He secures a modest teaching position in order to send money to his mother, but falls ill again and is unable to work. The final entries document his last days, confined to his room without money or food, as the last leaf trembles on the birch tree outside his window. The diary trails off as the student loses consciousness. As in the case of Nekrasov's vanished poet, the older wiser narrator grants the fallen provincial the posthumous status of a writer, but in this case without mocking his aspirations. Ironically, however, the framing narrator, a stand-in for Grebenka himself, publishes the diary in the popular journal *Notes of the Fatherland* as a warning to other naïve hopefuls in the provinces.[54]

Ivan Goncharov's 1847 novel *An Ordinary Story* (*Obyknovennaia istoriia*) is perhaps the best-known work of Russian literary fiction about a provincial in Petersburg. The epithet of nondistinctiveness that Goncharov's novel assigns to itself acknowledges the preexisting tradition of such Petersburg tales and anticipates many more to come. What is more, the term "story" (*istoriia*) in Russian evokes both fictional and real-life narratives, thus explicitly blurring the boundary between art and biography that this corpus so often calls into question.

At the time of his arrival, Goncharov's young hero Alexander Aduev personifies the dated and banal romanticism associated with his dreams of literary fame. His development over the course of the novel juxtaposes abstract idealism with ironic pragmatism without privileging either. The novel operates according to a zero-sum literary economy, making the young hero change places with his hard-nosed bourgeois-industrialist uncle in a cycle of literary and psychic evolution. At the novel's conclusion, Uncle Petr sells his business and goes abroad to devote himself to his ailing wife, while his nephew Alexander enters government service and marries for money.

Upon Alexander's arrival in Petersburg, he gazes at people "with provincial curiosity," but soon wearies of the well-dressed citizens and the oppressively uniform architecture, and longs for his native town, where he can "read" so much in the eyes of every person he meets, acquaintance or stranger. Alexander participates in what the narrator intimates is an unavoidable rite: "The first impressions of a provincial visitor weigh him down" and "his provincial pride declares war on everything he sees here and didn't see at home." After visiting the Bronze Horseman, the Neva, and Nevsky Prospect, however, Alexander's spirits rise, and he loses himself in dreams of "ennobling activity."[55] The material city of Petersburg is rarely evoked again, however, over the course of Goncharov's novel. The hero's experience is rather one of words—conversations, letters, thoughts, and literary efforts. An Ordinary Story tells the story of learning *not* to be a writer.

The Petersburg part of An Ordinary Story begins by associating the provinces with bad writing. After reading a letter Alexander writes to a friend, Petr Aduev reconceives these hackneyed impressions, dictating "the truth" to his nephew. Alexander's youthful poetry is similarly subjected to critical assessment, as his uncle reads the mediocre verses aloud, providing ruthless editorial commentary. Like Gogol's Akakii Akakievich, Alexander's first job in Petersburg requires him to copy documents. In response to his uncle's intercession, he receives a "literary" project as well—a German article on manure, to be translated into Russian for the agriculture section of a journal. Goncharov's novel ironically redirects its young protagonist away from the tired literary forms associated with the provincial aspirant and toward the demonstratively "down-to-earth" writing that will better serve a life apprenticeship.

Two years later, the narrator "reads" the changes in Alexander, as reflected in the protagonist's face: "The sketched-in picture had yielded a finished portrait."[56] Alexander is still prone to transports of bad taste, however, most particularly on the subject of love. After listening to his nephew's impassioned disquisition on conventional marriages, Petr Aduev declares disgustedly, "It's wild, it's not good, Alexander! You've been writing for two years now about fertilizer and potatoes and other serious subjects that require a severe, compressed style, and you still speak in this wild way. For Heaven's sake, don't give way to ecstasy, or at least when this foolishness comes over you, just be still and let it pass."[57] Alexander writes poetry to his beloved Nadenka at night, and publishes his verses pseudonymously. He sends several prose pieces to the journals, but they are rejected, and his writing is criticized for its "superfluous fervor," "unnaturalness," and "pompous rhetoric."[58]

When Alexander writes a story set in the provinces, Petr Aduev sends it to an editor friend, whose diagnosis of the story is as follows: "The author must be a young man. He is not stupid, but somehow angry at the whole world. In what an enraged and furious spirit he writes! Probably he's disillusioned. . . . What a pity that so much talent in this country is lost through a false view of life in empty, fruitless dreams, in vain strivings toward that for which they lack the calling."[59] Most important, declares the editor, "talent is necessary and there isn't a trace of it here." At this devastating blow, Alexander consigns his writings to the fireplace.

In the face of his growing disillusionment, Alexander decides to return to life in the country. As his carriage reaches the city limits, he cultivates a "melancholy mood" by expressing his emotions in an "internal monologue" that inadvertently reveals the same literary flaws noted by the journal editor. "Farewell," Alexander declares, "Farewell, oh city of false hair, false teeth, cotton imitations of nature, round hats, city of polite haughtiness, artificial feelings, lifeless bustle! Farewell, magnificent morgue of the soul's deep, strong, tender, and warm movements. Here I stood face to face with contemporary life . . . but with my back to nature, which turned away from me."[60] In the country, Alexander watches peasants work in the fields and "learned from experience things about which he had often written and translated for the magazine."[61] He gives himself over to a large writing project on agricultural problems—his true magnum opus.

Alexander, however, finds himself missing St. Petersburg. His final literary effort consists of eloquent, yet touchingly honest letters to his aunt and uncle that offer his reasons for wanting to return. He promises, "Not a scatterbrain, not a dreamer, not a disillusioned man, nor a provincial boy will come to you, but just a person, the kind of which there are so many in Petersburg, and such as I long since should have been."[62] To his uncle, Alexander writes, "Who hasn't been young and stupid? . . . I thought creative talent had been instilled in me from on high and I wanted to disclose new unknown secrets to the world, not suspecting that these were not secrets and that I was not a prophet. We're all ridiculous."[63] This embrace of the middle range of life—the ordinary experiences of a working adult—is the literary and aesthetic culmination of Goncharov's novel.

When Alexander appears in the Epilogue four years later, he is bald and ruddy, with a "little protruding belly," happily contemplating his marriage to a rich girl.[64] Alexander presents his uncle with an "ancient, almost ruined, yellowed little sheet of paper," a silly love letter that attests to the time when Petr Aduev, too, produced "sincere outpourings" and wrote with "special inks." Petr Aduev is mortified by these memories, but admits that in his youth he had indeed loved, raged, wept, and plucked yellow flowers. In return for this concession, Alexander gives his uncle the scrap of paper, which the latter promptly burns. With this final destruction of an immature "artistic" text, the novel ends, as the two men embrace and talk about money. With its resolute rejection of melodrama and equally firm commitment to prosaism and real-life commitments, Goncharov's novel represents one of the more unusual "provincial in Petersburg" tales. In transcribing the story of not becoming a writer, *An Ordinary Story* parodoxically lauds the principles of the novel as a form.

Aleksei Pisemskii's novel *A Thousand Souls* (*Tysiacha dush*, 1858) complements Goncharov's *An Ordinary Story* in depicting a provincial protagonist who resists embracing the cultural middle space to which he rightfully belongs, and instead yearns for entry into higher literary and social orders. Pisemskii himself was from Kostroma and studied at Moscow University, moving in 1854 to Petersburg, where he felt himself very much the uncouth provincial. In Pisemskii's novel, the ambitious provincial Kalinovich comes to Petersburg after having a story accepted by a journal. Although he initially hopes to become a professional writer, once in the capital, Kalinovich marries a wealthy woman he does not love and devotes himself to a career in state service.

When Kalinovich first arrives in the capital, he hires a cabdriver to take him "past all of the palaces and cathedrals."[65] He goes on foot to see the monument to Peter the Great: "He stood by the monument for a little while, walked around it a couple of times, and then took a look at St. Isaac's. All of this had a somehow irritating effect on him." He walks down Voznesenskii Prospect, where the sight of drunks emerging from the taverns and the smell of frying onions depress his spirits. As twilight falls, Kalinovich returns to his hotel, and, hearing the music of an organ-grinder on the street, thinks, "This is the crying and moaning of a human soul, imprisoned amidst the gloom and snows of this sepulchral city." As he lies down to sleep, he is overcome by the psychic state proper to Petersburg: "an incomprehensible and unbearable anguish," in conjunction with an "unaccountable terror." Kalinovich has arrived. His would-be writer's mind, like the narrating voice, struggles to formulate a response to the unfamiliar surroundings.

Kalinovich receives a smaller sum than expected for his published story. Still, he has high hopes for a second literary effort, until his old university friend Zykov—ill and skeletal—rebukes Kalinovich for treating only high-society characters in his writing: "Drama seethes in the lives of our simple people and in those of the middle estate. . . . This one perishes in poverty, this one is innocently but constantly humiliated . . . This one, among scoundrels and villain-bureaucrats, himself becomes a villain. But you go around all of this and take some high-society people, and relate how they suffer from strange relationships. I spit on them!"[66]

Kalinovich's central failing as a writer is his inability to tell his own story, that of a middling sort. He decides to abandon literature and stands on the Anichkov Bridge, gazing at the activity on the Fontanka and envying the peasant haulers, who, he feels, are far more necessary to Petersburg's existence than a "thinking person" like himself. The arrival of Nastenka, his true love from the provinces, briefly revives him, but he grows restless in her orbit of modest domestic comfort. He peers longingly through the *belle-étage* windows of apartment houses at "flowers, chandeliers, candelabras, and enormous paintings in gold frames," still pining for the milieu he ascribed to his own fictional protagonists.[67] Soon, in a perfect response to both Kalinovich's desire and Zykov's proposed literary plots, the scheming Prince Ivan appears to lead Kalinovich astray, granting him entrée to the best drawing-rooms at the cost of his provincial ideals. Kalinovich's subsequent unhappiness, like Pisemskii's, is exactly that of a provincial *raznochinets* who has wandered into the wrong fictional drawing room.

Even when the arriving provincial keeps to his appointed course, the results are not encouraging. The writer Ivan Kushchevskii arrived in Petersburg in 1864, after completing his gymnasium studies in Tomsk. He managed to complete the novel *Nikolai Negorev, or The Successful Russian* (*Nikolai Negorev, ili, Blagopoluchnyi rossiianin*) while he lay ill in a hospital in 1871, but died in 1876, before his thirtieth birthday. Kushchevskii's feuilleton "To Petersburg! To the river of honey, Neva!" (*V Peterburg! Na medovuiu reku Nevu!*), from the early 1870s, retells the familiar story. The narrator, a Petersburg resident, finds himself at the Nikolaevskii railway station one day and notices the crowd of young men disembarking from the train. He remembers that "it is now that time of the year, that month, when provincial youth, having completed its final examinations, hurries to Petersburg with mountains of the most shining hopes and rosy dreams."[68] The narrator recalls his own arrival, years earlier, with thirty-two rubles in his pocket. Unable to afford the university, he earns occasional money as a laborer, but succumbs to typhus and lands in the hospital. While languishing there, he writes an urban-ethnographic sketch and submits it to *The Contemporary*. To his surprise, he receives a note from Nekrasov, informing him that his sketch will be published. Kushchevskii's narrator reproduces his own youthful rapture: "Him—he himself—that genius, whose compositions I know by heart, whom I worship. Once I have seen him, I will probably fall at his feet and lick the wax from his boots. He himself writes with his own hand to pathetic, poor, and insignificant me!"[69] The narrator professes to remember nothing of Nekrasov's visit to him in the hospital, only that "involuntary tears" trickled down his cheeks, and that he did not dare take the great writer's outstretched hand. This stagy moment of literary baton-passing is treated ironically, however, as the older narrator has not attained literary glory, but simply become a middling literary professional.

Now the narrator mourns his long-lost ability to experience such transports. He exclaims, "How good it would be now, in the old way, like a youth, to carry a three-*pood* suitcase on one's shoulders from the Nikolaevskii railway station. . . . For what did I work so hard?" The narrator watches one provincial hopeful exiting the station, and predicts his future—starving in a tiny apartment on the Petersburg Side with seven friends from his old gymnasium. One by one, the gymnasium friends will move on, until the aspirant is left with a single friend, who will die in his arms from tuberculosis. Kushchevskii's sketch presents an endless regress of provincial youths who come to Petersburg and write about their experiences. The young idealist and the tiredly knowing narrator are a perfectly matched literary set. Writing pays badly and costs the provincial youth nearly everything else in return, including the self that originally longed to be a writer.

In Kushchevskii's story "The Errors of Youth" (*Oshibki molodosti*), published in an 1881 posthumous collection, the starving provincial Stubefaktov presents himself at a Petersburg police station, declaring he has eaten nothing for three days, and demanding that he be dealt with via official channels. He refuses the baffled station officer's offer of food, pompously insisting that he be sent to a prison or workhouse, and expecting the police to be shocked by the indigent circumstances of a person such as himself. Kushchevskii's worldly narrator offers the familiar "provincial in Petersburg" master plot as one of self-misrepresentation, in a tirade devoted to Stubefaktov's ilk: "The poor seminary student was only one of the thousands of those little Lomonosovs, who come in droves each year from the provinces to the capital... Like all of his fellows, he naively considered himself one of the chosen, 'set apart by a heavenly finger,' ... and therefore entitled to special attention and respect from all sides. Alas!"[70] Young men like Stubefaktov, he claims, are actually self-interested individuals "who do not wish to be country priests," in no way distinct from their fellows as "the simplest and most ordinary seekers of happiness." Kushchevskii's narrator mourns the collective fate of all Stubefaktovs nonetheless: "Having appeared in Petersburg without a penny, with nothing but a naïve faith in their greatness and the childish daring of the inexperienced, these unfortunates become disillusioned upon their first steps in the capital, suffer terrible poverty, and, not finding anywhere the expected warm sympathy and dedicated aid, they perish, die in the hospitals, and get lost in the crowd, having forgotten lofty dreams in their concerns over a piece of daily bread. The more weak-spirited of them return on foot to their native provinces, to spend the rest of their lives cursing inhospitable Petersburg."[71] The "provincial in Petersburg" tale is one of unrealized potential—for writing, for narrative, and for individuality. It is a subgenre that longs to obliterate itself by evolving from cautionary tale into creative biography, but one that, like its provincial protagonists, inevitably falls victim to inadequate potential and to the requisite deflation that is one of its essential traits. The narrator is guilty of the same grandstanding exhibited by Stubefaktov, and thus, while criticizing the latter's self-importance, his vehemence suggests that he is also invoking his own youthful experiences. The rhetoric infused with a self-conscious sense of Belinsky's "bitter truth" gives him away.

The tale of the provincial in Petersburg is sometimes rendered as autobiography, thus conflating the categories of jaded narrator and youthful acolyte. Accordingly, some of these autobiographical accounts invent a double-figure, a venerable tradition in the Petersburg Text, to reintroduce the element of literary fiction. Vladimir Korolenko's voluminous autobiography *The History of My Contemporary (Istoriia moego sovremennika,* 1904–18), for example, relates the author's experiences as a young man in Petersburg during the first half of the 1870s through the estranging device of treating his younger self as a compatriot. The chapter "In Petersburg!" describes Korolenko's arrival by train, at the requisite "young provincial" moment when summer turns to fall, and the brief vacation after lycée examinations has ended: "My heart trembled from joy. Petersburg! Here was concentrated all that I considered best in life, because all of Russian literature emerged from here, the true motherland of my soul."[72]

Korolenko's prior knowledge of the city is *literary,* and it is against this literary Petersburg that he measures his own experience. When he sees Nevsky Prospect, he thinks, "This is where Gogol's Colonel Pirogov once strolled. . .And somewhere there, in that confused mass of buildings, Belinsky lived, and Dobroliubov thought and worked. Here he wrote with stiffening hand, 'My dear friend, I am dying because I was honorable'. . . Here Nekrasov lives still, and thus I am breathing the same air as he." The older Korolenko claims that this moment of arrival "imprinted itself forever" in his memory "as one of the landmarks that distinguishes the retreating spaces of life." As is usual in the provincial tale, however, this exaltation is immediately dispelled, when he is treated rudely by a pastry-seller.

The next morning, Korolenko looks out his hotel window onto the Ligovka, a "slimy little canal" under the gray and overcast sky. "That's how it should be," he thinks contentedly. "Not for nothing do they compare this sky with a gray soldier's overcoat. . . There it is. It really looks like that. The creeping gloom has traveled from Nevsky to the tip of the Znamenskaia Church. Marvelous. After all, this is the 'Petersburg fog' that has so often been described. It is all the way they said! I am, without a doubt, in Petersburg." Korolenko knows Petersburg intimately from reading about it that he is able to lead his comrade Korzhenevskii confidently along Nevsky Prospect, down Sadovaia Street to Haymarket Square. Korolenko wishes to clamber aboard the top of a horse-drawn streetcar, seeking "knowledge of every sort of Petersburg thing, as Pavel Ivanovich Chichikov would have said," but Korzhenevskii hesitates. Korolenko remarks that the two of them resembled Goliadkin climbing the staircase to the home of Doctor Rutenspitz in Dostoevsky's novella "The Double": "Korzhenevskii was timid Goliadkin, doubting his right to be there, while I was the haughty Goliadkin, assuring himself that 'like everyone,' we were not without the right to ride on the imperial of this magnificent streetcar."[73] Here, Korolenko's narrative spawns yet another double, for good measure.

Korolenko finds lodging with a group of students in a garret space near the Technological Institute. Unable to sleep, he writes to his brother, describing his new comrades, in particular one Veselitskii: "He is from Kostroma, the son of a priest, from a seminary. You can tell that he is a *raznochinets,* the same type as Pomialovskii. . . . I sense in him a great potential strength that is destined to manifest itself in some striking way. He reads all of the time, rarely tearing himself away from his book."[74] Korolenko is perfectly aware of his own tendency to view Petersburg in terms of Russian literature. At this point in his narrative, he remarks, "The reader has probably noticed from the preceding text that my contemporary was particularly receptive to the influence of literary motifs and types." This he attributes to "the life of a little town, ordinary and monotonous, which did not correspond to literary categories," and which therefore caused everything connected to the world illuminated by literature to take on, in his eyes, "a rather fantastical and thus alluring light."[75] Initially, the imperial capital pleased him, "even the dull brick walls that blocked that sky, because they were familiar from Dostoevsky. . . I even liked the insecurity and prospect of hunger. . . After all, this is also encountered in descriptions of student life, and I looked at life through the prism of literature." Korolenko leads an unproductive, dissipated student life, but does so in a kind of literary reverie. After a year of poverty, he finds work coloring in the drawings on botanical atlases, contributing in a minor way to the textual production of the capital, not unlike Goncharov's Alexander with his journal articles about manure.

At one point, an acquaintance proposes that Korolenko become a correspondent for *Russian World*. Korolenko cannot fall asleep, so ecstatic is he at the prospect:

> From earliest childhood I had dreamed about literature. . . I tried to express every notable impression and striking image in appropriate words and could not rest until I had found the most suitable expression. Even my dreams took the alternating form of pictures and narration about them. Several times I awakened in a kind of exalted state. It seemed I had written a superb story or poem. Fragments of the last pictures and the last lines of verse still burned in my brain, quickly disappearing, like the traces of breath on crystal glass. Only, alas, I could not remember the contents of what I had written, and if I recalled a few of the final verses of this resonant poem, then, upon closer examination, they were found to lack both meter and form.[76]

Korolenko dreams the collective fantasy of the "provincial in Petersburg" tale, of artistic genius that manifests itself in predestined perfect form. The provincial aspirant longs to create a literary masterwork, and in so doing, to author himself as a distinctive exception. The master plot requires, however, that the Holy Grail should remain forever beyond reach. This distancing is almost always underscored by self-parody, which creates an even wider gap between wishful thinking and the "ordinary story" of self that the older narrator ends up writing.

In any case, Korolenko can scarcely believe that he might become a newspaper writer. When he visits the newspaper office, however, he is met with indifference, and told that he may write something if he wishes, and if his work is deemed suitable, the newspaper will print it. This, Korolenko observes, is precisely what he himself would subsequently tell the uncountable "bashful youths" who would come to his office "with the same naïve proposals of collaboration."

At the end of the school year, Korolenko returns home, stopping along the way to visit his uncle, who finds him much altered. Korolenko attempts to explain the change in himself, which he characterizes as the dissolution of his "rosy fog." He confesses, "Life in the capital during this year did not raise me to its level. Quite the opposite—it seemed to me that this life descended to my level. I am dim and not interesting. . . And so is this life."[77] Nikolai Antsiferov nevertheless points to the continuity of Korolenko's central image—the glistening chain of gas streetlights under the nighttime summer sky that he encounters when he disembarks from the train that first time, and again, when his Petersburg period reaches its end. The chain of lights then provides a painful reminder of his former naïve expectations. The streetlamps are a specifically literary image for Korolenko, evoking the textual chain of narrative, and the recurrence of literary motif. This defining moment is equivalent to the middle meeting place created by literature over the preceding decades—the formative points in a writer's creative biography viewed in self-conscious retrospective.

Dmitri Mamin-Sibiriak's autobiographical fiction *Traits from the Life of Pepko* (*Cherty iz zhizni Pepko*, 1894) follows Nekrasov in making use of the author's own experience, in this case as a provincial in 1870s Petersburg. From a distance of twenty years, Mamin-Sibiriak's first-person narrator chronicles his experiences as a casual journalist struggling to break into more serious literary circles and describes the bohemian excesses of his threadbare existence. At the end of the novel, the narrator boards a train and returns to the provinces, where he finally becomes a writer. In this same spirit of retrospection, *Pepko* can be characterized as an "eventual" novel, since it was initially published in the journal *Russian Riches* as a self-identified series of sketches, and was reconceived as a novel with chapter divisions only in 1895.

Pepko opens on a gloomy autumn morning in a remote part of the Petersburg Side, with the narrator's admission that he has skipped his university lectures in order to finish "the seventh chapter of the third part of my first novel."[78] The narrator's best friend purportedly shares the surname Popov, but calls himself "Pepko," and is openly acknowledged by the narrator as "my double, my alter ego," with whom he traversed the "thorny path" of youth "hand in hand," a figure not unlike Korolenko's "contemporary."[79] Pepko hails from the northeast provinces, however, while the narrator comes from the south.

"If the Bronze Horseman didn't stand on Senate Square," Pepko tells his friend, "we would never have met." Thus the consummate symbol of the modernizing Russian empire, the Peter statue, marks the decidedly unmonumental meeting place of middling provincial aspirations. Pepko continues, "And do you know what has brought us here? . . . You will say: love of knowledge. . . thirst for education. . . . The essence of the matter is much simpler. Education is all very well, but it is good to get one's piece of the pie."[80] Pepko unfurls the collective narrative in the well-established denunciatory moment of such tales, in which Belinsky's "bitter truth" becomes an excuse for self-dramatization:

> I have a passion for wandering about the cemeteries in the spring... Here is an instructive picture: how many of our brother provincials who dragged themselves to Petersburg with good intentions instead of luggage are laid here?... And how many of those who did not even manage to show the worth of their talents, strong people, perhaps geniuses, are rotting in these cemeteries? You look at these graves and sense that you yourself are walking the path of these dead failures, that you are repeating the same mistakes, submitting to the simple physical law of centripetal force. And new battalions appear to replace these dead men, meaning us, and new Petyas and Kolyas are being readied to replace us in some unknown provincial backwoods.

Despite this lofty rhetoric, Pepko characterizes himself ingenuously as "an average (*srednii*) person," the type from which the "fabric of life" is woven. He claims, however, to have discovered the secret of becoming a great writer. He takes a short story from each of the most famous Russian authors and performs upon it what he calls "the most precise chemical analysis," or more accurately, "an anatomical post-mortem."[81] In this way, he calculates the number of lines devoted to such features as "Description of a Summer Morning," "Action Scene," "Development of the Protagonist," and "Lyrical Digressions." He then determines the proportions devoted to each category for each celebrated author, as well as the ordering of these elements in their works. Pepko similarly analyzes one of the narrator's own literary efforts—recently rejected by a well-known journal—and decides that the deep structure of the narrator's writing most resembles that of Gogol, a revelation he urges the narrator to turn to his advantage by making the coincidence of proportions even closer. When the narrator fails to become a serious writer, however, he himself mentally advises young would-be writers quite differently: "Better not even to try... because Pushkin, Lermontov, Gogol, Turgenev, Goncharov, Dostoevsky, and Lev Tolstoy have said it all, and not even allowed you the leftovers."[82] Herein lies the tragedy of the provincial tale, but also its ironic twist. Would that literary "classics" could yield up their secrets so readily!

Toward the end of the novel, Mamin-Sibiriak's narrator revisits the familiar topos of the "provincial in Petersburg" tale with heightened self-awareness: "Now I left the house only in the evenings and loved to take long rambles along the streets. Generally I left the detested Petersburg Side and walked into the city center. How many rich houses there were, what magnificent carriages hurtled past, as I took pleasure in my own insignificance, stopping in front of the windows of luxurious shops, by the brightly illuminated entranceways, in places where the idle public gathered."[83] The narrator's Dostoevskian relish of his own humiliation becomes part of the tale, the very impetus for writing. Petersburg is a crucible for writers—and not necessarily great ones—who then perpetuate the city's mythology ever after in their texts.

Alexander Kuprin made one of the final contributions to the "provincial in Petersburg" text with his 1905 story "Black Fog: A Petersburg Incident" (*Chernyi tuman: peterburgskii sluchai*), which employs the nineteenth-century device of the "Petersburg" subtitle. Originally from the Penza province, Kuprin studied in Moscow, served in the military, and worked as a journalist in Kiev before moving to Petersburg in 1901.

The protagonist of Kuprin's story, Boris, appears at the narrator's furnished room in Petersburg early one winter morning, as the latter recalls with grudging admiration: "I remember very well when he came to Petersburg for the first time from his lazy, hot, sensual south. It even emanated from him, that black-soil strength, the dry and sultry smell of needle grass, the simple poetry of quiet sunsets fading out beyond the trees of the little cherry orchards. It seemed that there could be no end to his inexhaustible steppe-dweller health and his fresh, naïve directness."[84] Boris finds a position with the railway administration and devises a detailed plan for the coordinated movements of passenger and freight trains. Unlike his many literary semblances, Boris does not aspire to be a writer, but rather, it seems, to be of practical use to the capital. The "provincial" in Petersburg tale is nevertheless so established, even fossilized, at this point, that Boris's fate is predetermined.

Boris gradually loses his enthusiasm for the capital, becoming "melancholy, irritated, and completely undone by the white nights, which caused him insomnia and an anguish approaching despair."[85] An evening on the town with the narrator only makes him gloomier, and the two return home, passing butcher shops in which hang "upended red carcasses of revolting dead beef." The narrator sees "five-story buildings drowning in the gloom, which, exactly like the flaccid belly of a black snake, descended into the corridor of the street, hiding and growing still, hanging there as if preparing to snatch someone."[86] At this point, the language that reflects the narrator's urban-artist consciousness becomes Boris's property as well, since he has earned the right to this literary medium with his Petersburg spiritual crisis. Boris declares agitatedly that the city is breathing: "This is no fog, but the exhalations of these stones with holes. Here is the stinking dampness of the laundry and the soot of hard coal, here is the sin of people, their malice and hatred, the effluvium of their mattresses, the smell of sweat and rotting mouths... Curse you, anathema, you beast, beast—I hate you!" Boris breaks into a fit of coughing and shows his friend the bloody handkerchief—the oft-rendered tubercular moment in the provincial tale, here simultaneous with the moment of denunciation. "It has devoured me... the fog," he mutters. In actuality, Boris has been engulfed by a literary tradition that is too powerful for him to resist.

Back in Ukraine, under the "caressing blue sky," Boris briefly revives, as if his soul were waking from a "long, clinging, icy nightmare," but the black fog has killed off "something essential in him, which gives both life and the desire to live." On the day before his death, Boris assures the narrator, "after me will come others, hundreds and thousands of others" from the southern provinces, and these warriors cannot fail to defeat the city of black fog. The narrator's own writing grows more and more lyrical as the story's end approaches, and in the final lines he describes himself placing a branch of white lilac blossoms on his dead friend's breast, as the thrushes sing in the garden and church prayer-bells sound from across the river. The canonical plot of the "provincial in Petersburg" tale can accommodate diverse writers and writing styles, including Kuprin's hyperbolically Manichaean juxtaposition of Petersburg north and Ukrainian south. The return to the provinces seems, however, a reversion to a tired romanticism. The city of black fog may have killed Boris, but the trip south has done nothing to sharpen the narrator's own literary sensibility.

The "provincial in Petersburg" tale is a literary tradition that is by definition self-perpetuating. Like Korolenko in the 1870s, the young would-be writer reads autobiographical accounts and fictional works by writers before him and is moved to imitate their experience by setting off for Petersburg. In this spirit, Nikolai Antsiferov's memoirs, written during the 1940s-1950s, describe his 1908 arrival in autumnal Petersburg in the very terms that he used to characterize the "Petersburg" writings of so many prerevolutionary Russian writers. In *The Soul of Petersburg* (*Dusha Peterburga*, 1922), Antsiferov writes, "Petersburg! Straight lines, right angles. Gray granite. White shroud of the wide motionless Neva. Frost on the columns of St. Isaac's. What cold! Terrible Peter congealed in his burst of movement. The Tsarist sphinxes also frozen in their places."[87] Petersburg has not merely frozen at the beginning of the long northern winter, but has become similarly fixed in cultural memory, an impression anticipated by the young Antsiferov, received by him as expected, and finally, conveyed telegraphically in a literary code that felt like home to his readers.

In an eccentrically situated city such as Petersburg, defining margins against center in terms of literary and urban topography becomes a creative challenge. Petersburg literature champions the urban underprivileged, but only those who inhabited central parts of the city. The literature of the palace-parks itself is exclusive—a series of expensively illustrated albums and elegant memoirs produced for the cultural elite. The literary middle ground of the Petersburg Text can be found, however, in the shared intelligentsia fantasy of distinctive, all-conquering uniqueness, manifested as literary genius. Sometimes the provincial tale represents the writer's biography (Nekrasov, Panaev, Kushchevskii, Korolenko, Mamin-Sibiriak), while in other cases, this tale constitutes a writer's antibiography—the story of *not* becoming a writer (Goncharov, Pisemskii). Each time the common story—in Goncharov's phrasing, the "ordinary story"—is repeated, its author claims to have discovered a new truth. The literary middle can thus be characterized as a loose association of autodidacts who teach themselves the same lesson. The Petersburg Text instructs its authors as well as its readers.

CHAPTER SEVEN

The City's Memory: Public Graveyards and Textual Repositories

PETERSBURG's chroniclers have long been preoccupied by this young city's history and memory, or, to put it another way, many chroniclers have underscored Petersburg's paradoxes of preservation and loss. Count Francesco Algarotti was among the first to exhibit this conflation of old and new, noting the dilapidated state of the city's grand palaces, hastily constructed by courtiers whom Peter the Great had compelled to establish residency in the new capital: "Their walls are all cracked, quite out of perpendicular, and ready to fall. It has been wittily enough said, that ruins make themselves in other places, but that they were built at Petersburg."[1]

Algarotti attributed Petersburg's "ruins" to shoddy building practices exacerbated by the inhospitable topographical situation. Similarly, William Kinglake, who visited Petersburg in the mid-1840s, scornfully advised travelers to admire the city by moonlight, so as to avoid seeing, "with too critical an eye, plaster scaling from the white-washed walls, and frost-cracks rending the painted wooden columns." Comparing Peter's project to Solomon's obstinacy in creating Tadmor, Kinglake evoked the city's "huge, staring masses of raw whitewash," which, to him, had "the air of gigantic models, abandoned on the site intended to be hereafter occupied by more substantial structures."[2] These Petersburg ruins are seen as inadvertent, but as nevertheless symptomatic of the city's need to create a past for itself while hastily erecting an all too provisional present. Built ruins like Yuri Velten's 1771 Ruined Tower at Tsarskoe Selo and the Apollo Collonade created by Charles Cameron at Pavlovsk encouraged their viewers to meditate upon the work of time by staging a contemplative moment during a landscaped stroll. Algarotti and Kinglake both propose Petersburg's crumbling palaces as monuments to human vanity and ill-conceived imperial aspirations, and in this sense as not unlike the defeat of the Turks at Ochakov invoked by Velten's project.

Algarotti and Kinglake viewed the Russian imperial capital with the critical assessing gaze of foreign visitors, exposing practices of Petersburg sham and

scam. For Russian writers during the nineteenth century, in contrast, the notion of premature ruins came to be associated with metaphysical and moral-
ethical issues. The image of the imperial capital in ruins reflects the eschatological thinking of Pushkin, Gogol, Dostoevsky, and Bely, as discussed in
contemporary writing about the "Petersburg mythology." What is less often acknowledged, however, is that this imagery also responds to real historical processes of urban destruction and reconstruction. Although imperial Petersburg
was not an old city, by the nineteenth century its urban topography constituted
a much-overwritten and rewritten cultural text, subject to cycles of overlay
long before the well-known early-Soviet and post-Soviet remapping projects.
The quintessential twentieth-century Petersburg project of replacing, renaming, and reclaiming city structures finds many counterparts in nineteenth-
century literature that illustrate the continuous remapping—that is, the intertwined process of forgetting and remembering—that constitutes both the life
and death of the city. It is this selfsame twinned process, with its particular
omissions and emphases, which produced the Petersburg myth as we know it
today.

Beginning in the nineteenth century, Petersburg's memory has been maintained by diverse institutions, events, and practices. Monuments and memorial
plaques around the city physically figure a past proposed to contemporary viewers as simultaneously present and absent. The Museum of Old Petersburg and
its successors, as well as the city's historical archives, have provided paper repositories for memory, while cemeteries preserve both inscriptions and material
"remains," albeit not very reliably. Material and written tributes memorialize aspects of city life that fell victim to the gradual passage of time, as well as those
erased in a single day by disasters such as flood and fire. This sort of remembering is necessarily selective and mythological, however, and it is also true that
in imperial St. Petersburg, old structures were intentionally destroyed to make
way for the new. During the Soviet period, of course, extensive changes of this
sort were imposed on the city by the Bolshevik government. The on-going project of remapping Petersburg has thus often resembled a kind of willed amn-
esia, occasioned by imperial caprice, political revolution, and rehabilitative efforts that can be by turns cynical, simply expedient, or quixotic. Petersburg
proves the counterintuitive but ancient rule that writing, a seemingly ephemeral
medium, offers the most reliable material for building an enduring monument
to the past. But all of this writing about imperial Petersburg requires the physical resources of the city for its continued preservation in libraries, museums,
and archives.

It has been said that literature may be, at its origins, a lapidary object or an
inscription. Literary language of a sort is often inscribed upon an architectural
work in decorative symbols, narrative bas-reliefs, coats-of-arms, dedications,
and proclamations, and the existence of an architectural object is entwined with
the various texts that are written before, in, around, and about it. In fact, an ed-

ifice is by nature "forgetful" and can only reacquire its lost meaning through the agency of historians' studies, guidebooks, and plaques.[3]

Cemeteries: The Topos of Memory

Throughout the city's history, eloquent pens have consigned Petersburg to an early grave. In his memoirs of Petersburg of the early 1820s, O. A. Przhetslavskii commented on the "melancholy character" of the famous masquerades at the Engelhardt house, which "had the appearance of a funeral procession and wearied one with their uniform-like monotony of costumes."[4] During his 1839 visit, the Marquis de Custine gloomily noted the twin identities (prison and tomb) of the Peter-Paul Fortress and thus of the city as a whole. Political prisoners languished in the underground fortress dungeons, while the tombs of the Romanov monarchs, from Peter the Great through Alexander I, stood on display in the fortress church. "In this funereal citadel, the dead appeared to me more free than the living," remarked the Marquis, adding, "If it had been a philosophical idea which suggested the inclosing in the same tomb the prisoners of the emperor and the prisoners of death—the conspirators and the monarchs against whom they conspired—I should respect it; but I see in it nothing more than the cynicism of absolute power."[5] In the essay "Winter Rainbows" (*Zimnie radugi*, 1907), Dmitri Merezhkovskii recalled Petersburg's "face of death" in 1905, which, to him, reflected both the social unrest and the cholera epidemic sweeping the city at the time. Merezhkovskii claimed that Petersburg bore the mark of inescapable doom evident on a soon-to-be-dead-man's countenance, just like that evoked by Lermontov's Pechorin in the 1840 novel *A Hero of Our Time* (*Geroi nashego vremeni*).[6]

In the 1990s, the writer Alexander Skidan acknowledged Petersburg's primary function as the "sepulcher of imperial Russian culture." The "museum principle" as everywhere manifested in Petersburg "gives rise to the nauseating sensation of unceasing *déjà vu*," he wrote.[7] Even the most recent of events are "conserved," "surrendered before our eyes into an archive," and transformed into "reminiscence" and "petrified ruins." Petersburg's dead, fixed quality could then be attributed to the Bolsheviks' neglect of the imperial capital, compounded by the lack of funds during the post-Soviet period for renovating shabby palaces and formerly grand apartment houses. For many imperial-era commentators, however, Petersburg was already a city of loss, a cemetery-like site of much-regretted change and destruction. Indeed, there have been moments in Petersburg's prerevolutionary history when the city as a whole might have been seen as a tombstone marking its own grave. These periods include an interlude following Peter the Great's death when the capital temporarily shifted back to Moscow (1728–31), as well as the years after the 1881 assassination of Alexander II, when both Alexander III and Nicholas II preferred to reside in Moscow or at the Gatchina and Tsarskoe Selo palace-parks outside of Petersburg.[8]

As Lewis Mumford points out, "Mid the uneasy wanderings of paleolithic man, the dead were the first to have a permanent dwelling." Since the site of ancestral graves often provided an incentive for the living to form a settlement, "The city of the dead antedates the city of the living . . . is the forerunner, almost the core, of every living city."[9] In the Petersburg Text, the cemetery provides one of the most common figures for the city's memory, as well as a favorite subject for cultural historians, who use tombstones to chronicle city life.[10] Vladimir Saitov's massive project of 1907–11 took precisely this approach to Petersburg cemeteries, compiling more than 40,000 epitaphs from fifty-seven different burial places in a four-volume reference that he termed a "dictionary of individuals."[11] Petersburg's cemeteries as a group also compose a cultural text that speaks to phenomena such as the haphazard nature of cemetery planning in eighteenth-century Russia, the lurching evolution of cemeteries' relationship to the nineteenth-century city, and the postrevolutionary relocation of individual graves to the Masters of Art cemetery (*Nekropol' Masterov Iskusstv*) and the Volkovo Writers' Footway (*Literatorskie mostki*)—museum-like collections of dead Russian cultural luminaries.

In 1939, all of the city sculpture, including monuments and memorials inside cemeteries, came under the supervision of the "Museum of City Sculpture"—an abstraction more than an institution that signaled the increasingly museum-like atmosphere of St. Petersburg as a whole.

According to the statistical data regarding Petersburg's population and its cemeteries from the imperial period, the city could be characterized, in Toporov's words, as "a gigantic and well-functioning factory for the production and intake of dead people." The death rate far exceeded the birth rate in Petersburg until the 1880s, and near the end of the nineteenth century, the number of dead buried in Volkovo, one of the city's large public cemeteries, numbered well over half the living population of the capital.[12] As Vsevolod Garshin wrote in his "Petersburg Letters" (*Peterburgskie pis'ma*, 1882), "Dead Petersburg is bigger than live Petersburg." He noted that the cemeteries within the city proper had long since been filled up, and that the dead were being transported to new cemeteries along the railroad lines outside of the city limits: "Entire funeral trains depart daily from Petersburg, conveying dozens of coffins; some are placed in a heap in one train car, while other coffins occupy entire cars, standing out vividly on mourning catafalques. The whistle blows, the train begins to move with its lifeless load, and from the other direction arrive trains filled with the living, with a new supply of people, many of whom will return back only as far as the first station—the Preobrazhenskii or Udel'nyi cemeteries. Hello to the living! Farewell to the dead!"[13]

Recasting Petropolis as Nekropolis was a favorite sally of Petersburg-hating nineteenth-century Russian writers. Nikolai Nekrasov, for example, frequently

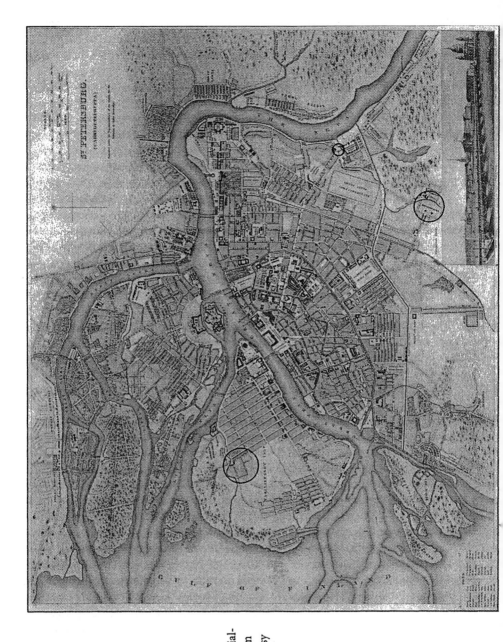

Figure 7.1. Imperial-Era Cemeteries from 1853 Map. (Courtesy of Harvard Map Collection.)

characterized Petersburg in his urban poetry with reference to graveyards, comparing the nighttime Neva to "an enormous coffin" that lay within its illuminated banks, and evoking the "boundless cemeteries" that surrounded the city's luxuries and entertainments.[14] Yakov Polonskii's 1862 poem "White Night" (*Belaia noch*') picks out the gold dome of St. Isaac's Cathedral as the only feature of the cityscape that stands out among the "grizzled palaces," gleaming "like a corpse's funeral wreath before an icon lamp." In Ivan Turgenev's story "Phantoms" (*Prizraki*, 1864), the narrator and his spirit-guide fly over Petersburg, a "sick city" whose pale night is indistinguishable from its ailing day, surveying the empty gray streets, with their "petrified yardmen" and cabdrivers "crumpled in a deathlike sleep."[15] Petr Iakubovich's 1883 poem-tirade "Fantastic City" (*Skazochnyi gorod*) terms Petersburg "a cemetery of the best people." Thus, as Toporov observes, "One of the indubitable functions of the Petersburg Text is that of an ecclesiastical death bill (*pominal'nyi sinodik*) for those who perished in Petropolis, which became for them a genuine Nekropolis."[16]

Despite the prevalence of the cemetery topos in the Petersburg Text, however, the history of Petersburg's burial places is a confusing account of the interpolating, supplementing, and overwriting of memory sites. During the first decades of St. Petersburg's existence, the dead were buried at random, with workers' graves dug on unconsecrated ground, and other graves simply attached to local churches scattered about the city territory.[17] The first official cemetery grounds were formally established in 1710 on the Vyborg Side and the territory of Bol'shaia Okhta, and in 1717, at the Alexander-Nevskii Monastery. The burial of the dead soon became a pressing issue, however, since the swampy ground and shallow graves constituted a public health hazard. In 1746, Empress Elizabeth issued a decree requiring the comprehensive regulation of cemeteries in Petersburg; she also closed several cemeteries inside the city proper, and forbade further burials on the grounds of small parish churches. A Senate decree of 1756 formally established the Volkovo Cemetery to the southeast of where the Obvodnyi Canal would later be excavated, the Smolenskoe Cemetery in the midpart of Vasilievskii Island, and a cemetery by the old Sampsonievskaia Church burial grounds on the Vyborg road. Members of the city's elite were laid to rest in the Lazarevskoe Cemetery at the Alexander-Nevskii Monastery, as well as the newer Tikhvinskoe (formerly Novoe Lazarevskoe) and Nikol'skoe cemeteries. Lazarevskoe housed members of powerful families such as Sheremetev, Apraksin, Golytsin, and Stroganov, and high-ranking persons who had performed valuable service to the state. In contrast, the Smolenskoe cemetery offered a final home to modest merchants and humble people of the "middle estate."[18] Later, Smolenskoe became known as the burial place for the intelligentsia, because of the many Academy of Sciences members, university professors, and artists from the Academy of Fine Arts who lived on Vasilievskii Island near their institutions. By the middle of the nineteenth century, Petersburg was once again suffering from a shortage of cemetery space, and a city commission commandeered additional burial ground along the Nikolaevskaia, Varshavskaia, and Finliandskaia railway lines leading out of the city, as per Garshin.

During the nineteenth century, Rasstannaia Street (from the verb *rasstat'sia*, to part company), down which funeral processions traveled to the Volkovo cemetery, was lined with artisan workshops specializing in tombstones, shops selling flowers and wreaths, and small businesses that sold provisions for funeral feasts. These artisans and small merchants from the burial industry provided Petersburg physiologists with a vivid subject for sketches. Alexander Bashchutskii's 1840 "Coffin-maker" (*Grobovoi master*) is an early effort of this sort, rendered in a somewhat heavy-handed comic mode typical of the time.[19] Anatoly Bakhtiarov included a series of journalistic sketches called "Petersburg Gravediggers" (*Peterburgskie grobokopateli*) in his 1895 collection *The Proletariat and Street Types of Petersburg* (*Proletariat i ulichnye tipy Peterburga*). Bakhtiarov's subgroupings within this series included undertakers, gravediggers, wreath-sellers, and torchbearers, each sketch replete with mordant conversational snippets and unsavory trade secrets.[20]

While the emphasis on the logistical aspects of burying the dead was satirically realist in the sketches by Bashchutskii and Bakhtiarov, the material markers placed in cemeteries were imbued with solemn meaning in their time and are accorded an equally weighty semiotic significance by those who study them now. The specific forms of imperial-era monuments—marble sarcophagi, obelisks, steles, pyramids, pylons, urns, allegorical figures from classical mythology, and decorative symbols such as butterflies, anchors, and Masonic crosses—preserve the visual language for commemorating the dead.[21] Cemetery monuments might include specifically Petersburgian details such as bas-reliefs depicting the Rostral Columns, the Admiralty, or the Kazan Cathedral.[22] One particularly distinctive Petersburg monument style, "Peter-Mound" (*Petrovskaia gorka*), used a scaled-down copy of the Bronze Horseman pedestal, topped with an Orthodox cross. The historicism and eclecticism of Petersburg architecture beginning in the 1830s was reflected in the movement away from classical motifs in cemetery markers, and the increasing use of pseudo-Russian elements in graves from the period 1830s–1890s.

Like the tombstones themselves, epitaphs reflect the trends of their day. The earliest Petersburg inscriptions, from the second decade of the eighteenth century, are in prose rather than verse, detailing the departed one's rank and titles. During the 1740s, however, epitaphs appeared in syllabic verse, even though the syllabo-tonic system for Russian poetry was already in force, in this way illustrating the conservative nature of cemetery verse as a genre.[23] By the middle of the eighteenth century, the biographical format had yielded to a panegyric or elegiac approach to the departed subject. With the confluence of epigrammatic and epitaph forms during the second decade of the nineteenth century, the intimate four-line verse became dominant, but there were also longer verses that proffered metaphysical meditations to cemetery strollers. "Petersburg" verse epitaphs became popular throughout Russia, among them Karamzin's 1792 "Repose, dear remains, until the joyful morning!" (*Pokoisia, milyi prakh, do radostnogo utra!*), Pankratii Sumarokov's 1802 "Epitaph to Myself" (*Epitafiia samomu sebe*), and Pushkin's 1828 "Epitaph for an Infant" (*Epitafiia mladentsu*). It was common, moreover, for tombstones to display verses not specifically composed as epigraphs, excerpted from Russia's leading poets—Derzhavin's "River of times. . ." (*Reka vremen. . .*), Zhukovskii's translation of Thomas Gray's "Elegy Written in a Country Churchyard," or Pushkin's "Monument" (*Pamiatnik*), for example.[24] During the second half of the nineteenth century, all-purpose sentimental inscriptions gave way to expressive verse evoking the specific historical circumstances, civic achievements, and unofficial particulars of individual biography.

Despite well-developed burial practices, the explicit transformation of selected Petersburg cemeteries into museums during the 1930s occasioned an immense loss of grave-markers from the imperial period. These cemetery-museums oddly represent at once an acknowledgement and a violation of hallowed cultural ground. Up to this time, logical groupings of graves—according to family ties, close friendships, area of residence, professions, and circumstances of death—had evolved in many of the city's cemeteries.[25] Many literary and cultural luminaries had been interred in the Lazarevskoe Cemetery at the Alexander-Nevsky Monastery as a result of organically evolving burial practices.[26] The 1930s plan, however, sought to establish a formal pantheon of dead Russian cultural heroes modeled after the national pantheon in Paris, and to this end the Lazarevskoe and Tikhvinskoe cemeteries at the Alexander-Nevsky Monastery, and Volkovskoe Cemetery in the city's southern territory were reconceived and remapped. While tombstones of the greatest historical and artistic interest were transferred from various graveyards to the new cemetery-museums—often without the human remains whose location they marked—many other markers were simply destroyed in the process of liquidating old burial grounds throughout the city.

The "Masters of Art" cemetery was opened on the grounds of Tikhvinskoe in 1937, and, in 1939, the "Cemetery of the Eighteenth Century" (*Nekropol' XVIII veka*) was established on the territory of Lazarevskoe. The Eighteenth Century cemetery houses the graves of the writers Lomonosov and Fonvizin; the architects Quarenghi, Starov, Voronikhin, Zakharov, Toma de Thomon, and Rossi; and the painter Borovikovskii, among others. The Masters of Art cemetery includes the graves of the writers Karamzin, Zhukovskii, Gnedich, Krylov, Baratynskii, Viazemskii, and Dostoevsky, the composers Glinka, Serov, Dargomyzhskii, Mussorgsky, Rubinstein, Borodin, Tchaikovsky, and Rimsky-Korsakov, the sculptor Klodt, and cultural notables such as the critic Vladimir Stasov and the actress Vera Komissarzhevskaia. It is true that many of these luminaries *were* originally buried in the Lazarevskoe Cemetery, but their numbers were significantly augmented by new arrivals during the 1930s. As a 1970s guidebook to the "Museum of City Sculpture" explains, "[T]he cemetery was liberated of monuments that possessed no artistic value or historical significance. At the same time . . . many gifted prominent figures were transferred here from other cemeteries in Leningrad." The cemetery was converted into a "shady park with wide alleys" and well-tended vegetation. As a rule, continues the guidebook, "the graves are grouped according to the principle of the intellectual and creative affinity between the interred: writers, musicians, representatives of the theater, and masters of the plastic arts. This particularity of the necropolis significantly facilitates the study of its historical-artistic collection."[27] In a lengthy piece from the late 1930s titled "A Thought Describing a Circle" (*Mysl', opisavshaia krug*), Lydia Ginzburg contemplates the new cemetery-museum at the monastery, with its posted signs forbidding bicycling, playing musical instruments, or consuming alcoholic beverages. Where poorly preserved monuments or lesser personages have been removed to make the cemetery-museum less crowded, she notes the presence of identifying markers on sticks, "like those used in botanical gardens," whose textual presence mirrors and supplements the job of the tour-guide. "What constitutes the exhibit of this museum?" wonders Ginzburg. "The monument, the name, or the empty space, on which it is written that here a particular (historical) person turned to ashes?" Our incomprehension of death is so immense, she argues, that it overpowers the habits of professional museum-workers, who know that, in general, explanatory text with no accompanying exhibit object does not enlighten and merely irritates the public. In this case, however, respectful visitors fill these marked empty spaces with their mental "cultural baggage."[28] Graveside memorials, like the cemetery-museum's absurd markers of absence, may include text engraved or inscribed on their physical surfaces, but these objects are no more than placeholders for a different kind of writing—the invisible, pervasive, and shared cultural text of commemoration.

The transfer of tombstones and remains effected a rearrangement of the Petersburg cultural text, making it at once more coherent and less historically accurate. Conveying human remains to a new location to underscore their emblematic cultural significance, not to mention the import of their new resting place, parallels Peter the Great's 1724 decision to transfer the relics of thirteenth-century Prince Alexander Nevsky from a monastery in Vladimir to the Petersburg Alexander-Nevsky Monastery, in commemoration of this Russian hero's 1240 victory over the Swedes at the confluence of the rivers Izhora and Neva.[29] Like the "translation" of religious relics, the resettlement of Petersburg's dead writers and artists established a place of pilgrimage and a locus of moral and cultural authority. The cemetery-museums of the 1930s also suggested the extent to which the imperial era as a historical and literary construct had become the property of the Soviet cultural establishment.

The "Writers' Footway" of the Volkovo Cemetery constitutes Petersburg's other cemetery-museum of the imperial period, also officially established during the 1930s. Beginning with Radishchev's burial at Volkovo in 1802 (although the precise site of his grave has been lost), there evolved a tradition of burying Petersburg's "civic-minded" writers in a community of their literary brethren. Belinsky was buried at Volkovo in 1848, and Dobroliubov in 1861.[30] Also buried in the Writers' Footway are Saltykov-Shchedrin, Leskov, Goncharov, Pomialovskii, Grigorovich, Pisarev, Reshetnikov, Mamin-Sibiriak, Garshin, and Gleb Uspenskii.[31] As in the Alexander-Nevsky cemetery-museums, a considerable number of literary luminaries had originally been buried in this same part of the Volkovo Cemetery; other writers, Turgenev and Kavelin among them were transferred during the 1930s from liquidated sections of Volkovo and from various city cemeteries slated for destruction. The Writers' Footway as a twentieth-century institution appropriated and augmented a nineteenth-century development that proved fortuitously convenient for the Soviet establishment—the canonization of the "Belinsky line" of Russian literature.[32] In this sense, Soviet cultural policy might be said to have fulfilled the wishes of the Petersburg democratic intelligentsia of the latter nineteenth century, as expressed in their writings.

In Nikolai Nekrasov's "Morning Stroll" (*Utrenniaia progulka*), in the first part of his long poem "About the Weather" (*O pogode,* 1859), the morose narrator happens upon a funeral procession. He idly follows the lonely coffin conveyed by a dray-cart hearse to the Volkovo Cemetery, where he searches for the "inconspicuous grave" that constitutes the resting place of "a great force" (Belinsky). The cemetery watchman does not know where his friend lies, but advises him on navigating the cemetery: crosses mark the graves of petty-bourgeois, officers, and lower gentry; tombstone slabs stand above the graves of government officials, while slabs cover the ground over teachers' burial-places. The watchman concludes, "Where there is neither a slab nor a cross / There, most probably, lies a writer (*sochinitel'*)."[33] Nekrasov's poem fashions itself as a substitute grave-marker for Belinsky, whose resting place the narrator fails to find.

Garshin, who would himself be buried in the Writers' Footway, described a stroll through Volkovo in his "Petersburg Letters." Explicitly echoing Pushkin's 1836 poem "When pensive, I stroll outside the city. . ." (*Kogda za gorodom, zadumchiv, ia brozhu. . .*), Garshin takes himself off to the cemetery for a quiet walk, noting that city cemeteries such as Smolenskoe, Mitrofanievskoe, and Volkovo still accept new "residents," even though the dead have already been stacked one on top of another and in tight rows.[34] "Cemeteries are the shadiest parks in the city," declares Garshin with dark humor, because vegetation grows beautifully in the "rich soil."[35] He evokes the "Poets' Corner" in Westminster Abbey as a reproach to his own countrymen: "We do not take care of our great dead as the English do. We do not take care of them even while they are alive." Petersburg's own "Poets' Corner" is not actually a corner for poets, but rather houses "journalists" (*publitsisty*) such as Belinsky, Dobroliubov, and Pisarev. These great men inhabit their cramped corner, "surrounded by a numberless crowd of obscure names. . . . The crowd, which they loved and taught and which suffocated them, has not left them in peace even after death, and has crowded and constricted their little corner so that there was no place for a new friend to lie down."[36] Belinsky is now forgotten, mourns Garshin, and not a single wreath adorns his simple black-granite tombstone, in shameful contrast to the ornate surrounding monuments erected to merchants. Long-ago visitors have simply inscribed their own "naïve prose with expressions of love and grief" on the wooden railings around the writers' graves. Garshin's emphasis on Russian prose, as opposed to English verse, implicitly proposes his "Letters" as the true monument to Belinsky, even as he deplores the poverty of physical commemoration.

The eulogy "Oration on Lomonosov" (*Slovo o Lomonosove*) that concludes Alexander Radishchev's "Journey from Petersburg to Moscow" (*Puteshestvie iz Peterburga v Moskvu,* 1790) represents a significantly earlier contribution to such meditations on public memory—one that proves oddly prescient of the postrevolutionary fate suffered by Petersburg cemeteries. Radishchev describes an evening stroll to the Alexander-Nevsky Monastery, where he finds the 1765 grave of Mikhail Lomonosov, whose marble tombstone erected by Count Vorontsov bears inscriptions in both Latin and Russian. In contrast to Garshin, Radishchev disputes the power of a graveside monument (mere "cold stone") to preserve cultural memory, arguing that such majestic structures merely commemorate human vanity. "A stone with your name inscribed will not carry your fame into future centuries," intones Radishchev. "Your words, living always and forever in your creations, in the words of the Russian tribe, made new again by you in our language, will fly on people's lips beyond the boundless horizon of the centuries." He adds, "Let the elements, raging together, open the earthly abyss and swallow this splendid city, from which your great song resounded to all of the corners of vast Russia . . . but as long as the Russian language can be heard, you will be alive and will not die."[37] Radishchev's evocation of the Petersburg apocalypse notwithstanding, he could hardly have anticipated the neglect and indignities that the later nineteenth century, not to mention the twentieth, would inflict upon the city's cemeteries, and the extent to which we must now rely on written accounts of "dead Petersburg."

Although burial sites themselves represent an institution of memory, Petersburg has needed special efforts such as Vladimir Saitov's immense catalogue in order to remember its cemeteries and markers. The preservationists of the early twentieth century protested the disrepair into which many historical cemeteries had fallen, most particularly N. N. Vrangel' in his famous 1907 piece "Forgotten Graves" (*Zabytye mogily*).[38] Thirty years before the institution of the Masters of Art cemetery, Vrangel' wrote passionately of the destruction wrought by time, the elements, and vandals on the expressive Lazarevskoe tombstone sculpture created by Petersburg Academy artists such as Mikhail Kozlovskii, Ivan Martos, and Dominique Rachette. Vrangel' pointed out the painful irony in the motifs of remembering that pervade the epitaph verse on these forgotten graves and warned that on-going neglect would lead to the loss of historical knowledge about Petersburg's burial practices. Thirty years later, however, the 1930s saw the destruction of entire cemeteries in a mass exercise in historical forgetting. During the 1970s, several more imperial-era cemeteries were liquidated, resulting in the loss of thousands of gravesites, and hundreds of marble tombstones, not to mention the handmade decorative metalwork fencing that surrounded them. This process was halted only after the intervention of prominent city intellectuals headed by Dmitri Likhachev of the Academy of Sciences.

During the early years of the twentieth century, Saitov and Vrangel' worked to capture on paper the collective memory that a cemetery, with its monuments and inscriptions, is intended to preserve. The more recent efforts of cemetery historians have extended this prerevolutionary project, and perhaps this is only proper. As Pushkin's famous "Monument" poem—by way of Horace and Derzhavin—asserts, material commemoration is doomed to fail in its goal of guarding against the loss of memory: "I have raised myself a monument not made by human hands. . . . Its insubordinate head has risen higher than the Alexandrian Pillar." Only writing, that seemingly fragile but well-developed Petersburg practice, can hope to succeed in a monument's place. So goes the intelligentsia conceit, in any case, although the general public surely considered a physical monument a more substantial memorial than a printed text.

Memory as Antidote: Remembering Disaster

The recurrent floods and fires in texts about Petersburg attest to historical realities, but also to the city's fondness for prematurely aligning itself with the famous ruined cities of world civilization—Babylon, Sodom and Gomorrah, Carthage, Troy, Pompeii, and even mythological cities such as Atlantis and Kitezh. The poetics of disaster figures throughout Petersburg cultural history in the apocalyptic presentiments that skulk like an evil twin alongside the city's imperial posturing.[39] The idea of the end lies at the essence of Petersburg's existence in the form of a "catastrophic consciousness"—a constant awareness of the sword of Damocles hanging over the city in the here and now, and a sense of impending doom that is itself as terrible as the anticipated cataclysm.[40]

As a low-lying city without a system of protective dikes, Petersburg was vulnerable to the elements, although flood, fire, and even disease in the Petersburg Text also embody specific cultural and political threats to the city, such as revolutionary terrorists, unruly mobs, or foreign invasion. Occasionally, these threats come together at historical, rather than allegorical, junctures. The civil unrest of summer 1831, for example, was stirred up by rumors about who was responsible for the city's cholera epidemic, and groups as disparate as medical doctors and Polish nationals were blamed.[41]

Flood as a literary trope in the Petersburg Text signals a metaphysical unease in connection with the ocean, despite the affinity asserted by the sea-theme sculpture on two major architectural structures in the city center—the Admiralty and the Stock Exchange. Joseph Brodsky maintains that the "idea of the sea" is alien to the Russian sensibility and that "the notions of freedom, open space, of getting the hell out of here, are instinctively suppressed and consequently surface in the reverse forms of fear of water, fear of drowning."[42] Similarly, Andrei Martynov's lithographs of Petersburg from the early 1820s show "the utterly unformed emptiness of the world abyss," in which "everything solid in the city seemed ready to drown."[43] The Rostral Columns in Martynov's 1821–22 lithograph "View of the Winter Palace and the Admiralty" resemble the Pillars of Hercules at the border of the inhabited world. According to Plato's dialogues "Timaeus" and "Critias," the island of Atlantis was located just outside the Pillars, also known as the Straits of Gibraltar, and thus beyond the familiar Mediterranean Sea in the mysterious Atlantic Ocean, which swallowed up the "Lost City" after earthquakes and floods over the course of a single day and night.[44] Russian variants on the Atlantis myth by Russian literary figures such as Count Dmitri Khvostov, Mikhail Lermontov, Vladimir Odoevsky, and Mikhail Dmitriev—not to mention Alexander Pushkin—illustrate the potency of the flood trope in the Petersburg Text during the 1820–1840s.[45]

During its first century, Petersburg found itself subject to as much as an eight-meter rise in water when powerful westerly winds reversed the flow of the tributary that normally emptied into the Gulf of Finland. After 1703, floods occurred with ominous regularity in 1706, 1715, 1721, 1723, 1725, and 1727, most often during the fall. Accounts in letters and memoirs by inhabitants, including Peter the Great himself, describe residents paddling about the streets in small boats, sitting on their roofs, and perching in trees.[46] The worst Petersburg flood of the eighteenth century occurred in September 1777, taking many lives and famously destroying the linden trees and fountains in the Summer Garden. The construction of the Ekaterininskii Canal, during the reign of Catherine the Great, and the Obvodnyi Canal, initiated by Alexander I in 1805, reduced the threat of flood as hoped, at least for a time. There was nothing to equal 1777 until the 1824 deluge of "Bronze Horseman" fame—the worst in the city's history, responsible for thousands of deaths, although the official toll was only five hundred. According to recent calculations, Petersburg has experienced between two and three hundred dangerous floods, three of them ranked as "catastrophic" (the floods of 1777, 1824, and 1924).[47] In these worst cases, the reverse movement of the Neva caused Petersburg's internal waterways—its canals and hydraulic systems—to join forces with the advancing deluge from the sea and turn against the city. All of this lends a special poignancy to the annual Russian Orthodox January Feast of the Blessing of the Waters and its accompanying ceremony on the frozen river, commemorating the baptism of Christ in the river Jordan with an offering to the Neva.[48]

Literary invocations of the flood trope in the Petersburg Text illustrate the rhetorical purposes to which this flexible figure can be turned.[49] Ivan Born's 1803 poem "On the Occasion of the Flood of 27 September 1802, at Night" (*Na sluchai navodneniia 27 sentiabria 1802 goda, v nochi*) solemnly reminds "wrathful Poseidon" that Petersburg is not Troy and implores him to heed the despairing moans of the populace. "Why . . . do you make war?" asks the poet, reversing the customary vector of the eighteenth-century ode. Instead of describing battling armies with reference to the natural world and the elements, Born's faux-classical prayer denies Petersburg's connection to the heroic past of the ancient Greeks in hopes of saving the city (*Se slavnyi grad Petrov—ne Ilion*). Born's invocation ends with a plea to Apollo, urging the sun god to pour his healing rays upon Petersburg's suffering. Thus the annual flooding of Peter's city also serves the poet as a late-Enlightenment allegory for the first years of Alexander I's reign.

The Petersburg sunset idyll described in the second part of Nikolai Gnedich's 1822 poem "The Fishermen" (*Rybaki*) links the spires of the magnificent city with the purple and gold of the sky, which subsides peacefully, in thrall to the moonless night. This sort of harmonious meeting of city and natural surroundings is invoked ironically by the "Idyll" subtitle to Mikhail Dmitriev's 1847 poem "The Underwater City" (*Podvodnyi gorod*), which prophecies that Petersburg will disappear from the face of the earth. An old fisherman and a little boy spread their nets from a dilapidated boat. All is silent around them, save the anguished moaning of the sea. The old fisherman points to a spire just visible above the water's surface (now useful as a mooring for their boat) and tells the boy stories of the rich city built by a "warrior-hero" (*bogatyr'*), who sacrificed untold lives to his project. The city's demise comes as divine retribution, meted out by the elements to its unfeeling, wealthy inhabitants. At the story's conclusion, the boy asks the name of the drowned city, and the old fisherman replies that the name is "alien" (*chuzhoe*) and "long-forgotten." The poem closes with his remark, "Because [the name] was not native (*rodnoe*) / It was not memorable (*pamiatno*)." Dmitriev's poem writes Petersburg out of the textual tradition entirely, leaving nothing behind but the material "evidence" of the steeple-tip and the oral fragments that consign the now-nameless city to folkloric prehistory, the poet's verse text notwithstanding. With a single, repeated gesture, the water, like time, effaces cultural memory: "As soon as [the sea] touches the shore's loose soil / It rushes away with a groan." But the water's work of concealment and erasure is redundant, since, as the fisherman observes, cultural memory cannot inscribe what is "alien." Overwriting, obliteration, and forgetting are especially significant cultured as well as natural processes for Petersburg, as revealed by the obsessive focus on the fact of loss by so many writers and artists.[50]

The 1824 flood in particular created a distinct literary tributary—an entire corpus of verse and memoir tributes, Pushkin's "Bronze Horseman" among them, flowing into the Petersburg Text.[51] Count Dmitri Khvostov, the frequent

object of parodic assaults by the Pushkin circle, looked back to classical literature for poetic figures to fit the occasion in his 1824 "Epistle to NN: On the Flood
of Petropolis that Transpired on the Seventh of November in 1824" (*Poslanie k
NN o navodnenii Petropolia, byvshem 1824 goda 7 noiabria*). Khvostov penned
his descriptive verses immediately following the disastrous flood, if not the very
next morning, a fact noted snidely in Pushkin's own, far more famous flood-
poem of 1833. Khvostov's "Epistle" unleashes a deluge of hackneyed images and
raging vocabulary upon its reader over the course of its 150-odd lines.[52]

There exist two main ideological lines in depictions of the 1824 flood: the first
views the flood as nature's response to Peter's presumptuously situated city,
while the second casts the flood allegorically in connection with the Decembrist
or Polish uprisings.[53] Stepan Shevyrev's 1829 poem "Petrograd" exemplifies the
first literary type, in which the sea "argues" with Peter over which of them is the
mightier. Mikhail Lermontov's 1839 poem "A Tale for Children" (*Skazka dlia
detei*), in contrast, evokes the "mute" palace columns, which crowd along the
Neva banks "like shades," and the foaming waves that have "washed the fateful
traces of the past years' ill-fated events" from the wide steps of the city. With this
oblique reference to the Decembrists, the poet-visionary flying overhead explains the madness and suffering that characterize the city.[54]

The most dramatic example of a post-Decembrist allegory is V. S. Pecherin's
1833 mystery verse-drama "The Triumph of Death" (*Torzhestvo smerti*), which
exacts an imaginary retribution on the city with a scourge-wielding Nemesis.
The second part of the poem, which Mikhail Gershenzon called "a mighty symphony of Beethoven-like power and gloom," depicts the destruction of an "ancient capital" by flood, an event overseen by choruses of "bloody hearts pierced
by daggers," "smoking extinguished torches," "pale shades of soldiers covered in
blood and ash, with crowns of thorns interwoven with laurels on their heads,
and broken swords in their arms," and "five dimmed stars"—this last a reference to the executed Decembrist leaders.[55] The scene of destruction concludes
as "all people, present, past, and future" join the spirits for a grand-scale ballet,
which is followed by the appearance of Death himself, a "beautiful youth on a
white horse," and by general cries of "Vive la mort!" and "Hallelujah!" Pecherin's
drama ends with the dying words of the Poet, the last figure on stage, who too
must perish to make way for the coming new order.

A vast body of prose writing, much of it memoiristic, also treats the watery
onslaughts endured by Petersburg. Alexander Griboedov, who was living in
Kolomna at the time, wrote about his experience on November 7, 1824 in a
sketch titled, "Particulars of the Petersburg Flood" (*Chastnye sluchai peterburgskogo navodneniia*), apparently intended for a planned volume of materials
never approved by the censor. Griboedov vividly described the fearsome sight
from the upper-story of a house, where he took refuge after his own apartments
had been completely submerged, and he surveyed the damage on the day after
the flood, carefully noting the state of specific streets, bridges, and homes.

"Extraordinary events inspire the spirit to activity," noted Griboedov, but he refused to shape his observations into polished literary form or political allegory, and even made this disavowal part of his sketch: "I hastily collected several features that most struck me in the picture of enraged nature's fury and the deaths of individuals. There was no place here for the colors of oratory, and I similarly restrained myself from ruminations: to allow these would have meant putting my own person in place of a great event."[56]

The poetics of flooding is one of dislocation. Many flood memoirs thus evoke the stream of displaced and bizarrely juxtaposed objects carried by the waters.[57] In this sense, the flood's activity is democratic, in line with Decembrist mythology. But floods must also be considered in their sociocultural significance— their effects were most sharply felt by the city's poor, who tended to occupy basements or rickety one-story wooden dwellings.

Przhetslavskii noted with disgust that the censor forbade accurate accounts of the 1824 disaster: "It is remarkable that not a single newspaper printed information about the flood, making a secret of an event to which there were 400,000 witnesses. This quite sufficiently characterizes the times."[58] Beginning during the Great Reform era, however, personal accounts of the 1824 flood by Petersburg old-timers appeared regularly in the "memory journals." In an 1870 edition of *Russian Archive*, memoirist K. K. Boyanus recounted his experience of the flood as a seven-year-old child living on Vasilievskii Island.[59] A. Romanovskii's jocular "Reminiscences of the 1824 Flood" (*Vospominaniia o navodnenii 1824 g.*), which appeared in a 1905 edition of *Russian Antiquity*, relates the events of November 1824 in connection with the receipt of his officer's rank the day before.[60] To celebrate, he ordered a sumptuous meal from a German restaurant for the evening of the seventh and paid in advance. When he ventured onto the street the next day, however, he saw a section of the Isaakievskii Bridge torn loose and carried away, with pedestrians on it crying for help. The flood stranded the hungry Romanovskii at the Senate, where he improvised a sleeping place on a chancellery table. He concludes by noting that all has been forgotten, and nothing remains of the 1824 flood but the chronicles of old men like himself, who now write from the provinces. It is curious that disasters such as floods, which obliterated and damaged many structures from Petersburg's past, themselves became the anxious objects of preservationist and memoirist efforts in a paradoxical reversal of the rebuilding that remembering ostensibly entails.[61]

P. P. Karatygin's 1888 "Chronicle of Petersburg Floods, 1703–1879" (*Letopis' peterburgskikh navodnenii, 1703–1879*) draws an explicit parallel between the written and material traces of disaster and the working of collective urban memory:

Eyewitnesses of the 1777 flood assured their children that it was much more disastrous than the flood of 1824, but nevertheless, the latter has engraved itself much more deeply upon the memory of Petersburg inhabitants, for many years leaving ineradicable sad traces of itself. Remembrance of the flood has been, perhaps, facilitated by the notations on building walls in the form of metal, sometimes even marble plaques with the inscription "7 November 1824," which have been preserved to this day; by broken flagstones on the embankments of the Fontanka, Moika, Ekaterininskii and Kriukov canals, which were leveled and repaved only ten years ago; and finally by a multitude of terrible episodic stories, as well as by legends about the secret connection of this flood with the Emperor Alexander I: the flood preceded his death by twelve months and twelve days, and the flood of September 10, 1777 preceded his birth by three months and two days.[62]

Karatygin links the events "engraved" in citizens' memory with commemorative plaques and remaining physical traces of the damage. Implicitly, of course, his chronicle serves the same purpose, inscribing the flood upon the Petersburg Text, just as the flood left its marks upon city topography and urban psyche. Karatygin's chronicle transcribes the still-circulating corpus of oral lore connected with the flood, in self-conscious observance of the Petersburg Text's conventions. In seemingly credulous spirit, he records a number of "portents" reportedly observed from the months preceding the 1824 disaster, as well as anecdotes "heard from trustworthy individuals," such as the story of a coffin buried in Smolenskoe Cemetery two days before the flood, which was washed back into the late occupant's former apartment. Karatygin balances these anecdotes by including the full text of a broad geographical and climate-based account by academic Friedrich-Theodore Shubert, as well as numerous "narratives of contemporaries."[63] Thus Karatygin's "chronicle" of 1824 is actually a textual anthology of flood stories in diverse genres, both literary and oral—a text of texts, a compendium and not a primitive form of event chronology, as the term "chronicle" (*letopis'*) implies. Put another way, Karatygin chronicles the heterogeneous *writing* generated by the flood—the true subject of his historical survey.

Fires also punctuate the history of Petersburg, reversing the processes of expansion and growth, but simultaneously creating new possibilities within the urban topography. Urban fire, after all, is not an entirely natural disaster, since the physical composition of cities cannot help but generate regular incendiary crises.[65] Major fires occurred in the Petersburg city center in 1736 and 1737, for example, destroying hundreds of wooden buildings between the Neva and the Moika Canal, and thereby making way for new stone constructions.[64] Major structures such as the Gostinyi Dvor in its various locations (1710, 1763, 1780), the Winter Palace (1737, 1837), the Admiralty (1783), and the Stone Theater (1811) were all periodically damaged or destroyed by fire and repeatedly rebuilt.

Petersburg did not suffer any of the truly major fires in urban history, as did London in 1666 or Chicago in 1871, and experienced nothing like the Moscow fire of 1812, which looms large in Russian cultural history as a patriotic act of self-immolation that saved the city from Napoleon.[66] Fires, like floods, nevertheless served as objects of collective memory in Petersburg with increasingly regularity during the second half of the nineteenth century.[67] An 1865 edition of the journal *Russian Archive,* for example, includes a substantial selection of reminiscences under the rubric "Eyewitness Accounts of the Burning of the Winter Palace in 1837" (*Rasskazy ochevidtsev o pozhare Zimnego Dvortsa v 1837-m godu*).[68] Retired Major-General Baranovich recalled the Preobrazhenskii and Pavlovskii regiments carrying furniture and valuables out of the burning palace and piling them up by the Alexander Column in Palace Square. Cavalry officer Baron Mirbach also noted the grand-scale effort to save the material legacy of the Winter Palace, recounting the burning of a gilded chandelier with great emotion, and describing a vivid scene in which the Tsar commandeered a crowd of guard chasseurs to remove an enormous mirror from the wall, as flames surrounded them. Mirbach also recalls with horror the spectacle of the Empress's things spread on the ground outside the Palace: "Paintings by the best masters, malachite objects, wall and table clocks, bronze, and many other diverse valuables lay strewn about on the snow. A musical clock, set in motion by its fall, suddenly began to play a lovely aria in an ironic contrast to the surrounding scene."[69] These stories of a major Petersburg conflagration, in contrast to flood narratives, emphasize the threatened or actual loss of national treasures and important city structures, rather than human lives.

Fires, like floods, were often rendered metaphorical in the discourse of imperial Petersburg, as in the case of several suspicious blazes during the the spring of 1862. These fires, which destroyed the Apraksin arcade, the Tolkuchii market, the Ministry of the Interior building, and various houses and palaces along the left bank of the Fontanka, were reputedly set by nihilist-arsonists in a burning opposition of impressionable youth to the state. Disaster inscribes itself on the city and lends itself to the rich collective project of interpretation. Even without disaster, however, the urban topography constitutes a vast writing surface that variously commemorates and obscures the history of the city.

Walking on Words: Topography, Place Names, and Oral History

The explicit meeting points of urban terrain and text—that is, the words that are part of the city, constituting its toponymy—are those proper names identifying structures such as streets, squares, canals, bridges, islands, and parks. Place names may be conferred officially on parts of the city, but they can also arise spontaneously from physical and cultural circumstances and be granted official recognition long after the fact. Urban toponymy is shaped by the interplay of official and unofficial city practices, as well as the relationship between written and oral cultures.[70]

Urban toponyms preserve the specific history of place even when they outlive their physical referents, as in the case of Troitskaia Square, whose name speaks the memory of the eponymous church that once stood there. Place names can also impose a topographically unrelated memory upon a place by paying homage to national rulers, heroes, and artists, or perhaps by reminding citizens of a battle that occurred on foreign territory, as in the case of Petersburg's Ochakovskaia ulitsa, named for the taking of a Turkish fortress in 1788. Most interestingly, place names can transform physical city space into the space of metaphor—in Petersburg's case, the Russian Empire, and later, World Communism. Place names can overwrite the past, but they can just as easily recover it. Today, in toponymical terms, the Petersburg cityscape is highly eclectic, with all periods in its history reflected according to a complex pattern of overlapping layers representing different cultural moments.

According to Gorbachevich and Khablo, authors of the popular Petersburg reference work *Why Are They So Named?* (*Pochemu tak nazvany?*), place names should be protected against the vicissitudes of time by being accorded the status of historical and cultural monuments.[71] There are, however, ways of thinking about urban toponymy apart from fixing histories in "place." Place names are also part of oral history and "urban folklore." The Petersburg neighborhood called Kolomna, for example, may refer to laborers sent from the village of Kolomenskoe near Moscow, or to *koloniia,* the Russian word for a settlement of foreigners, of which there were many in Petersburg, or to a mispronunciation by the architect Domenico Trezzini, who apparently referred to the swaths he was cutting through swampy forestland as *kolonny,* meaning "rows or columns," but pronounced it *kolomny.*[72]

Nikolai Antsiferov declared that urban place names in their particular style, pattern, and sound provide access to a city's "*genius loci*"—that is, to the guardian spirit of a particular place, its essential nature—and represent "the language of the city." "What do the place names of Petersburg give us?" asks Antsiferov. "We won't find anything vivid or particularly expressive in them. And doesn't that fact itself characterize Petersburg? Isn't this appropriate for a stern, restrained city?"[73] Antsiferov cites place names he considers "most characteristic for Petersburg"—those utterly devoid of imagery such as the various Big (*Bol'shie*), Little (*Malye*), and Middle (*Srednie*) prospects, and the infinite series of numbered "lines" (*linii*) and "military companies" (*roty*). This characterization is not entirely accurate, since it is also true that a more colorful class of toponyms reflected the presence of specific military regiments, barracks, and encampments throughout the city, preserving the identities of regiments such as Belozerskii, Izmailovskii, and Semënovskii, as well as the specific functions that shaped life in the imperial military corps, just as they structured the street-layout of an encampment area: Artilleriiskaia (artillery), Batareinaia (battery), Strel'bishchinskaia (shooting range), Poligonnaia (proving ground), Lazaretnaia (military hospital), Ofitserskaia (officer), Kadetskaia (cadet), and Konnogvardeiskii (Horse Guards). Perhaps these street names once seemed purely functional, but over time they have become richly evocative.[74]

Many Petersburg place names seem very close to the ground and to everyday urban life, informally reflecting strictly local concerns. In this sense, toponyms can be said to narrate the cityscape from a particular angle of vision. Petersburg street names reflect the movement of goods into and around the city, the need to store materials in various places, and the particular locations where traders did business: Customs tax from merchants was gathered on Mytnyi Lane; traders from outside the city stayed on Posadskaia Street. Perevoznaia, Telezh-naia, and Skladskoi identify transport routes and warehouse districts; and Khlebnaia, Sennaia, and Miasnaia refer to areas where bread, hay, and meat were traded. A large number of Petersburg toponyms refer to trades and occupations at every social and economic level, among them Stremiannaia (court groom), Iamskaia (coachmen), Glazurnaia (glazer), Bocharnaia (cooper), Stoliarnaia (joiner), Liteinyi (foundry), Goncharnaia (potter), and Pod'iachii (scrivener). In this litany of preindustrial trades and occupations, the humbler inhabitants of Petersburg left their mark upon the city. Petersburg place names from the eighteenth century and the early nineteenth century also paid informal tribute to homeowners and inhabitants, quite apart from famous members of the no-bility who were close to the court. Merchants' names such as Shchukin, Tuchkov, and Kokushkin became attached to streets where they lived and did business.

A substantial class of toponyms designates streets and squares adjacent to re-ligious institutions, often with the specific vocabulary of Eastern Orthodoxy, which embedded itself in the Petersburg cityscape as did toponymical subsys-tems related to trade or the military, and inscribed spiritual life upon the mate-rial surface of the earthly city: Blagoveshchenskaia (annunciation), Voskresen-skaia (resurrection), Vvedenskaia (presentation), Vosnesenskaia (ascension), Znamenskaia (cross, baptize), Pokrovskaia (shroud), Preobrazhenskaia (trans-figuration), Rozhdestvenskaia (birth), Spasskaia (salvation), Troitskaia (trin-ity), and Uspenskaia (assumption).

Despite the seemingly straightforward nature of so many toponyms from the imperial period, however, nineteenth-century writers often found the system of Petersburg street names impenetrable. In his 1844 "Jottings of a Petersburg Idler" (*Zametki peterburgskogo zevaka*), Apollon Grigor'ev declares that it is nearly impossible to discover the reasons behind most Petersburg street names: "In certain names, there seems to glimmer something resembling an idea, seri-ous or mocking; in others, there is no logical significance whatsoever."[75] Some of the names that left Grigor'ev at a loss refer to topographical features or cul-tural landmarks no longer extant by the mid-nineteenth century, such as Sadovaia (once lined with gardens, turned into a street of markets), Karavan-naia (a defunct mid-eighteenth-century settlement of Persian elephant drovers, established a gift from the Persian shah), and, most famously, Fontanka, the site of the fountains of the Summer Garden installed by Peter the Great during the first part of the eighteenth century, destroyed by the flood of 1777, and never replaced.

The broader toponymical history of Petersburg helps to explain why the cityscape might have seemed illegible to residents of the capital at different periods in its history. For one thing, despite Petersburg's reputation as one of the most planned cities in world history, changes in place names date back to the earliest years of the city's existence. The very first renamings occurred immediately after St. Petersburg was founded in 1703, when new Russian names overlaid the Finnish or Swedish names already attached to the topography. In subsequent decades, streets were created and destroyed, tributaries were filled in, new canals were constructed, names were lost, unnecessarily duplicated, or transferred to other objects.[76] City plans from this period also include many "quasitoponyms"—designations such as "the canal leading from the Neva to the Fontanka."[77]

The 1738 Commission on St. Petersburg Construction conferred the first batch of official toponyms on the city, naming eighteen main streets and prospects—including Nevsky Prospect, Sadovaia Ulitsa, and Zagorodnyi Prospect, which last reflected the Fontanka Canal as city limit—as well as five squares, and several canals and bridges. Eventually, this commission conferred upward of 250 different names. The 1753 Makhaevskii plan from the Academy of Sciences shows 200 streets named, but many more Petersburg place names simply emerged out of the life of the city. Particularly common during the eighteenth and nineteenth centuries were names that spoke to a street's function, as in Shestilavochnaia, a street on which there were six shops, or Zverinskaia (from beast, or *zver'*), the street near the zoo.

Petersburg toponymy during the first half of the nineteenth century was a study in contrasts. Upscale street names such as Millionnaia (million), Dvortsovaia (palace), Dvorianskaia (aristocrat), Kniazheskii (prince), and Paradnaia (military parade), which conveyed the requisite cachet for an imperial capital, existed alongside decidedly inelegant street names, some of which dotted the cityscape many times over, such as Griaznaia (dirty) and Bolotnaia (swampy). Street names seemed to deny the very existence of the street they purported to identify, among them Glukhaia (lonely and overgrown), Pustaia (empty), Bezymiannaia (nameless), and Ordinarnaia (ordinary). Imperial Petersburg toponymy, like that of any city, was littered with simple self-descriptive names such as Bol'shoi (big), Shirokaia (wide), Pesochnaia (sandy), Lugovaia (meadow), and Roshchinskaia (grove). Many of these names reflect the perspective of people who must not have been particularly conscious of living in the capital city, caught up as they would have been in their daily business. One might also argue that "upscale" place names such as Millionnaia convey an admiring, even gaping quality that reflects the street-level perspective of the disenfranchised, more the desire of the well-off to advertise their status.

Most diverting of all are the strangely redundant Petersburg toponyms that describe the trajectory, placement, or nature of a particular byway: Odnostoronniaia (houses only on one side), Poperechnaia (diametrical), Prokhod-

naia (through-street), Razvodnaia (branching), Parallel'naia (parallel), Razdel'-
naia (separating), Tupikovaia (dead end), Bokovaia (side), Krivoi and Kosoi
(crooked), Kruglaia (circular), Lomanaia (bent or fractured), Pogranichnaia
and Rubezhnaia (border), Okrainaia (outlying), and Zarechnaia (across the
river). These names show how quasitoponyms in the form of oral directions can
"morph" into true toponyms, even if such names are informative in only the
most local sense imaginable. In contrast to truly functional place names that
specify where a street goes, such as Tsarskosel'skii, Petergofskii, and Kamennoostrovskii Prospects, street names like Poperechnaia and Bokovaia seem almost perversely local designations that clash with the image of a perfect, classical city.

   During the second half of the nineteenth century, a more official written toponymy established by Senate decrees of the latter 1850s replaced many of the
eighteenth- and nineteenth-century names that were integrally connected with
everyday speech and everyday life. Petersburg toponyms evoking major Russian
rivers and provincial cities date from this period, during which the city was
blanketed by place names such as Donskaia, Volkhovskii, Kazanskaia, Sara-
tovskaia, Tverskaia, and Voronezhskaia, to name only a few. Such imperial toponyms reminded Petersburg residents of the Russian Empire's vast proportions, now conveyed by analog in the official topography of the capital. In this
way, Senate decrees renamed the dozens of modest streets and alleys called Griaznaia, Pesochnaia, and Bolotnaia, instead of simply modifying these local place
names informally with prefixes such as Bolshaia (Big), Malaia (Little), Sredni-
aia (Middle), Vtoraia Malaia (Second Little), Staraia Malaia (Old Little), Novaia
Malaia (New Little), and so forth. The increasingly grand imperial sweep of
these new patterns coincided with the growth of the city population during the
second half of the nineteenth century.

   Naming Petersburg places in honor of Russian rulers and their family members became widespread beginning in the first half of the nineteenth century,
resulting in many structures such as bridges, major canals, and theaters named
Nikolaevskii, Alexandrinskii, Mikhailovskii, Ekaterininskii, or Mariinskii. The
so-called ideological naming for cultural figures, national heroes, and major
events in national history that was so closely associated with Petersburg place
names during the Soviet period actually began during the final decades of the
imperial period, usually in connection with jubilee celebrations or new monuments. Pushkinskaia Street marked the unveiling of the 1880 monument to Russia's national poet in Moscow (this street then got its own Pushkin monument
in 1884), and a street was named for Gogol in 1902, on the fiftieth anniversary
of his death. In 1887, Otechestvennaia (fatherland) Street commemorated the
seventy-five year anniversary of 1812, the end of the Napoleonic wars.

   As in the case of Troitskaia Square, some of the imperial toponyms that have
survived to the present have become artifacts. Now, names that would *not* have
seemed confusing to Grigor'ev possess for *us* that strange and mocking poetry

of near-sense.[78] Thus, over time, official written toponymy devolves back into the realm of oral culture whence place names often originate. True, official commissions wage war against unofficial naming practices, trying to stave off the inevitable process of toponymical entropy. The lessons of history show, however, that city residents inhabit their urban toponymy in a subversive poetic spirit quite different from the proud citizen-consciousness legislated by naming commissions.

Under the Soviets, even the most official imperial toponyms came to seem mysterious and incantatory—the voice of the urban landscape's repressed memory, in response to the frenetic naming and renaming that attempted to create an entirely new ideological toponymy. Out of 1,500 names noted on a 1917 Petrograd map, for example, more than 500 were changed after the Revolution. Beginning in 1918, the new city government eliminated most references to the Romanov dynasty and those close to them. It also did away with place names referring to "capitalist" types such as merchants, entrepreneurs, and factory-owners, replacing these with the names of approved prerevolutionary and Soviet scientists, engineers, war heroes, academicians, writers, and artists. Bolshevik revolutionary toponymy replaced that associated with the imperial military and the Orthodox Church, or simply with the flavor of tsarist times. In this way, Karetnaia (carriage) Street became Sovetskaia (soviet) Street, Kniazheskii (prince) Lane became Rabochii (worker) Lane, and Troitskaia (Trinity) Square became Revoliutsionnaia (revolution) Square. But it is also true that under the Soviets, Petersburg became more than ever a city of imperial Russian arts and culture, with streets in central parts of the city newly named for Lomonosov, Radishchev, Griboedov, Belinsky, Nekrasov, Herzen, Chernyshevsky, Dobroliubov, Pisarev, Shevchenko, Ostrovsky, Turgenev, Tolstoy, Dostoevsky, Saltykov-Shchedrin, Chekhov, Repin, Tchaikovsky, and Rimsky-Korsakov, among others. All of these renamings—those that appropriate the imperial past as well as those that seek to obliterate it—offer a poetics of translation and cultural transformation, suggesting that the urban object itself could be fundamentally changed along with its name.

Well before Stalin began pulling down imperial-era churches in the 1930s, the Soviet authorities overwrote large portions of Petersburg's toponymical system in keeping with the city's new identity as Leningrad. Even so, the waves of toponymical reconfiguration in 1918, 1924, 1939–41, and 1952 could not fully eliminate place names evoking prerevolutionary culture. Furthermore, the process of renaming sometimes reversed, itself when imperial Petersburg toponyms were reinstated as a concession from the Soviet government. In 1944, twenty major streets and squares had their historical prerevolutionary names returned in acknowledgement of the suffering and loss endured by the "Hero-City." This reverse translation was performed on some of the city's most prominent streets and squares, those very urban landmarks that had been given the shrillest new revolutionary names after 1917.

After the city's name change from Leningrad back to St. Petersburg in 1991, officials reinstituted historical names bearing information about city history, among them Shpalernaia (imperial textile manufacturing works), Galernaia, Bol'shaia Morskaia, and Malaia Morskaia (all three attesting to Petersburg shipbuilding and the naval fleet), even if that meant getting rid of names associated with important cultural figures such as Herzen and Gogol. Famous toponyms that occur in "Golden Age" Russian literature were also restored, among them Angliiskaia, Millionnaia, Gorokhovaia, Ital'ianskaia, Kamennoostrovskii, Koniushennaia, and Sennaia. The city finally made official those cases where Soviet renamings had never quite "taken" and paid toponymical respects by returning street or square names associated with structures the Soviets had destroyed, such as the Vvedenskaia and Voznesenskaia churches demolished during 1930s. Toponyms established for *new* streets, squares, and bridges from the Soviet period have remained in place, however, since there were no imperial names to restore. Just as the Soviets were not able to eliminate all traces of imperial toponymy in Leningrad, the Soviet period cannot be eradicated from the cityscape of today's St. Petersburg (although officials did rename streets called "Sovetskaia"). This collective, often internally divisive effort has combined to produce a vast collage, a blend of oral and literary artifacts from different periods that perhaps best of all represents the history of place names in the former Russian imperial capital.[79]

Cultural Memory and Monumental Loss

In his 1844 essay "Petersburg and Moscow" (*Peterburg i Moskva*), Vissarion Belinsky argued with those who characterized Petersburg as a city without ancient historical monuments. "Yes, dear sirs, there are no such monuments in Petersburg, and there can be none because Petersburg has existed since the day of its founding for only 141 years," he granted. However, "Petersburg *itself* is a great historical monument" in the extraordinary fact of its existence.[80] In Belinsky's view, Petersburg thus bears cultural memory, by standing as a physical monument to itself.

The city, as it turns out, however, is *not* an apt visual analog for either individual or cultural memory. As Sigmund Freud took pains to show in *Civilization and Its Discontents*, forgetting is an operation quite distinct from destroying, since an idea once formed in the human mind can in theory be retrieved or reconstructed. To support his point, Freud constructed an elaborate metaphor, hypothesizing that if Rome were a human consciousness "with just as long and varied a past history," it would look quite different from the modern city of Rome:

> This would mean that in Rome the palaces of the Caesars were still standing on the Palatine and the Septizonium of Septimius Severus was still towering to its old

height; that the beautiful statues were still standing in the colonnade of the Castle of St. Angelo, as they were up to its siege by the Goths, and so on. But more still: where the Palazzo Cafferelli stands there would also be, without this being removed, the Temple of Jupiter Capitolinus, not merely in its latest form, moreover, as the Romans of the Caesars saw it, but also in its earliest shape, when it still wore an Etruscan design and was adorned with terra-cotta antifixae. Where the Coliseum stands now we could at the same time admire Nero's Golden House; on the Piazza of the Pantheon we should find not only the Pantheon of to-day as bequeathed to us by Hadrian, but on the same site also Agrippa's original edifice; indeed, the same ground would support the church of Santa Maria sopra Minerva and the old temple over which it was built. And the observer would need merely to shift the focus of his eyes, perhaps, or change his position, in order to call up a view of either the one or the other.[81]

For Freud, this metaphor proves that mental life cannot be adequately rendered by visual representation, since only one structure can occupy any given space in an artistic depiction. What Freud does not acknowledge—although he performs this very operation in elaborating Rome as metaphor—is that a city's memory, like the memories of a person, may receive a full representation in writing, at least in theory. The seemingly infinite contemporary Petersburg project of textual commemoration strives for precisely this articulation, in its never-ending reconstruction of the city's past. While cities may not be an adequate analog for the human mind, text serves very well as a model of the city.

As Umberto Eco declares, "Remembering is like constructing and then traveling again through a space. . . . Memories are built as a city is built."[82] Structures such as libraries, museums, and archives make this connection explicit, realizing in physical form the "containers for the documents that represent the memory of a civilization" no less than architectural monuments.[83] Aarchitectural models of memory are common in treatises dating back to the ancient Greeks, who first articulated the practice of mnemonics for mentally creating loci for objects, concepts, and events to be remembered.[84] Thus the creation of textual as well as physical architecture aids greatly in developing the faculties of memory.

A certain amount of change and loss in a cityscape over time is to be expected. Few Petersburg residences from the early baroque period have survived, for example, except for the Men'shikov Palace on the University Embankment and the restored Kikin house not far from the Tauride Palace. The beautiful Stock Exchange building by Thomas de Thomon (1805–10) replaced Giacomo Quarenghi's partially completed Stock Exchange from the 1780s. The present St. Isaac's cathedral is actually the *fourth* cathedral by that name constructed in more or less the same place—two of these from the first half of the eighteenth century, and a third designed by Antonio Rinaldi during the reign of Catherine the Great and completed by Vincenzo Brenna under Paul. Similarly, there were four different Winter Palaces. The third and fourth were built by Bartolomeo Rastrelli, the former for Anna Ioannovna during the 1730s, and the latter for Elizabeth during the 1750s. Catherine's Tsaritsyn Meadow became Paul's Field of Mars. Elizabeth's Summer Palace was torn down to make way for Paul's Mikhailovskii Castle. Petersburg cultural historians have treated these major architectural "rewritings" as a normative, if regrettable part of the city's history during the eighteenth century and the first part of the nineteenth-century. As discussed in chapter 1, however, many of Petersburg's most prominent cultural commentators were enraged by the destruction of small homes and other structures from the eras of Catherine the Great and Alexander I in order to make room for eclectic-style apartment buildings during the later nineteenth century.

Beginning in the final years of the nineteenth century, Petersburg lost a number of its architectural monuments, owing to unfortunate decisions by city officials. The neoclassical Bolshoi Theater by Thomas de Thomon was almost entirely demolished and turned into a conservatory of music with nothing to recommend it architecturally. The famous Stroganov dacha on Chernaia rechka was torn down in 1898 to make room for an apartment building and is preserved only in a well-known painting by the architect Andrei Voronikhin that hangs in the Russian Museum. The Iakovlev residence by the Obukhov Bridge, built in the 1760s by Rastrelli, was torn down in 1901 to accommodate the expansion of the Haymarket. The greater part of Trezzini's early eighteenth-century Gostinyi Dvor on Vasilievskii Island was destroyed to make room for the construction of the Academy of Sciences library in the second decade of the twentieth century, in a clear manifestation of presumed cultural precedence that might well be questioned today.

During this period, Petersburg preservationists actively protested the "vandalism" of the imperial capital's older buildings, initially in the journal World of Art and most particularly in the journal Past Years (Starye gody, 1907–16), which regarded saving Russia's architectural legacy as one of its primary missions.[85] A 1907 article in Past Years mourned Petersburg's old chain bridges, the Panteleimonovskii and Egipetskii bridges across the Fontanka, dating from the last years of Alexander I's reign, and both defunct by the first decade of the twentieth century.[86] A 1915 article deplored the loss of gardens adjoining various palaces.[87] The preservationist movement—a union of artists and architectural specialists—made major textual contributions to the cult of "Old Petersburg" in the form of books, articles, and catalogues, and sponsored public lectures and exhibitions.[88] The work of the preservationists at the end of the imperial period thus took a consummately Petersburgian form, a fusion of literature and architecture. Like the journal Past Years, the Museum of Old Petersburg—eventually incorporated into the City Museum, and later called the Museum of the History of Petersburg—dates from the late 1910s. The Museum, which included a large collection of original architectural drawings and photographs, had many different homes over the years, including the residence of Count Siuzor, the Anichkov

Palace, the Rumiantsev House on the English Embankment, and the Peter-Paul Fortress.[89]

The cult of Old Petersburg established at the beginning of the twentieth century did not die out after the 1917 Revolution, but continued through the 1920s. Among the longest-lived efforts directed at preserving Petersburg's memory of itself were the excursionist school of Ivan Grevs and Nikolai Antsiferov, specializing in the study of local lore (discussed in chapter 3), and the "Old Petersburg" Society (1921–38), in which Petr Stolpianskii played a major part.[90] Both of these groups survived the early Soviet era by directing their work toward the cultural enrichment of city workers, in a departure from the elitist orientation of the prerevolutionary organizations. With the onset of the Stalinist 1930s, however, the collective project of remembering and preserving Petersburg was largely put aside. Many of the city's most beautiful buildings were turned into headquarters for various Bolshevik organs, while others became Soviet museums, veterans' hospitals, and "cultural centers" for teachers. (It must be acknowledged, however, that physical changes to the actual cityscape were much more extensive in Moscow, the new capital.)

Toward the end of the Soviet period, the project of remembering that had been broken off by the 1930s resumed once more. The 1988 exhibition catalogue *Lost Architectural Monuments of Petersburg-Leningrad* (*Utrachennye pamiatniki arkhitektury Peterburga-Leningrada*) accompanied brief descriptions of defunct structures with images from old photographs and postcards in order to commemorate approximately 150 lost civil structures and church buildings, monuments, engineering projects, and minor architectural forms such as bridges, gates, and railings from the imperial period. The compilers conceded that all cities are subject to an on-going and organic process of change, but they distinguish this inevitable work of time from "malevolent" forces that degrade the cityscape. The center of then-Leningrad, they argue, should be considered a cultural "preserve" (*zapovednik*).[91] To this proposed city-museum, *Lost Architectural Monuments* added in textual and photographic form those structures that should still by rights be present.

Where as the nineteenth-century construction of apartment buildings caused the demise of old homes and dachas, the early Soviet period, in particular the 1930s, saw the demolition of many churches in an attempt to change the essential face of the city. Among the churches destroyed were Znamenskaia, torn down to make way for the metro station opposite the Moscow railway station; Pokrova Bogoroditsy, the church invoked by Pushkin in his poem "A Little House in Kolomna"; Uspenskaia, dating from the mid-1700s and called Spasna-Sennoi during the nineteenth century; the Church of St. Matvei, built in 1720 to commemorate the 1704 Russian victory at Narva on that apostle's day; Preobrazhenskaia from Peter's time on the left bank of the Neva; and the Troitskii Cathedral, which dated from the very earliest period in the city's history, although it had burned down and been restored more than once. The Sergiev-

skaia, Voznesenskaia, Rozhdestvenskaia, Vvedenskaia, Vladimirskaia, Ekaterininskaia, and Panteleimonovskaia churches were similarly demolished—the
Ekaterininskaia ignominiously pulled down to make way for a movie theater.
Most of these churches dated in their earliest wooden forms from the eighteenth
century, and, although all of them had undergone remodeling and rebuilding
over the years, most had retained their original period style and appearance. It
is fair to say, however, that churches from every period in Petersburg's history
suffered at Stalin's hands. Several nineteenth-century churches by Constantine
Thon were torn down during the 1930s, as were a number from the eclectic period of the later nineteenth century, including some in the pseudo-Russian style,
which might have been expected to escape the wrecking ball.[92]

After the October Revolution of 1917, busts depicting Russia's imperial rulers
were removed from their places at public institutions such as the Obukhovskaia
and Mariinskaia hospitals and the Alexandrovskii Lyceum. Several sculptures of
Peter the Great erected for Petersburg's bicentennial celebration in 1903 were
moved to unobtrusive places in the city or destroyed. The large statue of Alexander III on Znamenskaia Square was moved to a courtyard of the Russian Museum. One major monument was entirely demolished—the 1880s victory column in front of the Troitskii Cathedral commemorating Russian soldiers and
officers of the Izmailovskii regiment who fought in the 1877–78 war with
Turkey. As shown in period postcards, the monument was constructed from
dozens of captured Turkish cannons forming five vertical "rings" and crowned
with a winged Nike. Photographs, drawings, and written accounts are all that
remain of this victory monument, however, despite its vivid emphasis on the
material spoils of war. Reading the cityscape, the task of so much Petersburg literature from the imperial period, thus becomes in these cases an *exclusively* textual practice.[93]

Like the catalogue of *Lost Architectural Monuments,* memorial plaques serve
as an antidote to the losses of time, affixed to buildings and other landmarks,
literally inscribing stories upon the cityscape. As evidenced by a substantial body
of secondary literature, Petersburg memorial plaques dating back to the eighteenth and nineteenth centuries themselves constitute an object of study—an
exercise of metarecollection—within the larger project of reconstructing cultural memory.[94]

It is hard to miss the irony and paradox that infuse the history, preservation,
and loss of cultural memory in St. Petersburg. Memory journals of the nineteenth century, like all periodicals, were easily lost or destroyed, leaving an incomplete series. The Museum of St. Petersburg scarcely resembles a permanent
institution, with its dizzying succession of names and locations. The Museum
of City Sculpture, in transferring graveside monuments and human remains
from all over Leningrad, and in converting the city's oldest cemetery into a cultural park, violates the notion of a final resting place. Some of the most serious
and sustained efforts at preserving the past, or at least its memory, have been

made by *temporary* exhibitions, such as those staged by the preservationists through the Society of Architect-Artists during the early 1910s, or by the *Lost Architectural Monuments* project of the 1980s. To a great extent, the continuity in the project of preserving Petersburg cultural memory comes most demonstrably from the frequency with which new efforts have been mounted.

CONCLUSION

Timely Remembering and the
Tricentennial Celebration

St. Petersburg's tricentennial year of 2003 found the city at a moment that could not have been anticipated during the celebrations of 1803 and 1903. Each of these three celebrations marks a cultural moment—the hopeful beginning of Alexander I's reign in 1803, the sense of a waning culture under siege in 1903, and the "Rip van Winkle" experience of 2003, as Petersburg reclaimed its past while simultaneously confronting the lag in its development as a modern city. Preparations for the tricentennial entailed the most extensive physical renovations and festivities planning—not to mention the most concerted stream of commemorative Petersburg projects and publications—that the city has ever seen.

The May 1803 centennial festivities were relatively modest compared with the coronation celebrations that would be staged to honor a new Russian monarch. The main embankments of the Neva were decorated with flags.[1] Four elderly men born before the death of Peter the Great stood guard over the city founder's boat, known as "Grandfather of the Russian Navy Fleet," as it stood upon the battleship "Archangel Gabriel" stationed across from Senate Square. Twenty thousand troops gathered on Palace Square and paraded past the Bronze Horseman, accompanied by cannon and artillery salutes from the Neva. The young Tsar Alexander paid his respects to Peter's statue and was presented with a gold commemorative medallion by a city deputation. In the evening, there was a special performance at the Bolshoi Theater.

By May 1903, the population of St. Petersburg had increased nearly four times over, and the bicentennial festivities were correspondingly more extensive, despite the fact that Nicholas II had little interest in them.[2] The city was lavishly festooned with hangings and coats of arms, including a series of painted panels depicting events in Peter the Great's much-mythologized biography. Several hundred citizens in early eighteenth-century period costumes strolled about the Summer Garden, and traditional folk entertainments such as carousels and fairground booths filled the Ekaterinhof and Tauride gardens as well as the Field of

Mars. Church bells pealed throughout the city as a procession crossed the new Troitskii Bridge to visit Peter the Great's little house. The 1903 bicentennial celebration venerated Petersburg's past, but also turned this past—into theater and mass culture, an example that would be followed in 2003. Most notably, however, the 1903 festivities involved the city's cultural, religious, and military institutions along with its diverse populations in a show of unity at what was actually a highly divisive moment in the city's history, characterized by dissatisfied constituencies and crises of modernization that had not been at all in evidence in 1803.

Ever since the restoration of its historic name in the early 1990s, St. Petersburg, the "city without a history," has been eager to remember as much as it can, and this project expanded at an accelerating rate as 2003 approached. Along with many new publications detailing aspects of the city's imperial-era past came a flood of reprints, and Petersburg chroniclers such as Bogdanov, Georgi, Svin'in, Pushkarev, Bakhtiarov, Pyliaev, Kurbatov, Lukomskii, Stolpianskii, and Antsiferov were all once again in print. Literary as well as physical Petersburg thus served as the object of rehabilitation. New perspectives on familiar cultural terrain were also proposed. In a modern-day revision of the Sadovnikov and Bozherianov "panoramas," for example, a CD-ROM allowed the viewer to traverse Nevsky Prospect by means of nearly 500 drawings and engravings, hundreds of pages of hypertext, and interactive vistas that permit close approaches to individual structures. A series of twelve new guidebooks with accompanying videocassettes, each devoted to a particular "route" through Petersburg's topographical and cultural history, heralded a tricentennial project called "St. Petersburg at the Crossroads of Culture. Tours are available in Russian, English, and in the language particular to their subject matter: French, Italian, Dutch, German, Japanese, Swedish, Finnish, Arab, Spanish, Hebrew, and Chinese. This project reemphasized St. Petersburg's historical cosmopolitanism, an aspect of the city's public image denigrated during aggressively nationalist periods of the nineteenth century and under the Soviets, but in 2003 a major potential asset.

As Governor of St. Petersburg Vladimir Yakovlev declared on the official tricentennial website *www.spb300.ru,* "The period leading up to the celebration of St. Petersburg's tercentenary is, above all, a time for implementing . . . projects in the fields of science, technology, construction, and culture" that will "serve as the bases for St. Petersburg's economic and cultural prosperity in the twenty-first century." To this end, "Russian and foreign investors wishing to take part in preparations for the tercentenary to the benefit of both the city and themselves will have the advantage of especially favorable conditions. The city authorities will do everything they can to see that St. Petersburg is integrated into the Russian and global economies." In an article subtitled "How To Sell Petersburg Most Profitably" (*Kak vygodnee prodat' Peterburg*), one journalist wrote, "The jubilee is not a goal, but a means. The city does not exist to serve the jubilee celebration, but rather the jubilee exists for the city's benefit."[3] The Promako advertising agency, responsible for publicizing Petersburg and its tricentennial in foreign airline magazines, proposed the former imperial capital as "an attractive place for leisure and business with major tourist opportunities and high investment potential, a city with 'a European face' . . . a city of high intellect . . . of open and cultured people."[4] Thus were the familiar Petersburg tropes incorporated into an entirely new discourse for the twenty-first century—that of the international service city.

In 2001, in order to help Russian and foreign investors "buy into" this new image of Petersburg, Governor Yakovlev established a set of corporate sponsor packages, each tied to a specific monetary contribution, ranging from "general sponsorship" for three million U.S. dollars and "official sponsorship" for one million, down to "patron" status, which cost the donor only five thousand. There existed an ample sufficiency of tricentennial projects needing such underwriting. Official documents from the early stages of preparation stated that approximately one-half of the city's 5,748 "monuments of history and culture," 300 works of "monumental sculpture," and 600 works of "decorative sculpture" were in need of restoration and repair. In addition to projects of moderate proportions, tricentennial preparations also included extensive renovations of twenty-one major imperial-era structures, among them the Peter-Paul Fortress, Alexander Column, Aleksandrinskii Theater, Summer Garden, Admiralty, Stock Exchange, and Russian National Library. Haymarket Square, long the site of an open-air flea market, was cleaned up to prepare for the construction of a multimillion-dollar business center and the possible reconstruction of the Holy Virgin Assumption Church, destroyed in 1961.

The ten-day tricentennial during the spring of 2003 represented the culmination of several years' worth of projects and events, as manifested by Petersburg tricentennial calendars for the period 2000–2003, which featured innumerable festivals, performances, exhibitions, commemorative gatherings, sports events, competitions, and conferences taking place each month. A database of Petersburg tricentennial projects tracked dozens of new efforts, among them an international conference on "The Petersburg Style," a reenactment of a Winter Palace ball, the commissioning of a "triumphal march" in honor of the tricentennial, and a competition for schoolchildren researching "The History of My Family" in connection with the history of Petersburg.

Aeroflot underwrote the restoration of the monuments to 1812 war heroes Field-Marshall Kutuzov and Barclay de Tolly. The third annual Petersburg international rock festival was held in June 2003 under the Petersburgian rubric "Open the windows!" (*Okna otkroi!*) in the spirit of Algarotti and Pushkin. A student of the Moscow Aviation Institute prepared for a contemporary "Journey from Petersburg to Moscow" following the eighteenth-century writer Alexander Radishchev, but this time in a motorized capsule with a parachute-like wing (called a *paralyot*), in hopes of breaking the world record for distance in such a craft. There were concurrent competitions for best monument, best play, and best congratulatory "toast" (*pozdravleniie*) in honor of the tricentennial.[5]

Activity in St. Petersburg came to a head during the week of May 23–June 1, dedicated to a ten-day series of events under the rubric "300 Years to the Glory of Russia" (*300 let vo slavu Rossii*), with May 27 as the city's official "founding date." Day One saw the opening of a museum in the Marble Palace, a conference at the Pribaltiiskaia Hotel for the mayors of Petersburg's city-partners, a World Congress at the Tauride Palace for cultural, scientific, and business leaders ("St. Petersburg—Cultural Capital of the World"), Jubilee Races at the Ocean Yacht-Club, and the Russian Academy of Sciences' affirmation of a resolution to name a minor planet "St. Petersburg–300." The opening of a large public park by the gulf and the installation of a Peter the Great statue at Sampsonievskii Cathedral marked Day Two, titled "Grateful Descendants." Deputations placed wreaths at Piskarevskoe and other cemeteries, the Pavlovsk palace-park hosted a historical festival in honor of "Petersburg—Military Capital," and the renovated Alexander Column was unveiled.

Day Five was devoted to the "City's Birthday," whose commemoration followed traditional forms such as laying flowers at the pedestal of the Bronze Horseman, presenting a jubilee medallion at Peter the Great's tomb, and holding ceremonial prayers at city churches, including a special service at Kazan Cathedral, from which there was a religious procession (*krestnyi khod*). The Governor reviewed the cadet corps on Palace Square in conjunction with the opening of the new main entrance to the Hermitage from that side. Day Nine was international in focus, titled "All Flags Come to Visit Us" (*Vse flagi v gosti k nam*) pace Pushkin, and included a summit of foreign leaders at the renovated Konstantinovskii Palace at Strelna. (The same group of leaders also visited the restored Amber Room at Tsarskoe Selo.)

The tricentennial festivities were far too numerous for more than a mention of intriguing highlights, among these the premiere of the musical "Anna Karenina," a fashion show called "St. Petersburg Silhouette," a citywide competition for local goods and services called "Made in Petersburg," a variety show at Petrovskii Stadium, and a fifty-hour dance marathon in honor of Peter the Great's birthday. Thus St. Petersburg's tricentennial staged collisions of old and new, high art and mass culture, the boldly esoteric and the confidently commercial.

One spectacular tricentennial project in the spirit of twenty-first-century fusion came to naught, however, for lack of funds. The artist Eduard Kochergin proposed the resurrection of a tsarist-era ceremony performed every spring beginning in Peter the Great's time, celebrating the moment when the Neva was cleared of ice and free for vessels. Each year, the Russian monarch was conveyed to the center of the aquatic square in a rowboat, and met there by the commander of the Peter-Paul Fortress and the head officer of the Admiralty; the monarch would drink a silver goblet of Neva water, as cannons fired from the Fortress. According to Kochergin's vision, President Putin would have welcomed visiting ships from all over the world from a floating stage bearing an immense baroque-style statue of Neptune. In the evening, the Neptune statue would have been converted into a giant fountain and lit up by fireworks, as enormous portraits of Peter the Great and Alexander Nevsky would unfurl, suspended by balloons over the Fortress.

In the absence of this grand plan, it was not clear where in the city the Russian President could place himself to address the public. Petersburg lacks a major gathering place such as Moscow's Red Square, which can accommodate 1.5 million people. Palace Square holds under 100,000 and was intended for reviewing elite military forces, rather than for assembling a huge crowd. In 1803, Alexander I addressed the public on Senate Square, and in 1903, Nicholas II made a formal appearance on the Field of Mars, but the city's population was much smaller on both occasions than it was in 2003. Access to the various tricentennial celebrations posed a major problem, even events held in open spaces such as major squares, embankments, or palace-parks. After all, the most famous public massings in Petersburg (1825, 1905) ended not in jubilation, but in bloodshed. In 2003, video-screens were installed on the streets and some major ceremonies and closed functions were televised. A host of local, neighborhood-based festivities proliferated outside the city center.

Alongside the official tricentennial celebrations, however, there existed a local countermovement in Petersburg expressing frustration at the many inconveniences and disruptions to normal local life, protesting the exclusion of ordinary residents from so many of the events. During the festivities, important driving routes were closed to regular traffic to guarantee smooth passage for dignitaries and foreign visitors. The renovations were termed Potemkin-like, providing attractive face-lifts to select buildings, but leaving structural and interior problems unaddressed. Also, as many noted, sprucing-up efforts were limited to the city center, while the rest of Petersburg remained its usual shabby self. In short, the tricentennial was deemed a return to the founding attitudes of imperial Petersburg—a hollow city-for-show that cared more about impressing the rest of the world than the quality of life for its inhabitants.

The tricentennial countermovement reversed the number "3" in "*300-letie*" (tricentennial), and local opposition united under the rubric of "*zoo-letie,*" a messy and chaotic farce that had little in common with the celebration's official incarnation. The countermovement mounted its own websites—*anti300.spb. ru, 300.cartoon.ru,* and *fuckoff.spb.ru.* These offered practical tips to residents on how to survive the official ten-day festivities, provided space for individual rants (*vzryv emotsii*), collected wild rumors and wilder facts, and performed postmortem analyses of the proceedings, reporting anticlimactic moments and other assorted contretemps with great relish.

Thanks to the Internet, even the unofficial countermovement was able to add its voice to the tricentennial throng. Measured official rhetoric notwithstanding, the discourse of the 2003 Petersburg celebrations was messy and plural, with journalists contentiously speaking their minds, commercial interests asserting themselves, and events staged in many different "genres" in addition to the traditional formal exercises. In this sense, tricentennial Petersburg manifested the cultural "middleness" that was always one of its most salient features as a living city, in spite of the persistent mythology of extremes and the habit of evoking middle ground solely in terms of its absence.

Through diverse and colorful exercises in commemoration, St. Petersburg made amends for the past. If 1903 was a cultural moment marked by preservationist calls to arms, 2003 celebrated a Petersburg that has learned many sad lessons about forgetting. The collective project of recollection, having gone underground to a large extent during the Soviet era, when it became the province of individual eccentrics and intelligentsia research-workers, was back in full swing.

❧ NOTES ❧

Introduction

1. See, for example, Solomon Volkov, *St. Petersburg: A Cultural History*, trans. Antonina W. Bouis (New York: The Free Press, 1995), which recounts the city's history as the story of a great artistic legacy—Pushkin, Glinka, Gogol, Dostoevsky, Mussorgsky, Tchaikovsky, Benois, Diaghilev, Stravinsky, Meyerhold, Blok, Mandelstam, Akhmatova, Nabokov, Balanchine, Shostakovich, and Brodsky. See also the Petersburg sections of Suzanne Massie, *Land of the Firebird: The Beauty of Old Russia* (New York: Simon & Schuster, 1980).

2. W. Bruce Lincoln declares in this vein, "Blended with images of poverty, suffering, and heroism on a monumental scale, opulence, raw political power, and artistic brilliance make up the historical persona of St. Petersburg." W. Bruce Lincoln, *Sunlight at Midnight: St. Petersburg and the Rise of Modern Russia* (New York: Basic Books, 2000), pp. 12, 31.

3. Yuri Egorov, *The Architectural Planning of St. Petersburg*, trans. Eric Dluhosch (Athens: Ohio University Press, 1969), pp. 86–91.

4. Joseph Brodsky, "Guide to a Renamed City," in *Less Than One: Selected Essays* (New York: Farrar, Straus, Giroux, 1986), pp. 93–94.

5. V. N. Toporov, "Peterburg i 'Peterburgskii text russkoi literatury' (Vvedenie v temu)." *Mif. Ritual. Simvol. Obraz: Issledovaniia v oblasti mifopoeticheskogo* (Moscow: Prog ress, 1995).

6. The snake may thus refer to the reactionary opponents of Peter the Great's reforms, but also to the Antichrist and the coming end of the world. Iu. M. Lotman, "Simvolika Peterburga i problemy semiotiki goroda," *Izbrannye stat'i: Stat'i po istorii russkoi literatury XVIII—pervoi poloviny XIX veka*, vol. 1 (Tallinn: Aleksandra, 1992), p. 13.

7. Elise Kimerling Wirtschafter, *Social Identity in Imperial Russia* (Dekalb: Northern Illinois University Press, 1997), p. 79.

8. See, for example, Pavel Buryshkin, *Moskva kupecheskaia* (Moscow: Vysshaia shkola, 1991), and James L. West and Iurii A. Petrov, eds., *Merchant Moscow: Images of Russia's Vanished Bourgeoisie* (Princeton: Princeton University Press, 1998). See also the remarks on this subject by Vissarion Belinskii in his essay "Peterburg i Moskva," in *Fiziologiia Peterburga*, ed. V. I. Kuleshov (Moscow: Nauka, 1991), pp. 26–27. For general information about this class in Russia, see Alfred J. Rieber, *Merchants and Entrepreneurs in Imperial Russia* (Chapel Hill: University of North Carolina Press, 1982). For literary images of the merchant, see the chapter "The Problem of the Merchant in Russian Literature" in Beth Holmgren, *Rewriting Capitalism: Literature and the Market in Late Tsarist Russia and the Kingdom of Poland* (Pittsburgh: University of Pittsburgh Press, 1998).

9. Elise Kimerling Wirtschafter, *Structures of Society: Imperial Russia's "People of Diverse Ranks"* (Dekalb: Northern Illinois University Press, 1994), p. xi.

10. For background on the emergence of the professions in late imperial Russia, see

Harley D. Balzer, ed., *Russia's Missing Middle Class: The Professions in Russian History* (Armonk: M. E. Sharpe, Inc., 1996).

11. Samuel D. Kassow, James L. West, and Edith W. Clowes, "Introduction: The Problem of the Middle in Late Imperial Russian Society," in *Between Tsar and People: Educated Society and the Quest for Public Identity in Late Imperial Russia*, Edith W. Clowes, Samuel D. Kassow, and James L. West, eds. (Princeton: Princeton University Press, 1991), pp. 3–14.

12. Kassow, West, and Clowes nevertheless stress the "precariousness and fragility" of the social and cultural middle and the "widening gulf between the possible forming of a cohesive urban public and a real growing discord, faltering communication, and difficult definition of common political and economic ground." Alfred J. Rieber, too, invokes "the vast splintered middle of Russian society—merchants, professionals, clerks, petty shopkeepers, and artisans," who possessed "no sense of class consciousness and no ability to unify politically." See Rieber's "The Sedimentary Society" in *Between Tsar and People*, p. 356.

13. Foucault's early interdisciplinary archeology represents, in his words, "The history not of literature but of that . . . everyday, transient writing that never acquires the status of an oeuvre, or is immediately lost . . . concerned with all that insidious thought, that whole interplay of representations that flow anonymously between men; in the interstices of the great discursive monuments, it reveals the crumbling soil on which they are based. It is the discipline of fluctuating languages (*langages*), of shapeless works, of unrelated themes." Michel Foucault, *The Archaeology of Knowledge and The Discourse on Language*, trans. A. M. Sheridan Smith (New York: Pantheon Books, 1972), pp. 136–37.

14. Edward Soja attributes the modern emphasis on time to Marx's reaction against Hegel's emphasis on states and territories. See *Postmodern Geographies: The Reassertion of Space in Critical Social Theory* (New York: Verso, 1989), pp. 46, 86.

15. See Foucault's complaints on this score in "Questions on Geography" in *Power/Knowledge*, ed. Colin Gordon (New York: Pantheon Books, 1980). He wonders why space has been treated as fixed and nondialectical, while time is seen as rich and complex (p. 70).

16. For an excellent survey of these developments, see Stephen Kern, *The Culture of Time and Space 1880–1918* (Cambridge, MA: Harvard University Press, 1983).

17. Henri Lefebvre, *The Production of Space*, trans. Donald Nicholson-Smith (Oxford: Blackwell, 1991), pp. 94, 102. See also Louis Althusser and Etienne Balibar, *Reading Capital*, trans. Ben Brewster (London: New Left Books, 1977), and Manuel Castells, *The Urban Question: A Marxist Approach* (London: Edward Arnold, 1977).

18. Place (*lieu*) is "the order . . . in accord with which elements are distributed in relationships of coexistence." Space (*espace*), in contrast, is "actuated by the ensemble of movements deployed within it." Michel de Certeau, *The Practice of Everyday Life*, trans. Steven Rendall (Berkeley: University of California Press, 1984), p. 117. Terminological inconsistencies abound in this debate, with "space" and "place" occupying different positions in the bold statements of social theorists. While de Certeau privileges space as the location of the everyday, John Agnew proposes "place" as a more productive analytic category than "space," indeed as a "counter-representation" to space that conveys the local, the social, and the heterogeneous. See "Representing Space: Space, Scale and Culture in Social Science," *Place/Culture/Representation*, pp. 261–64. Similarly, Allan Pred defines place as "an appropriation and transformation of space and nature that is inseparable

from the reproduction and transformation of society in time and space," and as "what takes place ceaselessly, what contributes to history in a specific context through the creation and utilization of a physical setting." See "Place as Historically Contingent Process: Structuration and the Time-Geography of Becoming Places," *Annals of the Association of American Geographers* 74, 1984, p. 279.

19. Burton Pike, *The Image of the City in Modern Literature* (Princeton: Princeton University Press, 1981), p. 119.

20. Lewis Mumford highlights the essential connection between text and city, even in ancient times, with reference to the written records that all cities maintained. The city was thus a "container" and a "storehouse" for goods and services, but also the site of inscription for memory, tradition, and law. See *The City in History: Its Origins, Its Transformations, and Its Prospects* (New York: Harcourt, Brace & Jovanovich, 1961), pp. 97–98.

21. Raymond Williams, *The Country and the City* (London: The Hogarth Press, 1985), p. 154.

22. See Georg Simmel, "The Metropolis and Mental Life," in Kurt Wolff, ed., *The Sociology of Georg Simmel* (Glencoe: Free Press, 1950), and Simmel's 1900 *The Philosophy of Money*.

23. Henri Lefebvre, "The Specificity of the City," in *Writings on Cities*, trans. and eds. Eleonore Kofman and Elizabeth Lebas (Oxford: Blackwell Publishers Ltd, 1996), p. 101.

24. Brodsky, p. 72.

25. James Cracraft, *The Petrine Revolution in Russian Imagery* (Chicago: University of Chicago Press, 1997), pp. 273–75. For additional information on early Russian mapmaking, see A. V. Postnikov, *Karty zemel' rossiiskikh: Ocherki istorii geograficheskogo izucheniia i kartografirovanniia nashego otechestva* (Moscow: Nash Dom—L'Age d'Homme, 1996). See also L. S. Bagrov, *A History of the Cartography of Russia up to 1600*, H. W. Castner, ed. (Ontario: Walker Press, 1975) and *A History of Russian Cartography up to 1800*, H. W. Castner, ed. (Ontario: Walker Press, 1975).

26. Denis Cosgrove and Mona Domosh, "Author and Authority: Writing the New Cultural Geography," in *Place/Culture/Representation*, James Duncan and David Ley, eds. (New York: Routledge, 1993), p. 30. For an extended discussion of the shift in spatial and geographical paradigms across traditional Marxism, humanistic geography, and postmodernist thought, see the chapter "Geography and the Cartographic Anxiety" in Derek Gregory, *Geographical Imaginations* (Oxford: Blackwell Publishers Ltd., 1994).

27. See, for example, the following articles by J. B. Harley: "Deconstructing the Map," *Cartographica* 26 (1989); "Historical Geography and the Cartographic Illusion," *Journal of Historical Geography* 15 (1989); and "Maps, Knowledge, and Power," in Denis Cosgrove and Stephen Daniels, eds., *The Iconography of Landscape: Essays on the Symbolic Representation, Design, and Use of Past Environments* (Cambridge, UK: Cambridge University Press, 1988). See also Denis Wood, *The Power of Maps* (New York: Guilford, 1992) and James Duncan and David Ley, "Representing the Place of Culture," in Duncan and Ley, eds., *Place/Culture/Representation* (London: Routledge, 1993).

28. J. Hillis Miller, *Topographies* (Stanford: Stanford University Press, 1995), pp. 3–19.

29. Miller's literary approach to cartography counters Michel de Certeau's critique of Renaissance- and Enlightenment-era mapmaking, which, de Certeau claims, caused the map to disengage from "the itineraries that were the condition of its possibility." The map thus constitutes space as "a formal ensemble of abstract places" and "a totalizing stage on

which elements of diverse origin are brought together to form the tableau of a 'state' of geographical knowledge." See de Certeau, pp. 119–21.

30. Tom Conley, *The Self-Made Map: Cartographic Writing in Early Modern France* (Minneapolis: University of Minnesota Press, 1996), pp. 2–3.

31. Iu. M. Lotman and B. A. Uspenskii, "Binary Models in the Dynamics of Russian Culture (to the End of the Eighteenth Century)," in *The Semiotics of Russian Cultural History*, Alexander D. Nakhimovsky and Alice Stone Nakhimovsky, eds. (Ithaca: Cornell University Press, 1984), pp. 31–33, 52–57.

32. William Mills Todd III, *Fiction and Society in the Age of Pushkin: Ideology, Institutions, and Narrative* (Cambridge, MA: Harvard University Press, 1986).

33. V. G. Belinskii, "Vstuplenie," in *Fiziologiia Peterburga*, V. I. Kuleshov, ed. (Moscow: Nauka, 1991), p. 13.

34. Ibid., pp. 8–10.

35. V. O. Mikhnevich, "Peterburzhtsy," in *Zhivopisnaia Rossiia: Otechestvo nashe v ego zemel'nom, istoricheskom, plemennom, ekonomicheskom i bytovom znachenii*, P. P. Semenov, ed., t. 1, ch. 2, Severnaia Rossiia: Ozernaia ili Drevne-Novgorodskaia Oblast' (SPb: M. O. Vol'f, 1881), p. 65.

36. For a general survey of the publishing industry in Petersburg, see I. E. Barenbaum and N. A. Kostyleva, *Knizhnyi Peterburg-Leningrad* (Leningrad: Lenizdat, 1986), which includes a useful bibliography. See also Gary Marker, *Publishing, Printing, and the Origins of Intellectual Life in Russia, 1700–1800* (Princeton: Princeton University Press, 1985).

37. See also the Supplement (Prilozhenie) to N. I. Sveshnikov's reprinted *Vospominaniia propashchego cheloveka* (Moscow: Novoe literaturnoe obozrenie, 1996), for additional nineteenth-century descriptions of the Petersburg book "market," including an excerpt from G. F. Kurochkin's unpublished *Vospominaniia starogo bukinista*, as well as sketches from the 1860s by A. D. Shtukin ("Knizhniki") and V. V. Krestovskii ("Bukinist"). See also *Ocharovannye knigoi : Russkie pisateli o knigakh, chtenii, bibliofilakh*, ed. A. V. Blium (Moscow: Kniga, 1982), and P. K. Simoni, "O knizhnoi torgovle i tipakh torgovtsev na Starom Apraksinom rynke," *Starye gody*, 1907, no. 2. Note also the brief sketch "Bukinist" in Anatoly Bakhtiarov's *Briukho Peterburga* (SPb: Fert, 1994).

38. See also the short chapter devoted to secondhand booksellers in Anatolii Bakhtiarov's 1887 *Briukho Peterburga*. This chapter treats books much like the other consumable goods described in this series of sketches, providing figures on the number of booksellers, the number of books purveyed by each bookseller at any given time, and so forth. This chapter's main source of interest is the reported conversations between bookseller and customer, rendered in the same rough-and-tumble tone as any other market exchanges. This chapter also anticipates Bakhtiarov's later interest in the publishing industry, about which he authored several books, including *Slugi pechati: Ocherki knigopechatnogo dela* (1893), *Kak delaiut bumagu i kak pechataiut knigi* (1901), and *Istoriia bumazhnogo lista* (1906).

39. Louise McReynolds claims that the mass daily newspaper provided the urban middle readership with "a place for a modicum of cultural cohesion," and that the very existence of a newspaper industry implies the existence of "a middle class that is substantial enough to provide the combined prerequisites of a large readership and advertising capable of sustaining it." Louise McReynolds, *The News Under Russia's Old Regime: The Development of a Mass-Circulation Press* (Princeton: Princeton University Press, 1991), pp. 5–7.

40. My study grounds itself in the imperial period. Elena Hellberg-Hirn, in contrast, examines the complexities of Petersburg cultural space through the lens of the present in her highly informative study, *Imperial Imprint: Post-Soviet St. Petersburg* (SKS Finnish Literature Society, 2003).

41. For a discussion of Lotman's view of "everyday life" in contrast to those of Foucault and de Certeau, see Jonathan Bolton, "Writing in a Polluted Semiosphere: Everyday Life in Lotman," in *Yuri Lotman and Cultural Theory*, Amy Mandelker and Andreas Schönle, eds., (forthcoming, University of Wisconsin Press, 2005).

42. Michael L. Ross, *Storied Cities: Literary Imaginings of Florence, Venice, and Rome* (Westport: Greenwood Press, 1994), p. 1, 9–11. That Alexander Pushkin gave birth to the Petersburg mythology as the city's literary paradigm with his poem "The Bronze Horseman" (1833) and short story "The Queen of Spades" (1834) is a commonplace of Russian literary history. As Nikolai Antsiferov declared, "Pushkin is the creator of the *image* of Petersburg in the same measure as Peter the Great was the builder of the city itself.". . N. P. Antsiferov, *Dusha Peterburga. "Nepostizhimyi gorod . . ."* (Leningrad: Lenizdat, 1991), pp. 58–59. Donald Fanger similarly asserts that Pushkin is responsible for the "atmosphere" that permeates Petersburg literature: "a constant, equivocal mixing of the soberly realistic with the apparently fantastic," which creates "the image of an unreal city." See Donald Fanger, *Dostoevsky and Romantic Realism* (Chicago: University of Chicago Press, 1965), pp. 104–5.

43. Further literature on the subject of this much-enunciated myth includes Ettore Lo Gatto, *Il mito di Pietroburgo: Storia, leggenda, poesia* (Milan: Feltrinelli Editore, 1960), Johannes Holthusen, "Petersburg als literarischer Mythos," in *Russland in Vers und Prosa* (Munich: Verlag Otto Sagner, 1973), R. G. Nazirov, "Peterburgskaia legenda i literaturnye traditsii," in *Traditsii i novatorstvo*, vyp. 3: *Uchenye zapiski Bashkirskogo Gosudarstvennogo Universiteta*, vyp. 80. Seriia filologicheskikh nauk, 26 (Ufa, 1975), L. K. Dolgopolov, "Mif o Peterburge i ego preobrazovanie v nachale XX veka," in *Na rubezhe vekov: O russkoi literature kontsa XIX-nachala XX veka* (Leningrad: Sovetskii pisatel', 1977), Sidney Monas, "Unreal City: St. Petersburg and Russian Culture," in *Russian Literature and American Critics*, Kenneth N. Brostrom, ed. (Ann Arbor: University of Michigan Press, 1984), the articles by Iu. M. Lotman, V. N. Toporov, Z. G. Mints, M. V. Bezrodnyi, and A. A. Danilevskii, and R. G. Timenchik in *Semiotika goroda i gorodskoi kul'tury (Peterburg). Trudy po znakovym sistemam*, vol. 18 (Tartu, 1984), and G. P. Makogenenko, "Tema Peterburga u Pushkina i Gogolia," in *Izbrannye raboty: O Pushkine, ego predshestvennikakh i naslednikakh* (Leningrad: Khudozhestvennaia literatura, 1987).

44. Antsiferov, p. 44.

45. Toporov, p. 278.

46. Ibid., pp. 260–61.

47. Thomas Raikes, *A Visit to St. Petersburg in the Winter of 1829–30* (London: Richard Bentley, 1838), p. 319.

48. N. V. Gogol, "Dozhd' byl prodolzhitel'nyi . . ." *PSS*, t. 3 (Moscow: Izdatel'stvo AN SSSR, 1938), pp. 331–32.

49. F. M. Dostoevskii, *Dvoinik. PSS*, t. 1 (Leningrad: Nauka, 1972), p. 109.

50. Ibid., p. 138.

51. F. M. Dostoevskii, *Unizhennye i oskorblennye. PSS*, t. 3 (Leningrad: Nauka, 1972), p. 300.

52. N. A. Nekrasov, "Preferans i solntse," *PSSiP*, (Leningrad: Nauka, 1981–), t. 12, p. 175.

53. N. A. Nekrasov, "O pogode." *PSS*, t. 2 (Moscow: Khudozhestvennaia literature, 1948), p. 61.

54. K. G. Isupov claims that writers invoked Moscow with "tenderness and gratitude" but evinced "a tortured love" for Petersburg. K. G. Isupov, "Dialog stolits v istoricheskom dvizhenii," *Moskva-Peterburg: Pro et Contra* (SPb: Izdatel'stvo Russkogo Khristianskogo Gumanitarnogo Instituta, 2000), p. 55.

55. Letter, A. S. Pushkin to N. N. Pushkina, no later than May 29, 1834, as cited in Toporov, p. 271.

56. V. G. Belinskii, *PSS*, t. 11 (Moscow: Izdatel'stvo AN SSSR, 1953–), p. 418.

57. Alexander Herzen, "Moskva i Peterburg." *Peterburg v russkom ocherke XIX veka*, M. V. Otradin, ed. (Leningrad: Izdatel'stvo Leningradskogo Universiteta, 1984), p. 57.

58. Dostoevsky, too, polemicized with Pushkin, citing the famous "I love you" declaration, and adding, "I'm sorry, but I don't love it," followed by his rewritten version of Pushkin's line: "Windows, godforsaken holes—and monuments." N. N. Strakhov, ed., "Iz zapisnoi knizhki F. M. Dostoevskogo," *Biografiia, pis'ma i zametki iz zapisnoi knizhki F. M. Dostoevskogo* (St. Petersburg, 1883), p. 359.

59. In this vein, Kornei Chukovskii was reportedly wont to remark, "When he wasn't depressed, Nekrasov was not a poet" (*Nekrasov ne khandriashchii—ne poet*). See Stanislav Rassadin, *Russkie, ili Iz dvorian v intelligenty* (Moscow: Knizhnyi sad, 1995), p. 297.

60. See, respectively, V. A. Sleptsov, *Sochineniia v dvukh tomakh*, t. 1 (Moscow, 1957), p. 324, and V. Garshin, "Peterburgskie pis'ma," *Rasskazy*, kn. 3 (St. Petersburg: Tip. M. M. Stasiulevich, 1902), p. 54.

61. Toporov, pp. 313–14.

62. V. V. Krestovskii, "Khandra," *Stikhi* (SPb: A. Ozerov, 1862).

63. Similarly, see the six verses of Count Arsenii Golenishchev-Kutuzov, the poetic monologues of a depressed and isolated narrator, set to music by Modest Mussorgsky in his 1874 song cycle "Sunless" (*Bez solntsa*): "Inside Four Walls," "You Did Not Recognize Me in the Crowd," "The Idle, Noisy Day Is Done," "Languish," "Elegy," and "Above the River." The progression takes the narrator from feeling trapped in his room to contemplating suicide.

64. Julia Kristeva, *Black Sun: Depression and Melancholia*, trans. Leon S. Roudiez (New York: Columbia University Press, 1989), pp. 147, 151.

65. Ibid., p. 33.

66. S. Ia. Nadson, "Ditia stolitsy, s iunykh dnei . . .," *Stikhotvoreniia* (SPb: Tip. I. N. Skorokhodova, 1898), pp. 253–54.

67. N. V. Gogol', "Peterburgskie zapiski 1836 goda," *Sobranie sochinenii v vos'mi tomakh*, t. 7 (Moscow: Pravda, 1984), pp. 179–80.

68. F. M. Dostoevskii, "Peterburgskie snovedeniia v stikhakh i proze," in *Polnoe sobranie khudozhestvennykh sochinenii*, B. Tomashevskii and K. Khalabaev, eds., t. 13 (Moscow: Gosudarstvennoe izdatel'stvo, 1926–30), pp. 155–56.

69. Svetlana Boym, *Common Places: Mythologies of Everyday Life in Russia* (Cambridge: Harvard University Press, 1994), p. 67.

70. Furthermore, as Beth Holmgren argues, the two groups did share certain overlapping social and moral values, even though the *meshchantstvo* exhibited the more capitalist orientation. In this context, Holmgren discusses the rise of an "incipient middlebrow literature" that catered to this audience in Russia and Poland during the early years of the twentieth century. See *Rewriting Capitalism*, pp. 94–98.

71. For an account of Belyi's novel in this regard, see Pekka Pesonen, "Semiotics of a City: The Myth of St. Petersburg in Andrey Bely's novel *Petersburg*," *Slavica Helsingiensia* 18, 1997.

72. V. Serkova, "Neopisuemyi Peterburg: Vykhod v prostranstvo labirinta," *Metafizika Peterburga* (Spb: Eidos, 1993), p. 96.

73. I would like to mention two superb book-length projects currently in manuscript form, which both represent major contributions to re-visioning St. Petersburg: Katia Dianina, *A Nation on Display: Russian Museums and Print Culture in the Age of the Great Reforms* (Harvard University, dissertation, 2002), and Emily Johnson, *The Science of Local Sentiment: How Early Twentieth-Century Petersburg Learned to Study Its Self* (book manuscript, 2004).

Chapter One

1. See, for example, Grigorii Kaganov's discussion of the baroque-style swath through Petersburg left by Empress Elizabeth to mark the nocturnal route taken during the 1741 military coup that brought her to power, in *Peterburg v kontekste barokko* (Spb: Stella, 2001).

2. As the Marquis de Custine exclaimed, "Singular taste! Temples erected to clerks!" See Marquis de Custine, *Empire of the Czar: A Journey through Eternal Russia* (New York: Doubleday, 1989), p. 152.

3. See the introduction to Monika Greenleaf and Stephen Moeller-Sally, eds., *Russian Subjects: Empire, Nation, and the Culture of the Golden Age* (Evanston: Northwestern University Press, 1998). For a discussion of the harmonious principles governing literature, music, and architecture of this period, see T. F. Savarenskaia, "Evritmiia v arkhitekture Peterburga pushkinskoi pory," in *Arkhitektura v istorii russkoi kul'tury*, I. A. Bondarenko, ed. (Moscow: RAN, 1996).

4. Moisei Kagan declares the Empire style to be a synthesis of geometrical classicism and plastic, dynamic, and highly ornamental baroque. See his *Grad Petrov v istorii russkoi kul'tury* (SPb: Slaviia, 1996), p. 272.

5. "Vospominaniia O.A. Przhetslavskogo." *Russkaia starina*, no. 11, 1874, p. 465.

6. Peter Collins, *Changing Ideals in Modern Architecture 1750–1950* (London: Faber & Faber), p. 117.

7. *Ocherki istorii Leningrada*, t. 2 (Period kapitalizma—vtoraia polovina XIX veka) (Moscow: AN SSSR, 1957), pp. 793–809 ("Arkhitektura Peterburga").

8. For an incisive account of the architectural debates and developments of the period as a prelude to the emergence of moderne, see "The Quest for a National Style," in William Craft Brumfield, *The Origins of Modernism in Russian Architecture* (Berkeley: University of California Press, 1991).

9. In contrast, it has been proposed that the increasingly reactionary tsarist politics of the mid-nineteenth century are directly responsible for the onset of eclecticism. Monuments of this period have lost "the depth of principled content" and have assumed a merely "decorative" aspect, it is said. This view extends the familiar denigration of Nikolaian-era classicism to cover architectural eclecticism. See B. N. Kalinin and P. P. Iurevich, *Pamiatniki i memorial'nye doski Leningrada* (Leningrad: Lenizdat, 1979), p. 4.

10. As Renate Lachmann puts it, "In order to be what it truly is, the classical has to ini-

tiate an act of destruction." Renate Lachmann, *Memory and Literature: Intertextuality in Russian Modernism*, trans. Roy Sellars and Anthony Wall (Minneapolis: University of Minnesota Press, 1997), p. 193.

11. Francesco Algarotti, "Letters from Count Algarotti to Lord Hervey and the Marquis Scipio Maffei," Letter IV, June 30, 1739. (London: Johnson and Payne, 1769; Reprint in Goldsmiths'-Kress Library of Economic Literature, no. 10500). For more information about Algarotti's "Russian Journeys" and commentary on his letters, see M. G. Talalaia, "Franchesko Al'garotti: Russkie puteshestviia. Perevod s ital'ianskogo, predislovie i primechaniia," in *Nevskii arkhiv* III (SPb: Atheneum Feniks, 1997). See also M. S. Nekliudova and A. L. Ospovat, "Okno v Evropu: Istochnikovedcheskii etiud k 'Mednomu Vsadniku," *Lotmanovskii sbornik* 2 (Moscow: RGGU, 1997).

12. W. Bruce Lincoln also suggests something of this sort when he describes Peter the Great's 1697 Grand Embassy of the Russians to the West: "Everything Peter saw during his first trip to the West helped him create an eclectic image of what Russia might become." See his *Sunlight at Midnight: St. Petersburg and the Rise of Modern Russia* (New York: Basic Books, 2000), p. 22.

13. See Lindsey Hughes, *Russia in the Age of Peter the Great* (New Haven: Yale University Press, 1998), pp. 224–28. Hughes declares the blanket designation "Petrine Baroque" inadequate to describe the "composite nature of architectural practice" from this period, which produced a "hybrid style."

14. Custine, pp. 87–89.

15. The same might be true of the image of Petersburg as a "city of stone." During a 1908 visit to St. Petersburg, the English travel-writer A. Maccullum Scott strolled along Nevsky Prospect, "the pride and boast of St. Petersburg." Scott noted the "uninspired copying of classical and Renaissance forms" and observed, "Stucco and plaster are universal, not boldly avowing itself as such, but ruled and squared into a miserable counterfeit of dressed stone." See A. Maccullum Scott, *Through Finland to St. Petersburg* (London: Grant Richards, 1909), pp. 227–28. Note that this use of plaster and stucco was also widespread in the eighteenth century, used on wooden building facades to create the effect of stonemasonry.

16. The most significant buildings in the neoclassical style from Catherine's time include the Grand Gostinyi Dvor, Small Hermitage, Academy of Arts, Marble Palace, Academy of Sciences, and Tauride Palace. None are structures that can be said to dominate or define Petersburg architectural style. Some of the finest exemplars of this architecture are grand residences at some distance from the city center, among them the Kamennyi Island Palace.

17. Petr Chaadaev, "First Letter," in *Russian Philosophy*, vol. 1, James M. Edie, James P. Scanlan, and Mary-Barbara Zeldin, eds. (Knoxville: University of Tennessee Press, 1976), pp. 112, 116.

18. Petr Chaadaev, "Apology of a Madman," in *Readings in Russian Civilization*, vol. II, Thomas Riha, ed. (Chicago: University of Chicago Press, 1969), pp. 311–12. Of course, the irony of this shift in viewpoint must be noted. The 1836 publication of Chaadaev's first philosophical letter resulted in the author's being declared officially insane and placed under house arrest for more than a year. Thus the "madman" of the 1837 Apology's title was an independent thinker who became receptive to cultural eclecticism after being tormented by the repressive tsarist regime.

19. F. M. Dostoevskii, "Peterburgskaia letopis," in *Polnoe sobranie khudozhestvennykh*

sochinenii, B. Tomashevskii and K Khalabaev, eds. , t. 8 (Moscow: Gosudarstvennoe izdatel'stvo, 1926–1930), p. 23. For more information about Dostoevsky's response to the Marquis de Custine's account, see E. I. Kiiko, "Belinskii i Dostoevskii o knige Kiustina 'Rossiia v 1839'" in *Dostoevskii: Materialy i issledovaniia*, vol. 1 (Leningrad: Nauka, 1974), pp. 196–200.

20. F. M. Dostoevskii, "Malen'kie kartiny," in *Polnoe sobranie sochinenii v tridtsati tomakh* (Leningrad: Nauka, 1980), vol. 21, pp. 106–7.

21. V. V. Stasov, "Dvadtsat' piat' let russkogo iskusstva," in *Izbrannye sochineniia v trekh tomakh*, vol. 2 (Moscow: Iskusstvo, 1952), p. 499. Translation to English from William Craft Brumfield, *The Origins of Modernism in Russian Architecture* (Berkeley: University of California Press, 1991), p. 6.

22. Custine, p. 88.

23. E. Viollet Le Duc, *L'art russe: ses origines, ses elements constitutifs, son apogee, son avenir* (Paris, Ve. A. Morel, 1877), pp. 184–85.

24. See N. Ia. Danilevskii, *Rossiia i Evropa* (Moscow: Kniga, 1991).

25. Stasov, p. 510.

26. Alexander Benois, "Zhivopisnyi Peterburg." *Mir iskusstva*, no. 1, 1902, p. 1.

27. This originary conception of St. Petersburg as a stern geometrical city exists as part of the city's mythology rather than its history. As historian Yuri Egorov points out, with the abandonment of Leblond's model plan for the city, "the growing capital had no coherent master plan and developed instead according to local planning efforts centering around the Peter and Paul Fortress and the Admiralty." Since the central part of the city was so "poorly balanced," later eighteenth-century and nineteenth-century planners tried to reintegrate the "disparate fragments" that constituted St. Petersburg at the beginning of Catherine's reign and afterward. See Yuri Egorov, *The Architectural Planning of St. Petersburg*, trans. Eric Dluhosch (Athens: Ohio University Press, 1969), p. 179.

28. Alexander Benois, "Krasota Peterburga." *Mir iskusstva*, no. 8, 1902, p. 141.

29. Benois's exhortation recalls Konstantin Batiushkov's characterization of St. Petersburg as an ideal subject for artists as well as an art academy in itself nearly a century earlier in his 1814 sketch "Progulka v Akademiiu khudozhestv." See chapter 3 for a discussion of this work.

30. "Zhivopisnyi Peterburg," p. 2.

31. Alexander Benois, "Materialy dlia istorii vandalizma v Rossii." *Mir iskusstva*, no. 12, 1903, p. 118. Similarly, Vladimir Kurbatov, a leading member of the preservationist movement, acknowledged eclecticism's existence in his 1913 architectural history of Petersburg, but only in negative terms as the revivalist progression from "false" Nikolaian classicism, to false Renaissance, false gothic, false baroque, and false Russian styles. See V. Kurbatov, *Peterburg* (SPb: Lenizdat, 1993), pp. 149–50. Louis Réau, Director of the St. Petersburg French Institute, published a rapturous volume about the city in 1913 as part of the series "Les Villes d'Art célèbres," and, applauding the work of the preservationists, similarly deplored the "banal" disfiguration of the cityscape by European-style eclecticism and dissonant Russian revivalism. See Louis Réau, *Saint-Pétersbourg* (Paris: Librairie Renouard, 1913), pp. 10–13. In a 1917 study of the older parts of Petersburg, Georgy Lukomskii evoked the "epoch of indifference towards the image of St. Peter's city, which lasted from the 1850s almost up until the 1900s." See G. K. Lukomskii, *Staryi Peterburg: Progulki po starinnym kvartalam stolitsy* (Petrograd: Svobodnoe iskusstvo, 1917), p. 7. It should be noted, however, that Benois's stance had softened noticeably in a 1913

jubilee retrospective of Nicholas I's reign. At this time, Benois declared himself able to look upon the pseudogothic style with a certain "tenderness," although this rapprochement extended only to structures built before 1855. See "Dvortsovye stroitel'stva imperatora Nikolaia I," *Starye gody* July–September 1913, p. 173.

32. N. I. Glinka, "Krasuisia, grad Petrov . . ." *Zolotoi vek arkhitektury Sankt-Peterburga* (SPb: Lenizdat, 1996).

33. I. E. Grabar', *Peterburgskaia arkhitektura v XVIII i XIX vekakh* (SPb: Lenizdat, 1994).

34. Interestingly, the nineteenth-century perspective on the Petersburg cityscape may not have been so uniformly antieclectic. Vladimir Mikhnevich's 1874 popular reference guidebook *Peterburg ves' na ladoni*, for example, includes a relatively short list of the city's "Remarkable Buildings," which lists the notably eclectic Moscow Railroad Station and the Beloselskii-Belozerskii Palace alongside such Petersburg "classics" as the Peter-Paul Fortress, Senate and Synod, Gostinnyi Dvor, Stock Exchange, and New Admiralty. See Vladimir Mikhnevich, *Peterburg ves' na ladoni* (SPb: Izdanie K. N. Plotnikova, 1874), pp. 240–51.

35. Kurbatov, pp. 149–50. Kurbatov's views are echoed by a contemporary cultural history of St. Petersburg. In a chapter called "The Search for a New Style," Yurii Ovsiannikov declares that Stakenschneider, like Thon, was "a typical architect from the epoch characterized by social stagnation and the lack of an authentic style." See his *Tri veka Sankt-Peterburga: Istoriia. Kul'tura. Byt* (Moscow: Galart, 1997), p. 217.

36. An exception to this rule is a reference work that provides article-length biographies for sixty Petersburg architects associated with three different, but equally weighted periods in the city's history: the first half of the nineteenth century, the second half of the nineteenth century, and the early twentieth century. See V. G. Isachenko, ed., *Zodchie Sankt-Peterburga XIX—nachalo XX veka* (SPb: Lenizdat, 1998).

37. See, for example, W. Bruce Lincoln's *Sunlight at Midnight*, which evokes the "nouveaux riches of late-nineteenth-century St. Petersburg" as the force behind the trend according to which "From the mid-1860s to the late 1870s, a passion for redesigning facades swept the city and defaced a number of beautiful buildings as men and women with more money than taste sought to leave a mark." Only in the 1890s did city architects find a style "that matched artistic integrity to modern needs" (pp. 159–60). For an example of the cultural appeal and prestige of moderne in Petersburg, see I. A. Murav'eva, *Vek moderna* (from the series *Byloi Peterburg: Panorama stolichnoi zhizni*) (SPb: Pushkinskii fond, 2001).

38. Alexander Solzhenitsyn, "The City on the Neva," in *Stories and Prose Poems* (The Bodley Head, 1970), p. 233.

39. Joseph Brodsky, "A Guide to a Renamed City," in *Less Than One: Selected Essays* (New York: Farrar, Strauss, & Giroux, 1986), p. 81.

40. Joseph Brodsky, "Less Than One," in *Less Than One: Selected Essays*, p. 5.

41. Yuri Lotman, "Simvolika Peterburga i problemy semiotiki goroda," in *Stat'i po istorii russkoi literatury XVIII—pervoi poloviny XIX veka* (Tallinn: Aleksandra, 1992). Translated text from *Universe of the Mind: A Semiotic Theory of Culture*, trans. Ann Shukman (Bloomington: Indiana University Press, 1990), pp. 191–214.

42. Lotman, pp. 16–17.

43. Ibid., pp. 20–21.

44. In a similar spirit of selective remembering, the cultural historian Moisei Kagan

claims that St. Petersburg has lived by one essential principle since its founding in the early eighteenth century, namely "unity in diversity" and "spatio-plastic harmony," as each new architectural style integrates itself into the cityscape without negating its older neighbors. The seeming inclusiveness invoked by Kagan, however, may cloak a familiar Petersburg elitism. Kagan believes that the ornamental tendencies of baroque architecture in Petersburg were muted in order to harmonize with the city's classical dominant, as were those of later Empire and moderne styles. He also claims that the great spirit of the Petersburg architectural tradition softened the vulgar effects of bourgeois decorative excesses (read eclecticism) and thus prevented these newer structures from degrading the cityscape as a whole. See Moisei Kagan, *Grad Petrov v istorii russkoi kul'tury* (SPb: Slaviia, 1996), pp. 112, 275–76.

45. V. V. Antonov and A. V. Kobak, eds., *Utrachennye pamiatniki arkhitektury Peterburga-Leningrada* (Leningrad: Khudozhnik RSFSR, 1988), p. 3.

46. A. L. Punin, *Arkhitekturnye pamiatniki Peterburga—vtoraia polovina XIX veka* (Leningrad: Lenizdat, 1981). Other important Russian work on architectural eclecticism includes E. A. Borisova, *Russkaia arkhitektura vtoroi poloviny XIX veka* (Moscow: Nauka, 1979), E. I. Kirichenko, *Russkaia arkhitektura 1830–1910-kh godov* (Moscow: Iskusstvo, 1978), and A. L. Punin, *Arkhitektura Peterburga serediny XIX veka* (Leningrad: Lenizdat, 1990). These three authors have also produced a number of articles on this topic (see bibliography).

47. B. M. Kirikov, "Stil'—Zhanr—Sreda (K voprosu o formoobrazovanii v arkhitekture Peterburga 1830–1910-kh gg.)." *Antsiferovskie chteniia: Materialy i tezisy conferentsii* (Leningrad: Leningradskoe Otedelenie Sovetskogo Fonda Kul'tury, 1989), p. 148.

48. E. I. Kirichenko, *Russkaia arkhitektura 1830–1910-kh godov*, p. 8. For a careful analysis of many different trends and pronouncements concerning architecture in Russia during the nineteenth century, see E. I. Kirichenko, *Arkhitekturnye teorii XIX veka v Rossii* (Moscow: Iskusstvo, 1986). See also E. I. Kirichenko, "Romantizm i istorizm v russkoi arkhitekture XIX veka (K voprosu o dvukh fazakh razvitiia eklektiki)," *Arkhitekturnoe nasledstvo* 36 (1988).

49. Kirichenko, *Russkaia arkhitektura 1830–1910-kh godov*, p. 36.

50. N. B. Ivanova, "Zagadka i taina v literature 'peterburgskogo stilia'," in *Fenomen Peterburga* (SPb: Blits, 2000), p. 96. Ivanova calls Petersburg "the most postmodern of the important world cities" because it combines entire epochs, and not merely different tendencies.

51. I. V. Sakharov, "Stolitsa Rossiiskoi imperii kak proobraz ob"edinennoi Evropy: vzgliad etnodemografa i genealoga," in *Fenomen Peterburga* (SPb: BLITS, 2000), pp. 143, 150–51.

52. K. G. Isupov, "Dialog stolits v istoricheskom dvizhenii," in *Moskva-Peterburg: Pro et Contra* (SPb: Izdatel'stvo Russkogo Khristianskogo Gumanitarnogo Instituta, 2000), p. 17.

53. Ibid, pp. 18–19.

54. Mikhail N. Epstein, *After the Future: The Paradoxes of Postmodernism and Contemporary Russian Culture*, trans. Anesa Miller-Pogacar (Amherst: The University of Massachusetts Press, 1995), pp. 189–94. Epstein himself notes the parallel with Custine, arguing that Russian civilization has attempted similar production of reality ever since Prince Vladimir adopted Christianity in A.D. 988. See also Jean Baudrillard, "Simulacra and Simulations," in *Jean Baudrillard: Selected Writings*, Mark Poster, ed. (Stanford: Stanford University Press, 1988).

55. As Renato Poggioli observed, in primitive ages, there are *only* unwritten poetics, whereas in eclectic or composite epochs, unwritten poetics "predominate over the written ones." See Renato Poggioli, *The Spirit of the Letter: Essays in European Literature* (Cambridge: Harvard University Press, 1965), p. 345.

56. Donald J. Olsen, *The City as a Work of Art: London, Paris, Vienna* (New Haven: Yale University Press, 1986), pp. 254–69.

57. In fact, in his article "Architecture in Nineteenth-Century Russia: The Enduring Classic," Albert Schmidt links Russian neoclassical architecture *with* romanticism, declaring that the style he terms "romantic classicism" arose in late eighteenth-century Russia and "claimed an authenticity based on historical and archeological research" (including the work of Johann Joachim Winkelmann and Giovanni Battista Piranesi). In Schmidt's view, the medieval revival of the 1840s thus represents a new phase of romanticism's fundamental approach to the architectural past, and not at all a break with an established tradition of classicism. See *Art and Culture in Nineteenth-Century Russia*, Theofanis George Stavrou, ed. (Bloomington: Indiana University Press, 1983), pp. 172–73.

58. Per Palme, "Ut Architectura Poesis," in *Idea and Form: Studies in the History of Art*, Ake Bengtsson, et al. (Stockholm: Almqvist & Wiksell, 1959), p. 105. The citation from Aristotle as given here is from VIII, 4, quoted from S. H. Butcher, *Aristotle's Theory of Poetry* (New York, 1951), p. 35.

59. Cicero in *De oratore* invokes architecture as an analog for oratory in order to prove that the useful is also often the most beautiful: "In temples and colonnades, the pillars are to support the structure, yet they are as dignified in appearance as they are useful." In the same way, "virtually unavoidable practical requirements" in speech such as periodic structure and pauses "produce charm of style as a result." See Cicero, *De oratore* III, xiv, 180–xlvii, p. 182.

60. Judith Wolin thus elaborates a series of extremely literary architectural figurations, including rhythmic repetition, synecdoche, natural-world metaphor, and hyperbole. See Judith Wolin, "The Rhetorical Question," in *VIA 8: Architecture and Literature: The Journal of the Graduate School of Fine Arts, University of Pennsylvania* (New York: Rizzoli, 1986), p. 30.

61. Wightwick, "The Principles and Practice of Architectural Design" (Essay 7, 1850), in *Detached Essays of the Architectural Publication Society* (London, 1853), p. 37.

62. Eclecticism, moreover, emerged from the relationship between Greece and Rome, once Greece had become part of the Roman Empire. The Romans were prone to eclectic borrowing, not having developed independent philosophical systems, and in this, they are paralleled by the nineteenth-century Russian Empire's cultural predicament.

63. For a detailed study of this phenomenon, see John I. Brooks III, *The Eclectic Legacy: Academic Philosophy and the Human Sciences in Nineteenth-Century France* (Newark: University of Delaware Press, 1998), especially pp. 13–66.

64. Claude Mignot, *Architecture of the Nineteenth Century in Europe* (New York: Rizzoli, 1984), p. 100.

65. *L'Encyclopédie, ou dictionnaire raisonné des sciences, des arts et des métiers*, vol. 5 (Stuttgart: Verlag, 1966), p. 271.

66. Lachmann, pp. 122–23.

67. In fact, Diderot's own pronouncements in his 1755 article, "Encyclopedia," suggest that this massive project itself follows an eclectic aesthetics. As he declares, the decision

to use a purely conventional alphabetical ordering for the individual entries creates certain inadvertent "burlesque contrasts" in the juxtaposition of articles on extremely diverse topics. Diderot compares the Encyclopedia's structure to "the foundation of a city," since buildings should not all be constructed according to a single model. "The uniformity of the buildings, bringing with it a uniformity in public passages, would give to the whole city a sad and tiring appearance," he notes. See Denis Diderot, "Encyclopédie" in Denis Diderot and Jean le Rond D'Alembert, eds., *L'Encyclopédie, ou dictionnaire raisonné des sciences, des arts et des métiers* (New York, 1969), vol. 1, p. 642.

68. N. V. Kukol'nik, "Novye postroiki v Petergofe," *Khudozhestvennaia gazeta*, 1837, no. 11–12, p. 176. See also future Slavophile Ivan Kireevskii's 1831 essay "Deviatnadtsatyi vek," which characterizes the nineteenth century in terms of heterogeneity and fragmentation, in *Kritika i estetika* (Moscow: Iskusstvo, 1979).

69. The notion of "intelligent," or motivated, aesthetic choice gradually evolved into the "rational" architectural principles of the 1850s–1860s, most fully elaborated by engineer and pedagogue Apollinarius Krasovskii, who advocated a harmonious fusion of aesthetics and technology. During the first half of the nineteenth century, the relative meanings of "eclectic" and "rational" were close, united against the common enemy, reactionary classicism. By the final quarter of the nineteenth century, however, "rational" architecture connoted a turn towards functionalism, in response to eclecticism's purported overemphasis on surface ornamentation. See the introduction to Krasovskii's 1851 *Grazhdanskaia arkhitektura: Chasti zdanii* (SPb, 1851).

70. V. G. Belinskii, *Izbrannye filosofskie sochineniia* (Moscow: Gosudarstvennoe izdatel'stvo politicheskoi literatury, 1941), p. 267.

71. In a study of eclecticism in American architecture 1880–1930, Walter C. Kidney calls the movement "learnedly if selectively imitative of historic architecture in all aspects of its appearance, and using historic styles as expressions of various cultural institutions." For Kidney, the orientation to historic styles is a distinguishing feature between eclecticism and modernism, which is "tenuously unified by abstention from the historic styles." See *The Architecture of Choice: Eclecticism in America, 1880–1930* (New York: G. Braziller, 1974), p. viii.

72. A. L. Punin, *Arkhitekturnye pamiatniki*, p. 39.

73. For descriptions of eighteenth-century palace pavilions in the classical, gothic, Turkish, Chinese, and Egyptian styles, see Margrethe Floryan, *Gardens of the Tsars: A Study of the Aesthetics, Semantics and Uses of Late 18th- Century Russian Gardens* (Aarhus: Aarhus University Press, 1996), especially pp. 102–35. See also Priscilla R. Roosevelt, *Life on the Russian Country Estate: A Social and Cultural History* (New Haven: Yale University Press, 1995).

74. The transitional period from retrospective stylization to true eclecticism also had recourse to national folkloric elements, as in the stylized peasant huts (*izby*), which joined the other stylized pavilions on the grounds of imperial residences. The best-known stylized huts include those along the road to Tsarskoe Selo by Montferrand, the dacha-like Nikol'skii house at Peterhof by Stakenschneider, and the village Glazovo near Pavlovsk by Rossi. Stylized huts similarly proliferated in the dacha communities to the north and southwest of the city.

75. Constantine Thon's now defunct Church of St. Catherine on Peterhof Prospect, built during the 1830s, is often cited as an exemplar of the neo-Russian style, as is the similarly nonextant Church of the Annunciation (Blagoveshchenskaia). Neo-Russian

decorative window frames and facade detailing distinguish the 1845 Novodevichii Convent and the 1846 Trinity-Sergiev Monastery Hostel.

76. A second such revival appeared during the early years of the twentieth century, when "classical" facades appeared alongside buildings in the new moderne style. Kirikov has, in a perhaps unwittingly eclectic spirit, termed this second neoclassical revival (1900–25) the "Petersburg Renaissance." See B. M. Kirikov, "Peterburgskaia neoklassika nachala XX veka." *Nevskii Arkhiv: Istoriko-kraevedcheskii sbornik*, III (SPb: Atheneum Feniks, 1997), p. 345. For a discussion of the neoclassical revival of this period, see Katerina Clark, *Petersburg, Crucible of Cultural Revolution* (Cambridge: Harvard University Press, 1995), pp. 57–73.

77. Stakenschneider's neobaroque Beloselskii-Belozerskii Palace (1846–48) at the intersection of Nevsky Prospect and the Fontanka attests to the eclectic tendencies of its day with its segmental bow-shaped pediments, oval windows, and bare-torso atlantes supporting the portico pilasters of the upper level. Curiously, the Beloselskii-Belozerskii Palace represented one of the first efforts of St. Petersburg architecture to stylize and revive *itself*, since it very much recalled the old Stroganov Palace by Rastrelli on the corner of the Moika and Nevsky Prospect.

78. For an account of the Mariinskii Palace as a locus of Russian cultural, civic, and political history from its inception up to the year 2000, see Gennadii Petrov, *Dvorets u Sinego mosta: Mariinskii dvorets v Sankt-Peterburge* (SPb: Logos, 2001). Note that Petrov gives an upbeat accounting of the palace's synthetic architectural style, distinguishing Stakenschneider's work from that of later nineteenth-century excesses (p. 90).

79. Georgy Butikov, introduction to *St. Isaac's Cathedral*, trans. David and Judith Andrews (Leningrad: Aurora Art Publishers, 1980), p. 11.

80. See Grabar', *Peterburgskaia arkhitektura v XVIII and XIX vekakh*, pp. 376–77.

81. Théophile Gautier, *Voyage en Russie* (Paris: La Boîte à Documents, 1990), pp. 193–238.

82. For a discussion of the church "Savior on the Blood" within the general contexts of eclecticism and the "Russian style," see B. M. Kirikov, "Khram Voskreseniia Khristova (K istorii 'russkogo stilia' v Peterburge)," in *Nevskii arkhiv: Istoriko-kraevedcheskii sbornik* (St. Petersburg: Atheneum Feniks, 1993). See also Michael S. Flier, "At Daggers Drawn: The Competition for the Church of the Savior on the Blood," in *For SK: In Celebration of the Life and Career of Simon Karlinsky*, Michael S. Flier and Robert P. Hughes, eds. (Berkeley: Berkeley Slavic Specialties, 1994), and "The Church of the Savior on the Blood: Projection, Rejection, Resurrection," in *Christianity and the Eastern Slavs*, vol. II, Robert P. Hughes and Irina Paperno, eds. (Berkeley: University of California Press, 1994).

83. During the latter part of the nineteenth century, a few private homes in the neo-Russian style were built in the city proper, among them the residence of the writer Aleksei Suvorin, constructed by architect Fedor Kharlamov in the late 1880s on what is now Chekhov Street, as well as a large apartment building on Liteinyi from the late 1870s by the same architect. See V. G. Isachenko, *Osobniak Suvorina* (St.Petersburg: Beloe i chernoe, 1996), especially pp. 22–33. There also exist two pseudo-Russian-style apartment houses by N. N. Nikonov from the very end of the nineteenth century, one on Ostrovskaia Square and the other on Kolokolnaia Street.

84. The Nikolaevskii (Moscow) Railway Station, for example, blends neo-Renaissance and neoclassical styles.

85. Examples of this trend include the Grand Prince Vladimir's Palace by Rezanov

from the late 1860s (on the Palace embankment), and the Grand Prince Aleksei's Palace by Messmacher from the 1880s (on the Moika).

86. For a fuller account of this late-imperial phenomenon, see Boris M. Kirikov, "The Architecture of Petersburg Banks in the Late Nineteenth and Early Twentieth Centuries," in *Commerce in Russian Urban Culture, 1861–1914*, William Craft Brumfield, Boris V. Anan'ich, and Yuri A. Petrov, eds. (Washington: Woodrow Wilson Press, 2001). Kirikov traces architectural trends beginning with the last quarter of the nineteenth century, from "mature eclecticism" (sometimes manifested as a "classicist eclecticism," as in Viktor Shreter's St. Petersburg Municipal Credit Society building) to "a transitory and incomplete turn towards modernist style," and finally to "modernized neoclassicism."

87. Petersburg's eclecticism may well thus be related to what has more generally been identified as a nineteenth-century poetics of "expositions," whose aspects include "a delight in the encyclopedia of novelties and in the universal exposition of knowledge and products," and the creation of "a site for eclecticism." See Philippe Hamon, *Expositions: Literature and Architecture in Nineteenth-Century France*, trans. Katia Sainson-Frank and Lisa Maguire (Berkeley: University of California Press, 1992), pp. 9–10.

88. While detractors have argued that eclecticism's recourse to the architectural past invoked superficial features only, and not larger forms and underlying design, Evgenia Borisova claims that eclecticism manifested the general influence of literature on art during this period, in that such buildings required their audience to process complex, allegorical associations conveyed by details of structure and ornamentation. See "Znak stilia," *Arkhitektura SSSR*, no. 1, January-February, 1984, p. 21.

89. Similarly, the Aleksandrinskii Theater exhibited Apollo, leader of the muses, in his quadriga. Above the arch of the General Staff building rode the triumphal chariot of winged Nike, the goddess of Victory. Athena, goddess of wisdom, graced the front of the Russian National Library. Mars leaned on his sword near the portico of the Horse Guard regimental barracks. The redone Admiralty was a riot of marine-associated sculptural figures—nymphs, gods, and famed seafaring heroes.

90. Examples include the 1860s metalworks factory by Rachau on Ligovskii Prospect, the Russian Textile Works by Anisimov on the Obvodnyi Canal, the 1870 apartment house by Shreter and Kitner on Sadovaia Street, the 1877 Rat'kov-Roznov house by Rachau on Millionnaia Street, the 1897 Russo-Asiatic Bank by Ershovich on Nevskii Prospect, and the 1903 Eliseev store by Baranovskii on Nevskii. See Iurii Rakov, *Skul'pturnyi olimp Peterburga* (SPb: Iskusstvo-SPB, 2000), pp. 75–77, 131–33, 142, 146.

91. For comparative purposes, see Carl Schorske's discussion of ascendant bourgeois values given eclectic architectural expression in the chapter "The Ringstrasse, Its Critics, and the Birth of Urban Modernism" from his book *Fin-De-Siècle Vienna: Politics and Culture* (New York: Alfred A. Knopf, 1980).

92. Sharon Marcus, *Apartment Stories: City and Home in Nineteenth-Century Paris and London* (Berkeley: University of California Press, 1999), p. 17. For a study of this phenomenon on America, see Elizabeth Blackmar, *Manhattan for Rent, 1785–1850* (Ithaca: Cornell University Press, 1989).

93. See, for example, Frédéric Soulié, "Les Drames invisibles," in *Le Diable à Paris* (Paris: Hetzel, 1845).

94. For a survey of the work's reception in the mid-1840s, see Peter Hodgson, *From Gogol to Dostoevsky: Jakov Butkov, A Reluctant Naturalist in the 1840s* (Munich: Wilhelm

Fink Verlag, 1976), pp. 75–79. For an account of Butkov's life and works, see Alexander Miliukov, "Jakov Petrovich Butkov," *Istoricheskii vestnik*, no. 2, 1881.

95. Yakov Butkov, *Peterburgskie vershiny*, kn. pervaia (SPb: N. Grech, 1845), pp. vii–xvi.

96. The "heights" of Butkov's title, in fact, refer to wordplay rather than to socioeconomic or even physical specification, and to a parodic polemic that swoops between levels of rhetoric. Butkov's characters represent what Hodgson calls "sham realia"—exaggerated physiological types depicted by means of hackneyed conventions for humorous or stylistic effect. While often counted among those who provided literary documentation of Petersburg's underside, Butkov seems to have been just as interested in exploring the spatial properties of rhetoric as in illuminating the dark corners of urban life.

97. Kirichenko, *Russkaia arkhitektura 1830–1910-kh godov*, pp. 40–50. See also Kirichenko's series of articles from the 1960s in the journal *Arkhitekturnoe nasledstvo*, nos. 14, 15, and 16, entitled "Dokhodnye zhilye doma Moskvy i Peterburga (1770–1830-e gg)" (1962), "O nekotorykh osobennostiakh evoliutsii gorodskikh mnogokvartirnyikh domov vtoroi poloviny XIX—nachala XX vv. (Ot otdel'nogo doma k kompleksu)" (1963), and "Zhilaia zastroika Peterburga epokhi klassitsizma i ee vliianie na razvitie arkhitektury" (1967). See also A. L. Punin, *Arkhitektura Peterburga serediny XIX veka*, pp. 250–77. For the "official" account of this architectural trend, see *Ocherki istorii Leningrada*, vol. 2 (Moscow: AN SSSR, 1957), pp. 796–97, 803.

98. William C. Brumfield, "Building for the Bourgeoisie: The Quest for a Modern Style in Russian Architecture," in *Between Tsar and People: Educated Society and the Quest for Public Identity in Late Imperial Russia*, Edith W. Clowes, Samuel D. Kassow, and James L. West, eds. (Princeton: Princeton University Press, 1991), pp. 308–9.

99. Dostoevsky, "Malen'kie kartinki," p. 107. Evgenia Borisova warns against confusing these apartment houses with the famous slum dwellings of Dostoevsky's urban protagonists. The Dostoevskian building is a huge construction in the style of exhausted classicism, whose symmetrical facade contrasted grotesquely with the bizarre, haphazard fashion in which interior space was carved up into rooms, punctuated by depressing dark stairways and thick firewalls. According to Borisova, the newer eclectic apartment houses must have seemed liberating in their freedom of style, more oriented toward human comfort and individual preference. E. A. Borisova, "Nekotorye osobennosti vospriiatiia gorodskoi sredy i russkaia literatura vtoroi poloviny XIX veka," in *Tipologiia russkogo realizma vtoroi poloviny XIX veka* (Moscow: Nauka, 1979), p. 279.

100. See A. V. Ikonnikov, *Tysiacha let russkoi arkhitektury: Razvitie traditsii* (Moscow: Iskusstvo, 1990), p. 323.

101. See, for example, V. G. Isachenko and G. A. Ol', *Fedor Lidval* (Leningrad: Lenizdat, 1987). Basic information about many imperial-era Petersburg apartment houses, both surviving and defunct, can be found in the superb reference *Arkhitektory-stroiteli Sankt-Peterburga serediny XIX—nachala XX veka*, B. M. Kirikov, ed. (SPb: Piligrim, 1996).

102. For a complete cultural history of the Muruzi building, see I. I Lisaevich, ed., *Doma rasskazyvaiut* (Leningrad: Lenizdat, 1991), pp. 126–60. This building is also discussed in Anna Benn and Rosamund Bartlett, *Literary Russia: A Guide* (London: Papermac, 1997), pp. 232–35.

103. Joseph Brodsky, "In a Room and a Half," in *Less Than One: Selected Essays* (New York: Farrar, Straus, & Giroux, 1986).

104. A late sketch by Ivan Goncharov called "May in Petersburg" (*Mai mesiats v Peterburge*, 1891), for example, written the year of his death, uses the diverse apartment house inhabitants as the material for the literary work, introducing the reader to an assortment of characters from different parts of the building. Goncharov's sketch thus consists of miniplots, each of which might have opened out into a fully developed story. A Count-General and a prominent government official occupy the big apartments in the belleétage, while two genteel orphaned sisters, a merchant, and three bachelor clerks with a cook inhabit the more modest parts of the building. Goncharov's sketch takes an approach similar to that of Gogol's "Nevsky Prospect," describing the life of the house over the course of a day. This sketch is reprinted in M. V. Otradin, ed., *Peterburg v russkom ocherke XIX veka* (Leningrad: Izdatel'stvo Leningradskogo Universiteta, 1984).

Chapter Two

1. Analogies between literature and architecture remained widespread in the nineteenth century, in spite of what Ellen Eve Frank calls "the fracturing and collapsing of levels of literary style" and the parallel "shifts in architectural values." Prescriptive statements on architecture from the period of eclecticism tended to aim for a middle ground, as in an 1839 issue of *The Civil Engineer* and *Architect's Journal* in London, which advised, "[The architect] should sculpture in a style analogous to blank verse, avoiding the prose of conversation, and the rhyme of French tragedy." See *Literary Architecture: Essays Toward a Tradition: Walter Pater, Gerard Manley Hopkins, Marcel Proust, Henry James* (Berkeley: University of California Press, 1979), p. 253.

2. See A. P. Sumarokov, "Dve epistoly (v pervoi predlagaetsia o russkom iazyke, a vo vtoroi o stikhotvorstve)," in *Izbrannye proizvedeniia*, A. P. Berkov, ed. (Leningrad: Sovetskii pisatel', 1957), pp. 115–25. "Know the distinctions of genres in poetic art," cautions Sumarokov in the second Epistle. "Forsake the pompous voice in your idylls, / And amid the flocks, do not mute their reed pipe with your trumpet."

3. M. V. Lomonosov, "Kratkoe rukovodstvo k krasnorechiiu. Kniga pervaia, v kotoroi soderzhitsia ritorika, pokazuiushchaia obshchie pravila oboego krasnorechiia, to est' oratorii i poezii, sochinennaia v pol'zu liubiashchikh slovesnye nauki," *Polnoe sobranie sochinenii*, t. 7 (Moscow: Izdatel'stvo Akademii Nauk SSSR, 1952).

4. Mikhail Bakhtin relates genre and memory, declaring that literary genres always include elements of the archaic, which are renewed by being made contemporary: "A genre is always the same and yet not the same, always old and new simultaneously. . . . A genre lives in the present, but always *remembers* its past, its beginning. Genre is a representative of creative memory in the process of literary development." See M. M. Bakhtin, *Problems of Dostoevsky's Poetics*, ed. and trans. Caryl Emerson (Minneapolis: University of Minnesota Press, 1984), p. 106.

5. For the full text, see A. A. Shakhovskoi, *Komedii. Stikhotvoreniia*, ed. A.A. Gozenpud (Leningrad: Sovetskii pisatel', 1961), pp. 683–711.

6. Claudio Guillén writes, "The air of unreality one finds in the tradition of classical and neoclassical poetics has to be ascribed to this most widespread assumption, to wit, that genres are sharply delimited objects that are 'out there,' confronting the critic or the reader, requiring above all an effort of verbal definition." Forms cannot be "taken over," according to Guillén, but rather must be "achieved" anew with each individual work. See

Claudio Guillén, "On the Uses of Literary Genre," in *Literature as System: Essays toward the Theory of Literary History* (Princeton: Princeton University Press, 1971), p. 129.

7. Bakhtin, *The Dialogic Imagination*, p. 5.

8. Guillén, pp. 12–13.

9. Ibid., p. 109.

10. Tsvetan Todorov, *Genres in Discourse*, trans. Catherine Porter (Cambridge: Cambridge University Press, 1990), p. 10.

11. "The norm," argues Todorov, "becomes visible—lives—only by its transgressions." Tsvetan Todorov, "The Origin of Genres," *New Literary History*, vol. 8, no. 1, Autumn 1976, pp. 160–61.

12. Thomas Beebee, *The Ideology of Genre: A Comparative Study of Generic Instability* (University Park: The Pennsylvania State University Press, 1994), p. 264.

13. The combination (horizontal or syntagmatic) and selection (vertical or paradigmatic) axes in literature correspond in theory to the principles of metonymy and metaphor, or, put differently, to contiguity and equivalence. In Roman Jakobson's famous formulation, "The poetic function projects the principle of equivalence from the axis of selection into the axis of combination." Eclecticism, from that perspective, seems a very literary strategy indeed. See "Linguistics and Poetics" in *Language in Literature*, Krystyna Pomorska and Stephen Rudy, eds. (Cambridge: Harvard University Press, 1987), p. 71. See also chapters 5–7 of Iu. M. Lotman, *Struktura khudozhestvennogo teksta* (Providence: Brown University Press, 1971).

14. Beebee, p. 283.

15. Jacques Derrida, "The Law of Genre," *Glyph* 7 (1980), pp. 212–13.

16. Note, however, that Gary Rosenshield finds the opposite to be true. Instead of making prose more like poetry, he claims, Dostoevsky's "The Double" works to depoeticize and demythologize the Petersburg theme as posited by Pushkin. See "*The Bronze Horseman* and *The Double*: The Depoeticization of the Myth of Petersburg in the Young Dostoevskii," *Slavic Review*, vol. 55, no. 2, Summer 1996.

17. V. G. Belinskii, "Vstuplenie," in *Fiziologiia Peterburga*, V. I. Kuleshov, ed. (Moscow: Nauka, 1991), p. 6.

18. I. Iakovlev, "Doch' bednogo chinovnika," *Sovremennik*, v. 70, 1858, pp. 9–60.

19. Vladimir Toporov, "Peterburg i peterburgskii tekst russkoi literatury," *Mif. Ritual. Simvol. Obraz: Issledovaniia v oblasti mifopoeticheskogo* (Moscow: Izdatel'skaia gruppa "Progress"—"Kul'tura," 1995), p. 336 (footnote 39).

20. In Gary Saul Morson's discussion of the feuilleton as a "boundary genre," he declares that the attributes of "Petersburg" and "feuilleton" are perfectly suited to one another, as Dostoevsky's narrator discovers in his "Petersburg Chronicle" series: "These feuilletons discuss Petersburg in the Petersburg style—that is, haphazardly and formlessly—and so their title does, in a sense, finally answer to the text: though not a Petersburg *chronicle*, they are a *Petersburg* chronicle." Gary Saul Morson, *The Boundaries of Genre: Dostoevsky's Diary of a Writer and the Traditions of Literary Utopia* (Evanston: Northwestern University Press, 1981), p. 20.

21. Russian scholars have not considered literary "eclecticism" a term of merit, but rather as a synonym for "epigonism"—the practice of a second-rate imitator. In discussing Nekrasov's early prose works from the 1840s, for example, Grigorii Gukovskii insists that the young writer was *not* an "eclectic," by which he means "an unprincipled collector of fragments (*oskolki*) from other people's art." The problem with eclectic writers,

declares Gukovskii, is that "they come late," expressing ideas and using forms from the preceding epoch, that of their teachers. Although Nekrasov borrowed material from other writers, his art was deeply rooted in his own time, and thus "original." See "Neizdannye povesti Nekrasova v istorii russkoi prozy sorokovykh godov," in *Zhizn' i pokhozhdeniia Tikhona Trosnikova*, V. Evgen'ev-Maksimov and K. Chukovskii, eds. (Moscow: Khudozhestvennaia literatura, 1931), pp. 374–75.

22. L. V. Pumpianskii, "'Mednyi vsadnik' i poeticheskaia traditsiia XVIII veka," *Vremennik pushkinskoi komissii*, nos. 4–5, 1939, p. 98.

23. Ibid., p. 110.

24. Waclaw Lednicki, *Pushkin's 'Bronze Horseman': The Story of a Masterpiece* (Berkeley: University of California Press, 1955), p. 46.

25. M. V. Otradin, introduction to *Peterburg v russkoi poezii XVIII-nachala XX veka: Poeticheskaia antologiia* (Leningrad: Izdatel'stvo Leningradskogo Universiteta, 1988), p. 5.

26. Sidney Monas, "St. Petersburg and Moscow as Cultural Symbols," in *Art and Culture in Nineteenth-Century Russia*, Theofanis George Stavrou, ed. (Bloomington: Indiana University Press, 1983), p. 37.

27. Other urban literary traditions do not insist on the unity of the eighteenth-century corpus in this regard. For a discussion of the diverse literary invocations of eighteenth-century London, for example, see Max Byrd, *London Transformed: Images of the City in the Eighteenth Century* (New Haven: Yale University Press, 1978). Byrd treats apocalyptic visions of the city by Defoe and Blake, as well as images of London in works by Pope, Johnson, and Wordsworth, emphasizing the ways in which eighteenth-century London is variously "humanized" by literature.

28. This section concerns only those literary texts from the eighteenth century that explicitly render the city of St. Petersburg as the object of discourse. I am in no way proposing this characterization to flatten out official eighteenth-century Russian literature, about which there have been several excellent new studies. For a recent study situating works such as Vasilii Petrov's 1775 ode on the conclusion of a treaty with the Turks within a complex political and literary context, for example, see Andrei Zorin, *Kormia dvuglavogo orla . . . Literatura i gosudarstvennaia ideologiia v Rossii v poslednei treti XVIII—pervoi treti XIX veka* (Moscow: Novoe literaturnoe obozrenie, 2001).

29. N. P. Antsiferov, *Dusha Peterburga* in *"Nepostizhimyi gorod . . ."* (Leningrad: Lenizdat, 1991), pp. 49–50. Sumarokov made substantial later contributions to this tradition with his 1769 "Ody o gosudare imperatore Petre Pervom" and 1781 "Oda torzhestvennaia na pobedy gosudaria imperatora Petra Velikogo," as well as the 1755 ode to Elizabeth on the occasion of her birthday, and "Slovo na otkrytie Akademii khudozhestv."

30. See Tiutchev's "Gliadel ia, stoia nad Nevoi" (1844), "Na Neve" (1850), and "Opiat' stoiu ia nad Nevoi" (1868).

31. For the text of Buzhinsky's oration with commentary by eighteenth-century Petersburg chronicler A. I. Bogdanov, see Bogdanov, *Opisanie Sanktpeterburga 1749–1751* (SPb: S.-Peterburgskii filial Arkhiva RAN, 1997), pp. 373–404.

32. This method of praise by analogue is a convention of the time. See, for example, Feofan Prokopovich's 1725 oration at the funeral of Peter the Great, in which Samson, Solomon, and Moses are invoked in reference to Peter's physical strength and resistance to "Philistines," his establishment of new laws, and the high value he placed on learning. The mixing of classical and Christian motifs is typical of the baroque style in literature

and art, while the linking of Peter to an eclectic collection of biblical, classical, and historical heroes serves the cause of *translatio imperii.*

33. Perhaps this abrupt swing to a more colloquial register is a feature of Petersburg literature. Feofan Prokopovich's 1716 oration on the birth of Peter's son (Petr, who did not survive) marvels at the speed with which Petersburg was constructed, declaring that Peter's efforts counter the old Polish proverb, "Cracow wasn't built all at once." See F. Prokopovich, *Sochineniia*, I. P. Eremin, ed. (Moscow: AN SSSR, 1961), p. 45.

34. The full text of the poem is as follows:

> V pustyniakh khizhina sostroena siia,
> Ne dlia zatvornika sostroili eia:
> V porfire, s skipetrom, s derzhavoi i koronoi
> Velikii gosudar' imel zhilishche v onoi.
> L'zia l' pyshnyi bylo grad sim domom obeshchat'?
> Nikto ne mog togo v to vremia predveshchat';
> No to ispolnilos'; stal gorod skoro v tsvete . . .
> Kakoi sei domik mal, tak Petr velik na svete.

35. For a detailed history of the Bronze Horseman, see G. S. Knabe, *Voobrazhenie znaka: Mednyi vsadnik Fal'kone i Pushkina* (Moscow: Rossiiskii Gos. Gumanitarnyi Universitet, 1993), A. L. Kaganovich, *"Mednyi vsadnik": Istoriia sozdaniia monumenta* (Leningrad: Iskusstvo, 1975) and D. Arkin, *Mednyi vsadnik: Pamiatnik Petru I v Leningrade* (Leningrad: Iskusstvo, 1958).

36. For a contemporary account, see Marinos Charboures, *Monument elevé à la gloire de Pierre-le-Grand; ou, Relation des travaux et des moyens mechaniques qui ont été employés pour transporter à Petersbourg un rocher de trois millions pesant, destiné à servir de base à la statue equestre de cet empereur; avec un examen physique et chymique du même rocher* (Paris, 1777).

37. In Alexander Schenker's phrasing, "the dignified neoclassical posture of the tsar coexists with the baroque restlessness of the rearing horse and the fluid, wavelike shape of the pedestal." See his comprehensive *The Bronze Horseman: Falconet's Monument to Peter the Great* (New Haven: Yale University Press, 2003) p. 265.

38. See also M. N. Mikishat'ev, "Obraz Peterburga v peterburgskoi povesti A. S. Pushkina 'Mednyi vsadnik." *Antsiferovskie chteniia: Materialy i tezisy konferentsii* (Leningrad: Leningradskoe Otdelenie Sovetskogo Fonda Kul'tury, 1989).

39. Walter Vickery, for example, demonstrates that Pushkin deliberately emulates the prosodic features of the ode to underscore this affinity. Walter N. Vickery, "Mednyj vsadnik and the Eighteenth-Century Heroic Ode," *Indiana Slavic Studies* 3, 1963, pp. 140–62.

40. For a survey of works related to floods, see chapter 7. See also Pumpianskii, pp. 101–9 (on floods) and 109–12 (on monuments).

41. Pumpianskii, p. 93.

42. Lednicki, pp. 11–24. See also pp. 43–84 for an exploration of imperial themes and their genesis in Pushkin's poem. For a discussion of the elastic properties of the *poema* as a genre and of the work as polyphonic, see Andrew Kahn, *Pushkin's The Bronze Horseman* (London: Bristol Classical Press, 1998), pp. 29–34. This monograph treats Pushkin's depiction of Petersburg via diverse literary associations on pp. 89–97. For a discussion of stylistic diversity in lexical terms, see V. D. Levin, "O stile 'Mednogo vsadnika,'" *Izvestiia Akademii Nauk SSSR. Seriia literatury i iazyka*, 33, 3 (1974). See also N. A. Riabinina, "K

probleme literaturnykh istochnikov poemy A. S. Pushkina *Mednyi vsadnik,*" in *Boldinskie chteniia* (Gor'kii: Volgo-Viatskoe knizhnoe izdatel'stvo, 1977).

43. A. L. Ospovat, R. D. Timenchik, *"Pechal'nu povest' sokhranit'* . . .: *Ob avtore i chitateliakh Mednogo vsadnika* (Moscow: Kniga, 1987), p. 11.

44. Ibid, p. 13.

45. Abram Terts (Andrei Sinyavsky), *Progulki s Pushkinym* (London: Overseas Publications Interchange Ltd., 1975), pp. 134–48.

46. This tendency is not unique to "The Bronze Horseman," of course. Pushkin's poetry (and fictional prose, for that matter) has been treated more generally in terms of its innovative and creative synthesis of elements (lexical, stylistic, generic) unexpectedly combined within a single text. See, for example, the chapter "Poeziia deistvitel'nosti" in Lidiia Ginzburg, *O lirike* (Moscow: Intrada, 1997). See also V. V. Vinogradov, *Iazyk Pushkina: Pushkin i istoriia russkogo literaturnogo iazyka* (Moscow: Nauka, 2000) and *Stil' Pushkina* (Moscow: Nauka, 1999).

47. There also exists the occasional prose rendering of the monument, as in Alexander Radishchev's letter "Pis'mo k drugu zhitel'stvuiushchemu v Tobol'ske po dolgu zvaniia svoego" of August 1782. Radishchev describes the unveiling of the Falconet monument in lofty tones that, in his opinion, provide only "a weak depiction of what I feel, gazing upon Peter's image." See A. N. Radishchev, *Sochineniia* (Moscow: Khudozhestvennaia literatura, 1988), p. 202. Radishchev's letter is an interesting example of a middle-range genre turned to high-style purpose.

48. Antsiferov, *Dusha Peterburga*, p. 87.

49. For Nekrasov's response, see "Zametki o zhurnalakh za sentiabr' 1855 goda," *Sovremennik* 53 (1855). Nekrasov objects strenuously to Benediktov's "tone," which he finds inappropriate to Peter's great deeds, and to the legacy of Pushkin's "Bronze Horseman."

50. Henri Lefebvre objects to semiology's claim that space is "susceptible" of a reading, and that the space of the city embodies a discourse or language. He writes, "[S]ocial space can in no way be compared to a blank page upon which a specific message has been inscribed (by whom?). Both natural and urban spaces are, if anything, 'over-inscribed': everything therein resembles a rough draft, jumbled and self-contradictory. Rather than signs, what one encounters here are directions—multifarious and overlapping instructions." See *The Production of Space,* trans. Donald Nicholson-Smith (Oxford: Blackwell Publishers Ltd., 1991), p. 142. So, too, does the literary discourse constituting and surrounding the Bronze Horseman provide mixed instructions for decoding the monument.

51. W. Bruce Lincoln, *Sunlight at Midnight: St. Petersburg and the Rise of Modern Russia* (New York: Basic Books, 2000), p. 44.

52. As Susanne Fusso declares, "A work whose apparent fragmentation and discontinuity mask an inner unity takes as one of its major subjects the need to combine close examination of individual parts with a panoramic survey of the whole." Susanne Fusso, "The Landscape of *Arabesques*," in *Essays on Gogol: Logos and the Russian Word,* Susanne Fusso and Priscilla Meyer, eds. (Evanston: Northwestern University Press, 1992), p. 117.

53. Other major literary and philosophical figures also expressed a great interest in medieval styles of architecture as the most "natural" and thus "national," among them Chateaubriand, Goethe, Schlegel, Hegel, Sir Walter Scott, and Petr Chaadaev. For a summary of their pronouncements, see Ronald Bradbury, *The Romantic Theories of Architecture of the Nineteenth Century, in Germany, England and France (together with a brief survey of the Vitruvian School)* (New York: The Dorothy Press, 1934).

54. The "edifice metaphor" can be traced back to the literature of rhetorical theory from ancient Greece and Rome, through rhetoricians of the eighteenth and early nineteenth centuries. Leland M. Griffin, "The Edifice Metaphor in Rhetorical Theory," *Speech Monographs*, vol. 27, no. 5, November 1960.

55. Fusso, pp. 120–25.

56. Custine, p. 219.

57. Note that Andrei Sinyavsky asserts something quite different, claiming that Gogol's pronouncements on the ideal of architecture advocate the baroque style, although this period and style designation is never named. In Sinyavsky's view, the architectural principles that Gogol espoused apply equally well to the author's own literary style with its hyperbole and strikingly unorthodox juxtapositions of stylistic elements. See *V teni Gogolia* (London: Overseas Publications Interchange Ltd., 1975), pp. 347–52.

58. For Chaadaev's fourth philosophical letter, see "Nechto iz perepiski N. N," *Teleskop*, 1832, no. 11, pp. 351–52.

59. N. V. Gogol, "Ob arkhitekture nyneshnego veka," *Polnoe Sobranie Sochinenii* t. 8 (Leningrad: Nauka, 1937–1952), p. 80.

60. For a study of Gogolian aesthetics, see Melissa Frazier, *Frames of the Imagination: Gogol's Arabesques and the Romantic Question of Genre* (New York: Peter Lang, 2000).

61. Fourierist Victor Considérant similarly declared in 1834, "Architecture is the pivotal art that sums up all other arts, and consequently sums up society itself: architecture writes history." See Victor Considérant, *Considérations socials sur l'architectonique* (Paris: Librairies du Palais-Royal, 1834), p. 6.

62. Such a street—the "Rue des Nations"—was constructed for the 1878 Paris World's Fair. Pavilions for foreign nations featuring architecturally distinct facades made up a central promenade through the exhibition. See Erik Mattie, *World's Fairs* (New York: Princeton Architectural Press, 1998), pp. 43–51.

63. English critic John Ruskin's 1849 essay "The Lamp of Memory" warns that a culture would be unable to remember without its architecture: "How cold is all history, how lifeless all imagery, compared to that which the living nation writes, and the uncorrupted marble bears! . . . there are but two strong conquerors of the forgetfulness of men, Poetry and Architecture; and the latter in some sort includes the former, and is mightier in its reality." John Ruskin, "The Lamp of Memory," in *The Book-Worm*, April 1885, pp. 3–4.

64. Melissa Frazier characterizes Gogol's hypothetical chronicle as a "one-way street," illustrating the effect of time on genre. Beyond the second gate, however, there seems the potential that "diachronism is resolved in synchronism" with the incorporation of "all the achievements of the past." See *Frames of the Imagination*, pp. 110–11.

65. See, for example, Donald Fanger, *The Creation of Nikolai Gogol* (Cambridge: The Belknap Press of Harvard University Press, 1979), pp. 111–13, and Vsevolod Setchkarev, *Gogol: His Life and Works*, trans. Robert Kramer (New York: New York University Press, 1965), pp. 128–32.

66. Setchkarev, p. 132.

67. For an account of Gogolian narrative as possible "only under the limited regime of the picturesque," in terms of "a stylistic implementation of the picturesque's roughness, abrupt chance, and intricacy" (p. 612), see Andreas Schönle, "Gogol, the Picturesque, and the Desire for the People: A Reading of 'Rome,'" *The Russian Review*, 59 (October 2000).

68. For a discussion of Gogol's extreme preference for contiguity rather than similarity relations, see "Gogol's Tropological Vision" in Michael and Marianne Shapiro, *Figuration in Verbal Art* (Princeton: Princeton University Press, 1988).

69. P. N. Stolpianskii, *Staryi Peterburg: Admiralteiskii ostrov, Sad Trudiashchikhsia* (Moscow: Gosudarstvennoe izdatel'stvo, 1923), p. 73.

70. P. N. Stolpianskii, *Peterburg: Kak voznik, osnovalsia i ros Sankt-Peterburkh* (SPb: Nega, 1995), pp. 227–29.

71. Yuri Egorov, *The Architectural Planning of St. Petersburg*, trans. Eric Dluhosch (Athens: Ohio University Press, 1969), pp. 204–5.

72. Stolpianskii points out, however, that this is not due to Petersburg's admirable tolerance toward other faiths, as Gautier assumed, but to the fact that Nevsky, in its non-central location and status, offered a convenient out-of-the-way location for these churches. See *Staryi Peterburg: Admiralteiskii ostrov, Sad Trudiashchikhsia*, p. 72.

73. Théophile Gautier, *Voyage en Russie* (Paris: La Boîte à Documents, 1990), pp. 92–95.

74. This fragment was originally published in the journal *Russkaia starina* in 1880, and more recently in *Belye nochi* (Leningrad: Lenizdat, 1974), pp. 326–44.

75. An 1820–21 feuilleton series entitled "Chuvstvitel'noe puteshestvie po Nevskomu Prospektu" by P. L. Iakovlev in the journal *Blagonamerennyi* accomplished something similar by taking a satirical stance toward sentimentalism and, in so doing, surveying a heterogeneous literary field. The text is reprinted in *Progulki po Nevskomu prospektu v pervoi polovine XIX veka*, A. M. Konechnyi, ed. (SPb: Giperion, 2002), pp. 55–87.

76. A. S. Pushkin, *Polnoe sobranie sochinenii v deviati tomakh* (Moscow: Khudozhestvennaia literatura, 1938), p. 701.

77. For background information about Sadovnikov and his Nevsky project, see Grigory Kaganov, *Images of Space: St. Petersburg in the Visual and Verbal Arts*, trans. Sidney Monas (Stanford: Stanford University Press, 1997), pp. 80–86.

78. To this last category belongs Bashchutskii's account of "A Petersburg Day in the Year 1723," which opens with a scene-setting passage: "The sun burned fiercely in the sky; but the fog, barely rising from the damp land, absorbed its yellow rays and still pulled at the sharp summits of the tiled roofs. Cows meandered by the houses, loudly mooing; they greedily ate the fresh grass that poked through by the sides of the streets, where there was no pavement. . . ." See Alexander Bashchutskii, *Panorama Sanktpeterburga*, Part II (SPb: Tipografiia vdovy Pliushara s synom, 1834), p. 193.

79. Gogol's story itself served as the inspiration for Nekrasov's parodic poem of 1845, titled "Obyknovennaia istoriia" (this title anticipating Goncharov's novel of the same name by only two years). The epigraph to Nekrasov's poem is a long excerpt from the final chapter of Gogol's "Nevsky Prospect," and the poem retells Piskarev's story in comic colloquial terms. In this spirit, the poet declares that only the romantic epigone Benediktov would be equal to the task of describing the lovely girl gliding past like the moon across the heavens. The poet does catch up to the girl, but receives a box on the ears for his pains. It seems strangely appropriate that Gogol's unique generic pastiche should become the object of parody, a fate usually reserved for well-established literary forms. See N. A. Nekrasov, *PSSiP*, t. 1 (Leningrad: Nauka, 1981), pp. 438–39.

80. Bashchutskii, Part III, pp. 85–86.

81. Leonid Grossman characterizes Dostoevsky's Petersburg in *Crime and Punishment* as a "panorama" of "Petersburg types," rendered in detail that recalls graphic art of the

1840s–1860s by Gavarni, Agin, and Nevakhovich. In this spirit of eclectic panorama, Grossman also notes the stylistic variety of characters' speech. See "Dostoevskii-khudozhnik," in *Tvorchestvo F.M. Dostoevskogo*, N. L. Stepanov, ed. (Moscow: Izdatel'stvo Akademii Nauk SSSR, 1959).

82. See I. N. Bozherianov, *Nevskii Prospekt:kul'turno-istoricheskii ocherk dvukhvekovoi zhizni S.-Peterburga* (St. Petersburg: A.I. Vilborg, 1903).

83. V. F. Odoevskii, "Skazka o tom, kak opasno devushkam khodit' tolpoiu po Nevskomu Prospektu," in *Pestrye skazki s krasnym slovtsom sobrannye Irineem Modestovichem Gomozeikoiu*, M. A. Tur'ian, ed. (Moscow: Kniga, 1991).

84. Vladimir Dal', "Zhizn' cheloveka, ili progulka po Nevskomu Prospektu," *Povesti, rasskazy, ocherki, skazki* (Moscow: Khudozhestvennaia literatura, 1961), p. 116.

85. The narrator of Yakov Butkov's 1845 story "An Esteemed Gentleman" (*Pochtennyi chelovek*), from his collection *Petersburg Heights*, denies the eclectic literary potential of Nevsky Prospect. "There," he reflects, "they say you can find good literary *plots*; but this is untrue: on Nevsky you encounter the same creditors and friends as everywhere else." See Yakov Butkov, *Peterburgskie vershiny*, book 1 (SPb: Tipografiia N. Grecha, 1845), p. 85. This narrator's jaded assertion is, however, contradicted by another Butkov story, a hefty piece from 1848 called "Nevsky Prospect, or the Journey of Nestor Zaletaev" (*Nevskii Prospekt, ili Puteshestvie Nestora Zaletaeva*), discussed in chapter 3. See *Otechestvennye zapiski*, no. 60, 1848, pp. 101–76. Despite its length, Butkov's story belongs to the subcategory of "Nevsky anecdote" by virtue of its simple, catchy premise. The eponymous "Journey" along the Prospect represents the longed-for vindication of Zaletaev, an insignificant little man who has won a carriage in a lottery. From his new, elevated position, Zaletaev visits the homes of those who slighted him in the past.

86. Gleb Uspenskii, "Vstrecha na Nevskom," *Polnoe sobranie sochinenii Gleba Uspenskogo*, vol. 5 (SPb: 1908), p. 279.

87. Ibid, p. 281.

88. Rastorguev's strolls are reprinted in A. M. Konechnyi, ed., *Progulki po Nevskomu prospektu v pervoi polovine XIX veka*, pp. 121–204.

89. D. Iu. Sherikh, *Byli i nebylitsy Nevskogo Prospekta: Istoricheskaia progulka* (SPb: Ivanov i Leshchinskii, 1996), p. 168.

90. Ibid, p. 8.

Chapter Three

1. Because this book examines the Russian project of mapping St. Petersburg, travel accounts by foreigners are not treated, for the most part. Reference sources on this vast literature include Harry W. Nerhood, *To Russia and Return: An Annotated Bibliography of Travelers' English-Language Accounts of Russia from the Ninth Century to the Present* (Ohio State University Press, 1968), Regina Stürickow, *Reisen nach St. Petersburg. Die Darstellung St. Petersburgs in Reisebeschreibungen (1815–1861)* (Frankfurt: Peter Lang, 1990), and Francesca Wilson, *Muscovy: Russia through Foreign Eyes 1553–1900* (London: George Allen & Unwin Ltd., 1970). See also Iu. N. Bespiatykh, *Peterburg Petra I v inostrannykh opisaniiakh* (Leningrad: Nauka, 1991) and *Peterburg Anny Ioannovny v inostrannykh opisaniikh* (SPb: BLITS, 1997).

2. In Joseph Brodsky's formulation, "If it's true that every writer has to estrange him-

self from his experience to be able to comment upon it, then the city, by rendering this alienating service, saved them a trip." Joseph Brodsky, "A Guide to a Renamed City," in *Less Than One: Selected Essays* (New York: Farrar, Straus, & Giroux, 1986), pp. 79, 89.

3. John Murray III issued the first in an extensive series of travel guidebooks in 1836, his own *A Hand-Book for Travellers on the Continent.* Karl Baedeker's series of guidebooks began in 1839 with a guide to Holland and Belgium (based largely on Murray's earlier work) and soon branched out beyond Europe as well. Thomas Cooke made the genteel traveler's project even simpler by offering packages of guided tours, lodging, and transport; he began his business in England and Scotland, expanded to the continent in the 1860s, and then moved on to developing popular tourism in far-flung locations.

4. For a study of the specific discourse of travel writing about the Grand Tour, see Chloe Chard, *Pleasure and Guilt on the Grand Tour: Travel Writing and Imaginative Geography 1600–1830* (Manchester: Manchester University Press, 1999).

5. In fact, textual "tours" of London constituted a much older literary tradition, whose examples include John Stow's 1598 *Survey of London*, and the London sections of both John Macky's 1714 *Journey through England* and Daniel Defoe's 1724–27 *Tour thro' the Whole Island of Great Britain.*

6. For a description of the changing presentation of Paris in nineteenth-century guidebooks, see Claire Hancock, "*Capitale du plaisir:* The Remaking of Imperial Paris," in *Imperial Cities: Landscape, Display, and Identity,* Felix Driver and David Gilbert, eds. (Manchester: Manchester University Press, 1999). For comparative purposes, see Jill Seward, "The Potemkin City: Tourist Images of Late Imperial Vienna" in the same volume. For information about New York guidebooks, see Hans Bergmann, *God in the Street: New York Writing from the Penny Press to Melville* (Philadelphia, Temple University Press, 1995), pp. 50–53. As Bergmann points out, these guidebooks often combined factual information with ethnography, also providing entertainment (sometimes fictional) and advice for the visitor.

7. Travel writer Heinrich Reichard did feature a side trip to St. Petersburg in his 1801 road itinerary to Germany and Switzerland (*Itinéraire de poche de l'Allemagne et de la Suisse, avec les routes de Paris et de Petérsbourg*). Ironically, Napoleon's officers carried the second edition of this guidebook (1809) with them on the ill-fated Russian campaign of 1812. John Murray initially documented St. Petersburg relatively briefly in his two-part *Hand-Book for Northern Europe; Including Denmark, Norway, Sweden, Finland, and Russia,* and by the middle of the nineteenth century, he had produced a *Hand-Book for Travellers in Russia, Poland, and Finland* with substantial coverage of the imperial capital, which went through five updated editions by the turn of the century, and was expanded to include "The Crimea, Caucasus, Siberia, and Central Asia." Murray's coverage of St. Petersburg evolved into an increasingly businesslike and tightly organized presentation of the city's attractions. The most consummately professional and comprehensive foreign guidebook for travelers to St. Petersburg is Baedeker's 1914 *Russia: A Handbook for Travelers,* which unlike Murray's voluminous tomes, was designed to accompany the tourist on expeditions.

8. Marquis de Custine, *Empire of the Czar: A Journey through Eternal Russia* (New York: Doubleday, 1989), pp. 128–29.

9. V. G. Belinskii, *PSS,* t. 9 (Moscow: Izdatel'stvo AN SSSR, 1953–), p. 217.

10. See V. V. Shaposhnik, "Novaia literature ob A. I. Bogdanove," in *Peterburgskie chteniia 96* (SPb: BLITS, 1996). See also I. N. Koblents, *Andrei Ivanovich Bogdanov.*

1692–1766. Iz proshlogo russkoi istoricheskoi nauki i knigovedeniia (Moscow: Izdatel'stvo Akademii Nauk SSSR, 1958) and K. I. Logachev and V. S. Sobolev, *"Opisanie Sanktpeterburga."* Preprint (Leningrad: Leningradskoe Otd-nie Arkhiva Akademii Nauk SSSR, 1987).

11. See I. G. Georgi, *Opisanie rossiisko-imperatorskogo stolichnogo goroda Sankt-Peterburga i dostopamiatnostei v okrestnostiakh onogo, s planom* (SPb: 1996). For another contemporary account, see Henry Storch, *The Picture of Petersburg*, translated from the German (London: T. N. Longman & O. Rees, 1801). For the original Storch text in German, see Heinrich Friedrich von Storch, *Gemaehlde von St. Petersburg* (Riga: J. F. Hartknoch, 1794).

12. Granted, Georgi devotes a few intriguing sections—titled "About the Contemporary Way of Life" and "Mores of Residents"—to the texture of life in the capital, noting, for example, the extremes of hospitality and obsession with rank characteristic of Petersburg. See Georgi, pp. 477–78.

13. For an elaboration of this distinction, see Michel de Certeau, *The Practice of Everyday Life*, trans. Steven Rendall (Berkeley: University of California Press, 1984), pp. 118–122.

14. For a summary of the early exemplars of the Petersburg guidebook, see O.S. Ostroi, "S chego nachinalas' peterburgiana: Opisanie putevoditelei po gorodu s momenta ikh vozniknoveniia do serediny XIX stoletiia" in *Nevskii arkhiv* III (SPb: Atheneum Feniks, 1997).

15. F. A. Shreder, *Noveishii putevoditel' po Sanktpeterburgu* (SPb, 1820).

16. Moreover, Shreder, by his own admission, used as sources the limited number of texts already available on St. Petersburg—eighteenth-century "descriptions" by Bogdanov, Georgi, and Storch, as well as Svin'in's three existing volumes and Konstantin Arsenev's 1819 statistical study. See Konstantin Arsenev, *Nachertanie statistiki Rossiiskago gosudarstva* (SPb: Tip. Imperatorskogo vospitatel'nogo doma, 1819). Oddly, Shreder includes one foreign-language source on St. Petersburg—Theodore Faber's *Bagatelles: Promenades d'un Désoeuvré dans la Ville de St. Pétersbourg* (Paris, 1812), which he describes as more humanistic than the eighteenth-century descriptions, and more attentive to the city-dwellers themselves, but inadequate for visiting tourist attractions. It seems unlikely that "trifling" strolls by an "idler" could have provided a model for Shreder's buttoned-up guide to St. Petersburg.

17. P. P. Svin'in, *Dostopamiatnosti S.-Peterburga i ego okrestnostei* (SPb, 1816, 1817, 1818, 1821, 1828). Svin'in would seem to have been well qualified to produce an all-purpose travel guide to St. Petersburg. He served as the editor of the journal *Otechestvennye zapiski* during the period 1818–30, had previously traveled to England and America, and published English-language literary "sketches" about Moscow and St. Petersburg during the 1810s. But an article in the journal *Vestnik Evropy* accused Svin'in of propagating historical inaccuracies about the two Russian cities, and thus his credibility was suspect, at least at home. Undaunted, Svin'in published equally questionable Russian-language accounts of his travels in North America and London, which inspired A. E. Izmailov to compose "The Liar" (*Lgun*, 1824), a fable that lampooned Svin'in as a prevaricating tourist.

18. Unfortunately, an enormous number of engravings and drawings prepared in England for Bashchutskii's *Panorama* were lost in a shipwreck while on their way to Petersburg. As these were uninsured, Bashchutskii incurred a tremendous financial loss.

Bashchutskii himself describes these circumstances in the preface to the third part of his *Panorama*.

19. A. P. Bashchutskii, *Panorama Sanktpeterburga* (SPb, 1834), pp. iv–v, vi, vii.

20. "Literaturnaia letopis," *Biblioteka dlia chteniia*, 1835, t. 8, no. 4, otd. VI, pp. 45–48.

21. In fact, according to Vissarion Belinsky, as noted in his introduction to Nekrasov's 1845 compendium *Fiziologiia Peterburga*, Bashchutskii's *Panorama* was to have provided a much more extensive description of Petersburg's "everyday life and customs," in addition to treating the city's physical structures, creating a city-wide reference (*ukazatel'*) and providing a series of historical excursions, but the disastrous financial consequences of the shipwreck brought the project to a premature conclusion. Belinsky dismissed Bashchutskii's much-censored 1841–42 volume of illustrated sketches, *Nashi spisannye s natury russkimi*, as woefully inadequate. For more information about *Nashi*, as well as a biography of Bashchutskii, see N. G. Okhotin, "A. P. Bashchutskii i ego kniga," *Nashi spisannye s natury russkimi: Prilozhenie k faksimil'nomu izdaniiu* (Moscow: Kniga, 1986).

22. With Bur'ianov in hand, "the schoolteacher, fond papa, or visiting provincial could combine a survey of Petersburg sights with natural-science observations and 'ideologemes' (*ideologemy*) in the spirit of the Uvarov 'triad.'" L. Ia. Lur'e and A. V. Kobak, "Zametki o smysle peterburgskogo kraevedeniia," *Antsiferovskie chteniia* (Leningrad: Leningradskoe Otdelenie Sovetskogo Fonda Kul'tury, 1989), p. 72. Tsar Nicholas I's reactionary Minister of Education, Sergei Uvarov, had declared in an 1833 report to the tsar that education must be conducted with faith in the principles of Autocracy, Orthodoxy, and Nationality.

23. See Aleksei Grech, *Ves' Peterburg v karmane: Spravochnaia kniga dlia stolichnykh zhitelei i priezzhikh, s planami Sanktpeterburga i chetyrekh teatrov* (SPb: Tip. A. Grecha, 1851) and V. O. Mikhnevich, *Peterburg ves' na ladoni: S planom Peterburga, ego panoramoi . . . i s pribavleniem kalendaria* (SPb: Tip. K.N. Plotnikova, 1874).

24. See Mikhnevich, pp. 66–69 for the best panoramic vistas. The rest of the information mentioned is in *Pribavlenie: Kalendar' na 1874 god*, pp. iv–xii, xlvii–liv, lxxi–lxxx.

25. Petr Petrov's *Istoriia Sankt-Peterburga 1703–1782* (1885) does, however, constitute a comprehensive approach to the city as a serious history that attempts to provide a full "description"—a "complete, coherent, reliable" historical work "suitable for any type of reference"—like those that exist for major capital cities in Europe, "the enlightened part of the world." Petrov's *Istoriia*, which elides the nineteenth century completely, concluding with the unveiling of Catherine's monument to Peter I, asserts that the true Petersburg guidebook is a historical narrative that surpasses the nonnarrative genres of description and reference. Petrov begins with a survey-tour of existing literature, invoking the work of Bogdanov, Storch, Georgi, Svin'in, Shreder, Bashchutskii, Arsen'ev, Pushkarev, Grech, and Mikhnevich, all of whom he criticizes, in the usual way, for incompleteness, inaccuracy, lack of seriousness, or lack of originality. See P. N. Petrov, "Vstuplenie," *Istoriia Sankt-Peterburga s osnovaniia goroda do vvedeniia v deistvie vybornogo gorodskogo upravleniia 1703–1782* (SPb: Tip. Glazunova, 1885).

26. See Solomon Volkov's account of Tchaikovsky's symphonies, as well as his ballets and the opera "Pikovaia dama," as reflecting his darkening view of Petersburg from the mid-1860s through the early 1890s. Solomon Volkov, *St. Petersburg: A Cultural History*, trans. Antonina W. Bouis (New York: The Free Press, 1995), pp. 111–29.

27. D. N. Loman, *Dostoprimechatel'nosti S.-Peterburga. Chtenie dlia naroda* (SPb, 1898).

28. For another example of this type directed at soldiers and simple "folk," see V. V. Zherve, *Pamiatka o Peterburge i ego primechatel'nostiakh: s risunkami: dlia voisk i naroda* (SPb: Voennaia Tip., 1897).

29. For a discussion of Russians' own travels abroad and to the outer areas of the Russian empire and a study of the writing they produced about their experiences, see Andreas Schönle, *Authenticity and Fiction in the Russian Literary Journey, 1790–1840* (Cambridge: Harvard University Press, 2000).

30. T. Roboli, "The Literature of Travel," in *Russian Prose*, B. Eikhenbaum and Iu. Tynianov, eds., and Ray Parrott, trans. (Ann Arbor: Ardis, 1985), p. 46.

31. These imperial-era literary journeys are distinct from the later, twentieth-century genre of meditative Petersburg "strolls" by writers such as the Acmeists, who contributed to what V. N. Toporov calls "the spiritualization and humanization of the city" by connecting their text's subjective, contemporary consciousness with the city's past. See "Peterburg i 'peterburgskii tekst russkoi literatury,'" *Mif. Ritual. Simvol. Obraz: Issledovaniia v oblasti mifopoeticheskogo* (Moscow: Kul'tura, 1995), p. 288. These later works create an "atmosphere of heightened, even hypertrophied signification" within Petersburg by means of the supersaturated cultural-historical trajectory they trace, and their purpose is to review, remember, and impart.

32. Batiushkov's piece complements his unfinished 1811 "Stroll about Moscow" and is, in fact, subtitled "A Letter from an Old Moscow Resident to a Friend at His Village N."

33. K. N. Batiushkov, "Progulka v Akademiiu khudozhestv," in *Sochineniia*, ed. D. D. Blagoi (Moscow: Academia, 1934), p. 320.

34. For an earlier example of this discourse on art and essential nature, albeit not in excursion form, see A. P. Sumarokov's 1764 speech to commemorate Catherine's reorganization of the Academy, "Na otkrytii imperatorskoi sanktpeterburgskoi akademii khudozhestv," in *Polnoe sobranie vsekh sochinenii v stikhakh i proze*, Nikolai Novikov, ed. (Moscow: Universitetskaia tipografiia u N. Novikova, 1781–1782), t. 2, pp. 307–22.

35. Ibid., p. 322.

36. Ibid., pp. 323–24.

37. Ibid., p. 325. Note that the riding hall (Manezh) mentioned in this passage as one of the masterworks in the aestheticized cityscape was aptly transformed into an exhibition space during the twentieth century.

38. For example, the friends examine a painting by the Russian artist Egorov depicting the torture of Christ in prison. Starozhilov insists that the painting is unoriginal, since Rubens and Poussin have already painted the same subject with greater skill, but the young artist disagrees, emphasizing Egorov's potential. The narrator closes this debate by declaring that Egorov will bring honor to the Academy and to his countrymen in the future.

39. Ibid., p. 334.

40. Ibid., p. 339.

41. In this same regard, see "Progulka v Tavricheskom sadu," *Severnaia Minerva*, no. 10, 1832, p. 221. The narrator of "A Stroll in the Tauride Garden" passes through the palace "pantheon" and describes the classical statues in white marble—Cleopatra, Endymion and Diana, Laocoön and his sons, Cupid and Psyche, Venus, and Bacchus. These allegorical figures lead the narrator to reflect upon the past glories of Catherine's reign, Alexander's name-day celebration, Nicholas's recent victory over the Ottomans, and visits by Persian and Swedish princes—state events all associated with the Tauride

Palace and evoked in a suitably lofty register. A stroll through the Tauride Gardens thus constitutes a promenade through imperial Russian history and cultural literacy.

42. Donald Fanger, *Dostoevsky and Romantic Realism: A Study of Dostoevsky in Relation to Balzac, Dickens, and Gogol* (Chicago: University of Chicago Press, 1967), pp. 135–136. Fanger claims that the "more serious form" of the feuilleton as it developed in France and Russia is "a kind of romantic realism" in "the highly personal discovery of the strange in the familiar, of lyrical resonances in the urban 'elements of prose'" (p. 151).

43. Many of these journalistic pieces were written hastily out of financial necessity and therefore received little attention after their initial appearance. Later, scholars were hampered from making proper authorial attributions by the fact that feuilletons from this period were often published anonymously or pseudonymously. The 1920s marked the discovery of several such feuilletons, including the 1847 "Peterburgskaia letopis'" series by Dostoevsky and Goncharov's 1848 "Pis'ma stolichnogo druga k provintsial'nomu zhenikhu." For more information, see Iu. G. Oksman, ed., *Fel'etony sorokovykh godov* (Moscow: Academia, 1930). For a broad discussion of Russian feuilletons from the nineteenth and twentieth centuries, see E. I. Zhurbina, *Teoriia i praktika khudozhestvenno-publitsisticheskikh zhanrov (Ocherk. Fel'eton)* (Moscow: Mysl', 1969). For an excellent treatment of the newspaper feuilleton in Russia, see Katia Dianina, "The Feuillton: An Everday Guide to Public Culture in the Age of the Great Reforms," *Slavic and Eastern European Journal*, vol. 47, no. 2, Summer 2003.

44. Dana Brand disagrees with the Benjaminian notion that the *flâneur* as a "type" that originated in 1830s Paris and argues that this figure can be found in English literature as early as the beginning of the seventeenth century (despite the lack of a "widely current" English word for *flâneur*), as well as in American antebellum culture. See *The Spectator and the City in Nineteenth-Century American Literature*, pp. 1–13. For information about mid-century New York flaneurs, see Bergmann, *New York Writing from the Penny Press to Melville*, pp. 57–67.

45. Entry for 1 June in F. M. Dostoevsky, "Peterburgskaia letopis'," in *Polnoe sobranie khudozhestvennykh sochinenii*, B. Tomashevskii and K Khalabaev, eds., t. 8 (Moscow: Gosudarstvennoe izdatel'stvo, 1926–1930), p. 23.

46. The feuilleton in fact constituted a meta-genre, at least according to nineteenth-century writer Alexander Druzhinin, who joked that "soon . . . writers . . . will pen nothing but feuilletons" and that the elimination of specific forms would simplify the future production of literature. A. V. Druzhinin, "Pis'ma inogorodnego podpischika o russkoi zhurnalistike," *Sochineniia A. V. Druzhinina*, T. VI (SPb, 1865), p. 223. Druzhinin's characterization speaks to the heterogeneous nature of the feuilleton as a literary form, or more accurately, as a compendium of literary forms. Druzhinin himself wrote feuilletons during the period 1850–1863, which he published under the rubric "Observations of a Petersburg Tourist" (*Zametki peterburgskogo turista*). This guidebook-like series title could not mask the cannibalistically self-regarding nature of the feuilleton form, as evidenced by an 1855 piece from Druzhinin's cycle called "A Dramatic Feuilleton about the Feuilleton and about Feuilletonists." See *Russkie pisateli 1800–1917*, vol. 2 (Moscow: Bol'shaia Rossiiskaia Entsiklopediia, 1992), p. 188, for precise information on the journals, years, and issues in which these feuilletons appeared.

47. F. M. Dostoevsky, "Peterburgskaia letopis'," p. 21. For excellent background information on these feuilletons in the Russian cultural context, see V. L. Komarovich, "Peterburgskie fel'etony Dostoevskogo," in *Fel'etony sorokovykh godov*.

48. Ibid., p. 12.

49. Dostoevsky's "Petersburg Chronicle" has been characterized as an antifeuilleton, whose author hijacks the conventions of the form from its earlier, more aristocratic manifestation in order to develop his writer's craft at a critical stage in his creative biography. For a magnificent reading of the series, see Donald Fanger, *Dostoevsky and Romantic Realism*, pp. 134–48. See also Gary Saul Morson, *The Boundaries of Genre: Dostoevsky's Diary of a Writer and the Traditions of Literary Utopia* (Evanston: Northwestern University Press, 1981), pp. 17–20. For yet another reading of Dostoevsky's Petersburg feuilletons, see Joseph Frank, *Dostoevsky: The Seeds of Revolt 1821–1849* (Princeton: Princeton University Press, 1976), pp. 217–38. Frank emphasizes Dostoevsky's oblique treatment of key social and political issues in Russia of the 1840s.

50. See chapter 1 for a more extended discussion of the third feuilleton and Dostoevsky's early positive views on St. Petersburg architecture and the ongoing construction project for what he then saw as a city of an essentially contemporary spirit.

51. Ibid., p. 15.

52. Ibid., p. 20.

53. For a history of the scholarly investigations that resulted in the proper attribution of these feuilletons to Nekrasov, beginning with Kornei Chukovskii in the 1920s, see N. A. Nekrasov, *Polnoe sobranie sochinenii i pisem v piatnadtsati tomakh*, t. 12 (SPb: Nauka, 1995), pp. 361–79. For an overview of Nekrasov's feuilletons from the 1840s, see O. V. Loman, *Nekrasov v Peterburge* (Leningrad: Lenizdat, 1985), pp. 53–59.

54. Ibid., pp. 54–55. Apparently, the elevated opening is a parodic reference to Gogol's "Strashnaia mest," which begins with a similar description of the Dniepr River.

55. Petr Stolpianskii, writing about Nekrasov's Petersburg poetry from the second part of the nineteenth century, asserted that anyone wishing to understand the city's life from that period would find it essential to study Nekrasov. Stolpianskii denied that the poet gathered his material on Petersburg corners and slums by descending "to the depths of life in the capital like a tourist," and claimed instead that Nekrasov had experienced these horrors himself. See "Staryi Peterburg v proizvedeniiakh Nekrasova," *Kniga i revoliutsiia*, no. 2 (14), 1921, pp. 17–18.

56. As Evgenii Ol'khovskii observes, although much has been written about *Fiziologiia Peterburga*, the "urban studies" (*gorodovedcheskaia*) theme of the collection remains largely unexplored, including its treatment of everyday life. See *Peterburgskie istorii: Gorod i intelligentsiia v minuvshem stoletii (1810-e-1910-e gody)* (SPb: Kul'tInformPress, 1998), p. 18.

57. V. G. Belinskii, "Vstuplenie," in *Fiziologiia Peterburga*, V. I. Kuleshov, ed. (Moscow: Nauka, 1991), p. 7.

58. Ibid, p. 12.

59. The *Charakteristik*, as defined by Friedrich Shlegel, is a written fragment that contains the very essence of a (dramatic, dynamic) work, from which the whole can be adduced. Schlegel defines the term in his 1804 *Lessings Geist aus seinem Schristen*, as discussed in chapter 2 of Melissa Frazier, *Frames of the Imagination: Gogol's Arabesques* and the Romantic Question of Genre (New York: Peter Lang, 2000). The *Charakteristik* is small in length, but large in scope, for it "is intended as a small window which gives out onto a large world, a small lens which focuses the reflection of an infinitely large view" (p. 71). Frazier specifically treats the relationship between *Charakteristik* and literary physiology (pp. 83–87), asserting that the physiology is more like an anatomy that ren-

ders its human subject merely representative, rather than living and dynamic. What about the physiology's depiction of a living *city?*

60. N. A. Nekrasov, *PSSiP*, t. 12, p. 146.

61. Belinsky himself hinted at something along the same lines in his 1842 article, "A Speech about Criticism," in which he declared, "the world needs not the motley kaleidoscope of imagination, but the microscope and telescope of reason, which draws [the world] close to what is distant, and makes the unseen visible." See *Polnoe sobranie sochinenii v trinadtsati tomakh* (Moscow, 1953–59), t. 6, p. 268.

62. E. P. Grebenka, "Peterburgskaia storona," in *Fiziologiia Peterburga*, V. I. Kuleshov, ed. (Moscow: Nauka, 1991), p. 72.

63. Ibid, p. 81.

64. I. S. Turgenev, *Dokumenty po istorii literatury i obshchestvennosti*, vyp. 2 (Moscow: GIZ, 1923), p. 37. See also I. S. Turgenev, *Polnoe sobranie sochinenii i pisem*, t. 1 (Moscow, 1960), p. 454.

65. In fact, Ivan Panaev published an 1857 sketch titled "Galernaia Port" (*Galernaia gavan'*) that effectively realizes the plan for the first item on Turgenev's list. See I. I. Panaev, "Galernaia gavan," in *Peterburg v russkom ocherke XIX veka*, M. V. Otradin, ed. (Leningrad: Izdatel'stvo Leningradskogo Universiteta, 1984), p. 177. The narrator takes his readers on a tour along Bol'shoi Prospect on Vasilievskii Island, past the elegant embankment, the fashionable "First Line," and the beautiful Stock Exchange to the other end of the island, out by the Smolenskoe Cemetery, where the neighborhoods are unpaved, sparsely settled with tiny wooden houses, swampy, and overgrown.

66. Ivan Antsiferov, *Peterburg iz moego okna. Putevye zapiski moskvicha, avgust 1852 goda* (Moscow, 1853), p. 6.

67. Ibid., p. 46.

68. Nikolai Sveshnikov maps a different sort of unconventional personal journey in his drunken picaresque, *Memoirs of a Fallen Man* (*Vospominaniia propashchego cheloveka*), describing the many jobs he held in the city as an itinerant youth during the 1850s. Sveshnikov weighed heavy goods at the Stock Exchange, worked at a dairy shop in Chernaia Rechka, kneaded bread in a shop at the corner of Malaia Sadovaia and Ital'ianskaia Streets, served in a summer tavern on Serdobol'skaia Street, assisted at skittles matches on the Lanskoe highway, was a watchman at Simonson's balagan, and worked as a cook for a tailor in the Passazh Arcade. The striking specificity of Sveshnikov's odd jobs is complemented by whatever random turn of events prompts each new change of scene. See N. I. Sveshnikov, *Vospominaniia propashchego cheloveka* (Moscow: Novoe literaturnoe obozrenie, 1996), pp. 51–55.

69. N. N. Zhivotov, *Peterburgskie profili*, vyp. 1, "Na izvoshchich'ikh kozlakh: Shest' dnei v roli izvoshchika" (SPb: A. Vineke, 1894), p. 1.

70. Ibid., p. 2.

71. A. F. Koni, *Peterburg: Vospominaniia starozhila* (Atenei, 1922), p. 7.

72. Ibid., p. 8.

73. Ibid., pp. 22–23.

74. Ibid., p. 69.

75. G. K. Lukomskii, *Staryi Peterburg: Progulki po starinnym kvartalam stolitsy* (Petrograd: Svobodnoe iskusstvo, 1917), p. 10.

76. Ibid., p. 12.

77. Ibid., p. 48.

78. All of Lukomskii's cultural guidebooks similarly represent an exercise in time travel. Even Lukomskii's 1917 *Sovremennyi Petrograd* surveys what the book's subtitle describes as "The History of the Origin and Development of Classical Construction 1900–1915." In this study, Lukomskii sweeps aside the pseudo-Renaissance style of Alexander III's time, the "decadent" eclectic tendencies of late-imperial architecture, and unusual structures such as the Petersburg mosque in order to celebrate an architectural return to the Petersburg ideal in "the new classical architecture."

79. Stolpianskii complained in 1926 that nineteenth-century guidebooks and cultural histories by authors such as Shreder, Bur'ianov, Pushkarev, and Pyliaev culled from printed sources and did not test or investigate this textual legacy about St. Petersburg. See P. N. Stolpianskii, *Bibliografiia Sankt-Piter-Burkha (nyne Leningrada): Opisanie i plany po ekzempliaram Publichnoi Biblioteki* (typewritten manuscript, held in reference section of St. Petersburg Public Library) (Leningrad, 1926). In this sense, the nineteenth-century tradition of Russian-language guidebooks resembles the oral transmission of city "lore" so often cited as a defining feature of St. Petersburg culture.

80. For an assessment of Stolpianskii's contribution to the study of Petersburg and a call to complete work on his archive and produce a complete bibliography of his works, see I. A. Golubeva, "Neizvestnyi P.N. Stolpianskii," in *Fenomen Peterburga*, Iu. N. Bespiatykh, ed. (SPb: BLITS, 2000). This article also describes Stolpianskii's unfinished multivolume project, "The History of Petersburg." See also I. A. Golubeva, "Istorik-peterburgoved Petr Nikolaevich Stolpianskii (1872–1938): Biograficheskii ocherk," *Zhurnal liubitelei iskusstva*, nos. 8–9, 1997.

81. P. P. Stolpianskii, *Staryi Peterburg: Admiralteiskii ostrov (Sad Trudiashchikhsia)* (Moscow: Gosudarstvennoe izdatel'stvo, 1923), p. 7.

82. The notion of "Old Petersburg" (*Staryi Peterburg*) that structured preservationist texts was distinct from that employed during the late nineteenth century by Mikhail Pyliaev and cultural historians of his age in order to distinguish between eighteenth-century and nineteenth-century St. Petersburg, or between the "Pushkin period" and the latter part of the nineteenth century.

83. A good deal of Grevs's work remains unpublished. His published writing about cities includes "Gorod, kak predmet kraevedeniia," *Kraevedenie*, 1924, no. 3, and "Monumental'nyi gorod i istoricheskie ekskursii: Osnovnaia ideia obrazovatel'nykh puteshestvii po krupnym tsentram kul'tury," *Ekskursionnoe delo*, 1921, no. 1. See also the untitled chapter from the unpublished monograph *Razvitie kul'tury v kraevedcheskom issledovanii*, prepared by F. F. Perchenko in *Antsiferovskie chteniia: Materialy i tezisy konferentsii* (Leningrad: Leningradsoe Otedelenie Sovetskogo Fonda Kul'tury, 1989), pp. 28–36.

84. For an excellent background survey of humanist excursions within the context of Antsiferov's biography, see A. M. Konechnyi and K. A. Kumpan, "Peterburg v zhizni i trudakh N. P. Antsiferova," in *"Nepostizhimyi gorod . . ."* (Leningrad: Lenizdat, 1991). See also A. M. Konechnyi, "N. P. Antsiferov—issledovatel' Peterburga," in *Peterburg i guberniia: Istoriko-etnograficheskie issledovaniia* (Leningrad, 1989). This latter piece includes a bibliography of Antsiferov's works about Petersburg.

85. In parallel with the work of this society, Grevs and his associates established a research institute for excursionists (1921–24) and produced a journal called *Ekskursionnoe delo* (1921–23).

86. L. Ia. Lur'e and A. V. Kobak, "Zametki o smysle peterburgskogo kraevedeniia," p. 72.

For a full account of the discipline of *kraevedenie* in its various manifestations, see Emily D. Johnson, *The Science of Local Sentiment: How Early Twentieth-Century Petersburg Learned to Study Its Self* (forthcoming).

87. Veinert, Ia. A., "Vospominaniia o Nikolae Pavloviche Antsiferove." Mashinopis', 1958 (sobranie M. B. Verblovskoi). Cited in Konechnyi and Kumpan, p. 14.

88. See Grevs's preface to Antsiferov's *Dusha Peterburga*, in *"Nepostizhimyi gorod . . ."* For a complete elaboration of Antsiferov's views on the subject, see his treatise *O metodakh i tipakh istoriko-kul'turnykh ekskursii* (Petrograd, 1923).

89. *Dusha Peterburga*, pp. 29–30.

90. Ibid, p. 46.

91. In "Slovo o Pushkine," Anna Akhmatova notes the happy irony in the designation "Pushkin," which has subsumed the cynical Petersburg high society that destroyed Russia's national poet. Pushkin "conquered both time and space," asserts Akhmatova, in that everyone speaks now of "pushkinskaia epokha" (the Pushkin period) and "Pushkinskii Peterburg" (Pushkin's Petersburg), caring nothing for the former owners of a particular palace, for example, but only wondering whether Pushkin had ever been there (the all-important "zdes' byval Pushkin" or "zdes' ne byval Pushkin"). See Anna Akhmatova, *Sochineniia*, t. 2 (Munich: Inter-Language Literary Associates, 1968), pp. 275–76.

92. N. P. Antsiferov, *Peterburg Dostoevskogo*, in *"Nepostizhimyi gorod . . ."* (Leningrad: Lenizdat, 1991), pp. 240–54. Antsiferov's "territory" for his Dostoevsky project includes the areas bordering Voznesenskii Prospect from the Fontanka past St. Isaac's Square and up to the Admiralty. Antsiferov's route similarly covers the adjoining parts of the narrow and winding Ekaterininskii Canal, areas near Obukhovskii Prospect south of the Fontanka, and along the Fontanka as far as Nevsky Prospect. Through literary and historical detective work, Antsiferov identifies the building in which Raskolnikov lived—an apartment house that actually stood at the intersection of Voznesenskii Prospect and the present Gogol Street, but which Dostoevsky "moved" to the intersection of Stoliarnyi Lane and Meshchanskaia Street (pp. 248–51). Antsiferov similarly "finds" the building in which the old woman pawnbroker lived, but on the opposite side of the Ekaterininskii Canal from the spot to which Dostoevsky's literary route leads. Antsiferov and many Dostoevsky scholars after him also lovingly culled descriptions of squalid apartment houses from the writer's other works, among them "Khozaika," *Unizhennye i oskorblennye*, and *Idiot* (pp. 201–5).

93. For contemporary examples of this genre, see Iurii Rakov, *Lestnitsa Raskol'nikova: Zapiski literaturnogo sledopyta* (Leningrad: self-published, 1990) and *Peterburg—gorod literaturnykh geroev* (SPB: Khimiia, 1997).

94. M. Iu. Lermontov, "Kniaginia Ligovskaia." *Polnoe sobranie sochinenii*, vol. 5 (Moscow: Academia, 1937), p. 110.

95. N. A. Nekrasov, "Zhizn' Aleksandry Ivanovny: Povest' v chetyrekh ekipazhakh," *PSSiP*, t. 7 (Leningrad: Nauka, 1983).

96. N. P. Antsiferov, "Predislovie," *Byl i mif Peterburga* (SPb: Brokgauz-Efron, 1924), p. 5.

97. See "Ulitsa rynkov (Sadovaia, nyne ulitsa 3-ogo Iiuliia v Leningrade): Kraevedcheskii material dlia ekskursii po sotsial'nomu i ekonomicheskomu bytu," *Po ochagam kul'tury: Novye temy dlia ekskursii po gorodu* (Leningrad, 1926), and "Raion morskogo porta (epokha torgovogo kapitalizma): Ekskursiia po Vasil'evskomu ostrovu (Strelka i Tuchkova naberezhnaia)," *Teoriia i praktika ekskursii po obshchestvovedeniiu* (Leningrad,

1926). See also *Prigorody Leningrada: Goroda Pushkin, Pavlovsk, Petrodvorets* (Moscow: Gosudarstvennyi literaturnyi muzei, 1946).

98. A recent reference work displays an awareness of this tradition in its title: *Istoriia Sankt-Peterburga-Petrograda 1703–1917: Putevoditel'* [emphasis mine] *po istochnikam,* t. 1, vyp. 1 (Istoricheskie istochniki, raboty obshchego kharaktera, spravochnye i bibliograficheskie materialy) (SPb: Filologicheskii Fakul'tet Sankt-Peterburgskogo Gosudarstvennogo Universiteta, 2000).

99. Examples of the "Pushkinskii Peterburg" genre with their precise Pushkin geographies and accounts of high-society life in the capital include Andrei Iatsevich, *Pushkinskii Peterburg* (Leningrad: Pushkinskoe obshchestvo, 1935), B. V. Tomashevskii, ed., *Pushkinskii Peterburg* (Leningrad: Leningradskoe gazetno-zhurnal'noe i knizhnoe izdatel'stvo, 1949), N. P. Antsiferov, "Peterburg Pushkina" (1950) in *"Nepostizhimyi gorod . . .",* Moisei Kagan, "Vremia rastsveta: pushkinskii Peterburg" in his *Grad Petrov v istorii russkoi kul'tury* (SPb: Slaviia, 1996), and A. M. Gordin and M. A. Gordin, *Pushkinskii vek,* kn. 1 and 2, from series "Byloi Peterburg: Panorama stolichnoi zhizni" (SPb: Pushkinskii fond, 1999). Representatives of the "Peterburg Dostoevskogo" genre, most with the requisite topographical tour of *Prestuplenie i nakazanie,* include N. P. Antsiferov, "Peterburg Dostoevskogo" (1923) in *"Nepostizhimyi gorod . . .",* Vera Biron, *Peterburg Dostoevskogo* (Leningrad: Svecha, 1991), Moisei Kagan, "Vremia dramaticheskogo dialoga: Peterburg Dostoevskogo," in *Grad Petrov,* O. G. Dilaktorskaia, *Peterburgskaia povest' Dostoevskogo* (SPb: Dmitri Bulanin, 1999), and S. V. Belov, *Peterburg Dostoevskogo* (SPb: Aleteiia, 2002).

100. For a small sampling of this enormous body of work, see, for example, A. I. Bashmakov, *Ia idu po Millionoi* (SPb: Vsemirnyi klub peterburzhtsev, 2000); V. G. Isachenko and V. N. Pitanin, *Liteinyi Prospekt* (Leningrad: Lenizdat, 1989); E. Z. Kufershtein, K. M. Borisov, and O. E. Rubinchik, *Ulitsa Pestelia (Panteleimonovskaia)* (Leningrad: Svecha, 1991); I. I. Lisaevich, *Doma rasskazyvaiut* (SPb: Lenizdat, 2001); T. L. Pashkova, *Dom arkhitektora Briullova* (SPb: Almaz, 1997); Nataliia Perevezentseva, *Ia vyshla iz doma . . . Kniga o pushkinskoi ulitse i ne tol'ko o nei* (SPb: Ostrov, 2001), G. F. Petrov, *Dvorets u Sinego mosta: Mariinskii dvorets v Sankt-Peterburge* (SPb: Logos, 2001); T. A. Solov'eva, *K prichalam Angliiskoi naberezhnoi* (SPb: IKAR, 1998); and P. Suvorkov, *Prospekt Chernyshevskogo* (SPb: Beloe i chernoe, 1999).

101. N. R. Levina and Iu. I. Kirtsideli, *Po etim ulitsam, po etim beregam . . . : Peterburgskie progulki* (SPb, Papirus, 1997), p. 3.

102. *Po etim ulitsam, po etim beregam . . .* attempts a cultural synthesis, documenting a landscape that includes nineteenth-century and Silver Age imperial artifacts, as well as Soviet sites such as the ship "Aurora" and the mass graves of "Victims of the Revolution" on the Field of Mars. An inclusive post-*perestroika* approach to Petersburg culture is this guidebook's true innovation.

103. I. G. Proskuriakova and N. S. Volchek, *Besedy o Sankt-Peterburge* (SPB: Astra-Liuks, 1992), p. 5.

104. See *Sankt-Peterburg. Zanimatel'nye voprosy i otvety* (SPb: Paritet, 2001) and B. K. Pukinskii, *1000 voprosov i otvetov o Leningrade* (Leningrad: Lenizdat, 1981).

105. *Azbuka Peterburga,* A. D. Margolis, sost. (SPb: Mezhdunarodnyi blagotvoritel'nyi fond spaseniia Peterburga-Leningrada, 1995).

106. See D. Iu. Sherikh, *Peterburg den' za dnem: Gorodskoi mesiatseslov* (SPb: Peterburg—XXI vek, 1998).

107. Mikhail Kuraev, "Puteshestvie iz Leningrada v Sankt Peterburg," *Novyi mir*, no. 10 (1996).

Chapter Four

1. For an account of the conditions under which workers built the city, see P. N. Stolpianskii, *Peterburg: Kak voznik, osnovalsia i ros Sankt-Peterburg* (SPb: Nega, 1995), pp. 28–33. For a discussion of the non-Slavic peoples who inhabited this area before the Russians and the myths and legends from these substrata that made their way into the Petersburg semiosphere, see D. L. Spivak, *Severnaia stolitsa: Metafizika Peterburga* (SPb: Tema, 1998).

2. Walter Benjamin, "The Storyteller: Reflections on the Works of Nikolai Leskov." *Illuminations*, trans. Harry Zohn (New York: Schocken Books, 1969), p. 91.

3. Gillian Bennett and Paul Smith, "Introduction" to *Contemporary Legend: A Reader* (London: Garland Publishing, Inc., 1996), pp. xxii–xxiv, xxxvi–xxxix.

4. See Roland Barthes, "Structure of the *Fait-Divers*," in *Critical Essays*, Richard Howard, trans. (Evanston: Northwestern University Press, 1972). For Barthes, the *fait-divers* lies at the ambiguous crossroads of causality and coincidence.

5. See for example Noel Williams, "Problems in Defining Contemporary Legend," in *Perspectives on Contemporary Legend*, Paul Smith, ed. (Sheffield: CECTAL Conference Papers Series, 1984).

6. Michel de Certeau, *The Practice of Everyday Life*, trans. Steven Rendall (Berkeley: University of California Press), pp. 35, 131–132.

7. Harold Schechter attempts to counter this prejudice in the American context by merging traditional folk and contemporary pop objects of study in *The Bosom Serpent: Folklore and Popular Art* (Iowa City: University of Iowa Press, 1988).

8. P. Viazemskii, *Staraia zapisnaia knizhka*, ed. L. Ginzburg (Leningrad: Izdatel'stvo pisatelei v Leningrade, 1929), p. 94.

9. Iu. M. Lotman, "K funktsii ustnoi rechi v kul'turnom bytu pushkinskoi epokhi," *Izbrannye stat'i*, vol. 3 (Tallinn: Alexandra, 1993), p. 430.

10. B. N. Putilov, "Peterburg—Leningrad v ustnoi traditsii stoletii." Introduction to Naum Sindalovskii, *Peterburgskii fol'klor* (SPb: Maksima, 1994), p. 7.

11. Iu. M. Lotman, "Ustnaia rech' v istoriko-kul'turnoi perspektive," *Izbrannye stat'i*, vol. 1 (Tallinn: Alexandra, 1992), pp. 186–87.

12. There also exist legend "clusters" of a different type—namely, those collected and associated with a particular grouping of individuals. The most famous example is the Pushkin family, whose encounters with apparitions—in Moscow, Petersburg, and the country—are relayed by the poet's nephew, L. Pavlishchev in his 1890 memoirs. See his *Iz semeinoi khroniki: Vospominaniia ob A.S. Pushkine* (Moscow: Universitetskaia tipografiia na Strastn. bul'v., 1890).

13. A. S. Pushkin, *Dnevniki. Avtobiograficheskaia proza*, ed. S.A. Fomichev (Moscow: Sovetskaia Rossiia, 1989), p. 55.

14. *Ostaf'evskii arkhiv*, t. III, pp. 254–55, as cited in A. S. Pushkin, *Dnevniki*, p. 289.

15. N. V. Gogol', "Nos," *Sobranie sochinenii v vos'mi tomakh*, t. 3 (Moscow: Pravda, 1984), p. 61.

16. V. F. Odoevskii, "Prividenie," *Romanticheskie povesti* (Leningrad, 1929), p. 206.

17. My thanks to Julia Bekman for this one.

18. Anthony Vidler, *The Architectural Uncanny: Essays in the Modern Unhomely* (Cambridge, MA: The MIT Press, 1992), p. 6.

19. Sigmund Freud, "The Uncanny," in *Art and Literature*, from the Penguin Freud Library, vol. 14 (Middlesex, England: Penguin Books, 1985), p. 370. For a reading of Freud's own uncanny discourse on this subject, see Hélène Cixous's reading of Freud's essay, "Fiction and Its Phantoms: A Reading of Freud's *Das Unheimliche* (the 'uncanny')" in *New Literary History*, vol. 7, no. 3 (Spring 1976).

20. This "substantiating" phrase appears in the first account: Tar-ov, "Mysli i fakty," *Grazhdanin*, no. 348, December 16, 1890, and also in the reprinted version, "Tainstvennyi fakt," *Peterburgskii listok*, no. 345, December 17 (29), 1890, as per William Edgerton's "The Ghost in Search of Help," in *Readings from the Journal of the Folklore Institute. European Folklore*, Felix J. Oinas, ed. (Bloomington: Trickster Press, 1981).

21. Safonov's article, "V poiskakh za chudom," appears in *Novosti i birzhevaia gazeta*, ed. 1, no. 352, December 22, 1890.

22. William B. Edgerton, "A Ghostly Urban Legend in Petersburg: Was N. S. Leskov Involved?" in *The Supernatural in Slavic and Baltic Literature: Essays in Honor of Victor Terras*, Amy Mandelker and Roberta Reeder, eds. (Columbus: Slavica Publishers, 1988). The article in question is "Plokhi shutki," *Peterburgskaia gazeta*, no. 3, January 4, 1891.

23. Thus the *Acta diurna* of ancient Rome—announcements of daily political and cultural events posted around the city—were an early precursor to the newspaper.

24. For a study of New York's own internal texts and of New York's becoming its own literary subject, see Hans Bergmann, *God in the Street: New York Writing from the Penny Press to Melville* (Philadelphia, Temple University Press, 1995). Bergmann begins with the establishment of the first "penny" New York paper, the *Sun*, in 1833, and concludes with Melville's 1857 novel, *The Confidence-Man*. He documents what he calls "New York narratives of urban encounter in the antebellum period," emphasizing the discursive efforts of middle-class observers at "normalizing the alien and finding (often supernatural) 'meaning' in it" (p. 10).

25. For examples of Ksenia's remarkable predictions, see V. N. Toporov, "Peterburgskie teksty i Peterburgskie mify (Zametki iz serii)," *Mif. Ritual. Simvol. Obraz* (Moscow: Progress, 1995), p. 393.

26. M. I. Pyliaev, *Staryi Peterburg* (Leningrad:Titul, 1990), p. 167.

27. For examples of this sort of oral testimony, see E. Rakhmanin, *Raba Bozhiia Blazhennaia Kseniia*, as reproduced in *Blazhennaia Kseniia Peterburgskaia*, pp. 26–69. See also S. I. Opatovich, "Smolenskoe kladbishche v S.-Peterburge: Istoricheskii ocherk," *Russkaia starina*, August 1873, p. 195.

28. Liudmila Iakovleva, "Svetlyi lik Ksenii," *Blazhennaia Kseniia Peterburgskaia: Sovremennye chudesa. Zhitie. Akafist* (Moscow: 1994), p. 3.

29. For additional accounts of Ksenia's life, which largely repeat the same information, see "Zhitie sv. Ksenii Peterburgskoi," *Kanonizatsiia sviatykh* (Troitse-Sergieva lavra, 1988); D. Bulgakovskii, *Raba Bozhiia Kseniia, ili iurodivyi Andrei Fedorovich* (SPb, 1893); F. Belorus, *Iurodivyi Andrei Feodorovich ili Raba Bozhiia Kseniia, pogrebennaia na Smolenskom kladbishche v Peterburge* (SPb, 1893); E Rakhmanin, *Raba Bozhiia Kseniia, pochivaiushchaia na Smolenskom provoslavnom kladbishche v SPb*, izd. 4 (SPb, 1913).

30. E. P. Grebenka, "Peterburgskaia storona," in *Peterburg v russkom ocherke*, M. V. Otradin, ed. (Leningrad: Izdatel'stvo Leningradskogo Universiteta, 1984), p. 136.

31. V. N. Toporov, "Peterburgskie teksty i Peterburgskie mify (Zametki iz serii)," p. 370.

32. Joseph Brodsky, "A Guide to a Renamed City," in *Less Than One: Selected Essays* (New York: Farrar, Straus, & Giroux, 1986), p. 74.

33. P. N. Stolpianskii, "Legendy, predaniia i skazaniia starogo Peterburga," Petrograd, 1924, No. 2.

34. Stolpianskii, *Peterburg*, pp. 171–73.

35. O. G. Ageeva, "Peterburgskie slukhi (K voprosu o nastroeniiakh peterburgskogo obshchestva v epokhu petrovskikh reform)," in *Fenomen Peterburga*, Iu. N. Bespiatykh, ed. (SPb: BLITS, 2000), pp. 299–300. See also O. G. Ageeva, "*Velichaishii i slavneishii bolee vsekh gradov v svete*"—*Grad Sviatogo Petra: Peterburg v russkom obshchestvennom soznanii nachala XVIII veka* (SPb: BLITS, 1999), pp. 78–81.

36. Iu. M. Lotman, "Simvolika Peterburga i problemy semiotiki goroda," *Izbrannye stat'i v trekh tomakh*, t. 2 (Tallinn: Aleksandra, 1992), p. 14.

37. The information about Del'vig is seemingly confirmed by the memoirs of his cousin A. I. Del'vig, who attests to A. A. Del'vig's superstitious nature, his vivid imagination, and love of strange stories. A. I. Del'vig also relates the story about Del'vig's own ghost appearing to his friend N. V. Levashev shortly after his death, which Lotman obtains from a second source, the account of E. G. Levasheva. See *Polveka russkoi zhizni: Vospominaniia A. I. Del'viga 1820–1870* (Moscow: Academia, 1930), pp. 108, 169–71.

38. Dobroliubov does mention his interest in rumors in a letter of February 1, 1854, noting that they were especially rife on Mondays, when ecclesiastical academy students returned from Sunday overnight visits. The collective authorship of rumors, embellished with additional contributions by listeners, seemed to interest him most. In this letter, Dobroliubov jokes about writing a "feuilleton" on the subject of these rumors. See *Materialy dlia biografii N. A. Dobroliubova sobrannye v 1861–1862 godakh*, t. 1 (Moscow: V. F. Rikhter, 1890), pp. 79–80.

39. Lotman, pp. 15–16.

40. See also Naum Sindalovskii, *Peterburgskii fol'klor* (SPb: Maksima, 1994) for all manner of orally transmitted Petersburgiana, including proverbs and sayings, particular phraseology, and unofficial names from the eighteenth century up to the 1990s.

41. V. N. Toporov, "Peterburg i 'Peterburgskii tekst russkoi literatury' (Vvedenie v temu)," *Mif. Ritual. Simvol.* (Moscow: Progress, 1995), p. 348, footnote 59.

42. V. N. Toporov, "Peterburgskie teksty i Peterburgskie mify (Zametki iz serii)," p. 369.

43. Naum Sindalovskii, *Peterburg v fol'klore* (SPb: Zhurnal "Neva," ITD "Letnii sad," 1999), pp. 366–67.

44. V. D. Kuznetsov, "Predaniia i legendy Sankt-Peterburga v kontse XIX-nachale XX vv," *Psikhologiia Peterburga i peterburzhtsev za tri stoletiia* (SPb: Nestor, 1999), p. 61.

45. See the chapter "Science and Superstition" in Jeffrey Brooks, *When Russia Learned to Read: Literacy and Popular Culture 1861–1917* (Princeton: Princeton University Press, 1985).

46. See Parts V and VI of Thomas E. Berry, *Spiritualism in Tsarist Society and Literature* (Baltimore: Edgar Allan Poe Society, 1985).

47. My thanks to Richard Freeman for this fascinating observation.

48. Mary Wollstonecraft Shelley, *Frankenstein, or The Modern Prometheus*, James Rieger, ed. (Chicago: University of Chicago Press, 1982), p. 9.

49. For a discussion of how "information" (oral and written) circulated *between* cities before and after the invention of the telegraph in 1844, see Allan R. Pred, *Urban Growth*

and the Circulation of Information: The United States System of Cities, 1790–1840 (Cambridge: Harvard University Press, 1973).

50. Jean-Noel Kapferer, Rumor: Uses, Interpretations, and Images (New Brunswick: Transaction Publishers, 1990), p. 1.

51. In more contemporary parlance, an urban legend might well correspond to a "meme," a viruslike idea that evolves into a large-scale cultural preoccupation by virtue of its Darwinistic success in infecting people's thoughts and lives. See Richard Brodie, Virus of the Mind: The New Science of the Meme (Seattle: Integral Press, 1994).

52. See Peter Brooks's work on plot in "Freud's Masterplot: A Model for Narrative," in Reading for the Plot: Design and Intention in Narrative (Cambridge: Harvard University Press, 1992). Brooks finds that the middle space of "retard, postponement, error, and partial revelation" is the "place of transformation" in narrative (p. 92), which delays the final moment of "the death of the reader in the text" (p. 108).

53. M. I. Pyliaev, Zamichatel'nye chudaki i originaly (Moscow: Orbita, 1990), pp. 387–91.

54. See P. V. Annenkov, Literaturnye vospominaniia (Moscow: Khudozhestvennaia literature, 1983), p. 64.

55. N. V. Gogol, "Shinel'," Polnoe sobranie sochinenii, t. 3 (Moscow: Izdatel'stvo Akademii Nauk, 1938), p. 169.

56. Ibid., p. 173.

57. Vladimir Nabokov, Lectures on Russian Literature, ed. Fredson Bowers (New York: Harcourt Brace Jovanovich, 1981), pp. 58–59.

58. Ibid., p. 60.

59. Gogol, "Nos," PSS, t. 3, p. 75. Translation by Andrew R. MacAndrew in The Diary of a Madman and Other Stories (New York: Signet Classic Penguin Books, 1960), p. 55.

60. Yakov Butkov, "Nevskii Prospekt, ili Puteshestvie Nestora Zaletaeva," Otechestvennye zapiski, no. 60, 1848, p. 148.

61. The story, "Prividenie," was originally published in Literaturnoe pribavlenie k Russkomu Invalidu na 1838 g., no. 40, pp. 781–85. Citations here are taken from V. F. Odoevskii, Romantichestkie povesti (Leningrad, 1929). The same Romantic principle of multiple narrators is used by A. K. Tolstoi in his 1841 vampire tale "Upyr'," set in and around Moscow, and in Italy.

62. Odoevskii, p. 206.

63. For examples, see N. V. Izmailov, "Fantasticheskaia povest'," in Russkaia povest' XIX veka: Istoriia i problematika zhanra, B. S. Meilakh, ed. (Leningrad: Nauka, 1973), p. 140. On occasion, a collection of this type could gather together the multiple oral narrations of an actual gathering in the manner of Boccaccio. During the winter of 1879, for example, when Petersburg was in a panic over an epidemic "plague" and no one could talk of anything else, G. P. Danilevskii, as he notes in an author's preface, spent his evenings with a circle of friends who would meet "at the home of an amiable, cultured Petersburg old-timer." To distract themselves from the epidemic, the group agreed that each member would recount a fantastic tale, and that Danilevskii would keep a written record of the "proceedings," which eventually became a collection of Yuletide stories included in his collected works. The sixth story, "Progulki domovogo," explicitly elaborates the hermeneutic challenge posed by urban legend, making its narrator function as a thwarted detective. See G. P. Danilevskii, "Ot avtora," Sochineniia G.P. Danilevskogo, t. 19 (SPb: Izdanie A. F. Marksa, 1901).

64. Benjamin, "The Storyteller," p. 108.

65. Sigmund Freud, "The Uncanny," p. 340.

66. Friedrich Wilhelm Joseph Schelling, *Philosophie der Mythologie*, (Darmstadt: Wissenschaftliche Buchgesellschaft, 1966), vol. 2, p. 649.

67. Vidler, pp. 17–18.

68. R. G. Nazirov, "Peterburgskaia legenda i literaturnye traditsii," in *Traditsii i novatorstvo*, vyp. 3: *Uchenye zapiski Bashkirskogo Gosudarstvennogo Universiteta*, vyp. 80. Seriia filologicheskikh nauk, 26 (Ufa, 1975), p. 123.

69. Sharon Marcus, *Apartment Stories: City and Home in Nineteenth-Century Paris and London* (Berkeley: University of California Press, 1999), pp. 88–89.

70. Marcus, p. 120. Richard Lehan also links the popularity of the gothic novel with the rise of the "new city," as well as the decline of the landed estate. Gothic novels, he claims, are permeated by a growing sense of doubt about whether the estate constituted a secure refuge from the evils of the big city. The supernatural forces inhabiting the ancestral home thus represent a disruption of the "natural" order of things. See *The City in Literature: An Intellectual and Cultural History* (Berkeley: University of California Press, 1998), pp. 37–39.

71. Marcus, p. 127.

72. This aspect of Petersburg urban legend resembles Charles Dickens's novels *Oliver Twist, The Old Curiosity Shop, Our Mutual Friend*, and *Great Expectations*—in which, in Richard Lehan's view, "there is a sense of the uncanny." Lehan explains, "Between the country and the city is a strange, eerie, primitive world of the marshes—a world of water and mire with houses sinking into the mud, a world of sluice gates and mills. The narrative flash points in Dickens's fiction occur where water and land meet, or where the country and the city intersect, or where the past and the present converge. Here we find the return of the repressed: out of this world emerges a primitive evil, slinking in the form of various almost mutant outcasts." See *The City in Literature*, p. 44.

73. Sindalovskii, *Peterburg v fol'klore*, pp. 374–75.

74. Sindalovskii mentions several individual buildings that were known to be haunted—in the Peski region, on Kamennyi Island, on Bol'shaia Dvorianskaia Street, and on the Petersburg Side. Mikhail Pyliaev similarly describes urban legends connected with buildings on Kazanskaia Street, Malaia Morskaia Street, and along the Ekaterininskii Canal, as well as on Koltovskaia Street (Petersburg Side), Priadil'naia Street (Kolomna), and by the Blagoveshchenskaia Church (Vasilievskii Island), in his "Iz mira tainstvennogo: Starye i novye rasskazy o mediumakh, dukhakh, privideniiakh," *Trud*, 1894, no. 4, pp. 82–84.

75. For an account of this shift as reflected in visual representations of the city, see the chapter "'A Secret Inwardness'" in Grigory Kaganov, *Images of Space: St. Petersburg in the Visual and Verbal Arts*, trans. Sidney Monas (Stanford: Stanford University Press, 1997).

76. A. F. Koni, *Peterburg: Vospominaniia starozhila* (Atenei, 1922), pp. 24–25. Koni's comment about the atmosphere of the repressive final years of Nicholas I's rule resembles nineteenth-century theater chronicler A. I. Wolf's comment that Russian citizens lived for opera and ballet because the autocracy discouraged them from pursuing other civic interests. See *Khronika peterburgskikh teatrov (1826–84)* (St. Petersburg: Tip. R. Golike, 1877, 1884), p. 170. Thus high culture and urban legend may be said to have served similar purposes in the absence of a well-developed "public sphere."

77. For a description of this plan for Vasilievskii Island, see Yuri Egorov, *The Architec-*

tural Planning of St. Petersburg, trans. Eric Dluhosch (Athens: Ohio University Press, 1969), pp. 11–25.

78. For a history of Vasilievskii Island's development, see P. N. Stolpianskii, *Peterburg: Kak voznik, osnovalsia i ros Sankt-Peterburkh* (SPb: Nega, 1995), pp. 111–54.

79. Sindalovskii, *Peterburg: Ot doma k domu*..., p. 279.

80. D. Gubin, L. Lur'e, I. Poroshin, *Real'nyi Peterburg: O gorode s tochki zreniia nedvizhimosti i o nedvizhimosti s tochki zreniia istorii* (SPb: Limbus Press, 1999), p. 129.

81. For discussions of this controversy, see Naum Sindalovskii, *Peterburg: Putevoditel'* (SPb: Norint, 2000), pp. 266–67; K. Gorbachevich and E. Khablo, *Pochemu tak nazvany?* (SPb: Norint, 1998), pp. 284–85; and "Ot chego i kogda proizoshlo nazvanie Vasil'evskogo ostrova?" Smes'. *Syn otechestva*, 1837, no. 185, pp. 105–8.

82. N. V. Gogol, *PSS*, t. 3, pp. 329–30.

83. For more information about this area, see Viktor Annenkov, *Znakomaia i neznakomaia Vyborgskaia storona: Progulki po ulitsam i naberezhnym byvshei peterburgskoi okrainy* (SPb: Sudarynia, 1998).

84. N. A. Sindalovskii, *Peterburg: Ot doma k domu*... *Ot legendy k legende*, pp. 189–90, 195.

85. N. V. Gogol', "Portret," *PSS*, t. 3, p. 119.

86. See V. Sh. Krivonos's treatment of Kolomna in Gogol's story "The Portrait" as "non-space" and "non-being," and simultaneously the space of the demonic in "'... Tut ne stolitsa i ne provintsiia...' (Peterburgskaia okraina u Gogolia)." See *Russkaia provintsiia: Mif—Tekst—Real'nost'*, A. F. Belousov and T. V. Tsiv'ian, sost. (Moscow: "Kollektiv avtorov," 2000), pp. 215–27.

87. Vsevolod Krestovskii, *Peterburgskie trushchoby*, (St. Petersburg, 1996), p. 345.

88. This rumor is discussed in an article by P. Usov, *Novoe vremia*, 1883, no. 2603, as cited in A. Iatsevich, *Pushkinskii Peterburg* (Leningrad: Pushkinskoe obshchestvo, 1935), p. 338.

89. Naum Sindalovskii, *Peterburg: Putevoditel'*, p. 44.

90. Naum Sindalovskii, *Legendy i mify Sankt-Peterburga* (SPb: Norint, 1997), p. 97.

91. For a complete account, see M. I. Pyliaev, *Staryi Peterburg* (Leningrad: Titul, 1990), pp. 378–403.

92. Indeed, the inscription has forty-seven letters, and Paul lived from 1754 until 1801.

93. O. A. Medvedkova, "Predromanticheskie tendentsii v russkom iskusstve rubezha XVIII–XIX vekov. Mikhailovskii zamok," *Russkii klassitsizm vtoroi poloviny XVIII–nachala XIX veka* (Moscow: Izobrazitel'noe iskusstvo, 1994), pp. 166–74.

94. Marquis de Custine, *Empire of the Czar: A Journey through Eternal Russia* (New York: Doubleday, 1989), pp. 105–6.

95. N. S. Leskov, "Prividenie v Inzhenernom zamke (iz kadetskikh vospominanii)," *Sobranie sochinenii v odinatsati tomakh* (Moscow: Khudozhestvennaia literatura, 1958), vol. 7, pp. 110–24.

96. The basis for Leskov's story was an incident related to him by an acquaintance, Engineering Captain Zaporozhskii, in 1881. See the notes to "Prividenie" on pp. 518–19. Zaporozhskii's story concerned the death of General Lomnovskii, while Leskov's story features a General "Lamnovskii." It is not clear whether this slight difference represents Leskov's attempt at fictionalization or perhaps reflects the mishearings and shifts that are so much a part of the transmission of such stories. Similarly, the real Lomnovskii died in January 1860, not in November, as Leskov's story indicates.

97. Toporov, "Peterburgskie teksty i Peterburgskie mify," pp. 386–89.

98. In fact, Sindalovskii claims the well was located in the entrance-hall of the Polovtsov House, but that after the suicide, the well was filled in and the statue moved to the spot in commemoration. See N. A. Sindalovskii, *Peterburg: Ot doma k domu . . . Ot legendy k legende* (SPb: Norint, 2000), p. 256.

99. Stolpianskii, *Peterburg*, p. 263.

100. Veronica Shapovalov, "A. S. Pushkin and the St. Petersburg Text," in *The Contexts of Aleksandr Sergeevich Pushkin*, ed. Peter I. Barta and Ulrich Goebel (Lewiston: The Edwin Mellen Press), p. 45.

101. Iurii Rakov devoted a slim volume to collecting this lore. See his *Pikovyi perekrestok Peterburga* (SPb: Ostrov, 2001).

102. The serial detective story found its way into the street literature of the early twentieth century in Russia, often in adaptations of stories about well-known literary detectives like Sherlock Holmes, Nat Pinkerton, and Nick Carter that made use of foreign settings. See Jeffrey Brooks, *When Russia Learned to Read*, pp. 142–46, 151–53. For a broad study of contemporary Russian detective fiction, a genre that has flourished during the post-Soviet period, see Anthony Olcott, *Russian Pulp: The Detektiv and the Russian Way of Crime* (Lanham, MD: Rowman & Littlefield Publishers, Inc., 2001). Also note the phenomenon of Boris Akunin (pseudonym of Grigory Chkhartishvili), who, beginning in 1998, has produced a series of writerly historical crime novels set at the end of the nineteenth century, featuring the detective Erast Petrovich Fandorin.

103. Lehan, *The City in Literature*, pp. 96–97.

104. Dana Brand argues that the detective as a literary character in urban fiction arose when "the flaneur's method of interpretation became inadequate to the needs of a nineteenth-century audience because it denied what that audience had come to believe, that faces in the urban crowd were illegible and, because of this threatening." See *The Spectator and the City in Nineteenth-Century American Literature* (Cambridge: Cambridge University Press, 1991), pp. 101–5. In discussing Poe's detective-protagonist C. Auguste Dupin, Brand declares, "In order to allow a controlled exposure to urban anxiety, Poe invented the ratiocinative detective, a figure capable of mastering the urban environment without inhibiting its capacity to produce anxiety or terror" (pp. 93–94).

105. Richard Maxwell, *The Mysteries of Paris and London* (Charlottesville, University Press of Virginia, 1992), p. x. An account of similar works about New York by writers such as George Lippard and Ned Buntline is provided by Hans Bergmann in *God in the Streets*, pp. 124–30. The popularity of "urban mysteries" in the West has been attributed to the population's inability to grasp the complex pattern of market relations that organized urban space over the course of the nineteenth century. Commodities seemed to acquire a magical quality because they appeared completely separated from their origins in production. See Alan Trachtenburg, *The Incorporation of America: Culture & Society in the Gilded Age* (New York: Hill and Wang, 1982), pp. 22, 132–39.

106. For an excellent background sketch on Shkliarevskii's life and works, see A. I. Reitblat, "'Russkii Gaborio' ili uchenik Dostoevskogo?," the introductory article to A. Shkliarevskii, *Chto pobudilo k ubiistvu? (Rasskazy sledovatelia)*, A. I. Reitblat, ed. (Moscow: Khudozhestvennaia literatura, 1993). For a broader treatment of the incompatibility between the Western detective genre and the Russian cultural context, see Reitblat's "Detektivnaia Literatura i russkii chitatel' (vtoraia polovina XIX—Nachalo XX vv.)," *Knizhnoe delo v Rossii vo vtorio polovine XIX—Nachale XX veka*, vyp. 7 (SPb: Rossiiskaia Natsional'naia biblioteka, 1994).

107. Four exemplars of this genre, including Shkliarevskii's "Kak on prinudil sebia ubit' ee?" and one story each by A. Mel'nikov, N. Zhivotov, and N. Ponomarev are reprinted in *Peterburgskie pauki*, B. Gertsenzon, ed. (SPb: Lira, 1994).

108. Tsvetan Todorov, "The Secret of Narrative," in *The Poetics of Prose*, trans. Richard Howard (Ithaca: Cornell University Press, 1977), pp. 155–56.

109. Tsvetan Todorov, *The Fantastic: A Structural Approach to a Literary Genre*, trans. Richard Howard (Cleveland: The Press of Case Western Reserve University, 1973), p. 31.

110. V. A. Zhukovskii, *Polnoe sobranie sochinenii v dvadtsati tomakh*, ed. A. S. Arkhangel'skii, t. 10 (SPb: Izdanie A.F. Marksa, 1902), pp. 83–98.

111. For example, see "Prilozhenie. Uedinennyi domik na Vasil'evskom" in A. S. Pushkin, *Polnoe sobranie sochinenii v desiati tomakh*, t. 9 (Moscow: Nauka, 1965), pp. 507–40. This volume also contains "Istoriia Petra" and "Zametki o Kamchatke"—completely unrelated nonfictional works. On the other hand, see N. Brodskii's protest against the inclusion of "The Lonely Cottage" among Pushkin's canonical prose works in his "Novoe o Pushkine," *Golos minuvshego*, 1913, no. 4, p. 271.

112. As with any urban legend, misinformation is part of the story. The memoirs of A. P. Kern mistakenly name *Podsnezhnik* as the 1820s Del'vig almanac in which the story was published. Kern claims to have been present when Pushkin recounted to a small circle of friends the story of "a devil that rides about in a cab on Vasil'evskii Island." See A. P. Kern, *Vospominaniia* (Leningrad: Academia, 1929), p. 253.

113. A. I. Del'vig, *Polveka russkoi zhizni 1820–1870*, vol. I (Moscow: Academia, 1930), pp. 85–86. See also P. E. Shchegolev's article in *Den'*, nos. 81–83, 22, 23, and 24 December, 1912, and N. O. Lerner's article in *Severnye zapiski*, January 1913.

114. For a detailed study of this unrealized theme in Pushkin's oeuvre (including his drawings and doodles), see T. G. Tsiavlovskaia, "'Vliublennyi bes' (Neosushchestvlennyi zamysel Pushkina)." *Pushkin: Issledovaniia i materialy*, t. III (Moscow: Izdatel'stvo AN SSSR, 1960). See also V. Pisnaia, "Fabula 'Uedinennogo domika na Vasil'evskom," *Pushkin i ego sovremenniki*, vyp. XXXI–XXXII, 1927, with which Tsiavlovskaia polemicizes on p. 127 of her article.

115. Vladislav Khodasevich, "Peterburgskie povesti Pushkina," in Pushkin-Titov, *Uedinennyi domik na Vasilievskom* (Moscow: Universal'naia biblioteka, 1915), pp. 3–33.

116. N. V. Izmailov expresses doubt as to whether Pushkin truly made "many" corrections to Titov's manuscript and believes that Pushkin's changes must have concerned matters of plot alone, since "the manner of exposition and style of the story, in which the manner and style of Pushkin's prose are not at all ascertainable (except in individual details), could hardly have been corrected by him. For that, it would have been necessary to rewrite the entire story from scratch, and Pushkin, who evidently had no intention of publishing this oral novella and who had given it away to Titov, could not have had any desire to rework someone else's written transcription." Izmailov notes that V. V. Vinogradov had prepared a lengthy analysis of "The Lonely Cottage" in terms of its relationship to Pushkin's prose style, but that this chapter was ultimately not included in Vinogradov's 1961 *Problema avtorstva i teoriia stilei*. See N. V. Izmailov, "Fantasticheskaia povest'," p. 146. Note also that contemporary critics objected precisely to the story's verbosity. *Severnaia pchela*, for example, pronounced "The Lonely Cottage" "not bad" and the events depicted "rather entertaining," but claimed the story was spoiled by "too many details." See "Novye al'-manakhi na 1829 god," *S.P.*, 1829, no. 6, 12 January. A critic from *Galateia* similarly compared the story with German "ravings" about demonic forces from the previous quarter-

century and called it the weakest prose work in Del'vig's almanac. This same critic alluded to the story's many "inconsistencies," uneven language, and tiresome method of exposition and declared the author to be without talent. See *Galateia*, 1829, ch. 1, no. 5, pp. 272–73. According to A. I. Del'vig's account, Zhukovskii found the story "long and undistinguished" and said as much to Titov, not realizing he was the work's author.

117. A. S. Pushkin, "Uedinennyi domik na Vasil'evskom," *PSS*, t. 9 (Moscow: Nauka, 1965), p. 507. Translation (and subsequent excerpts) taken from *Alexander Pushkin: Complete Prose Fiction*, trans. Paul Debreczeny (Stanford: Stanford University Press, 1983), pp. 470–92.

118. Ibid., p. 537.

119. Tsiavlovskaia, p. 130.

120. V. G. Belinskii, *Polnoe sobranie sochinenii* (Moscow: Izdatel'stvo AN SSSR, 1953–), t. 1, p. 303 and t. 6, p. 426.

121. A. S. Suvorin referred explicitly to Gogol's "Portret" in his 1895 Yuletide story "'Ten' Dostoevskogo," a story about a mysterious portrait of the dead author lying in state and a visitation from the spirit of Dostoevsky himself, who mutters incoherently about Alyosha Karamazov, Tolstoy, and Nietzsche. The story is reprinted in *Peterburgskii sviatochnyi rasskaz*, E. V. Dushechkina, ed. (Leningrad: Petropol', 1991), pp. 139–44.

122. Gogol, "Portret," *PSS*, t. 3, p. 116.

123. Ibid., p. 122.

124. Ibid., p. 125. Note that the earlier version of "The Portrait" does not include this litany of stories that have attached themselves to the moneylender and, by extension, to his portrait.

125. N. V. Gogol, "Portret (Redaktsiia Arabesok)." *PSS*, t. 3, pp. 444–45.

126. Ibid., p. 128.

127. E. A. Sushkova-Khvostova, *Zapiski* (Leningrad, 1928), pp. 351–52, as cited in M. Iu Lermontov, *Sobranie sochinenii v chetyrekh tomakh*, t. 4 (Moscow: Izdatel'stvo Akademii Nauk SSSR, 1959), p. 658.

128. Lermontov, p. 485.

129. Ibid., p. 495.

130. In fact, it seems that the pseudonymous Prince Indostanskii published a supernatural ending for the story in 1897. See K. Indostanskii, *Prizraki—Okonchanie povesti Lermontova* (Moscow: I. N. Kushnerev, 1897), as cited in Thomas E. Berry, *Spiritualism in Tsarist Society and Literature*, p. 60.

Chapter Five

1. Spiro Kostof, *The City Assembled: The Elements of Urban Form through History* (Boston: Little, Brown and Company, 1992), p. 11.

2. These developments stimulated a new valuation of the historical urban border areas by preservationist writers and artists, who romanticized smaller architectural forms and older industrial structures located at the city's former periphery, considering them a last refuge of "Old Petersburg" untouched by the vulgarities of urban-bourgeois life. See I. Iu. Paukov, "Pereferiinye raiony stolitsy glazami peterburzhtsev nachala XIX v," *Antsiferovskie chteniia: Materialy i tezisy konferentsii* (Leningrad: Leningradskoe Otedelenie Sovetskogo Fonda Kul'tury, 1989), pp. 167–69.

3. Note the numerous historical studies by Western scholars on Russian urban culture and social life that emphasize the earliest years of the twentieth century, the so-called "twilight" period of the imperial era. Examples include Laura Engelstein, *The Keys to Happiness: Sex and the Search for Modernity in Fin-de-Siècle Russia* (Ithaca: Cornell University Press, 1992); Stephen P. Frank and Mark D. Steinberg, eds., *Cultures in Flux: Lower-Class Values, Practices, and Resistance in Late Imperial Russia* (Princeton: Princeton University Press, 1994); Louise McReynolds, *Russia at Play: Leisure Activities at the End of the Tsarist Era* (Ithaca: Cornell University Press, 2003); Joan Neuberger, *Hooliganism: Crime, Culture, and Power in St. Petersburg, 1900–1914* (Berkeley: University of California Press, 1993); and Reginald E. Zelnik, ed., *Workers and Intelligentsia in Late Imperial Russia: Realities, Representations, Reflections* (Berkeley: University of California Press, 1999).

4. David Harvey sees urban studies as examining the process that is capital (as Marx conceived it) "as it unfolds through the production of physical and social landscapes and the production of consciousness." See his *Consciousness and the Urban Experience: Studies in the History and Theory of Capitalist Urbanization* (Baltimore: The Johns Hopkins University Press, 1985), p. xviii. Harvey's analysis emphasizes the changing meanings of space and time produced by money as a mediator of commodity exchange, most particularly in Paris, 1850–70.

5. N. A. Sindalovskii, *Istoriia Sankt-Peterburga v predaniiakh i legendakh* (SPb: Norint, 1997), p. 69.

6. For a discussion of the gardens at Peterhof, Tsarskoe Selo, and Pavlovsk, see Margrethe Floryan, *Gardens of the Tsars: A Study of the Aesthetics, Semantics and Uses of Late Eighteenth-Century Russian Gardens* (Aarhus: Aarhus University Press, 1996).

7. William Kinglake, "A Summer in Russia," *The New Monthly Magazine and Humorist*, no. 3, 1846, pp. 30–31.

8. Georgi's 1794–96 description of St. Petersburg and its environs notes that at the time of his writing, the Strelna palace was in such a sorry state that "it is impossible to tour the inside without apprehension." See I. G. Georgi, *Opisanie Rossiisko-Imperatorskogo stolichnogo goroda Sankt-Peterburga i dostopamiatnostei v okrestnostiakh onogo* (SPb: Liga, 1996), p. 517.

9. The notorious Count D. I. Khvostov even composed an 1823 ode entitled "Na pererozhdenie Ekateringofa" (On the Rebirth of Ekaterinhof). See also S. I. Velikanova, "Graviura K. Gampel'na 'Ekateringofskoe gulianie 1-go maia' kak istochnik dlia izucheniia arkhitektury i byta Peterburga 1820-kh godov," in *Staryi Peterburg: Istoriko-etnograficheskie issledovaniia*, N. V. Iukhneva, ed. (Leningrad: Nauka, 1982).

10. See M. I. Mil'chik, "Ropshinskii dvorets—zabytyi pamiatnik arkhitektury XVIII v," *Nevskii arkhiv: Istoriko-kraevedcheskii sbornik* III (SPb: Atheneum-Feniks, 1997).

11. For an account of efforts at one of the palace-parks, see Ia. I. Shurygin, *Petergof: Letopis' vosstanovleniia* (SPb: Abris, 2000).

12. A significant part of Nikolai Antsiferov's work for the Excursion Institute during the early 1920s was devoted to Tsarskoe Selo and Pavlovsk, which were precisely the kind of cultural "organisms" he loved to study. See Antsiferov's monographs *Detskoe Selo* (Moscow-Leningrad, 1927), *Okrestnosti Leningrada. Putevoditel'* (Moscow-Leningrad, 1927), and *Pushkin v Tsarskom Sele (Literaturnaia progulka po Detskomu Selu)* (Leningrad, 1929).

13. E. Gollerbakh, *Gorod muz: Povest' o Tsarskom Sele* (Leningrad, 1930, as reprinted

by LEV in Paris, 1980), p. 20. For an anthology of Tsarskoe Selo poetry, see Boris Chulkov, ed., *Tsarskoe Selo v poezii 1750–2000* (SPb: Fond russkoi poezii, 1999).

14. The earlier "Recollections" poem is the very one whose 1815 reading before the elderly poet Derzhavin provoked much-mythologized raptures over the artistic talents of the young Pushkin, conferring an official eighteenth-century blessing on the future nineteenth-century cultural icon. For an account of Pushkin's 1814 "Recollections" as a "stroll" through the great past works of Derzhavin that turn the older poet into a kind of palace-park monument, see Anna Lisa Crone, "What Derzhavin Heard When Pushkin Read 'Vospominaniia v Tsarskom Sele' in 1815," *Pushkin Review*, vol. 3, 1999.

15. As Roman Jakobson expresses it, "Aside from patriotic pride in the Russian victories, the poet's lyceum memories are the most passable road to a reconciliation with the court." See Roman Jakobson, "The Statue in Pushkin's Poetic Mythology," in *Language in Literature*, Krystyna Pomorska and Stephen Rudy, eds. (Cambridge: Belknap Press of Harvard University Press, 1987), p. 335. For information about the social and literary culture of the Lycée during Pushkin's time, see K. Ia. Grot, *Pushkinskii litsei (1811–1817)* (SPb, 1911), which also includes "Bumagi I-go kursa, sobrannye akademikom Ia. K. Grotom" (Prilozhenie).

16. See the section "'Istoricheskie' teksty Tsarskogo Sela" in V. N. Toporov, "Peterburgskie teksty i peterburgskie mify (Zametki iz serii)," pp. 376–81. For a description of the Tsarskoe Selo elegy as a form celebrating a sacred place of higher life as well as a space for experiencing loss and return, see Anna Lisa Crone, "Akhmatova and the Passing of the Swans," in *A Sense of Place*, Lev Loseff and Barry Scherr, eds. (Columbus: Slavica Publishers, 1993). Note, however, that Osip Mandelstam's 1912 poem "Tsarskoe Selo" departs from this tradition, with its fantasy of military officers' dissolute amusements.

17. Charles Masson, *Secret Memoirs of the Court of Petersburg*, second edition (London: T. N. Longman and O. Rees, 1801), pp. 91–92. For the verses inscribed on the dog Zemira's tombstone and an account of the circumstances under which Count de Ségur composed them for Catherine, see the excerpt from his memoirs in P. E. Mel'gunova, K. V. Sivkovyi, N. P. Sidorovyi, eds., *Russkii byt po vospominaniiam sovremennikov. XVIII vek*, ch. II, (Moscow: Zadruga, 1918), pp. 82–83.

18. The curious combination of premature nostalgia and museum-guide pride became explicitly manifest during the second half of the nineteenth century when the palace-parks became accessible to the general Petersburg public for day-trips. Alexander Geirot's 1868 *Opisanie Petergofa*, for example, provides a guidebook for visitors who come from Petersburg by rail or on the steamers that departed from the English Embankment. Note that there exists a vast Russian-language literature produced after 1917 detailing the features and treasures of each palace-park, which lies outside the scope of this project.

19. *Zapiski Imperatritsy Ekateriny Vtoroi* (SPb: Izdanie A.S. Suvorina, 1907), p. 109.

20. Ibid., p. 131.

21. Ibid., pp. 134–35.

22. For an account of Strelna's early days, see S. Gorbatenko, "Dva petrovskikh ansamblia Strel'ny," *Nevskii arkhiv: Istoriko-kraevedcheskii sbornik* III (SPb: Atheneum-Feniks, 1997). See also P. N. Stolpianskii, *Petergofskaia pershpektiva* (Petrograd, 1923), pp. 35–46.

23. P. P. Svin'in, *Dostopamiatnosti Sankt-Peterburga i ego okrestnostei* (SPb: Liga Plius, 1997), pp. 177–78. Note that Stolpianskii scornfully dismisses Svin'in's "romantic" de-

scription of Strelna in ruins, insisting that historical documents show some use of the palace by Catherine during the 1770s. See *Petergofskaia pershpektiva*, pp. 41–42.

24. See the literary "tour" in V. V. Gerasimov, *Bol'shoi dvorets v Strel'ne—bez chetverti tri stoletiia* (SPb: Almaz, 1997), pp. 86–113.

25. The palace exterior and interior renovations were carried out, up to a point, in accordance with photographs from the imperial period. The new, updated Strelna also included a helicopter landing pad, a colony of VIP bungalows, and an international press center, all constructed for the summit of foreign leaders who met at Strelna to affirm a series of collaborative cultural enterprises. Further wide-ranging restoration and development of the palace grounds are anticipated.

26. Svin'in, p. 38.

27. Note, however, that in monographs from the first part of the twentieth century, preservationists Kurbatov and Lukomskii focused on Pavlovsk as a locus of endangered cultural legacy. See V. Kurbatov, *Pavlovsk: Ocherk-putevoditel'* (SPb, 1912) and G. Lukomskii, *Pavlovsk i Gatchina* (SPb, 1922).

28. Suzanne Massie's study of Pavlovsk details the creation and early days of Pavlovsk, as well as its subsequent fate during the nineteenth century, after the 1917 Revolution, during the Nazi siege of Leningrad, and over the course of the subsequent restoration efforts. Massie thus draws her readers' attention to the peculiarly beloved official status of former imperial residences during Soviet times, although she does not account for this cultural phenomenon. Suzanne Massie, *Pavlovsk: The Life of a Russian Palace* (Boston: Little, Brown, 1990), p. 4.

29. The anniversary volume is entitled *Pavlovsk: Ocherk, istorii, i opisanie 1777–1877* (Sostavleno po porucheniiu Ego Imperatorskogo Vysochestva Gosudaria Velikogo Kniazia Konstantina Nikolaevicha) (SPb, 1877). This volume includes a valuable bibliography "Istochniki k istorii i opisaniiu Pavlovska 1777–1877," pp. 579–92.

30. These are included in the anthology *Tsvetoslov uteshnoi stolitsy: Poeticheskaia istoriia Pavlovska ot dnei ego osnovaniia, pisannaia imenitymi i bezvestnymi stikhotvortsami*, S. V. Vyzhevskii, ed. (Spb: Bip, 1997), pp. 64–69.

31. N. A. Leikin, *Neunyvaiushchie rossiiane: Rasskazy i kartinki s natury* (SPb: N. A. Khana, 1881), p. 137. Leikin is doubtless referring to the Grand Duke Constantine's habit of reviewing lists of applicants for summer dacha rentals in the town of Pavlovsk and refusing anyone who did not meet with his approval.

32. Ibid., p. 144.

33. Aleksandr Benua (Alexander Benois), *Moi vospominaniia v piati knigakh*, kn. 1 (Moscow: Nauka, 1990).

34. Yuri Lotman characterizes dacha culture as such in his posthumously published "Kamen' i trava," *Lotmanovskii sbornik* 1 (Moscow: ITS-Garant, 1995).

35. For a history of Kamennyi Island, see P. Stolpianskii, "Kamennyi Ostrov," in *Stolitsa i usad'ba*, nos. 14–15, 1914.

36. Custine, p. 119.

37. K. Maksimov, "Krestovskii ostrov (Iz vospominanii petrogradskogo starozhila)," *Nasha starina*, no. 7, 1915.

38. M. I. Pyliaev, *Zabytoe proshloe okrestnostei Peterburga* (SPb: Lenizdat, 1996), p. 29.

39. The Islands became prominent sites of mass entertainment after the Revolution—to wit, the Central Park of Culture and Rest established on Elagin alongside the beautiful architectural ensemble created by Carlo Rossi during the first quarter of the nine-

teenth century. See V. P. Ivanova, ed., *Sady i parki Leningrada* (Leningrad: Lenizdat, 1981), pp. 138–59.

40. V. O. Mikhnevich, "Peterburgskie sady i ikh etnografiia," *Iazvy Peterburga: Sbornik gazetnogo fel'etona kontsa XIX—nachala XX vv.* (Leningrad: Leningradskoe Otdelenie Sovetskogo Fonda Kul'tury, 1990).

41. K. G. Isupov, "Dialog stolits v istoricheskom dvizhenii," *Moskva-Peterburg: Pro et Contra* (SPb: Izdatel'stvo Russkogo Khristianskogo Gumanitarnogo Instituta, 2000), p. 45.

42. Stephen Lovell, "Between Arcadia and Suburbia: Dachas in Late Imperial Russia," *Slavic Review*, vol. 61, no. 1, Spring 2002, p. 87... Lovell provides an excellent historical survey of this expanding culture during its final decades. For a full-scale survey of modern Russian dacha culture, see his *Summerfolk: A History of the Dacha, 1710–2000* (Ithaca: Cornell University Press, 2003).

43. E. B. Iakovleva, "Dachnaia arkhitektura severnykh okrestnostei Sankt-Peterburga vo vtoroi polovine XIX—nachale XX v," *Peterburgskie chteniia—97: Peterburg i Rossiia* (SPb: Petrovskii fond, 1997), p. 233.

44. S. V. Svetlov, *Peterburgskaia zhizn' v kontse XIX stoletiia (v 1892 godu)* (SPb: Giperion, 1998), p. 21.

45. Faddei Bulgarin, "Dachi," *Severnaia pchela*, 176, 9 August 1837, p. 703.

46. See the cycle "Peterburgskie dacha i okrestnosti" in *Literaturnaia gazeta* for 1844, no. 17 (4 May), no. 18 (11 May), no. 23 (15 June), no. 27 (13 July), no. 28 (20 July), and no. 30 (3 August).

47. N. A. Nekrasov, "Peterburgskie dachi i okrestnosti (4 May 1844)," *Polnoe sobranie sochinenii i pisem v piatnadtsati tomakh*, vol. 12 (SPb: Nauka, 1995), pp. 87–88.

48. "Peterburgskaia khronika (24 August 1844)," *PSS*, vol. 12, p. 129.

49. A three-part story-feuilleton by Alexander Druzhinin published in *Sovremennik* in 1850 reflects the continued evolving life of the "dacha theme." Druzhinin's narrator searches the dacha colonies for an elusive beauty named Tanya, and the story traces his picaresque wanderings from one social misadventure to the next. See "Santimental'noe puteshestvie Ivana Chernoknizhnikova po peterburgskim dacham," *Sovremennik*, 1850, vol. 22 (pp. 54–75, 177–257) and 23 (193–97).

50. Nekrasov's journalistic efforts are a prelude to a long tradition of fictional works that situate themselves in the dacha regions, that literary crossroads of nature and culture. Other works include Ivan Kushchevskii's stories "Dlia popravki zdorov'ia" and "Predmet vseobshchei zavisti" (both published posthumously in 1881), Chekhov's story "Dachniki" (1885), the lengthy "dacha" interlude (chapters XIV–XXV) in D. N. Mamin-Sibiriak, *Cherty iz zhizni Pepko* (1894), and Gorky's 1904 play "Dachniki."

51. For more on Petersburg dacha culture of this period, see *Peterburgskie dachi i dachniki* (SPb, 1867); N. Fedotov, *Putevoditel' po dachnym mestnostiam, vodolechebnym zavedeniiam i morskim kupan'iam v okrestnostiakh S.-Peterburga i po zheleznym dorogam* (SPb, 1889) and *Peterburgskie dachnye mestnosti v otnoshenii ikh zdorovosti* (SPb, 1881, 1892); V. Mikhnevich, *Peterburgskoe leto* (SPb, 1887); P. N. Stolpianskii, *Dachnye okrestnosti Peterburga* (Petrograd, 1923). The prolific N. A. Leikin published several collections about dacha life: *Na lone prirody: Iumoristicheskie ocherki podgorodnoi derevenskoi dachnoi zhizni* (SPb, 1893), *Dachnye stradal'tsy* (SPb, 1897), and *Na dachnom proziabanii* (SPb, 1900). See also Deotto Patricia, "Peterburgskii dachnyi byt XIX v. kak fakt massovoi kul'tury," in *Europa Orientalis*, 1991, no. 1.

52. Lovell, *Summerfolk*, pp. 116–17.

53. Bater, pp. 156–57.

54. See, for example, Kagan, pp. 284–85.

55. For a survey of the entire literature of poverty in the Petersburg tradition, see Gian Piero Piretto, *Derelitti, bohémiens e malaffari: il mito povero di Pietroburgo* (Bergamo: P. Lubrina, 1989).

56. For a study of "the poetics of the perception of poverty" in Russian literature that includes works by Gogol and Dostoevsky, see David Herman, *Poverty of the Imagination: Nineteenth-Century Russian Literature about the Poor* (Evanston: Northwestern University Press, 2001).

57. The 1840s also saw the publication of landmark journal articles such as the 1848 piece on Petersburg real estate by K. Veselovskii that included a lengthy section on the living conditions of the city's humblest residents. See "Statisticheskie issledovaniia o nedvizhimykh imushchestvakh v Sanktpeterburge," *Otechestvennye zapiski*, 1848, t. LVII, otd. II, pp. 1–27.

58. James H. Bater, "Between Old and New: St. Petersburg in the Late Imperial Era," in *The City in Late Imperial Russia*, Michael F. Hamm, ed. (Bloomington: Indiana University Press, 1986), pp. 56–57.

59. Donald Fanger, *Dostoevsky and Romantic Realism; A Study of Dostoevsky in Relation to Balzac, Dickens, and Gogol* (Chicago: University of Chicago Press, 1967), p. 189. Fanger acknowledges his debt on this topic to Leonid Grossman, who discusses the many nonfiction periodical articles devoted to social problems from the same period. See "Gorod i liudi *Prestupleniia i nakazaniia*," which provides the introduction to F. M. Dostoevsky, *Prestuplenie i nakazanie* (Moscow, 1935). Another useful source on this aspect of the novel is F. I. Evnin, "Roman *Prestupleniie i nakazanie*" in *Tvorchestvo F. M. Dostoevskogo*, N. L. Stepanov, ed. (Moscow, 1959).

60. For a cultural "case study" of the Haymarket as site of interaction and symbol of urban blight, see Hubertus F. Jahn, "Der St. Petersburger Heumarkt im 19. Jahrhundert. Metamorphosen eines Stadtviertels," *Jahrbücher für Geschichte Osteuropas* 44 (1996).

61. James H. Bater, *St. Petersburg: Industrialization and Change*, (London: E. Arnold, 1976), pp. 326–27.

62. The Viazemskii slums also housed the ironically named "Crystal Palace" tavern featured in *Crime and Punishment*—the site of a dramatic confrontation between Raskolnikov and Svidrigailov.

63. G. H. Kudriavtseva, "Siuzhetnye situatsii i motivy romana V. Krestovskogo 'Peterburgskie trushchoby,'" *Voprosy khudozhestvennogo metoda, zhanra i kharaktera v russkoi literature XVIII-XIX vekov* (Moscow, 1975), pp. 205–6.

64. Krestovskii's was not the first full-scale attempt in Russian literature to match Sue's success. In 1845–46, Egor Kovalevskii—a writer known more for travel writing than for urban fictional prose—published his *Mystères*-inspired *Peterburg dnem i noch'iu* in six installments of the journal *Biblioteka dlia chteniia*. Indeed, Sue cast a long shadow in Russian literature; Dostoevsky's 1861 retrograde roman-feuilleton *Unizhennye i oskorblennye* harks back to Sue's *Mystères* with recourse to familiar elements such as the abandoned little girl Nellie, her mother ruined and cast aside by the evil Prince Valkovskii, and the dark apartment stairways and corridors along which the narrator must follow the story's improbably interconnected plots.

65. Irina Sobkowska Ashcroft finds a "remarkable resemblance" between Krestovskii's

Peterburgskie trushchoby and Sue's *Mystères de Paris* "in almost all respects," including subplots, characters, serialized narrative structure, "documentary" technique, stylistics, and the specific social themes and conditions. See Irina Sobkowska Ashcroft, "*Peterburgskie Trushchoby*: A Russian Version of *Les Mystères de Paris*," *Revue de Littérature Comparée*, t. LIII, no. 2, April–June 1979, pp. 163–64.

66. Kudriavtseva, pp. 210–20.

67. Prior to beginning his novel, Krestovskii published three cycles of sketches about life in the capital—"Peterburgskie tipy," "Peterburgskie zolotokopateli," and "Fotograficheskie kartiny peterburgskoi zhizni"—thus undergoing a literary apprenticeship in depicting Petersburg.

68. V. V. Krestovskii, *Peterburgskie trushchoby (Kniga o sytykh i golodnykh)*, kn. 1 (SPb: Sankt-Peterburgskaia tip. no. 6, 1996), p. 3.

69. Ibid., p. 4.

70. In a letter written twenty-five years after the novel's publication, Krestovskii claimed that in preparation for writing *Peterburgskie trushchoby*, he "devoted nearly nine months to a preliminary acquaintance with the world of the slums, visited the chambers of police detectives, prisons, courts, the dens of Haymarket Square (the Viazemskii slums), and so forth." See "Pis'mo A.V. Zhirkevichu, 25 February 1892," *Istoricheskii vestnik*, 1895, no. 3, p. 880.

71. V. V. Krestovskii, *Peterburgskie trushchoby (Kniga o sytykh i golodnykh)*, kn. 2, p. 536.

72. N. Smirnov, "Slova i vyrazheniia vorovskogo iazyka, vybrannye iz romana Vs. Krestovskogo—'Peterburgskie trushchoby,'" *Izvestiia otdeleniia russkogo iazyka i slovestnosti Imperatorskoi Akademii Nauk*, t. 4 (SPb, 1899).

73. Ibid., p. 359.

74. N. I. Sveshnikov, *Vospominaniia propashchego cheloveka* (Moscow: Novoe literaturnoe obozrenie, 1996), p. 55.

75. Ibid., p. 132.

76. A condensed summary of these articles is included in Sveshnikov's memoirs, pp. 153–63.

77. Other contributions from this earlier period include the anonymous *Sinks of London Laid Open* (1848), Thomas Beames's *The Rookeries of London* (1852), John Garwood's *The Million-Peopled City, or One-Half of the People of London Made Known to the Other Half* (1853), and John Hollingshead's *Ragged London in 1861*.

78. For more on this literature of urban exploration, see the chapter "Urban Spectatorship" in Judith R. Walkowitz, *City of Dreadful Delight: Narratives of Sexual Danger in Late-Victorian London* (Chicago: University of Chicago Press, 1992).

79. Lev Lur'e has characterized the marginal yet ubiquitous Petersburg journalists as "omnipresent, persistent, badly dressed individuals, who interspersed the completion of editorial commissions with sessions at journalists' taverns, jacks-of-all-trades, who were just as prepared to write a novel and sequel from the life of some exotic pirate as a feuilleton about the predicament of the national grain trade, or reportage of fistfights." L. Ia. Lur'e, "Predislovie," *Iazvy Peterburga: Sbornik gazetnogo fel'etona kontsa XIX—nachala XX vv.* (Leningrad: Leningradskoe Otdelenie Sovetskogo Fonda Kul'tury, 1990), p. 5.

80. In an earlier collection called *Malen'kie kartiny peterburgskoi zhizni* (1884), whose lengthy first part was devoted to "Brodiachii Peterburg," Mikhnevich provided a series of "fleeting observations" concerning the "habits and customs" of Petersburg itinerants. In *Malen'kie kartiny*, "vagabondage" (*brodiazhnichestvo*) referred to eccentric idlers from

the intelligentsia, and not to the poor and homeless. The marginal figures in *Little Pictures* were thus merely literary and social curiosities. In his other writings, Mikhnevich did not focus exclusively on the urban poor and even published a *roman-feuilleton* in the tradition of Sue and Krestovskii, *V peterburgskom omute* (1879), which follows the maximal "social canvas" approach of his two predecessors instead of using the slums as primary setting.

81. V. O. Mikhnevich, "Vvedenie," *Iazvy Peterburga: Opyt istoriko-statisticheskogo issledovaniia nravstvennosti stolichnogo naseleniia* (SPb, 1886), pp. xxviii–xxix.

82. A. Bakhtiarov, "Nochlezhniki i nochlezhnye doma," "Nishchie," "Peterburgskie raznoschiki," "Triapichniki," *Proletariat i ulichnye tipy Peterburga: Bytovye ocherki* (SPb, 1895).

83. N. N. Zhivotov, "Sredi brodiazhek: Shest' dnei v roli oborvantsa," *Peterburgskie profili*, vyp. II (SPb: A. Vineke, 1894), p. 43.

84. Maxim Gorky would dramatize such characters on stage in his play *Na dne* (1902), set in a flophouse, albeit not in Petersburg.

85. Zhivotov, p. 61.

86. N. V. Nikitin, "Predislovie," *Peterburg noch'iu: Bytovye ocherki* (SPb, 1903).

87. Note, however, that this neglect is beginning to correct itself. Mikhnevich, Bakhtiarov, and Zhivotov have all merited lengthy entries in the recent multivolume reference work *Russkie pisateli 1800–1917: biograficheskii slovar'* (Moscow: Sovetskaia entsiklopediia, 1989–).

88. Grigory Kaganov, *Images of Space: St. Petersburg in the Visual and Verbal Arts*, trans. Sidney Monas (Stanford: Stanford University Press, 1997) p. 108.

89. See chapter 14 of M. I. Pyliaev, *Staryi Peterburg* (Leningrad: Titul, 1990 reprint), as well as N. A. Leikin, *Stseny iz kupecheskogo byta* (SPb, 1871) and *Apraksintsy: Stseny i ocherki iz byta i nravov peterburgskikh rynochnykh torgovtsev i ikh prikazchikov polveka nazad* (SPb, 1864). See also G. T. Polilov-Severtsev, *Nashi dedy-kuptsy: Bytovye kartiny nachala XIX stoletiia* (SPb, 1907).

90. In Peter's time, vessels were built at the prominently situated Admiralty, and a cannon foundry called the Liteinyi Dvor (later the Arsenal) stood on the Neva bank near the Summer Garden. There is a substantial body of scholarship describing manufacturing facilities and other industries in Petersburg during the time of Peter the Great. Examples include the chapter "Industrializatsiia po-Petrovski" in E. Anisimov, *Vremia petrovskikh reform* (Leningrad: Lenizdat, 1989), the chapter "Promyshlennost' i torgovlia" in V. V. Mavrodin, *Osnovanie Peterburga* (Leningrad: Lenizdat, 1983). See also P. N. Stolpianskii's chapter "Rabochii Peterburg" in *Peterburg: Kak voznik, osnovalsia i ros Sankt-Peterburkh* (SPb: Nega, 1995), which describes a number of fanciful manufacturing projects from the eighteenth century.

91. James H. Bater, *St. Petersburg: Industrialization and Change* (London: Edward Arnold, 1976), p. 92. For more information about Petersburg's emerging urban proletariat, see T. M. Kitanina, "Rabochie Peterburga v period razlozheniia i krizisa krepostnichestva (1800–1861 gg.)" and I. A. Baklanova, "Formirovanie i polozhenie promyshlennogo proletariata. Rabochee dvizhenie (60-e gody—nachalo 90-kh godov)" in *Istoriia rabochikh Leningrada*, t. 1 (Leningrad: Nauka, 1972).

92. For a detailed discussion of St. Petersburg industrialization during the second half of the nineteenth century, see "Promyshlennost'" in *Ocherki istorii Leningrada*, t. 2 (Moscow-Leningrad: Izdatel'stvo Akademii Nauk SSSR, 1957).

93. Bater, p. 222.

94. See V. V. Pokshishevskii, "Territorial'noe formirovanie promyshlennogo kompleksa Peterburga v XVIII–XIX vekakh," *Voprosy geografii*, t. 20 (Moscow: Gosudarstvennoe izdatel'stvo geograficheskoi literatury, 1950).

95. See Stolpianskii, *Peterburg: Kak voznik, osnovalsia i ros Sanktpiterburkh* (SPb: Nega, 1995), pp. 361–62.

96. Bater, p. 322.

97. The same seems to be true for Russian intellectual history in general. For a discussion of the paucity of pronouncements on industrialization and economic development among imperial Russia's foremost intelligentsia until the very end of the nineteenth century, see Alexander Gerschenkron, "Economic Development in Russian Intellectual History of the Nineteenth Century," in *Economic Backwardness in Historical Perspective: A Book of Essays* (Cambridge: The Belknap Press of Harvard University Press, 1962). Gerschenkron declares, "As the industrialization of the country gathered momentum, the process was either overlooked or viewed as transitory, and deplored withal," and thus "what must appear to those interested in literature, sociology, perhaps philosophy, as the golden age of the Russian intelligentsia appears far from brilliant to the economist" (p. 181).

98. Indeed, by the end of the 1830s, St. Petersburg periodicals regularly included descriptions of new factories, as well as commentary on the changing face of the industrializing city. Given the dearth of belletristic writing about nineteenth-century industrial workers' lives prior to the 1870s, police and public health reports, as well as city directories and street maps, statistics on industrial enterprises, and census materials also constitute major sources of information about this aspect of Petersburg, confirming the significant presence of factories and factory-workers. P. N. Stolpianskii, for example, relies upon reports by medical officials to convey the living conditions of factory workers during the latter part of the nineteenth century. See chapter 4 of his *Zhizn' i byt peterburgskoi fabriki, 1704–1914 gg.* (Leningrad: Izdanie Leningradskogo Gubernskogo Soveta Professional'nykh Soiuzov, 1925).

99. "O novom manufakturnom gorode voznikaiushchem v predmestiiakh S.-Peterburga," *Severnaia pchela*, no. 274, 4 December 1839. For historical background on the Aleksandrovskaia complex beginning in the eighteenth century, see P. N. Stolpianskii, *Peterburg*, pp. 358–61.

100. See also the earlier piece in the "Statistika" section, "Aleksandrovskaia manufaktura v nachale 1831 goda," *Severnaia pchela*, nos. 109, 110, 111, 112, and 113, May 1831.

101. For a detailed discussion, see Evel G. Economakis, *From Peasant to Petersburger* (New York: St. Martin's Press, 1998).

102. Bater, p. 257

103. Rose Glickman believes that the Russian intelligentsia evinced little interest in the factory worker prior to the reign of Alexander II because serfdom and the plight of the rural peasant were considered far more pressing issues. See Rose L. Glickman, "Industrialization and the Factory Worker in Russian Literature," *Canadian-Slavic Studies*, vol. 4, no. 4, 1970, pp. 629–30.

104. For background on the contact between the populist intelligentsia and the proletariat, see Reginald E. Zelnik, "Workers and Intelligentsia in the 1870s: The Politics of Sociability," in *Workers and Intelligentsia in Late Imperial Russia: Realities, Representations, Reflections*, Reginald E. Zelnik, ed. (Berkeley: University of California International and Area Studies, 1999).

105. See "Aleksandrovskaia manufaktura v nachale 1831 goda," *Severnaia pchela*, no. 112, May 1831 for an account of the Foundling Home boys and girls employed at the factories, whose living conditions are presented in entirely positive terms.

106. D. S. Mirsky, *A History of Russian Literature* (New York: Alfred A. Knopf, 1949), p. 291.

107. Mirsky, p. 333.

108. M. S. Stieglitz, *Promyshlennaia arkhitektura Peterburga*, 2nd edition (SPb, 1996). Brodsky noted the affinity between Petersburg's traditional architecture and its industrial facilities, albeit ironically, in his characterization of the rapidly growing city in 1900: "Industry was booming and smokestacks rose around the city like a brick echo of its colonnades." See "A Guide to a Renamed City," p. 84.

109. Factories were part of the Petersburg cityscape from the earliest years, as Stieglitz observes. Among the first industrial structures, both state and private, were the Kronwerk shipyard (1703), Admirality (1704), Izhorskii factory (1706), Sestroretskii factory (1721), Porokhovoi (gunpowder) factory (1710), Liteinyi (foundry) and Pushechnyi (gun) facilities (1711–12), Galernaia shipyard (1712), Partikuliarnaia shipyard (1718), Shpalernaia textile plant (1718), Isaev tannery (1718), and Peterhof lapidary works (1725). None of these original structures have survived, although their images remain in the engravings of Zubov and Makhaev, among others.

110. Stieglitz, p. 6.

111. Stieglitz, Introduction by Valentina Lelina, pp. 3–4.

112. Lelina asks pointedly, "If we do not have the means to create a museum of the history of technology and industrial design, then perhaps we should not hurry to smelt down these unique exemplars? Perhaps it might be more profitable to sell them to already-existing museums in Europe?" (p. 4). Lelina also suggests that these buildings might be put to other uses, for trade, exhibitions, and community centers. Stieglitz suggests that the "picturesque" old factories lying in the outskirts of Petersburg, with their fascinating and aesthetically pleasing obsolete technology, might well serve as special museum-parks. See Stieglitz, p. 52.

113. *Handbook for Northern Europe* (London: John Murray, 1849), p. 506. Murray notes that these "industrial establishments" all belong either to the crown or to foreign proprietors. Strangely, this section on "Factories" is absent from the 1868 and 1875 editions of what was then Murray's *Handbook for Travellers in Russia, Poland, and Finland*.

114. Vasilii Mikhnevich's 1874 *Peterburg ves' na ladoni*, in contrast, features a large section titled "Industry and Trade," filled with tables and statistics, locations of trade and retail sites, and listings of manufacturing facilities for the production of foodstuffs, household goods, clothing, building supplies, metalwork and instruments, chemicals, and paper products. See pp. 447–543.

115. I. A. Goncharov, *Obyknovennaia istoriia, Sobranie sochinenii*, t. 1 (Moscow: Khudozhestvennaia literatura, 1952), pp. 59–60.

116. N. A. Nekrasov, "O pogode (Komu kholodno, komu zharko)," *PSS*, t. 2 (Moscow: Khudozhestvennaia literatura, 1948), p. 214.

117. For purposes of comparison, see the large body of English verse on industrial themes (mid-1700s to mid-1900s) anthologized in *The Industrial Muse: The Industrial Revolution in English Poetry*, compiled by Jeremy Warburg (London: Oxford University Press, 1958).

118. L. A. Mei, "Dym," *Izbrannye proizvedeniia* Biblioteka poeta. Bol'shaia Seriia. (Leningrad: Sovetskii pisatel', 1972), pp. 102–5.

119. Catherine Gallagher, *The Industrial Reformation of English Fiction: Social Discourse and Narrative Form, 1832–1867* (Chicago: University of Chicago Press, 1985), p. xi.

120. See Raymond Williams's chapter "The Industrial Novels," in *Culture and Society, 1780–1950* (London: Hogarth Press, 1993).

121. Adrienne Siegel, *The Image of the American City in Popular Literature 1820–1870* (Port Washington: Kennikat Press, 1981), p. 77. For a study of the evolving discourse on industrialization, see Leo Marx, *The Machine in the Garden: Technology and the Pastoral Ideal in America* (New York: Oxford University Press, 1964).

122. According to Rose Glickman, Reshetnikov's magnum opus is "the only Russian novel of the nineteenth century which can be compared in scope and detail with the industrial novels of nineteenth-century England, such as those of Mrs. Gaskell, Disraeli, Kingsley, and others." See Glickman, pp. 634–35.

123. Reshetnikov's diary from 1868 states, "On the embankment of the Obvodnyi canal, I was for the first time compelled to make closer acquaintance than anyone yet had with the Petersburg workers. These are a crushed people, unable to raise a protest because there is no unity among the workers . . ." *Iz literaturnogo naslediia F. M. Reshetnikova*, I. I. Veksler, ed. (Leningrad: Akademiia Nauk SSSR, Institut Russkoi Literatury, 1932), p. 281.

124. Reshetnikov's earlier novels *Gornorabochie* (1866) and *Glumovy* (1866–67, pub. 1880) treat the conditions of the Ural mineworkers, but do not take their peasant protagonists out of the provinces. See also D. N. Mamin-Sibiriak's novel about Ural industrialists and workers, *Gornoe gnezdo* (1884).

125. A few obscure nineteenth-century Russian populist novels take up industrialization as seen through the eyes of a socially conscious *raznochinets* hero in locations other than Petersburg—examples include I. V. Omulevskii's *Shag za shagom* (1869–70), set in a state glass and textile factory near a Siberian village, and K. M. Staniukovich's *Bez iskhoda* (1871), set in a fictitious manufacturing town.

126. F. M. Reshetnikov, *Izbrannye proizvedeniia*, t. 2 (Moscow: Khudozhestvennaia literature, 1956), pp. 611–12.

127. For a discussion of writers from the worker class during the early part of the twentieth century, see Mark D. Steinberg, "The Injured and Insurgent Self: The Moral Imagination of Russia's Lower-Class Writers," in *Workers and Intelligentsia in Late Imperial Russia*, Zelnik, ed.

128. N. A. Blagoveshchenskii, "Na liteinom zavode," *Russkie ocherki*, B. O. Kostelianets and P. A. Sidorov, eds., t. 2 (Moscow: Khudozhestvennaia literature, 1956), p. 447. This collection includes other nineteenth-century sketches that describe factory environments, but none of these are set in Petersburg. See A. P. Golitsynskii, "Ocherki fabrichnoi zhizni" (1861), F. M. Reshetnikov "Gornozavodskie liudi" (1863), N. N. Zlatovratskii, "Gorod rabochikh" (1885), V. G. Korolenko, "Pavlovskie ocherki" (1890), and A. S. Serafimovich, "Na zavode" (1899), as well as Blagoveshchenskii's "Na tkatskoi fabrike" (1870), "Na bolote" (1870), and "Sel'skie farforovye zavody" (1871). *Russkie ocherki*, a three-volume collection of sketches, exemplifies the new lease on life given to this loosely defined body of work by the Soviet literary establishment, which appropriated these populist writings for its own ideological and cultural context.

129. Ibid., p. 451.

130. Ibid., p. 453.

131. Gleb Uspenskii, "S konki na konku," *PSS*, t. 3 (1908), p. 163.

132. F. M. Lur'e, Introduction to A. A. Bakhtiarov, *Briukho Peterburga* (SPb: Fert, 1994), p. 8. The title of Bakhtiarov's collection of sketches evokes Émile Zola's novel *The Belly of Paris* (*Le Ventre de Paris*), published in 1873 as the third novel in his naturalist series *Les Rougon-Macquart*. Like Bakhtiarov's sketches, Zola's novel takes as its settings the food markets of a big city, but with a more explicitly critical social consciousness.

133. Bakhtiarov, p. 15.

134. Ibid., p. 148.

135. Ibid., p. 177.

136. A. A. Bakhtiarov, *Proletariat i ulichnye tipy Peterburga*, p. 110.

137. Ibid., pp. 113–17.

138. Ibid., p. 136.

139. V. G. Korolenko, *Istoriia moego sovremennika*, t. 2, ch. 1 (Moscow: Zadruga, 1920), p. 61.

140. Ibid., pp. 62–64.

141. Andrei Bely, *Petersburg*, translated, annotated, and introduced by Robert A. Maguire and John E. Malmstad (Bloomington: Indiana University Press, 1978), p. 9.

142. Ibid., p. 11.

143. Ibid., pp. 51–52.

144. Ibid., p. 66.

145. Ibid., p. 273.

146. Ibid., p. 288.

Chapter Six

1. Iu. M. Lotman, *Universe of the Mind: A Semiotic Theory of Culture*, trans. Ann Shukman (Bloomington: Indiana University Press, 1990), p. 141. (Translation of "Simvolika Peterburga i problemy semiotiki goroda.")

2. Marika Fazolini, "Vzgliad na usad'bu, ili Predstavlenie provintsialov o russkoi stolichnoi zhizni," in *Russkaia provintsiia: Mif—Tekst—Real'nost'*, A. F. Belousov and T. V. Tsiv'ian, ed. (Moscow: "Kollektiv avtorov," 2000), p. 177. See also *Mir russkoi provintsii i provintsial'naia kul'tura*, G. Iu. Sternin, ed. (SPb: Dmitri Bulanin, 1997).

3. V. A. Koshelev, "O 'literaturnoi' provintsii i literaturnoi 'provintsial'nosti' novogo vremeni," *Russkaia provintsiia*, pp. 40–41. In a similar vein, Lotman defines a semiosphere as "the semiotic space necessary for the existence and functioning of languages," and sees language as "a cluster of semiotic spaces and their boundaries, which, however clearly defined these are in the language's grammatical self-description, in the reality of semiosis are eroded and full of transitional forms." See *Universe of the Mind*, pp. 123–24, 134.

4. See Kaganov's discussion of Quarenghi's work in *Images of Space: St. Petersburg in the Visual and Verbal Arts*, Sidney Monas, ed. (Stanford: Stanford University Press, 1997), pp. 30–38.

5. Koshelev, p. 54.

6. For a discussion of post-*perestroika* Petersburg as a "cosmopolitan province" re-

flecting and renewing the earlier postrevolutionary "nostalgia for world culture" that was invoked by poet Osip Mandelstam, see chapter 9 in Svetlana Boym, *The Future of Nostalgia* (New York: Basic Books, 2001).

7. V. N. Toporov, "Peterburg i 'Peterburgskii text russkoi literatury' (Vvedenie v temu)," *Mif. Ritual. Simvol. Obraz: Issledovaniia v oblasti mifopoeticheskogo* (Moscow: Progress, 1995), p. 319.

8. K. G. Isupov identifies another trend in this subgenre deriving from the *lubok* print tradition, including anonymous works such as "Fomushka in Piter" that are hybrids of oral and print cultures. K. G. Isupov, "Dialog stolits v istoricheskom dvizhenii." *Moskva-Peterburg: Pro et Contra* (SPb: Izdatel'stvo Russkogo Khristianskogo Gumanitarnogo Instituta, 2000), pp. 40–41.

9. See, for example, K. F. Ryleev, "Provintsial v Peterburge," *Polnoe sobranie sochinenii* (Academia, 1934); Faddei Bulgarin, "Pis'ma provintsialki iz stolitsy (Pis'mo pervoe)," *Severnaia pchela*, June 10, 1830, no. 69 through August 26, no. 102; A. I. Kronenberg, "Perepiska mezhdu peterburgtsem i provintsialom," *Sovremennik*, 1848, t. VIII (Mody), pp. 1–12; t. IX, pp. 1–6; and t. X, otd. V, pp. 7–11, published under the pseudonym "Vladimir Chulkov"; I. A. Goncharov, "Pis'ma stolichnogo druga k provintsial'nomu zhenikhu," *Sobranie sochinenii*, t. 7 (Moscow: Pravda, 1952); M. E. Saltykov-Shchedrin, "Dnevnik provintsiala v Peterburge," *Sobranie sochinenii*, t. 10 (Moscow: Khudozhestvennaia literatura, 1970); and Gleb Uspenskii, "Peterburgskie pis'ma. Pis'mo pervoe," *Nesobrannye proizvedeniia*, t. 1 (Moscow: Khudozhestvennaia literatura, 1936).

10. S. N. Krivenko, *M. E. Saltykov. Ego zhizn' i literaturnaia deiatel'nost'* (Petrograd, 1914), p. 91.

11. M. E. Saltykov-Shchedrin, "Dnevnik provintsiala v Peterburge," *Sobranie sochinenii*, t. 10 (Moscow: Khudozhestvennaia literatura, 1970), p. 271.

12. Toporov, p. 277.

13. N. A. Verderevskaia, *Stanovlenie tipa raznochintsa v russkoi realisticheskoi literature 40–60kh godov XIX veka* (Kazan: Kazanskii Gosudarstvennyi Pedagogicheskii Institut, 1975), p. 4.

14. J. J. van Baak, "On Space in Russian Literature: A Diachronic Problem," in *Dutch Contributions to the Ninth International Congress of Slavists*, A.G.F. van Holk, ed. (Amsterdam: Rodopi, 1983), p. 40. Sometimes the plot moves in the opposite direction, with the Petersburg-trained *raznochinets* hero going to the provinces—as a tutor or a teacher, or perhaps as a guest at a friend's country estate. Works by Herzen, Turgenev, and Chekhov, among others, treat this reverse trajectory.

15. Joseph Brodsky notes, "all these writers belonged, to use an economic stratification, to the middle class: the class which is almost solely responsible for the existence of literature everywhere. With two or three exceptions, all of them lived by the pen, i.e., meagerly enough to understand without exegesis or bewilderment the plight of those worse off as well as the splendor of those at the top." Joseph Brodsky, "A Guide to a Renamed City," in *Less Than One: Selected Essays* (New York: Farrar, Straus, & Giroux, 1986), p. 79.

16. For examples of nineteenth-century usages of the term in connection with writers and other cultural figures, see Elise Kimerling Wirtschafter, *Structures of Society: Imperial Russia's "People of Various Ranks"* (DeKalb: Northern Illinois University Press, 1994), pp. 98–109.

17. For a treatment of this sociocultural dynamic, see William Mills Todd III, *Fiction*

and Society in the Age of Pushkin: Ideology, Institutions, and Narrative (Cambridge: Harvard University Press, 1986).

18. Harry Levin, *The Gates of Horn* (New York, 1963), p. 85.

19. As Sidney Monas points out, the story of the "provincial fledgling" coming to the great city tends to parallel the biography of Napoleon—"the gifted provincial who arrives there to enact his dreams" with concomitant "standard themes" such as "talent corrupted." Sidney Monas, "St. Petersburg and Moscow as Cultural Symbols," in *Art and Culture in Nineteenth-Century Russia,* Theofanis George Stavrou, ed. (Bloomington: Indiana University Press, 1983), p. 36. The reference to Napoleon evokes Russian literature's perhaps most notorious "provincial in Petersburg" tale—Dostoevsky's 1866 *Crime and Punishment,* in which Rodion Raskolnikov comes to Petersburg from the provinces to study law at the university, descends into abject poverty, and conceives a bold plan to murder an elderly pawnbroker. This chapter primarily concerns provincial protagonists with dreams of literary fame, and for that reason, Dostoevsky's novel is not treated here.

20. In this spirit, Burton Pike invokes the "figure of the alienated and isolated middle-class individual, frequently an artist," that develops in "the fragmented word-city" in modern European literature, as an outgrowth of the eighteenth century and the romantic period. Burton Pike, *The Image of the City in Modern Literature* (Princeton: Princeton University Press, 1981), p. 100.

21. Nadezhda Durova's memoir "A Year of Life in Petersburg, or The Disadvantages of a Third Visit" (*God zhizni v Peterburge, ili Nevygody tret'ego poseshcheniia*), however, instantiates the familiar male-centered paradigm in describing its author's 1836–37 social and literary misadventures. Durova famously served in the cavalry dressed as a man during the Napoleonic wars and twice spent time in Petersburg during this period. The purpose of her third trip was to bring her notes to Petersburg and, under the literary patronage of Alexander Pushkin, to publish her memoirs in *The Contemporary.* Durova's gender-ambiguous identity and her connection to the already-antiquated Alexandrine past merely underscore the elements of the archetypal tale that her memoir reiterates— the experience of a provincial visitor who is a poor "reader" of Petersburg social and cultural topography.

22. A descendant of the recipient, I. I. Sreznevskii, prepared selections from these letters for publication in the journal *Russkaia starina* in 1900. See "Peterburg v 1831–1832 gg. (Po pis'mam provintsiala)," *Russkaia starina,* 1–3, 1900.

23. Similarly, in a letter from June 1840, Alexander Herzen characterized Petersburg as "a city of six-story buildings and six-mast ships, a mill in which passions, money, and sometimes even water are ground down, unceasingly crushed amidst noise and grating sounds." See A. I. Gerzen, Pis'mo k Iu. F. Kurute (11 iiunia 1840), *PSS,* t. 2 (Petersburg: Literaturno-Izdatel'skii Otdel Narodnogo Komissariata po Prosveshcheniiu, 1919), p. 368.

24. N. V. Gogol, Pis'mo 52, *PSS,* t. 10 (Izdatel'stvo Akademii Nauk SSSR, 1940), p. 83.

25. Pis'mo 59, p. 101.

26. Pis'mo 84, pp. 136–37.

27. Pis'mo 89, p. 146.

28. Note also the wild claims of Khlestakov in "The Inspector General," among them that he and Pushkin are best pals.

29. N. V. Gogol, *Mertvye dushi, Sobranie sochinenii* (Moscow: Pravda, 1984), t. 5, p. 242.

30. Similarly, in the unfinished prose work "Rome" (*Rim,* 1842), Gogol conveys the

perspective of the provincial Italian protagonist amazed by his first sight of the materialist-capital Paris: "And here he is in Paris, incoherently embraced by its monstrous exterior, struck by the movement, the glitter of the streets, the disorder of roofs, the thicket of chimneys, the close-packed multitude of buildings in no particular architectural style covered with a dense graft of shops, the ugliness of naked non-supporting side walls, the infinite muddled crowd of golden letters . . ." With these breathless sentences, Gogol improves upon his own disappointing early impressions of Petersburg and restages his inauspicious entry into the capital. The reference to the muddled lettering of the shop signs nevertheless suggests that this visiting provincial will find it no easier to decipher the city-text. N. V. Gogol, "Rim," *PSS*, t. 3, p. 222.

31. N. G. Chernyshevskii, Pis'mo 10 iiulia 1846, *PSS*, t. 14 (Moscow: Khudozhestvennaia literatura, 1949), p. 29.

32. N. A. Dobroliubov, *Dnevniki, 1851–59* (Moscow: Izdatel'stvo Vsesoiuznogo Obshchestva Politkatorzhan i Ssylno-Poselentsev, 1932), p. 89.

33. N. A. Dobroliubov, Pis'mo k ottsu i materi (10 August 1853), *Materialy dlia biografii N. A. Dobroliubova*, t. 1 (Moscow: Tip. V. F. Rikhter, 1890), pp. 18–19.

34. V. G. Belinskii, "Peterburg i Moskva," *Peterburg v russkom ocherke XIX veka*, M. V. Otradin, ed. (Leningrad: Izdatel'stvo Leningradskogo Universiteta, 1984), pp. 96–100.

35. Ibid., p. 104.

36. After writing society tales during the 1830s, Panaev himself abandoned his civil service career in 1844 to become a full-time professional writer. Unlike his nameless feuilletonist, however, Panaev's literary career working with Nekrasov on *The Contemporary* was successful by the standards of the time. His feuilletonist character is based on the writer Vasilii Mezhevich, who underwent a similar decline during the mid-1840s.

37. I. I. Panaev, "Peterburgskii fel'etonist," in *Fiziologiia Peterburga*, V. I. Kuleshov, ed. (Moscow: Nauka, 1991), pp. 213–14.

38. For more information, see E. G. Bushkanets, "U istokov memuarnoi literatury o N. A. Nekrasove," *Voprosy istochnikovedeniia russkoi literatury*, vyp. 112 (Kazan', 1973).

39. V. Evgen'ev-Maksimov, *Zhizn' i deiatel'nost' N. A. Nekrasova*, t. 1 (Moscow: Khudozhestvennaia literatura, 1947), p. 155.

40. Nekrasov did not always use the perspective of the visiting provincial to dramatic or autobiographical effect, but also mined this theme for its comic potential in his early works. Nekrasov earned a first positive critical response from Belinsky for his 1840 "Provintsial'nyi pod'iachii v Peterburge," a comic Petersburg feuilleton in verse, in which the narrator-clerk Feoklist Bob arrives in Petersburg from his native Pskov. The familiar discourse on the capital's attractions is conveyed in a completely new idiom—naively coarse, highly stylized *skaz* verse.

41. V. A. Egorov, "Rasskaz Nekrasova 'Bez vesti propavshii piita' v literaturnoi polemike nachala 1840-kh godov," *Nekrasov i ego vremia*, vyp. IV (Kaliningrad: Kaliningradskii Gosudarstvennyi Universitet, 1975–1983).

42. N. A. Nekrasov, "Bez vesti propavshii piita," *PSSiP*, t. 7 (Leningrad: Nauka, 1983), p. 64.

43. For more information about the autobiographical elements in *Tikhon Trosnikov*, see K. Chukovskii, "Trosnikov-Nekrasov (Cherty avtobiografii v naidennykh proizvedeniiakh Nekrasova)," in *Zhizn' i pokhozhdeniia Tikhona Trosnikova*, Evgen'ev-Maksimov and Chukovskii, eds. (Moscow: Khudozhestvennaia literatura, 1931).

44. For details, see *PSSiP*, t. 8, pp. 718–24. Note, however, that Nekrasov's novel-length project was a quixotic one. Owing to the censor's objections, Nekrasov was able to pub-

lish only two fragments of *Tikhon Trosnikov,* and he then abandoned the work, most likely anticipating more problems with its publication. The two fragments are "Neobyknovennyi zavtrak," published in *Otechestvennye zapiski* in 1843, and "Peterburgskie ugly," which was included in the 1845 collection *Fiziologiia Peterburga.*

45. O. V. Loman, *Nekrasov v Peterburge* (Leningrad: Lenizdat, 1985), p. 46. For another account of Nekrasov's life viewed through the prism of Petersburg, see V. E. Evgen'ev-Maksimov, *Nekrasov i Peterburg* (Leningrad: Leningradskoe Gazetno-Zhurnal'noe i Knizhnoe Izdatel'stvo, 1947).

46. "Speaking about himself, Nekrasov at the same time speaks about the entire social layer to which he belonged, about the hundreds and thousands of young people of diverse callings and diverse ranks (*'raznochintsy'*), who directed themselves from the provinces to the capital during the 1830s–40s in hopes of attaining 'career and fortune.'" See V. Evgen'ev-Maksimov, "Ispoved' rannego raznochintsa," in *Zhizn' i pokhozhdeniia Tikhona Trosnikova,* V. Evgen'ev-Maksimov and K. Chukovskii, eds. (Moscow: Khudozhestvennaia literatura, 1931), p. 12.

47. Grigorii Gukovskii, "Neizdannye povesti Nekrasova v istorii russkoi prozy sorokovykh godov," *Zhizn' i pokhozhdeniia Tikhona Trosnikova,* p. 347.

48. V. E. Evgen'ev-Maksimov, *Nekrasov i Peterburg,* p. 161.

49. "Zhizn' i pokhozhdeniia Tikhona Trosnikova," *PSSiP,* t. 8, pp. 250–51.

50. E. P. Grebenka, "Zapiski studenta," *Polnoe sobranie sochinenii,* t. 2 (SPb: N.F. Merts, 1902), p. 48.

51. Ibid., p. 66.

52. Ibid., p. 70.

53. Ibid., p. 72.

54. Sardonic literary "farewells" to the imperial capital by visiting provincials, fictional and otherwise, represent another textual type within the larger corpus. Apollon Grigor'ev's 1846 lyric "Farewell to Petersburg" (*Proshchanie s Peterburgom*) bids adieu to the "magnificent city of slaves, barracks, brothels, and palaces." In the longer poem "The City" (*Gorod*) from the same period, Grigor'ev declares himself "alien" to Petersburg. The poet mourns the many who have fallen victim to the city's evil atmosphere, in which the "chosen ones" of his age perish. In the final stanza, he directly addresses idealist youth throughout Russia, urging young provincials to strive toward the capital "with hope and love" as their weapons against vice, anger, slavish fear, or death. In Grigor'ev's proposed beginning lies the predetermined, already-written end.

55. I. A. Goncharov, *Sobranie sochinenii,* t. 1 (Moscow: Khudozhestvennaia literatura, 1952), p. 39.

56. Ibid., p. 63.

57. Ibid., p. 78.

58. Ibid., p. 102.

59. Ibid., p. 179.

60. Ibid., p. 269.

61. Ibid., p. 291.

62. Ibid., pp. 292–93.

63. Ibid., p. 295.

64. Ibid., p. 307.

65. A. F. Pisemskii, *Tysiacha dush. Sobranie sochinenii v deviati tomakh,* t. 3 (Moscow: Pravda, 1959), p. 226.

66. Ibid., p. 246.

67. Ibid., p. 303.

68. I. A. Kushchevskii, "V Peterburg! (na medovuiu reku Nevu!)," *Peterburg v russkom ocherke XIX veka*, p. 308.

69. Ibid., p. 311.

70. I. A. Kushchevskii, "Oshibki molodosti," *Neizdannye rasskazy* (St. Petersburg, 1881), pp. 108–9.

71. Ibid., pp. 110–11.

72. V. G. Korolenko, *Istoriia moego sovremennika*, t. 2, ch. 1 (Moscow: Zadruga, 1920), p. 50.

73. Ibid., p. 53.

74. Ibid., pp. 59–60.

75. Korolenko, t. 2, ch. 2, p. 88.

76. Ibid., pp. 140–41.

77. Ibid., p. 145.

78. D. M. Mamin-Sibiriak, *Cherty iz zhizni Pepko* (Sverdlovsk: Sredne-Ural'skoe Knizhnoe Izdatel'stvo, 1984), p. 5.

79. Ibid., p. 16.

80. Ibid., p. 26.

81. Ibid., p. 203.

82. Ibid., pp. 223–24.

83. Ibid., pp. 221–22.

84. A. I. Kuprin, "Chernyi tuman (peterburgskii sluchai)," *Sobranie sochinenii*, t. 3 (Moscow: Khudozhestvennaia literatura, 1957), p. 270.

85. Ibid., p. 278.

86. Ibid., p. 280.

87. N. P. Antsiferov, *Iz dum o bylom* (Moscow: Feniks, 1992), p. 130.

Chapter Seven

1. Francesco Algarotti, "Letters from Count Algarotti to Lord Hervey and the Marquis Scipio Maffei," Letter IV, June 30, 1739. (London: Johnson and Payne, 1769; reprint in Goldsmiths'-Kress Library of Economic Literature, no. 10500).

2. William Kinglake, "A Summer in Russia," *The New Monthly Magazine and Humorist*, no. 2, 1846, pp. 278–79.

3. Philippe Hamon, *Expositions: Literature and Architecture in Nineteenth-Century France*, trans. Katia Sainson-Frank and Lisa Maguire (Berkeley: University of California Press, 1992), pp. 45–50.

4. "Vospominaniia O. A. Przhetslavskogo, 1818–1831," *Russkaia starina*, no. 11, 1874, p. 469.

5. Marquis de Custine, *Empire of the Czar: A Journey through Eternal Russia*, p. 111. Nearly a century later, in 1926, Georgy Fedotov declared that Petersburg had become a museum of the Russian Empire, or its graveyard, which he considered "the same thing." "When you walk about the Winter Palace, which has been transformed into the Museum of the Revolution, or around the Peter-Paul Fortress," observed Fedotov, "you begin to be confused: Whose monuments are these and whose burial vaults—the tsar-killers' or

the tsars'?" See E. Bogdanov (G. P. Fedotov), "Tri stolitsy," *Novyi Mir*, no. 4, April 1989, p. 210. Two of Petersburg's major architectural structures from the imperial period also offered themselves to viewers as ambiguous monuments to the death of a Russian tsar: the former Mikhailovskii Castle, where Pavel had been murdered, and the lavish Cathedral of the Resurrection of Christ (Savior on the Blood), which commemorated the site of Alexander II's murder.

6. D. Merezhkovskii, "*Bol'naia Rossiia*" (Leningrad: Izdatel'stvo Leningradskogo Universiteta, 1991), p. 115.

7. Aleksandr Skidan, "O pol'ze i vrede Peterburga dlia zhizni," *Russkii zhurnal*, July 6, 1999. Like Brodsky, Skidan declares that the Bolsheviks are to be thanked for the city's transformation into a cemetery-museum after the transfer of the capital back to Moscow.

8. For details on the latter period, see Richard Wortman, "Moscow and Petersburg: The Problem of Political Center in Tsarist Russia, 1881–1914," in Sean Wilentz, ed., *Rites of Power: Symbolism, Ritual, and Politics since the Middle Ages* (Philadelphia: University of Pennsylvania Press, 1985).

9. Lewis Mumford, *The City in History: Its Origins, Its Transformations, and Its Prospects* (New York: Harcourt, Brace, 1961), p. 7.

10. A. V. Kobak and Iu. M. Piriutko, "Ot sostavitelei," *Istoricheskie kladbishcha Peterburga: Spravochnik-putevoditel'* (SPb: Izdatel'stvo Chernysheva, 1993), p. 5. For a historical survey of Petersburg's cemeteries, see their "Ocherk istorii peterburgskogo nekropolia" in the same volume.

11. V. I. Saitov, Introduction to *Peterburgskii nekropol'* (SPb, 1912–1913), t. 1–4.

12. V. N. Toporov, "Peterburg i 'Peterburgskii tekst russkoi literatury' (Vvedenie v temu)," *Mif. Ritual. Simvol. Obraz: Issledovaniia v oblasti mifopoeticheskogo* (Moscow: Progress, 1995), pp. 284–85. Toporov's data on the relationship between birth and death rates, which are based on several late prerevolutionary sources, are confirmed by the information in James H. Bater, *St. Petersburg: Industrialization and Change* (London: Edward Arnold, 1976), pp. 160–63, 185–87, 311–13. Until the very late imperial period, Petersburg's population grew only by means of migration, and these selfsame itinerant workers and provincial arrivals contributed more to the death rate than any other segment of the city's residents.

13. Vsevolod Garshin, "Peterburgskie pis'ma," *Rasskazy*, kn. 3 (SPb: Tip. M. M. Stasiulevicha, 1902), p. 61. Vasilii Mikhnevich's 1874 *Ves' Peterburg na ladoni* confirms Garshin's account, providing a description of the scheduled trains departing for these cemeteries and the procedures for sorting the coffins by religious faith (pp. 177–79). Mikhnevich also lists prices for burial services (LXIX).

14. The first reference is from Part II of "O pogode" (1865), from the section titled "Komu kholodno, komu zharko!" The second is from "Neschastnye" (1856).

15. I. S. Turgenev, "Prizraki," *Sobranie sochinenii* (Moscow: Russkaia kniga, 1994), pp. 440–41. Critics were bewildered and displeased by the dark tone of this story, causing Turgenev to write in a letter to P. B. Annenkov, "By all accounts, 'Prizraki' has suffered a general fiasco. And still, it seems to me that the departed one (*pokoinik*) was not a bad sort." See Letter of 21 May/2 June 1864.

16. Toporov, p. 283.

17. For an overview of the early period, see V. N. Mullin, "Kladbishche v sisteme petrovskoi kul'tury nachala XVIII veka," *Russian Studies: Ezhekvartal'nik russkoi filologii i kul'tury*, I, 4, 1995 (SPb).

18. For a historical sketch of the Smolenskoe Cemetery from the imperial period, see S. I. Opatovich, "Smolenskoe kladbishche v S.-Peterburge: Istoricheskii ocherk," *Russkaia starina*, August 1873.

19. Bashchutskii's sketch was originally published in *Biblioteka dlia chteniia* (1840, t. 42, ch. 10, otd. I) and was then included in the 1841–42 collection *Nashi spisannye s natury russkimi*.

20. For a description of traditional Petersburg funeral practices at the end of the nineteenth century, see S. F. Svetlov, *Peterburgskaia zhizn' v kontse XIX stoletiia (v 1892 godu)* (SPb: Giperion, 1998), pp. 14–17. For an account of personal experiences as a Peterburg funeral torchbearer, see N. N. Zhivotov, *Peterburgskie profili: Sredi fakel'shchikov. Shest' dnei v roli fakel'shchika* (SPb: 1895).

21. For a survey of these material forms, see Iu. M. Piriutko, "Nadgrobnye pamiatniki: Stil', mastera, zakazchiki," in *Istoricheskie kladbishcha Peterburga*.

22. T. S. Tsar'kova, "Memorial'nyi zhanr: obraztsy i podrazhaniia," *Fenomen Peterburga*, Iu. N. Bespiatykh, ed. (SPb: BLITS, 2000), p. 247.

23. T. S. Tsar'kova and S. I. Nikolaev, "Epitafii peterburgskogo nekropolia," *Istoricheskie kladbishcha Peterburga*, p. 114.

24. For a discussion of the "circumtextually framed" quality of epigraphs as a defining generic feature, see Ian Reid, "Genre and Framing: The Case of Epitaphs," *Poetics* 17 (1988). For an excellent historical survey of Russian epitaph poetry, see S. I. Nikolaev and T. S. Tsar'kova, "Tri veka russkoi epitafii," *Russkaia stikhotvornaia epitafiia* (SPb: Akademicheskii proekt, 1998). For a sampling of eighteenth-century Petersburg tombstone inscriptions made during the 1890s, see S. N. Shubinskii, "Kladbishchenskaia literatura (Epitafii XVIII veka)," *Istoricheskie ocherki i rasskazy* (reprint of 1908 edition; Moscow: Moskovskii rabochii, 1995).

25. Iu. M. Piriutko, "Leningradskii panteon," *Antsiferovskie chteniia: Materialy i tezisy konferentsii* (Leningrad: Leningradskoe Otdelenie Sovetskogo Fonda Kul'tury, 1989), p. 162.

26. For detailed historical information about Lazarevskoe, see the section on "Kladbishcha Aleksandro-Nevskoi lavry" by Iu. M. Piriutko in *Istoricheskie kladbishcha Peterburga*. See also Iu. M. Piriutko, "Lazarevskaia usypal'nitsa—pamiatnik russkoi kul'tury XVIII–XIX vv.," *Pamiatniki kul'tury. Novye otkrytiia* (Moscow: Nauka, 1989).

27. G. D. Netunakhina and N. I. Udimova, *Muzei gorodskoi skul'ptury: Kratkii putevoditel'* (Leningrad: Lenizdat, 1972), pp. 109–10.

28. Lidiia Ginzburg, "Mysl', opisavshaia krug," *Zapisnye knizhki. Vospominaniia. Esse* (SPb: Iskusstvo-SPB, 2002), pp. 557–58.

29. For a description of the official ceremonies accompanying the transfer of the relics, see M. I. Pyliaev, *Staryi Peterburg* (Leningrad: Titul, 1990), p. 23

30. Note also the parallel tradition of burying nineteenth-century radical thinkers (Vera Zasulich among them) in the Literatorskie mostki. For a description of the notorious funeral of populist Pavel Chernyshev at Volkovo, see Tom Trice, "Rites of Protest: Populist Funerals in Imperial St. Petersburg, 1876–1878," *Slavic Review*, vol. 60, no. 1, Spring 2001.

31. Note that the Literatorskie mostki is also home to the gravesites of Petersburg cultural historians Mikhail Pyliaev and Petr Stolpianskii—a characteristic detail of Petersburg's metacommentary upon its own history.

32. For a historical survey, see A. I. Kudriavtsev and G. N. Shkoda, "Pravoslavnoe klad-

bishche i nekropol'-muzei Literatorskie mostki," in *Istoricheskie kladbishcha Peterburga.* For a Soviet-era description, see *Leningrad: Putevoditel'* (Leningrad: Lenizdat, 1988), pp. 194–95.

33. N. A. Nekrasov, *PSSiP*, t. 2 (Moscow: Kudozhestvennaia literature, 1949), p. 64.

34. Most scholars concur that Pushkin's famous stroll through a depressing "public cemetery" took place at the Blagoveshchenskoe Cemetery on Kamennyi Island, since the poem was written during the author's visit to this island. The notion has also been advanced that this poem captures the impressions of a visit to his friend Anton Del'vig's grave at the Volkovo Cemetery, known for its diverse mix of representatives from the Petersburg population. See M. P. Alekseev, *Pushkin i mirovaia literatura* (Leningrad, 1987), p. 148.

35. Garshin, pp. 62–64.

36. This last is a reference to the writer Afanas'ev-Chuzhbinskii, who had requested that he be buried near Belinsky and Dobroliubov, but was laid to rest at some distance from them because of the lack of space.

37. A. N. Radishchev, *Puteshestvie iz Peterburga v Moskvu*, V. A. Zapadov, ed. (SPb: Nauka, 1992), p. 115. Ironically, in 1783 Radishchev had composed an epitaph for his late wife and wished to have it inscribed upon her tombstone at the monastery cemetery, but was forbidden by the authorities on the grounds that the verses showed "insufficient certainty in the immortality of the soul." See A. N. Radishchev, *Sochineniia* (Moscow: Khudozhestvennaia literatura, 1988), p. 650.

38. N. N. Vrangel', "Zabytye mogily," *Starye gody*, February 1907.

39. As Lotman declared, "One might have expected that the medieval tradition of visions and prophecies would be more a part of the Moscow tradition than of 'rationalist' and 'European' Petersburg. But it was Petersburg where such things flourished." See Yuri M. Lotman, *Universe of the Mind: A Semiotic Theory of Culture*, trans. Ann Shukman (Bloomington: Indiana University Press, 1990), p. 195. For an overview of apocalyptic thinking about Petersburg during the Silver Age, see K. G. Isupov, "Dialog stolits v istoricheskom dvizhenii" (the section titled "Nachalo poslednego veka. Pripominanie puti i apokalipsis nadezhdy"), in *Moskva-Peterburg: Pro et Contra*, pp. 46–69. See also David Bethea, *The Shape of Apocalypse in Modern Russian Fiction* (Princeton: Princeton University Press, 1989).

40. Toporov, p. 295.

41. Tsar Nicholas—as depicted on the bas-relief sculpture of his monument on St. Isaac's Square—personally quelled a rioting crowd that had destroyed a temporary cholera hospital at the Haymarket. See Richard S. Wortman, *Scenarios of Power: Myth and Ceremony in Russian Monarchy*, vol. 1 (Princeton: Princeton University Press, 1995), pp. 300–2. For more on this subject, see Roderick E. McGrew, *Russia and the Cholera, 1823–1832* (Madison: University of Wisconsin Press, 1965).

42. Joseph Brodsky, "A Guide to a Renamed City," p. 75.

43. Grigory Kaganov, *Images of Space: St. Petersburg in the Visual and Verbal Arts*, trans. Sidney Monas (Stanford: Stanford University Press, 1997), pp. 76–79. In this sense, writes Kaganov, the structures of the Russian imperial city "become a pure symbol of the Northern Palmyra," since "The uninhabited ruins of ancient Palmyra were cut off in precisely the same way from the wild locale surrounding them. Their endless rows of columns, continuing to stand amidst the wasteland, also remained a mere symbol of the city that had lived around them and whose best ornament they had at one time been."

44. For a recent perspective on the Atlantis myth, see Richard Ellis, *Imagining Atlantis* (New York: Alfred A. Knopf, 1998).

45. Russia's most famous marine painter, Ivan Aivazovskii, who studied at the Petersburg Academy of Arts, produced many nineteenth-century canvasses depicting raging seas, several of which belong to Petersburg's Russian Museum. Although Aivazovskii's work is representative of romantic seascape painting in general and is by no means limited to the Petersburg environs, major works such as "The Ninth Wave," "The Deluge," and "The Creation of the World" also point to biblical motifs that easily lend themselves to Petersburg by allegory. Note, as literary precedent for such an allegory, the depiction of the Flood in Ovid's *Metamorphoses*, which served Pushkin, among others, as a model for treating the 1824 disaster in verse. See L. V. Pumpianskii, "'Mednyi vsadnik' i poeticheskaia traditsiia XVIII veka," *Vremennik pushkinskoi komissii*, nos. 4–5, 1939, pp. 103–4.

46. See, for example, the description of the 1721 flood in the diary of diplomat F. V. Berkhgol'ts, published in Russian as *Dnevnik kamer-iunkera F.V. Berkhtol'tsa v 4 chasti-akh*, ch. 1 (Moscow, 1902–3). This passage is also excerpted in P. E. Mel'gunova, K. V. Sivkovyi, and N. P. Sidorovyi, eds., *Russkii byt po vospominaniiam sovremennikov. XVIII vek*, ch. 1 (Moscow: Zadruga, 1914), pp. 166–71. See also Dmitri Merezhkovskii's fictional account of the 1715 flood in *Antikhrist (Petr i Aleksei)*, the third novel in his historical trilogy, which includes a vision of the Summer Garden Venus statue, whose pedestal is submerged, rising from the Styx-like waters.

47. Kim Pomeranets, "Dva navodnen'ia, s raznitsei v sto let . . ." *Peterburg trushchobnyi*, Neva, no. 7, 1998, p. 231. See also Alexander Kushner's poem "Dva navodnen'ia," which begins by evoking 1824 and 1924: "Two floods, a hundred years apart."

48. Each year, a pavilion-shrine was constructed on the river, and a hole made in the ice, through which the Metropolitan plunged a silver cross into the water, an act witnessed by the court and city population. The fortress guns fired a salute and regiment standards were sprinkled with the holy water. The Empress was then sent silver containers of Neva water, and the Petersburg populace was allowed to draw water once the procession of priests had departed. For descriptions of the ceremony during the 1820s as observed by foreign visitors, see Marie Cornélie de Wassenaer, *A Visit to Petersburg*, Igor Vinogradoff, trans. and ed. (Norwich: Michael Russell, 1994), pp. 74–75, Théophile Gautier, *Voyage en Russie* (Paris: La Boîte à Documents, 1990), pp. 129–31, and Thomas Raikes, *A Visit to St. Petersburg in the Winter of 1829–1830* (London: Richard Bentley, 1838), pp. 154–57.

49. Note, for example, an anthology of literature on the subject of Petersburg floods, S. A. Prokhvatilova and E. V. Anisimov, eds., *"Gorod pod morem" ili blistatel'nyi Sankt-Peterburg* (SPb: Lenizdat, 1996). For a fuller historical chronicle and more comprehensive references to literary writing about Petersburg floods (as well as an anthology of excerpts from the same), see K. S. Pomeranets, *Navodneniia v Peterburge, 1703–1997* (SPb: Baltrus-buk, 1998).

50. As the memoirs of Count Vladimir Sollogub attest, Mikhail Lermontov, too, was fascinated by images of Petersburg lost beneath the waters and "loved to draw with pen, and even brush, the view of a frenzied sea, out of which rose the tip of the Alexander Column with its crowning angel. His gloomy imagination . . . was reflected in this depiction." See *Peterburgskie stranitsy vospominanii Grafa Solloguba* (SPb: Afina, 1993), pp. 66. As Lotman points out, the image of the protruding steeple that obsessed Lermontov links

Petersburg to the eschatological mythology connected with Constantinople, whose inundation by God's wrath, which left only a single steeple visible through the waves, was predicted by Methodius of Patara. Iu. M. Lotman, "Simvolika Peterburga i problemy semiotiki goroda," pp. 10–11.

51. Strangely, however, the 1777 flood did not give rise to a body of literary texts, although there do exist a few straightforward descriptions of the disaster by eyewitnesses and historians. See, for example, the anonymous September 1777 letter, recopied by a chancellery clerk and published much later as "Peterburgskoe navodnenie ekaterininskogo vremeni v opisanii ochevidtsa," *Russkii arkhiv*, nos. 1–3, 1916.

52. In fact, Pushkin draws upon the same jumble of poetic tropes as Khvostov, if more sparingly. Pushkin, too, has recourse to roaring, preying waves and rebellious elemental forces, and to the heartsick tsar surveying the destruction from his palace window. Note that Pumpianskii attributes this shared lexicon to the use of common sources—V. N. Berkh's account of the 1824 flood, which Pushkin invokes in the prefatory statement to "The Bronze Horseman," as well as contemporary accounts in Russian journals, to which both Khvostov and Pushkin refer. See Pumpianskii, p. 101.

53. V. E. Vatsuro, "Pushkin i problemy bytopisaniia v nachale 1830-kh godov," *Pushkin: Issledovaniia i materialy*, t. 6 (Leningrad, 1969), p. 160. Note that the eighteenth-century Russian ode also uses the flood trope to invoke specific historical circumstances, as in Lomonosov's odes of 1742 and 1746, which equate flooding with the *bironovshchina*— the dominant influence of Biron under Anna Ioannovna, before the reign of Elizabeth. See Pumpianskii, pp. 104–5.

54. Nikolai Ogarev's 1859 poem "Pamiati Ryleeva" more obviously exemplifies this second type of Petersburg flood poem. Similarly, an anonymous poem entitled "Navodnenie," which has been attributed to Lermontov, contains references to a despotic tsar who finds he can no longer subdue the rebellious waters. See *Lermontovskaia entsiklopediia* (Moscow, 1981), pp. 446–47, as cited in Antsiferov, *Dusha Peterburga*, p. 305, 137n.

55. M. Gershenzon, *Zhizn' V.S. Pecherina* (Moscow, 1910), p. 72. Note that Gershenzon includes lengthy excerpts from Pecherin's verse-play.

56. A. S. Griboedov, "Chastnye sluchai peterburgskogo navodneniia," in *Polnoe sobranie sochinenii*, N. K. Piksanov, ed. (Petrograd, 1917), vol. 3, pp. 109–10.

57. In this context, see also Vladimir Odoevskii's 1833 story "Nasmeshka mertvetsa" from his cycle *Russkie nochi*, in which flood waters burst into a high-society ball, bearing a black coffin in reproach and punishment for the soulless participants.

58. "Vospominaniia O. A. Przhetslavskogo, 1818–1831," *Russkaia starina*, vol. II, 1874, pp. 672–73.

59. "Vospominanie o navodnenii v Peterburge, 7 noiabria 1824 goda," *Russkii arkhiv*, 1870.

60. A. Romanovskii, "Vospominaniia o navodnenii 1824 g," *Russkaia starina*, no. 122, 1905.

61. A bibliographical item in an 1827 edition of the journal *Moskovskii telegraf* strikes a similar note, in relation to the recent publication of two works about Petersburg floods—V. N. Berkh's *Podrobnoe istoricheskoe izvestie o vsekh navodneniiakh, byvshikh v Sankt-Peterburge (1691–1824)* and Samuil Aller's *Opisanie navodneniia, byvshego v Sanktpeterburge 7 chisla noiabria, 1824 goda*, criticized for including trivial or humorous anecdotes in connection with the event. The editor declared, "The disastrous event suffered by the great capital of Russia should be conveyed to posterity in detailed descrip-

tion. The traces of devastation have been erased by the beneficent activities of the State and by the energetic application of capital in St. Petersburg; but the memory of this terrible phenomenon of nature in all its details must be preserved in the annals of St. Petersburg." See "Bibliografiia," *Moskovskii telegraf*, no. 1, 1827, p. 151.

62. P. P. Karatygin, "Letopis' peterburgskikh navodnenii, 1703–1879," *Istoricheskii vestnik*, vol. 33, 1888, p. 33. Karatygin's survey was published as a separate edition by A. S. Suvorin the following year.

63. The account by Fridrikh-Teodor Shubert was originally published as "O prichinakh navodneniia 1824 goda," in *Russkaia starina*, vol. 20, 1877.

64. Yuri Egorov points out that the fires of 1736 and 1737 were well timed in eliminating the old wooden structures located in the Admiralty district "with remarkably methodical speed and precision," since the suburbs in this area "were not in keeping with the splendor of the newly emerging city center." After the fire, new laws prevented the old suburbs from reestablishing themselves, and a royal decree permitted only stone structures to be constructed in the Admiralty area. See Yuri Egorov, *The Architectural Planning of St. Petersburg*, Eric Dluhosch, trans. (Athens, Ohio: Ohio University Press, 1969), pp. 29–30.

65. For a chronicle of major Petersburg fires in the eighteenth and nineteenth centuries, see chapter 5 in M. I. Pyliaev, *Staryi Peterburg* (Leningrad: Titul, 1990).

66. For a study of fire imagery in Griboedov's play "Gore ot uma," see Stephen Baehr, "Is Moscow Burning? Fire in Griboedov's *Woe from Wit*," in *Russian Subjects: Empire, Nation, and the Culture of the Golden Age*, Monika Greenleaf and Stephen Moeller-Sally, eds. (Evanston: Northwestern University Press, 1998). In Baehr's reading, "fire" refers not only to the purgative fire of 1812, but also to the revolutionary Decembrist sentiments circulating in Russian aristocratic society, as well as to a satirically "hellish" Moscow that repels new ideas.

67. For a description of fire brigades during the early part of the nineteenth century, see A. M. Gordin and M. A. Gordin, *Pushkinskii vek*, kn. 1 (from the series *Byloi Peterburg: Panorama stolichnoi zhizni*) (SPb: Izdatel'stvo Pushkinskogo Fonda, 1999), pp. 26–27.

68. "Rasskazy ochevidtsev o pozhare Zimnego Dvortsa v 1837-m godu," *Russkii arkhiv*, no. 9, 1865.

69. Ibid., pp. 1110–11.

70. As Roland Barthes declares, "We speak our city . . . merely by inhabiting it, walking through it, looking at it." Roland Barthes, *Architecture d'aujord'hui*, no. 153, December 1970–January 1971, pp. 11–13. For more of Barthes on place names and proper names, see "Proust and Names" in his *New Critical Essays*, trans. Richard Howard (New York: Hill and Wang, 1980).

71. K. Gorbachevich and E. Khablo, *Pochemu tak nazvany? O proiskhozhdenii nazvanii ulits, ploshchadei, ostrovov, rek, i mostov Sankt-Peterburga* (St. Petersburg: Norint, 1998), pp. 5–7. In fact, the project of *Pochemu tak nazvany?* has already contributed substantially to establishing the cultural significance of Petersburg place names, beginning with the first edition in 1960, and delving ever deeper into Petersburg's toponymical history in subsequent editions of 1962, 1967, 1975, 1985, 1996, and 1998. Each of these editions provides a toponymical snapshot of Petersburg at a particular moment in time, with the 1975 and 1985 editions documenting a high-Soviet Leningrad, and the 1990s editions striving for comprehensive imperial, Soviet, and post-Soviet minihistories treating each

street, square, bridge, or island entry. The synchronic focus of the individual entries in this reference work does indeed posit each street in Petersburg as a monument, along with its associated cluster of names.

72. N. A. Sindalovskii, *Legendy i mify Sankt-Peterburga* (St. Petersburg: Norint, 1997), p. 105.

73. N. P. Antsiferov, *Dusha Peterburga. "Nepostizhimyi gorod . . ."* (Leningrad: Lenizdat, 1991), p. 46.

74. It should be noted that in his specific excursionist studies of Petersburg market districts and the area around the Stock Exchange on Vasilievskii Island, Antsiferov did explore the functional naming practices that have become a valuable source of information for the urban cultural historian.

75. A. A. Grigor'ev, "Zametki peterburgskogo zevaka," *Peterburg v russkom ocherke XIX veka*, M. V. Otradin, ed. (Leningrad: Izdatel'stvo Leningradskogo Universiteta, 1984), p. 62.

76. For a summary, see V. V. Kukushkina and N. K. Shablaeva, "Plany Peterburga kak istochniki po toponimii goroda XVIII v.," in *Fenomen Peterburga*, Iu. N. Bespiatykh, ed. (SPb: BLITS, 2000).

77. In fact, Gorbachevich and Khablo claim there were no street names at all in 1710s–1720s, and that residents simply used such descriptive directions.

78. As Michael de Certeau remarks, "Disposed in constellations that hierarchize and semantically order the surface of the city, . . . these words . . . slowly lose, like worn coins, the value engraved on them, but their ability to signify outlives its first definition. . . . A rich indetermination gives them, by means of a semantic rarefaction, the function of articulating a second, poetic geography on top of the geography of the literal." Michel de Certeau, *The Practice of Everyday Life*, trans. Steven Rendall (Berkeley: University of California Press, 1984), p. 105.

79. For comparative purposes, see G. P. Smolitskaia, *Nazvaniia moskovskikh ulits* (Moscow: Izdatel'skii Dom "Muravei," 1996). Moscow street names have their own associative logic.

80. V. G. Belinskii, "Peterburg i Moskva," *Peterburg v russkom ocherke XIX veka*, p. 89.

81. Sigmund Freud, *Civilization and Its Discontents*, trans. Joan Rivière (New York: Jonathan Cape & Harrison Smith, 1930), pp. 17–18.

82. Umberto Eco, "Architecture and Memory," *VIA* 8, 1986, p. 89.

83. See, in this regard, V. N. Zaitsev, "Bibliotechnoe-informatsionnoe prostranstvo Sankt-Peterburga," in *Fenomen Peterburga*.

84. For a detailed historical exposition of these practices from antiquity up to Leibniz, see Frances Yates's classic study of "mnemotechnics" in *The Art of Memory*, vol. 3 in *Selected Works* (London: Routledge, 1966). For a fascinating particular case, see "Building the Palace" (chapter 1) in Jonathan D. Spence, *The Memory Palace of Matteo Ricci* (New York: Viking Penguin, 1984).

85. Alexander Benois's best-known articles in this regard are "Zhivopisnyi Peterburg," *Mir iskusstvo*, no. 1, 1902; "Krasota Peterburga," *Mir iskusstvo*, no. 8. 1902; and "Vandalizmy," *Mir iskusstvo*, no. 10, 1904. For a brief historical sketch of *Starye gody*, see F. M. Lur'e, "Golosa 'serebrianogo veka': knigi, zhurnaly, vystavki," *Fenomen Peterburga*, pp. 183–87. For a memoiristic account of the founding of *Starye gody* written during the mid-1920s, see M. A. Vitukhnovskaia, "Vospominaniia P. P. Veinera o zhurnale 'Starye gody,'" *Pamiatniki kul'tury. Novye okrytiia. Ezhegodnik 1984* (Leningrad: Nauka, 1986).

86. S. Troinitskii, "O tsepnykh mostakh Peterburga," *Starye gody*, March 1907.

87. V. Kurbatov, "Unichtozhenie petrogradskikh sadov," *Starye gody*, January–February 1915.

88. For an overview of preservationist activities, see Katerina Clark, *Petersburg, Crucible of Cultural Revolution* (Cambridge: Harvard University Press, 1995), pp. 59–65.

89. Sources on the Museum include *Muzei Goroda: K oktiabriu 1927 g.* (Leningrad: Izdatel'stvo Muzeiia Goroda, 1928); A. M. Blinov, "Muzei 'Staryi Peterburg,' 1907–1918 g.," *Leningrad ves' na ladoni* 1990; A. N. Andreeva, "Muzei Goroda," *Peterburgskie chteniia* 96 (SPb: BLITS, 1996); and R. I. Shpiller, "Gosudarstvennyi Muzei Istorii Leningrada (1918–1985 gg.)," *Muzei i vlast': Iz zhizni muzeev: Sbornik nauchnykh trudov* (Moscow, 1991).

90. See A. M. Konechnyi, "Obshchestvo 'Staryi Peterburg—Novyi Leningrad,'" *Muzei* no. 7, 1987.

91. V. V. Antonov and A. V. Kobak, eds., *Utrachennye pamiatniki arkhitektury Peterburga-Leningrada* (Leningrad: Khudozhnik RSFSR, 1988), p. 4.

92. Sources on Petersburg churches, past and present, include V. V. Antonov and A. V. Kobak, *Sviatyni Sankt-Peterburga: Istoriko-tserkovnaia entsiklopediia v trekh tomakh* (SPb: Izdatel'stvo Chernysheva, 1994–96), A. P. Pavlov, *Khramy Sankt-Peterburga: Khudozhestvenno-istoricheskii ocherk* (SPb: Lenizdat, 1995), and S. S. Shul'ts, *Khramy Sankt-Peterburga (istoriia i sovremennost'): Spravochnoe izdanie* (SPb: Glagol, 1994). See also *Kul'tovye zdaniia Peterburga: Ukazatel' russkoi literatury 1717–1917 gg*, vyp. 1 and 2 (SPb: Rossiiskaia Natsional'naia Biblioteka, 1994, 1999).

93. This checkered history also includes unexpected chapters, when cycles of restoration undid some of the recent work of destruction. See, for example, V. Iu Korovainikov, "Okhrana i restavratsiia pamiatnikov arkhitektury Petrograda-Leningrada v 1920-e gody (po dokumentam Tsentral'nogo Munitsipal'nogo Arkhiva Moskvy)," in *Peterburg i Moskva: Dve stolitsy Rossii v XVIII-XX vekakh*, Iu. V. Krivosheev, A. S. Fedotov, and M. V. Khodiakov, eds. Universitetskie Peterburgskie chteniia (SPb: Izdatel'stvo S.-Peterburgskogo Universiteta, 2001).

94. See V. N. Timofeev, E. N. Poretskina, and N. N. Efremova, eds., *Memorial'nye doski Sankt-Peterburga: Spravochnik* (SPb: Art-Biuro, 1999), and B. N. Kalinin and P. P. Iurevich, eds., *Pamiatniki i memorial'nye doski Leningrada: Spravochnik* (Leningrad: Lenizdat, 1979).

Conclusion

1. Sources on 1803 include V. Sreznevskii, "Prazdnovanie stoletiia Peterburga," *Russkaia starina*, kn. 5, 1903; V. A. Nikol'skii, "Kak prazdnovalas' stoletiia Peterburga," *Peterburgskaia starina*, I. Bozherianov, and V. Nikol'skii, eds. (SPb: 1903); and O. A. Khodiakova, "Iz istorii prazdnovaniia 100-letiia i 200-letiia osnovaniia Sankt-Peterburga," *Peterburgskie chteniia*, 96.

2. For a description, see V. G. Avseenko, *Istoriia goroda S.-Peterburga v litsakh i kartinkakh, 1703–1903* (reprint of 1903 *200 let Sankt-Peterburga. Istoricheskii ocherk*) (SPb: Sotis, 1995), pp. 218–20.

3. http://www.300online.ru/articles1/4401.html, accessed April 2, 2004.

4. Ibid.

5. The winner of the last was one Evgenii Bukin, who expressed himself in the follow-

ing, not always harmonious fusion of classical and contemporary lexicon: "Ostrosh-pil'nyi, khladnokrovnyi, seksapil'nyi, liubvipolnyi, belonochnyi, vshtormprilivnyi, bud' ty moshchnym, bud' schastlivym, bud' vekami nagrazhdennym, bud' vsegda novorozh-dennym" [Sharp-spired, cold-blooded, sex-appealing, full-of-love, white-nighted, in-storm high-tiding, may you be mighty, may you be happy, may you be rewarded for cen-turies, may you be always newborn].

⟞ BIBLIOGRAPHY ⟝

Ageeva, O. G. *"Velichaishii i slavneishii bolee vsex gradov v svete . . ."—Grad Sviatogo Petra: Peterburg v russkom obshchestvennom soznanii hachala XVIII veka.* SPb: BLITS, 1999.

———. "Peterburgskie slukhi (K voprosu o nastroeniiakh peterburgskogo obshchestva v epokhu petrovskikh reform)." *Fenomen Peterburga,* ed. Iu. N. Bespiatykh. SPb: BLITS, 2000.

Agnew, John. "Representing Space: Space, Scale and Culture in Social Science." In *Place/ Culture/Representation,* James Duncan and David Ley, eds. New York: Routledge, 1993.

Akhundov, Murad D., *Conceptions of Space and Time: Sources, Evolution, Directions,* trans. Charles Rougle. Cambridge, MA: MIT Press, 1986.

Alekseev, M. P. *Pushkin i mirovaia literatura.* Leningrad, 1987.

Alianskii, Iurii. *Uveselitel'nye zavedeniia starogo Peterburga.* SPb: AOZT "PF," 1996.

Althusser, Louis and Etienne Balibar. *Reading Capital,* trans. Ben Brewster. London: New Left Books, 1977.

Andreeva, A. N. "Muzei Goroda." *Peterburgskie chteniia 96.* SPb: BLITS, 1996.

Andrews, Howard F. "Nineteenth-Century St. Petersburg: Workpoints for an Exploration of Image and Place." In *Humanistic Geography and Literature: Essays on the Experience of Place,* Douglas C. D. Pocock, ed. London: Croom Helm, 1981.

Anisimov, E. *Vremia petrovskikh reform.* Lenizdat, 1989.

Annenkov, P. V. *Literaturnye vospominaniia.* Moscow: Khudozhestvennaia literature, 1983.

Annenkov, Viktor. *Znakomaia i neznakomaia Vyborgskaia storona: Progulki po ulitsam i naberezhnym byvshei peterburgskoi okrainy.* SPb: Sudarynia, 1998.

Antalov, V. *Mikrotoponimika Leningrada. Vestnik soveta po ekologii kul'tury.* Leningradskoe Otdelenie Sovetskogo Fonda Kul'tury, 1989.

Antonov, V. V. and A. V. Kobak. *Utrachennye pamiatniki arkhitektury Peterburga-Leningrada: Katalog vystavki.* Leningrad: Khudozhnik RSFSR, 1988.

———. *Sviatyni Sankt-Peterburga: Istoricheskaia tserkovnaia entsiklopediia v 3-kh tomakh.* SPb: Izdatel'stvo Chernysheva, 1994–1996.

Antsiferov, Nikolai. *Byl i mif Peterburga.* Petrograd: Brokgauz-Efron, 1924.

———. *O metodakh i tipakh istoriko-kul'turnykh ekskursii.* Petrograd, 1923.

———. "Raion morskogo porta (epokha torgovogo kapitalizma): Ekskursiia po Vasil'evskomu Ostrovu (Strelka i Tuchkova Naberezhnaia)." *Teoriia i praktika ekskursii po obshchestvovedeniiu.* Leningrad, 1926.

———. "Ulitsa rynkov (Sadovaia, nyne Ulitsa 3-ogo Iiuliia v Leningrade): Kraevedcheskii material dlia ekskursii po sotsial'nomu i ekonomicheskomu bytu." *Po ochagam kul'tury: Novye temy dlia ekskursii po gorodu.* Leningrad, 1926.

———. *Prigorody Leningrada: Goroda Pushkin, Pavlovsk, Petrodvorets.* Moscow: Gosudarstvennyi Literaturnyi Muzei, 1946.

————. *Dusha Peterburga.* "Nepostizhimyi gorod . . ." Leningrad: Lenizdat, 1991.

————. *Peterburg Dostoevskogo.* "Nepostizhimyi gorod . . ." Leningrad: Lenizdat, 1991.

————. *Peterburg Pushkina.* "Nepostizhimyi gorod . . ." Leningrad: Lenizdat, 1991.

————. *Iz dum o bylom: Vospominaniia.* Moscow: Feniks, 1992.

Arkin, D. *Mednyi vsadnik: Pamiatnik Petru I v Leningrade.* Leningrad: Iskusstvo, 1958.

Arkin, David. "Grad Obrechennyi" (1917). Reprinted in *Novyi Zhurnal,* kn. 184–85, 1991.

Arsenev, Konstantin. *Nachertanie statistiki Rossiiskago gosudarstva.* SPb: Tip. Imperatorskogo Vospitatel'nogo Doma, 1819.

Ascherson, Neal. *Black Sea.* London: Jonathan Cape, 1995.

Ashcroft, Irina Sobkowska. "*Peterburgskie Trushchoby:* A Russian Version of *Les Mystères de Paris.*" *Revue de Littérature Comparée,* t. LIII, no. 2, April–June 1979.

Ashukin, N. S. *Pushkinskaia Moskva.* SPb: Akademicheskii proekt, 1998.

Avseenko, V. G. *Istoriia goroda S.-Peterburga v litsakh i kartinkakh, 1703–1903* (reprint of 1903 *200 let Sankt-Peterburga. Istoricheskii ocherk*). SPb: Sotis, 1995.

Bachelard, Gaston. *The Poetics of Space,* Maria Jolas, trans. Boston: Beacon Press, 1994.

Baehr, Stephen. "Is Moscow Burning? Fire in Griboedov's *Woe from Wit.*" In *Russian Subjects: Empire, Nation, and the Culture of the Golden Age,* Monika Greenleaf and Stephen Moeller-Sally, eds. Evanston: Northwestern University Press, 1998.

Bagrov, L. S. *A History of the Cartography of Russia up to 1600,* H. W. Castner, ed. Ontario: Walker Press, 1975.

————. *A History of the Cartography of Russia up to 1800,* H. W. Castner, ed. Ontario: Walker Press, 1975.

Bakhtiarov, A. A.. *Briukho Peterburga: Ocherki stolichoi zhizni* (reprint of 1887). St. Petersburg: Fert, 1994.

————. *Proletariat i ulichnye tipy Peterburga. Bytovye ocherki.* St. Petersburg, 1895.

————. *Sovremennyi Peterburg.* Rodnik, 1903.

Bakhtin, M. "Vremia i prostranstvo v romane." *Voprosy literatury* 3, 1979.

————. *Problems of Dostoevsky's Poetics,* Caryl Emerson, trans. and ed. Minneapolis: University of Minnesota Press, 1984.

————. "Formy vremeni i khronotopa v romane." *Literaturno-kriticheskie stat'i.* 1986.

Bakhtin, V. S. *Pesni, skazki, chastushki, prislov'ia Leningradskoi oblasti.* Leningrad, 1982.

Baklanova, I. A. "Formirovanie i polozhenie promyshlennogo proletariata. Rabochee dvizhenie (60-e gody—nachalo 90-kh godov)." *Istoriia rabochikh Leningrada,* t. 1. Leningrad: Nauka, 1972.

Balzer, Harley D., ed. *Russia's Missing Middle Class: The Professions in Russian History.* Armonk: M. E. Sharpe, Inc., 1996.

Barenbaum, I. E. and Kostyleva, N. A. *Knizhnyi Peterburg-Leningrad.* Leningrad: Lenizdat, 1986.

Bartenev, I. N. and Batatkova, V. N. *Russkii inter'er XIX veka.* Leningrad: Khudozhnik RSFSR, 1984.

Barthes, Roland. *Architecture d'aujord'hui,* no. 153, December 1970–January 1971.

————. "Structure of the *Fait-Divers.*" In *Critical Essays,* Richard Howard, trans. Evanston: Northwestern University Press, 1972.

————. "Proust and Names." In *New Critical Essays,* Richard Howard, trans. New York: Hill and Wang, 1980.

Bashchutskii, Alexander. *Panorama Sanktpeterburga.* SPb: Tipografiia vdovy Pliushara s synom, 1834.

Bashmakov, A. I. *Ia idu po Millionoi.* SPb: Vsemirnyi klub peterburzhtsev, 2000.

Bater, James H. *St. Petersburg: Industrialization and Change.* London: E. Arnold, 1976.

————. "Between Old and New: St. Petersburg in the Late Imperial Era." In *The City in Late Imperial Russia,* Michael F. Hamm, ed. Bloomington: Indiana University Press, 1986.

Batorevich, N. I. *Chesmenskii dvorets.* SPb: Beloe i chernoe, 1997.

Baudelaire, Charles. "The Painter of Modern Life." In *The Painter of Modern Life and Other Essays,* Jonathan Mayne, trans. and ed. London: Phaidon Publishers, 1964.

Baudrillard, Jean. "Simulacra and Simulations." In *Jean Baudrillard: Selected Writings,* Mark Poster, ed. Stanford: Stanford University Press, 1988.

Beebee, Thomas O. *The Ideology of Genre: A Comparative Study of Generic Instability.* University Park: The Pennsylvania State University Press, 1994.

Belinskii, V. G. *Izbrannye filosofskie sochineniia.* Moscow: Gosudarstvennoe Izdatel'stvo Politicheskoi Literatury, 1941.

Belorus, F. *Iurodivyi Andrei Feodorovich ili Raba Bozhiia Kseniia, pogrebennaia na Smolenskom kladbishche v Peterburge.* SPb, 1893.

Belov, I. *Russkaia istoriia v narodnykh pogovorakh i skazaniiakh. Russkii arkhiv,* vyp. 1, 1990.

Belov, S. V. *Peterburg Dostoevskogo.* SPb: Aleteiia, 2002.

Benjamin, Walter. "The Storyteller: Reflections on the Works of Nikolai Leskov." In *Illuminations,* Harry Zohn, trans. New York: Schocken Books, 1969.

————. *Charles Baudelaire: A Lyric Poet in the Era of High Capitalism,* Harry Zohn, trans. London: New Left Books, 1973.

Benn, Aènna and Rosamund Bartlett. *Literary Russia: A Guide.* London: Papermac, 1997.

Bennett, Gillian and Paul Smith, eds. *Contemporary Legend: A Reader.* London: Garland Publishing, Inc., 1996.

Benois, Alexander. "Zhivopisnyi Peterburg." *Mir iskusstva,* no. 1, 1902.

————. "Krasota Peterburga." *Mir iskusstva,* no. 8, 1902.

————. "Materialy dlia istorii vandalizma v Rossii." *Mir iskusstva,* no. 12, 1903.

————. *Moi vospominaniia v piati knigakh,* kn. 1. Moscow: Nauka, 1990.

Berelowitch, Vladimir, and Olga Medvedkova. *Histoire de Saint-Pétersbourg.* Paris: Fayard, 1996.

Bergmann, Hans. *God in the Street: New York Writing from the Penny Press to Melville.* Philadelphia, Temple University Press, 1995.

Berkh, V. N. *Podrobnoe istoricheskoe izvestie o vsekh navodneniiakh, byvshikh v Sankt-Peterburge.* SPb, 1826.

Berkhtol'ts, F. V. *Dnevnik kamer-iunkera F. V. Berkhtol'tsa v 4 chastiakh,* ch. 1. Moscow, 1902–3.

Berlin, P. A. *Russkaia burzhuaziia v staroe i novoe vremia,* 2nd ed. Leningrad-Moscow: Kniga, 1925.

Berman, Marshall. *All That Is Solid Melts into Air: The Experience of Modernity.* New York: Penguin Books, 1982.

Berry, Thomas E. *Spiritualism in Tsarist Society and Literature.* Baltimore: Edgar Allan Poe Society, 1985.

Bespiatykh, Iu. N. *Peterburg Petra I v inostrannykh opisaniiakh.* Leningrad: Nauka, 1991.

————. *Peterburg Anny Ioannovny v inostranniiakh opisanniiakh.* SPb: BLITZ, 1997.

————, ed. *Fenomen Peterburga.* SPb: Russko-Baltiiskii Informatsionnyi Tsentr BLITS, 2000.

Bethea, David. *The Shape of Apocalypse in Modern Russian Fiction.* Princeton: Princeton University Press, 1989.

Biron, Vera. *Peterburg Dostoevskogo.* Leningrad: Svecha, 1991.

Blackmar, Elizabeth. *Manhattan for Rent, 1785–1850.* Ithaca: Cornell University Press, 1989.

Blackwell, William L. *The Beginnings of Russian Industrialization, 1800–1860.* Princeton: Princeton University Press, 1968.

Blanchot, Maurice. *The Space of Literature,* Ann Smock, trans. Lincoln: University of Nebraska Press, 1982.

Blinov, A. M. "Muzei 'Staryi Peterburg', 1907–1918 g." *Leningrad ves' na ladoni,* 1990.

Blium, A. V., ed. *Ocharovannye knigoi : Russkie pisateli o knigakh, chtenii, bibliofilakh.* Moscow: Kniga, 1982.

Blumenfeld, Hans. "Russian City Planning of the Eighteenth and Early Nineteenth Centuries." *Journal of the Society of Architectural Historians* IV (1944).

Blumin, Stuart M. *The Emergence of the Middle Class: Social Experience in the American City, 1760–1900.* Cambridge, UK: Cambridge University Press, 1989.

Bogdanov, A. I. *Istoricheskoe, geograficheskoe i topograficheskoe opisanie Sanktpeterburga, ot nachala zavedeniia ego, s 1703 po 1751 god. . . Reprint entitled Opisanie Sanktpeterburga. Polnoe izdanie unikal'nogo rossiiskogo istoriko-geograficheskogo truda serediny XVIII veka.* SPb: Severo-Zapadnaia Bibleiskaia Komissiia, S-Peterburgskii Filial Arkhiva RAN, 1997.

Bogdanov, E. (Fedotov, G. P.). *Tri stolitsy. Novyi mir,* 1989, No. 4.

Bogdanov, I. A. *Tri veka peterburgskoi bani.* SPb: Iskusstvo-SPB, 2000.

Boime, Albert. *Thomas Couture and the Eclectic Vision.* New Haven: Yale University Press, 1980.

Bolotov, A. T. *Peterburg pri Petre III.* SPb: A. S. Suvorin, 1901.

Borges, Jorge Luis. "On Exactitude in Science." In *Collected Fictions.* New York: Viking, 1998.

Borisova, E. A. "Nekotorye osobennosti vospriiatiia gorodskoi sredy i russkaia literatura vtoroi poloviny XIX veka." *Tipologiia russkogo realizma vtoroi poloviny XIX veka.* Moscow: Nauka, 1979.

———. *Russkaia arkhitektura vtoroi poloviny XIX veka.* Moscow: Nauka, 1979.

———. "Znak stilia." *Arkhitektura SSSR,* no. 1, January–February, 1984.

Boyarin, Jonathan, ed. *Remapping Memory: The Politics of TimeSpace.* Minneapolis: University of Minnesota Press, 1994.

Boyer, M. Christian. *The City of Collective Memory: Its Historical Imagery and Architectural Entertainments.* Cambridge: MIT Press, 1994.

Boym, Svetlana. *Common Places: Mythologies of Everyday Life in Russia.* Cambridge, MA: Harvard University Press, 1994.

———. *The Future of Nostalgia.* New York: Basic Books, 2001.

Bozherianov, I. N. *Nevskii Prospekt: Kul'turno-istoricheskii ocherk dvukhvekovoi zhizni S.-Peterburga.* SPb: A. I. Vilborg, 1900.

Bozherianov, I. N. and V. A. Nikol'skii. *Peterburgskaia starina. Ocherki i rasskazy.* SPb, 1909.

Bradbury, Ronald. *The Romantic Theories of Architecture of the Nineteenth Century, in Germany, England and France (Together with a Brief Survey of the Vitruvian School).* New York: Dorothy Press, 1934.

Brand, Dana. *The Spectator and the City in Nineteenth-Century American Literature.* Cambridge: Cambridge University Press, 1991.

Braudel, Fernand. *Capitalism and Material Life: 1400–1800.* New York: Harper & Row, 1975.

Broadbent, Geoffrey, Richard Bunt, and Charles Jencks, eds. *Signs, Symbols, and Architecture.* Chichester: John Wiley & Sons, 1980.

Brodie, Richard. *Virus of the Mind: The New Science of the Meme.* Seattle: Integral Press, 1994.

Brodskii, N. "Novoe o Pushkine." *Golos minuvshego,* 1913, no. 4.

Brodsky, Joseph. "A Guide to a Renamed City," "Less Than One," and "In a Room and a Half." In *Less Than One.* New York: Farrar, Straus, & Giroux, 1986.

Brooks, Jeffrey. *When Russia Learned to Read: Literacy and Popular Literature, 1861–1917.* Princeton: Princeton University Press, 1985.

Brooks, John I. III. *The Eclectic Legacy: Academic Philosophy and the Human Sciences in Nineteenth-Century France.* Newark: University of Delaware Press, 1998.

Brooks, Peter. "Freud's Masterplot: A Model for Narrative." In *Reading for the Plot: Design and Intention in Narrative.* Cambridge: Harvard University Press, 1992.

Brower, Daniel. "Urbanization and Autocracy: Russian Urban Development in the First Half of the Nineteenth Century." *Russian Review,* vol. 42 (1983).

Brown, Dona. *Inventing New England: Regional Tourism in the Nineteenth Century.* Washington, D.C.: Smithsonian Institution Press, 1995.

Brown, Lloyd A. *The Story of Maps.* New York: Dover Publications, 1979.

Brumfield, William Craft. "Urban Russia on the Eve of World War One: A Social Profile." *Journal of Social History* 13 (1980).

———. "Building for the Bourgeoisie: The Quest for a Modern Style in Russian Architecture." In *Between Tsar and People: Educated Society and the Quest for Public Identity in Late Imperial Russia,* Edith W. Clowes, Samuel D. Kassow, and James L. West, eds. Princeton: Princeton University Press, 1991.

———. *The Origins of Modernism in Russian Architecture.* Berkeley: University of California Press, 1991.

———. *A History of Russian Architecture.* Cambridge, UK: Cambridge University Press, 1993.

———. *Lost Russia: Photographing the Ruins of Russian Architecture.* 1995.

———, Boris V. Anan'ich, and Yuri A. Petrov, eds. *Commerce in Russian Urban Culture, 1861–1914.* Washington: Woodrow Wilson Center Press, 2001.

Buck-Morss, Susan. *The Dialectics of Seeing: Walter Benjamin and the Arcades Project.* Cambridge, MA: MIT Press, 1989.

Buickerood, James G. "Pursuing the Science of Man: Some Difficulties in Understanding Eighteenth-Century Maps of the Mind." *Eighteenth-Century Life* 19 (May 1996).

Bulakh, A. G. and N. B. Abakumova. *Kamennoe ubranstvo tsentra Leningrada.* Leningrad: Izdatel'stvo Leningradskogo Universiteta, 1987.

———. *Kamennoe ubranstvo glavnykh ulits Leningrada.* SPb: Izdatel'stvo S.-Petersburgskogo Universiteta, 1993.

Bulgakovskii, D. *Raba Bozhiia Kseniia, ili iurodivyi Andrei Fedorovich.* SPb, 1893.

Burbank, Jane and David L. Ransel. *Imperial Russia: New Histories for the Empire.* Bloomington: Indiana University Press, 1998.

Bur'ianov, V. *Progulka s det'mi po Sankt-Peterburgu i ego okrestnostiam.* SPb, 1838.

Burlak, Vadim. *Tainstvennyi Peterburg: Legendy severnoi stolitsy.* Moscow: OOO "AiF-Print," 2002.

Buryshkin, Pavel. *Moskva kupecheskaia.* Moscow: Vysshaia shkola, 1991.

Bushkanets, E. G. "U istokov memuarnoi literatury o N. A. Nekrasove." *Voprosy istochnikovedeniia russkoi literatury,* vyp. 112. Kazan', 1973.

Butikov, Georgy. Introduction to *St. Isaac's Cathedral,* David and Judith Andrews, trans. Leningrad: Aurora Art Publishers, 1980.

Butkov, Ia. *Peterburgskie vershiny* (Parts I and II). Spb: Tipografiia N. Grecha, 1845, 1846.

Buzinov, Viktor. *Dvortsovaia ploshchad': Neformal'nyi putevoditel'.* SPb: Ostrov, 2001.

Byrd, Max. *London Transformed: Images of the City in the Eighteenth Century.* New Haven: Yale University Press, 1978.

Campbell, John. *Past, Space, and Self.* Cambridge, MA: MIT Press, 1994.

Castells, Manuel. *The Urban Question: A Marxist Approach.* London: Edward Arnold, 1977.

Caws, Mary Ann, ed. *City Images: Perspectives from Literature, Philosophy, and Film.* New York: Gordon and Breach, 1991.

Charboures, Marinos. *Monument elevé à la gloire de Pierre-le-Grand; ou, Relation des travaux et des moyens mechaniques qui ont été employés pour transporter à Petersbourg un rocher de trois millions pesant, destiné à servir de base à la statue equestre de cet empereur; avec un examen physique et chymique du même rocher.* Paris, 1777.

Chard, Chloe. *Pleasure and Guilt on the Grand Tour: Travel Writing and Imaginative Geography 1600–1830.* Manchester: Manchester University Press, 1999.

Chukovskii, Kornei. "Trosnikov-Nekrasov (Cherty avtobiografii v naidennykh proizvedeniiakh Nekrasova)." In *Zhizn' i pokhozhdeniia Tikhona Trosnikova,* Evgen'ev-Maksimov and Chukovskii, eds. Moscow: Khudozhestvennaia literatura, 1931.

Chulkov, Boris, ed. *Tsarskoe Selo v poezii 1750–2000. Antologiia.* SPb: Fond Russkoi Poezii, 1999.

Cixous, Hélène. "Fiction and Its Phantoms: A Reading of Freud's *Das Unheimliche* (the 'uncanny')." *New Literary History,* vol. 7, no. 3, Spring 1976.

Clark, Katerina. *Petersburg: Crucible of Cultural Revolution.* Cambridge, MA: Harvard University Press, 1995.

Clayton, Jay and Eric Rothstein, eds. *Influence and Intertextuality in Literary History.* Madison: University of Wisconsin Press, 1991.

Clowes, Edith W., Samuel D. Kassow, and James L. West, eds. *Between Tsar and People: Educated Society and the Quest for Public Identity in Late Imperial Russia.* Princeton: Princeton University Press, 1991.

Cobley, Evelyn. "Mikhail Bakhtin's Place in Genre Theory." *Genre* XXI (Fall 1988).

Colie, Rosalie L. *The Resources of Kind: Genre-Theory in the Renaissance,* Barbara K. Lewalski, ed. Berkeley: University of California Press, 1973.

Colley, Ann C. *The Search for Synthesis in Literature and Art: The Paradox of Space.* Athens: University of Georgia Press, 1990.

Collins, Peter. *Changing Ideals in Modern Architecture 1750–1950.* London: Faber and Faber, 1965.

Colomina, Beatriz, ed. *Sexuality and Space.* Princeton Architectural Press, 1992.

Confino, Alon. *The Nation as a Local Metaphor: Wfrttemberg, Imperial Germany, and National Memory, 1871–1918.* Chapel Hill: University of North Carolina Press, 1997.

Conley, Tom. *The Self-Made Map: Cartographic Writing in Early Modern France.* Minneapolis: University of Minnesota Press, 1996.

Connolly, Peter. *The Ancient City: Life in Classical Athens and Rome*. Oxford: Oxford University Press, 1998.

Considérant, Victor. *Considérations socials sur l'architectonique*. Paris: Librairies du Palais-Royal, 1834.

Cosgrove, Denis. *Social Formation and Symbolic Landscape*. Madison: University of Wisconsin Press, 1998.

Cosgrove, Denis and Stephen Daniels, eds. *The Iconography of Landscape: Essays on the Symbolic Representation, Design, and Use of Past Environments*. Cambridge: Cambridge University Press, 1988.

Cosgrove, Denis and Mona Domosh. "Author and Authority: Writing the New Cultural Geography." In *Place/Culture/Representation*, James Duncan and David Ley, eds. New York: Routledge, 1993.

Cracraft, James. *The Petrine Revolution in Russian Architecture*. Chicago: University of Chicago Press, 1988.

———. *The Petrine Revolution in Russian Imagery*. Chicago: University of Chicago Press, 1997.

Crone, Anna Lisa. "Petersburg and the Plight of Russian Beauty: The Case of Mandelstam's Tristia." In *New Studies in Russian Language and Literature*, Anna Lisa Crone and Catherine V. Chvany, eds. Columbus, OH: Slavica, 1986.

———. "Echoes of Nietzsche and Mallarme in Mandelstam's Metapoetic 'Petersburg.'" *Russian Literature*, 1991 Nov 15, 30:4.

———. "Akhmatova and the Passing of the Swans." In *A Sense of Place*, Lev Loseff and Barry Scherr, eds. Columbus, OH: Slavica, 1993.

———. "Tiutchev and Identification of Self with Space in Petersburg Poetics of the Twentieth Century." In *Literary Tradition and Practice in Russian Culture*, Valentina Polukhina, Joe Andrews, and Robert Reid, eds. Amsterdam: Rodopi, 1993.

———. "What Derzhavin Heard When Pushkin Read 'Vospominaniia v Tsarskom Sele' in 1815." *Pushkin Review*, vol. 3, 1999.

Crossick, Geoffrey and Heinz-Gerhard Haupt. *The Petite Bourgeoisie in Europe 1780–1914: Enterprise, Family and Independence*. New York: Routledge, 1995.

Curry, Michael R. *The Work in the World: Geographical Practice and the Written Word*. Minneapolis: University of Minnesota Press, 1996.

Custine, Marquis de. *Empire of the Czar: A Journey through Eternal Russia*. New York: Doubleday, 1989.

Danilevskii, N. Ia. *Rossiia i Evropa*. Moscow: Kniga, 1991.

Darinskii, A. V. and V. I. Startsev. *Istoriia Sankt-Peterburga XVIII–XIX vv*. SPb: Glagol, 2000.

de Certeau, Michel. *The Practice of Everyday Life*, Steven Rendall, trans. Berkeley: University of California Press, 1984.

———. *Heterologies: Discourse on the Other*. Minneapolis: University of Minnesota Press, 1986.

———. *Culture in the Plural*. Minneapolis: University of Minnesota Press, 1997.

de Coulanges, Fustel. *The Ancient City: A Study on the Religion, Laws, and Institutions of Greece and Rome*. Baltimore: Johns Hopkins University Press, 1980.

Del'vig, A. I. *Polveka russkoi zhizni: Vospominaniia A. I. Del'viga 1820–1870*. Moscow: Academia, 1930.

Denitskii, V. N., ed. *M. Gor'kii. Materialy i issledovaniia*. Moscow: Izdatel'stvo AN SSSR, 1934–51.

Derrida, Jacques. "The Law of Genre." *Glyph*, 7, 1980.

De Wassenaer, Cornélie. *A Visit to St. Petersburg, 1824–1825*, Igor Vinogradoff, trans. and ed. Norwich: Michael Russell, 1994.

Dianina, Katia. "The Feuilleton: An Everyday Guide to Public Culture in the Age of the Great Reforms." Slavic and East European Journal, vol. 47, no. 2, summer 2003.

Diderot, Denis and Jean le Rond D'Alembert, eds. *L'Encyclopédie, ou dictionnaire raisonné des sciences, des arts et des métiers*. Stuttgart-Bad Cannstatt: Frommann, 1966.

Dilaktorskaia, O. G. *Peterburgskaia povest' Dostoevskogo*. Studiorum Slavicorum Monumenta, Tomus 17. SPb: Dmitri Bulanin, 1999.

Dobuzhinskii, M. *Vospominaniia*. Moscow: Nauka, 1987.

Dokusov, A. M. *Literaturnye pamiatnye mesta Leningrada*. Leningrad: Leninzdat, 1968.

Dolgopolov, L. K. "Mif o Peterburge i ego preobrazovanie v nachale XX veka." In *Na rubezhe vekov: O Russkoi literature kontsa XIX-nachala XX veka*. Leningrad: Sovetskii pisatel', 1977.

Dolgorukov, P. *Peterburgskie ocherki: Pamflety emigranta, 1860–1867*. Moscow: Novosti, 1992.

Dubiago, T. B. *Letnii sad*. Moscow: Gosudarstvennoe Izdatel'stvo Literatury po Stroitel'stvu i Arkhitekture, 1951.

Dubrow, Heather. *Genre*. London: Methuen, 1982.

Duncan, James. *The City as Text: The Politics of Landscape Interpretation in the Kandyan Kingdom*. Cambridge: Cambridge University Press.

Duncan, James and David Ley, eds. "Representing the Place of Culture." In *Place/Culture/Representation*. New York: Routledge, 1993.

Dushechkina, E. V., ed. *Peterburgskii sviatochnyi rasskaz*. Leningrad: Izdatel'stvo Petropol' LO SFK, 1991.

Eco, Umberto. "Architecture and Memory." *VIA* 8, 1986.

Economakis, Evel G. *From Peasant to Petersburger*. New York: St. Martin's Press, 1998.

Edgerton, William B. "The Ghost in Search of Help." In *Readings from the Journal of the Folklore Institute. European Folklore*, Felix J. Oinas, ed. Bloomington: Trickster Press, 1981.

———. "A Ghostly Urban Legend in Petersburg: Was N. S. Leskov Involved?" In *The Supernatural in Slavic and Baltic Literature*, Amy Mandelker and Roberta Reeder, eds. 1988.

Edwards, Catherine. *Writing Rome: Textual Approaches to the City*. Cambridge: Cambridge University Press, 1996.

Egorov, Yuri. *The Architectural Planning of St. Petersburg*, Eric Dluhosch, trans. Athens, Ohio: Ohio University Press, 1969.

Egorov, V. A. "Rasskaz Nekrasova 'Bez vesti propavshii piita' v literaturnoi polemike nachala 1840-kh godov." *Nekrasov i ego vremia*, vyp. IV. Kaliningrad: Kaliningradskii Gosudarstvennyi Universitet, 1975–1983.

Ellis, Richard. *Imagining Atlantis*. New York: Alfred A. Knopf, 1998.

Engelstein, Laura. *The Keys to Happiness: Sex and the Search for Modernity in Fin-de-Siècle Russia*. Ithaca: Cornell University Press, 1992.

Entrikin, J. Nicholas. *The Betweenness of Place: Towards a Geography of Modernity*. Baltimore: Johns Hopkins University Press, 1991.

Epstein, Mikhail N. *After the Future: The Paradoxes of Postmodernism and Contemporary*

Russian Culture, Anesa Miller-Pogacar, trans. Amherst: University of Massachusetts Press, 1995.

Evgen'ev-Maksimov, V. E. "Ispoved' rannego raznochintsa." In *Zhizn' i pokhozhdeniia Tikhona Trosnikova,* V. E. Evgen'ev-Maksimov and K. Chukovskii, eds. Moscow: Khudozhestvennaia literatura, 1931.

———. *Nekrasov i Peterburg.* Leningrad: Leningradskoe Gazetno-Zhurnal'noe i Knizhnoe Izdatel'stvo, 1947.

———. *Zhizn' i deiatel'nost' N. A. Nekrasova.* Moscow: Khudozhestvennaia literatura, 1947.

Evnin, F. I. "Roman *Prestupleniie i nakazanie.*" *Tvorchestvo F. M. Dostoevskogo,* N. L. Stepanov, ed. Moscow, 1959.

Faber, Theodore. *Bagatelles: Promenades d'un Désoeuvré dans la Ville de St. Pétersbourg.* Paris, 1812.

Fanger, Donald. "Dostoevsky's Early Feuilletons: Approaches to the Myth of a City." *Slavic Review,* 22, 1963.

———. *Dostoevsky and Romantic Realism.* Chicago: University of Chicago Press, 1965.

———. "The City of Russian Modernist Fiction." In *Modernism, 1890–1930,* Malcolm Bradbury and James Walter McFarlane, eds. Hassocks, UK: Harvester, 1978.

———. *The Creation of Nikolai Gogol.* Cambridge, MA: Belknap Press of Harvard University Press, 1979.

Fazolini, Marika. "Vzgliad na usad'bu, ili Predstavlenie provintsialov o russkoi stolichnoi zhizni." *Russkaia provintsiia: Mif—Tekst—Real'nost',* A. F. Belousov and T. V. Tsiv'ian, eds. Moscow: "Kollektiv avtorov," 2000.

Fedetov, N. *Petersburgskie dachnye mestnosti v otnoshenii ikh zdorovosti.* SPb, 1881, 1892.

———. *Putevoditel' po dachnym mestnostiam, vodolechebnym zavedeniiam i morskim kupan'iam v okrestnostiakh S.-Peterburga i po zheleznym dorogam.* SPb, 1889.

Fernandez, James W., ed. *Beyond Metaphor: The Theory of Tropes in Anthropology.* Stanford: Stanford University Press, 1991.

Field, Andrew. "The Nabokovs: Radical Chic in St. Petersburg: Wearing White Gloves." *Quadrant,* 31:16, June 1987.

Finke, Michael C. *Metapoesis: The Russian Tradition from Pushkin to Chekhov.* Bloomington: Indiana University Press, 1995.

Finnegan, Ruth. *Tales of the City: A Study of Narrative and Urban Life.* Cambridge: Cambridge University Press, 1998.

Fishelov, David. *Metaphors of Genre: The Role of Analogies in Genre Theory.* University Park: The Pennsylvania State University Press, 1993.

Flier, Michael S. "At Daggers Drawn: The Competition for the Church of the Savior on the Blood." In *For SK: In Celebration of the Life and Career of Simon Karlinsky,* Michael S. Flier and Robert P. Hughes, eds. Berkeley: Berkeley Slavic Specialties, 1994.

———. "The Church of the Savior on the Blood: Projection, Rejection, Resurrection." In *Christianity and the Eastern Slavs,* vol. II, Robert P. Hughes and Irina Paperno, eds. Berkeley: University of California Press, 1994.

Floryan, Margrethe. *Gardens of the Tsars: A Study of the Aesthetics, Semantics and Uses of Late Eighteenth Century Russian Gardens.* Aarhus: Aarhus University Press, 1996.

Foucault, Michel. *The Archaelogy of Knowledge and The Discourse on Language,* A. M. Sheridan Smith, trans. New York: Pantheon Books, 1972.

———. "Questions on Geography." In *Power/Knowledge,* Colin Gordon, ed. New York: Pantheon Books, 1980.

————. "Of Other Spaces." *Diacritics* 16.1 (1986).

Frank, Ellen Eve. *Literary Architecture: Essays toward a Tradition: Walter Pater, Gerard Manley Hopkins, Marcel Proust, Henry James.* Berkeley: University of California Press, 1979.

Frank, Joseph. "Spatial Form in Modern Literature." In *The Widening Gyre: Crisis and Mastery in Modern Literature.* New Brunswick: Rutgers University Press, 1963.

————. *Dostoevsky: The Seeds of Revolt 1821–1849.* Princeton: Princeton University Press, 1976.

Frank, Stephen P. and Mark D. Steinberg, eds. *Cultures in Flux: Lower-Class Values, Practices, and Resistance in Late Imperial Russia.* Princeton: Princeton University Press, 1994.

Frazier, Melissa. "*Arabesques*, Architecture, and Printing." In *Russian Subjects*, Monika Greenleaf and Stephen Moeller-Sally, eds. Evanston: Northwestern University Press, 1998.

————. *Frames of the Imagination: Gogol's Arabesques and the Romantic Question of Genre.* New York: Peter Lang, 2000.

Freud, Sigmund. *Civilization and Its Discontents*, Joan Rivière, trans. New York: Jonathan Cape & Harrison Smith, 1930.

————. "The Uncanny." In *Art and Literature*, from the Penguin Freud Library, vol. 14. Middlesex, UK: Penguin Books, 1985.

Fried, Michael. *Absorption and Theatricality: Painting and Beholder in the Age of Diderot.* Chicago: University of Chicago Press, 1988.

Fritzsche, Peter. *Reading Berlin 1900.* Cambridge, MA: Harvard University Press, 1996.

Frow, John. "Intertextuality and Ontology." In *Intertextuality: Theories and Practices*, Michael Worton and Judith Still, eds. Manchester: Manchester University Press, 1990.

Frye, Northrop. *Anatomy of Criticism.* Princeton: Princeton University Press, 1957.

Fusso, Susanne. "The Landscape of *Arabesques*." In *Essays on Gogol: Logos and the Russian Word*, Susanne Fusso and Priscilla Meyer, eds. Evanston: Northwestern University Press, 1992.

Gallagher, Catherine. *The Industrial Reformation of English Fiction: Social Discourse and Narrative Form, 1832–1867.* Chicago: University of Chicago Press, 1985.

Gautier, Théophile. *Voyage en Russie.* Paris: La Boîte à Documents, 1990.

Genette, Gérard. *The Architext: An Introduction*, Jane E. Lewin, trans. Berkeley: University of California Press, 1992.

————. *Fiction and Diction*, Catherine Porter, trans. Ithaca: Cornell University Press, 1993.

————. *Palimpsests: Literature in the Second Degree*, Channa Newman and Claude Doubinsky, trans. Lincoln: University of Nebraska Press, 1997.

Georgi, I. G. *Opisanie rossiisko-imperatorskogo stolichnogo goroda Sankt-Peterburga i dostopamiatnostei v okrestnostiakh onogo, 1794–1796.* SPb: Liga, 1996.

Georgiev, I. I., et al. *Sankt-Peterburg. Zanimatel'nye voprosy i otvety.* SPb: Paritet, 2001.

Gerasimov, V. V. *Bol'shoi dvorets v Strel'ne—Bez chetverti tri stoletiia.* SPb: Almaz, 1997.

Germont, G. *Reshetki Leningrada i ego okrestnostei.* Moscow: Izdatel'stvo Vsesoiuznoi Akademii Arkhitektury, 1938.

Gerschenkron, Alexander. "Economic Development in Russian Intellectual History of the Nineteenth Century." In *Economic Backwardness in Historical Perspective: A Book of Essays.* Cambridge, MA: Belknap Press of Harvard University Press, 1962.

Gershenzon, M. *Zhizn' V. S. Pecherina.* Moscow, 1910.

Gilloch, Graeme. *Myth and Metropolis: Walter Benjamin and the City.* Cambridge, UK: Polity Press, 1996.

Ginzburg, Lidiia. *O lirike.* Moscow: Intrada, 1997.

———. "Mysl', opisavshaia krug." *Zapisnye knizhki. Vospominaniia. Esse.* SPb: Iskusstvo-SPb, 2002.

Glickman, Rose L. "Industrialization and the Factory Worker in Russian Literature." *Canadian-Slavic Studies,* vol. 4, no. 4, 1970.

Glinka, N. I. *Derzhavin v Peterburge.* Leningrade, 1985.

———. "*Krasuiska, grad Petrov . . .*" *Zolotoi vek arkhitektury Sankt-Peterburga.* St. Petersburg: Lenizdat, 1996.

Gogin, Alexander, et al. *Metafizika Peterburga,* Vyp. I. SPb: EIDOS, 1993.

Gollerbakh, E. *Gorod muz: Povest' o Tsarskom Sele.* Leningrad, 1930, as reprinted by LEV in Paris, 1980.

Golubeva, I. A. "Istorik-peterburgoved Petr Nikolaevich Stolpianskii (1872–1938): Biograficheskii ocherk." *Zhurnal liubitelei iskusstva,* nos. 8–9, 1997.

———. "Neizvestnyi P. N. Stolpianskii." *Fenomen Peterburga,* Iu. N. Bespiatykh, ed. SPb: BLITS, 2000.

Gorbachevich, K. and E. Khablo. *Pochemu tak nazvany? O proiskhozhdenii nazvanii ulits, ploshchadei, ostrovov, rek, i mostov Sankt-Peterburga.* SPb: Norint, 1998.

Gorbatenko, S. B. "Dva petrovskikh ansamblia Strel'ny." *Nevskii arkhiv: Istoriko-kraevedcheskii sbornik III.* SPb: Atheneum-Feniks, 1997.

———. *Petergofskaia doroga: Oranienbaumskii istoriko-landshaftnyi kompleks.* SPb: Dmitri Bulanin, 2001.

Gordin, A. M. *Pushkinskii Peterburg* (album). SPb: Khudozhnik RSFSR, 1991.

Gordin, A. M., Iu. M. Denisov, N. M. Kozyreva, et al, eds. *Gorod glazami khudozhnikov: Peterburg—Petrograd—Leningrad v proizvedeniiakh zhivopisi i grafiki.* Izdatel'stvo Khudozhnik RSFSR, 1978.

Gordin, A. M. and M. A. Gordin. *Pushkinskii vek: Panorama stolichnoi zhizni* (series *Byloi Peterburg*), books 1 and 2. SPb: Pushkinskii fond, 1999.

Gottdiener, M. *The Social Production of Urban Space,* 2nd ed. Austin: University of Texas Press, 1985.

Grabar', Igor. *Peterburgskaia arkhitektura v XVIII i XIX vekakh.* SPb: Lenizdat, 1994.

Grach, A. D. *Arkheologicheskie raskopki v Leningrade: k kharakteristike kul'tury i byta naseleniia Peterburga XVIII veka.* Moscow: AN SSSR, 1957.

Grech, Aleksei. *Ves' Peterburg v karmane: Spravochnaia kniga dlia stolichnykh zhitelei i priezzhikh, s planami Sanktpeterburga i chetyrekh teatrov.* SPb: Tip. A. Grecha, 1851.

Greenleaf, Monika and Stephen Moeller-Sally, eds. *Russian Subjects: Empire, Nation, and the Culture of the Golden Age.* Evanston: Northwestern University Press, 1998.

Gregory, Derek. *Geographical Imaginations.* Oxford: Blackwell, 1994.

Gregory, Derek and John Urray, eds. *Social Relations and Spatial Structures.* Basingstoke: Macmillan, 1985.

Grevs, Ivan. "Monumental'nyi gorod i istoricheskie ekskursii: Osnovnaia ideia obrazovatel'nykh puteshestvii po krupnym tsentram kul'tury." *Ekskursionnoe delo,* no. 1, 1921.

———. "Gorod, kak predmet kraevedeniia." *Kraevedenie,* no. 3, 1924.

Griffin, Leland M. "The Edifice Metaphor in Rhetorical Theory." *Speech Monographs,* vol. 27, no. 5, November 1960.

Grossman, Leonid. "Gogol'—urbanist." In N. V. Gogol', *Povesti*. Moscow, 1935.

———. "Gorod i liudi." In F. M. Dostoevskii, *Prestuplenie i nakazanie*. Moscow: Goslitizdat, 1935.

———. "Dostoevsky-Khudozhnik." In *Tvorchestvo F. M. Dostoevskogo*, N. L. Stepanov, ed. Moscow: Izdatel'stvo Akademii Nauk SSSR, 1959.

Grot, K. Ia. *Pushkinskii litsei (1811–1817)*. SPb, 1911.

Groth, Paul and Todd W. Bressi, eds. *Understanding Ordinary Landscapes*. New Haven: Yale University Press, 1997.

Gubin, D., L. Lur'e, and I. Poroshin. *Real'nyi Peterburg: O gorode s tochki zreniia nedvizhimosti i o nedvizhimosti s tochki zreniia istorii*. SPb: Limbus, 1999.

Guillén, Claudio. *Literature as System: Essays Toward the Theory of Literary History*. Princeton: Princeton University Press, 1971.

Gukovskii, Grigorii. "Neizdannye povesti Nekrasova v istorii russkoi prozy sorokovykh godov." In *Zhizn' i pokhozhdeniia Tikhona Trosnikova*, Evgen'ev-Maksimov and Chukovskii, eds. Moscow: Khudozhestvennaia literatura, 1931.

Hamm, Michael F., ed. *The City in Russian History*. Lexington: University Press of Kentucky, 1976.

———. *The City in Late Imperial Russia*. Bloomington: Indiana University Press, 1986.

Hamon, Philippe. *Expositions: Literature and Architecture in Nineteenth-Century France*, Katia Sainson-Frank and Lisa Maguire, trans. Berkeley: University of California Press, 1992.

Hancock, Claire. "*Capitale du plaisir:* The Remaking of Imperial Paris." In *Imperial Cities: Landscape, Display, and Identity*, Felix Driver and David Gilbert, eds. Manchester: Manchester University Press, 1999.

Handlin, Oscar and John Burchard, eds. *The Historian and the City*. Cambridge, MA: M.I.T. and Harvard University Presses, 1963.

Harley, J. B. "Maps, Knowledge, and Power." In *The Iconography of Landscape: Essays on the Symbolic Representation, Design, and Use of Past Environments*, Denis Cosgrove and Stephen Daniels, eds. Cambridge: Cambridge University Press, 1988.

———. "Deconstructing the Map." *Cartographica* 26, 1989.

———. "Historical Geography and the Cartographic Illusion." *Journal of Historical Geography* 15, 1989.

Harvey, David. *Consciousness and the Urban Experience: Studies in the History and Theory of Capitalist Urbanization*. Baltimore: Johns Hopkins University Press, 1985.

———. *The Condition of Postmodernity: An Enquiry into the Origins of Cultural Change*. Oxford: Blackwell, 1990.

Harvey, Milton E. and Brian P. Holly, eds. *Themes in Geographic Thought*. London: Croom Helm, 1981.

Heidegger, Martin. "Building, Dwelling, Thinking" and "The Origin of the Work of Art." In *Poetry, Language, Thought*, Albert Hofstadter, trans. New York: Harper & Row, 1971.

———. *Being and Time: A Translation of Sein und Zeit*, Joan Stambaugh, trans. Albany: State University of New York Press, 1996.

Hellberg-Hirn, Elena. *Imperial Imprints: Post-Soviet St. Petersburg*. SKS Finnish Literature Society, 2003.

Herman, David. *Poverty of the Imagination: Nineteenth-Century Russian Literature about the Poor*. Evanston: Northwestern University Press, 2001.

Hernadi, Paul. *Beyond Genre: New Directions in Literary Classification*. Ithaca: Cornell University Press, 1972.

Higonnet, Patrice. *Paris: Capital of the World*, Arthur Goldhammer, trans. Cambridge, MA: Belknap Press of Harvard University Press, 2002.

Hill, Ida Carleton Thallon. *The Ancient City of Athens: Its Topography and Monuments*. Cambridge, MA: Harvard University Press, 1953.

Hirsch, E. D., Jr. *Validity in Interpretation*. New Haven: Yale University Press, 1967.

Hodgson, Peter. *From Gogol to Dostoevsky: Jakov Butkov, A Reluctant Naturalist in the 1840s*. Munich: Fink Verlag, 1976.

Holmgren, Beth. *Rewriting Capitalism: Literature and the Market in Late Tsarist Russia and the Kingdom of Poland*. Pittsburgh: University of Pittsburgh Press, 1998.

Holthusen, Johannes. "Petersburg als literarischer Mythos." In *Russland in Vers und Prosa*. Munich: Verlag Otto Sagner, 1973.

Howlett, Jana. "Petersburg—Moscow—Petropolis." In *Unreal City: Urban Experience in Modern European Literature and Art*, Edward Timms and David Kelley, eds., Manchester: Manchester University Press, 1985.

Hughes, Lindsey. *Russia in the Age of Peter the Great*. New Haven: Yale University Press, 1998.

Iakovleva, E. B. "Dachnaia arkhitektura severnykh okrestnostei Sankt-Peterburga vo vtoroi polovine XIX—nachale XX v." *Peterburgskie chteniia—97: Peterburg i Rossiia*. SPb: Petrovskii fond, 1997.

Iakovleva, Liudmila. "Svetlyi lik Ksenii." *Blazhennaia Kseniia Peterburgskaia: Sovremennye chudesa. Zhitie. Akafist*. Moscow, 1994.

Iatsevich, A. *Pushkinskii Peterburg*. Pushkinskoe obshchestvo, Leningrad, 1935.

Iezuitova, R. V. *Pushkin v Peterburge*. Leningrad, 1991.

Ignatova, Elena. *Zapiski o Peterburge: Ocherk istorii goroda*. SPb: Kul'tInformPress, 1997.

Ikonnikov, A. V. "Peterburg i Moskva (k voprosu o russkoi gradostroitel'noi traditsii)." *Esteticheskaia vyrazitel'nost' goroda*. Moscow, 1986.

———. *Tysiacha let russkoi arkhitektury: Razvitie traditsii*. Moscow: Iskusstvo, 1990.

Indostanskii, K. *Prizraki—Okonchanie povesti Lermontova*. Moscow: I. N. Kushnerev, 1897.

Isachenko, G. *Okno v Evropu. Istoriia i landshafty*. Spb: Sankt-Peterburgskogo Gosudarstvennogo Universiteta, 1998.

Isachenko, V. G. and G. A. Ol'. *Fedor Lidval*. Leningrad: Lenizdat, 1987.

Isachenko, V. G. and V. N. Pitanin. *Liteinyi Prospekt*. Leningrad: Lenizdat, 1989.

———. *Osobniak Suvorina*. St.Petersburg: Beloe i chernoe, 1996.

———, ed. *Zodchie Sankt-Peterburga XIX—nachalo XX veka*. SPb: Lenizdat, 1998.

Istoricheskie rasskazy i anekdoty iz zhizni russkikh gosudarei i zamechatel'nykh liudei XVIII i XIX stoletii. SPb, 1885.

Istorizm v Rossii: Stil' i epokha v dekorativnom iskusstve 1820-e—1890-e gody. SPb: Slaviia, 1996.

Isupov, K. G. "Dialog stolits v istoricheskom dvizhenii." *Moskva-Peterburg: Pro et Contra*. SPb: Izdatel'stvo Russkogo Khristianskogo Gumanitarnogo Instituta, 2000.

———, ed. *Moskva-Peterburg: Pro et Contra*. SPb: RKHGI, 2000.

Iukhneva, N. V., ed. *Peterburg i guberniia: Istoriko-etnograficheskie issledovaniia*. Leningrad: Nauka, 1989.

Ivanov, A. A. *Doma i liudi: Iz istorii peterburgskikh osobniakov*. SPb: Lenizdat, 1997.

Ivanov, V. V. "K semioticheskomu izucheniiu kul'turnoi istorii bol'shogo goroda." *Semiotika prostranstva i prostranstvo semiotiki: Trudy po znakovym sistemam* 19 [Uchenye Zapiski Tartuskogo Universiteta, 720], 1986.

Ivanova, N. B. "Zagadka i taina v literature 'peterburgskogo stilia.'" *Fenomen Peterburga.* SPb: BLITS, 2000.

Ivanova, V. P., ed. *Sady i parki Leningrada.* Leningrad: Lenizdat, 1981.

Ivask, George. "The Vital Ambivalence of Petersburg." *Texas Studies in Literature and Language,* vol. 17, 1975.

Izmailov, N. V. "Fantasticheskaia povest'." *Russkaia povest' XIX veka: Istoriia i problematika zhanra,* B. S. Meilakh, ed. Leningrad: Nauka, 1973.

Jackson, John Brinckerhoff. *Discovering the Vernacular Landscape.* New Haven: Yale University Press, 1984.

Jackson, Peter, ed. *Maps of Meaning: An Introduction to Cultural Geography.* London: Unwin Hyman, 1989.

Jahn, Hubertus F. "Der St. Petersburger Heumarkt im 19. Jahrhundert. Metamorphosen eines Stadtviertels." *Jahrbfcher ffr Geschichte Osteuropas,* 44, 1996.

Jakobson, Roman. "On Realism in Art." In *Readings in Russian Poetics: Formalist and Structuralist Views,* Ladislav Matejka and Krystyna Pomorska, eds. Ann Arbor: Michigan Slavic Publications, 1978.

———. "The Statue in Pushkin's Poetic Mythology." In *Language in Literature,* Krystyna Pomorska and Stephen Rudy, eds. Cambridge, MA: Belknap Press of Harvard University Press, 1987.

Jakobson, Roman and Yurii Tynianov. "Problemy izucheniia literatury i iazyka." *Novyi Lef,* 12, 1928.

Jameson, Frederic. "Magical Narratives: On the Dialectical Use of Genre Criticism." In *The Political Unconscious: Narrative as a Socially Symbolic Act.* Ithaca: Cornell University Press, 1981.

Jammer, Max. *Concepts of Space: The History of Theories of Space in Physics,* 3rd ed. New York: Dover Publications, 1993.

Jarvis, Robin. *Romantic Writing and Pedestrian Travel.* New York: St. Martin's Press, 1997.

Johnston, William M. "William Kinglake's 'A Summer in Russia': A Neglected Memoir of St. Petersburg in 1845." *Texas Studies in Literature and Language,* 9, 1967.

Kachurin, M. G., G. A. Kudyrskaia, and D. N. Murin. *Sankt-Peterburg v russkoi literature: Uchebnik-khrestomatiia,* 2 volumes. SPb: Svet, 1996

Kagan, Moisei. *Grad Petrov v istorii russkoi kul'tury.* St. Petersburg: Slaviia, 1996.

Kaganov, Grigory. "Sight Riven and Restored: The Image of Petersburg Space, 1850–1900. *Russian Review,* April 1995.

———. *Images of Space: St. Petersburg in the Visual and Verbal Arts,* Sideney Monas, trans. Stanford: Stanford University Press, 1997.

———. *Peterburg v kontekste barokko.* SPb: Stella, 2001.

Kaganovich, A. L. *Mednyi vsadnik: Istoriia sozdaniia monumenta.* Leningrad: Iskusstvo, 1975.

Kahn, Andrew. "Readings of Imperial Rome from Lomonosov to Pushkin." *Slavic Review,* vol. 52, no. 4, Winter 1993.

———. *Pushkin's The Bronze Horseman.* London: Bristol Classical Press, 1998.

Kalinin, B. N. and P. P. Iurevich. *Pamiatniki i memorial'nye doski Leningrada.* Leningrad: Lenizdat, 1979.

Kann, P. Ia. *Progulki po Peterburgu: Vdol' Moiki, Fontanki, Sadovoi.* SPb: Palitra, 1994.

Kapferer, Jean-Noel. *Rumor: Uses, Interpretations, and Images.* New Brunswick: Transaction Publishers, 1990.

Karatygin, P. P. "Letopis' peterburgskikh navodnenii, 1703–1879." *Istoricheskii vestnik,* vol. 33, 1888.

Kassow, Samuel D., James L. West, and Edith W. Clowes. "Introduction: The Problem of the Middle in Late Imperial Russian Society." In *Between Tsar and People: Educated Society and the Quest for Public Identity in Late Imperial Russia,* Edith W. Clowes, Samuel D. Kassow, and James L. West, eds. Princeton: Princeton University Press, 1991.

Keating, P. J. *The Working Classes in Victorian Fiction.* London: Routledge & Kegan Paul, 1971.

Kedrinskii, A. A., et al. *Vosstanovlenie pamiatnikov arkhitektury Leningrada.* Leningrad: Stroizdat, 1983.

Kellman, Steven G. "Circles, Squares, and the Mind's Ear in St. Petersburg." *Papers on Language and Literature: A Journal for Scholars and Critics of Language and Literature,* 14, 1978.

Kent, Thomas. *Interpretation and Genre: The Role of Generic Perception in the Study of Narrative Texts.* London: Associated University Presses, 1986.

Kern, A. P. *Vospominaniia.* Leningrad: Academia, 1929.

Kern, Stephen. *The Culture of Time and Space 1800–1918.* Cambridge, MA: Harvard University Press, 1983.

Khodasevich, Vladislav. "Peterburgskie povesti Pushkina." *Uedinennyi domik na Vasilievskom.* Moscow: Universal'naia biblioteka, 1915.

Khodiakova, O. A. "Iz istorii prazdnovaniia 100-letiia i 200-letiia osnovaniia Sankt-Peterburg," 96, *Peterburgskie chteniia.*

Kidney, Walter C. *The Architecture of Choice: Eclecticism in America, 1880–1930.* New York: George Braziller, 1974.

Kiiko, E. I. "Belinskii i Dostoevskii o knige Kiustina 'Rossiia v 1839.'" *Dostoevskii: Materialy i issledovaniia,* vol. 1. Leningrad: Nauka, 1974.

Kinglake, William. "A Summer in Russia." *The New Monthly Magazine and Humorist,* nos. 2 and 3, 1846.

King, Ross. *Emancipating Space: Geography, Architecture, and Urban Design.* London: Guilford Press, 1996.

Kirichenko, E. I. "Dokhodnye zhilye doma Moskvy i Peterburga (1770–1830-e gg)." *Arkhitekturnoe nasledstvo,* no. 14, 1962.

———. "O nekotorykh osobennostiakh evoliutsii gorodskikh mnogokvartirnyikh domov vtoroi poloviny XIX—nachala XX vv. (Ot otdel'nogo doma k kompleksu)." *Arkhitekturnoe nasledstvo,* no. 15, 1963.

———. "Zhilaia zastroika Peterburga epokhi klassitsizma i ee vliianie na razvitie arkhitektury." *Arkhitekturnoe nasledstvo,* no. 16, 1967.

———. *Russkaia arkhitektura 1830–1910-kh godov.* Moscow: Iskusstvo, 1978.

———. "Prostranstvenno-vremennye kharakteristiki v russkoi arkhitekture serediny i vtoroi poloviny XIX veka." *Tipologiaa russkogo realizma vtoroi poloviny XIX veka,* G. Iu. Sternin, ed. Moscow: Nauka, 1979.

———. *Arkhitekturnye teorii XIX veka v Rossii.* Moscow: Iskusstvo, 1986.

———. "Romantizm i istorizm v russkoi arkhitekture XIX veka (K voprosu o dvukh fazakh razvitiia eklektiki)." *Arkhitekturnoe nasledstvo 36,* 1988.

Kirikov, B.M. "Stil'—Zhanr—Sreda (K voprosu o formoobrazovanii v arkhitekture Pe-terburga 1830–1910-kh gg.)." *Antsiferovskie chteniia: Materialy i tezisy conferentsii.* Leningrad: Leningradskoe Otedelenie Sovetskogo Fonda Kul'tury, 1989.

———. "Khram Voskreseniia Khristova (K istorii 'russkogo stilia' v Peterburge)." *Nevskii arkhiv: Istoriko-kraevedcheskii sbornik,* I. St. Petersburg: Atheneum Feniks, 1993.

———, ed. *Arkhitektory-stroiteli Sankt-Peterburga serediny XIX—nachala XX veka.* SPb, Piligrim, 1996.

———. "Peterburgskaia neoklassika nachala XX veka." *Nevskii Arkhiv: Istoriko-kraeved-cheskii sbornik,* III. SPb: Atheneum Feniks, 1997.

Kitanina, T. M. "Rabochie Peterburga v period razlozheniia i krizisa krepostnichestva (1800–1861 gg.)." *Istoriia rabochikh Leningrada,* t. 1. Leningrad: Nauka, 1972.

Knabe, G. S. *Voobrazhenie znaka: Mednyi vsadnik Fal'kone i Pushkina.* Moscow: Rossiiskii Gosurdarstvennyi Gumanitarnyi Universitet, 1993.

———, ed. *Moskva i "moskovskii tekst" russkoi kul'tury: Sbornik statei.* Moscow: Rossi-iskii Gosudarstvennyi Gumanitarnyi Universitet, 1998.

Kniazevskaia, T. B., ed. *Russkaia intelligentsia. Istoriia i sud'ba.* Moscow: Nauka, 1999.

Kobak, A. V., Stefan Kotkin, and Alla Sevast'ianova, eds. *Metodologiia regional'nykh is-toricheskikh issledovanii: Materialy mezhdunarodnogo seminara.* SPb: Notabene, 2000.

Kobak, A. V., S. Emmrikh, M. Mil'chik, and B. Iangfel'dt, eds. *Shvedy na beregakh Nevy: Sbornik statei.* Stockholm: Swedish Institute, 1998.

Kobak, A. V. and Iu. M. Piriutko, eds. "Ocherk istorii peterburgskogo nekropolia." *Is-toricheskie kladbishcha Peterburga: Spravochnik-putevoditel'.* SPb: Izdatel'stvo Cherny-sheva, 1993.

Koblents, I. N. *Andrei Ivanovich Bogdanov. 1692–1766. Iz proshlogo russkoi istoricheskoi nauki i knigovedeniia.* Moscow: Izdatel'stvo Akademii Nauk SSSR, 1958.

Kocka, Jürgen and Allan Mitchell, eds. *Bourgeois Society in Nineteenth-Century Europe.* Providence: Berg, 1993.

Komarovich, V. "Peterburgskie feletony Dostoevskogo." In *Feletony sorokovykh godov,* Yu. Oksman, ed. Moscow-Leningrad, 1930.

Komelova, G. N. "'Panorama Peterburga'—graviura raboty A. F. Zubova." *Kul'tura i iskusstvo petrovskogo vremeni: Publikatsii i issledovaniia.* Leningrad: Avrora, 1977.

Konechnyi, A. M. "Obshchestvo 'Staryi Peterburg—Novyi Leningrad.'" *Muzei* no. 7, 1987.

———. "N. P. Antsiferov—issledovatel' Peterburga." *Peterburg i guberniia: Istoriko-etno-graficheskie issledovaniia.* Leningrad, 1989.

———, ed. *Peterburgskie balagany.* SPb: Giperion, 2000.

———, ed. *Progulki po Nevskomu prospektu v pervoi polovine XIX veka.* SPb: Giperion, 2002.

———, ed. *Peterburgskoe kupechestvo v XIX veka.* SPb: Giperion, 2003.

Konechnyi, A. M. and K. A. Kumpan. "Peterburg v zhizni i trudakh N.P. Antsiferova." *"Nepostizhimyi gorod. . ."* Leningrad: Lenizdat, 1991.

Koni, A. F. *Peterburg: Vospominaniia starozhila.* Petrograd: Atenei, 1922.

Koshelev, V. A. "O 'literaturnoi' provintsii i literaturnoi 'provintsial'nosti' novogo vre-meni." *Russkaia provintsiia: Mif—Tekst—Real'nost',* A. F. Belousov and T. V. Tsiv'ian, eds. Moscow: "Kollektiv avtorov," 2000.

Koshevaia, L. E., ed. *Peterburgskie vstrechi Pushkina.* Leningrad: Lenizdat, 1987.

Kostelianets, B. O. "Podrobnee ob ocherke, ego zarozhdenii i razvitii v Rossii." *Russkie ocherki* (multivolume collection).

Kostof, Spiro. *The City Shaped: Urban Patterns and Meanings through History.* Boston: Little, Brown, 1991.

————. *The City Assembled: The Elements of Urban Form through History.* Boston: Little, Brown, 1992.

Krampen, Martin. *Meaning in the Urban Environment.* London: Pion, 1979.

Krasovskii, Apollinarii. *Grazhdanskaia arkhitektura: Chasti zdanii.* SPb, 1851.

Kristeva, Julia. *Black Sun: Depression and Melancholia,* Leon S. Roudiez, trans. New York: Columbia University Press, 1989.

Kriukovskikh, A. P. *Dvortsy Sankt-Peterburga: Khudozhestvenno-istoricheskii ocherk.* SPb: Lenizdat, 1997.

Krivenko, S. N. *M. E. Saltykov. Ego zhizn' i literaturnaia deiatel'nost'.* Petrograd, 1914.

Krivonos, V. Sh. "'. . . Tut ne stolitsa i ne provintsiia . . .' (Peterburgskaia okraina u Gogolia)." *Russkaia provintsiia: Mif—Tekst—Real'nost',* A. F. Belousov and T. V. Tsiv'ian, eds. Moscow: "Kollektiv avtorov," 2000.

Krivosheev, Iu. V., A. S. Fedotov, and M. V. Khodiakov, eds. *Peterburg i Moskva: Dve stolitsy Rossii v XVIII–XX vekakh.* Universitetskie Peterburgskie Chteniia. SPb: Izdatel'stvo S.-Peterburgskogo Universiteta, 2001.

Kubler, George. *The Shape of Time: Remarks on the History of Things.* New Haven: Yale University Press, 1962.

Kudriavtsev, A. I. and G. N. Shkoda. "Pravoslavnoe kladbishche i nekropol'-muzei Literatorskie mostki." *Istoricheskie kladbishcha Peterburga: Spravochnik-putevoditel',* A. V. Kobak and Iu. M. Piriutko, eds. SPb: Izdatel'stvo Chernysheva, 1993.

Kudriavtseva, G. H. "Siuzhetnye situatsii i motivy romana V. Krestovskogo 'Peterburgskie trushchoby.'" *Voprosy khudozhestvennogo metoda, zhanra i kharaktera v russkoi literature XVIII–XIX vekov.* Moscow, 1975.

Kufershtein, E. Z., K. M. Borisov, and O. E. Rubinchik. *Ulitsa Pestelia (Panteleimonovskaia).* Leningrad: Svecha, 1991.

Kukushkina, V. V. and N. K. Shablaeva. "Plany Peterburga kak istochniki po toponimii goroda XVIII v." *Fenomen Peterburga,* Iu. N. Bespiatykh, ed. SPb: BLITS, 2000.

Kul'tovye zdaniia Peterburga: Ukazatel' russkoi literatury 1717–1917 gg, vyp. 1 and 2. SPb: Rossiiskaia Natsional'naia Biblioteka, 1994, 1999.

Kuraev, Mikhail. "Puteshestvie iz Leningrada v Sankt Peterburg." *Novyi mir,* no. 10 (1996).

Kurbatov, V. *Pavlovsk: Ocherk-putevoditel'.* SPb, 1912.

————. *Peterburg.* SPb: Lenizdat, 1993 (abridged reprint of SPb, 1913).

————. "Unichtozhenie petrogradskikh sadov." *Starye gody,* January–February 1915.

Kurgatnikov, A. V. *Russkaia starina: Putevoditel' po XVIII veku.* Moskva: RIK "Kul'tura," 1996.

Kutsenogii, M. V. *Peterburg: Konspekty po istorii i kul'ture 1703–1917.* SPb: Papirus, 2003.

Kuznetsov, V. D. "Predaniia i legendy Sankt-Peterburga v kontse XIX-nachale XX vv." *Psikhologiia Peterburga i peterburzhtsev za tri stoletiia.* SPb: Nestor, 1999.

Lachmann, Renate. *Memory and Literature: Intertextuality in Russian Modernism,* Roy Sellars and Anthony Wall, trans. Minneapolis: University of Minnesota Press, 1997.

Lander, Sarah W. *Spectacles for Young Eyes: St. Petersburg.* Boston: Walker, Wise, 1862.

Laverychev, V. Ia. *Krupnaia burzhuasiia v poreformennoi Rossii, 1861–1900.* Moscow: Mysl', 1974.

Lebedev, G. S. *Meta-Peterburg (Osnovaniia programmy).* SPb: Peterburgskie chteniia, 1992.

Lebrun, Richard A. "St. Petersburg Nightmares? Joseph de Maistre's Soirees de Saint-Petersbourg." *Studies on Voltaire and the Eighteenth Century,* 303, 1992.

Lednicki, Waclaw. *Pushkin's "Bronze Horseman": The Story of a Masterpiece.* Berkeley: University of California Press, 1955.

Lefebvre, Henri. *Writings on Cities,* Eleonore Kofman and Elizabeth Lebas, trans. and ed. Oxford: Blackwell, 1996.

————. *The Production of Space,* Donald Nicholson-Smith, trans. Oxford: Blackwell, 1997.

Lehan, Richard. "Urban Signs and Urban Literature: Literary Form and Historical Processes." *New Literary History,* 18:1, Autumn 1986.

————. *The City in Literature: An Intellectual and Cultural History.* Berkeley: University of California Press, 1998.

Leikin, N. A. *Apraksintsy: Stseny i ocherki iz byta i nravov peterburgskikh rynochnykh torgovtsev i ikh prikazchikov polveka nazad.* SPb, 1864.

————. *Stseny iz kupecheskogo byta.* SPb, 1871.

————. *Neunyvaiushchie rossiiane: Rasskazy i kartinki s natury.* SPb: N. A. Khana, 1881.

Leiter, Sharon. "Mandelstam's Petersburg: Early Poems of the City Dweller." *Slavic and East-European Journal,* 22, 1978.

Lelina, V. I. Introduction to Stieglitz, M. S. *Promyshlennaia arkhitektura Peterburga,* 2nd ed. SPb, 1996.

————. *V prostranstve Peterburga.* SPb: Beloe i chernoe, 1997.

Leonov, V. P., ed. *Istoriia Sankt-Peterburga-Petrograda 1703–1917: Putevoditel' po istochnikam,* t. 1, vyp. 1 (Istoricheskie istochniki, raboty obshchego kharaktera, spravochnye i bibliograficheskie materialy). SPb: Filologicheskii Fakul'tet Sankt-Peterburgskogo Gosudarstvennogo Universiteta, 2000.

Levin, Harry. *The Gates of Horn.* New York, Oxford University Press, 1963.

Levin, V. D. "O stile 'Mednogo vsadnika'." *Izvestiia Akademii Nauk SSSR. Seriia literatury i iazyka,* vol. 33, no. 3 (1974).

Levina, N. P. and Iu. I. Kirtsideli, *Po etim ulitsam, po etim beregam: Peterburgskie progulki.* SPb: Papirus, 1997.

Levine, Lawrence W. *Highbrow/Lowbrow: The Emergence of Cultural Hierarchy in America.* Cambridge, MA: Harvard University Press, 1988.

Likhachev, D. S. *Poeziia sadov: K semantike sadovo-parkovykh stilei: Sad kak tekst.* Moscow: Soglasie, 1998.

Lilly, Ian K. "Imperial Petersburg, Suicide, and Russian Literature." *Slavonic and East European Review,* 72, 1994.

Lincoln, W. Bruce. *Between Heaven and Hell: The Story of a Thousand Years of Artistic Life in Russia.* New York: Viking Penguin, 1998.

————. *Sunlight at Midnight: St. Petersburg and the Rise of Modern Russia.* New York: Basic Books, 2000.

Lisaevich, I. I. *Doma rasskazyvaiut.* Leningrad: Lenizdat, 1991.

Lobell, Mimi. "Spatial Archetypes." *ReVision,* vol. 6, no. 2, Fall 1983.

Logachev, K. I. and V. S. Sobolev. "*Opisanie Sanktpeterburga.*" Leningrad: Leningradskoe Otd-nie Arkhiva Akademii Nauk SSSR, 1987.

Lo Gatto, Ettore. *Il mito di Pietroburgo: Storia, leggenda, poesia.* Milan: Feltrinelli Editore, 1960.

Loman, D. N. *Dostoprimechatel'nosti S.-Peterburga. Chtenie dlia naroda.* SPb, 1898.

Loman, O. V. *Nekrasov v Peterburge*. Leningrad: Lenizdat, 1985.

Lotman, Iu. M. "Problema khudozhestvennogo prostranstva v proze Gogolia." *Trudy po russkoi i slavianskoi filologii*, XI: Literaturovedenie. Tartu: Tartu University Press, 1968.

————. *Struktura khudozhestvennogo teksta*. Providence: Brown University Reprints, 1971.

————. "On the Metalanguage of a Typological Description of Culture." *Semiotica*, 14:2, 1975.

————. "Zametki o khudozhestvennom prostranstve." *Semiotika prostranstva i prostranstvo semiotiki: Trudy po znakovym sistemam* 19 [Uchenye Zapiski Tartuskogo Universiteta, 720], 1986.

————. *Universe of the Mind: A Semiotic Theory of Culture*, Ann Shukman, trans. Bloomington: Indiana University Press, 1990.

————. *Kul'tura i vzryv*. Moscow: Gnosis, 1992.

————. "Simvolika Peterburga i problemy semiotiki goroda." *Izbrannye stat'i: Stat'i po istorii russkoi literatury XVIII—pervoi poloviny XIX veka*, vol. 1. Tallinn: Aleksandra, 1992.

————. "Ustnaia rech' v istoriko-kul'turnoi perspective." *Izbrannye stat'i*, vol. 1. Tallinn: Alexandra, 1992.

————. "K funktsii ustnoi rechi v kul'turnom bytu pushkinskoi epokhi." *Izbrannye stat'i*, vol. 3. Tallinn: Alexandra, 1993.

————. "Kamen' i trava." *Lotmanovskii sbornik* 1. Moscow: ITS-Garant, 1995.

Lotman, Iu. M. and B. A. Uspenskii. "Binary Models in the Dynamics of Russian Culture (to the End of the Eighteenth Century)." In *The Semiotics of Russian Cultural History*, Alexander D. Nakhimovsky and Alice Stone Nakhimovsky, eds. Ithaca: Cornell University Press, 1984.

Lovell, Stephen. "Between Arcadia and Suburbia: Dachas in Late Imperial Russia." *Slavic Review*, vol. 61, no. 1, Spring 2002.

————. *Summerfolk: A History of the Dacha, 1710–2000*. Ithaca: Cornell University Press, 2003.

Lowenthal, David. *The Past Is a Foreign Country*. Cambridge: Cambridge University Press, 1985.

Lukomskii, G. K. *Sovremennyi Peterburg: Ocherk istorii vozniknoveniia i razvitiia klassicheskogo stroitel'stva 1900–1915 gg*. Petrograd, 1917.

————. *Staryi Peterburg. Progulki po starinnym kvartalam stolitsy*. Petrograd: Svobodnoe iskusstvo, 1917.

————. *Pavlovsk i Gatchina*. SPb, 1922.

Lur'e, F. M. *Peterburg 1703–1917: Istoriia i kul'tura v tablitsakh*. SPb: Zolotoi vek, Diamant, 2000.

————. "Golosa 'Serebrianogo veka': knigi, zhurnaly, vystavki." *Fenomen Peterburga*, Iu. N. Bespiatykh, ed. SPb: BLITS, 2000.

Lur'e, L., ed. *Iazvy Peterburga: Sbornik gazetnogo fel'etona kontsa XIX—nachala XX vv*. Leningrad, 1990.

Lur'e, L. Ia. and A. V. Kobak. "Zametki o smysle peterburgskogo kraevedeniia." *Antsiferovskie chteniia: Materialy i tezisy konferentsii*. Leningrad: Leningradskoe Otdelenie Sovetskogo Fonda Kul'tury, 1989.

Lutwack, Leonard. *The Role of Place in Literature*. Syracuse: Syracuse University Press, 1984.

Lynch, Kevin. *The Image of the City*. Cambridge, MA: MIT Press, 1960.

―――. *A Theory of Good City Form.* Cambridge, MA: MIT Press, 1981.

Makhlina, S. T., ed. *Peterburgskaia pushkiniana: Sbornik statei po materialam nauchnoi konferentsii 17 iiunia 1999 goda.* SPb: Sankt-Peterburgskii Gosudarstvennyi Universitet Kul'tury i Iskusstv, 2000.

Makogonenko, G. P. "Tema Peterburga u Pushkina i Goglia." *Izbrannye raboty.* Leningrad: Khudozhestvennaia literatura, 1987.

Maksimov, K. "Krestovskii ostrov (Iz vospominanii petrogradskogo starozhila)." *Nasha starina,* no. 7, 1915.

Malia, Martin. *Russia Under Western Eyes: From the Bronze Horseman to the Lenin Mausoleum.* Cambridge, MA: Harvard University Press, 1999.

Marcus, Sharon. *Apartment Stories: City and Home in Nineteenth-Century Paris and London.* Berkeley: University of California Press, 1999.

Margolis, A. D., ed. *Azbuka Peterburga.* SPb: Mezhdunarodnyi Blagotvoritel'nyi Fond Spaseniia Peterburga-Leningrada, 1995.

―――. *Peterburg Dekabristov.* SPb: Kontrfors, 2000.

Margolis, Joseph, ed. *Philosophy Looks at the Arts: Contemporary Readings in Aesthetics,* 3rd ed. Philadelphia: Temple University Press, 1987.

Marker, Gary. *Publishing, Printing, and the Origins of Intellectual Life in Russia, 1700–1800.* Princeton: Princeton University Press, 1985.

Marx, Leo. *The Machine in the Garden: Technology and the Pastoral Ideal in America.* New York: Oxford University Press, 1964.

Massie, Suzanne. *Land of the Firebird: The Beauty of Old Russia.* New York: Simon & Schuster, 1980.

―――. *Pavlovsk: The Life of a Russian Palace.* Boston: Little, Brown, 1990.

Masson, Charles F. *Secret Memoirs of the Court of Petersburg.* London: T. N. Longman and O. Rees, 1801.

Materialy dlia biografii N.A. Dobroliubova sobrannye v 1861–1862 godakh, t. 1. Moscow: V. F. Rikhter, 1890.

Mattie, Erik. *World's Fairs.* New York: Princeton Architectural Press, 1998.

Matveev, P. N. *Atlanty i kariatidy Peterburga.* SPb: Iskusstvo—SPb, 2001.

Mavrodin, V. V. *Osnovanie Peterburga* (2nd ed.). Leningrad: Lenizdat, 1983.

Maxwell, Richard. *The Mysteries of Paris and London.* Charlottesville: University Press of Virginia, 1992.

McGrew, Roderick E. *Russia and the Cholera, 1823–1832.* Madison: University of Wisconsin Press, 1965.

McReynolds, Louise. *The News under Russia's Old Regime: The Development of a Mass-Circulation Press.* Princeton: Princeton University Press, 1991.

―――. *Russia at Play: Leisure Activities at the End of the Tsarist Era.* Ithaca: Cornell University Press, 2003.

Medvedkova, O. A. "Predromanticheskie tendentsii v russkom iskusstve rubezha XVIII-XIX vekov. Mikhailovskii zamok." *Russkii klassitsizm vtoroi poloviny XVIII—nachala XIX veka.* Moscow: Izobrazitel'noe iskusstvo, 1994.

Mel'gunova, P. E., K. V. Sivkov, and N. P. Sidorov, eds. *Russkii byt po vospominaniiam sovremennikov.* Moscow: Zadruga, 1914, 1918.

Melnick, Arthur. *Space, Time, and Thought in Kant.* Dordrecht: Kluwer Academic, 1989.

Merezhkovskii, D. *"Bol'naia Rossiia."* Leningrad: Izdatel'stvo Leningradskogo Universiteta, 1991.

Metter, I. M. "*Na beregu pustynnykh voln. . .*" *Istoricheskie ocherki o Peterburge XVIII veka.* SPb: Kul't-inform-press, 1999.

Mignot, Claude. *Architecture of the Nineteenth Century in Europe.* New York: Rizzoli, 1984.

Mikhailova, S. B. *Gleb Uspenskii v Peterburge.* Leningrad: Lenizdat, 1987.

Mikhnevich, V. O. *Peterburg ves' na ladoni.* SPb: Izdanie K. N. Plotnikova, 1874.

———. "Peterburzhtsy" and "Okrestnosti Peterburga." *Zhivopisnaia Rossiia: Otechestvo nashe v ego zemel'nom, istoricheskom, plemennom, ekonomicheskom i bytovom znachenii,* P. P. Semenov, ed., t. 1, ch. 2, Severnaia Rossiia: Ozernaia ili Drevne-Novgorodskaia Oblast'. SPb: M. O. Vol'f, 1881.

———. *Iazvy Peterburga: Opyt istoriko-statisticheskogo issledovaniia nravstvennosti stolichnogo naseleniia.* SPb, 1886.

———. *Peterburgskoe leto.* SPb, 1887.

———. "Peterburgskie sady i ikh etnografiia." *Iazvy Peterburga: Sbornik gazetnogo fel'etona kontsa XIX–nachala XX vv.* Leningrad: Leningradskoe Otdelenie Sovetskogo Fonda Kul'tury, 1990.

Mikishat'ev, M. N. "Obraz Peterburga v peterburgskoi povesti A. S. Pushkina 'Mednyi vsadnik.'" *Antsiferovskie chteniia: Materialy i tezisy konferentsii.* Leningrad: Leningradskoe Otdelenie Sovetskogo Fonda Kul'tury, 1989.

Mil'chik, M. I. "Ropshinskii dvorets—zabytyi pamiatnik arkhitektury XVIII v." *Nevskii arkhiv: Istoriko-kraevedcheskii sbornik III.* SPb: Atheneum-Feniks, 1997.

Miliukov, Alexander. "Iakov Petrovich Butkov." *Istoricheskii vestnik,* no. 2, 1881.

Miller, David C. *Dark Eden: The Swamp in Nineteenth-Century American Culture.* Cambridge: Cambridge University Press, 1989.

Miller, J. Hillis. *Topographies.* Stanford: Stanford University Press, 1995.

Mironov, Boris N. with Ben Eklof. *The Social History of Imperial Russia, 1700–1917* (2 v.). Boulder: Westview Press, 2000.

Mirsky, D. S. *A History of Russian Literature.* New York: Alfred A. Knopf, 1949.

Missac, Pierre. *Walter Benjamin's Passages,* Shierry Weber Nicholsen, trans. Cambridge, MA: MIT Press, 1995.

Mitchell, W.J.T. "Spatial Form in Literature: Toward a General Theory." In *The Language of Images,* W.J.T. Mitchell, ed. Chicago: University of Chicago Press, 1980.

Mochulsky, K. *Dostoevsky: Zhizn' i tvorchestvo.* Paris, 1947.

Mohr, Hans-Ulrich. "The Picturesque: A Key Concept of the Eighteenth Century." In *The Romantic Imagination: Literature and Art in England and Germany,* Frederick Burwick and Jürgen Klein, eds. Amsterdam-Atlanta, GA: Rodopi, 1996.

Monas, Sidney. "St. Petersburg and Moscow as Cultural Symbols." In *Art and Culture in Nineteenth-Century Russia,* Theofanis George Stavrou, ed. Bloomington: Indiana University Press, 1983.

———. "Unreal City: St. Petersburg and Russian Culture." In *Russian Literature and American Critics: In Honor of Deming B. Brown,* Kenneth N. Brostrom, ed. Ann Arbor: University of Michigan, 1984.

———. "Derzhavin's Petersburg." *Russia and the World of the Eighteenth Century,* R. P. Bartlett, A. G. Cross, and Karen Rasmussen, eds. Columbus: Slavica Publishers, 1986.

Morson, Gary Saul. *The Boundaries of Genre: Dostoevsky's Diary of a Writer and the Traditions of Literary Utopia.* Evanston: Northwestern University Press, 1981.

Mowitt, John. *Text: The Genealogy of an Antidisciplinary Object.* Bloomington: Indiana University Press, 1992.

Mullin, V. N. "Kladbishche v sisteme petrovskoi kul'tury nachala XVIII veka." *Russian Studies: Ezhekvartal'nik russkoi filologii i kul'tury*, vol. I, no. 4, 1995 (SPb).

Mumford, Lewis. *The Culture of Cities*. New York: Harcourt Brace, 1938.

————. *The City in History: Its Origins, Its Transformations, and Its Prospects*. New York: Harcourt, Brace, & Jovanovich, 1961.

Murav'eva, I.A. *Vek moderna* (from the series Byloi Peterburg: Panorama stolichnoi zhizni). SPb: Pushkinskii fond, 2001.

Muzei Goroda: K Oktiabriu 1927 g. Leningrad: Izdatel'stvo Muzeiia Goroda, 1928.

Nabokov, Vladimir. *Lectures on Russian Literature*, Fredson Bowers, ed. New York: Harcourt, Brace, & Jovanovich, 1981.

Nash, Gary B. *The Urban Crucible: Social Change, Political Consciousness, and the Origins of the American Revolution*. Cambridge, MA: Harvard University Press, 1979.

Nazirov, R. G. "Peterburgskaia legenda i literaturnye traditsii." *Traditsii i novatorstvo*, vyp. 3: Uchenye zapiski Bashkirskogo Gosudarstvennogo Universiteta, vyp. 80. Seriia filologicheskikh nauk, 26. Ufa, 1975.

Nekliudova, M. S. and A. L. Ospovat. "Okno v Evropu: Istochnikovedcheskii etiud k 'Mednomu Vsadniku." *Lotmanovskii sbornik 2*. Moscow: RGGU, 1997.

Nerhood, Harry W. *To Russia and Return: An Annotated Bibliography of Travelers' English-Language Accounts of Russia from the Ninth Century to the Present*. Columbus: Ohio State University Press, 1968.

Nesin, Vadim. *Zimnii dvorets v tsarstvovanie poslednego imperatora Nikolaia II (1894–1917)*. SPb: Zhurnal "Neva," ITD Letnii sad, 1999.

Nesterov, V. V. *L'vy steregut gorod*. Leningrad, 1972.

Netunakhina, G. D. and N. I. Udimova. *Muzei gorodskoi skul'ptury: Kratkii putevoditel'*. Leningrad: Lenizdat, 1972.

Neuberger, Joan. *Hooliganism: Crime, Culture, and Power in St. Petersburg, 1900–1914*. Berkeley: University of California Press, 1993.

Nikitin, N. V. *Peterburg noch'iu*. SPb, 1903.

Nikolaev, S. I. and T. S. Tsar'kova. "Tri veka russkoi epitafii." *Russkaia stikhotvornaia epitafiia*. SPb: Akademicheskii proekt, 1998.

Nikol'skii, V. A. "Kak prazdnovalas' stoletiia Peterburga." In *Peterburgskaia starina*, I. Bozherianov and V. Nikol'skii, eds. SPb: 1903.

Ocherki istorii Leningrada, 6 vols. Moscow-Leningrad: AN SSSR, 1955–.

O'Connell, Shaun. *Imagining Boston: A Literary Landscape*. Boston: Beacon Press, 1990.

Okhotin, N. G. "A. P. Bashchutskii i ego kniga." *Nashi spisannye s natury russkimi: Prilozhenie k faksimil'nomu izdaniiu*. Moscow: Kniga, 1986.

Oksman, Iu. G., ed. *Fel'etony sorokovykh godov*. Moscow: Academia, 1930.

Okuriur'e, M. "Smert' Peterburga." *Sankt-Peterburg: Okno v Rossiiu 1900–1935*. SPb: Feniks, 1997.

Olcott, Anthony. *Russian Pulp: The Detektiv and the Russian Way of Crime*. Lanham, MD: Rowman & Littlefield, 2001.

Ol'khovskii, E. P. *Peterburgskie istorii: Gorod i intelligentsiia v minuvshem stoletii (1810-e–1910-e gody)*. SPb: Kul't-inform-press, 1998.

Olsen, Donald J. *The City as a Work of Art: London, Paris, Vienna*. New Haven: Yale University Press, 1986.

Opatovich, S. I. "Smolenskoe kladbishche v S.-Peterburge: Istoricheskii ocherk." *Russkaia starina*, August 1873.

Ospovat, A. L. "Vokrug 'Mednogo vsadnika.'" *Izvestiia Akademii Nauk SSSR. Seriia literatury i iazyka*, t. 43, no. 3, May–June 1984.

Ospovat, A. L. and Timenchik, R. D. "*Pechal'nu povest' sokhranit'*": *Ob avtore i chitateliakh Mednogo vsadnika*. Moscow: Kniga, 1985.

Ostroi, O. S. "S chego nachinalas' peterburgiana: Opisanie putevoditelei po gorodu s momenta ikh vozniknoveniia do serediny XIX stoletiia." *Nevskii arkhiv* III. SPb: Atheneum Feniks, 1997.

———. *Gorod mnogolikii: Ocherki o knigakh i izobrazitel'nykh materialakh, posviashchennykh Sankt-Peterburgu (XVIII–XX vv.)*. SPb: Rossiiskaia Natsional'naia Bibioteka, 2000.

Otradin, M. V., ed. *Peterburg v russkom ocherke XIX veka*. Leningrad: Izdatel'stvo Leningradskogo Universiteta, 1984.

———. *Peterburg v russkoi poezii (XVIII—nachalo XX veka)—poeticheskaia antologiia*. Leningrad: Izdatel'stvo Leningradskogo Universiteta, 1988.

Ovsiannikov, Iurii. *Tri veka Sankt-Peterburga*. Moscow: Galart, 1997.

Owen, Thomas C. *Capitalism and Politics in Russia: A Social History of the Moscow Merchants, 1855–1905*. New York: Cambridge University Press, 1981.

Palme, Per. "Ut Architectura Poesis." In *Idea and Form: Studies in the History of Art*, by Ake Bengtsson, et al. Stockholm: Almqvist & Wiksell, 1959.

Park, Robert E., Ernest W. Burgess, and Roderick D. McKenzie. *The City*. Chicago: University of Chicago Press, 1925.

Pashkova, T. L. *Dom arkhitektora Briullova*. SPb: Almaz, 1997.

Patricia, Deotto. "Peterburgskii dachnyi byt XIX v. kak fakt massovoi kul'tury." *Europa Orientalis*, no. 1, 1991.

Paukov, I. Iu. "Pereferiinye raiony stolitsy glazami peterburzhtsev nachala XIX v." *Antsiferovskie chteniia: Materialy i tezisy konferentsii*. Leningrad: Leningradskoe Otedelenie Sovetskogo Fonda Kul'tury, 1989.

Pavlishchev, L. *Iz semeinoi khroniki: Vospominaniia ob A. S. Pushkine*. Moscow: Universitetskaia tipografiia na Strastn. bul'v., 1890.

Pavlov, A. P. *Khramy Sankt-Peterburga: Khudozhestvenno-istoricheskii ocherk*. SPb: Lenizdat, 1995.

Pavlovsk: Ocherk, istorii, i opisanie 1777–1877 (Sostavleno po porucheniiu Ego Imperatorskogo Vysochestva Gosudaria Velikogo Kniazia Konstantina Nikolaevicha). SPb, 1877.

Pearson, Michael Parker and Colin Richards, eds. *Architecture and Order: Approaches to Social Space*. London: Routledge, 1994.

Peet, Richard. *Modern Geographical Thought*. Blackwell, 1998.

Perevezentseva, Nataliia. *Ia vyshla iz doma. . . Kniga o pushkinskoi ulitse i ne tol'ko o nei*. SPb: Ostrov, 2001.

Perlina, N. M. "Ivan Mikhailovich Grevs i Nikolai Pavlovich Antsiferov: K obosnovaniiu ikh kul'turologicheskoi pozitsii." *Antsiferovskie chteniia: Materialy i tezisy konferentsii*. Leningrad: Leningradskoe Otedelenie Sovetskogo Fonda Kul'tury, 1989.

Pesonen, Pekka. "Bitov's Text as Text: The Petersburg Text as Context in Andrey Bitov's Prose." In *Literary Tradition and Practice in Russian Culture*, Valentina Polukhina, Joe Andrews, and Robert Reid, eds. Amsterdam: Rodopi, 1993.

———. "Semiotics of a City: The Myth of St. Petersburg in Andrey Bely's novel *Petersburg*." *Slavica Helsingiensia* 18, 1997.

"Peterburg v 1720 godu." *Russkaia starina*, 1879.

Petrov, G. F. *Dvorets u Sinego mosta: Mariinskii dvorets v Sankt-Peterburge.* SPb: Logos, 2001.

Petrov, P. *Istoriia Sanktpeterburga, s osnovaniia goroda do vvedeniia v deistvie vybornogo gorodskogo upravleniia po uchrezhdeniiam o guberniiakh, 1703–1782.* SPb, 1885.

Pike, Burton. *The Image of the City in Modern Literature.* Princeton: Princeton University Press, 1981.

Pile, Steve and Nigel Thrift. *Mapping the Subject: Geographies of Cultural Transformation.* London: Routledge, 1995.

Piretto, Gian Piero. *Derelitti, bohémiens e malaffari: il mito povero di Pietroburgo.* Bergamo: P. Lubrina, 1989.

Piriutko, Iu. M. "Lazarevskaia usypal'nitsa—pamiatnik russkoi kul'tury XVIII–XIX vv." *Pamiatniki kul'tury. Novye otkrytiia.* Moscow: Nauka, 1989.

———. "Leningradskii panteon." *Antsiferovskie chteniia: Materialy i tezisy konferentsii.* Leningrad: Leningradskoe Otdelenie Sovetskogo Fonda Kul'tury, 1989.

———. "Nadgrobnye pamiatniki: Stil', mastera, zakazchiki." *Istoricheskie kladbishcha Peterburga: Spravochnik-putevoditel',* Koback, A. V. and Iu. M. Piriutko, eds. SPb: Izdatel'stvo Chernysheva, 1993.

Pisnaia, V. "Fabula 'Uedinennogo domika na Vasil'evskom." *Pushkin i ego sovremenniki,* vyp. XXXI–XXXII, 1927.

Poggioli, Renato. *The Spirit of the Letter: Essays in European Literature.* Cambridge, MA: Harvard University Press, 1965.

Pogosian, E. A. "Traditsionnaia odicheskaia frazeologiia v tvorchestve Derzhavina." *Lotmanovskii sbornik* 2. Moscow: Izdatel'stvo RGGU, 1997.

Pokshishevskii, V. V. "Territorial'noe formirovanie promyshlennogo kompleksa Peterburga v XVIII–XIX vekakh." *Voprosy geografii,* t. 20. Moscow: Gosudarstvennoe Izdatel'stvo Geograficheskoi Literatury, 1950.

Polilov-Severtsev, G. T. *Nashi dedy-kuptsy: Bytovye kartiny nachala XIX stoletiia.* SPb, 1907.

Pomeranets, K. S. "Dva navodnen'ia, s raznitsei v sto let. . ." *Peterburg trushchobnyi.* Neva, no. 7, 1998.

———. *Navodneniia v Peterburge, 1703–1997.* SPb: Baltrus-buk, 1998.

Postnikov, A. V. *Karty zemel' rassiskikh: Ocherki istorii geograficheskogo izucheniia i kartografirovanniia nashego otechestva.* Moscow: Nash Dom—L'age d'Homme, 1996.

Pozzi, Dora C. and John M. Wickersham, eds. *Myth and the Polis.* Ithaca: Cornell University Press, 1991.

Pred, Allan. *Urban Growth and the Circulation of Information: The United States System of Cities, 1790–1840.* Cambridge, MA: Harvard University Press, 1973.

———. "Place as Historically Contingent Process: Structuration and the Time-Geography of Becoming Places." *Annals of the Association of American Geographers* 74, 1984.

———. *Lost Words and Lost Worlds: Modernity and the Language of Everyday Life in Late Nineteenth-Century Stockholm.* Cambridge, UK: Cambridge University Press, 1990.

Predtechenskii, A. V., ed. *Peterburg petrovskogo vremeni.* Leningrad: Lenizdat, 1948.

Prokhvatilova, S. A. and E. V. Anisimov, eds. *"Gorod pod morem" ili blistate'nyi Sankt-Peterburg.* SPb: Lenizdat, 1996.

Proskuriakova, Irina and Nataliia Volchek. *Besedy o Sankt-Peterburge.* SPb: Astra-Luks, 1992.

Pukinskii, B. K. *1000 voprosov i otvetov o Leningrade*. Leningrad: Lenizdat, 1981.

Pumpianskii, L. V. "'Mednyi vsadnik' i poeticheskaia traditsiia XVIII veka." *Vremennik pushkinskoi komissii*, nos. 4–5, 1939.

Punin, A. L. *Povest' o leningradskikh mostakh*. Leningrad, 1971.

———. *Arkhitekturnye pamiatniki Peterburga—vtoraia polovina XIX veka*. Leningrad: Lenizdat, 1981.

———. *Arkhitektura Peterburga serediny XIX veka*. Leningrad: Lenizdat, 1990.

Pushkarev, I. I. *Nikolaevskii Peterburg*. SPb: Liga Plius, 2000 (abridged reprint of 1839–42 *Opisanie Sankt-Peterburga i uezdnykh gorodov S.-Peterburgskoi gubernii*).

Pushkariov, V., ed. *The Neva Symphony: Leningrad in Works of Graphic Art and Painting*. Aurora Art Publishers in Leningrad, 1975.

Putilov, B. N. "Peterburg—Leningrad v ustnoi traditsii stoletii." Introduction to Naum Sindalovskii, *Peterburgskii fol'klor*. SPb: Maksima, 1994.

Pyliaev, M. I. *Staryi Peterburg*. Leningrad: Titul, 1990 (reprint of 1889 edition).

———. *Zabytoe proshloe okrestnostei S. Peterburga*. SPb: A. S. Suvorin, 1889.

———. *Staraia Moskva*. Moscow: Svarog, 1995 (reprint of 1891 edition).

———. *Staroe zhitie*. SPb, 1892.

———. "Iz mira tainstvennogo: Starye i novye rasskazy o mediumakh, dukhakh, privideniiakh." *Trud*, no. 4, 1894.

———. *Zamechatel'nye chudaki i originaly*. SPb: A. S. Suvorin, 1898.

Raevskii, F. *Peterburg s okrestnostiami*. SPb, 1902.

Raikes, Thomas. *A Visit to St. Petersburg, in the Winter of 1829–30*. London: Richard Bentley, 1838.

Rakhmanin, E. *Raba Bozhiia Kseniia, pochivaiushchaia na Smolenskom pravoslavnom kladbishche v SPb*, izd. 4. SPb, 1913.

Rakov, Iu. A. *Lestnitsa Raskol'nikova: Zapiski literaturnogo sledopyta*. Leningrad: self-published, 1990.

———. *Antichnye strazhi Peterburga*. SPb: Khimiia, 1996.

———. *Peterburg—gorod literaturnykh geroev*. SPB: Khimiia, 1997.

———. *Skul'pturnyi olimp Peterburga: Puteshestvie v antichno-mifologicheskii Peterburg*. SPb: Iskussvo—SPB, 2000.

———. *Pikovyi perekrestok Peterburga*. SPb: Ostrov, 2001.

Ram, Harsha. *The Imperial Sublime: A Russian Poetics of Empire*. Madison: University of Wisconsin Press, 2003.

Raskin, A. G. *Triumfal'nye arki Leningrada*. Leningrad: Lenizdat, 1985.

Rassadin, Stanislav. *Russkie, ili Iz dvorian v intelligenty*. Moscow: Knizhnyi sad, 1995.

Réau, Louis. *Saint-Pétersbourg*. Paris: Librairie Renouard, 1913.

Reid, Ian. "Genre and Framing: The Case of Epitaphs." *Poetics* 17, 1988.

Rein, Yevgenii. "Sotoye Zerkalo: Zapozdalye vospominaniya." *Zvezda* no. 12, 1991.

Reitblat, A. I. "'Russkii Gaborio' ili uchenik Dostoevskogo?" In A. Shkliarevskii, *Chto pobudilo k ubiistvu? (Rasskazy sledovatelia)*, A. I. Reitblat, ed. Moscow: Khudozhestvennaia literatura, 1993.

———. "Detektivnaia literatura i ruskii chitatel' (vtoraia polovina XIX—Nachalo XX VV.)," *Knizhnoe delo v Rossii vo vtoroi polovine XIX—Nachale XX veka*, vyp. 7. SPb: Rossiiskaia Natsional'naia biblioteka, 1994.

Riabinina, N. A. "K probleme literaturnykh istochnikov poemy A. S. Pushkina *Mednyi vsadnik*." *Boldinskie chteniia*. Gor'kii: Volgo-Viatskoe knizhnoe izdatel'stvo, 1977.

Rieber, Alfred J. *Merchants and Entrepreneurs in Imperial Russia.* Chapel Hill: University of North Carolina Press, 1982.

———. "The Sedimentary Society." In *Between Tsar and People: Educated Society and the Quest for Public Identity in Late Imperial Russia,* Edith W. Clowes, Samuel D. Kassow, and James L. West, eds. Princeton: Princeton University Press, 1991.

Ripellino, Angelo Maria. *Magic Prague,* David Newton Marinelli, trans. Berkeley: University of California Press, 1994.

Rivosh, Ia. N. *Vremia i veshchi: Ocherki po istorii material'noi kul'tury v Rossii nachala XX veka.* Moscow: Iskusstvo, 1990.

Rober, P. *Ves' Peterburg v karrikaturakh.* St. Petersburg: Golike i Vil'borg, 1903–.

Roboli, T. "The Literature of Travel." In *Russian Prose,* B. Eikhenbaum and Iu. Tynianov, eds., and Ray Parrott, trans. Ann Arbor: Ardis, 1985.

Romanovskii, A. "Vospominaniia o navodnenii 1824 g." *Russkaia starina,* no. 122, 1905.

Roosevelt, Priscilla R. *Life on the Russian Country Estate: A Social and Cultural History.* New Haven: Yale University Press, 1995.

Rosenberg, Daniel. "An Eighteenth-Century Time Machine: The *Encyclopedia* of Denis Diderot." *Historical Reflections/Reflexions Historiques,* vol. 25, no. 2, 1999.

Rosenshield, Gary. "*The Bronze Horseman* and *The Double:* The Depoeticization of the Myth of Petersburg in the Young Dostoevsky." *Slavic Review,* Summer 1996.

———. *Pushkin and the Genres of Madness: The Masterpieces of 1833.* Madison: University of Wisconsin Press, 2003.

Rosmarin, Adena. *The Power of Genre.* Minneapolis: University of Minnesota Press, 1985.

Ross, Kristin. *The Emergence of Social Space: Rimbaud and the Paris Commune.* Minneapolis: University of Minnesota Press, 1988.

Ross, Michael L. *Storied Cities: Literary Imaginings of Florence, Venice, and Rome.* Westport: Greenwood Press, 1994.

Rotikov, K. K. *Drugoi Peterburg.* SPb: Liga Plius, 1998.

Rozanov, A. S. *Muzykal'nyi Pavlovsk.* Leningrad, 1978.

Rudnitskaia, I. "Otkrytie Severnoi Venetsii: Frantsuzskie pisateli XVIII–XIX vekov v Peterburge." *Belye nochi.* Leningrad, 1973.

Ruskin, John. "The Lamp of Memory." *The Book-Worm,* April 1885.

Rybczynski, Witold. *Looking Around: A Journey through Architecture.* New York: Viking, 1993.

———. *City Life: Urban Expectations in a New World.* New York: Scribner, 1995.

Rykwert, Joseph. *The Idea of a Town: The Anthropology of Urban Form in Rome, Italy and the Ancient World.* Princeton: Princeton University Press, 1976.

Saitov, V. I. *Peterburgskii nekropol'.* SPb, t. 1–4, 1912–13.

Sakharov, I. V. "Stolitsa Rossiiskoi imperii kak proobraz ob"edinennoi Evropy: vzgliad etnodemografa i genealoga." *Fenomen Peterburga.* SPb: BLITS, 2000.

Samuilikovich, S., N. Shmitt-Fogelevich, and S. Mianik. *Peterburg-Petrograd-Leningrad v otkrytkakh.* Leningrad: Institut Istorii SSSR Akademii Nauk SSSR, 1984.

Savarenskaia, T. F. "Evritmiia v arkhitekture Peterburga pushkinskoi pory." In *Arkhitektura v istorii russkoi kul'tury,* I. A. Bondarenko, ed. Moscow: RAN, 1996.

Schechter, Harold. *The Bosom Serpent: Folklore and Popular Art.* Iowa City: University of Iowa Press, 1988.

Schelling, Friedrich Wilhelm Joseph. *Philosophie der Mythologie,* vol. 2. Darmstadt: Wissenschaftliche Buchgesellschaft, 1966.

Schenker, Alexander M. *The Bronze Horseman: Falconet's Monument to Peter the Great.* New Haven: Yale University Press, 2003.

Schivelbusch, Wolfgang. *The Railway Journey: The Industrialization of Time and Space in the 19ᵗʰ Century.* Hamburg: Berg, 1986.

Schmidt, Albert. "Architecture in Nineteenth-Century Russia: The Enduring Classic." In *Art and Culture in Nineteenth-Century Russia,* Theofanis G. Stavrou, ed. Bloomington: Indiana University Press, 1983.

SchÜnle, Andreas. *Authenticity and Fiction in the Russian Literary Journey, 1790–1840.* Cambridge, MA: Harvard University Press, 2000.

———. "Gogol, the Picturesque, and the Desire for the People: A Reading of 'Rome.'" *The Russian Review,* 59, October 2000.

———. "Prostranstvennaia poetika Tsarskogo Sela v ekaterininskoi prezentatsii imperii." *Tynianovskii sbornik,* vyp. 11. Ob"edinennoe Gumanitarnoe Izdatel'stvo, 2002.

Schorske, Carl E. *Fin-De-Siècle Vienna: Politics and Culture.* New York: Alfred A. Knopf, 1980.

Scott, A. Maccallum. *Through Finland to St. Petersburg.* London: Grant Richards, 1909.

Sears, John. *Sacred Places: American Tourist Attractions in the Nineteenth Century.* New York: Oxford University Press, 1989.

Sem(e)evskii, M. I. *Pavlovsk.* SPb, 1877.

———. *Ocherki i rasskazy iz russkoi istorii XVIII veka. Slovo i delo 1700–1725.* SPb, 1884.

Semenov, P. P., ed. *Zhivopisnaia Rossiia: Otechestvo nashe v ego zemel'nom, istoricheskom, plemennom, ekonomicheskom i bytovom zhachenii,* t. 1, ch. 2: Severnaia Rossiia. SPb: M. O. Vol'f, 1881 (reprint, SPb: Logos-SPb, 1994).

Semenova, L. N. *Byt i naselenie Sankt-Peterburga (XVIII vek).* Moscow: Ves' mir, 1998.

Semiotika goroda i gorodskoi kul'tury (Peterburg). Trudy po znakovym sistemam. vol. 18, Tartu: Tartu University Press, 1984.

Sennett, Richard. *The Uses of Disorder: Personal Identity and City Life.* New York, Norton, 1970.

———. *Flesh and Stone: The Body and the City in Western Civilization.* New York: W. W. Norton, 1994.

Serkova, V. "Neopisuemyi Peterburg: Vykhod v prostranstvo labirinta." *Metafizika Peterburga.* SPb: Eidos, 1993.

Setchkarev, Vsevolod. *Gogol: His Life and Works,* Robert Kramer, trans. New York: New York University Press, 1965.

Seward, Jill. "The Potemkin City: Tourist Images of Late Imperial Vienna." In *Imperial Cities: Landscape, Display, and Identity,* Felix Driver and David Gilbert, eds. Manchester: Manchester University Press, 1999.

Shapiro, Michael and Marianne Shapiro. *Figuration in Verbal Art.* Princeton: Princeton University Press, 1988.

Shaposhnik, V. V. "Novaia literatura ob A.I. Bogdanove." *Peterburgskie chteniia 96.* SPb: BLITS, 1996.

Shapovalov, Veronica. "A. S. Pushkin and the St. Petersburg Text." In *The Contexts of A. S. Pushkin,* Peter I. Barta and Ulrich Goebel, eds. New York: Mellen, 1988.

Shchuchenko, V. A., ed. *Peterburg v russkoi kul'tury: Tezisy dokladov.* SPb: Sankt-Peterburgskaia Gosudarstvennaia Akademiia Kul'tury, 1997.

Sherikh, D. Iu. *Byli i nebylitsy Nevskogo prospekta: Istoricheskaia progulka.* SPb: Ivanov i Leshchinskii, 1996.

————. *Peterburg den' za dnem: Gorodskoi mesiatseslov.* SPb: Peterburg XXI veka, 1998.

Shevyrev, A. P. "Kul'turnaia sreda stolichnogo goroda. Peterburg i Moskva." *Ocherki russkoi kul'tury XIX veka,* vol. 1. Obshchestvenno-kul'turnaia sreda. Moscow: Izdatel'stvo Moskovskogo Universiteta, 1998.

Shields, Rob. *Places on the Margin: Alternative Geographies of Modernity.* London: Routledge, 1991.

Shpiller, R. I. "Gosudarstvennyi muzei istorii Leningrada (1918–1985 gg.)." *Muzei i vlast': Iz zhizni muzeev: Sobrnik nauchnykh trudov.* Moscow, 1991.

Shreder, F. A. *Noveishii putevoditel' po Sanktpeterburgu.* SPb, 1820.

Shubinskii, S. N. "Kladbishchenskaia literature (Epitafii XVIII veka)." *Istoricheskie ocherki i rasskazy.* Moscow: Moskovskii rabochii, 1995 (reprint of 1908 edition).

Shul'ts, S. S. *Khramy Sankt-Peterburga (istoriia i sovremennost'): Spravochnoe izdanie.* SPb: Glagol, 1994.

Shurygin, Ia. I. *Petergof: Letopis' vosstanovleniia.* SPB: Abris, 2000.

Siegel, Adrienne. *The Image of the American City in Popular Literature 1820–1870.* Port Washington: Kennikat Press, 1981.

Simmel, Georg. "The Metropolis and Mental Life." In Kurt Wolff, ed., *The Sociology of Georg Simmel.* Glencoe: Free Press, 1950.

Simoni, P. K. "O knizhnoi torgovle i tipakh torgovtsev na starom Apraksinom rynke." *Starye gody,* no. 2, 1907.

Sindalovskii, N. A. *Legendy i mify Sankt-Peterburga.* Fond Leningradskaia Galereia, 1994.

————. *Peterburgskii fol'klor.* SPb: Maksima, 1994.

————. *Istoriia Sankt-Peterburga v predaniiakh i legendakh.* SPb: Norint, 1997.

————. *Peterburg v fol'klore.* SPb: Zhurnal "Neva," ITD "Letnii sad," 1999.

————. *Peterburg: Ot doma k domu. . . Ot legendy k legende.* SPb: Norint, 2000.

————. *Legendy i mify prigorodov Sankt-Peterburga.* SPb: Norint, 2001.

Skidan, Alexander. "O pol'ze i vrede Peterburga dlia zhizni." *Russkii zhurnal,* July 6, 1999.

Skorikov, Iu. A. *Peterburg i Nevskaia guba v XXI stoletii.* SPb: Stroiizdat SPb, 2000.

Smart, J.J.C., ed. *Problems of Space and Time.* New York: Macmillan, 1964.

Smirnov, N. "Slova i vyrazheniia vorovskogo iazyka, vybrannye iz romana Vs. Krestovskogo—'Peterburgskie trushchoby.'" *Izvestiia otdeleniia russkogo iazyka i slovestnosti Imperatorskoi Akademii Nauk,* t. 4. SPb, 1899.

Smirnov, S. B. *Peterburg—Moskva: summa istorii.* SPb: Izdatel'stvo RGPU im. A. I. Gertsena, 2000.

Smolitskaia, G. P. *Nazvaniia moskovskikh ulits.* Moscow: Izdatel'skii Dom "Muravei," 1996.

Soja, Edward. *Postmodern Geographies: The Reassertion of Space in Critical Social Theory.* New York: Verso, 1989.

Sollogub, V. A. *Peterburgskie stranitsy vospominanii Grafa Solloguba.* SPb: Afina, 1993.

Solov'ev, L. F. *Tainy Peterburgskoi storony.* SPb, 1908.

Solov'eva, T. A. *K prichalam Admiralteiskoi naberezhnoi.* SPb: IKAR, 1999.

————. *K prichalam Angliiskoi naberezhnoi.* SPb: IKAR, 1998.

Solzhenitsyn, Alexander. "The City on the Neva." In *Stories and Prose Poems.* London: Bodley Head, 1970.

Soulié, Frédéric. "Les Drames invisibles." In *Le Diable à Paris.* Paris: Hetzel, 1845.

Spence, Jonathan D. *The Memory Palace of Matteo Ricci.* New York: Viking Penguin, 1984.

Spivak, D. L. *Severnaia stolitsa: Metafizika Peterburga.* SPb: Tema, 1998.

Sreznevskii, V. "Prazdnovanie stoletiia Peterburga." *Russkaia starina*, kn. 5, 1903.

Srzednicki, T. J. *The Place of Space and Other Themes: Variations on Kant's First Critique*. The Hague: Martinus Nijhoff, 1983.

Stambaugh, John. *The Ancient Roman City*. Baltimore: Johns Hopkins University Press, 1988.

Startsev, V. I., L. B. Boriskovskaia, and T. V. Partenenko, eds. *Psikhologiia Peterburga i Peterburzhtsev za tri stoletiia*. SPb: Nestor, 1999.

Stasov, V. V. "Dvadtsat' piat' let russkogo iskusstva." *Izbrannye sochineniia v trekh tomakh*, vol. 2. Moscow: Iskusstvo, 1952.

Stein, Howard F. and William G. Niederland, eds. *Maps from the Mind: Readings in Psychogeography*. Norman: University of Oklahoma Press, 1989.

Steinberg, Mark D. "The Injured and Insurgent Self: The Moral Imagination of Russia's Lower-Class Writers." *Workers and Intelligentsia in Late Imperial Russia: Realities, Representations, Reflections*, Reginald E. Zelnik, ed. Berkeley: University of California International and Area Studies, 1999.

Sternin, G. Iu., ed. *Mir russkoi provintsii i provintsial'naia kul'tura*. SPb: Dmitri Bulanin, 1997.

Stieglitz, M. S. *Promyshlennaia arkhitektura Peterburga*, 2nd ed. St. Petersburg, 1996.

Stolpianskii, P. N. "Kamennyi Ostrov." *Stolitsa i usad'ba*, nos. 14–15, 1914.

———. *Peterburg: Kak voznik, osnovalsia i ros Sanktpiterburkh*. SPb: Nega, 1995 (reprint of 1918 book).

———. "Staryi Peterburg v proizvedeniiakh Nekrasova." *Kniga i revoliutsiia*, no. 2 (14), 1921.

———. *Dachnye okrestnosti Peterburga*. Petrograd, 1923.

———. *Petergofskaia pershpektiva*. Petrograd, 1923.

———. *Staryi Peterburg: Admiralteiskii ostrov, Sad Trudiashchikhsia*. Moscow: Gosudarstvennoe Izdatel'stvo, 1923.

———. *Legendy, predaniia i skazaniia starogo Peterburga*. Petrograd, no. 2, 1924.

———. *Zhizn' i byt peterburgskoi fabriki za 210 let ee sushchestvovaniia, 1704–1914 gg.* Leningrad, 1925.

Storch, Henry. *The Picture of Petersburg*, translated from the German. London: T. N. Longman & O. Rees, 1801.

Strakhov, N. N., ed. "Iz zapisnoi knizhki F.M. Dostoevskogo." *Biografiia, pis'ma i zametki iz zapisnoi F. M. Dostoevskogo*. SPb, 1883.

Strelka, Joseph P., ed. *Theories of Literary Genre*. University Park: The Pennsylvania State University Press, 1978.

Stroll, Avrum. *Sketches of Landscapes: Philosophy by Example*. Cambridge, MA: MIT Press, 1998.

Struc, Roman S. "St. Petersburg: The Phases of a Literary Myth." *Research Studies*, 43, 1975.

Stürickow, Regina. *Reisen nach St. Petersburg. Die Darstellung St. Petersburgs in Reisebeschreibungen (1815–1861)*. Frankfurt am Main: Peter Lang, 1990.

Sukhodrev, V. M. *Peterburg i ego dostoprimechatel'nosti*. SPb, 1901.

Sushkova-Khvostova, E. A. *Zapiski*. Leningrad, 1928.

Suvorkov, P. *Prospekt Chernyshevskogo*. SPb: Beloe i chernoe, 1999.

Sveshnikov, N. I. *Peterburgskie Viazemskie trushchoby i ikh obitateli*. SPb, 1900.

———. *Vospominaniia propashchego cheloveka*. Moscow: Novoe literaturnoe obozrenie, 1996.

Svetlov, S. V. *Peterburgskaia zhizn' v kontse XIX stoletiia (v 1892 godu)*. SPb: Giperion, 1998.

Svin'in, P. P. *Dostopamiatnosti Sankt-Peterburga i ego okrestnostei*. SPb: Liga Plius, 1997.

Sweet, Rosemary. *The Writing of Urban Histories in Eighteenth-Century England*. Oxford: Clarendon Press, 1997.

Taborsky, Edwina. *The Architectonics of Semiosis*. London: Macmillan Press, 1998.

Talalaia, M. G. "Franchesko Al'garotti: Russkie puteshestviia. Perevod s ital'ianskogo, predislovie i primechaniia." *Nevskii arkhiv* III. SPb: Atheneum Feniks, 1997.

Terts, Abram (Andrei Sinyavsky). *Progulki s Pushkinym*. London: Overseas Publications Interchange, 1975.

———. *V teni Gogolia*. London: Overseas Publications Interchange, 1975.

Thesing, William B. *The London Muse: Victorian Poetic Responses to the City*. Athens: University of Georgia Press, 1982.

Thrower, Norman J. W. *Maps and Civilization: Cartography in Culture and Society*. Chicago: Universtity of Chicago Press, 1996.

Timofeev, V. N., E. N. Poretskina, and N. N. Efremova, eds. *Memorial'nye doski Sankt-Peterburga: Spravochnik*. SPb: Art-Biuro, 1999.

Tkhorzhevskii, I. I. *Poslednii Peterburg: Vospominaniia kamergera*. SPb: Aleteiia, 1999.

Todd, William Mills III. *Fiction and Society in the Age of Pushkin: Ideology, Institutions, and Narrative*. Cambridge, MA: Harvard University Press, 1986.

Todorov, Tsvetan. *The Fantastic: A Structural Approach to a Literary Genre*, Richard Howard, trans. Ithaca: Cornell University Press, 1975.

———. "The Origin of Genres." *New Literary History*, vol. 8, no. 1, Autumn 1976.

———. *The Poetics of Prose*, Richard Howard, trans. Ithaca: Cornell University Press, 1977.

———. *Genres in Discourse*, Catherine Porter, trans. Cambridge, UK: Cambridge University Press, 1990.

Tomashevskii, B. V., ed. *Pushkinskii Peterburg*. Leningrad: Leningradskoe gazetno-zhurnal'noe i knizhnoe izdatel'stvo, 1949.

Toporov, V. N. "Aptekarskii ostrov kak gorodskoe urochishche (obshchii vzgliad)." *Noosfera i khudozhestvennoe tvorchestvo*. Moscow: Nauka, 1991.

———. "Peterburg i 'Peterburgskii text russkoi literatury'," "O structure romana Dostoevskogo v sviazi s arkhaicheskimi skhemami mifologicheskogo myshleniia ('Prestuplenie i nakazanie')," and "Peterburgskie teksty i Peterburgskie mify (Zametki iz serii)." *Mif. Ritual. Simvol. Obraz: Issledovaniia v oblasti mifopoeticheskogo*. Moscow: Progress, 1995.

Toulmin, Stephen. *Cosmopolis: The Hidden Agenda of Modernity*. Chicago: University of Chicago Press, 1990.

Trachtenburg, Alan. *The Incorporation of America: Culture and Society in the Gilded Age*. New York: Hill and Wang, 1982.

Trice, Tom. "Rites of Protest: Populist Funerals in Imperial St. Petersburg, 1876–1878." *Slavic Review*, vol. 60, no. 1, Spring 2001.

Trinder, Barrie. *The Making of the Industrial Landscape*. London: Phoenix, 1997.

Troinitskii, S. "O tsepnykh mostakh Peterburga." *Starye gody*, March 1907.

Tsar'kova, T. S. "Memorial'nyi zhanr: obraztsy i podrazhaniia." *Fenomen Peterburga*, Iu. N. Bespiatykh, ed. SPb: BLITS, 2000.

Tsar'kova, T. S. and S. I. Nikolaev. "Epitafii peterburgskogo nekropolia." In *Istoricheskie kladbishcha Peterburga: Spravochnik-putevoditel'*, Kobak, A. V. and Iu. M. Piriutko, eds. SPb: Izdatel'stvo Chernysheva, 1993.

Tsiavlovskaia, T. G. "'Vliublennyi bes' (Neosushchestvlennyi zamysel Pushkina)." *Pushkin: Issledovaniia i materialy*, t. III. Moscow: Izdatel'stvo AN SSSR, 1960.

Tumilovich, E. V. and Altunin, S. E. *Mosty i naberezhnye Leningrada*. Moscow, 1963.

Turgenev, I. S. *Dokumenty po istorii literatury i obshchestvennosti*, vyp. 2. Moscow: GIZ, 1923.

Uspenskii, L. V. *Zapiski starogo peterburzhtsa*. Leningrad, 1970.

van Baak, J. J. "On Space in Russian Literature: A Diachronic Problem." In *Dutch Contributions to the Ninth International Congress of Slavists (Literature)*, A.G.F. van Holk, ed. Amsterdam: Rodopi, 1983.

Vance, James E. Jr. *The Continuing City: Urban Morphology in Western Civilization*. Baltimore: Johns Hopkins University Press, 1990.

Vanchugov, Vasilii. *Moskvosofiia i Peterburgologiia. Filosofiia goroda*. Moscow: RITS "PILIGRIM," 1997.

van Pelt, Robert Jan and Carroll William Westfall. *Architectural Principles in the Age of Historicism*. New Haven: Yale University Press, 1991.

Vatsuro, V. E. "Pushkin i problemy bytopisaniia v nachale 1830-kh godov." *Pushkin: Issledovaniia i materialy*, t. 6. Leningrad: Nauka, 1969.

Vdovin, Gennadii. *Obraz Moskvy 18 veka: gorod i chelovek*. Moscow: Nash Dom—L'Age d'Homme, 1997.

Vedenin, Iu. A. *Ocherki po geografii iskusstva*. St. Petersburg: Rossiiskii NII kul'turnogo i prirodnogo naslediia, 1997.

Veksler, I. I., ed. *Iz literaturnogo naslediia F.M. Reshetnikova*. Leningrad: Akademiia Nauk SSSR, Institut Russkoi Literatury, 1932.

Velikanova, S. I. "Graviura K. Gampel'na 'Ekateringofskoe gulianie 1-go maia' kak istochnik dlia izucheniia arkhitektury i byta Peterburga 1820-kh godov." *Staryi Peterburg: Istoriko-etnograficheskie issledovaniia*, N. V. Iukhneva, ed. Leningrad: Nauka, 1982.

Verderevskaia, N. A. *Stanovlenie tipa raznochintsa v russkoi realisticheskoi literature 40–60kh godov XIX veka*. Kazan: Kazanskii Gosudarstvennyi Pedagogicheskii Institut, 1975.

Veselovskii, K. "Statisticheskie issledovaniia o nedvizhimykh imushchestvakh v Sanktpeterburge." *Otechestvennye zapiski*, t. LVII, otd. II, 1848.

Viazemskii, P. *Staraia zapisnaia knizhka*, ed. L. Ginzburg. Leningrad: Izdatel'stvo pisatelei v Leningrade, 1929.

Vickery, Walter N. "*Mednyj vsadnik* and the Eighteenth-Century Heroic Ode." *Indiana Slavic Studies* 3, 1963.

Vidler, Anthony. *The Architectural Uncanny: Essays in the Modern Unhomely*. Cambridge, MA: MIT Press, 1992.

Vilibakhov, G. V. "Osnovanie Peterburga i imperskaia emblematika." *Semiotika goroda i gorodskoi kul'tury (Peterburg). Trudy po znakovym sistemam*, vol. 18, Tartu: Tartu University Press, 1984.

Vinogradov, V. V. *Stil' Pushkina*. Moscow: Nauka, 1999.

———. *Iazyk Pushkina: Pushkin i istoriia russkogo literaturnogo iazyka*. Moscow: Nauka, 2000.

Viollet le Duc, E. *L'art russe: ses origines, ses elements constitutifs, son apogee, son avenir*. Paris, Ve. A. Morel, 1877.

Vitiazeva, V. A. and B. M. Kirikov. *Leningrad: Putevoditel'*. Leningrad: Lenizdat, 1988.

Vitukhnovskaia, M. A. "Vospominaniia P.P. Veinera o zhurnale 'Starye gody.'" *Pamiatniki kul'tury. Novye okrytiia. Ezhegodnik 1984*. Leningrad: Nauka, 1986.

Vol'f, A. I. *Khronika peterburgskikh teatrov (1826–84)*. St. Petersburg: Tip. R. Golike, 1877, 1884.

Volkov, Solomon. *St. Petersburg: A Cultural History*, Antonina W. Bouis, trans. New York: The Free Press, 1995.

Vrangel', N. N. "Zabytye mogily." *Starye gody*, February 1907.

Vyzhevskii, S. V., ed. *Tsvetoslov uteshnoi stolitsy: Poeticheskaia istoriia Pavlovska ot dnei ego osnovaniia, pisannaia imenitymi i bezvestnymi stikhotvortsami*. SPb: Bip, 1997.

Walkowitz, Judith R. *City of Dreadful Delight: Narratives of Sexual Danger in Late-Victorian London*. Chicago: University of Chicago Press, 1992.

Wall, Cynthia. "Details of Space: Narrative Description in Early Eighteenth-Century Novels." *Eighteenth-Century Fiction*, vol. 10, no. 4, July 1998.

Wallace, Anne D. *Walking, Literature, and English Culture: The Origins and Uses of Peripatetic in the Nineteenth Century*. Wutton-under-Edge, Clarendon Press, 1993.

Wallace, Donald Mackenzie. *Russia on the Eve of War and Revolution*. Princeton: Princeton University Press, 1984.

Warburg, Jeremy, comp. *The Industrial Muse: The Industrial Revolution in English Poetry*. London: Oxford University Press, 1958.

Ward, Charles A. *Moscow and Leningrad: A Topographical Guide to Russian Cultural History. Volume 1: Buildings and Builders*. Munchen: K. G. Saur, 1989.

Waterhouse, Alan. *Boundaries of the City: The Architecture of Western Urbanism*. Toronto: University of Toronto Press, 1993,

Weber, Max. *The City*, Don Martindale and Gertrud Neuwirth, trans. and eds. New York: Free Press, 1958.

Weimer, David R. *The City as Metaphor*. New York: Random House, 1966.

West, James L. and Iurii A. Petrov, eds. *Merchant Moscow: Images of Russia's Vanished Bourgeoisie*. Princeton: Princeton University Press, 1998.

Whitehill, Walter Muir. *Boston: A Topographical History*, 2nd ed. Cambridge, MA: Belknap Press of Harvard University Press, 1982.

Whiteside, Anna and Michael Issacharoff, eds. *On Referring in Literature*. Bloomington: Indiana University Press, 1987.

Wightwick, "The Principles and Practice of Architectural Design" (Essay 7, 1850). In *Detached Essays of the Architectural Publication Society*. London, 1853.

Williams, Noel. "Problems in Defining Contemporary Legend." In *Perspectives on Contemporary Legend*, Paul Smith, ed. Sheffield: CECTAL Conference Papers Series, 1984.

Williams, Raymond. *The Country and the City*. London: Hogarth Press, 1985.

———. *Culture and Society, 1780–1950*. London: Hogarth Press, 1993.

Wilson, Francesca. *Muscovy: Russia through Foreign Eyes, 1553–1900*. London: George Allen & Unwin, 1970.

Wirtschafter, Elise Kimerling. *Structures of Society: Imperial Russia's "People of Various Ranks."* DeKalb: Northern Illinois University Press, 1994.

———. *Social Identity in Imperial Russia*. DeKalb: Northern Illinois University Press, 1997.

Wolfreys, Julian. *Writing London: The Trace of the Urban Text from Blake to Dickens*. New York: St. Martin's Press, 1998.

Wolin, Judith. "The Rhetorical Question." *VIA 8: Architecture and Literature: The Journal of the Graduate School of Fine Arts, University of Pennsylvania.* New York: Rizzoli, 1986.

Wood, Denis. *The Power of Maps.* New York: Guilford, 1992.

Wortman, Richard S. "Moscow and Petersburg: The Problem of a Political Center in Tsarist Russia." In *Rites of Power: Symbolism, Ritual, and Politics since the Middle Ages,* Sean Wilentz, ed. Philadelphia: University of Pennsylvania Press, 1985.

————. *Scenarios of Power: Myth and Ceremony in Russian Monarchy: Volume One* (From Peter the Great to the Death of Nicholas I). Princeton: Princeton University Press, 1995.

————. *Scenarios of Power: Myth and Ceremony in Russian Monarchy: Volume Two* (From Alexander II to the Abdication of Nicholas II). Princeton: Princeton University Press, 2000.

Worton, Michael and Judith Still, eds. *Intertextuality: Theories and Practices.* Manchester: Manchester University Press, 1990.

Yates, Frances. *The Art of Memory,* vol. 3 in *Selected Works.* London: Routledge, 1966.

Zabelin, Ivan. *Istoriia goroda Moskvy,* 1990 (reprint of 1905 book).

Zaitsev, V. N. "Bibliotechnoe-informatsionnoe prostranstvo Sankt-Peterburga." In *Fenomen Peterburga,* Iu. N. Bespiatykh, ed. SPb: BLITS, 2000.

Zapiski Imperatritsy Ekateriny Vtoroi. SPb: Izdanie A. S. Suvorina, 1907.

Zasosov, D. A. and V. I. Pyzin. *Iz zhizni Peterburga 1890–1910 godov.* Leningrad, 1991.

Zelnik, Reginald E. *Labor and Society in Tsarist Russia: The Factory Workers of St. Petersburg, 1855–1870.* Stanford: Stanford University Press, 1971.

————. "Workers and Intelligentsia in the 1870s: The Politics of Sociability." In *Workers and Intelligentsia in Late Imperial Russia: Realities, Representations, Reflections,* Reginald E. Zelnik, ed. Berkeley: University of California International and Area Studies, 1999.

Zherve, V. V. *Pamiatka o Peterburge i ego primechatel'nostiakh: s risunkami: dlia voisk i naroda.* SPb: Voennaia Tip., 1897.

Zhivotov, N. N. *Peterburgskie profili* (4 vypuski: *Na izvozchich'ikh koslakh, Sredi brodiazhek, Sredi fakel'shchikov, Sredi ofitsiantov*). SPb, 1894–96.

Zhurbina, E. I. *Teoriia i praktika khudozhestvenno-publitsisticheskikh zhanrov (Ocherk. Fel'eton).* Moscow: Mysl', 1969.

Zorin, Andrei. *Kormia dvuglavogo orla. . . Literatura i gosudarstvennaia ideologiia v Rossii v poslednei treti XVIII—pervoi treti XIX veka.* Moscow: Novoe literaturnoe obozrenie, 2001.